Henrik Ibsen and the

Henrik Ibsen (1828–1906) is the foun̶ ̶ ̶ ̶ ̶ ̶ ̶ ̶ ̶ ̶ ̶ ̶ ̶ ̶ theater, and his plays
are performed all over the world. Yet in spite of his unquestioned status as
a classic of the stage, Ibsen is often dismissed as a boring old realist, whose
plays are of interest only because they remain the gateway to modern theater.
In *Henrik Ibsen and the Birth of Modernism*, Toril Moi makes a powerful case
not just for Ibsen's modernity, but also for his modernism.

Henrik Ibsen and the Birth of Modernism situates Ibsen in his cultural context, emphasizes his position as a Norwegian in European culture, and shows how important
painting and other visual arts were for his aesthetic education. The book rewrites literary history, reminding modern readers that idealism was the dominant aesthetic
paradigm of the nineteenth century. Modernism was born in the ruins of idealism,
Moi argues, thus challenging traditional theories of the opposition between realism
and modernism.

By reading Ibsen's modernist plays as investigations of the fate of love in an
age of skepticism, Moi shows why Ibsen still matters to us. In this book,
Ibsen's plays are showed to be profoundly concerned by theater and theatricality, both on stage and in everyday life. Ibsen's unsettling explorations of
women, men, and marriage here emerge as chronicles of the tension between
skepticism and the everyday, and between critique and utopia in modernity.

This radical new account places Ibsen in his rightful place alongside Baudelaire,
Flaubert, and Manet as a founder of European modernism.

Henrik Ibsen and the Birth of Modernism

Art, Theater, Philosophy

TORIL MOI

OXFORD
UNIVERSITY PRESS

OXFORD
UNIVERSITY PRESS

Great Clarendon Street, Oxford OX2 6DP

Oxford University Press is a department of the University of Oxford.
It furthers the University's objective of excellence in research, scholarship,
and education by publishing worldwide in

Oxford New York

Auckland Cape Town Dar es Salaam Hong Kong Karachi
Kuala Lumpur Madrid Melbourne Mexico City Nairobi
New Delhi Shanghai Taipei Toronto

With offices in

Argentina Austria Brazil Chile Czech Republic France Greece
Guatemala Hungary Italy Japan Poland Portugal Singapore
South Korea Switzerland Thailand Turkey Ukraine Vietnam

Oxford is a registered trademark of Oxford University Press
in the UK and in certain other countries

Published in the United States
by Oxford University Press Inc., New York

© Toril Moi 2006

First published 2006
First published as an Oxford University paperback 2008

British Library Cataloguing in Publication Data
Data available

Library of Congress Cataloging in Publication Data

Typeset by SPI Publisher Services, Pondicherry, India
Printed in Great Britain
on acid-free paper by
Clays Ltd., St Ives plc

ISBN 978–0–19–920259–1

Cover image: William Quiller Orchardson, *The First Cloud*, 1887.
National Gallery of Victoria, Melbourne, Australia.

For David
Der er—forvandling i dette her!

and in memory of Inga-Stina Ewbank:
Ibsen scholar, Ibsen translator, friend.

Acknowledgments

Several institutions have generously supported this book. In 2001 I received a John Simon Guggenheim Memorial Fellowship. Dean Drew Faust offered me a Senior Fellowship at the Radcliffe Institute for Advanced Study at Harvard University, for the spring of 2003. Duke University granted me research leave in 2002 and in the spring of 2003, and in May 2005 the Rockefeller Foundation's Bellagio Residency provided ideal working conditions.

In 2000 and in 2002, Duke University's Arts and Sciences Research Council gave me grants to travel to Oslo to do research at the Center for Ibsen Studies. A 2005 grant from the Norwegian National Ibsen Committee (*Nasjonalkomiteen for Ibsen-satsingen*) have helped to pay for the color illustrations in this book.

I have received much assistance from many libraries. At Duke University Library, I want specially to thank Sara Seten Berghausen and Yunyi Wang, as well as the whole Inter-Library Loan office. At Harvard I profited from the Widener Library's extensive collections of nineteenth-century Scandinavian materials. Mária Fáskerti, the head librarian at the Center for Ibsen Studies, mailed photocopies to me for years. Without her, it would have been much harder to work on Ibsen in North Carolina. The London Library was a terrific place to work during the summer of 2004. The library at the National Gallery in Oslo, the National Art Library at the Victoria and Albert Museum, and the Tate Library at Tate Britain's Hyman Kreitman Research Centre in London all helped me to understand Ibsen's visual world

Over the years I have been lucky to have excellent research assistants. At the Radcliffe Institute my two undergraduate research assistants, Sarah Thomas and Natalia A. J. Truszkowska, made life in Cambridge more efficient, and more pleasant, too. At Duke, Erin Post, Abby Salerno, Fiona Barnett, Ka Man Calvin Hui, and Tess Shewry took care of all the boring jobs I gave them without a single complaint. It has been a privilege to work with such brilliant young intellectuals.

I thank people who have helped me in particular ways in the notes. But here I must acknowledge a special gratitude to Erik Henning Edvardsen, Director of the Ibsen Museum in Oslo, who provided more help than I had any right to expect. Vigdis Ystad, the principal editor of *Henrik Ibsens Skrifter*, the much awaited new edition of Ibsen's writings, has patiently answered all my questions. My dear friend and colleague Sarah Beckwith and I have been reading Wittgenstein, Austin, and Cavell together for years. My students at Duke and at the 2005 School of Criticism and Theory at Cornell University have made me think more clearly about philosophy, theater, and Ibsen.

I am honored to acknowledge the feedback and encouragement I have received from Stanley Cavell and Michael Fried. Early on, Michael Fried told me that I really was writing about Ibsen's modernism. He was right. Stanley Cavell's friendship and intellectual generosity are exemplary. His comments on various chapters have been invaluable, always revealing that matchless ear for the wrong note—and for the right note, too—that is so characteristic of his own writing.

Two friends will never read these acknowledgments. Naomi Schor was for many years my colleague at Duke University. Without Naomi's pioneering work on idealism, this book would not exist in the form it has now. Inga-Stina Ewbank read some of my early drafts and helped me to find my way in Ibsen scholarship. She was a magnificent woman: warm, generous, and very funny, a brilliant Ibsen scholar, and a great friend. I miss her. This book is dedicated to Inga-Stina's memory.

I am happy that I have finally managed to write "something Norwegian" for my mother, Nora Moi, and my father, Georg Seval Moi. I owe them more than I can ever say. My dear brother, Geir Arne Moi, read several chapters for me. His daughter, Marlene Nora Diana Moi, is the most delightful niece I could imagine. I am lucky also to have two wonderful American step-children. I want to thank Gabriel M. Paletz and Susannah B. F. Paletz for reading drafts, reading Ibsen, going to the theater to see Ibsen plays, and for having faith in the book, and in me.

My husband, David L. Paletz, has lived with this book since its first beginnings. He sat through five hours of *Emperor and Galilean* in Norwegian in Bergen and claimed to enjoy it. He also cheerfully went to the theater with me in Oslo, London, New York, New Haven, Los Angeles, and Greensboro, NC. Without the slightest murmur of complaint he weathered spring in Oslo and summer in Munich, and even put up with Sorrento and Amalfi in June. This book is also dedicated to him. Nobody deserves it more.

An excerpt from an earlier version of Chapter 1 was published as "Ibsen, Theatre and the Ideology of Modernism", *Theater Survey*, 45/2 (2004), 247–52.

Some of the ideas that now appear at the end of Chapter 6 and in Chapter 8 were first tried out in "Ibsen's Anti-Theatrical Aesthetics: *Pillars of Society* and *The Wild Duck*", in Pål Bjørbye and Asbjørn Aarseth (eds.), *Proceedings:*

IX International Ibsen Conference, Bergen 5–10 June 2000 (Øvre Ervik: Akademisk Forlag, 2001), 29–47.

An earlier version of Chapter 8 was published as " 'It was as if he meant something different from what he said—all the time': Language, Metaphysics and the Everyday in *The Wild Duck*", *New Literary History*, 33/4 (2002), 655–86. © Johns Hopkins University Press, 2002.

Some parts of Chapter 9 appear in "Expressive Freedom: Melodrama in *Rosmersholm*", in Gunnar Foss (ed.), *I skriftas lys og teatersalens mørke: Ein antologi om Ibsen og Fosse* (Kristiansand: Høyskoleforlaget, 2005), 81–107.

Toril Moi

Durham, NC
September 2005

We begin to feel, or ought to, terrified that maybe language (and understanding, and knowledge) rests upon very shaky foundations—a thin net over an abyss.

Stanley Cavell, The Claim of Reason

Contents

Contents

List of Illustrations

Color Plates

1. Anne Louis Girodet de Roucy-Trioson (1767–1824), *The Flood*, 1806 (oil on canvas), Musée Girodet, Montargis, France, Peter Willi; Bridgeman Art Library.

2. Hippolyte (Paul) Delaroche (1797–1856), *The Execution of Lady Jane Grey*, 1833 (oil on canvas), National Gallery, London, Bridgeman Art Library.

3. Eilif Peterssen, *Christian II Signing the Death Warrant of Torben Oxe*, 1876. Photo by J Lathion: © The National Museum of Art, Architecture and Design, Oslo.

4. Arnold Böcklin, *Im Spiel der Wellen*, Bayerische Staatsgemäldesammlungen, Neue Pinakothek Munich and Kunstia-Archiv ARTOTHEK, D-Weilheim.

Black and White Illustrations

1. Johan Christian Clausen Dahl, *Winter at the Sognefjord*, 1827. Photo by J Lathion: © The National Museum of Art, Architecture and Design, Oslo.

2. Erik Werenskiold, *Portrait of the Poet Henrik Ibsen*. © DACS 2005. Photo by J Lathion: © The National Museum of Art, Architecture and Design, Oslo.

3. Olaf 'Filou' Krohn, *Norwegian Poets*, National Library, Oslo.

4. Christian Krogh, *August Strindberg*, Photo: Anne-Lise Reinsfelt, Norsk Folkemuseum, Oslo.

5. Théodore Géricault (1791–1824), *The Raft of the Medusa*, 1819 (oil on canvas), Louvre, Paris, France/Bridgeman Art Library.

6. Adolph Tidemand and Hans Gude, *Bridal Procession in Hardanger*, 1848. Photo by J Lathion: © The National Museum of Art, Architecture and Design, Oslo.

7. Arthur C. Payne and Harry Payne, Illustration from Robert Browning, *Der Rattenfänger von Hameln*, ca 1889. University Library of Braunschweig.

8. Arnold Böcklin, *Isle of the Dead* (first version), 1880. Kunstmuseum Basel. Permanent loan of the Gottfried Keller Foundation 1920. Photo; Kunstmuseum Basel, Martin Bühler.

9. Anonymous, *Master Böcklin with the Ugly Mugs of his Critics*, photographic postcard, ca. 1872. Photo; Kunstmuseum Basel.

10. Knud Bergslien, *An Evening at the High Mountain Farm*. The Syndics of Cambridge University Library, from Christian Tønsberg and Adolph Tidemand, *Norske folkelivsbilleder efter malerier og tegninger* (1858). Waddleton.bb.11.17.

A Note on the Text

All references to texts by Ibsen are to the Norwegian centenary edition: Henrik Ibsen, *Hundreårsutgave: Henrik Ibsens samlede verker*, ed. Francis Bull, Halvdan Koht, and Didrik Arup Seip, 21 vols. (Oslo: Gyldendal, 1928–57). References to this edition are included in the text without any preceding abbreviation. Thus (1: 220) means *Hundreårsutgaven*, volume 1, page 220.

When the reference is to a letter from Ibsen, the date and addressee of the letter are included in a note, if such information is not given in the text.

Unless otherwise indicated, all translations are mine. I have usually not anglicized the names of Ibsen's characters, except occasionally in spelling (I write Johannes Rosmer, not John Rosmer, but Rebecca West, not Rebekka West). I have reproduced the characteristic nineteenth-century Norwegian usage in which wives and lovers call their husbands and lovers by their last name. Sometimes the list of references adds information about an English translation of a Scandinavian work. In such cases, unless I specify otherwise, the references are always to the original Scandinavian text, and the translation is my own.

References in the notes have been abbreviated throughout. This means that full references can be found *only* in the Bibliography. When a work is quoted frequently in a specific chapter, page references are given in the text after the first note-cue. When there is no page reference after a quotation, it comes from a web site, and the URL will be found both in the note and in the Bibliography.

To keep the book to a manageable length, I have had to remove quotations in foreign languages (an exception has been made for poetry). Readers who wish to see the original Danish and Norwegian texts will find them in *Ibsens modernisme*, the Norwegian translation of this book, published by Pax Forlag in Oslo in the spring of 2006.

An Ibsen Chronology

For a wealth of information on Ibsen online, use the Ibsen portal:
<http://www.ibsen.net>. To see Ibsen's own paintings, go to
<http://www.ibsen.net/index.gan?id=37400&subid=0> ("Ibsen as Painter").
The pictures are downloadable.

1828	(20 March) Henrik Johan Ibsen born.
1828–43	*Skien*
	1835 Father's bankruptcy. The Ibsen family moves to Venstøp, just outside town.
1844–50	*Grimstad, pharmacist's assistant*
	1846 Ibsen's illegitimate son, Hans Jacob Henriksen Birkedalen, was born on 9 October. The mother was Else Sophie Jensdatter Birkedalen, a maid servant at the pharmacist's house, ten years Ibsen's senior. Ibsen paid child maintenance with difficulty and reluctance until June 1862. (He may have met his son once, in 1892.)
	1849 Writes first play: *Catiline* (published 1850).
1850–1	*Christiania*, to take his student's exams*
	1850 *The Burial Mound* (September, first Ibsen production ever) Ibsen writes for various short-lived magazines.
1851–7	*Bergen, theater director and writer at Det norske teater*
	1852 First trip abroad, to Copenhagen and Dresden. Probably sees Shakespeare for the first time.
	1853 *St John's Night*
	1854 *The Burial Mound* (revised version)
	1855 *Lady Inger* (published 1857)
	1856 *The Feast at Solhoug*
	1857 *Olaf Liljekrans*
1857–64	*Christiania, artistic director at Kristiania* Norske Theater*
	1858 Marries Suzannah Daae Thoresen from Bergen.
	1858 *The Warriors of Helgeland*
	1859 Two programmatic poems: "Paa vidderne" ("On the Heights") and "I billedgalleriet" ("In the Picture Gallery")

* The city now called Oslo was called Oslo until 1624; in this year, after a devastating fire, the town was largely rebuilt and renamed Christiania by King Christian IV. In 1877, the spelling was officially changed to Kristiania. This was the result of a long political struggle for a more "Norwegian" (as opposed to "Danish") orthography, which many radicals, including Ibsen, had used for years before it became official. In 1925, the name was changed back to Oslo.

1859 (December) Birth of Sigurd Ibsen.

1861–3 Money trouble. Sued for debts; barely escapes debtors' prison. Deteriorating living conditions. Moves seven times in four years.

1862 Kristiania Norske Theater goes bankrupt.

1862 "Terje Vigen", epic poem, one of the best-loved poems in Norwegian literature.

1863 *Love's Comedy*

1864 *The Pretenders*

1864–8   Rome

1864 (June) Ibsen's belongings sold at public auction in Christiania, to cover debts.

1866 *Brand* is published and becomes a success. Ibsen gets annual state stipend.

1867 *Peer Gynt*

1868–75   Dresden

1869 *The League of Youth*

1869 Visits Egypt, present at opening of Suez Canal.

1871 *Poems*

1873 *Emperor and Galilean*

1873 Member of art jury at Universal Exhibition in Vienna.

1874 Visits Norway for the first time since 1864.

1875–8   Munich

1877 *Pillars of Society*

1878–9   Rome

1879 *A Doll's House*

1879–80   Munich

1880–5   Rome

1881 *Ghosts*

1882 *An Enemy of the People*

1884 *The Wild Duck*

1885–91   Munich

1885 Visits Norway for the second time since 1864.

1886 *Rosmersholm*

1888 *The Lady from the Sea*

1890 *Hedda Gabler*

1891–1906   Kristiania

1891 Moves back to Kristiania.

1892 *The Master Builder*

1894 *Little Eyolf*

1896 *John Gabriel Borkman*

1899 *When We Dead Awaken*

1900 First stroke.

1906 (23 May) Ibsen dies.

Introduction

In this book I first explain how Ibsen became a modernist (Parts I and II), and then I analyze the kind of modernism that was uniquely his (Part III). To show that Ibsen actually was a modernist, it has been necessary to expose a theoretical rigidity, uncover a case of historical amnesia, and develop a historically and culturally grounded understanding of Ibsen's aesthetic development.[1]

A theoretical rigidity: The ideology of modernism

I began to write this book because I was struck by the discrepancy between Ibsen's unquestioned status as a classic of the stage and the relative absence of interest in his work among academic critics. Equally striking were the incessant references to Baudelaire, Flaubert, and Manet as the great founders of modernism. Why, I wondered, was Ibsen's name not included? Why would intellectuals and critics ritually refer to modernism in relation to poetry, narrative prose, and painting, but not theater? Was it because of Ibsen? Or because of something to do with theater as an art form? Whatever the reasons, I soon noticed that in Anglophone academic circles the bare mention of Ibsen's name tended to elicit responses marked by boredom, disdain, or condescension. I cannot count the number of times otherwise well-read people have told me that they have never read and never bothered to see any plays by Ibsen, or that they haven't read any since they were students. They do not seem to mind telling me this. In the Anglophone world it is still shameful for a literary critic to reveal that he or she knows nothing about Baudelaire and Flaubert. Why, then, are so many critics convinced that ignorance of Ibsen is just fine?

Although one or two of Ibsen's plays remain required reading in introductory courses on modern theater, they are there mostly as obligatory historical markers, hurdles to be got over as soon as possible, so as to get to the really exciting stuff, whether that is taken to begin with Chekhov, Artaud, and Brecht, or Beckett. This attitude reveals Ibsen's ambiguous status: on the one hand, he represents the unquestioned beginning of modernism in the theater; on the other, there is a widespread feeling that however important he was for the development of modernism, Ibsen himself was not a modernist. Ibsen thus comes to occupy a strangely liminal position as an artist at once essential and irrelevant to the theory and history of modernism. This book begins by exposing the theoretical and aesthetic positions that produce this picture of Ibsen's place in history.

In Chapter 1, I show that the widespread neglect of Ibsen's achievement is caused by the specific set of aesthetic beliefs that rose to dominance in the Western world after 1945. Drawing on Fredric Jameson's work in *A Singular Modernity*, I name these aesthetic assumptions the *ideology of modernism*. The ideology of modernism produces a characteristic theoretical and literary rigidity, most clearly evident in the belief that there is a fundamental opposition between realism and modernism, in which realism figures formally as modernism's abjected other, and historically as modernism's necessary precursor. The effect is to categorize realism as at once formally naïve and historically passé, and in any case as incompatible with modernism, which, in contrast, shines forth as formally self-reflexive and sophisticated, and as historically still relevant. The same theoretical rigidity explains why the ideology of modernism has a great deal of difficulty dealing with theater as an art form.

Chapter 1, then, provides a theoretical analysis of the ideology of modernism, and shows that its fundamental aesthetic categories inevitably construct a picture of Ibsen as a boring old realist, incapable of self-conscious metatheatrical reflection. This picture is simply wrong: if this book shows anything at all, it is that Ibsen's theater offers an unmatched series of superbly sustained metatheatrical reflections. But although he was highly formally self-conscious, Ibsen's modernism was not a formalism. When I go on to establish the key features of Ibsen's modernism in Chapter 6, it becomes clear that his concern with the question of theater, what it can do and what it can be, is only one aspect of his path-breaking theatrical modernism.

A historical amnesia: The forgetting of idealism

The theoretical analysis in Chapter 1 aims to unsettle the belief that there is a fundamental opposition between realism and modernism. Formally, this is easy to do: if realism is taken to mean the "representation of reality", then James Joyce is surely not less realistic than Honoré de Balzac. The historical version of this belief is the idea that realism precedes modernism. To displace this belief, it is necessary to propose an alternative account of the birth of modernism, which is what I set out to do in Chapter 3. Here I show that we (literary critics, literary historians) have suffered from an amazing case of historical amnesia: we have forgotten all about the importance of aesthetic idealism throughout the nineteenth century. To be more specific, literary historians know, of course, that romanticism was idealist and that modernism was not. What we have forgotten is that idealism did not simply die with romanticism, but that it remained a powerful aesthetic norm for most of the nineteenth century, and that weak, degraded forms of idealism lasted until well into the twentieth century. By showing that idealism was a key factor in just about all the aesthetic conflicts that raged in Europe throughout the century, and particularly in the bitter struggles that mark the period after 1870, *Henrik Ibsen and the Birth of Modernism* makes a fundamentally new contribution to the understanding of nineteenth-century literary history.

Most of the numerous nineteenth-century struggles over realism had nothing at all to do with modernism, and everything to do with idealism. On this point, my work draws on the pioneering analysis of Naomi Schor in *George Sand and Idealism*, where she shows that in France in the 1830s idealism and realism, as embodied in the novels by George Sand and Balzac, were taken to be two aesthetic paths leading towards the same idealist goal. Much later in the century, idealist critics would still praise some kinds of realism (for example, Dostoevsky's and Tolstoy's) and pile invectives upon others (for example, Ibsen's and Zola's). Realism, then, is not *one*; to cast something called "realism" as modernism's negative other simply will not do.

Chapter 3 charts the rise and fall of aesthetic idealism, from its exuberant, revolutionary romantic origins, exemplified in Schiller's aesthetics, to its inglorious decline into a conservative moralism, embodied in the decisions of the Nobel Committee of the Swedish Academy in the period before World War I. The chapter has two key arguments: that the works of Henrik Ibsen provide a near-perfect genealogy of the emergence of modernism from the demise of idealism; and that by reintroducing the concept of idealism, we can see that what we usually call modernism is the result of a historical development that only really gathers pace after 1914. To project this relatively narrow notion of modernism back to the last decades of the nineteenth century is both anachronistic and unhelpful.

In this book, I do not set out to provide one, new definition of modernism. Rather, I show that modernism, like realism, is not *one*. In Chapter 3, in particular, I claim that in the period from around 1870 to around 1914 the various kinds of early modernism can be defined only negatively: what they have in common is not what they *are*, but what they are *against*. Since late idealism was a complex and incoherent phenomenon, challenges to it also take many and quite dissimilar forms. (Just think of the differences between Émile Zola and Stéphane Mallarmé, or between Oscar Wilde and Henrik Ibsen, for that matter.) In Chapter 3, then, I show that the end of idealism is the birth of modernism. This is not intended as a definition of modernism, but a foundation for further work on early modernism. My contribution to such a task is to account for the important features of *Ibsen's* modernism. That some of these features will turn out to be quite different from the features privileged by the ideology of modernism is not surprising. (That some of them will turn out to be quite similar to those preferred by the ideology of modernism is not surprising either.)

In this book "idealism" is used as a synonym for "idealist aesthetics" or "aesthetic idealism", understood as the belief that the task of art (poetry, writing, literature, music) is to uplift us, to point the way to the Ideal. Idealists thought that beauty, truth, and goodness were *one*. Artistic beauty thus simply could not be immoral; to call a work ugly—in nineteenth-century Norwegian, the word is often *uskjønt* ("unbeautiful")—was to question its ethics as well as its aesthetics. Idealism thus seamlessly merged aesthetics and ethics, and usually religion too, since most (but not all) ideal-ists also believed that God was the highest incarnation of the trinity of beauty, goodness, and truth. Although it could coexist with certain kinds of realism, idealism required writers and artists to idealize women and sexual-ity. If these things could not be idealized, they had to be demonized. The result was a long line of literary women who sacrifice their life for love, opposed to an equally long line of demonic temptress-figures: the madonna/ whore opposition is everywhere in idealist works. Ibsen's greatest modernist achievement is surely his unique capacity not simply to destroy idealist notions of femininity, but to avoid falling into the opposite trap of demon-izing women and sex (this is what happens to Zola's women, and to most women in modernism, too).

By reintroducing the concept of idealism, we can make sense of the long period in literary and aesthetic history that stretches from the end of roman-ticism as a living artistic movement to the rise of modernism. Much of what is currently lumped together under the general heading of "Victorianism", for example, could be analyzed historically and theoretically as the many-faceted effects of the specifically British appropriation of idealist aesthetics. The concept of idealism is perhaps even more illuminating when it comes to grasping the aesthetically confusing period from 1870 to 1914, which I see as a moment marked by a great number of different, highly self-conscious aesthetic attempts to *negate idealism*. In this respect this period can be understood as what Thomas Kuhn would call a period of *crisis*, a transitional period in which one paradigm has broken down and another has not yet become dominant. Kuhn writes that new theories usually emerge "only after a pronounced failure in the normal problem-solving activity".[2] The aesthetic failure of idealism, its incapacity to deal with modern life and modern problems, became increasingly obvious as the century wore on. For Ibsen, who lived in Germany at the time, the Franco–Prussian War of 1870–1 and the rise and fall of the Paris Commune in the spring of 1871 were events that confirmed the bankruptcy of idealism, occasioning in him an urgent need to forge something new out of the destruction of the old. (For Flaubert and Baudelaire, who lived in a more advanced society, 1848 performed a similar task.) The result was aesthetic crisis and, ultimately, the birth of a new paradigm: modernism.

In Chapter 6, I show that Ibsen's great work of crisis, the work that most profoundly registers the impact of the events of 1870–1 as well as his movement out of idealism, is *Emperor and Galilean*, the remarkable double play written in the immediate aftermath of the fall of the Paris Commune. In my analysis of this play, it emerges that for Ibsen, the negation of idealism leads to skepticism. While Ibsen considers skepticism as perhaps the most important existential and philosophical problem of modern life, he also represents it as death-dealing and destructive, and tries to find non-idealist ways to overcome it. (I shall return to this.)

I speak of the death of idealism. But did it really die? The argument of this book is that some time before World War I, idealism ceased to be artistically respectable even among established arbiters of taste (or, in terms inspired by Pierre Bourdieu: around this time idealism had lost the capacity to bestow cultural and artistic capital on serious artists). This is not to say that the literary establishment turned anti-idealist overnight. Many of the Nobel Prizes in the period from 1914 to 1945 went to latter-day idealists. Various kinds of aesthetic idealism flourished in the twentieth century: religious idealism, socialist realism, certain kinds of fascist aesthetics, and a great deal of popular literature and film. My point in Chapter 3 is simply that every single one of these belated incarnations of idealism was profoundly alien to the ideology of modernism. Thus, the ideology of modernism itself became the greatest promoter of the historical amnesia that has erased the long survival of idealism from literary history. The true aesthetic antithesis of modernism is not realism, but idealism. In all other ways, however, the history of the twentieth-century legacy of aesthetic idealism remains to be written.

A culturally grounded engagement with aesthetics: Biography and painting

In this book I have tried to find a way to understand Ibsen's works that engages with questions of form, style, tone, and aesthetic traditions without neglecting their cultural and historical significance. Works of art are not produced in a cultural vacuum. The fact that some of them transcend their own circumstances and still speak to us does not turn them into eternal expressions of essential humanity: their historicity is part of their continuing appeal to us.

Part I of this book is called "Ibsen's Place in History". In this part, the theoretical opening chapter is followed by three large, cultural, and historical chapters. Chapter 1, the most theoretical chapter of the book, explains how he is currently placed, and analyzes the theoretical positions that have led to the relative downgrading of Ibsen. Chapter 2, the most biographical chapter of the book, begins the analysis of Ibsen and his works by discussing his personal place in culture and history. Chapter 3, the chapter on idealism, makes the case for a new understanding of Ibsen's place in literary history; and Chapter 4 investigates Ibsen's interaction with the visual and theatrical traditions in which he found himself placed. Read as a whole, Part I is an effort to place Ibsen in the European context where he belongs.

In Chapter 2 I ask what it was about Ibsen's trajectory and career that enabled him to revolutionize European theater. This biographical chapter introduces the reader to Ibsen's highly unusual, and highly marginal, cultural position as a white, male, heterosexual writer from a peripheral and under-developed, more or less postcolonial European nation, who chose to live in exile in Italy and Germany for twenty-seven years. The focus of the chapter is on Ibsen's cultural resources, which I bring out by comparing Ibsen to his friends, the radical Danish critic Georg Brandes and the German idealist Paul Heyse, a figure whose power to reveal important aspects of Ibsen's character and work has never before been explored. Since Heyse was an influential idealist, this comparison also helps to prepare the ground for the full-scale investigation of Ibsen and idealism that follows in Chapter 3.

Anyone interested in Ibsen quickly learns that he originally wanted to become a painter, and that he always prided himself on his knowledge and understanding of visual arts. Critics have often referred to Ibsen's visual imagination, yet very little work has actually been done to establish what kind of visual imagination Ibsen is likely to have had. Nor has anyone elucidated the connection between painting, spectacles, and theater in the aesthetic traditions that Ibsen first made his own, and then went on to transform. These are the tasks I have taken on in Chapter 4. "Ibsen's Visual World" begins with Ibsen's experiences as a member of the jury for painting and sculpture at the 1873 Universal Exhibition in Vienna, and continues by comparing Ibsen's taste in the 1870s to that of another early modernist, Henry James. I then briefly discuss the aesthetic theories (of Diderot and Lessing) and the visual technologies and spectacles (panoramas, dioramas, attitudes, *tableaux vivants*, among others) that produced the European visual culture to which Ibsen belonged.

Inspired by *Realizations*, Martin Meisel's impressive study of painting, theater, and narrative in nineteenth-century Europe, Chapter 4 shows how close the relationship between painting and theater was in Ibsen's time, and how many traces of the European tradition in painting one can find in his works. This chapter establishes a number of possible connections between scenes and images in Ibsen's plays and painters from Anne-Louis Girodet to Arnold Böcklin, and, equally importantly, demonstrates that Ibsen's modern breakthrough both illuminates and is illuminated by contemporary painting. Particularly important for this part of the argument is a stunning 1887 canvas by the Scottish painter William Quiller Orchardson entitled *The First Cloud*. The painting has significant modernist features, and strongly parallels some of Ibsen's concerns at the time; yet Orchardson himself appears to have understood it in idealist terms. Orchardson's painting thus helps me to show that in the late nineteenth century, even art that considered itself traditional was beginning to outstrip the available aesthetic discourses. The chapter ends by considering Ibsen's use of visual elements in his satirical treatment of Gregers Werle's idealism in *The Wild Duck*. Ibsen has only to a very limited extent been connected to the broad visual traditions of the nineteenth century, and "Ibsen's Visual World" thus provides new perspectives on his plays.

Becoming modern

Part II is called "Ibsen's Modern Breakthrough", and deals with Ibsen's transition from idealism to modernism. Drawing on the broad historical and aesthetic findings of Part I, I show that right from the start, Ibsen never felt truly at home within the idealist aesthetic tradition, which in Norway in the 1850s was deeply nationalistic and dominated by the visual arts. Although this cultural milieu appears to have been inimical to Ibsen's specific talents, as long as he lived in Norway, he participated fully in its concerns, even writing a poem specially for a *tableau vivant* based on a national romantic painting.

Mid-nineteenth-century Norwegian culture was also deeply hostile to theater. I bring this out by looking at Bjørnstjerne Bjørnson's 1868 novella *The Fisher Maiden* (*Fiskerjenten*), in which Bjørnson (who in 1903 received the Nobel Prize that many thought Ibsen ought to have had) sets out to reconcile religion, nationalism, and theater. A masterpiece of idealist aesthetics, *The Fisher Maiden* reveals the depth of the divide between Bjørnson's sunny idealism and Ibsen's far more fraught struggles with the aesthetic tradition that dominated Norway in his early years.

This chapter traces Ibsen's constant discomfort with the demands of idealist aesthetics, in his early plays *St John's Night*, *Lady Inger*, *The Feast at Solhoug*, and *Love's Comedy*, as well as in the poems "In the Picture Gallery" and "On the Heights". In particular, I draw attention to Ibsen's constant meta-theatrical, or rather meta-aesthetic self-consciousness which, in the eyes of idealists, completely ruined the effect of many of his most promising works, but which today emerges as evidence of his immense artistic hunger for something new. Ibsen created only one undisputed idealist masterpiece: namely, the epic and highly pictorial poem "Terje Vigen" written in 1861–2. In the play published at the same time, *Love's Comedy*, Ibsen finally managed to turn idealism into his subject matter. In so doing, he took a decisive step on the path towards modernism, not least because *Love's Comedy* creates a thoroughly modern and thoroughly fascinating woman in the character of Svanhild.

To write a book on Ibsen, one has to quote him. Throughout this book I mostly use my own translations, which I have made as literal as possible. English-language readers and directors have sometimes found Ibsen's prose plays excruciatingly pedestrian. Like Arthur Miller, they feel that "Ibsen's language, lyrical as it may sound in Scandinavia, does not sing in translation".[3] I can understand this reaction, for translations of Ibsen often do make him sound flat-footed and boring. But this is not always the translator's fault. My own struggles with Ibsen's texts have taught me to respect the difficulties of the Ibsen translator. I have therefore included, as an appendix, a brief discussion of why it is so difficult to translate Ibsen's subtle and dramatic Norwegian into equally subtle and dramatic English.

Chapter 6 focuses on *Emperor and Galilean*, the vast double play about the life and death of Julian the Apostate, the fourth-century Roman emperor killed on the plains of Mesopotamia by a fanatical Christian hell-bent on martyrdom. For me—as for Ibsen himself—this is the pivotal play in Ibsen's production, the play in which he writes his way out of idealism and into modernism. In the same way, Chapter 6 is the pivotal chapter of this book, for this is the chapter in which I first set out the key features of Ibsen's modernism. Although most critics have failed to see why Ibsen always insisted that *Emperor and Galilean* was his *hovedverk* (principal work), I think he was right to do so, for this is the play in which the idealist trinity of truth, beauty, and goodness finally falls apart for Ibsen, and in which a quite modern skepticism carries the day.[4] (Although *Emperor and Galilean* is a fascinating play, it remains one of Ibsen's least read and least performed plays. I therefore include a synopsis as an appendix.)

Emperor and Galilean is a document of the historical moment in which Ibsen came to consciousness of the absolute bankruptcy of idealism, a consciousness which was already pushing its way to the surface in *Brand* and *Peer Gynt*, without reaching the maturity it does in *Emperor and Galilean*. In spite of its radical challenges to idealist aesthetics, however, *Emperor and Galilean* cannot escape idealism's demand for absolute idealization or absolute demonization of women: the play's contrast between the evil and lascivious Helena and the holy and pure Macrina would, unfortunately, shock no idealist. In this play, Ibsen nevertheless engages with the most burning intellectual and existential questions of his time, and above all with questions of faith and skepticism, of the meaning of life in a universe without God. But *Emperor and Galilean* also contains Ibsen's most advanced metatheatrical and meta-aesthetic reflections. This is why I consider this play absolutely central to Ibsen's transition to modernism, in a way that *Brand* and *Peer Gynt* are not.

I bring out the meta-aesthetic and metatheatrical dimensions of *Emperor and Galilean* by comparing the last act of Part I of Ibsen's play to Act 4 of Victor Hugo's breakthrough romantic drama *Hernani*, which Ibsen undoubtedly knew, and by showing that Ibsen's friend in Munich, the painter Eilif Peterssen, does something quite similar in his masterpiece *Christian II signs the Death Warrant of Torben Oxe*. I then go on to show that Part II of *Emperor and Galilean* is a veritable theater laboratory, packed with metatheatrical and meta-aesthetic scenes.

The key features of Ibsen's modernism, then, emerge from my reading of *Emperor and Galilean*. But *Emperor and Galilean* does not complete Ibsen's transition to modernism. At the end of Chapter 6, therefore, I turn briefly to *Pillars of Society*, to show that it provides the remaining features that, when combined, produced the sequence of modernist masterpieces that begins with *A Doll's House* and ends with *The Lady from the Sea*:

—there is a turn to realism and prose
—idealism is ironized or shown to be destructive

—skepticism is a central theme
—the everyday is represented as a possible alternative to skepticism
—theater as an art form is embraced and acknowledged
—antitheatricalism is rejected
—theatricality is criticized
—self-theatricalization in everyday life is a central theme
—love is shown to be destroyed by theatricality and skepticism
—the situation of women is seen as the key social question of modernity
—marriage is a central theme, often used as a figure for the everyday

This skeletal list does not convey the richness of Ibsen's vision of the conditions of modern art and modern life. The number of references to theater and theatricality nevertheless testifies to the depth of Ibsen's meta-aesthetic concerns. The list also conveys the characteristic themes of Ibsen's modernism: the situation of women; the relationship between idealism and skepticism; and the use of marriage as a figure for the ordinary and the everyday; and, not least, the fate of love in an age of skepticism. These, then, are the concerns that come to the fore in the third and last part of this book.

The language I use in this list—skepticism, the everyday, theater, and theatricality—says something about my own intellectual allegiances. My understanding of Ibsen is inspired by the profound and original work of Stanley Cavell, above all by his magnum opus *The Claim of Reason*. My analyses of theater and theatricality are particularly inspired by certain sections of "The Avoidance of Love", Cavell's astounding reading of *King Lear*, and by Michael Fried's epochal study of Diderot's aesthetics in *Absorption and Theatricality*, a book which itself has close affinities with Cavell's essay on *King Lear*. In this respect, much of this book stands as an attempt to develop something one might call an "ordinary language criticism": namely, a way of reading that looks to Cavell and the late Wittgenstein for its understanding of language, rather than to the tradition after Saussure.[5]

Ibsen's modernism: Theater, skepticism, love

By proposing that Ibsen's modernism can be understood as a set of features, I do not mean to say that every single one must be present in every work for the work to count as modernist; nor do all the features need to bear the same weight in every play. In *The Wild Duck*, for example, the situation of women is not the major concern (although it is a concern); and in *Rosmersholm*, the protagonists never manage to find their way back to the everyday. On the other hand, Ibsen's concern with idealism and skepticism, and with theater and theatricality, surfaces in some way in every play I discuss.

In Part III of this book, I read four plays in some detail to bring out the richness and complexity of Ibsen's modernism, to draw attention to his profound understanding of his medium, of the situation of women, and of the difficulty of human relationships in modernity. These plays are *A Doll's House*, *The Wild Duck*, *Rosmersholm*, and *The Lady from the Sea*. In the brief epilogue, I turn to *Hedda Gabler* and *When We Dead Awaken*, principally to trace the fate of idealism in Ibsen's later work, and to show that if *Hedda Gabler* inaugurates a new phase in Ibsen's writing, it is because this play exhibits a significant change in Ibsen's relation to the everyday.

I would have liked to write at length about every single one of Ibsen's contemporary plays, but that would have produced a book at least twice the size of this one. First of all, I decided to discuss Ibsen's plays and other works in chronological order, beginning, in Chapter 5, with some of the early works, and ending in the "Epilogue" with some comments on *When We Dead Awaken*. Even more than most writers, Ibsen had a strong sense of the development and the evolution of his thought. To mark his seventieth birthday in 1898, his collected works were published in Dano-Norwegian for the first time. Ibsen was unusually enthusiastic about the project. Younger readers, he wrote in his preface to the edition, knew his more recent plays far better than the older ones:

This has caused a break in the reader's awareness of the internal connections among the works, and to this break I attribute no small part of the strange, incomplete and misleading interpretations and constructions to which my more recent works have been subjected from many quarters.

Only if one apprehends and understands the totality of my production as one, coherent and continuous whole will one get the intended and appropriate impression of the individual parts.

In short, therefore, my friendly request to my readers is not to put any play aside for a while, not to skip anything just for now, but to take in the works—reading them and experiencing them (*gennemleve dem*)—in the same sequence as I created them.

(15: 381–2)

My choice of plays for detailed, chapter-long commentary has in part been decided by the historical logic of my argument: given the pivotal role it occupies in Ibsen's development towards modernism, *Emperor and Galilean* imposed itself. Having chosen to place *Emperor and Galilean* at the center of my argument, I needed to show how he got there. In Chapter 5, I therefore turn to Ibsen's early works, ending with a discussion of *Love's Comedy*, the most "proto-modernist" of the plays written before *Brand*. Since I consider *A Doll's House* to be Ibsen's first fully modernist play, *A Doll's House* was the obvious starting point for Part III. And since *The Lady from the Sea* answers some of the questions raised in *A Doll's House*, that play seemed to me to be the end of a cycle.

Between *A Doll's House* and *The Lady from the Sea* Ibsen wrote *Ghosts, An Enemy of the People, The Wild Duck*, and *Rosmersholm*. In Chapter 3, I show that *Ghosts* provoked perhaps the final intense flare-up of idealism in Europe. That is one reason why I did not return to it in Part III. The main reason, however, is that in Part III I want to foreground Ibsen's investigations of love. Both *Ghosts* and *An Enemy of the People* contain almost all of the features of Ibsen's modernism that interest me in this book. In particular, they are profoundly meta-aesthetic: *Ghosts* in its explicit thematization of idealism and its fascinating use of the final, theatrical tableau; *An Enemy of the People* in the great metatheatrical Act 4 featuring Dr Stockmann's speech. They are not, however, primarily concerned with love, which is why I decided to leave them out of Part III. Although *Ghosts* is about a miserable marriage, that marriage is never represented onstage. One of the central questions in *Ghosts*: "Was Helene Alving right to leave her depraved husband after barely a year of marriage?" In my view, that question receives a far more subtle treatment in *The Lady from the Sea* than it does in *Ghosts*.

In Chapter 7, I begin to analyze Ibsen's investigations of love by looking at the subtle intermingling of Ibsen's critique of idealism (embodied in the character of Torvald Helmer) and his unmatched understanding of women's situation in marriage and society. I also relate Ibsen's critique of idealism to the reception of the play in Norway and Denmark. My argument in this chapter is both that *A Doll's House* can be read as a rebuff of Hegel's conservative understanding of women's role in marriage and the family, and that in the famous tarantella scene, Ibsen shows us just why theater is the only antidote to theatricality. Reading the tarantella scene in the light of Wittgenstein's famous remark that "The human body is the best picture of the human soul", I show that this scene is revolutionary in its understanding of different ways of looking at a performing woman's body. Above all, however, I read *A Doll's House* as a play that asks what it will take for two modern individuals to build a relationship based on freedom, equality, and love. That question is one Ibsen returns to in many plays, but most intensely in *The Lady from the Sea*.

In Chapter 8, I turn to *The Wild Duck*. As the subtitle indicates, my main concern in this chapter is love and language. No other play by Ibsen gives such a moving account of love denied and rejected. The relationship between Hedvig and her father reminds me of *King Lear*: perhaps *The Wild Duck* is *King Lear* as it would have to be written after 1871. The main argument of the chapter is that Hjalmar Ekdal's theatricality and Gregers Werle's skepticism lead them to use language in ways that erode Hedvig's sense of the meaning of words. In so doing, they ultimately cause her death. I also show that *The Wild Duck* is deeply preoccupied with theater, idealism, skepticism, and the everyday, and wonder why Gina is represented as powerless to defend her daughter against the erosive skepticism of Gregers Werle.

Rosmersholm, the subject of Chapter 9, is Ibsen's darkest play of the period before 1890. Here there is hardly a trace of the redemptive powers of the everyday. All attempts to lead a meaningful public and personal life fail. Ibsen's astounding investigation of Rebecca's and Rosmer's relationship shows that this couple is doomed: mired in skepticism, they can only celebrate an ironic negation of marriage: their destiny is death. *Rosmersholm* is also, on my reading, a thoroughly self-conscious exploration of theater and theatricality. To me, the end of this play is Ibsen's most complex, and most bitter, analysis of idealism, and not, as some critics have claimed, an unbridled celebration of romantic heroism.

The Lady from the Sea rehearses almost all the themes found in *Rosmersholm*, but comes to a very different conclusion. In my view, Ibsen's account of Ellida's and Dr Wangel's conversations is a stunning attempt to ask what it takes to make a modern marriage—understood as a relationship between two equally free human beings—work. In this way, the play sets out to provide an answer to the question on which *A Doll's House* ends: namely, what it takes for a relationship to become a marriage. In order to follow Ibsen's analysis of this question, however, we also need to notice that the play can be read as Ibsen's rebuff to romantic tales of female sacrifice: namely, Richard Wagner's *The Flying Dutchman* and Hans Christian Andersen's "The Little Mermaid". This much underestimated play also intertwines the story of Ellida's achievement of freedom with a fascinating investigation of art, theater, and music, in which the main question is how painting, sculpture, and theater can express what some critics have called the "inner mind". Ultimately, I show, *The Lady from the Sea* is a stunning analysis of the perversion as well as the assertion of freedom and choice.

As I read Ibsen's modernist plays, they tell us that the death of idealism gave free reins to modern skepticism, and that skepticism makes us doubt the power of words. To Ibsen, love is bound up with faith in human language and expression, with our attempts to reveal ourselves to others, our wish to be known and understood by them, and with our wish to know and understand them. To doubt language, as Johannes Rosmer ends up doing, is to exile oneself from human community and from love. In Ibsen's theater the only alternative to love is an unbearable solitude that either destroys us or drives us to madness and melodramatic excess in a desperate attempt to make our existence heard and to have it acknowledged by others.

Ibsen's contemporary plays are concerned with the difficult task of finding a way to honor the dreams of freedom and creativity of revolutionary romanticism while at the same time negating idealist aesthetics. At his most optimistic, Ibsen thinks that our best chance of expressive freedom and of love comes in ordinary human relationships. At his most pessimistic, he shows that precisely those relationships can easily become the source of desperate meaninglessness. At all times, however, Ibsen sees that both the longing for the (romantic) absolute and the disappointed, skeptical recoil from that longing are existentially destructive. *Rosmersholm* in particular is a masterly investigation of the way in which the romantic yearning for full and free expression is thwarted by the equally romantic belief in perfect (wordless) communion between souls. The play implacably demonstrates that idealist notions of love, beauty, and sexuality will destroy human relationships, imprison us in skeptical isolation, and, in the end, make us fit only for death.

In this book, Ibsen's theater ultimately emerges as an exploration of the conditions of love in a world where the most genuine expressions of human feelings increasingly come across as theatrical. How can we love each other in a world where we no longer trust the power of language to convey our meanings, where the search for absolute truth and absolute faith just leads to absolute despair? This is the mature Ibsen's most fundamental question, the one to which his major plays keep returning. It is a question that resonates even more powerfully today than in Ibsen's time. This is why Ibsen's investigations of women, men, and marriage are crucial to our understanding of modernity, and why they still matter intensely.

Part I

Ibsen's Place in History

1

Ibsen and the Ideology of Modernism

Ibsen is the most important playwright writing after Shakespeare. He is the founder of modern theater. His plays are world classics, staged on every continent, and studied in classrooms everywhere. In any given year, there are hundreds of Ibsen productions in the world.[1] A 1998 Bangladeshi adaptation of *Ghosts* directed by Kamaluddin Nilu drew crowds to village squares all over the country. The same year a Hebrew production of *The Lady from the Sea* filled a theater a stone's throw from the Temple Mount in Jerusalem. In 1999 Mitsuya Mori staged a Japanese version of *An Enemy of the People* in the manner of a Kabuki play, while the 2002 Ibsen festival in Oslo presented a production of the same play from Upper Volta.[2]

The stars of film and stage still think of Ibsen's big parts as major challenges and major achievements. In 1998, Ian McKellen spellbound audiences in London and Los Angeles as Dr Stockmann, and the following year Annette Bening played Hedda Gabler to packed houses in Los Angeles. New Yorkers flocked to see Janet McTeer in *A Doll's House* in 1997 and Kate Burton in *Hedda Gabler* in 2001. In London in the summer of 2003, a dedicated Ibsen fan could see Ralph Fiennes in *Brand*, Natasha Richardson in *The Lady from the Sea*, and Patrick Stewart in *The Master Builder* in a single week.

At the same time, however, Ibsen is regularly dismissed, particularly by academics. In 1990, one scholar noted that Ibsen had become "one of the most underread of great writers".[3] For a classic writer of his stature there are remarkably few full-length studies of his work. Significantly, there are absolutely none by the current stars of literary criticism.[4] Outside Norway, no major literary theorist has written at length on Ibsen since Raymond Williams in 1969. The late cultural sociologist Pierre Bourdieu would surely have said that these are signs that in the English-speaking academy today Ibsen does not bestow much distinction on critics who work on him.[5]

Intellectuals started to experience Ibsen's plays as increasingly unexciting, old-fashioned, and boring after World War II. Already in 1945, the great German critic Theodor Adorno registered the change: "No sooner is a name like Ibsen's mentioned, than he and his themes are condemned as old-fashioned and outdated."[6] *Mimesis*, Erich Auerbach's classic study of the representation of reality in European literature, appeared in 1946. It bears out Adorno's perception, for Auerbach gives Ibsen's "naturalism" short shrift. Having helped to renew the theater at the end of the nineteenth century, after 1914 Ibsen became increasingly irrelevant, Auerbach claims. The result is that "we can now better see how calculated and contrived his art often is. . . . It is his misfortune, though perhaps it is also in a small degree due to him, that the bourgeoisie has since changed beyond recognition."[7] The same sentiment prevailed on the other side of the Atlantic. In 1947 Brooks Atkinson, the theater reviewer for *The New York Times*, felt that the end of *John Gabriel Borkman* "does give off a few turgid sentiments that now smack of sophomoric melodrama", and wrote of Borkman's "old-fashioned bombast" in the face of death; and in 1950, Eric Bentley noted that "Today the mention of the Norwegian's name elicits, in many quarters, a certain feeling of tedium".[8]

In 1952, in *Drama from Ibsen to Eliot*, Raymond Williams credited Ibsen with having fashioned naturalist theater out of romantic drama. For Williams, however, both genres were intrinsically mediocre: "Ibsen was a great artist," Williams concluded, "working in a tradition which was acutely inimical to art."[9] In 1969, in *Drama from Ibsen to Brecht*, in which Williams comes across more as a Marxist and less as a New Critic (the shift from Eliot to Brecht says it all), his conclusion was different, but, if anything, even more detrimental to Ibsen's claims to aesthetic relevance and appeal: "As a whole experience [his work] is still very powerful. It is still the crucial action of that movement of liberal tragedy which has been a central experience of modern Western civilization. It belongs to history now, but the actions are still valid, and still hold though they can no longer release the imagination."[10] In other words, while Ibsen's plays remained powerful incarnations of a certain moment in history, by 1969 they were no longer living art, but dead historical monuments.

Artists and writers too registered the climate change. In an essay on Ibsen written in 1956, Mary McCarthy, who reviewed theater in New York for two decades, considered Ibsen to be vastly overrated: "His work, viewed as a whole, seems at once repetitive and inchoate. Twice, in *Hedda Gabler* and *The Wild Duck*, he created a near-masterpiece. The rest of his career appears as a series of false starts and reverses in an interior conversation that keeps lapsing into reverie."[11] For McCarthy, Ibsen's major fault was not his naturalism or his realism, but his exaggerated symbolism and hollow emotional manipulation: "[In the later plays] a kind of corny symbolism replaces the specific fact in the mechanism of the plot—white horses, steeples, trolls, a sailor, a mermaid, and the sea and a ring."[12] All this, McCarthy suggests, amounts to a kind of "bathetic 'studio' art", common in late nineteenth-century writers, who allow themselves to "manipulate their emotions like a stage hand cranking out a snowstorm from a machine containing bits of paper. This effect of false snow falling on a dramatic scene is more noticeable in Ibsen than in any of his great coevals."[13] Ibsen is here accused of being excessively theatrical, and to McCarthy that means false, phony, and inauthentic.

In the theater, the 1950s was the decade of Brecht, Beckett, Ionesco, and the angry young men. It was a decade when theater people on the whole were happy to dismiss Ibsen (Kenneth Tynan was a great exception[14]). Michael Billington, the distinguished theater critic of the British *Guardian*, captures the attitude exactly when he writes of a "caricature idea of [Ibsen's] plays, all too accurately summed up by Tyrone Guthrie in *A Life in the Theatre* (1959): 'High thinking takes place in a world of dark-crimson serge tablecloths with chenille bobbles, black horsehair sofas, wall brackets and huge intellectual women in raincoats and rubbers.' "[15]

Naturalism, realism, romantic drama, melodramatic theatricality: by the 1950s these had become negative aesthetic terms, and they were all applied to Ibsen. In my view, we are seeing here the effects of what Fredric Jameson has called the "ideology of modernism", a set of aesthetic beliefs that became dominant shortly after World War II.[16] If Ibsen is to become alive and challenging again, we need to free ourselves from the effect of this aesthetics. Writing in 2003, Billington is optimistic: "Today a whole host of directors have freed us from the tyranny of furniture and shown us that Ibsen can be spare, ironic, witty and sexy. What also perennially strikes me about Ibsen is his raging modernity."[17] He is right. Ibsen is more modern than ever. To see Ibsen as the fresh, radical, modern playwright he actually is, we need to start by examining the aesthetic ideology that makes him look dead and boring.

Formalism and the Ideology of Modernism

In *A Singular Modernity*, Fredric Jameson defines the ideology of modernism as a set of aesthetic norms that arose as a response to the artistic practices of the Cold War generation of artists and writers. A wide umbrella concept, the ideology of modernism covers some salient aesthetic and theoretical beliefs shared by modernism, postmodernism, and various kinds of avant-gardisms in art, literature, and theory.

In general, the ideology of modernism produces formalist approaches to aesthetic works. I am thinking of the aesthetic canon and the ways of reading texts produced by schools and critics like the American New Critics, Maurice Blanchot, Theodor Adorno, Paul de Man, and deconstruction. Formalists love self-referential complexity, linguistic experimentation, self-deconstructing textuality, and texts that agonize on the limits of the unsayable. According to Jameson, the ideology of modernism has three foundational doctrines. The first and most important is the *autonomy of the aesthetic*. This is supported by two others: *depersonalization* and the *autonomization of language*. Ideologues of modernism are fundamentally concerned with justifying the autonomy of art, philosophically, existentially, and materially. Ultimately, Jameson writes, these efforts are always serving "a more fundamental aim, namely to endow the aesthetic with a transcendental value which is incomparable (and indeed which does not need to be completed with descriptions of the structure of other kinds of experience, social or psychological; which stands on its own and needs no external justification)" (*SM*, 162).

The "autonomy of the aesthetic", however, can be interpreted in two quite different ways (this is my point, not Jameson's). It can mean that art must be free from social, political, and religious pressures, or that art must, fundamentally, take art, not the "reflection" or "representation" of reality, as its subject matter. While the first interpretation is not necessarily culture-phobic, the second is. Because the second interpretation necessarily subsumes the first, ideologues of modernism often think that their preferred, anti-cultural, and self-reflexive formulation is the only one available. Inheriting the romantic (and idealist) desire for the absolute, the "high modernists" of the 1920s and 1930s turned art into the secular equivalent of a religion. As he struggled to write *Nausea*, the young Jean-Paul Sartre still passionately believed that he could be "saved" by literature. "Late modernists" (those who came to writing after 1945) opted for the dialectically opposite solution with the same absolutist fervor: the result was a cult of negativity, absence, and nothingness which nevertheless could only be reached through artistic practices. We find here an obsession with the fundamental failure of language, and a strong disdain for realism, understood simply as the result of a writer's naïve faith in the power of language to represent reality. The doctrine of autonomy is culture-phobic, for however different the various ideologues of modernism otherwise are, they agree that, as Jameson puts it, "the concept of culture is the true enemy of art as such and that if one opens the door to 'culture,' everything currently reviled under the term of cultural studies pours in and leaves pure art and pure literature irredeemably tainted" (*SM*, 177).

The doctrine of *depersonalization* takes a range of forms. Typical themes are impersonality, objectivity, the death of the author, and the decentering or emptying out of subjectivity. The insistence on the *autonomization of language* underpins the taboo on representation, the hatred of realism, the preference for language preoccupied with the unsayable, the unrepresentable, the impossibility of meaning, absolute negativity, and so on. Jameson writes of "the aesthetic foregrounding of a language beyond bourgeois consciousness, a language with the density of an existent, a language that wishes not to mean but to persist on the very limits of meaning, or beyond them" (*SM*, 72). It is easy to see that the doctrines of depersonalization and of the autonomization of language are in the service of the greater project: to reinforce the idea that art is autonomous with respect to everything else, particularly culture. All these values produce a strong predilection for poetry and poetic language, and an outright rejection of realism, which is turned into modernism's negated and abjected other.

As Jameson points out, the ideology of modernism was originally a response to late modernist practices. Its aesthetic values were quickly projected back onto the high modernists, however, and then from there the ideology of modernism went on to engulf the whole literary tradition. The ideologues of modernism thus succeeded in developing a "purely aesthetic or artistic canon", Jameson writes, "[which] on closer inspection, stands revealed as little more than modernism itself" (*SM*, 179). I shall show that this process inevitably leads to the construction of a canon in which theater in general, and Ibsen in particular, will rank low, if they rank at all, but first we need to consider the culturalist response to the ideology of modernism a little more closely.

The Culturalist Failure to Engage with the Aesthetic

Sooner or later someone is bound to ask whether it isn't a little too late to fight the ideology of modernism: Isn't the ideology of modernism *over*? After all, formalism has long been opposed by various trends that I shall broadly call "culturalism". By culturalism, I mean all the various approaches to literature and other cultural objects that reject the autonomy of art in its modernist formulation and stress the cultural, historical, social, and political aspects of aesthetic phenomena, such as Marxism, feminism, new historicism, and

cultural, postcolonial, and queer studies, as they have developed over the
past twenty-five years. All these trends share an insistence on the cultural
situatedness of all human forms of expression, which is entirely alien to the
formalist veneration of art as sacred and transcendental, or as the purest form
of negativity.

It is true that the ideology of modernism has found itself under severe
attack from culturalists for decades. Canon revision, in particular, has been
going on for more than thirty years, and brought about radical changes in
what students read in colleges and universities. We now read more women,
more postcolonial writers, more non-white writers—even, perhaps, more
working-class writers than before. Because the reasons for expanding the
canon have mostly been political and historical, however, culturalism has
failed to challenge the aesthetic doctrines of the ideology of modernism.[18]

To my great disappointment (for my own sympathies, after all, are with
culturalism), when culturalists *read*, they often simply translate formalist
concepts into politicized categories. Culturalist critics of film, theater, and
literature are still obsessed with high modernist and postmodernist themes
such as reflexivity, negativity, absence, the instability of boundaries, and the
breakdown of language. The difference is that theoretical constructs such as
the unsayable are relabeled as femininity, the abject, the marginal, or the
subversive; and textual self-deconstruction is read as a sign of revolutionary
undoing of established norms. When it comes to aesthetic strategies, then,
formalism and culturalism are not as different as they seem. In fact, they are
barely different at all. For how long are formalists and culturalists going to go
on tracking the same old fissures, breaks, and boundaries of signification or
losing themselves in the contemplation of the linguistic beyond?

Beneath contemporary culturalist forms of reading, then, the formalist
paradigm remains intact. This explains why a whole generation of canon
revision has not benefited Ibsen, and why it has not brought greater aesthetic
prestige to twentieth-century writers who fail to live up to the aesthetic
criteria of the ideology of modernism. Obvious examples are Rosamund
Lehmann, Simone de Beauvoir, Jean-Paul Sartre, Iris Murdoch, or, in a completely different vein, Anthony Powell. If we look back to the nineteenth
century, culturalism has done little to reclaim Madame de Staël, George
Sand, or—of course—Henrik Ibsen. If the ideology of modernism had been
entirely dismantled by culturalism, surely such writers would have been
brought in from the cold by now.

Contemporary culturalists do not deliberately promote the aesthetic
doctrines of the ideology of modernism. Instead, they largely leave them
alone, unquestioned and unchallenged. One example of this strategy of

non-engagement can be found in the fascinating and innovative *Modernism/ Modernity*. Founded in 1994, this journal encourages interdisciplinary work, favors history, sociology, and cultural studies, and regularly publishes essays dealing with questions of modernism and race, sexuality, gender, empire, and colonialism. *Modernism/Modernity* is dominated by essays on the social, historical, cultural, and political *circumstances* of modernist art. Nobody could accuse it of willfully upholding the autonomy of art, or of being culture-phobic. Yet, at the same time, it silently accepts the dominant definition of what modernism is, and on the question of who is to count as a modernist, it either toes the formalist line or tacitly abandons all aesthetic criteria of modernism, in order to admit anyone writing in the period of high modernism.[19] In my view, the journal's spirited challenge to the ideology of modernism can be only partly successful as long as it fails to engage with the category of the aesthetic itself. Significantly, I have not noticed any resurgence of interest in Ibsen in the pages of this otherwise innovative journal.

To complete the break with the ideology of modernism, we must insist on the importance of culture. But this is not enough. We also need to confront the ideology of modernism on its own ground: namely, that of aesthetics. We need to historicize aesthetics, to find ways of reading that are consonant with a commitment to a cultural and historical understanding of works of art, which nevertheless engages fully with aesthetic questions.

Realism Despised

The ideology of modernism produces an opposition between realism and modernism understood both as formal aspects of texts and as names for distinct literary and artistic periods. This opposition is fundamentally flawed. First of all, the word realism is often used condescendingly, to refer to a writer's naïve belief in "reference", or in other words, in the power of language to reflect reality. The idea is that the realist writer is too unsophisticated to realize that words never "catch" reality, that there will always be a gap between language and the world that no amount of earnest realistic description will fill. This only demonstrates that the modernist attack on realism is motivated by the need to defend the philosophical skepticism that underpins the ideology of modernism. (If there is no guarantee that language is reliably connected to the world, the skeptic asks, then how can we trust anything put into words?)

It is as if the ideologues of modernism fear that realism, with its faith in the power of language to signify *something*, is fundamentally threatening to their own enterprise. But literary realism does not have a built-in commitment to any particular philosophical position. There are many kinds of realism, and realist illusion can coexist with the deepest skepticism in relation to the power of words to make sense. In fact, such coexistence is a hallmark of many realist or representational texts of the twentieth century, and a crucial feature in works as different as Sartre's *Nausea* and Doris Lessing's *The Golden Notebook*.

It is impossible to banish all forms of reference from language. There is no modernist work, Jameson writes, that doesn't, at the very least, have a "realist core . . . which the various telltale modernist deformations . . . take as their pretext and raw material, and without which their alleged 'obscurity' and 'incomprehensibility' would not be possible. This . . . is the ultimate reason why the work of art and the realm of art itself can never become truly autonomous" (*SM*, 120). James Joyce's *Ulysses* is surely not *less* realistic than Honoré de Balzac's *La Cousine Bette*. Realism, in short, is neither modernism's predecessor nor its negative opposite.

When culturalists write about realism, they usually politicize the formalist critique. To them, realism is not just an example of artistic and philosophical naïvety, it is politically conservative. Here is an example from contemporary theater scholarship:

With Brechtian hindsight we know that realism, more than any other form of theater representation, mystifies the process of theatrical signification. Because it naturalizes the relation between character and actor, setting and world, realism operates in concert with ideology. And because it depends on, insists on a stability of reference, an objective world that is the source and guarantor of knowledge, realism surreptitiously reinforces (even if it argues with) the arrangements of that world.[20]

This passage is a good example of the widespread blend of formalism and culturalism obsessed with the "politics of form". (The philosophical assumptions that underpin such views owe at least as much to Roland Barthes and French poststructuralism as they do to Brecht.)

Positing that a particular literary form—namely, realism—is *intrinsically* reactionary, critics in the grip of this ideology are usually not swayed by evidence of a work's actual political effects. Although the critic I just quoted does admit that rebellious Victorian women both admired and identified with Rebecca West and Hedda Gabler as symbols of freedom and revolt, she nevertheless remains adamant in her refusal to concede that either Ibsen or his contemporary admirers may actually have been politically radical: "If the early texts of realism seem to gender its spectators, dividing men who snigger . . . and fail to understand Ibsen, from women who weep and do understand, realism is just doing its job, mirroring and reproducing society's most conservative ideological positions."[21]

For such critics—and there are many—there can be no difference between the sexual politics of Ibsen and those of Tolstoy, yet what, apart from the year of publication, does *Hedda Gabler* have in common with *The Kreutzer Sonata?* Such a theory of realism is in fact a particularly abstract formalism, which turns realism into an intrinsically reactionary and ahistorical form, thus making us quite unable to explain the difference between Balzac's, Flaubert's, and Zola's realisms.[22]

When we consider that Ibsen has always been associated with modernization, with modern cultural conflicts, and most particularly with the struggle for women's freedom and equality, such blanket denials of the radical potential of realism become incomprehensible. All over Europe in the 1880s and 1890s Ibsen was denounced by moralizing conservatives and championed by socialists and feminists. In China in the 1930s, *A Doll's House* (with Jiang Qing, the actress who was to become Chairman Mao's last wife, taking the part of Nora) was the site of the controversial beginnings of Chinese cultural modernity. General denunciations of realism are singularly unhelpful when it comes to accounting for Ibsen's radical impact in so many different societies.

Another effect of the formalist opposition between realism and modernism is the belief that while modernism is self-referential and formally self-conscious, realism is not. Postulating an untenable contrast between realistic "illusion" or "representation", on the one hand, and self-conscious modernist explorations of the relevant artistic medium (painting, poetry, theater), on the other, this opposition blinds us to what Ibsen is actually doing in his contemporary plays. In a review of three 2004 productions of *A Doll's House*, one self-confident Norwegian theater critic voiced this critical commonplace in exemplary fashion:

There is in these texts little reflection on theater as such and on the fact that the figures in the space are also actors on a stage. The absence of meta-theatrical reflection turns Ibsen into a quite peculiar, and from a theatrical point of view quite boring dramatist, if we disregard his romantic dramas and his touches of symbolism in the 1890s. Meta-theatrical reflection returned already with Chekhov, and since Beckett it has been a precondition for writing for the theater. The theatrical realism, on which Ibsen builds his plays, is a long since past stage in the art of theater.[23]

In this book, I shall show that there is no fundamental opposition between realism and metatheatrical reflection, between theater as illusion and representation, and theater as investigation of theater.[24] This is not an attempt to deny that a number of Ibsen's best plays are realist; it is, rather, an attempt to show that realism is perfectly compatible with aesthetic self-consciousness.

Ever since Diderot, in defiance of the artificiality of classical French tragedy, first wanted to have his actors take tea onstage, the appearance of the ordinary or the everyday has signaled a will to realism in art.[25] In 1959 Tyrone Guthrie condescendingly referred to the "cup-and-saucer school of realism".[26] Hjalmar Ekdal's cold beer and well-buttered sandwiches always annoy ideologues of modernism, who insist on contrasting realism with modernism, and see most realistic details as evidence that Roland Barthes's "reality effect" is at work.[27]

An illusion of reality, however, is not the same thing as a reference to reality, as Ibsen well knew: "The play [*Emperor and Galilean*] is, as you will have noticed, constructed in the most realistic form; the illusion I wanted to produce was that of reality; I wanted the reader to get the impression that what he was reading was something that had really happened" (17: 122).[28] This little passage shows more clearly than many tomes of theory that Ibsen knew that the impression of reality is just one of the many kinds of illusion available to the theater. In *The Wild Duck*, then, the herring salad, and the beer, and the butter are there at once to produce an illusion of reality and to make a meta-aesthetic point: namely, to mark Ibsen's distance from idealist notions of beauty, incarnated in genres such as classical tragedy and high romantic drama *à la* Victor Hugo's *Hernani*.

But there is more. Right from the beginning of his career, Ibsen placed obviously metatheatrical scenes in his plays (in Chapter 5, my first example comes from Ibsen's 1853 play *St John's Night* (*Sancthansnatten*)). Such scenes increase in power and importance in his most realistic phase (I am thinking of the whole last act of *Pillars of Society*, Nora's tarantella, the last scene of *Ghosts*, the loft in *The Wild Duck*, just to mention some of the most obvious cases). Because it believes that "reference" and "representation" are always naïve, the formalist understanding of realism—as widespread among culturalists as it is among formalists—remains blind to the patently obvious aesthetic self-consciousness of so many realist writers.

The Trouble with Theater: Antitheatricality and the Ideology of Modernism

If the ideology of modernism denigrates realism, it is at best ambivalent to the theater as an art form. The usual narratives of modernism start with

Baudelaire, Manet, and Flaubert—that is to say, with poetry, painting, and the novel. The omission is obvious, for where Ibsen's name ought to be, there is nothing.[29] This is symptomatic: most books on modernism do not mention theater at all, and the few that do, rarely mention Ibsen. Instead, they usually start with the little avant-garde theater houses in Berlin and Paris in the 1890s, and forget that precisely those theater houses considered Ibsen one of their own, usually being the first to stage his new plays.[30]

The reason for such silence is, as Michael Fried was the first to see, that modernism is profoundly antitheatrical. "Theater is now the negation of art," Fried declared in "Art and Objecthood", his famous 1967 critique of minimalism.[31] Fried here places the emphasis on "now". By the 1960s, the conflict between modernism and theater had become so intense that Fried was able to come up with a clear diagnosis: "Theater and theatricality are at war today, not simply with modernist painting (or modernist painting and sculpture), but with art as such—and to the extent that the different arts can be described as modernist, with modernist sensibility as such."[32]

By "theater" (or "theatricality") Fried understands art that is produced specifically to impress an audience, art that is, as it were, eager to make a spectacle of itself. "For theater has an audience—it exists for one—in a way that other arts do not; in fact, this more than anything else is what modernist sensibility finds intolerable in theater generally," Fried writes.[33] Within such an aesthetic framework, practically *nothing* presented onstage could ever hope to be "modernist". (That art and theater have not always been considered opposites is Fried's point in his works on art history, which I read as an attempt to establish the genealogy of modernism from the eighteenth century onwards. I return to this in Chapter 4.)

There are a number of reasons why theater usually fails to satisfy the ideologues of modernism. First of all, theater is a public art exposed to social and cultural pressures in a way that poetry is not. Moreover, whatever the bodies onstage do, they remain concrete bodies in space, and as such they can never come across as entirely autonomous of social, cultural, and political reality. Because audience and actors have to share a length of time together, and because the actors have to do *something* during that time, it is also difficult for them to avoid the taint of mimeticism and narrative. In his explanation of why theater has been problematic for modernism, Christopher Innes admirably summarizes the whole problem:

The theatre's intrinsic connection to physical reality and social existence (communicated at a minimum through the bodies of the actors and their relationships to each other) make some of the key modernist principles inapplicable. On the stage, art

could neither assert itself as an autonomous activity, independent of external experience, nor aspire to pure form. In sharp contrast to the modernist drive in poetry or
painting, imitation was always present, being the essential basis of acting. Simply
presenting a sequence of actions in a temporal and spatial frame evoked the "narrative method" that Eliot rejected . . . Abstraction too proved possible to only a very
limited degree.[34]

This is a fascinating passage, for it implies that the ideologues of modernism
have not truly confronted the fundamental questions about what theater is,
and what it can do. This is surely why they fail to find much of value in Ibsen,
for his plays provide a thoughtfulness about theater that is conspicuously
lacking in the ideology of modernism.

Ideologues of modernism hate realism. But they also detest melodrama,
usually because they take it to demonstrate a humanist belief in expression (as
opposed to the approved antihumanist belief in the failure of language),
which can lead to nothing but excessive, histrionic, inauthentic, and—worst
of all—unselfconscious theatricality. Directors in the grip of the ideology of
modernism often persuade themselves that Nora's final slamming of the door
in A Doll's House must be melodramatic. This shows that they have quite the
wrong idea about the artistic potential of melodrama, and also that they fail
to notice that the play ends on a question: namely, Torvald Helmer's
anguished "Det vidunderligste—?" ("The most wonderful thing—?")—
which leaves the audience to ask themselves exactly what it will take to make
a relationship between a man and a woman into something desirable for both
of them.

Confronted with what they consider to be Ibsen's unbearable theatricality,
such directors often choose either to delete or ironically to exaggerate the
ending that Ibsen actually wrote. In December 2002 in Ålborg in Denmark,
Nora left, slammed the door, turned around, and came straight back in.[35] In
November 2002 in Berlin, where the ultramodern stage set was dominated
by a huge aquarium, Nora drew a gun and shot Helmer, who fell into the
aquarium and sank down among the fish. (One reviewer thought that there
might be a Darwinist point to this.[36]) At the end, she remained huddled on
the doorstep, unable either to stay or to leave.[37]

And what about that highly pictorial tableau at the end of Ghosts, where
Oswald has gone mad and Mrs Alving freezes in horror at the thought of
having to kill her only son? Isn't this pure melodrama? Theatricality in the
worst sense of the word? But is it not conceivable that Ibsen actually knew
that he was writing a tableau, and did so for good aesthetic reasons? What
might we find out if we actually stopped to ask what Ibsen thought about the
artistic potential of melodramatic and pictorial modes of expression?

On the one hand, then, the ideology of modernism is profoundly *antitheatricalist*, by which I mean *against theater* as an art form and as an institution. On the other hand, the avant-garde factions of the modernist movement use the word "theatricality" as a term of praise, based on the highly modernist idea that the task of theater is to explore the resources of theater. By "theatricality" they understand something like "self-reflective theater" or "theater constantly aware that it is theater". The constant avant-garde praise of modernist theatricality, then, is simply another version of the belief that playwrights and directors somehow have to choose between realistic illusion and metatheatricality. Needless to say, apostles of modernist theatricality usually detest Ibsen.

In the theater, the sources of such views are to be found in Brecht and Artaud, both of whom used Ibsen as a whipping boy to promote their own projects. It is no coincidence that Fried singled out Brecht and Artaud for praise in 1967 precisely because they tried to *defeat* theater by "establishing a radically different relation to its audience".[38] Artaud's rejection of language in favor of the gesture is pointedly directed against Ibsen and his ilk. "To save theatre I would go as far as abolishing Ibsen," Artaud wrote as early as 1923, "because of all his discussions on philosophical and moral points which don't sufficiently affect, *as far as we are concerned*, the soul of his heroes."[39] Likewise, in an interview given in Copenhagen in 1934, Brecht declared that "Works by such people as Ibsen and Strindberg remain important historical documents, but they no longer move anybody. A modern spectator can't learn anything from them."[40] In general, Brecht presented his "epic" theater as the exact opposite of Ibsen's bourgeois and "dramatic" theater.[41]

For Brecht and Artaud, and for all the critics who have taken their cue from them, Ibsen was bourgeois, he was wordy, he had traditional plots, and his concerns were hopelessly passé. His was the theater of the text, not of the body, a theater which entirely failed to explore the potential of theater as such. Both Artaud and Brecht wanted to foreground their medium, to emphasize that their theater was theater; in contrast, Ibsen appeared to think that he was simply presenting a slice of life onstage. As we have seen, the many derogatory references to Ibsen's realism or naturalism share this view.

When it comes to the theater, then, the ideology of modernism appears to be split between a dominant antitheatrical modernism and a pro-theatrical avant-garde. This is borne out by Martin Puchner's study of the relationship between modernism and theater, which shows that while high modernism resisted theater, the avant-garde, including Brecht and Artaud, embraced it. "Just as contemporary theater studies tends to continue avant-garde theatricalism by virtue of its largely uncritical dedication to the value of theater,"

Puchner writes, "studies on literary modernism tend to perpetuate the modernist anti-theatricalism through an uncritical erasure of the category of theater."[42] This strikes me as entirely true. Late and high modernists neglect theater because it is a public art that simply cannot pretend to be as autonomous of "culture" as the ideology of modernism would like art to be; the avant-garde celebrates theatricality (if not actually existing plays and productions) because they think theatricality means some kind of self-referential exploration of the artistic medium of theater, a theatrical analogue to poetry about poetry. Ibsen, then, suffers a peculiar kind of double erasure, in which the antitheatricalist modernists find him too theatrical, and the pro-theatrical avant-garde does not find him theatrical enough.[43]

Postmodernism does no better than modernism and the avant-garde. I certainly have not found any postmodern celebrations of Ibsen.[44] When it comes to Ibsen, it really does not matter whether one prefers modernism, the avant-garde, or postmodernism. Aesthetically, they are all subsets of the ideology of modernism that exiles Ibsen into its own abjected others—namely, despised categories such as realism, naturalism, melodrama, and romantic drama, or in a different register: narrative, character, plot; or, again: mimesis and representation, or—even worse—expression and communication.

The result is that the high priests of the ideology of modernism do not write about Ibsen. Not so long ago, an extremely distinguished US literary critic told me that he had not read any Ibsen since he was in graduate school in the 1950s. This goes to show that ignorance of Ibsen is no bar to distinction in the US academy. Had the critic said the same thing about Baudelaire or Flaubert, he would simply not *be* so distinguished. For how long are we going to put up with an aesthetic ideology that reveals itself to be incapable of understanding the founding works of modern theater?

A Note on Realism

Before I turn to the way in which the ideologues of modernism read Ibsen, I want to pause to clarify my own view on realism. It should be clear by now that I object to the understanding of realism that emerges from the ideology of modernism. In particular, I object to the idea that realism is a period of aesthetic naïvety preceding modernism, defined formalistically as a highly self-conscious and sophisticated exploration of the relevant artistic medium.

In my view, there are all kinds of realisms: our task as literary critics is to account for their specificity, not to try to demonize them all as naïve "representationalism". (This is why I am not interested in attempts to elaborate general theories of realism.) If we follow Erich Auerbach and define realism as "representation of reality", then it becomes obvious that realism is neither a specific style nor a specific historical period, but rather an aspect or feature of all kinds of texts.[45] Critics have praised Homer's realism, Dante's realism, Racine's realism, and Joyce's and Woolf's realism, too. Even the ideologues of modernism manage to live with the representation of reality—for example, in *Ulysses*—as long as they are convinced that such representations are in the service of the greater goal: the autonomy of art.

Finally, I have been struck by a peculiar trend in mid-twentieth-century Norwegian Ibsen scholarship, arising in reaction to the modernist critique of realism. In his little book *Ibsens realisme* (*Ibsen's Realism*), published in 1957, the leading Ibsen scholar Daniel Haakonsen takes note of the new anti-realistic tendencies in literary scholarship, and admits that they might be quite detrimental to Ibsen's prestige. He worries particularly about the accusation that Ibsen's realism makes him so complicit with the period and the milieus he describes, that once they are no longer historically relevant, then Ibsen will fade into oblivion.[46]

As we have already seen, this was a typical critique of Ibsen at the time. What is fascinating, however, is Haakonsen's mode of defense. Ibsen, he declares, has eternal values. We just need to see beneath the realistic surface of his plays: "On a deeper level, the action has a different, deeper and freer ideality, or constantly tends towards it" (*IR*, 27). Ibsen's heroes, Haakonsen claims, always have an ideal; they aspire towards "a kind of state of perfection" marked by a strong "will to self-sacrifice" (*IR*, 28). This ideal goal is "clear-cut and sublime"; "it lifts itself *above* reality, into daydreams, illusions or a 'pure' spiritual apiration" (*IR*, 28, 33). For this reason, Ibsen has after all created a great dramatic form, a kind of "tragedy of destiny" characterized by the final confrontation between human beings and the "power of destiny itself" (*IR*, 33). Surely, Haakonsen here reinvents idealism as an antidote to realism, thus reenacting a battle fought for most of the nineteenth century (for details, see Chapter 3). Haakonsen's influence on Norwegian Ibsen scholarship was substantial. As a result, in the 1960s and 1970s there developed in Norway a curiously spiritually oriented trend in Ibsen criticism, a trend that sought to protect Ibsen's status as a great writer by stressing the eternal, timeless, and tragic aspects of his work, in an attempt to keep both the realist and the modernist wolves at bay.

Ibsen Read by Ideologues of Modernism

Even on the quickest perusal of the criteria for excellence of the ideology of modernism, it is obvious that Ibsen will be in trouble. His works do not confirm the doctrine of autonomy; on the contrary, he appears to be deeply immersed in "culture", and on the crucial question of the autonomy of art Ibsen is wobbly at best. He is not obsessed by the ultimate impossibility of meaning, and seems, rather, to think of language as expression and act, in a suspiciously non-Saussurean way. Although Ibsen's theater erases the author (no single character ever expresses the author's point of view, and the endings of his plays are usually thoroughly ambiguous), Ibsen does not hesitate to represent real people engaged in ordinary conversations onstage in ways that do not at all seem consonant with the death of the subject. Ibsen's theater is mostly mimetic, and some of his best plays privilege the ordinary and the everyday. Finally, Ibsen clearly believes that theater should be about more than just theater. For all these reasons, in the eyes of the ideologues of modernism, Ibsen comes across as old-fashioned and passé.

Ideologues of modernism who for some reason decide to read Ibsen anyway have only two options. Either they must reject him as unmodernist, as a tedious old representational realist and a purveyor of clunkily contrived plots with a penchant for melodrama, or they must recuperate the founder of modern theater for their own aesthetic ideology. The former is more common in the Anglophone world, the latter has lately become the attitude of choice in Norway.

Although the ideology of modernism came late to Norway, by the 1980s it was beginning to gain hegemony in literary studies, inevitably entering into conflict with the neo-idealist trend. The startling result was that no doctoral thesis was written on Ibsen in Norway for almost twenty years, from the early 1980s until 1998. (Of course, even during this period there was a steady stream of Norwegian books and essays on Ibsen.[47]) Doctoral dissertations are nevertheless a particularly significant barometer of intellectual climate, for they define the emerging trends in a field. It is as if the ideologues of modernism waited to establish themselves as the unchallenged keepers of the Norwegian canon, before turning to the massive task of recuperating Ibsen for their own aesthetic ideals.

The drought ended in January 1998, when Frode Helland defended his monumental thesis *Melankoliens spill* (*The Play of Melancholy*). Helland's brilliant and innovative readings of Ibsen's last four plays turn Ibsen into a nineteenth-century Adorno, a late modernist *avant la lettre*. Central to his argument is the idea that Ibsen himself embraced the autonomy of art. In the four last plays, Helland finds only "radical negativity" and "pervasive irony", which he interprets, with Adorno, as a kind of mourning over the alienation of modernity, in which authenticity has become impossible.[48] Balancing on the edge of silence, Ibsen's last plays barely overcome negativity. Ultimately, however, even in Helland's thoroughgoing cult of negativity, art is the only thing in life that has positive value: "These infinitely negative works of art *are* created, they *are* written, and thus express the defiance of creative productiv- ity."[49] The high modernist cult of art and the late modernist cult of negativity are here seamlessly merged.

Helland's work opened the floodgates. Since 2000 there has been an intense revival of scholarship on Ibsen in Norway. Although I draw on insights from many of these works throughout this book, my purpose here is not to discuss recent Ibsen scholarship in general, but to discuss the ideology of modernism's relationship to Ibsen. Among the most ambitious recent books on Ibsen in Norway, the trend is clear: the aim is to show that Ibsen fits the criteria of the ideology of modernism after all. This usually produces a strong predilection for the last four plays. So far, the high point of this trend has been Atle Kittang's *Ibsens heroisme* (*Ibsen's Heroism*) from 2002, which claims for Ibsen all the key features of the ideology of modernism. For Kittang, *Brand* is the key to what he considers Ibsen's career-long obsession with male heroism. As Ibsen's heroes become increasingly negative, Kittang too finds that Ibsen shares the cult of the autonomy of art and the obsession with the negativity of language and meaning.

If Helland turns Ibsen into Adorno, Kittang transforms him into a mix- ture of Maurice Blanchot and Jacques Derrida. Art is negativity, Kittang writes, yet it is our only hope: "Art—poetry—has 'eternal life' precisely because it does not have life."[50] The power of art in Ibsen is spectral, "as unreal, as negative, as 'extraterritorial' in our actual lives as death", yet immensely attractive—"pure promise of happiness with no guarantee of any- thing but loss".[51] This is Kittang's message, and, according to him, it is Ibsen's too.[52]

Such "late modernist" readings of Ibsen largely obscure his real concerns. I think, for example, that they are entirely wrong in their projection of an almost wholly negative view of the expressive possibilities of language onto Ibsen, and also in their assumption that Ibsen thought that art was the only transcendent value in a meaningless world. In my view, Ibsen's pre- occupation with language as act and expression led him to an impassioned investigation of speakers, listeners, the world they share, and their different attitudes towards language and communication. When he looks at the modern world of words, Ibsen finds a fundamental distrust of language and meaning, a deep-seated skepticism with regard to our possibilities of knowing another human being. Some of his best plays are obsessed with the disastrous consequences that such a failure of human attunement inevitably produces (*The Wild Duck, Rosmersholm, Hedda Gabler*). These plays masterfully explore the isolation, loneliness, and loss of meaning in modernity, yet they are not deaf to the yearning for expressive freedom, and the yearning for human understanding presupposed by that freedom. Ibsen's linguistic modernism, in short, is closer to that of Freud and Wittgenstein than to that of Lacan and Derrida.

The ideology of modernism's insistence that Ibsen's plays must demonstrate a commitment to the transcendence of art erases Ibsen's lifelong ambivalence about the meaning and value of being an artist. Helland, for example, invokes Ibsen's famous defense of *Peer Gynt* against the accusation of a Danish critic called Clemens Petersen, who claimed that *Peer Gynt* was not poetry. Ibsen's outburst came in a letter to Bjørnstjerne Bjørnson written in Rome on 9 December 1867:

My book *is* poetry, and if it isn't, then it shall become so. The concept of poetry shall in our country, in Norway, come to shape itself after the book. There is nothing stable in the world of concepts; Scandinavians in our century are not Greeks. He [Clemens Petersen] says that the Strange Passenger is the concept of dread! If I were standing at the place of execution and could save my life with that explanation, I would never have come up with it; I have never thought of it; I added the scene as a caprice. And isn't Peer Gynt a personality, finished, individualized? *I* know he is. Isn't the mother? . . . To sum it all up: I *don't* want to be an antiquarian or a geographer, I *don't* want to develop my talents for Monradian philosophy [Monrad was the leading Norwegian Hegelian] any further, in short, I really don't want to follow good advice.

(16: 198–9)

Thoroughly provoked by the idea that a character in *Peer Gynt* is no more than a philosophical allegory (in his review, Petersen had explicitly claimed that the Strange Passenger is an allegory of the Kierkegaardian concept of dread (*Angst*)), Ibsen expresses his outrage at the suggestion that his play was not a free, individual expression of his creativity, but a simple illustration of someone else's ideas.[53] Of course, the reaction is entirely typical of Ibsen's reluctance to acknowledge influence by other writers. Because people kept relating him to Kierkegaard, he kept insisting that he had read very little Kierkegaard and understood even less (see 16: 158, 179, 318). Although he may have read more than he lets on, the passion in this denial rings true.

Helland nevertheless take this passage as evidence of Ibsen's (formalist) modernism:

> Already in 1867 Ibsen espoused a specifically modern view of art. He rejects all external criteria for art. The work itself must declare and explain its own status as "Poetry". Normativity is taken to be immanent to the work; the work is its own norm. Not only does he think he has changed the concept of poetry by his work, but he also rejects all considerations external to art: no antiquarian, no geographer, no philosopher.[54]

But it is not obvious that the passage is evidence of Ibsen's faith in the autonomy of art in the orthodox modernist sense that Helland gives to the phrase: namely, as the work's fundamental autonomy from the surrounding world. Ibsen's formulations strike me, above all, as an impassioned defense of his own freedom of expression. They give voice to his romantic conviction that the artist is in some sense chosen, that his vocation and his privilege are to give objective form to feelings and thoughts that the people themselves cannot fully voice. Insofar as the poet is his people's prophet, he is also the sovereign arbiter of his poetry. (In Chapter 5, I show that Ibsen held such views in 1859, and probably continued to hold them as he was writing "Terje Vigen" in 1861–2.)

In his *next* letter to Bjørnson, Ibsen wrote, "Don't misunderstand my remarks in my previous letter so as to believe that I take the nature of poetry to be something different from what Clemens Petersen says it is. On the contrary; I understand and completely agree with him. But I think I have fulfilled the demand, he thinks not" (16: 202).[55] There is no sign here that Ibsen felt himself to be advocating a radically new theory of the autonomy of art. The most striking claim in Petersen's review, in fact, is his repeated insistence that true poetry must express the ideal, and that the reason why neither *Brand* nor *Peer Gynt* is poetry is that the ideal is missing (I discuss this further in Chapter 3). Ibsen's declaration of agreement with Petersen's "demand" makes it look as if he had no quarrel with Petersen's aesthetic idealism, which would make him about as unmodernist as it is possible to be.

But Ibsen's concession to idealism here might not go that deep. First of all, he does not mention the word "ideal" anywhere in his two letters about Petersen, and second, he was writing to Bjørnson, who was known to be a close friend of Petersen, and a card-carrying idealist to boot. As Ibsen was writing his letter in Rome, Bjørnson was in Copenhagen finishing *The Fisher Maiden*, a novella containing an impassioned idealist defense of theater (which I discuss in Chapter 5). Then there is the fact that it was extremely difficult for writers and critics in Scandinavia in the 1860s to talk about aesthetics in anything but an idealist vocabulary. It was not until Georg Brandes held his revolutionary lectures on literature in Copenhagen in 1871, published under the title *Emigrantlitteraturen* (*Emigré Literature*), that Scandinavians started to develop an anti-idealist aesthetic language. Whatever else we want to say about these two letters, I think it is safe to conclude that they do not prove that Ibsen was a formalist modernist *avant la lettre*.

When Ibsen is assimilated to the ideology of modernism, he is misunderstood. When Ibsen is excluded from sustained considerations of modernity in literature, it impoverishes our understanding both of Ibsen and of modernism. His exclusion blinds us to those aspects of modern literature that cannot be subsumed under the ideology of modernism, and leaves us powerless to explain the intense admiration that great modernists such as Rainer Maria Rilke and James Joyce had for Ibsen. We need to start afresh, to reconsider Ibsen's theatrical revolution in terms that made sense to him, not in the anachronistic terms offered by the ideology of modernism.

2

Postcolonial Norway?
Ibsen's Cultural Resources

Ibsen's biographers have been cowed by his self-representation as a man who never read a book, a genius untouched by the artistic and intellectual culture of his time, a writer influenced by nothing and nobody.[1] They have also happily followed Ibsen's lead when it comes to the importance of his nationality. The result is a picture of Ibsen the Norwegian, a natural genius emerging from the wild mountains of his homeland, uninfluenced by European cultural and intellectual life. This picture may have suited Ibsen (it would have protected him against more serious inquiries into his cultural and intellectual allegiances), but it has little to do with the truth. Since there is no intellectual biography that places Ibsen in relation both to the cultural situation in Norway and to the larger European cultural movements of his century, I begin by providing some elements towards a biographical analysis of Ibsen's cultural position.[2] I shall begin by asking what we are to make of his nationality.

In 1886, just after finishing *Rosmersholm*, Ibsen was adamant that his readers simply *had* to know something about the country he came from:

Anyone who wishes to understand me fully must know Norway. The spectacular but severe landscape which people have around them in the north, and the lonely shut-off life—the houses often lie miles from each other—force them not to bother about other people, but only their own concerns, so that they become reflective and serious, they brood and doubt and often despair. In Norway every second man is a philosopher. And those dark winters, with the thick mists outside—ah, they long for the sun![3]

It is true that to know Ibsen, one must know something about Norway. But we should definitely not follow this invitation to look at his relationship to his country through romantic spectacles, to the point of believing that there is a deep, organic connection between Norwegian nature and the Norwegian soul.

For what is Ibsen's picture of Norway? To judge from this statement, he is imagining a country where entirely non-urbanized individuals spend their time brooding in isolation, unable to connect with others, to the point that they start to suffer from a fatal tendency to philosophize. Although this is a brilliant description of some of Ibsen's most challenging characters (Julian in *Emperor and Galilean*, Gregers Werle in *The Wild Duck*, Johannes Rosmer in *Rosmersholm*), it remains a far better account of Ibsen's own innermost tendencies than of the Norwegian soul. Ibsen was indeed a brooding, philosophizing Norwegian, yet he did not grow up in the mountains, but in a small town on the south coast, and however Norwegian he was, he still needed to live in Rome, Dresden, and Munich in order to find his dramatic voice.

According to Ibsen, however, the vast, cold, inhospitable spaces, the looming mountains, the dark valleys, and the general human loneliness produced by the Norwegian landscape form the Norwegian soul. Ibsen here gives voice to a still powerful national myth, for I know highly urban, postmodern Norwegians who believe the same thing. As evidence from the late twentieth century, I submit the opening ceremony of the 1994 Winter Olympics at Lillehammer, crammed with trolls, "nisser" (a kind of leprechaun), and all the other supernatural beings ubiquitous in Norwegian national romantic art, including Ibsen's own early plays.

The idea that there is an ineffable, metaphysical bond between the land and the people, and above all between the land and the artist, was as widespread among the first modernists as it was among the romantics. *Modern Art*, Julius Meier-Graefe's passionately pro-Impressionist manifesto from 1904, for example, is packed with similar ideas. Belgian painters express Belgium. Scandinavians express Scandinavianness. Germans negotiate Germanness. Those who fail to stick to their national spirit are severely chastised: "English Pre-Raphaelitism, posturing before the Italian painters, was a wild aberration."[4] Because of his Italian origins, Dante Gabriel Rossetti nevertheless earns some grudging praise, for his "blood" is assumed to make him more intrinsically sensitive to the Italian mode. Rossetti's wholly British colleagues, on the other hand, are all equally bad, particularly Edward Burne-Jones, who "seldom rises above the art of the typographer".[5]

Such national essentialisms are unhelpful. If Norwegian mountains still loom large in the imagination even of the most determinedly urban Norwegian, it has less to do with Norwegian nature than with Norwegian culture and ideology. The powerful romantic *image* of the Norwegian landscape and the equally powerful belief in its metaphysical connection to the Norwegian soul was crucially important to Ibsen and to everyone else living in Norway in the 1840s and 1850s. At the time, the quest for national autonomy did in fact take the form of a quest for a highly idealized national identity and a veneration of the spontaneous expression of the Norwegian soul. That Ibsen was inspired by these trends is obvious, but to acknowledge that the young Ibsen at times saw himself as a national bard does not oblige us to consider his whole career from that point of view.

Ibsen's life, his trajectory in the world, is relevant to anyone interested in a culturally grounded understanding of his revolution of modern theater, for it anchors him in a specific historical and cultural situation.[6] Without knowing anything about Ibsen's circumstances it is impossible to grasp his cultural specificity. There is a difference between believing in national essences and believing, as I do, that human beings are shaped by their cultural, social, and economic situation, as well as by their individual reactions to that situation. We cannot grasp the significance and shape of Ibsen's life and work without seeing them against a broad, historical, and cultural background. This chapter, then, is intended both as an introduction to Ibsen's life and career, and as an attempt to discover what it might have meant for a writer and dramatist to be born in a small town on the south-east coast of Norway in 1828. My emphasis will therefore be on Ibsen's access to cultural resources. (For a checklist of important dates in Ibsen's life and work, see the brief Ibsen Chronology at the beginning of this book.)

Postcolonial Norway?

The most startling fact about the man who claimed that "Anyone who wishes to understand me fully must know Norway" is that he lived abroad for twenty-seven years and wrote most of his major works outside Norway. There were many reasons for this. Before looking in greater detail at Ibsen's specific trajectory, however, I shall present a few facts about the country he left behind in the early spring of 1864.

Politically, economically, and culturally, mid-nineteenth-century Norway was partly colonial, and partly postcolonial. Politically, it was neither quite dependent nor quite independent. The union between Denmark and Norway had begun in 1380 as a union of two separate kingdoms. The last king of a fully independent Norway died in 1319. The Black Death in 1349 further weakened Norway's position in Scandinavia. In 1536, with the advent of the Reformation, Norway was reduced to being a mere province of Denmark. (The plot of Ibsen's *Lady Inger*, set in 1528, turns precisely on events leading to the final loss of Norwegian self-rule.) Norway remained a part of Denmark until 1814.

The dissolution of the long union was caused, indirectly, by Napoleon. Denmark–Norway had been one of Napoleon's staunchest allies, while Sweden had supported the alliance against Napoleon. After Napoleon's defeat at the Battle of Leipzig in 1813, Sweden declared war against Denmark, and after being soundly defeated, Denmark ceded Norway to Sweden in the Treaty of Kiel, signed in January 1814. In response, the Norwegians, with covert Danish support, convened a Constitutive Assembly at Eidsvoll, which produced a new Constitution and elected a Danish prince as the new king of Norway on 17 May 1814. Norway had become a constitutional monarchy with a one-chamber parliament, the *Storting*. But Norwegian aspirations for independence were almost immediately quashed. In July 1814 Sweden declared war, and after only a few weeks of armed resistance, Norway was forced to enter a union with Sweden, which lasted until 7 June 1905. This time, however, the country was not turned into a province; rather, it was allowed to keep most of its Constitution and its own independent parliament, the *Storting*.

Economically, Norway was less developed than the two other Scandinavian countries, but by the mid-nineteenth century the Norwegian shipping fleet had started to expand rapidly. By 1900, Norway had the second largest merchant navy in the world. In Ibsen's childhood Norway was a largely rural country with extremely bad internal communications. In the 1820s steamships started to travel along the coast, but there were hardly any roads suitable for carriages. In 1800 it took ten days to travel from Christiania to Bergen. If one sent a letter from Christiania to Alta in Finnmark, one would have to wait eighteen weeks for a reply. In the 1830s road building took off, yet Lila Bulyovszky, a Hungarian actress who traveled around Norway in 1864, complained bitterly about the appalling roads.[7] The first railway in Norway was built by a British company in 1854. Norwegian agriculture started to move away from subsistence farming towards a market economy in the 1860s. Although the pace of industrialization increased rapidly after 1860, the industrial breakthrough in Norway did not really happen until after 1905. In short, economic modernization in Norway lagged far behind the leading European nations, and was only starting to gather speed around the time when Ibsen left Norway.[8]

Politically, however, Norway moved more rapidly towards a modern, democratic, and parliamentarian system than many other European countries. By the end of the century it was certainly more democratic than Sweden and Denmark. In 1821, the nobility was abolished. Already in 1837 extensive local self-government was introduced. In June 1884, after a long and extremely bitter struggle culminating in the impeachment of the Prime Minister, a parliamentary system of government was established. (*Rosmersholm* is, among other things, Ibsen's acerbic commentary on Norwegian politics in the wake of this great victory for the Left.) In 1898, universal suffrage for men was introduced, and, finally, in 1913 Norwegian women gained the right to vote.[9]

What makes Norway *look* postcolonial in the mid-nineteenth century, then, is not so much its political and economic situation—although it was not free to conduct its own foreign policy, it was in every other respect a self-governing country—as its striking lack of cultural institutions and resources. With the exception of the University of Christiania, founded in 1811, almost all the cultural institutions of the old kingdom of Denmark–Norway remained in Denmark.

Theater and publishing

Theater, the art that Ibsen was to make his own, was a typical case of under-development. The first permanent theater in Norway, Christiania Theater, was founded in 1827.[10] Outside Christiania, people still had to rely on traveling theater companies from Denmark, which used to tour Norway in the spring and summer. Ibsen might have seen some of their productions in Skien and Grimstad. Isak Dinesen's (Karen Blixen's) fine short story "Tempests" concerns precisely such a company on tour on the south coast of Norway.[11] There were also local dramatic societies in some towns, usually in higher social circles from which Ibsen was excluded.[12]

In a country without permanent theaters, there were naturally few play-wrights. When *Catiline* arrived from the printers in April 1850, it was the first serious play to be published in Norway for seven years.[13] As such, it deserved attention, and it did in fact receive three long, somewhat mixed reviews, which was not bad for Norway in 1850; yet *Catiline* was refused at Christiania Theater, and the book did not sell at all.[14] In his Grimstad isol-ation Ibsen was enthusiastic about the great European revolutionary move-ments. He saw no need to choose a Norwegian hero when a Roman hero had far greater European relevance. But in Christiania, the wake of 1848 had brought an intensification of nationalist fervor. In its belated, romantic way, *Catiline* may have been in touch with Europe, but it was thoroughly out of touch with Norwegian trends. In the first review of an Ibsen play ever written, Paul Botten-Hansen, who was to become a good friend of Ibsen's, complains that the author has "turned away from national matters".[15] Ibsen would not write about a Roman again until 1873, and then he proudly and deliberately gave *Emperor and Galilean* the subtitle "a world-historical play", as if fully to mark his distance from Norway.

The actors at Christiania Theater were Danes and Norwegians speaking Danish. In contrast, the two theaters where Ibsen worked, in Bergen (1851–7) and Christiania (1857–62), were "Norwegian" theaters, started in the 1850s in deliberate opposition to the "Danish" Christiania Theater. Both "Norwegian" theaters had a programmatic commitment to Norwegian pronunciation and Norwegian words onstage. The conflict between the dominant Christiania theater and the nationalist upstarts sparked several intense theater feuds in the 1850s and 1860s, in which Ibsen found himself thoroughly enmeshed. Particularly in his Christiania years, he participated vigorously in newspaper debates about theater. For the next fifteen years, from *The Burial Mound* to *The Pretenders*, with the sole exception of *Love's Comedy*, Ibsen took the subject matter for all his plays from Norwegian history, mythology, and folklore.[16]

For most of the century, the small publishers in Christiania were much less important than those in Copenhagen. When Ibsen published *Catiline* in 1850, the printer was paid by his friend Ole Schulerud. For a Norwegian writer at the time, the sign of success was a Danish publisher. Ibsen did not achieve this until 1866, when *Brand* was published by Frederik Hegel of Den Gyldendalske Boghandel. Hegel was to remain his friend and publisher for the rest of his life. After Hegel's death, Hegel's son continued to publish Ibsen. The rights to the works of the so-called four great Norwegian writers of the nineteenth century—Ibsen, Bjørnstjerne Bjørnson, Alexander Kielland, and Jonas Lie—remained in Danish hands until 1925, when Norwegian Gyldendal was founded.

In the 1850s Norwegian nationalism often merged harmoniously with Scandinavianism, particularly among intellectuals. Ibsen remained a committed Scandinavianist all his life. As opposition to the union with Sweden increased, close cultural ties with Denmark became politically more contentious. In the early 1870s Olaus Fjørtoft (1847–78) called for a struggle against the "two unions", by which he meant the political union with Sweden and the cultural union with Denmark. Fjørtoft, who died far too young, was a kind of utopian socialist, a great defender of the Paris Commune, and a leader in the struggle to develop an authentically Norwegian written language. He has entered literary history because he organized the whistles and catcalls that greeted the opening of Ibsen's comedy *The League of Youth* in

Christiania in October 1869. Fjørtoft and just about everyone else in Norway took Steensgaard, the play's spineless lawyer, to be a transparent caricature of Ibsen's colleague and friend Bjørnstjerne Bjørnson (1832–1910), and therefore a stab in the back of all young radicals in Norway. This goes to show that, regardless of where Ibsen actually lived, Norwegians did what they could to interpret his plays as comments on local circumstances.[17]

According to the Danish Brandes scholar Per Dahl, the "modern breakthrough" created closer cultural connections between the two countries than ever before.[18] According to one account, between 1860 and 1890 sixty Norwegian authors published books in Denmark.[19] The increase in numbers testifies at once to Danish cultural power and the increasing influence of Norwegian literature, for the last third of the nineteenth century was a golden age for Norwegian literature, a time when Ibsen, Bjørnson, Alexander Kielland, Jonas Lie, Arne Garborg, and Amalie Skram were producing their best work. By 1905, however, this era was drawing to a close. In the twentieth century no Norwegian writer could conquer Kristiania (let alone Oslo) by conquering Copenhagen first.

Art and Nationalism

In early nineteenth-century Norway, art and artistic institutions were, if possible, even less developed than the theater. When Ibsen was born, there was no art gallery and no art academy in the country. A drawing school was set up in the capital in 1818, the same year as the first art exhibition in Norwegian history was held there. This, I should add, was not an exhibition of new works, but of paintings lent by private citizens.[20]

The absence of museums and galleries gave Norwegians few opportunities to see the works of their own painters. The landscape painter J. C. Dahl (1788–1857), a fisherman's son from Bergen, was by far the most famous Norwegian artist of the first half of the century; yet by the mid-1830s his paintings were still generally unavailable in Norway. Dahl, a close friend of Caspar David Friedrich (1774–1840), was educated in Copenhagen, and had been a professor at the Art Academy in Dresden since 1824.

Such cultural poverty was deplored by the generation of young, nationalist Norwegians who came of age around 1830. In Andreas Munch's (1811–84) first collection of poetry, *Ephemerer* (1836), there is a sequence of poems entitled "Min første Reise" ("My first voyage"), dealing with his trip by boat from Christiania to Copenhagen and his experiences in the Danish capital.

The first stanza of an impassioned poem entitled "Ved et Maleri af Dahl" ("At a painting by Dahl") registers the poet's joy at recognizing a landscape from his homeland, and concludes, "Saadant maler kun en Norges Søn" ("Only a son of Norway paints such things"). The next stanza continues on a bitter note:

> Og i danske Sale skal jeg søge
> Disse Farver? Mellem danske Bøge
> Hængte man en Mindekrands for *Ham*,
> Medens Norge paa hver Stilling veier,
> Af sin egen Kunstner Intet eier,
> Intet, uden Mindet om sin Skam![21]

(And in Danish halls am I to seek / These colors? Among Danish beech-trees / A laurel wreath was hung for *Him* / While Norway debates every position / Owns nothing of her own artist / Nothing except the memory of its shame!)

The reference to Denmark's honoring of Dahl may have to do with the fact that in 1828 Dahl was offered a professorship at the Academy in Copenhagen, which he turned down.[22] I take it that Munch's reference to Norway "debat-[ing] every position" means that the Norwegian *Storting* had not offered Dahl a salaried position.

Belonging to the high romantic generation of Wergeland and Welhaven (and Turgenev, Bakunin, and Marx), Munch went on to have a successful career as a poet, playwright, and novelist. By 1860 he, not Bjørnson or Ibsen, was the best known and most widely respected writer in Norway.[23] In 1860, when Ibsen was hitting economic rock bottom, Munch was the first writer to receive an annual stipend from the Norwegian parliament.[24] Both Ibsen and Brandes, incidentally, saw and reviewed one of Munch's most important plays, the historical tragedy *Lord William Russell* (1857), a completely idealist concoction full of perfect aristocratic nobility, evil treachery, and female self-sacrifice.[25]

Andreas Munch's poetic outburst on behalf of Dahl obviously expressed a significant cultural concern, for that same year the Norwegian parliament decided that art had to be bought for a national gallery. Unlike most other European national galleries, the Norwegian one had no existing royal collection to build on: in 1836, the nation did not own a single painting. When Nasjonalgalleriet (The National Gallery) opened in Christiania in January 1842, it boasted seventy-two paintings and two busts exhibited in "three small rooms in the Royal Castle".[26]

The year 1836 was also when the Christiania Art Society was founded (the first thing it did was to buy a painting by Dahl).[27] To celebrate the event, the leading poet Johan Sebastian Welhaven wrote "En Tribut til Kunstforeningen" ("A Tribute to the Art Society"). Connecting art, nature, and national identity in a way typical of Norwegian culture in the 1830s and 1840s, he stresses the importance of art for a new nation:

> I Fjeldet boer vor Kunst og Poesi;
> den drømmer der endnu i Landets Bringe,
> der har den viist os Glimtet af sin Vinge
> i Dalens Sagn, i Dalens Melodi.
> Men for det unge, nylig vakte Folk
> den trænger til en Leder, til en Tolk,
> der i Naturens haardeste Forstening
> har fattet denne himmelbaarne Gnist,
> der klarer sig, og hæver sig tilsidst,
> og giver Formerne en aandig Mening.[28]

(In the mountains lives our art, our poetry; / there in the country's heart it still dreams, / there it has shown us a glimpse of its wings / in the valley's tales, in the valley's melody. / But for a young, / newly awakened people / art requires a leader, an interpreter, / who in nature's hardest stone / has grasped the heaven-born spark, / which, ever brighter, finally rises / to endow forms with spiritual meaning.)

Giving voice to the romantic theory of the artist as the God-given interpreter of the people's soul, Welhaven insists that a true national artist must find his inspiration in Norwegian nature. The transition from the plural "Kunst og Poesi" ("art and poetry") at the end of the first line, to the singular pronoun "den" ("it") at the beginning of the second line is particularly striking. The effect is strongly to stress the romantic belief in the unity of the arts: ultimately, painting is poetry, poetry is painting. Welhaven also singles out Dahl as the artist who most fully expresses the Norwegian soul:

> Saaledes digter dig vor gjæve *Dahl*
> en sjælfuld Stæmning i Naturens Skifter;
> i Himlens Smiil, i Uveirskyens Rifter,
> han maler kjækt din Glæde og din Kval.
> Saaledes adler dig den gyldne Kunst
> de dunkle Timer af din travle Vandring,
> og fanger Øieblikkets korte Gunst,
> og redder den i Tidernes Forandring.[29]

(Thus for you our noble *Dahl* creates / a soulful mood in nature's transformations; / in heaven's smile, in the storm cloud's breaks / he bravely paints your joy and your agony. / Thus for you the golden art ennobles / the dark hours of your busy wandering, / catching the brief bliss of the moment / saving it from time's changes.)

The bard of his nation, Dahl was entrusted with the mission of interpreting the inchoate yearnings of the people, comforting and upholding its spirit in times of trouble. As we shall see in Chapter 5, in the early 1850s, Ibsen was evidently inspired by Dahl and the artistic nationalism he represented (and also by Munch and Welhaven's way of praising him). In 1841, Dahl set forth his artistic principles in a letter to his Bergen protector and friend, Lyder Sagen:

A landscape must not just transport us to a particular country or region, but contain the characteristic aspects of this country and its nature; it must speak to the sensitive beholder in a poetic way; it must in addition so to speak tell him about the country's nature, its ways of building, its people and customs, now idyllic, now historical-melancholic—what they were and what they are, if I may put it that way. This is unfortunately what I so often miss in the otherwise quite good landscapes that are being produced in Norway—they do not sufficiently breathe Norwegian particularity.[30]

1. J. C. Dahl, *Winter at the Sognefjord*, 1827. Photo by J. Lathion: © The National Museum of Art, Architecture and Design, Oslo.

Embodying a "historic-melancholic" and "poetic" approach to the past and present of the Norwegian people, *Winter by the Sognefjord* (1827) exemplifies Dahl's aesthetic position (Fig. 1). The painting depicts the view across the fiord towards Fimreite, the scene of a famous 1184 battle in which King Sverre defeated his rival Magnus Erlingssøn. The landscape, which Dahl saw in the summer of 1826, is covered by snow, and the painting is dominated by a "bauta", a Viking memorial stone, in the foreground. Permeated by a melancholic sense of past greatness and contemporary desolation, the painting also conveys present natural grandeur. It is as if Dahl urges Norwegians to go on to produce new heroic deeds in remembrance of their past greatness. Ibsen's *The Vikings at Helgeland* (1857) certainly follows in Dahl's footsteps.

In 1836, when so many poets and politicians fueled a public debate about the importance of visual arts for the young nation, Ibsen was eight years old. Perhaps all the attention given to the arts inspired his ambition to become a painter. He certainly was taking painting lessons already as a boy in Skien. His first teacher was Mikkel Mandt (1822–82), who taught him basic oil painting techniques. Mandt himself went on to study with Johannes Flintoe in 1842, and in 1843 he became Adolph Tidemand's first student in Christiania. In 1847–8 Mandt studied in Düsseldorf. He specialized in portraits, and is said to have assisted Tidemand on *Haugianerne*. In the end, Mandt gave up painting in order to become sheriff of his home county in the south of Norway, not far from Skien.

Around 1850, when he arrived in Christiania, Ibsen still had thoughts of becoming a painter. But at that time an ambitious artist had to leave Norway to get serious art training, and Ibsen had no money. The revered Dahl had gone to Copenhagen in 1811, and Dresden in 1818, but by the 1840s, Norwegian painters preferred Düsseldorf. In the 1870s they went to Munich, where Ibsen met and became friendly with many of them, and in the 1880s and 1890s, they would seek out Paris, and so, eventually, impressionism and other modern forms.

When Ibsen lived in Bergen (1851–7), he painted quite a lot, and also made costume sketches for some of the productions he directed, including some for his own plays.[31] In this period, Ibsen took lessons from Johan Ludvig Losting (1810–76), a painter and photographer who painted stage sets for the theater in Bergen in its early years, and worked as a drawer and lithographer, in addition to running a shop where he sold art supplies, a versatility which brings the painter, hairdresser, brass band leader, and tourist guide Ballested in *The Lady from the Sea* to mind. All that is left of Losting's paintings today are some neoclassical landscapes.

In his second period in Christiania (1857–64), Ibsen took lessons from the landscape painter Magnus Thulstrup Bagge (1825–94). Bagge has been said to be a source of inspiration for the character of Hjalmar Ekdal in *The Wild Duck*, but this is by no means certain.[32] Of Ibsen's three art teachers, Bagge was the most talented and had the best education. He studied at the academy in Copenhagen from 1844 to 1847, and then, in the early 1850s, with August Leu at the academy in Düsseldorf. One of Bagge's finest paintings, *Labrofossen* (1847), now hangs in the National Museum of Art in Oslo.

In the late 1850s, when Ibsen's career was going particularly badly, he fantasized about giving up the theater in order to become a professional painter. Ibsen's daughter-in-law, Bergliot (*née* Bjørnson), writes, "It is no secret that he wanted to be a painter, but few people know that it cost Mrs. Ibsen many efforts to get him to give it up. Indeed, she herself says that 'I actually had to struggle with him.' "[33] Fru Suzannah was right to advise Ibsen to stay away from painting. His own paintings, now readily available on the web, don't show any spectacular talent. Ibsen nevertheless had some experience as an artist, for in 1851 he probably produced the illustrations for a short-lived magazine called *Andhrimner*. As Erik Henning Edvardsen has pointed out, if this is true, then Ibsen is the very first Norwegian magazine illustrator.[34]

Norway and Ibsen: Religion, Race, and Sex

It may be tempting to classify Ibsen as a "white, male, bourgeois" writer, and move on. To do so, however, would be to eradicate Ibsen's specificity. Undoubtedly, Ibsen was a white man in a white man's world, and nineteenth-century Norway was surely as racist as other European countries, and certainly more xenophobic. In the otherwise relatively liberal 1814 Constitution, for example, Jews, Jesuits, and all monastic orders were explicitly excluded from the realm. The original §2 of the Norwegian Constitution reads, "The evangelical-Lutheran religion remains the official religion of the state. The inhabitants who profess it, have a duty to raise their children in the same. Jesuits and monastic orders must not be tolerated. Jews still remain excluded from access to the realm."[35] Spearheaded by the poet Henrik Wergeland, opposition to the infamous "Jewish paragraph" first became vocal in the early 1830s, but it took four attempts before the *Storting* finally, in 1851, managed to muster the two-thirds majority required to change the Constitution. Monastic orders were allowed in 1897. As for the Jesuits, they remained constitutionally banned from Norwegian soil until 1956.

Nineteenth-century Norway was ethnically quite homogeneous. The exceptions to this rule were the nomadic Lapps (Sámi), and the relatively recently arrived Finns in the far north. Like other Scandinavian writers, Ibsen has a tendency to make the far north of Norway the location of the supernatural, of monsters and ghosts. The uncanny Irene in *When We Dead Awaken* is said to speak "pure, good Norwegian. Perhaps with the faintest trace of a northern accent" (13: 226). Rebecca West in *Rosmersholm* comes from Finnmark (the northernmost region of Norway on the Russian border, and north of Finland), and the Stranger in *The Lady from the Sea* is explicitly said to be a *kvæn*—that is to say, not a Lapp, but an immigrant to Finnmark from Finland (11: 88). In popular Norwegian ideology, *kven* and sami people were supposed to be particularly skilled in witchcraft and magic.[36]

There have been Romani travelers (gypsies) in Norway since the sixteenth century. In *Brand*, the first play Ibsen wrote in Italy, they have prominent roles. The wild mountain girl, Gerd, who dies with Brand, is a *tater* (gypsy), and Agnes dies of grief after Brand forces her to give all her treasured baby clothes, the only things she has left after the death of her baby son, to a gypsy woman. In both *Brand* and *Peer Gynt*, moreover, we hear about an ethnic Norwegian, a young man from the local village, who marries a gypsy, and follows her on her travels. In *Brand*, the young man in question is the rejected suitor of Brand's money-grabbing mother, and Gerd is their daughter. Gerd and Brand, then, are symbolic siblings, and in the final scene of the play, they share the same position as outcasts enamored of shining utopian visions, equally unfit to live in a society that has no place for people like them.

With the exception of his two Roman plays, *Catiline* and *Emperor and Galilean*, Ibsen's plays conjure up a thoroughly Norwegian world in which there are more supernatural beings than foreigners, for in the early plays as well as in *Peer Gynt*, we encounter a great many trolls, fairies, "nisser", and other magic creatures. The most flamboyantly foreign moment in all of Ibsen is the fourth act of *Peer Gynt* (written before Ibsen himself went to Egypt in 1869 to be present at the opening of the Suez Canal), where Peer rubs shoulders with representatives of modern imperialism, colonialism, and capitalism, as well as with modern Egyptians.[37] There are also some Scandinavians here and there, notably the Swedish capitalist Trumpeterstraale in *Peer Gynt* and the Danish painter and jack-of-all-trades Ballested in *The Lady from the Sea*, who has lived in Norway for many years. The outrageously sexy Fanny Wilton in *John Gabriel Borkman* has a British name, but nothing in the text indicates that she is anything but Norwegian. In this case, her name appears to mark her affinities with the great world outside Norway, rather than with any specific nationality.

Ibsen's sex was certainly essential to his career. Had Ibsen been born a woman, he would never have become a writer.[38] This is not just a general platitude, for in 1846, at the age of 18, Ibsen fathered a son, Hans Jacob Henriksen Birkedalen, born on 9 October 1846 to Else Sophie Jensdatter Birkedalen, a servant at the pharmacy in Grimstad where Ibsen was working as an assistant, and ten years his senior.[39] (Curiously enough, the name Birkedalen returns in Ibsen's play *St John's Night* as the name of a disputed farm that turns out to belong to the hero Birk, himself originally called Birkedalen.)

For a young, penniless woman, the birth of an illegitimate child would have meant the end of any hopes of an education, let alone of any chance to write. For a young man with no money, it meant a burdensome struggle to pay child support for a son he probably never met.[40] In this respect, Ibsen's career is the perfect contrast to that of Shakespeare's sister, as Virginia Woolf imagined her to be: a young girl, in every respect as talented and as eager to work in the theater as her brother, but who, thwarted by her sex, finally "found herself with child [and] killed herself one winter's night and lies buried at some cross-roads where the omnibuses now stop outside the Elephant and Castle".[41] I like to think (but there is of course no evidence for this) that Ibsen's astonishingly radical analysis of women's situation, his respect for women's independence, and his belief in their talents as thinkers and writers are tacit acknowledgments that he, even more than most men, owed his career to his sex.

Money

Ibsen is often called "bourgeois". The conventional image of the nineteenth-century bourgeois writer is that of a comfortably well-off man, living in or within easy reach of one of the great cultural capitals of Europe, writing in a major language (English, French, or German), and with ready access to all the resources of European culture. This image is disturbed but not displaced by the undeniable importance of Russian and Scandinavian writers to European culture in this century. In Ibsen's case there is also the image of the famous writer approaching the end of his illustrious career, someone like the man painted in 1895 by Erik Werenskiold (Fig. 2). The impression given by this painting is of Ibsen as a sharp-eyed cultural icon, a man who surely is comfortably settled in his own apartment in the capital of his country, financially cushioned by safe investments, a man who loved official honors, particularly if they were bestowed by the hands of royalty, and who did not shrink from soliciting them himself.[42]

Werenskiold's image does convey something important about Ibsen in 1895. But it does not even begin to capture the trajectory of the person called Henrik Johan Ibsen who started life on 20 March 1828 in Skien, a small port town on the south-east coast of Norway. Ibsen's mother, Marichen Altenburg, was of a good Skien family. His father, Knud Ibsen, was for a while a rich and respected merchant in the town. The very names Altenburg and Ibsen indicate their bourgeois status. To a Norwegian, it is striking how many of Ibsen's

2. Erik Werenskiold, *Portrait of the Poet Henrik Ibsen*, 1895. © DACS 2005. Photo by J. Lathion: © The National Museum of Art, Architecture and Design, Oslo.

protagonists have such upper-class, mostly German- or Danish-sounding names: Lone Hessel, Nora Helmer, Johannes Rosmer, Rebecca West, Hedda Gabler, Arnold Rubek, often contrasted with lower-class Norwegian names: Mrs Helmer is blackmailed by Mr Krogstad, Dr Stockmann is opposed by the printer Aslaksen, John Gabriel Borkman's foil is Vilhelm Foldal. The obvious exception is the master builder Halvard Solness, whose name reveals his status as a self-made man.

When the little Henrik Johan was 6, his father lost all his money, and in 1835 the Ibsen family had to move to a small farm outside town. Later, they also had to leave the farm. Ibsen, then, is a quintessential *déclassé*. For the next thirty years he had very little money. He had terrible trouble scraping together the child support for his son. Per Kristian Heggelund Dahl has discovered a touching letter from Ibsen dated 7 December 1846 addressed to *byfogd* (town judge) Preus in Grimstad, whose task it was to determine exactly how much Ibsen would have to pay in child support for the next fifteen years: "I am now in my twentieth year; I own absolutely nothing, except some shabby clothes, shoes and linen, and will shortly leave the Grimstad pharmacy where I have lived as an apprentice, that is to say without any other pay than my food and the previously mentioned necessities, since the summer of 1843."[43] Ibsen finally left Grimstad for Christiania in 1850. In 1851 he moved to Bergen, returning to Christiania in 1857. In 1858 he married Suzannah Daae Thoresen, in 1859 their only son Sigurd was born, and in 1864 the Ibsen family settled in Rome.

Ibsen's second stay in Christiania was marked by severe financial difficulties. Dahl has shown that in this period Ibsen was sued for debts no fewer than thirteen times (ten times in 1861 alone), at times barely escaping the usual punishment for debtors: namely, hard labor.[44] Increasingly alcoholic, he was sometimes seen drunk in the streets. Francis Bull writes that in 1864 the Christiania bourgeoisie was asked to contribute money so that the "drunken poet Henrik Ibsen" could go abroad.[45] The Ibsen family kept moving to ever cheaper and shabbier lodgings in ever worse locations, before they finally left for Rome early in 1864. The trip was financed by a government grant and by contributions from friends and supporters, organized, among others, by Ibsen's colleague and friend Bjørnstjerne Bjørnson.[46] But on 2 June 1864, only a few months after Ibsen's departure, all the furniture and other personal belongings he had stored in the attic of Christiania Theater were sold at an auction that failed to raise enough money to cover all his debts.

Ibsen knew nothing about this humiliating auction until 1866, when Bjørnson mentioned it in a letter, to which Ibsen replied, "I haven't cried over the loss of furniture and that sort of thing, but to know that my private letters, papers, drafts etc. are in the hands of just anyone is to the highest degree annoying to me" (16: 169).[47] Ibsen kept paying off his Norwegian debts for many years. He waited until 1885 before he risked buying furniture again. For the rest of his life Ibsen was extremely careful with money, and did his utmost to procure financial security for himself and his family.

Education

Social class is not just a matter of money. Culture and education are equally strong class markers. In Skien Ibsen got a rudimentary education, but his father could not afford to send him to a secondary school to prepare for university entrance. When Ibsen was a child, the population of Skien was about 2,000. Skien may have been a small town on the periphery of Europe, but it was not a closed-off, isolated community. The town had a lively commercial and economic life, fueled by lumber export. Over thirty ships were registered in Skien, ensuring its connections with the world.[48] Like the town in *Pillars of Society* where American ships are frequently docked in the harbor, but where people associated with the theater, let alone with the circus, are considered beyond the pale of respectable society, Skien must have been torn by the tension between deep-rooted suspicion of strangers and wild dreams of freedom in the great world outside Norway.

Ibsen, then, was not allowed to continue his education beyond the age of 15. This must have been a bitter disappointment to him, for he had ambitions to study at the University of Christiania. Instead, he was sent to work as a pharmacist's trainee in Grimstad, where he probably arrived in November 1843.[49] At the time the only regular communications between Skien and Grimstad were by boat. It is no coincidence that consul Bernick in *Pillars of Society* wants to construct a railway branch in order to improve the economic life of his home town.

With a population of only 800, Grimstad was much smaller than Skien, and dominated by a tiny coterie of ship-owning bourgeoisie, into whose circles the lowly pharmacist's assistant was never admitted.[50] The "pharmacist's boy" was badly lodged, badly fed, and not paid at all. For the first few years in Grimstad, Ibsen had no friends. He spent his spare time, such as it was, reading, painting, and writing, mostly at night. Many years later, Ibsen remarked that this was surely the unconscious reason why almost the whole of *Catiline* is set at night (1: 121).

In 1847 Ibsen's circumstances improved a little. He passed the exam to become a qualified pharmacist's assistant, the pharmacy was sold and moved to new premises, and as a result Ibsen got a better room in a better house. Above all, he acquired two friends, Christopher Due and Ole Schulerud. In this period we know that Ibsen read voraciously, that he was passionately interested in Voltaire, and that, like another literary pharmacist, Flaubert's Homais, he spent much time railing against Christianity.[51]

In the year of revolution 1848 Ibsen was enflamed with enthusiasm. In his scant spare time, he had been studying the Latin syllabus for the university entrance exams with a local clergyman, and here he encountered Sallust's account of the conspiracy of Catiline and Cicero's speeches against the rebel. The result was his first play, finished in Grimstad in 1849. As Halvdan Koht points out, *Catiline* shows how deeply inspired Ibsen was by revolutionary romanticism: "The whole play lives in the air produced by revolutionary romanticism from Schiller and Goethe to Victor Hugo, Lord Byron and Henrik Wergeland."[52]

In April 1850, at the age of 22, Ibsen finally managed to leave Grimstad. On his way to Christiania, he stopped in Skien. This was to be his last visit to his home town, and Ibsen never tried to see his family again. In 1850, the population of Norway was around 1.5 million.[53] Although the capital was growing fast, it was not exactly a metropolis; in 1845 it had a population of around 32,000.[54] In 1888, Ibsen's first biographer, Henrik Jæger, described the Norwegian capital as a cold-hearted provincial hellhole, inimical to art and artists:

Surely many things can be said in praise of the Norwegian capital; but nobody in their right mind would call it a town where art and literature thrive. With almost American speed it has grown from being a small town of 10,000 inhabitants at the beginning of the century to a city that already has exceeded the first hundred thousand inhabitants and is well on its way to the second. . . .

Kristiania is a settler's colony which pretends to be a cultural center. The conditions have improved to the point that people go around and claim to be a part of Europe, yet at the same time the place is so small that there is no elbow room. . . . Gossip and personal criticism flourish to an unbelievable degree. . . . And just as people are eager to drag others down, they are reluctant to acclaim them. In greater societies, where there is more room, there are also more generous hearts; there the acclaim of one does not prevent the acclaim of another. . . . And people are as harsh in their judgments as they are lacking in independence. They always wait to follow the latest slogan from outside. Still today, the writer who wants to conquer Kristiania has to start by conquering Copenhagen.

Of course such circumstances inhibit artistic and literary productivity. Faced with the indifference and lack of interest that they encounter everywhere, many tire and weaken. They lose their energy and courage, and give the whole thing up. Others become bitter and dissatisfied, and express their bitterness. Were one to collect all the attacks on Kristiania in the literature of this century, it would produce quite a fine little anthology.[55]

When Ibsen arrived in Christiania at the end of April 1850, he immediately joined the so-called Heltberg's student factory, a school where promising but penniless young men from the provinces came to cram for the university entrance exams. Many other literary giants of the Norwegian nineteenth century, such as A. O. Vinje and Bjørnstjerne Bjørnson, attended this famous crammer. In August Ibsen sat his exams. He did well in German, scraped through Latin, got mediocre results in Norwegian composition, and failed mathematics and Greek outright. Although he styled himself "student Ibsen" for a while, this was the end of Henrik Ibsen's formal education.

Had Ibsen wanted to matriculate at the university, he would have had to retake the exams in mathematics and Greek, but this he never did. Over the next year he nevertheless attended lectures of interest to him. We know that he was interested in philosophy, and he may have heard the lectures of the leading young Hegelian, Professor Marcus Jacob Monrad (1816–97), who had published some words in praise of *Catiline* in October 1850.[56] He certainly read and was influenced by the Danish Hegel-inspired philosopher and dramatist J. L. Heiberg, director of the Royal Theater in Copenhagen.

In his first year in Christiania Ibsen was also involved in radical politics. In 1850 he lived in the same house as Theodor Abildgaard, a close collaborator of Marcus Thrane, the first great Norwegian workers' leader. In 1850–1, Ibsen wrote some articles for *Arbeider-Foreningernes Blad* (*The Magazine of the Worker's Societies*), the paper of the Thrane movement. With Abildgaard, Ibsen even taught literacy classes for the Christiania Workers' Society that winter. In July 1851 the police arrested Abildgaard and Thrane, and Ibsen, who was never a brave man in person, was terrified that the police would come after him as well.[57] After spending seven years in prison, Thrane emigrated to the United States in 1863, and became politically active in the Chicago area.[58] Ibsen's involvement with Thrane and Abildgaard during this year must have taught him much about European socialism in the aftermath of 1848. Nevertheless, this was to be Ibsen's first and last brush with risky political activities, and just a few months later he left Christiania.

In 1851, the famous violinist Ole Bull (1810–80) offered Ibsen a job as a writer and director at the Norwegian Theater in Bergen, which he had founded in 1849. (At around this time Bull was also busy founding Oleanna, a utopian colony in Pennsylvania, whose miserable failure is immortalized in the song of the same name.) Given that Ibsen had no practical theater experience, this may sound surprising. But he was, after all, the author of

Catiline and *The Burial Mound*, and therefore one of the very few published and performed playwrights in Norway. Bull, an enthusiast if ever there was one, had arrived in Christiania to petition the *Storting* for money for his nationalist theater. His petition was refused, but the refusal caused much public debate, and during a heated debate in the University Literary Society, Ibsen defended Bull with passionate eloquence. Apparently, this was the event that first brought Ibsen's name to Bull's attention. The Christiania students protested against the decision of the *Storting*, and organized a grand national concert to raise money for Bull's theater, an event for which Ibsen wrote two well-received poems. Bull required no more: he had found his man, and took the 23-year-old penniless writer back to Bergen with him in late October 1851.[59]

After Ibsen's arrival in Bergen, all his education was linked to his practical work in the theater. In this respect, the most important single event was Ibsen's three and a half months long study trip to Copenhagen and Dresden in the spring and summer of 1852, paid for by the theater in Bergen. In both cities he went to the theater as much as he could, and for the first time in his life Ibsen saw Shakespeare performed. Thanks to Inga-Stina Ewbank's painstaking research we know that Ibsen was in Copenhagen from 20 April until 28 May 1852, and that in this period he probably saw *King Lear, Romeo and Juliet,* and *Hamlet,* as well as Oehlenschläger's romantic tragedy *Hakon Jarl.* He could also have seen Mozart's *Don Giovanni,* three comedies by Holberg, a great many Scribe comedies, lots of Danish vaudevilles, and many ballets. (At the time the Royal Theater's ballet master was the great August Bournonville.)[60]

In Dresden, where the Hoftheater "held some of the most exciting staging and acting of Shakespeare that Europe could offer in 1852", Ibsen could have seen *Hamlet, Richard III,* and *A Midsummer Night's Dream.*[61] He also discovered and devoured a book called *Das moderne Drama (Modern Drama),* which had just been published by a local intellectual, Hermann Hettner; met the revered J. C. Dahl; and, not least, spent hours and hours in the Dresden picture gallery, an experience that left a lasting impression, as is evident from the poem cycle entitled "I billedgalleriet" ("In the Picture Gallery").

At this stage of his life, then, Ibsen had reasonable German, schoolboy's Latin, a little French, and, as far as we know, no English.[62] Later in life he acquired some Italian, and became fluent in German. He learned some English on his own, but it is unclear whether he ever learnt more French.[63] Although he was interested in ideas, he had no formal training in philosophy, and was in any case never a great reader. In Bourdieu's terms, Ibsen's was a *miraculé*, a miraculous exception to the rules of recruitment to the European cultural elite.

Cultural capital: Ibsen, Brandes, Heyse

Throughout his life Ibsen took pride in his understanding of painting, yet in this domain, as in all others, Ibsen was essentially an autodidact who never acquired the cultural ease of a well-educated intellectual from the European urban bourgeoisie. What this means becomes evident if we compare him to his superbly educated Danish friend Georg Brandes (1842–1927), one of the leading European intellectuals of his day, fluent in French and German and with good English. Compared to Brandes, Ibsen clearly had very little "cultural capital", to use a Bourdieuian term. Both men must have felt the difference to be a burden on their relationship, and although Ibsen remained silent on the matter, Brandes left strong expressions of his views.

In late June 1874, Brandes was staying in Munich, in the brand new villa of the German writer Paul Heyse (1830–1914). Since Brandes had just returned from a brief visit to Ibsen in Dresden, his letters from the period are full of comparisons between Heyse and Ibsen. In a letter dated 21 June 1874 to his Danish friend C. J. Salomonsen, Brandes is outspoken about Ibsen's shortcomings:

The man sits there with poor inner productivity, unable to take in spiritual nourishment from the world around him because he lacks the relevant organs, and thus all kinds of prejudices and unreasonable ideas have become ossified in him. Only for one thing does he have a strong and sure eye, namely for the prejudices at home, for everything that is old and obsolete in Norway and Denmark, but his lack of any kind of solid cultural foundation makes him utterly limited.[64]

In a letter to his mother dated 18 June 1874, Brandes explicitly compares Ibsen and Heyse:

However cordial Ibsen was and always is towards me, I am nevertheless too culturally superior to him to find long conversations with him to be of any use. In Heyse, on the other hand, I have finally found a complete equal, superior in talent moreover, and even such a kindred spirit that we never need completely to finish a sentence in order to understand each other. In addition he is not like Ibsen spiritually raw, and therefore [a] paradox, but thoroughly mature and understands almost everything.[65]

Who was the man whom the brilliant young Brandes found so vastly superior to Ibsen? When I first came across Brandes's many passionately admiring references to him, I had never heard of Heyse at all. It turns out that Heyse's life and career offer an unusually dramatic and fascinating contrast between contemporary glory and posthumous oblivion. The fact that this destiny was the result of Heyse's lifelong adherence to aesthetic idealism makes his career a perfect foil for that of Ibsen, as we shall see in Chapter 3.

In 1874, Paul Heyse was not just a well-known writer; he was the unquestioned German *Dictherfürst* (poet prince) of the second half of the nineteenth century. The son of a Jewish mother and a Protestant father, Heyse was born into the liberal bourgeoisie in Berlin, and studied classical philology in Berlin and romance philology in Bonn. Among his early friends in Berlin were Jacob Burckhardt, Adolph Menzel, Theodor Fontane, and Theodor Storm, all of whom remained lifelong friends. Already in his early twenties Heyse was considered Germany's great literary hope, the long-awaited next Goethe. At the age of 24 he was called to be the court writer of Maxmilian II, king of Bavaria, who offered him an excellent salary for life in return for which he was expected to attend some literary functions at court, and otherwise devote himself entirely to his writing. As Sigrid von Moisy points out, this came at a time when most German writers could not earn any money at all from their writing.[66] Heyse's unusually strong allegiance to aesthetic idealism may have been strengthened by his anachronistic position as a court poet in the middle of the nineteenth century.

Heyse did not disappoint the expectations of his contemporaries. He was the golden boy of German literature, often referred to as the "favorite son of the Muses", enormously productive and extremely successful in every literary genre. He wrote 150 short stories, eight novels, more than 60 plays, innumerable poems, and also translated widely from Italian and Spanish. Brandes, who first wrote to Heyse in 1872, appears to have been almost in love with him, for his letters as well as his 1874 essay on Heyse are full of gushing admiration for the "elected favorite of the Gods, Fortuna's own cosseted child"; they all give the impression that Brandes was quite unable to stop praising Heyse's looks, cultured spirituality, and grace.[67] The polar opposite of the churlish, money-pinching, charmless Ibsen, the sociable and generous Heyse must have been Brandes's ideal ego, the person he would most want to be like in the world.

Irresistible to women, Heyse was a loyal friend to men, a veritable paragon of charm and friendliness combined with high moral principles and civic virtue. The splendid house he had built in the center of Munich was modeled on an Italian Renaissance villa, and filled with carefully selected art and furniture. Here Heyse enjoyed being the amiable host of large soirees and small coffee gatherings. He had innumerable guests. A master of friendship, he was close to a whole host of German artists and intellectuals, and founded the literary society *Krokodil*, devoted to the cultivation of idealism in literature. In Munich, both Arnold Böcklin and Georg Brandes became close, lifelong friends.

Heyse remained immensely popular with readers all his life, not least in Scandinavia. *Verdens Børn*, the Danish translation of his immensely successful 1872 novel *Kinder der Welt* (*Children of the World*) was published in 1874, and Brandes wrote to Heyse to assure him that everyone in Scandinavia was reading it, not least in Norway, where "all the young men and women have read *Children of the World* with curiosity and to some extent with enthusiasm".[68] When Fridtjof Nansen set off for his three-year-long expedition to the North Pole in 1893, the polar ship *Fram* stocked a wide selection of Heyse's books. In 1897, Hjalmar Johansen, Nansen's and Roald Amundsen's trusted companion, wrote a letter of gratitude to Heyse for having provided so much pleasure to the men aboard *Fram* as they were drifting across the ice-covered polar seas.[69] People traveled to Munich to see Heyse, just as they once had traveled to Weimar to see Goethe. Official accolades did not go missing, either: in 1910, when Heyse turned 80, he was ennobled in Bavaria, made an honorary citizen of Munich, and received the Nobel Prize for Literature.

Heyse died in 1914, just a few months before the outbreak of World War I, which destroyed the traditional German bourgeoisie to which he had given voice. His works were almost instantly forgotten; he had no followers and no admirers. Today his lovely villa has been turned into a lacquer factory, and the beautiful garden exists no more. There is not even a plaque on the wall, although there is one on the wall of the building where Ibsen lived from 1885 to 1891. In a final irony of history, the short and dreary Munich street that bears Heyse's name ends ignominiously in a railway underpass. The reason for this astounding fall from grace is not hard to find. Heyse was the last highly respected, widely successful, self-consciously idealist writer in Europe; his works were doomed to land on the dustheap of history the moment he died. As we shall see in Chapter 3, the tide started to turn in the early 1880s, when Heyse became the target of intense criticism from the emerging generation of German naturalists.

Heyse, then, is the perfect contrast to Ibsen, personally, aesthetically, and culturally. It is striking, to say the least, to learn that for a while the two men were close friends. Or rather, they were as close as Ibsen would ever get to most people, which is to say not very close at all. Ibsen cannot have been impervious to Heyse's fame, for he was keen to meet Heyse. He left his card at Heyse's villa as soon as he arrived in Munich in the spring of 1875, and even asked Brandes to put in a "couple of good words" for him with Dr Heyse (17: 183–4).[70]

The immensely productive Heyse was then at the height of his career, still basking in the success of the widely discussed and much translated *Children of the World*. Ibsen, on the other hand, had published *Emperor and Galilean* in Copenhagen in 1873, and was now living through his longest period of silence since the early 1860s. *Pillars of Society* was not published until 1877. At the time, Ibsen was known in Germany as the author of *The Vikings at Helgeland*, *The Pretenders*, *Brand*, and *Peer Gynt*; his cultural status simply could not be compared to Heyse's.

After his first meeting with Ibsen in July 1875, Heyse sent an immensely perceptive and revealing letter to Brandes:

I have indeed seen Ibsen for half an hour, but I cannot say much more about him than that I felt a deep human attraction to him in spite of all his oddness, the decorations in the velvet jacket, his unusually stiff, formal and yet not self-assured attitude, so that in spite of all his self-importance he practically seems to beg one for help to be delivered from himself. In part the foreignness of the language may have been a hindrance to him; he certainly *meant* to be very warm and intimate with me, his warm hand and the light in his eyes proved that we will have much to share with each other. But precisely his uneasiness of expression warns me not to draw any hasty conclusions about his mind. I will look him up again as soon as I get back into town and will keep seeing him through the winter, if I can and he wants to.[71]

There is a well-known photo of Ibsen taken in Munich around this time, in which he wears the very velvet jacket to which Heyse refers of (see 20: 83). In Heyse's eyes, Ibsen entirely lacked the easy and free ways (the *corporeal habitus*, Bourdieu would say) of a distinguished member of the European cultural elite.

Ibsen must have keenly felt the social, economic, and cultural gulf that separated him from the debonair Heyse. He also knew that he was not gifted for close, open-hearted friendship. In a letter to Bjørnson written in 1864, he analyzes his own character in a way that helps to explain Heyse's reaction to Ibsen, and Ibsen's constant concern, in his own plays, with the contrast between inner depths and outer surface, between authenticity and theatricality:

I know that I am unable to become deeply and closely intimate with the kind of people who demand complete and total self-disclosure. I suffer from something of the same as the Poet in *The Pretenders*, I can never really manage to bare myself completely, I have the feeling that in personal relationships I only dispose of false expressions of the things I carry deepest within me, which really are me, therefore I prefer to lock them up, and that is why we sometimes have been as it were observing each other at a distance.

(16: 101)[72]

Yet Ibsen was attracted to the cultural life of which Heyse was the center, and Sigrid von Moisy tells us that the two writers met frequently over the next few years, particularly in summer, when they saw each other almost every day as members of a group that regularly met at lunchtime in a local hotel, the Achatz, but that Ibsen was too withdrawn for a warm relationship to develop.[73]

In 1880 Ibsen moved back to Rome, and Heyse became the target of furious attacks from the very same naturalists who championed Ibsen's plays. Although he loved *A Doll's House*, Heyse hated both *Ghosts* and *An Enemy of the People*, and all the "symbolic" plays that followed, and when Ibsen moved back to Munich in 1885, the year after publishing *The Wild Duck*, the situation created difficulties for their friendship.[74] It appears to have been a topic much on Ibsen's mind during his conversations with William Archer in Sæby, Denmark, in August 1887:

[Ibsen] told me, what I had already read in the Norwegian papers, that there had been a regular Ibsen controversy in Berlin—that a certain set of critics had taken to exalting him to the skies and flinging him at the head of their own poets. They won't even hear of Spielhagen and Paul Heyse, being (Ibsen says) very unjust to the latter— which is particularly unpleasant for him (Ibsen), as he now lives near Heyse in Munich, and they are very good friends. Ibsen's account of Heyse is that he values himself on his plays, which are weak, while he despises his stories, many of which Ibsen holds to be masterpieces.

(19: 170)

Ibsen, then, was in all respects Heyse's antithesis. Until 1885, he lived in furnished apartments, which, visitors claimed, had no more individuality than a comfortable hotel, and assiduously scared away most of his guests. The more famous he became, the more isolated he chose to be. In Dresden and in his early days in Munich, he often went to the theater, but by the mid-1880s, he seems to have stopped going anywhere. He was shy and proud, and could be extremely touchy about criticism. He would thaw and become warm and charming on the relatively rare occasions when he felt at ease—that is to say, when he felt secure in the love and appreciation of his interlocutors.

Ibsen, moreover, was hardly irresistible to women. He was small and squat, with a big head and powerful shoulders. On the whole he appears to have found friendship to be a burden. On 6 March 1870, he wrote to Georg Brandes, who felt friendless and ostracized in Denmark: "Friends are a costly luxury; and when one has invested one's capital in a vocation and a mission here in life, then one cannot afford to keep friends. For the extravagance in keeping friends is not what one does for them, but what one avoids doing out of regard for them. In that way many spiritual germs are stunted. I have gone through it, and this is why I have behind me a number of years in which I could not succeed in becoming myself" (16: 283). No wonder, then, that most people found Ibsen charmless, and that he preferred to remain an outsider wherever he lived.

If Brandes (and surely the suave and sociable Heyse too) had such a keen sense of their own cultural superiority to Ibsen, we can be sure that the proud, sensitive, and supremely observant Ibsen knew it. And Brandes and Heyse were not the only ones. Even after Ibsen had started to write his greatest plays, his friends thought much the same thing. On 20 September 1884, Bjørnson, who had just spent three days with Ibsen, wrote to Jonas Lie:

Ibsen . . . was all amiability the few days he was here. He is chastened and well-intentioned.—He has an eye for fundamental issues, but only for some, the ones with a material basis. He hangs on more closely than we do, he is more careful, calculates better; yes, I would be tempted to say that his main talent is calculation; we see both more and better; our intellectual capacity is certainly larger. But he organizes his in such a way that it yields a greater percentage anyway.[75]

The next day Bjørnson wrote to Hegel, the publisher of both men:

The meeting with Ibsen (who has grown old!) was heartfelt; he is now a well-intentioned old gentleman, with whom I disagreed on many things when it came to world-view and what means to use in life; but with whom it was in the highest degree interesting to exchange opinions. The capacity for calculation, circumspection, cunning in his intelligence is unusually large. But neither his intelligence nor his knowledge is comprehensive.[76]

Only four years younger than Ibsen, Bjørnson was his opposite in almost everything: although he traveled widely (he even spent a year in the United States) and lived intermittently in Rome, Copenhagen, and Paris, he did not, like Ibsen, live continuously abroad. Bjørnson had a complicated, but fundamentally positive relationship to Christianity, remained a lifelong aesthetic idealist, engaged himself passionately in politics, knew everyone, stirred up cultural and political life in Denmark as well as Norway, and was preferred to Ibsen for the third Nobel Prize for Literature awarded in 1903.

Ibsen's cultural habitus, his understanding of his place in cultural and intellectual life, was essentially that of an autodidact and a social *déclassé*, who can never be sure that he has caught the "tone" of the cultural milieu in which he finds himself. This is surely one reason why he was always so careful not to reveal what he had and had not read, and why his increasing fame made him increasingly wary of social occasions.

Everyone who works on Ibsen soon discovers that it is impossible to get clear on whether he ever actually read Kierkegaard, Hegel, Nietzsche, and so on. The same is true for literature and art. Although he often mentions going to picture galleries, he hardly ever mentions any specific paintings or sculptures. By contrast, Ibsen frequently professed his love for the newspapers, particularly the small ads. In his letters, whenever an intellectual or literary topic comes up, Ibsen's usual strategy is to interrupt the discussion before it can begin, on the grounds that such matters would be better discussed in person. I get the impression that he was haunted by fear that people would believe he didn't own his own thoughts.

Ibsen's lack of education, as well as his often freely chosen outsider status, may have enabled him to understand women's situation in bourgeois society far more keenly than his colleagues. The cultured Georg Brandes thought very highly of the equally cultured Paul Heyse's fictional women, but on the evidence of *Children of the World*, his judgment was seriously flawed, for this is a novel in which the men discuss art, philosophy, religion, and the right to be a freethinker, while the women can find a sense of identity and a purpose in the world only through passionate, heterosexual love.[77]

Thus Toinette, a beautiful woman who cannot love, is on the brink of suicide. Having married an unpleasant count for the love of luxury, she finally discovers the meaning of life when she falls in love with Edwin, the smug, self-satisfied hero of the novel. Edwin, however, who loved Toinette when he was unmarried, is now married to a brilliant Jewish woman called Lea, and is, of course, far too noble and principled to consider leaving his wife. In the end, Toinette commits suicide because she cannot live without love. Fortunately, this leaves Edwin free to discover the true, passionate love of his wise and beautiful wife.

Heyse's idealism is most obviously present in the character of Balder, Edwin's brother, who is beautiful, noble, deeply good, and whose only function is to serve as a reminder of ideal humanity for the other characters. Mortally ill, Balder dies half-way through the book. Heyse is supposed to have thought of Balder as his finest creation.[78] At the end of the book there is an incredible scene in which an old family friend, Franzelius, persuades Lea to forgive Edwin for his flirtation with Toinette simply by showing her Balder's death mask. It is greatly to his credit that Ibsen could never have written anything remotely like this.

Why did Georg Brandes admire this novel so much? First of all, I suspect that Brandes had not yet fully worked out the consequences of the aesthetic program he announced in his lectures of 1871/2. But the main reason, surely, was that *Children of the World* did in fact "place problems under debate", as Brandes wanted literature to do, for its ostensible subject was the rights of freethinkers in a society dominated by state-sponsored Christianity, a theme close to the heart of the Jewish and radically antireligious Brandes.[79] Heyse's aim, however, was to show, as the English translator of the novel puts it, "that freethinking is compatible not merely with morality, but with the highest purity and self-sacrifice".[80] Heyse's idealism, his debt to Schiller and Goethe, can find no clearer expression.

Exile or Émigré?

An ambitious writer with Ibsen's cultural background may have had little choice: he could either stay at home, in a small country with extremely limited cultural resources, where he had never been able to earn a decent living, and where he always seemed to get bogged down in petty provincial squabbles, or go abroad where nobody knew or cared about him and his writing. The latter at least had the virtue of leaving him free to focus entirely on his work. Ibsen's outrage at the cowardice of the Norwegians and the Swedes, who did nothing to help Denmark in the war with Prussia over Schleswig-Holstein in 1864, may have tipped the scales: Ibsen left Norway in April 1864, shortly after his thirty-sixth birthday.

The very first summer in Rome Ibsen got the idea for two of his three great closet dramas—*Brand* and *Emperor and Galilean*—and with the publication in Copenhagen of *Brand* in 1866, his career finally took off. No wonder that he hesitated to return. Ibsen's years in voluntary exile were spent in Rome (1864–8, 1878–9, 1880–5), Dresden (1868–75), and Munich (1875–8, 1879–80, 1885–91). In this period he visited Norway only twice, in 1874 and 1885. In 1891, after twenty-seven years abroad, Ibsen finally moved back to Kristiania. *The Master Builder* (1892) was the first Ibsen play written in Norway since *The Pretenders* in 1863–4.

Ibsen's letters are full of references to the freedom of life abroad, to the larger vistas and wider scope offered by Europe. In 1879, while he was hard at work on *A Doll's House* (most of which was written in Amalfi), Ibsen wrote to Lie that he had no wish to move back to Kristiania: "Life out here in Europe is after all freer and more refreshing, and larger" (17: 348).[81] But his letters are equally full of references to his need to go somewhere to work in peace. He craved isolation, was a terrible letter-writer (his letters are short, always full of apologies for being written so late, and usually not particularly revealing of his personality, or rather: the personality they reveal is personally and emotionally unexpressive), and often contrived not to meet potentially congenial people living in the very same city. Although Ibsen lived for seven years in Dresden, for example, he appears not to have made any effort to meet Hermann Hettner, author of the book on drama that inspired him in 1852. Georg Brandes, on the other hand, sought out Hettner on his very first trip to see Ibsen in Dresden.

Ibsen's trajectory has some features in common with postcolonial writers, and some distinct differences. Like many postcolonial writers in the twentieth century, Ibsen wrote almost all his major works abroad. Unlike many postcolonial writers, however, he did not settle in the metropolitan capital, Copenhagen, where his own language would be understood.[82]

In Italy, Ibsen belonged to the Scandinavian Association, and socialized almost entirely with other Scandinavians. In Germany, this pattern continued. Although Ibsen's German was good, he did not have the linguistic ease of Brandes, who was writing articles in German by the mid-1870s. Unlike Brandes, Ibsen surrounded himself mostly with resident and visiting Scandinavians. His most sociable periods appear to have been during his first stay in Rome and his first period in Munich, when he saw quite a lot of Heyse and his extensive social circle, and also made some close friends among the Norwegian painters there.[83]

Ibsen wrote few letters to foreigners, and then mostly to men like Edmund Gosse and William Archer who endeavored to spread his works in other countries. As his fame increased, Ibsen's interactions with German culture grew; yet the more famous he became, the less he appears to have enjoyed ordinary social life. In all these respects, Ibsen abroad behaved more like a writer in political exile than a postcolonial intellectual trapped in an ambivalent relationship to the metropolitan culture.

In some ways Ibsen's cultural and social position is close to that of the great Irish writers emerging towards the end of the nineteenth century. It may be no coincidence that George Bernard Shaw and James Joyce both responded so spontaneously and strongly to Ibsen. Oscar Wilde, another Irishman, also appears to have admired Ibsen, albeit as a playwright essentially different from himself. Nineteenth-century Norway and Ireland shared many important traits: a geographical location on the North Atlantic fringe of Europe, a fast-growing, overwhelmingly rural population, an extremely high rate of emigration to the United States (when calculated in percentages of the total population, Norway's rate of emigration was the second highest in Europe after Ireland).[84]

The parallels between Ibsen and Joyce are particularly striking. The young Joyce admired Ibsen immensely. Joyce too lived and wrote in self-imposed European exile. Perhaps Joyce in Trieste, Zurich, and Paris is not so unlike

Ibsen in Rome, Dresden, and Munich?[85] Surely the young Joyce was attracted to Ibsen's trajectory as much as to his writing. For Ibsen was an example of the very thing Joyce wanted to become: a writer who had managed to escape from a stiflingly provincial background and imposed himself on world literature. Ibsen's way of doing this must also have been inspiring to Joyce, for Ibsen's relentless attacks on aesthetic idealism, and on religious and moralistic judgments of art and literature, must have felt like a profound liberation to a young Irishman in 1899.[86]

Yet here too there are significant differences: the social and religious situation in Ireland was entirely different from that in Norway; the violent and rapacious British colonization of Ireland had left a bitter legacy utterly unlike that of the Danes and Swedes in Norway. Joyce, moreover, wrote in a world language, and Ibsen did not. Finally, because Joyce was more than fifty years younger than Ibsen, he belongs to a different period of European modernity.

Ibsen's trajectory, then, is *sui generis*. It has something in common with that of postcolonial intellectuals, but also with that of political exiles. A writer from the periphery, Ibsen arrived in some of the great cities of Europe with little education and no cultural connections, and made no particular effort to gain access to cultural and artistic circles in his countries of residence.

During his first summer in Rome, Ibsen must have discovered that living anonymously, in linguistic and cultural isolation, he could take his work to unprecedented levels. His self-imposed cultural marginality surely helped to foster his radical critique of the existing social order, as well as his famous *dobbeltblikk*—his dual vision—his capacity to grasp the complexity of human behavior. Freeing him from the oppressively provincial atmosphere of Norway, Ibsen's voluntary exile turned him into a great writer. To know Ibsen, we must know Norway, but we must know Europe, too.

3

Rethinking Literary History
Idealism, realism, and the birth of modernism

A new genealogy of modernism

For anyone interested in the emergence of modernism, Ibsen's writings are a find: an undisturbed archaeological site concealing a perfectly preserved genealogy of modernism. Ibsen's career spans the whole of the second half of the nineteenth century. In the 1850s Ibsen wrote romantic tragedy and national romantic drama; by the 1890s he had become Europe's most famous avant-garde playwright, hailed by the emerging modernist generation as their leader and lodestar. To trace Ibsen's aesthetic transformations is to trace the birth of European modernism.

The genealogy of modernism that emerges from a close study of Ibsen's works is easily summarized: modernism is built on the negation of idealism. Realism—the representation of reality in writing and art—is neither modernism's opposite nor its historically necessary predecessor. If any one entity occupies that position, it is idealism. Realism, moreover, is not *one*: Balzac's realism is not Flaubert's; Ibsen's realism is not Zola's. Different realisms must be theorized differently. Idealists did not object to realism; they objected to realism that did not subscribe to idealist aesthetics. This kind of realism came increasingly to be called "naturalism", and in the 1880s, the question at the heart of the culture wars unleashed by naturalism was precisely whether anti-idealist realism (not realism in general) could be *art*.

In fact, the war against idealism was waged not just by naturalists, but by many other avant-garde movements: Oscar Wilde's radical aestheticism was as anti-idealist as Emile Zola's experimental novels. The movement away from idealism was a long, slow, piecemeal process, which is why the period from 1870 to 1914 produced such a profusion of widely different protomodernist (because anti-idealist) writing alongside the continuing stream of idealist works. Once idealism had been destroyed as a viable aesthetic position, avant-gardes of all kinds came to dominate the cultural scene, and eventually modernism achieved aesthetic hegemony. In the twentieth century, idealism nevertheless lived on, spectacularly so in the early decisions of the Nobel committee in Stockholm, and then, as the century wore on, in a more routine fashion in the middle- and low-brow literary genres which established themselves in opposition to the elitism of high modernism.[1]

This chapter will chart the rise and fall of nineteenth-century idealism, from Schiller's ecstatic, revolutionary romantic vision of human perfection to its final incarnation as a desiccated moralism embraced by religious and social conservatives all over Europe. I shall show that Ibsen's plays were crucial to the demise of idealism as an aesthetic norm, not just because of the battles fought over them, but because they thematize the very aesthetic conflicts raging around them. When we read references to the ideal in Ibsen exclusively as *ethical references*, rather than what they are, references to (or expressions of) an *aesthetic ideal in which ethics and aesthetics are one*, then we blind ourselves to the fact that discussions of the ideal in Ibsen are also always discussions of the nature and purpose of art in general and theater in particular. (Unless I specifically say something else, in this book *idealism* means this kind of *aesthetic idealism*.)

Naturally, more extensive discussions of how Ibsen's difficult and complicated relationship to idealist aesthetics appears in his texts will have to wait until Parts II and III of this book. The main task of this chapter is to rescue idealist aesthetics from oblivion, and to show why doing so is crucial to our understanding not just of Ibsen's modernism, but of the emergence of modernism in the period from 1870 to 1914 in general.

Idealism: A Forgotten Term

As an *aesthetic* term, "idealism" appears to have disappeared. It is absent from major dictionaries of literary terms.[2] I have never seen it discussed as a literary or aesthetic concept on a par with realism or modernism. We appear to have forgotten how important idealism was as a general way of understanding art and literature; how strong its hold on the hearts and minds of nineteenth-century writers, artists, critics, and audiences was; and what a long, slow, piecemeal task it was for a whole generation—the first generation of modernists—to work itself free of that hold.

Idealism's star status in the history of philosophy and the history of ideas makes its absence in literary criticism all the more striking. Or, to be more precise, when literary critics speak of idealism, they too have various aspects of philosophical or ethical (as opposed to aesthetic) idealism in mind. In Ibsen studies, for example, to examine idealism means to consider Ibsen's relationship to Hegel and Kierkegaard, or his treatment of characters who profess to hold high ideals, not specifically his relationship to idealist beliefs about the nature and purpose of art.[3] Insofar as idealist aesthetics is discussed at all, it is under the rubric of romanticism.[4] I shall show, however, that if we take idealism to be just another word for romanticism, we deprive ourselves of the resources we need to understand not just why naturalism and modernism provoked the most intense culture wars in European literary history, but also why the issues provoked by the death of idealism are still relevant today.

In his overview article "The Metaphysics of Modernism", Michael Bell rightly claims that modernism emerged as the result of the "collapse of idealism". On closer examination, however, it turns out that he means that modernists preferred Marx, Nietzsche, and Freud to Kant, Fichte, and Schelling's theories concerning the relationship between the mind and the world.[5] This is true. Nevertheless, it was not primarily philosophical idealism that had to collapse for modernism to arise, but the enormously powerful and influential idealist understanding of the nature and purpose of art. Modernism began when idealist aesthetics came under attack, not when writers and artists discovered Freud.

I owe my own discovery of idealism as a key aesthetic category in nineteenth-century art and literature to Naomi Schor's pioneering 1993 book *George Sand and Idealism*. In the introduction, Schor explains that she first realized the importance of idealism in 1985, when she found a dusty old book in a secondhand bookshop in Hay-on-Wye:

I flipped to the table of contents to see if [George Sand] was included. It was then that I made an important, indeed a decisive discovery: she was included, but under what struck me as a strange and unfamiliar heading, *Le Roman idéaliste.* . . . I knew, of course, in a general sort of way—as anyone working on Sand would—that an important idealistic strain existed in Sand's fiction. . . . But this moldy and outdated study aid suddenly made palpable for me the force of that category and the extent of its disappearance.[6]

Working on Ibsen, I have come to realize how right Schor was: idealism was indeed a tremendously powerful aesthetic force in the nineteenth century, and it has disappeared more thoroughly than any other aesthetic category of that century. Refusing to connect Sand's idealism to German aesthetics, Schor focuses on the presence of idealist categories in non-philosophical contexts, such as reviews, correspondence, and political debates. Following

Schor's lead, I started looking for signs of the presence of idealism in the literary debates provoked by Ibsen's plays. The results were spectacular. Not only was idealism everywhere, but it was clear that Ibsen's plays had been important battlefields for the all-out struggle between idealists and anti-idealists. Most importantly, Ibsen's plays explicitly and repeatedly dramatize the questions and assumptions at the heart of idealist aesthetics.

I think Schor was wrong to leave German philosophy out of her book, for the omission weakens her understanding of what idealist aesthetics was. We have to acknowledge that Kant, Hölderlin, Schiller, Novalis, Friedrich Schlegel, Hegel, and others laid the foundations of nineteenth-century idealist aesthetics, and that in the first decades of the nineteenth century distinguished interpreters such as Madame de Staël and Coleridge contributed powerfully to spread German aesthetic idealism throughout Europe. But Schor was right to focus on "idealism in action", idealism as it was expressed in French nineteenth-century debates. Truly original and inspiring, this aspect of her pioneering work teaches us to look for idealist aesthetics in places we would not necessarily have connected with German philosophy.

To put all this slightly differently: around 1800, German idealist aesthetics produced one of the most powerful and inspiring accounts of the nature and purpose of art and literature the world has ever seen. This is hardly news. What *is* news is that *some* version of this account, however debased, diluted, vulgarized, and simplified, shows up practically everywhere in nineteenth-century aesthetic discussions, not just in the 1810s and 1820s, but throughout the nineteenth and well into the twentieth century.

The Idealist View of Art and Literature

"Idealism" is a complex word. It has as much to do with the *idea* as with the *ideal*. Indeed, Plato's ideas *are* ideals: the timeless pattern and archetype of any class of things, as opposed to the lowly imitations we are condemned to live with here on earth. For a long time, *idea* simply meant *ideal*. The *Oxford English Dictionary* quotes Thomas Browne in 1682: "How widely we have fallen from the pure Exemplar and Idea of our Nature." In everyday usage we still speak of the idea of a thing in the sense of its general pattern or plan. We are bound, therefore, to concede that actual realizations may always fall short of the idea that spawned them, and thus we find ourselves treading a fine line between the idea and the ideal, and between the ideal and the real. Plato's contrast between the pure sphere of the idea and the messy realities of ordinary life is only a few steps away.

In contemporary philosophy idealism is often taken to mean the opposite of materialism: idealism is to materialism as Hegel is to Marx. In the late nineteenth century, however, anti-idealism took many forms. Marxist materialism was only one of them. Equally important was the rise of "free thought", that is to say, of secularism, agnosticism, and atheism, on the one hand, and of various forms of scientific determinism on the other. Strindberg's flirtations with Darwinism in a play like *The Father* are perfectly representative of the period.

Although psychoanalysis does not have much to say about idealism, it has produced a huge amount of work about *idealization*—that is, on how and why we idealize something or somebody in the first place. Because I am interested in the rise and fall of idealism in the nineteenth century, not in the reasons why individual authors and artists may have been more or less inclined to accept or reject idealism as an aesthetic norm, I shall not pursue that question further here.[7]

The *Oxford English Dictionary* defines idealism as the "practice of idealizing or tendency to idealize; the habit of representing things in an ideal form, or as they might be; imaginative treatment of a subject in art or literature; ideal style or character: opposed to *realism*. Also, aspiration after or pursuit of an ideal". If the ideal is imaginary—some would go as far as to call it chimerical—an idealist is not just someone who pursues ideals, but someone "who cherishes visionary or unpractical notions". In this sense, the opposite of idealism is surely realism.

Idealists, then, can be too unworldly, too high-minded for comfort. They can come across as more moral and more moralizing than the average human being, which is why they tend to make ordinary people feel petty-minded. There is definitely something utopian about idealists. The opposite of idealism, therefore, may not just be realism, but cynicism, for cynics are "disposed to disbelieve in human sincerity or goodness", which is exactly what many idealists *are* disposed to believe in. (The contrast between Gregers Werle and Dr Relling in *The Wild Duck* leaps to mind.) But we can go further. Perhaps the opposite of idealism is nihilism: "negative doctrines in religion or morals; total rejection of current religious beliefs or moral principles". The *OED*'s example is from 1881: "The hollow vacuities and negative absurdities of Atheism or Nihilism", which brings us back to the fact that because nineteenth-century idealists almost always fused morality and religion, anti-idealists were almost always taken to be freethinkers or worse (as we have seen, the freethinking German idealist Paul Heyse was a distinguished exception to this rule).

Just by reading the dictionary, then, we have arrived at a striking contrast between morally uplifting idealism and world-weary realism and cynical nihilism, a contrast which exactly captures the difference between idealism and naturalism as it was understood by last-ditch idealists in the 1880s and 1890s. To understand what was at stake in those cultural struggles, however, we need to return to the source: German idealist aesthetics.

In 1796 Friedrich Hölderlin—or rather, Hölderlin together with his two good friends G. W. F. Hegel and F. W. J. Schelling—admirably encapsulated the key ideas of idealist aesthetics in a very short paper entitled "Oldest Programme for a System of German Idealism".[8] Kant's distinction between *freedom* (the realm of reason, of the human will and imagination; the moral and creative world) and *necessity* (the realm of natural laws; the world of science) is as fundamental to Hölderlin as it is to all the other German idealist aesthetes. The world of necessity is the world of material objects, subjected to natural laws which are explained by science. The world of freedom is the world of consciousness, imagination, and the will, the world in which we make moral and aesthetic choices. It is against this conceptual background that Hölderlin goes on to discuss *beauty*, the key term of aesthetic idealism:

Finally, the idea which unites everyone, the idea of *beauty*, the word taken in the higher, platonic sense. I am now convinced that the highest act of reason, by encompassing all ideas, is an aesthetic act, and that *truth and goodness* are only siblings in *beauty*. The philosopher must possess as much aesthetic power as the poet. Those people without an aesthetic sense are our philosophers of literalness [*Buchstabenphilosophen*]. The philosophy of spirit is an aesthetic philosophy. One can be spiritually brilliant in nothing, one cannot even think about history—without an aesthetic sense. . . .

Thus poetry gains a higher honour, it finally becomes what it was at its inception— *the teacher of humanity*; for there is no longer any philosophy, any history; the art of poetry alone will outlive all other sciences and arts.[9]

Echoing Plato, aesthetic idealism considers the *beautiful*, the *true*, and the *good* to be one; but quite unlike Plato, idealism characteristically considers artistic beauty to be the highest expression of this trinity. Because beauty is both sensuous and spiritual—the idea made material through the use of the imagination—it overcomes the split between freedom and necessity, and offers us an image of our own lost wholeness. Because truth without beauty remains arid and soulless, a great poet is also a great philosopher, and the greatest philosopher will never be great unless he is a poet, too. (The echoes of this creed reverberated all the way down to the French 1930s, when Sartre and Beauvoir thought that literature was a greater and more noble pursuit than philosophy, and Sartre in particular still thought that he could be "saved" by literature.)

In order to reach the masses, we need to "make ideas aesthetic", Hölderlin writes. Only then will we transcend the opposition between art and philosophy, and create a new religion, or in Hölderlin's terms, a new mythology: "Mythology must become philosophical, to make the people rational, and philosophy must become mythological, to make philosophy sensuous. Then eternal unity will reign among us. . . . Only then will equal development of all of our powers await us, for the particular person as well as for all individuals. No power will again be suppressed, then general freedom and equality will reign among spirits!"[10] Fusing aesthetics with ethics and religion, the idealist program holds out to us all an optimistic, utopian vision of human perfection.

A few years later, in 1800, Friedrich Schlegel also considered religion to be the result of the fusion of poetry and philosophy: "Poetry and philosophy are, depending on one's point of view, different spheres, different forms, or simply the component parts of religion. For only try really to combine the two and you will find yourself with nothing but religion."[11] By advancing such a lofty image of the nature and purpose of poetry (and, to a slightly lesser extent, the other arts), German idealist aesthetics turned poets into prophets and mystics, and allowed artists of all kinds to claim that by pursuing beauty they were serving God. (As we shall see in Chapter 5, this is precisely Bjørnson's defense of theater in his 1868 novella *The Fisher Maiden*.) In its most radical political form, this utopian and perfectionist vision stayed with Ibsen throughout his life. In a speech in Stockholm in 1887, for example, he made it an article of faith: "I believe that poetry, philosophy and religion will blend into a new category and a new life power, of which we who live now can have no clear conception" (15: 411).

We have seen that Hölderlin connects ideas (and ideals) to freedom. Freedom is the great theme of Friedrich Schiller's aesthetics, not least in his masterly little treatise *On Naive and Sentimental Poetry* (*Über naive und sentimentalische Dichtung*) first published in installments in 1795 and 1796.[12] The ideas contained in this brilliant text circulated in one form or another throughout European aesthetic discussions for the next hundred years. I shall use it here as my principal example of full-blown idealist aesthetics, both because of the enormous influence of Schiller's ideas in the nineteenth century and because echoes of Schiller's formulations are so plentiful in Ibsen's own writings.

As the battles over idealism grew more intense, Schiller was often invoked as the positive counterbalance to Ibsen's negative example. In 1899, Carl David af Wirsén, permanent secretary of the Swedish Academy, soon to be the first chairman of the Nobel Committee, declared, "It is certainly undeniable that Ibsen is far more 'piquant' than Schiller; yet those who love a truly profound content, a noble essence in a drama, would gladly close *When We Dead Awaken*, and open *Wallenstein*, in which the grand clashes of a sombre heroic mind are so vigorously painted."[13] I shall draw on Schiller's *On Naive and Sentimental Poetry*, then, first to convey both what aesthetic idealism was in its full, romantic, radical, utopian glory and then to draw attention to its inner and ultimately destructive fault lines, which enabled Schiller's glorious vision of aesthetic freedom to be turned into a set of moralistic and deeply reactionary aesthetic norms.

By turning to Schiller, I do not wish to deny that Ibsen, like so many other Scandinavians at the time, was influenced by Hegel's aesthetics, whether directly or through the writings of J. L. Heiberg and M. J. Monrad.[14] The characteristic idealist conflation of truth and beauty is, if anything, stronger in Hegel's aesthetic than in Schiller's, and nineteenth-century Scandinavian critics often speak of the ideal in recognizably Hegelian terms.[15] But Hegel's lectures on aesthetics do not convey that burning, radical desire for freedom that still appealed powerfully to Ibsen and Brandes in 1871. (In his break-through lectures, Brandes invokes Schiller, but not Hegel.) In the late 1790s, Schiller became the theorist of aesthetic idealism at its most politically radical; in the 1820s, Hegel produced a philosophy of art that certainly contributed to setting aesthetic idealism on an altogether more moralistic and conservative path.

The key idea in Schiller's aesthetics is a utopian vision of human perfecti-bility. Humankind can become better, freer, more beautiful, more fulfilled. The task of art is to ennoble us, to help us overcome the split between nature and freedom, so that the whole of human nature can find full and free expression. Schiller's "Ideal"—the vision that poetry and art is supposed to convey to us—is an ample and generous one, a picture of a fully harmonious human being, fully free and fully at home in the world.

Long after the death of revolutionary, romantic idealism, this ideal had a strong afterlife in the Marxist tradition. Around 1900, the young Leon Trotsky declared, "As long as I breathe, I shall fight for the future, that radiant future in which man, strong and beautiful, will become master of the drifting stream of his history and will direct it towards the boundless horizon of beauty, joy and happiness."[16] As late as the mid-twentieth century, the great Marxist literary critic Georg Lukács still believed in the advent of the fully "harmonious human being", although he thought that such a perfected creature could only come into being under communism.[17]

Schiller's fundamental starting point is nature. Poets must always be the guardians of nature, he writes, for when we lose touch with nature, "moral and aesthetic degeneracy" follows.[18] Poets, therefore, "will either *be* nature or *seek* the lost nature" (p. 196). From this claim he derives his famous distinction between naïve and sentimental poets: the naïve poet *is* nature, the sentimental poet *seeks* nature. By nature, Schiller means above all human nature, which he sees as a unique combination of spirit and matter, or in other words: of freedom and necessity, infinity and finitude. The task of all poetry is to *give humanity its most complete possible expression*, Schiller writes (see p. 201). Poetry is to uplift and ennoble us, to give us concrete visions of a better world with better human beings in it. This is the heart of Schiller's idealist aesthetics. (There is an almost uncanny similarity between Schiller's aesthetics and Johannes Rosmer's doomed political project in *Rosmersholm*.)

By mapping the opposition between the naïve and the sentimental on to the opposition between the ancient and the moderns, Schiller develops an aesthetic theory balancing finely on the line between neoclassicism and romanticism. Ancient poets, Schiller writes, were at once natural and naïve, characterized by an innocence of heart that entirely escapes their modern colleagues. Their task, therefore, was to describe the world as they saw it, as fully and as well as possible. For the naïve poet still living in the "original condition of natural simplicity . . . the most complete possible *imitation of the actual is what necessarily makes someone a poet*" (p. 201). Naïve poets are specialists in realism, in other words.[19]

In the modern world, on the other hand, "nature has disappeared from our humanity, and we reencounter it in its genuineness only outside humanity in the inanimate world", Schiller writes (p. 194). This gives us a yearning for truth and simplicity unknown to the ancients who had never lost nature in the first place: "They felt naturally, while we feel the natural" (p. 195). Because the modern poet has lost touch with nature, he (all of Schiller's examples are male) cannot convey nature itself, but only the *idea* of nature. "The ancient poets touch us through nature, through sensuous truth, through living presence; the modern poets touch us through ideas" (p. 201). Since modern human beings are no longer at one with themselves, the mere description of reality is no longer poetic: "Here in the condition of culture . . . the elevation of actuality to the ideal, or, what comes to the same, *the portrayal of the ideal is what necessarily makes the poet*" (p. 201). Schiller's poetic idealism thus emerges out of his historicizing analysis of modern culture.

Because ideas are infinite and nature is finite (the Kantian foundations of Schiller's thought are everywhere apparent), the sentimental poet will always have to face the conflict between the limitations of the actual world and the unlimited soaring of which the imagination is capable. For the modern writer, then, poetry arises when the poet attempts to transcend the limits of the actual world; for the ancient writer, it was enough simply to describe that world.

Given this conflict, the sentimental poet can choose between two different aesthetic strategies, or what Schiller calls different "manner[s] of feeling" (p. 211 n.). He can focus on the actual and foreground the contrast between the actual and the ideal. This produces a mode of writing that Schiller calls *satire*: "In the satire, the actual world as something lacking is contrasted with the ideal as the supreme reality," Schiller writes, before stressing that the ideal need not be represented as long as the poet "knows how to awaken it in the mind" (p. 206). When satire is successful, "the magnificence of the idea we are filled with elevates us above all experience's limitations", Schiller declares (p. 206).[20]

But the modern poet can also contrast the actual world and the ideal in "such a way that the ideal dominates and the satisfaction taken in it becomes the predominant feeling" (p. 211). This is what Schiller calls *elegy*. Elegy has two subcategories: elegy proper and idyll: "Either nature and the ideal are objects of mourning, when the former is presented as something lost, the latter as something unattained, or both are objects of joy, because they are represented as something actual. The first class yields the *elegy* in the narrow sense, the second class the *idyll* in the broadest sense" (p. 211). Realism, then, is not at all excluded from Schiller's categories. What matters to Schiller is not whether one tries to represent reality, but the spirit in which one does so. While naïve and natural poets are realists by definition, Schiller's category of satire also gives wide scope to realism, as does the elegy proper.

That these categories were influential in nineteenth-century Norway is beyond doubt. We have already seen (in Chapter 1) that the leading Danish critic Clemens Petersen insisted that *Brand* and *Peer Gynt* were not poetry because they failed to convey "a complete, definite, clear and assured representation of the ideal".[21] When *Love's Comedy* was published in Christiania in 1862, the philosopher M. J. Monrad claimed that the end of the play constituted a "break with the Idea revolting to human feeling", and even Ibsen's good friend Paul Botten-Hansen thought that the play revealed an author "devoid of ideal faith and conviction".[22]

In 1875, in an overview of Ibsen's work published in the newspaper *Morgenbladet* on Ibsen's birthday to mark the twenty-fifth anniversary of the publication of *Catiline*, Monrad wrote that Ibsen considered himself to be living in a fallen world: "Truth, the idea, the ideal, has, as it were, fled the real conditions and now only reveals itself in negative form in noble spirits, as consciousness of the corruption of the times. This guilty conscience of the times reveals itself poetically in *Satire*, which thus is perfectly justified."[23]

This, of course, is Schiller's concept of satire. In Monrad's eyes, Ibsen was a fundamentally satirical poet, who never stopped expressing humanity's consciousness of its own fallenness. *Brand*, Monrad wrote elsewhere, was also a satire, in which the "higher demands of the idea and the spirit are . . . still present, but in conflict with reality".[24] Monrad's reading of *Brand* as a satire in which the "all or nothing" of the idea clashes with the "spirit of compromise" that dominates society is powerful because it is based on aesthetic norms that were still important to Ibsen himself.

Ideal Freedom and Vulgar Passions: Women, Sexuality, and Self-sacrifice

We now need to consider the connection between Schiller's theory of naïve and sentimental poetry and Hölderlin's claim that beauty encompasses truth and goodness. In Schiller's vision, beauty—the capacity to appreciate it as well as the capacity to create it—is an effect of freedom: "If we consider our natural condition to be an unlimited capacity for every human expression and the knack of being able to manage all our powers with equal freedom, then any separation and isolation of these powers is a violent condition," Schiller writes (pp. 244–5). Against the "ideal of humanity", Schiller places the "ideal of animality", by which he means the needs of "sensuous nature" alone (p. 245). Modern human beings have become more refined than the ancients, but the price humanity has paid for its increasing sophistication is a separation from what Schiller calls "genuine human nature". For Schiller, ideal or "genuine" human nature is always good: "Every moral baseness is part of human nature as it actually is, but hopefully it is not part of a human nature that is genuine, since this can never be anything but noble. It should not be overlooked that this confusion of actual human nature with genuine human nature has misled criticism as well as practice into all sorts of distastefulness" (p. 236).

Insisting on the contrast between "sensuous nature" and fully free and fully expressive "human nature", Schiller claims that true beauty can be appreciated only by someone who is not in thrall to mere material or sensuous needs: "Beauty is the product of the accord between mind and senses; it speaks to all the capacities of the human being at once. For this reason it can be felt and appreciated only on the supposition of a complete and free use of all the human being's powers" (p. 245). At once sensuous and ennobling, beauty overcomes the alienation (the split) created in human beings by modernity.

The incarnation of human freedom, poetic and artistic beauty lifts us up towards the ideal, which is precisely the full and free expression of human nature. In this way, truth, goodness, and beauty are united in the work of art, which itself is the highest expression of human freedom.

In its fullest and most generous formulation, this is an intoxicating vision of human freedom, a utopian vision of the ideal intended to inspire us to battle against all those forces that prevent us from realizing ideal freedom. Yet it is hardly without fault lines. Most prominent is the foothold it provides for narrowly moralistic judgments of poetry and art. Equally pernicious are the difficulties that Schiller's reliance on the Kantian opposition between nature and freedom causes for his treatment of sexuality in general and women in particular. Relying on the distinction between *actual* (*wirkliche*) human nature (which may be bad) and *genuine* or true (*wahre*) human nature (which is ideal—that is to say, always good, true, and beautiful), Schiller declares that outbreaks of sexual passion are always examples of actual and never of genuine nature (p. 236). Naïve poets, who depict nature as it is, therefore often produce vulgar representations of sex and sexuality.

If we wonder exactly what Schiller means by "vulgar", he explains it in a lengthy footnote concerning sex and women, inserted at the very point where he first uses the word. No naïve genius, Schiller claims, including Homer and Shakespeare, has ever entirely avoided vulgarity (pp. 237–8):

If . . . nature is vulgar, then the spirit . . . deserts their compositions. For example, in their portrayals of feminine nature, of the relations between both sexes, and of love in particular, every reader with refined feelings must sense a certain emptiness and a weariness that all genuineness and naiveté in the presentation cannot remove. . . . One will hopefully be allowed to assume that nature, as far as that relation of the sexes and the emotion of love are concerned, is capable of a nobler character than the ancients gave it. . . . Here, then, would have been the place for the ancients to render spiritual a material too crude on the outside and to do so from within, through the subject (*Subjekt*); that is to say, here would have been the place to recover, by means of reflection, the poetic significance missing in the feeling from the outside, to complete nature through the idea, in a word, to make something infinite out of a limited object by a sentimental operation.

(p. 237 n.)

It follows that sex and women—in the eyes of Schiller and his male comrades, women, not men, are the bearers of human sexuality—should never be treated realistically. The representation of human sexuality *requires* idealization, or it will be vulgar. In order to become properly poetic, sex must be sublimated, ennobled, and beautified, that is to say that it must be turned into highly idealized love. (Again Johannes Rosmer comes to mind.) In order to avoid the coarse and the vulgar, consciousness must transcend the body; morality, duty, and will must conquer mere material nature. This idea explains not only the proliferation of wildly idealized representations of women in nineteenth-century literature, but also the widespread tendency to require that the pure woman prove her purity by being ready to sacrifice her life for love. The motif of female self-sacrifice is extremely important to Ibsen. It is paramount in *Brand*, crucial in *Peer Gynt*, and even more important (in a completely different vein) in *Rosmersholm*, where Rosmer is fascinated and compelled by the thought that a woman would sacrifice her life for him. But it is also a significant concern in *Love's Comedy, A Doll's House, The Wild Duck, The Lady from the Sea*, and *Hedda Gabler*, and even in *When We Dead Awaken*, and therefore requires further discussion.

Schiller's view of sex is no different from Kant's. Since Kantian morality demands that we elevate ourselves above nature (since moral action is an exercise of freedom, to follow one's natural inclinations can never be a moral act), Kantian morality is extremely cautious with regard to human sexuality. Sex must always have the aim of procreation. If it is used for mere "animal pleasure", even heterosexual intercourse is immoral.[25] The only thing that can make sex morally permissible is the law—that is, marriage.

For Kant, unnatural sexual acts (by which Kant understands anything except procreative sex in marriage) are always vile and self-defiling. But even natural sexual acts may be immoral. If sex has no other aim than pleasure, for example, it turns the other person into a thing, a mere means to one's own enjoyment, and for Kant, it is never permissible to treat another human being as a means and not an end. But it is also immoral to treat *oneself* as a thing, for that is to violate one's duty to one's own humanity. To masturbate, in particular, is to give in to one's basest natural inclinations, to reduce oneself to a thing with the sole aim of pleasure. The resulting act, Kant writes, is so loathsome that it is repulsive even to "call this vice by its proper name".[26] Suicide may be more morally excusable than such self-defilement:

The *ground of proof* is, indeed, that by it [masturbation] man surrenders his personality (throwing it away), since he uses himself merely as a means to satisfy an animal impulse. But this does not explain the high degree of violation of the humanity in one's own person by such a vice in its unnaturalness, which seems in terms of its form (the disposition it involves) to exceed even murdering oneself. It consists, then, in this: that someone who defiantly casts off life as a burden is at least not making a feeble surrender to animal impulse in throwing himself away; murdering oneself requires courage, and in this disposition there is still always room for respect for the humanity in one's own person. But unnatural lust, which is complete abandonment of oneself to animal inclination, makes man not only an object of enjoyment, but still further, a thing that is contrary to nature, that is, a loathsome object, and so deprives him of all respect for himself.[27]

Although Kant thought that suicide was "impermissible and abhorrent", he also thought that it was better to kill oneself than to abdicate one's duties towards one's own person:[28]

Humanity, in our person, is an object of the highest respect and never to be violated in us. . . . If a man can preserve his life no otherwise than by dishonouring his humanity, he ought rather to sacrifice it. . . . At the moment when I can no longer live with honour, and become by such an action unworthy of life, I cannot live at all. It is therefore far better to die with honour and reputation, than to prolong one's life by a few years through a discreditable action. If somebody, for example, can preserve life no longer save by surrendering their person to the will of another, they are bound rather to sacrifice their life, than to dishonour the dignity of humanity in their person, which is what they do by giving themselves up as a thing to the will of someone else.[29]

These passages and others like them provide ample grounds to believe that a woman who prefers to kill herself rather than give in to a vile seducer is morally justified. One wonders whether Kant had G. E. Lessing's immensely popular *Emilia Galotti* (1772) in mind when he said this (the passage comes from lecture notes taken in 1784). In fact, mindful of the moral taint that clings to suicide, Lessing's heroine does not commit outright suicide in order to avoid the fiendish prince; instead, in a macabre *pas de deux*, she has her father drive a dagger through her heart.[30] It is surely no coincidence that when Goethe's Werther shoots himself in December 1772, he leaves a copy of the brand new *Emilia Galotti* open on his desk, thus inviting us to reflect on the similarities and differences between the high-minded Emilia and himself.

For thinkers like Kant and Schiller, women incarnate human sexuality. In order to lift them above the mere animal stage, poetry and painting need to idealize them far more intensively than they do men; they need, in short, to create the figure of the *pure woman*, which will become an icon of idealist aesthetics. When the woman is idealized, the feeling the man has for her can be represented as ideal love, rather than as a base expression of animal nature. If women were to be described as subjected to the same urges and needs as men, the foundation of idealist aesthetics would crumble. Only the extreme idealization of women enables Schiller to continue to believe in the perfectibility of human nature. As we have seen, he believes that this is the sole point on which modern poets always do better than the ancients.

The idea that it is better to sacrifice one's life than to give up one's moral self-respect (one's honor) is everywhere in nineteenth-century European literature. In the case of women, moral self-respect is almost always taken to be identical with bodily chastity. The result is that in a curious reversal of the hierarchy between body and spirit, a woman's honor comes to reside entirely in her sexuality. *A Doll's House* provides a caustic one-line dismissal of this whole tradition of thought:

HELMER. I would gladly work night and day for you, Nora—bear sorrow and deprivation for your sake. But nobody sacrifices his *honor* for the one he loves.
NORA. A hundred thousand women have done precisely that.

(8: 362)

By attacking the old clichés about sacrificing life for love, Ibsen hastened the modern de-idealization of women and powerfully contributed to the demise of idealism as an aesthetic theory. In an act of noble self-sacrifice, Nora intends to drown herself rather than let Helmer's reputation be sullied, but then realizes that Helmer would not have been worth the sacrifice; Hedvig's suicide makes Gregers Werle's conviction that love is proved through sacrifice look murderous; Rosmer's final request that Rebecca prove the value of his idealism by dying for his sake comes across as nothing short of monstrous. The obvious intertextual connections between *The Lady from the Sea* and Richard Wagner's *The Flying Dutchman* only serve to reinforce the gulf that separates Wagner's idealist, self-sacrificing Senta and Ibsen's modern, haunted Ellida. When Hedda Gabler encourages Ejlert Løvborg to kill himself, she appears to be inflamed by the idea that it is better to die than to live without honor; the same idea inspires her own suicide once she realizes that Brack has sexual power over her. The point, however, is that in 1890, an action that Hedda still thinks of as an expression of noble, heroic idealism, comes across as utterly baffling, both to Judge Brack and to the audience. Finally, the contrast between Irene and Maja in *When We Dead Awaken* dramatizes the contrast between noble, self-sacrificing but ultimately lunatic idealism and free-spirited, sensuous but spiritually empty vitalist modernism. The avalanche that sweeps away Rubek and Maja also sweeps away the literary tradition in which Ibsen was formed.

Idealism and Romanticism

There are, of course, non-romantic forms of idealism: literary idealism was born in the Renaissance; neoclassicism was always idealist.[31] Tragedy was an intrinsically idealist form, and when idealism died, tragedy died too.[32] Yet there can be no doubt that romanticism is the fullest and finest flourishing of the post-Kantian idealist aesthetics that permeates the nineteenth century. Whether Keats's " 'Beauty is truth, truth beauty,'—that is all / Ye know on earth, and all ye need to know" is meant to question or to reaffirm the thought it presents, that thought owes as much to Hölderlin and his German colleagues as it does to Plato.[33] What, then, is the point of distinguishing between idealism and romanticism? What are the advantages of speaking of idealism rather than romanticism?

The first and most important reason to resurrect the concept of idealism is that it provides a new lens through which to see the *second* half of the nineteenth century. If we are willing to distinguish between romanticism as an artistic and literary movement and idealism as a set of post-Kantian aesthetic principles that survived romanticism, and survived it for a very long time, we will gain a better understanding of the long period that separates the death of the romantic movement from the birth of modernism.

Another reason to reconsider idealism is that it allows us to escape from the confusion that arises when romanticism is contrasted with realism, for this always leads us to expect a profound difference in aesthetic views between the romantic generations and their successors the realists, a difference that is often extremely hard to find. The truth is that for half a century after the death of romanticism proper, an increasingly impoverished, moralizing, didactic form of idealism continued to function as a more or less compulsory master discourse about literature and art.

The long survival of idealism as the only legitimate discourse on art explains why so many writers and artists who really cannot be called romantics still talked about their work in idealist terms well into the last third of the nineteenth century. As the century wore on, there developed an increasingly strident dissonance between the works of art and literature actually being produced and the way the artists themselves chose to present them. In Chapter 4 I shall illustrate the point by looking at the way in which William Quiller Orchardson presented his painting *The First Cloud* (1887), but the phenomenon is widespread. (I can't help thinking that the intensely modern Gwendolyn Harleth far outstrips anything George Eliot might have said about her outside the novel, for example.)

To show that *both* these terms—idealism and romanticism—were important to European aesthetic discourse in general and to Ibsen's situation in particular around 1870, I shall take a look at one of the rare books known to have inspired Ibsen's aesthetic development: namely, *Emigrantlitteraturen* (*Emigré Literature*), the first volume of Georg Brandes's *Hovedstrømminger i det 19de Aarhundredes Litteratur* (*Main Currents in European Literature*). Ibsen read Brandes's lectures with elation as soon as they appeared in print in the spring of 1872, at a time when he himself was hard at work on *Emperor and Galilean*, the play in which he fully confronted his idealist inheritance and claimed his membership in European modernity.[34]

In his lectures, presented in Copenhagen in 1871–2, Brandes denounced Denmark as a cultural backwater and called for a new, modern literature to express the new, modern situation. Yet Brandes's firebrand of a book, which still stands as a landmark in Scandinavian cultural history, made its case by going back to the late eighteenth century, to the first generation of romantics. Brandes justifies beginning with the aftermath of the French Revolution by claiming, first, that the whole of nineteenth-century European literature has to be grasped in its relations to the French Revolution, and, second, that Danish literature in particular has much to learn from the "great drama" enacted by European literature in the period from 1789 to 1848, for "We are this time as usual about forty years behind Europe".[35] If Denmark was forty years behind Europe in 1871, its former colony Norway was surely no more advanced. (In 1861, Ibsen accused Norwegian theater audiences of being *fifty* years behind the times in their taste.[36])

Emigrantlitteraturen gives pride of place to Madame de Staël, the greatest intellectual woman of her age, theorist of German aesthetics, and a card-carrying aesthetic idealist if ever there was one. As a freethinking Jew, Brandes was suspicious of her flirtation with Catholicism, but he admired her resistance to the tyrant Napoleon and considered her novels quite radical.[37] While praising *Delphine* for its advanced understanding of marriage, Brandes reserved his greatest admiration for *Corinne*: "*Corinne, or Italy* is Mme de Staël's greatest poetic work. In the paradisaical nature [of Italy] her eyes were opened to nature. . . . Here her modern, revolutionary and melancholic mind opened itself to history" (*EL*, 113). Brandes's admiration for *Delphine* and *Corinne* is significant both because it places women and marriage at the center of the revolutionary literary tradition he wants to foster, and because he does not hesitate to canonize a woman writer.

Ibsen did not only read *Emigrantlitteraturen* (he wrote an enthusiastic letter to Brandes about it), he also read *Corinne, or Italy*.[38] This famous and much discussed novel went through seventy-five editions from 1807 to 1875 in French alone, and was widely used as a guidebook to Italy in general and Rome in particular. When Ibsen explored Rome in the 1860s, it was with the help of *Corinne*. (According to Daniel Haakonsen, Ibsen borrowed the Danish translation of Madame de Staël's novel from the Scandinavian library in Rome in 1864.[39])

In spite of all his admiration for Madame de Staël's revolutionary politics, Brandes never once mentions her *aesthetic* idealism. Yet there is an enormous amount of discussion of art in *Corinne, or Italy.* Corinne herself is a poet, dancer, actress, performer, and improviser of genius, and Corinne and Oswald incessantly visit museums, look at paintings, listen to music, go to the theater and the opera, and discuss aesthetics. When the protagonists are absorbed in contemplation of "the most perfect beauty" of the statues in the Vatican gallery, the narrator comments, "In this contemplation, the soul is uplifted to hopes filled with enthusiasm and virtue, for beauty is one in the universe, and whatever form it assumes, it always arouses a religious feeling in the hearts of mankind."[40] This is idealism in all its glory, for here beauty inspires feeling, enthusiasm, religion, and virtue all at once. The beautiful, the true, and the good are one; this goes to show that true beauty is harmonious and uplifting for the soul, however tragic the fate of the characters involved might be. In his long discussion of Madame de Staël, Brandes has nothing to say about any of this. I take this silence as a sign that Brandes in 1872 had not yet reached a consistent position in relation to idealism. (As we have seen in Chapter 2, Brandes's boundless admiration for Paul Heyse points in the same direction.)

There is nevertheless no doubt that Brandes detested the degenerate form of idealism that dominated Danish cultural life around 1870. *Emigrantlitteraturen* begins by complaining about the lofty idealism that prevented his fellow Danes from seeing reality as it was:

We vie with one another in erecting towering ideals from which reality is only visible as a distant, black point.

Where has this current ended? In figures like Paludan-Müller's Kalanus who in his ecstasy burns himself to death on a pyre, and like Ibsen's Brand, whose moral beliefs, were they to be realized, would lead half of mankind to starve to death for the love of the Ideal.

To this have we come: nowhere in all of Europe are there such exalted ideals, and in few places a more banal spiritual life. For one really has to be extremely naive to believe that our lives correspond to those types. So strong has the current been that even such a natural revolutionary as Ibsen has become caught up in it. Is *Brand* revolution or reaction? I can't tell, for there is so much of both in this poem.

(*EL*, 22)

Sick and tired of unrealistic and unlivable ideals, Brandes calls for reality, for the representation of "our life" in literature. For Brandes, as for the naturalists who followed his lead, *truth and reality are antidotes to idealism.*

The passage ends by asking whether *Brand* represents *revolution* or *reaction.*

These are the two "main currents of European literature" that provide the fundamental structure to Brandes's long lecture series. The reason why Brandes can't figure out whether *Brand* is reactionary or revolutionary is that *Brand* is the play in which Ibsen puts idealism on trial, exploring (but never affirming) the idea that idealism might be destructive and demoralizing, rather than uplifting and harmonizing. At the same time, however, Brand is a recognizably radical romantic hero, a prophet and outcast, the bearer of a new gospel, a new, utopian vision of humanity—that is to say, a type that in many ways appealed profoundly to Brandes.

In general, Brandes thinks of idealism as reactionary. His treatment of romanticism is more complex. On the one hand, there is a kind of romanticism that is radical, progressive, utopian, represented by Madame de Staël, Schiller, and Fichte (see *EL*, 164). On the other hand, there is reactionary, religious, German romanticism. In order to convey his point with greater power, Brandes decides to give the radical movement he admires a new name: namely, "Emigré literature, which can be considered a kind of Romanticism before Romanticism" (*EL*, 147). This move in effect splits Schiller's aesthetics in two, by drawing a wedge between his historical, political, and utopian vision of human perfectibility and the signature mix of ethics and aesthetics that by 1870 had led to the moralistic glorification of increasingly outlandish modes of self-sacrifice in literature.

Having introduced his signature term of "Émigré literature", Brandes can finally define romanticism as the intrinsically reactionary opposite of modern, progressive realism. Modern realism thus becomes the rightful inheritor of émigré radicalism, idealism the desiccated and superannuated survivor of reactionary romanticism. Or in other words, emigré literature is the revolutionary past, romanticism the reactionary past, and idealism the reactionary present. The empty fourth space is to be filled with the new, revolutionary literature of the future, a literature that Brandes will variously refer to as realism, naturalism, or the "modern breakthrough".

Idealism and Realism

In *On Naive and Sentimental Poetry* Schiller devotes a long passage to what he calls "a remarkable psychological antagonism between people in a century in the process of civilizing itself": namely, the opposition between idealists and realists (p. 249). Humankind is divided into two categories: realists, who judge only by experience, and idealists, who judge only by reason.

Realists risk becoming petty-minded positivists, idealists risk taking off into ungrounded flights of fancy, cut loose from every sense of morality. The two types each represent an aspect of ideal human nature, but neither reaches it completely. While it is clear that Schiller considers idealists to come closer to the ideal, he also shows that the "true realist" must ultimately agree with the "genuine idealist" (p. 259).

The same logic applies to the opposition between the naïve and the sentimental poet: although the naïve poet is a realist and the sentimental poet is an idealist, both work with the same goal in mind: to give full and free expression to ideal human nature. Schiller's division of sentimental poetry into satire and elegy works in the same way: while satire describes a world in which the ideal is absent, and elegy one in which it is still present, however problematically, the task of both poetic modes is to fill us with the "magnificence of the idea" (p. 206). What matters to Schiller, in short, is "the manner of feeling prevailing" in the various types of poetry (p. 211 n.). A realist technique is therefore perfectly compatible with idealist aesthetics, for the realist serves the ideal by pointing to the deleterious consequences of its absence. A generation later, the great French realist Honoré de Balzac explained the difference between his own novels and those of George Sand precisely in such terms.

In *Story of My Life*, George Sand sets out the principles of her own idealist aesthetics. First of all, she writes, a novel should be poetic, not analytical. Just like Schiller, she believes that the passion of love (and therefore also the character who feels it) must be idealized:

One must not be afraid to endow it [the passion] with exceptional importance, powers beyond the ordinary, or subject it to delight or suffering that completely surpass the habitual, human ones, and that even surpass what most intelligent people think is believable. In sum, the idealization of a sentiment yields the subject, leaving to the art of the storyteller the care of placing that subject within a situation and a realistic framework that is drawn sensitively enough to make the subject stand out.[41]

In conversations with Balzac, Sand writes, she learned that "one could sacrifice the idealized subject for the truth of the portrayal, or for the critique of society or humanity itself".[42] If this is right, at first glance it is difficult to see what the difference is between Balzac in the 1830s and Brandes and the naturalists of the 1880s. As George Sand continues, however, the difference becomes clear:

Balzac summed this up completely when he said to me later on, "You are looking for man as he should be; I take him as he is. Believe me, we are both right. Both paths lead to the same end. I also like exceptional human beings; I am one myself. I need them to make my ordinary characters stand out, and I never sacrifice them unnecessarily. But the ordinary human beings interest me more than they do you. I make them larger than life; I idealize them in the opposite sense, in their ugliness or in their stupidity. I give their deformities frightful or grotesque proportions. You could not do that; you are smart not to want to look at people and things that would give you nightmares. Idealize what is pretty and what is beautiful; that is a woman's job."[43]

That Balzac at his best was widely perceived to "combine the ideal and the real" is attested to by French criticism from the 1830s.[44]

Both Balzac and Sand believed that the task of literature was to draw attention to the shortcomings of ordinary human life by exaggeration; both were committed to the fundamental aims of aesthetic idealism: to uplift, ennoble, and transform humanity by filling us with a sense of the ideal. While Balzac chose Schiller's satirical mode, Sand settled on his elegiac mode, sometimes in the form of elegy (as in *Indiana*), sometimes in the form of idyll (as in the postscript to *Indiana*, or in *La petite Fadette*). As Schor points out, they both subscribe to an aesthetic theory in which idealism is the hierarchically superior and realism the subordinate term.[45]

This may seem an odd claim to make, for from the 1840s to the 1870s intense debates raged between realists and idealists in France. The quarrel started among painters and art critics, and soon spread to literature. Bernard Weinberg, however, has shown that most anti-realist critics did not object to the attempt to portray the real world; what they objected to was the absence of the ideal, for without the ideal and the immaterial, they claimed, truth was absent.[46] If the realist writers had style (beauty), the critics usually forgave them.

In the 1860s British critics vigorously debated the respective merits of idealism and realism in the same terms as Balzac had done in his conversations with George Sand. Mary Poovey finds that critics at the time are either straightforward idealists, or try to show that realism is compatible with idealism. Among the latter, we find George Eliot. Nobody defends a straightforwardly anti-idealist realism. Rather, Poovey writes, they "did not precisely prefer realism to idealism but tended to maintain that what critics called realism could also approach higher truths through detailed but imaginatively interpreted descriptions of everyday things".[47] In Norway, as usual a good number of decades behind the leading European nations, the battle between "realists" and "idealists" turns up in cartoons in the 1880s, after the publication of Ibsen's *Ghosts* (see Fig. 3).

It is only when the idealist trinity of truth, beauty, and goodness falls apart that realism becomes the outright enemy of idealism. (When critics and writers start thinking that the aim of art is to produce beauty, not truth, we

3. Olaf "Filou" Krohn, *Norwegian Poets*, National Library, Oslo. Cartoon published in *Vikingen* (Kristiania), no. 32 (7 August 1886), 28. The captions read: "The idealist", "The realist", "Economic Poets. Further Developments of Christopher Bruun's theories about frieze clothing and economy." Ibsen is playing the harp, Bjørnson is holding forth; on the far left is Alexander Kielland; on the far right Jonas Lie.

get various kinds of aestheticism; when they think it is to produce truth, but not beauty, we get naturalism.) Realism, then, is not *one*. The tendency among contemporary critics to theorize all kinds of realism in the same way—namely, as "reference" or "representation"—obscures the significant differences between Balzac's, Flaubert's, and Ibsen's realisms. One example of such differences is that Balzac, Flaubert, and Ibsen have a strikingly different relationship to the ordinary. As we have seen, Balzac is highly critical of the ordinary, which he tends to exaggerate, make grotesque, and infuse with melodrama. Flaubert, on the other hand, finds the ordinary indescribably dull, a place where no values, no thrills, no excitement can possibly be found. Ibsen, for his part, turns to the ordinary and the everyday, not as something that has to be overcome, exaggerated, or idealized, but as a sphere where we have to take on the task of building meaningful human relationships. If we fail at this task, the everyday becomes unbearable; if we succeed, it becomes a source of human values.

Because of his commitment to the ordinary, Ibsen is neither an idealist nor a straightforward anti-idealist. His most intensely anti-idealist—and, at the time, most controversial—play is *Ghosts*. Some of his most complex and thoughtful plays (*Rosmersholm* immediately comes to mind), however, convey an extremely nuanced and profound meditation on the legacy of idealism. On the one hand, Ibsen, like Brandes, deplored the shallow, positivistic moralism that kept harping on empty and unlivable ideals; on the other, he clearly regretted the passing of the utopian vision of human perfectibility that was such a seductive part of idealism. Ibsen's turn to the ordinary and the everyday was an attempt to maintain a balance between utopia and critique, between a positive and negative view of the world.

Truth Undoing Beauty: The War between Idealism and Naturalism

In France, the first signs of an emerging tension within the idealist trinity of truth, beauty, and goodness can be dated to the critical reactions to Balzac's works that surfaced in the 1840s.[48] Truth, however, was not the major issue in 1857, when the French public prosecutor Ernest Pinard took *Madame Bovary* to court for blasphemy, and *Les Fleurs du mal* for obscenity. Flaubert won his case, and Baudelaire lost his, with the result that six poems of *Les Fleurs du mal* remained officially prohibited until 1949. The underlying reasons for the prosecutor's outrage were very similar. These works shocked because they appeared to be beholden to no ultimate ethical and religious ideal. Baudelaire's attempt to produce beauty out of evil and Flaubert's nihilistic irony both attacked the very core of idealist aesthetics, and both proposed a new and unsettling understanding of the purpose of art, pointing in the direction of a modern, anti-idealist formalism, and not in the direction of the naturalist crusade for truth. This is why it is the story of modernism, not of naturalism, that starts with Baudelaire and Flaubert.[49] In other words, the development of the modern faith in the "autonomy of the aesthetic" begins when aesthetics is severed from ethics.

The trials of *Madame Bovary* and *Les Fleurs du mal* are significant because they show how powerful the idealist outrage could be against works in which truth, beauty, moral goodness, and religion were felt to come apart in a way that was threatening to the community. The idealists were right to feel threatened, for once the idealist trinity fell apart, the ground was cleared for all kinds of anti-idealist theories and beliefs: it is no coincidence that materialism, determinism, Darwinism, skepticism, nihilism, "free thought", and atheism were major naturalist themes, and that political movements like anarchism, socialism, communism, and feminism were all associated with the naturalist onslaught on idealism.

Late nineteenth-century anti-naturalist polemics conveys an overwhelming sense that beauty has been blemished, innocence defiled, womanhood dishonored, God defied. Idealists expressed their disgust at the ugliness of naturalism through an unusually insistent and widespread imagery of dirt, manure, sickness, boils, sores, infection, rotting corpses, and sexual depravation. In 1880 Paul Heyse wrote to Brandes that he was working on some Provençal stories in order to oppose the modern *Zolismus*, the craze for Zola, which he thought could not last: "Perhaps the world will soon return to the idea that the dirty washing of a courtesan in the long run looks uglier than clean linen and fine silks clinging to healthy and chaste limbs in beautiful airy folds."[50]

The true inheritor of Schiller's perfectionist aesthetics (and of George Sand's idealism, too), Heyse here produces a set of automatic connections between the ugly, the dirty, the sexual, and the "fallen woman", in every respect exemplary of late idealist polemics. Already in 1873, soon after their first meeting, Brandes wrote that Heyse "considers it a kind of duty to depict human beings as better and greater than they on average are; he would like to strengthen everyone's self-respect, give him courage to continue to live and hold up for him examples that show that even in a lowly human being there lies much beauty hidden, and that even in a philistine a hero may be slumbering."[51] In 1882 Heyse wrote a letter to Brandes in which he commented on the work of two Scandinavian novelists, the Dane J. P. Jacobsen and the Norwegian Alexander Kielland:

When they [the young Danish writers] establish a veritable clinic in which the wounds and boils of society are exposed, the eternal stench of disinfectant is so shocking that it drives away the unbiased and spiritually free friends of humanity, who until now were looking to the fine arts (to which I still think the art of writing belongs) to find comfort for the misery of the world. . . . I am completely convinced that a single work giving the sunny side of this wonderful world of sun and shade its due . . . would exert a deeper, warmer, more stimulating, more reformist influence than all these brilliant studies of putrefaction.[52]

While Heyse's wish for art and literature to represent a kinder, gentler view of the world, his desire to uplift and encourage people through art, may strike us as quaint and naïve, it expresses perfectly the feelings of embattled idealists in the 1880s and 1890s. Unlike some of his fellow idealists, however, Heyse was at pains not to dissociate himself from the freethinking aspects of naturalism; he did not wish to be taken for a reactionary religious spirit, he just believed that works with a more positive outlook on the world would have stronger political and moral effects than the dirt and stench of the naturalists. Lamenting the loss of the good and the beautiful in literature, Heyse continued to give voice to the utopian longings of idealism until he died in 1914.

"A Dunghill at Delphi": *Ghosts*

No Ibsen play challenged the idealists as deeply as *Ghosts*, perhaps because it dramatizes the conflict between the competing aesthetic norms that would rage in response to it:

PASTOR MANDERS. Is there not a voice in your mother's heart that forbids you to break down your son's ideals?
MRS. ALVING. Yes, but what about the truth?
PASTOR MANDERS. Yes, but what about the ideals?
MRS. ALVING. Oh—ideals, ideals! If only I weren't as cowardly as I am!

(9: 90)

Throughout *Ghosts*, Mrs Alving and pastor Manders embody the conflict between naturalists and idealists, faithfully reproduced and reenacted by outraged or exhilarated reviewers, all of whom deplored the shocking absence of reconciliation and uplift in the play. Ever since the publication of *Catiline*,

M. J. Monrad had been one of Ibsen's most intelligent and supportive reviewers, but when Ibsen broke with idealism, Monrad broke with Ibsen. Monrad began his 1882 review of *Ghosts* by complaining that idealist aesthetics was being threatened by truth:

The time is long gone when one turned to creative works in search of what one used to call poetry and beauty, when one sought refreshment for the spirit and the heart, to be uplifted above the messy, tiring confusion of everyday life, to find a reconciled and reconciling view of life. All such things are now only considered to be ghost-like matters; what poetry, like every other form of art, now wants to offer us, is only what it calls "truth," that is to say the naked, even stark naked reality in its most repellent form. It wants to smash all illusions, all so-called ideals.[53]

All *Ghosts* could teach us, Monrad ironically concluded, was that modern society actually requires a "religious foundation", and that the whole of humanity desires to be "liberated from the natural corruption and its consequences of natural corruption".[54]

Elsewhere the idealist response to *Ghosts* was simple outrage. The kindly Paul Heyse, who had admired *A Doll's House*, wrote to Brandes in December 1881 that when he read *Ghosts*, he felt as if he were sitting in a charnel house, incessantly smoking to keep the stench away, yet nevertheless succumbing to nausea at the abominable mixture of uneasiness, horror, and disgust that Ibsen had arranged with such consummate artistry.[55] In April 1882, the Norwegian novelist Amalie Skram, a radical who wrote a number of out-standing novels on women and marriage in the 1880s and 1890, described *Ghosts* as a description of "Earthly life's loudest lament, its darkest and most extreme distress, the ultimate consequence of its curse". Obviously shaken by the play, she exclaimed that the "sight of this mother and this son is unbearable".[56]

Ghosts, in short, was received as if it were the most horrible expression of naturalism ever produced. This was not least true in Britain, where the culture wars unleashed by the production of Ibsen's plays in the early 1890s laid the foundations for the advent of modernism. After the first London performance of *Ghosts* in 1891, *The Daily Telegraph* devoted a whole editorial to it. In the long article, the writer makes a point of denouncing a claim made by some of Ibsen's English defenders: namely, that *Ghosts* had the purity and simplicity of a Greek tragedy. The passion and the sense of outrage, as well as the language and the themes sounded here make this article particularly striking, and particularly representative of the feelings of the defenders of idealism all over Europe:

Ay! The play performed last night is "simple" enough in plan and purpose, but simple only in the sense of an open drain; of a loathsome sore unbandaged; of a dirty act done publicly; or of a lazar-house with all its doors and windows open. It is no more "Greek", and can no more be called "Greek" for its plainness of speech and candid foulness, than could a dunghill at Delphi, or a madhouse at Mitylene. It is not "artistic" even, in the sense of the anatomical studies of the Great Masters; because they, in carefully drawing the hidden things of life and nature, did it in the single and steadfast worship of Truth and Beauty, the subtle framework and foundation of which they thus reverently endeavoured to seize. . . .

But Morality, Criticism and Taste alike must certainly draw the line at what is absolutely loathsome and foetid. If Medea could not, according to Horace, kill her children upon the stage, still less can Art allow what common decency forbids. Realism is one thing, but the nostrils of an audience must not be visibly held before a play can be stamped as true to nature. It is difficult to expose indecorous words—the gross, and almost putrid, indecorum of this play of *Ghosts*. Suffice it to indicate that the central situation is that of a son exposing to a mother—herself, in past days, a would-be adulteress—his inheritance of a loathsome malady from a father whose memory the widow secretly execrates while she publicly honors and consecrates it. If this be Art—which word, be it remembered, is but the abbreviation of the Greek name for what is highest, most excellent, and best—then the masterpieces of English literature must be found in such vagaries as Ben Jonson's *Fleet Ditch Voyage*, Swift's mad scurrility, and Congreve's lewd coarseness.[57]

This passage has it all: the references to dirt, putrefaction, rotting bodies (the "lazar-house"), sexual depravation, and nihilism. This outraged and outrageous article brings out particularly clearly that by the end of the nineteenth century Schiller's aesthetic vision of human perfection had been reduced to a desiccated and moralistic demand for art to be decent, well-mannered, simple, and harmonious.

By 1890, then, many intellectuals and artists took idealism to be virtually identical with hypocritical, anti-artistic, moralistic conservatism. This is the image of idealism that emerges from George Bernard Shaw's *The Quintessence of Ibsenism* (1891), a book written in response to *The Daily Telegraph*'s attacks on Ibsen.[58] Shaw's despicable idealists have no connection to Schiller and Madame de Staël; they are simply trying to cover up the unpalatable reality of their own miserable lives. "The idealist . . . has taken refuge with the ideals because he hates himself and is ashamed of himself," Shaw declares.[59]

Because Shaw defends Ibsen by turning idealism into the expression of a personally and politically thwarted psyche, *The Quintessence of Ibsenism* conveys no sense of the illustrious origins of idealist aesthetics, no sense that idealism once had genuine claims to be taken seriously. By reducing idealism to an effect of psychological repression, Shaw accelerated the process that would lead readers and critics of Ibsen to forget idealism entirely. But when we forget all about the idealist tradition in aesthetics, we are no longer able to see that *Ghosts* is not just about family sickness and family secrets, but about aesthetic norms. Paradoxically, then, the death of idealism that Ibsen helped to bring about makes it more, not less, difficult to understand what Ibsen was doing in his modern plays.

Shaw's analysis of idealism, moreover, is entirely based on the opposition between ideals and truth. Realists face the truth of the human condition, idealists demand that people sacrifice themselves in the name of chimerical ideals. All over Europe, critics engaged in similar polemics. The battles over naturalism were in fact battles over idealism. At the time, it was impossible to avoid taking sides. The moralistic and conservative idealists kept harping on beauty, harmony, and uplift. The naturalists rightly revolted against the increasingly anachronistic, unrealistic, and reactionary demands of idealism. With truth and freedom on their side, they were not in a mood for compromise.

Published in 1886, Nietzsche's *Beyond Good and Evil* was in large parts a response to the debates over naturalism and idealism raging all over Germany. At the time, however, his provocative critique of the starry-eyed belief in the power of truth to set us free could gain him no support from the naturalists, while the very title of his book was enough to ensure that no self-respecting idealist would touch it. If they had opened it, Nietzsche's devastating denunciation of Christian slave morality and European herd morality would have made them throw the book across the room.

By casting idealists and naturalists together as equally misguided meta-physical moralists, Nietzsche's book far outstripped the cultural debates that surrounded it. The beginning of the following passage could have been written specially for Heyse; the middle is directed against naïve defenders of naturalism; and the end returns to a critique of the moralism usually associated with idealism:

Nobody is very likely to consider a doctrine true merely because it makes people happy or virtuous—except perhaps the lovely "idealists" who become effusive about the good, the true, and the beautiful and allow all kinds of motley, clumsy, and benevolent desiderata to swim around in utter confusion in their pond. Happiness and virtue are no arguments. But people like to forget—even sober spirits—that making unhappy and evil are no counterarguments. Something might be true while being harmful and dangerous in the highest degree. . . . But there is no doubt at all that the evil and unhappy are more favored when it comes to the discovery of certain *parts* of truth, and that the probability of their success here is greater—not to speak of the evil who are happy, a species the moralists bury in silence.[60]

Nietzsche's critique points beyond naturalism, to a kind of art that will reject metaphysics and place itself truly beyond good an evil, and art that understands that "the existence of the world is justified only as an aesthetic phenomenon", an art that will "fight at any risk whatever the *moral* interpretation and significance of existence".[61] This art, of course, turned out to be modernism.

One of the reasons why Ibsen so often reminds me of Nietzsche is that Ibsen, too, after what we may call his high naturalist phase of the early 1880s—*Ghosts* and an *Enemy of the People*—turned his back on the metaphysics of truth. Dr Stockmann's righteous pursuit of the truth in *An Enemy of the People* leads him into precisely the kind of elitism and arrogance that were to become widespread among modernists.[62] This is a route Ibsen chooses not to follow: there is no unchallenged admiration of supermen anywhere in Ibsen's 1880s and 1890s plays.

I have defined naturalism as an aesthetic movement obsessed with an anti-idealist quest for truth. Of course, the quest for truth expressed itself in different ways: in a turn towards science, a preference for critique over utopia, and, in general, a desire for literature to become less ideal and more real. But by the 1870s, realism in itself was not what the idealists objected to. At the beginning of Heyse's *Children of the World* the reader is slowly introduced to the inhabitants of a boarding house in Berlin, in a manner remarkably (and, surely, deliberately) reminiscent of the beginning of Balzac's *Père Goriot.* When Zola's *L'Assommoir* was published in 1877, a critic in *Le Figaro* wrote that the novel was "not realism, but filth; not crudity, but pornography".[63] The problem with Zola, then, was not that he was a realist, but that he was the wrong kind of realist, the kind that refused to deliver beauty and moral uplift to his readers. We have seen that *The Daily Telegraph* drew on the same distinction in order to condemn *Ghosts.* What is missing in objectionable realist works, in short, is reconciliation.

In 1893, the Swiss literary critic Ernest Tissot also stressed that realism in itself was not the problem. What was at stake, Tissot wrote, was the question of the "positive vision" that every self-respecting idealist expected from literature. Realism with a positive vision was fine; realism without was not. Commenting on the battle over naturalism, Tissot writes:

Ten years ago, assuming that it is possible to be precise about such dates, faced with the contemptible success of the naturalist novel, those who loudly proclaimed the rights of intelligence and the demands of conscience thought of invoking the great works of Tolstoy and Dostoevsky. They claimed that the life of the soul, the moral life, the inner life in short, was superior—even in beauty—to material life. As evidence, they produced *War and Peace, Crime and Punishment* and other works whose moral anxiety, passionate quest for the good, and for compassionate, almost evangelical meekness, demonstrated the disgraceful uselessness of novels like *Nana* and *L'Assomoir* all the more effectively since the aesthetics of both sides was equally realistic.[64]

For late nineteenth-century idealist aesthetics, realism was fine as long as it ended on a note of harmony. Art should never distress us, which Ibsen's plays increasingly did. According to Tissot, Ibsen wrote only "books of hatred or books of despair".[65]

No wonder that the same Tissot adored Bjørnstjerne Bjørnson ("Bjørnson's philosophy . . . is a philosophy of harmony and calm"), and thought that the problem in *The Wild Duck* was that the ignorant characters simply fail to grasp the uplifting message of the heroic Gregers Werle.[66] The duck was also a problem: "And then, is a crippled duck really a worthy symbol of the human soul? I prefer the eagle placed on the funeral pyres of the Roman emperors—the image was more beautiful. Thus, just as Hedda Gabler will later come to think, what is missing is above all beauty."[67] While Tissot's preference for the noble Roman eagle over the damaged Norwegian duck is representative of the increasingly absurd manifestations of a dying idealism, his apparently outmoded perspective nevertheless allows him to grasp, quite brilliantly, that the idealist cult of noble beauty, glorious heroism, and transcendent self-sacrifice is precisely what is at stake in *Hedda Gabler*.[68]

Idealism in Action: The Nobel Prize for Literature

When Alfred Nobel established the Nobel Prizes in his will of 1895, he specified that the prize for literature should be awarded to "the person who shall have produced in the field of literature the most outstanding work of an idealistic tendency".[69] There has been significant debate about what exactly Nobel meant by "idealistic tendency". Much evidence indicates that he probably wanted to keep faith with the utopian idealism of revolutionary romanticism, and in particular with the "religiously colored spirit of revolt" of his favorite author, Percy Bysshe Shelley (E, 4–5). But Nobel was out of touch with his time, for by the 1890s, "idealist" no longer meant revolutionary romanticism; it had become the slogan of the anti-naturalist, anti-modernist, moralizing lovers of uplifting beauty in literature, such as the permanent secretary of the Swedish Academy at the time, Carl David af Wirsén (1842–1912). Because of Wirsén's influence, the first Nobel Prizes for literature allow us to grasp with particular acuity the nature of late idealist aesthetics.

From 1901 to 1911, Wirsén made sure that the Nobel Prize went to works steeped in a "lofty and sound idealism", exhibiting "a true nobility not simply of presentation but of conception and of philosophy of life".[70] In his invaluable study of the aesthetic criteria governing the choice of the Nobel laureate in literature, Kjell Espmark tells us that in the Wirsén era the "literary quality of a work was weighed against its contribution to humanity's struggle 'toward the ideal' " (E, 10). Atheists and agnostics were automatically disqualified, unless they demonstrated an unusually strong "striving towards higher things and moral responsibility" (E, 12–13). Like most late nineteenth-century and early twentieth-century idealists, the early Nobel committees consistently praised clarity and simplicity, using words like "obscure" and "unclear" as terms of strong disapproval (see E, 14–15).

The outspoken commitment to rigidly conservative idealist principles explains why the list of the ten first Nobel laureates in Wirsén's era looks as strange as it does today:

1901   Sully-Prudhomme
1902   Theodor Mommsen
1903   Bjørnstjerne Bjørnson
1904   Frédéric Mistral, José Echegaray
1905   Henryk Sienkiewicz
1906   Giosuè Carducci
1907   Rudyard Kipling
1908   Rudolf Eucken
1909   Selma Lagerlöf
1910   Paul Heyse[71]

The first Nobel laureate was an establishment candidate, enthusiastically nominated by the Académie française. Honored "in special recognition of his poetic composition, which gives evidence of lofty idealism, artistic perfection and a rare combination of the qualities of both heart and intellect", Sully-Prudhomme was chosen in preference to that year's prime reject, Emile Zola, whose naturalism was dismissed as "spiritless, and often grossly cynical".[72] In 1902, the German historian Theodor Mommsen was preferred to Leo Tolstoy, "an author who in his otherwise magnificent *War and Peace* attributes to blind chance such a decisive role in the great events of world history . . . and who in countless of his works denies not only the church, but the state, even the right of property" (E, 17).

Wirsén, who was largely responsible for these decisions, was in fact something of an idealist activist. He had spent large parts of his career as a literary critic praising Bjørnson and panning Ibsen. At the end of Wirsén's brief review of *Little Eyolf,* he longs for the old, idealist Ibsen: "The three

works *Hedda Gabler, The Master Builder, Little Eyolf* nevertheless represent a
true decadence. Where is the author of *The Pretenders* and *The Vikings at
Helgeland*?" At the end of his review of *John Gabriel Borkman*, he complains
that "Everything is disconsolate, life is empty, human beings are grief-
stricken, or wretched—that is the overall impression." And at the beginning
of his review of *When We Dead Awaken*, Wirsén claims that everything
Ibsen has written from *A Doll's House* onwards is worse than "profound
masterpieces" like *Brand, Peer Gynt*, and *Emperor and Galilean*. Like all his
fellow idealists, Wirsén claimed Ibsen's great closet dramas for idealism, and
disliked virtually all of his contemporary plays.[73]

It is hardly surprising, then, that in 1903 the Nobel committee crowned
Bjørnson, and soundly rejected both Ibsen and Brandes. Brandes's view of
life and ethics was unacceptable to the committee, for he was considered to
be "negatively sceptical, totally atheistic", as well as far too lax on sexual
matters (E, 18). With the explicit exception of *The Pretenders, Brand*, and
Emperor and Galilean, Ibsen's works were criticized for being negativistic,
obscure, and generally repellent; about his later plays the committee wrote
that their "negative and enigmatic features have repelled even those who
would have willingly given the world-famous author a substantial recognition" (E, 18). Bjørnson, on the other hand, was lauded for his poetry, his
freshness of spirit, and above all for his positive and pure idealism in works
nobody, not even in Norway, reads anymore:

In *Laboremus* (1901) he has extolled the right of the moral life against the natural
forces of unrestrained passion. Finally, in *På Storhove* (1902) [At Storhove] he has paid
dramatic homage to the guardian forces of the home as represented by Margareta, the
faithful and constant support of her family. . . . Bjørnson's characters are of a rare
purity, . . . his genius is always positive and in no way negative. . . . He has never
ceased to combat the claim of the senses to dominate man.[74]

Possibly the most bizarre decision in the whole history of the Nobel Prize
for Literature was the 1908 award to the German philosopher Rudolf
Eucken, for his "lofty and scholarly idealism".[75] Even the committee itself
thought of Eucken as "an original but hardly an epoch-making thinker"
(E, 23). Wirsén himself was so upset at the choice that he refused to come to
the Nobel banquet. As with so many botched decisions, the choice of Eucken
was the result of a compromise. While Wirsén and his allies had supported
the British poet Algernon Swinburne, the rest of the committee wanted the
Swedish novelist Selma Lagerlöf. Although Wirsén's unexpected support for
Swinburne was mostly tactical (he would do almost anything to block
Lagerlöf), he enthusiastically invoked the poet's conversion from atheistic

hedonist to supporter of the status quo as evidence of his idealism: "The former intransigent republican now celebrates legitimate monarchy and . . . the singer whose lyre was previously tuned to pleasure now most beautifully lauds the innocence of childhood and makes the strings reverberate to the heart's purity" (E, 22). When the rest of the committee absolutely refused to embrace the erstwhile hedonist, and Wirsén's faction furiously rejected Lagerlöf, the compromise of Eucken was a fact.

"On or about December 1910 human character changed," Virginia Woolf famously declared.[76] The Nobel committee begged to differ, for in December 1910 it solemnly awarded the Nobel Prize to Paul Heyse. That year, the committee rejected Thomas Hardy, whose heroines were accused of being lacking in "character"—that is to say, in "religious and ethical firmness" (E, 22). Not surprisingly, precisely the qualities that make Hardy's women modern made Hardy unacceptable. Heyse, on the other hand, was praised as the greatest German poet since Goethe. In his presentation speech, Wirsén stressed Heyse's importance as a symbol of the idealist struggle against naturalism:

Naturalism, which burst forth in the eighties and dominated the scene for the next decade, directed its iconoclastic attack especially against Heyse, its most powerful opponent. He was too harmonious, too fond of beauty, too Hellenic and lofty for those who, slandering him at any price, demanded sensation, effect, bizarre licentiousness, and crass reproductions of ugly realities. Heyse did not yield. His sense of form was offended by their uncouth behaviour; he demanded that literature should see life in an ideal light that would transfigure reality.[77]

Heyse was also praised for his independence, which he had proved not least by disliking *Ghosts* and all the rest of Ibsen's late plays. In Wirsén's final peroration, he quotes Schiller, and thus gives full voice to the idealist aesthetics he had defended all his life:

Aesthetically [Heyse] has been faithful to truth, but in such a manner that he mirrored inner in external reality. Schiller's well known words, "Life is serious, art serene," properly understood, express a profound truth which can be found in the life and work of Heyse. Beauty should liberate and recreate: it should neither imitate reality slavishly nor drag it into the dust. It should have a noble simplicity. Heyse reveals beauty in this aspect. He does not teach morals, which would deprive beauty of its immediacy, but there is much wisdom and nobility in his works. He does not teach religion, but one would look in vain for anything that would seriously hurt religious feelings. Although he puts greater emphasis on the ethical than on the dogmatic side of religion, he has expressed his deep respect for every serious opinion. He is tolerant but not indifferent. He has praised love, but it was its heavenly and not its earthly aspect that he glorified. He likes men who are faithful to their nature, but the individuals to whom Heyse is most sympathetic adhere to their higher rather than their lower nature.[78]

Forlornly seeking harmony in an ever less harmonious world, Wirsén's aesthetics mixes fragments of Schiller's idealist romanticism with conservative German neoclassicism, and mounts a desperate last ditch defense of the spiritual over the material and—above all—over the sexual.

Modernism and Idealism

In 1918 idealism was dead; Paul Heyse was forgotten, and nobody remembered that *Ghosts* had once been a play about aesthetic conflicts. Soon Brecht would deride *Ghosts* as irrelevant to an age that had invented a cure for syphilis.[79] The rise of modernism started the process that was to turn Ibsen into a fuddy-duddy old realist or overly melodramatic symbolist.

The demise of idealism has turned the period from 1870 to 1914 into a puzzle for literary historians. After the horrors of the Franco–Prussian War and the Paris Commune in 1870–1, idealism was decidedly on the defensive in Europe. As we have seen, naturalism was its first prominent enemy. But in the shadow of naturalism, there flourished a plethora of other anti-idealist projects. The closer we get to the ultimate death of idealism, the more hectically different trends and movements flourish and die: symbolism, decadence, neo-romanticism, aestheticism, fin-de-siècle, and avant-garde are just some of the terms one regularly comes across in discussions of this period.

In spite of the proliferation of terms, many of the most important writers of the period remain exceedingly difficult to categorize. It is not just Ibsen who fails to conform to such labels. All the greatest writers of the period— just think of Oscar Wilde, Thomas Hardy, Henry James, and the young André Gide—are just as difficult to categorize. Thomas Hardy's fascination with the grotesque and the gruesome, his honesty about sex, and his uncanny grasp of women's complexity made his novels anathema to idealists.[80] In 1911, Wirsén's last year on the Nobel committee, Henry James's nuanced, careful, subtle weighing of human motivations, his fascination with the movements of human consciousness was deemed insufficiently clear and concentrated, and the prize went to Maurice Maeterlinck.[81] The very title of Gide's *L'Immoraliste* (1902) would have been enough to make the Nobel committee cringe, and Gide's fascination with transgressive action for action's sake (*Les Caves du Vatican*, 1914) would be completely outrageous to an idealist. (André Gide received the Nobel Prize in 1947.)

While finding him entirely alien to his own aesthetic preferences, Oscar Wilde admired Ibsen.[82] In fact, Wilde's brilliant paradoxes, his searing indictment of moralism, are as anti-idealist as Ibsen's turn to the ordinary. In its way, *The Picture of Dorian Gray* (first published in *Lippinscott's Monthly Magazine* in July 1890) is as preoccupied with the battle between idealism and realism as *Ghosts*. At the very beginning of Wilde's novel, the painter Basil Hallward explains that he is looking for a new aesthetic school, a school he finds embodied in the beauty of Dorian Gray: "Unconsciously he defines for me the lines of a fresh school, a school that is to have in it all the passion of the Romantic spirit, all the perfection of the spirit that is Greek. The harmony of soul and body—how much that is! We in our madness have separated the two, and have invented a realism that is vulgar, an ideality that is void."[83] Here realism is aligned with the body and vulgarity (as it was in contemporary discussions of Zola's and Ibsen's "naturalism"), and ideality with a hollowed-out notion of the soul. Hallward's diagnosis of the problems of contemporary aesthetics turns out to be a perfect description of Dorian Gray himself, for the uncanny paradox at the heart of *The Picture of Dorian Gray* is that Dorian's soul, forever captured in Basil's picture, is as visible, ugly, and material as can be, while his body, engaged in so many mysterious vices, remains perfect, the very embodiment of "void ideality", if ever there was one.[84]

A virulent opponent of idealism, Wilde detested its characteristic mingling of ethics and aesthetics. "There is no such thing as a moral or an immoral book," he declares in the Preface to *The Picture of Dorian Gray*, "Books are well written, or badly written. That is all."[85] In "The Critic as Artist" he reinforces the point: "The sphere of Art and the sphere of Ethics are absolutely distinct and separate. When they are confused, Chaos has come again."[86] Unlike Shaw, however, whose anti-idealism turned him into a fairly dry left-wing champion of realism and naturalism, Wilde remained a revolutionary romantic at heart, who adored historical novels full of exquisite and exotic details such as Flaubert's *Salammbô*, Charles's Reade's *The Cloister and the Hearth* ("as much above *Romola* as *Romola* is above *Daniel Deronda*"), and Alexandre Dumas's *The Vicomte de Bragelonne*.[87]

Sometimes Wilde sounds like a modernist Schiller, insisting that truth and goodness have nothing to do with beauty, while at the same time believing that "It is through Art, and through Art only, that we can realize our perfection."[88] The inheritor of Schiller's idealism, Wilde was a perfectionist sympathetic to socialism. No wonder, then, that in 1888 he praised the stalwart idealist George Sand for the spirit of "social regeneration" that is so characteristic of her novels: "This spirit . . . is the very leaven of modern life.

It is remoulding the world for us, and fashioning our age anew. If it is antediluvian, it is so because the deluge is yet to come; if it is Utopian then Utopia must be added to our geographies."[89] Wilde, in fact, appears to have found in Sand somewhat of a kindred spirit, a writer of genius fusing a passion for social transformation with a highly self-conscious awareness of the role of art in that transformation. Lauding Sand's "delightful treatment of art and the artist's life", he declares that "What Mr. Ruskin and Mr. Browning have done for England, she did for France. She invented an art literature."[90] Like Brandes before him, then, Wilde split the idealist tradition in two, so as to be able to combine the admiration for revolutionary romanticism with the rejection of moralistic idealism.

Once the idealist trinity of truth, goodness, and beauty started coming apart, Wilde chose to cultivate beauty; Brandes, Zola, and the naturalists who followed them settled for truth; and Nietzsche and Gide bravely attacked the good.

The Legacy of Idealism

The demise of idealism furthered the autonomization of art and literature. When idealism disappeared, ethical and religious claims on art lost their legitimacy. Left was politics. There has always been a great deal of tension between formalist modernism and politically committed forms of criticism. In 1871, Georg Brandes called for modern literature to "place problems under debate".[91] The naturalist generation that followed him—the "men of the modern breakthrough" as Brandes himself called them, thus conveniently erasing from his consciousness all the women writers he knew and sometimes even encouraged—took for granted that the purpose of literature was to work for radical social and political change. The idea that art and literature have to serve a political purpose, however, is a successor project to the idealist vision in which the ultimate task of art is to ennoble mankind.

With formalism, the separation of ethics and aesthetics is completed; art is perceived as fully autonomous of all moral, social, and political duties; its task is neither to uplift or improve us, nor to change society through its relentless uncovering of truth; it is to make us think about art. In so far as naturalism inherited the utopian and perfectionist project of idealism, modernism comes to stand as a negation of both. There is nevertheless an incipient conflict here. If we consider formalist modernism as the ultimate negation of both idealism and naturalism, it represents the final breakthrough of the autonomy of the aesthetic. If this is right, then modernism simply can have no political, social, or religious purpose. Yet there has always been a strong, political strand within modernism. Marxist modernists such as Erwin Piscator and Bertolt Brecht spearheaded the twentieth-century quest to combine aesthetic formalism with political commitment.

Inspired by Roland Barthes and Alain Robbe-Grillet, French poststructuralism and its American and Europeans avatars have generated a plethora of more or less sophisticated theories of the "politics of form" or the "politics of the signifier". These are only the most recent attempts to overcome the conflict between utopia and critique, between the desire for a positive project for change and the conviction that all art can do is to avoid, negate, hollow out, or undermine the contaminated, commodified, and fetishized forms of communication characteristic of modern society. In short, the more art negates and avoids modern society, the easier it is for astute critics to read the gesture of negation itself as a refusal of communication or commodification, thus as a statement of alienation from mass society and a protest against the degradation of art by market forces. It is not difficult, in other words, to turn the formalist negativity of late modernism into a powerful political statement. Here resides an important, but unacknowledged, legacy of idealism: just as Schiller and his friends thought of the artist as a seer, close to God in his understanding of the ideal, late modernism turns the artist, now perceived as a laborer of negativity, into a bearer of purity or authenticity in a corrupted world.

The demise of idealism made it increasingly impossible for artists, writers, and critics (as opposed to politicians, religious leaders, and school board members) to claim in public that art has a duty to promote social ideals, show us the beauty of life, help to uplift us in a difficult world. All these tasks, if they are to be performed at all, have been relegated to the category of entertainment, to the middle-brow, and the low-brow.[92] This was undoubtedly a fantastic victory for artistic freedom. With the death of idealism, political, religious, and ethical interference in the autonomy of art could no longer find aesthetic justification. Women, in particular, have had everything to gain from the death of the outlandish idealist requirements for the representation of women, sexuality, and love. These gains remain enduring legacies of the victory of modernism over idealism, and it is desperately ungrateful of us to forget how much they owe to Ibsen.

After modernism, however, critics and writers also routinely take for granted that anyone who reads to be consoled for the sorrows of the world has no understanding of literature. At the same time, the formalist, skepticist, ironic paradigms of modernism and postmodernism have come to seem increasingly empty. What can they tell us about the task of art in an era dominated by war, genocide, and terrorism? What can art do in an era in which secular liberalism, the modern defender of the autonomy of art and literature, is under pressure from militant religious fundamentalisms of every kind? Unless we find answers to these questions, we leave the way open for the return of the death-dealing "ideal demand" in ever more pernicious forms.

4

Ibsen's Visual World
Spectacles, Painting, Theater

Ibsen's Taste: Vienna 1873

In mid-June 1873, shortly after finishing *Emperor and Galilean*, Ibsen left Dresden for Vienna to spend a good part of the summer as the Dano-Norwegian representative on the jury for painting and sculpture at the Universal Exhibition.[1] On 30 August 1873, he published a short notice about the experience in *Morgenbladet*. After listing the members of the jury and discussing the distribution of medals among the different nations, he warns readers against drawing any conclusions about the strengths of each nation's art from the numbers: "In addition to this, medals could only be given to living artists, and only for works created after the year 1863, a circumstance to which some countries, notably England, had paid no heed. The consequence was that although the English exhibition consisted almost exclusively of masterpieces, it only received a relatively low number of medals" (19: 143). The passage dismayed Ibsen's biographer Michael Meyer:

It is a melancholy comment on Ibsen's taste in painting, which was always to remain curiously conservative (to the end of his life there is no record of his taking any interest in Impressionism), that he should have described this collection as "almost exclusively comprising masterpieces"; nor could they even be defended on the ground of realism; they were the visual equivalent of exactly the kind of sentimental melodrama that he was trying to lead the theatre away from.[2]

Meyer is right to pounce on Ibsen's reference to the British masterpieces, for this is one of the few places in which Ibsen utters any kind of judgment on art, but he is too quick to dismiss the British paintings as entirely irrelevant to Ibsen's modernism. By positing Impressionism as the only relevant standard for artistic taste in 1873, he is projecting the ideology of modernism backward in time, in the usual anachronistic fashion. The *Official Catalogue* for the British Section at the 1873 Vienna Universal Exhibition shows that there was a huge British presence: seventy-four oil paintings, fifty-five watercolors, seventy etchings and engravings, and thirty-two sculptures and medallions.[3] Was this just one big collection of sentimental kitsch, as Meyer claims? Or did Ibsen have a point?

It certainly was true, as Ibsen notes, that many of the British paintings were over ten years old, and that some of the painters had long been dead. The prime example is *Walton Bridges*, painted in 1807 by J. M. W. Turner, who died in 1851. Among artists included in the oil painting section were Charles West Cope (*Othello Relating His Adventures to Brabantio; The Marriage of Griselda*); William Powell Frith (*Ramsgate Sands* and *Lord Foppington Relating his Adventures*); George Harvey (*School Dismissing*); Edward Landseer (*The Sanctuary; The Arab Tent*, and others); John Millais (*Portrait of Miss Nina Lehmann; The Sisters*); Henry O'Neil (*Eastward Ho!*); William Orchardson (*Falstaff*); John Pettie (*Touchstone and Audrey*); Richard Redgrave (*A Way Through the Woods; The Woodland Mirror*); William Blake Richmond (*The Lament of Ariadne*); George Storey (*The Shy Pupil*); Henrietta Ward ("*The Tower, Aye, The Tower*") and her husband E. M. Ward (*The Last Sleep of Argyll*); G. F. Watts (*Portrait of the Poet Browning; The Angel of Death*); and William F. Yeames (*Queen Elizabeth and her Court Receiving the French Ambassadors after the News of the Massacre of St. Bartholomew Had Reached England*).

By the dominant standards of the time, the British section did deserve praise, for it contained strong selections in all the principal genres of painting of the pre-Impressionist nineteenth century. Landscapes, portraits, history paintings, genre paintings, and animal paintings were all richly represented. Landseer's *The Arab Tent* (1866), depicting a mare and her foal, is often considered one of the finest paintings of horses from the Victorian period. There were also a number of scenes from modern life. William Frith's large-scale *Ramsgate Sands* (1854) is justly famous as a particularly ambitious modern beach scene. Immensely successful in its day, it was bought by Queen Victoria and can now be seen in the Buckingham Palace Royal Collection. There were also plenty of orientalist genre paintings, which might have appealed to Ibsen, who visited Egypt for the opening of the Suez Canal in 1869.

These are indeed paintings marked by pathos and sentimentality, and imperialist ideology too. Yet at the same time, many exhibit a strong painterly desire to bear witness to contemporary events. The defense of the British Empire was the subject of one of the best-known paintings from the exhibition: namely, Henry O'Neil's *Eastward Ho!* (1857), which shows British troops embarking for India to quell the mutiny. In a painting like this, as in so many Victorian paintings, there is a striking coexistence of realism of detail with moral and aesthetic idealism. Ibsen was attuned to the relationship between these paintings and their time, for he concludes his dry account of the Vienna Universal Exhibition by stressing that the exhibition "offers extraordinarily rich material for casting the light of cultural history over our own time" (19: 144).

In 1873, Ibsen lived in Dresden, with its famous picture galleries. He had also lived in Rome, where he spent much time studying the treasures of ancient and baroque art. In September 1868 (the year before the great Courbet exhibition in that city), he spent a month in Munich, going intensively to the picture galleries there (see 16: 216). On his way home from the opening of the Suez Canal in 1869, he stopped in Paris to visit the art museums (see 17: 19). When he looked at the paintings in the British section, his brief was to rank them in relation to contemporary European painting. For this, his frame of reference is most likely to have been contemporary German art, which he would have seen both in Munich and Dresden. Today, the Schack Gallery in Munich offers a good overview of German art in the second half of the nineteenth century, with its collection of mostly romantic, literary, and idealist paintings by Moritz von Schwind, Carl Spitzweg, Moritz von Beckerath, Leopold von Bode, Rudolf Henneberg, and Ernst von Liphart, as well as (mostly) early works by better-known painters such as Arnold Böcklin, Anselm Feuerbach, Franz von Lenbach, and Hans von Marées. In my view, Ibsen was perfectly justified in thinking that the British paintings in Vienna represented a more contemporary perspective on the world than the German paintings he would have seen in Munich and Dresden.

The British "masterpieces" in Vienna comprised a striking number of literary paintings. In Vienna, visitors to the British section could see scenes from Shakespeare by the two Scottish painters and friends Orchardson and Pettie, and by Cope, who also contributed a scene from Chaucer. In addition to *Ramsgate Sands*, Frith was represented with a painting inspired by John Vandbrugh's Restoration comedy *The Relapse* (1696). There were paintings and watercolors referring to Greek mythology, the Old and New Testaments, Boccaccio, Milton, Wordsworth, and Dickens, and others. In the catalogue, many paintings, including landscapes, were introduced by a few lines of poetry.

There were also allegorical pictures, such as George Watts's moralizing and melodramatic *The Angel of Death*, showing Death gathering up people of all ages and from a wide variety of social backgrounds. In keeping with the romantic idea of the universality of art, Watts (1817–1904) thought of *The Angel of Death* as a "painted poem", as an embodiment of "poetic idea[s]".[4] In

1868, in an outburst of full-blown idealism, Watts declared that "The real mission of Art [is] not merely to amuse, but to illustrate . . . the beautiful and the noble, interpreting them as poetry does, and to hold up to detestation the bestial and brutal." In response a present-day art critic rightly speaks of Watts's "odd, old-fashioned artistic aims", but without noting that Watts's idealism was still in touch with the dominant aesthetic norm at the time.[5]

To judge from the Vienna exhibition, in 1873 the relations between litera-ture, theater, and painting were close. One of Ibsen's fellow judges in Vienna was the German history painter Karl Theodor von Piloty (1826–86), director of the Art Academy in Munich, and famous precisely for a literary painting: the dramatic *Seni before Wallenstein's Corpse* (1855), inspired by Schiller's *Wallenstein's Death* (see 19: 142). Ibsen must surely have seen this impressive canvas on his visit to Munich in 1868. (Piloty's monumental and hugely suc-cessful *Thusnelda in Germanicus's Triumphal Procession* was exhibited in Vienna in 1873, the year before it was shown in Munich.) Ibsen's experiences in Vienna would have confirmed him in a belief he shared with his century: namely, that theater and painting were closely allied sister arts, related in their search for visual beauty. Just as the theater provided painters with picturesque and poetic subjects, paintings provided dramatists with ideas for plays. In 1873, the modernist belief that the task of each art is above all to explore its own specific possibilities was an idea whose time had not yet come. If one wishes to criticize Ibsen for liking the British paintings in Vienna, one will also have to criticize just about everybody else who cared about paintings in Europe around 1875.

Henrik Ibsen, Henry James, and Impressionism

Did Ibsen's taste change over the years? The Ibsen Museum in Oslo preserves Ibsen's last apartment, and contains much of the artwork he owned at his death. The art on display here does not show any great changes in Ibsen's taste after 1873: when he died, Ibsen still owned paintings in the style of Italian Renaissance paintings, Dutch genre paintings, and all the conventional genres of the nineteenth century.[6]

By far the most modern work of art in Ibsen's study is Christian Krogh's striking painting of August Strindberg, which Ibsen called a "masterful pic-ture" when he bought it in 1895 "for the relatively speaking ridiculously cheap price of 500 crowns" (Fig. 4). But the painting was chosen not for its modern form, but for what Ibsen took to be its Gothic subject matter, for he referred to it as "Insanity Emergent" (19: 369).[7] The large canvas still dominates Ibsen's

4. Christian Krogh, *August Strindberg*, 1893, Photo: Anne-Lise Reinsfelt,
Norsk Folkemuseum, Oslo.

study in a most striking way. Ibsen used say that he worked better with the
portrait staring down at him. He especially liked its "demonic eyes", and
once remarked, "He is my mortal enemy; he shall hang there and watch
what I write."[8]

One has to agree with Meyer that all the evidence points to the same
conclusion: namely, that Ibsen thought very highly of precisely the kind of
painting that was to become entirely disreputable as soon as modernism
started to dominate artistic taste. Meyer appears to find this embarrassing:
"One would have supposed that the author of *The Lady from the Sea* and *The
Wild Duck* must have admired the Impressionists, especially as he himself was
painted by Edvard Munch."[9] The reference to Edvard Munch (1863–1944)
recurs in discussions of Ibsen and painting. Munch painted Ibsen in the
1890s, and scholars tend to agree that while Munch was inspired by Ibsen, it

is unlikely that the elderly Ibsen found much inspiration in Munch.[10] Although Munch's beautiful *Starry Night* from 1923 may owe something to the last act of *John Gabriel Borkman,* that play owes nothing to Munch.

Meyer and others who bemoan Ibsen's pictorial taste complain that Ibsen failed to notice the Impressionists. But is this truly an egregious error of judgment? Ibsen was not the only early modernist writer who failed to appreciate the new painters in Paris. He may not even have seen any Impressionist works until late in his life. Henry James, on the other hand, actually went to the second Impressionist exhibition in the spring of 1876. His verdict was harsh, but extremely perceptive:

The young contributors to the exhibition of which I speak are partisans of unadorned reality and absolute foes to arrangement, embellishment, selection, to the artist's allowing himself, as he has hitherto, since art began, found his best account in doing, to be preoccupied with the idea of the beautiful. The beautiful, to them, is what the supernatural is to the Positivists—a metaphysical notion, which can only get one into a muddle and is to be severely let alone.[11]

James rightly sees in Impressionism a new kind of art that deliberately rejects the idealist belief that the artist's task was to create beauty by embellishing life. As we have seen, for idealists it was axiomatic that the beautiful is also the morally good, and that a morally dubious work cannot be beautiful. In his comments on Impressionism, Henry James takes the connection between beauty, imagination, and virtue for granted:

[According to the Impressionists] the painter's proper field is simply the actual, and to give a vivid impression of how a thing happens to look, at a particular moment, is the essence of his mission. . . . The Impressionist doctrines strike me as incompatible, in an artist's mind, with the existence of first-rate talent. To embrace them you must be provided with a plentiful absence of imagination.[12]

James's "the actual" echoes Schiller's. The actual is that which happens to be the case, that which has not yet been transformed in the light of the ideal. Such raw realism is not yet art. For James, the aesthetically displeasing predilection for the "the actual" was something the Impressionists and the Pre-Raphaelites, whom James calls the "English realists", had in common.[13] Thirty years later, the German champion of Impressionism, Julius Meier-Graefe, compared the realism of the Pre-Raphaelites unfavorably to that of Gustave Courbet. Although he vastly preferred Courbet, he took for granted that the Pre-Raphaelites and Courbet were all realists.[14] To us, however, Courbet and the Pre-Raphaelites seem to be poles apart. And they are: not because the former is "more realistic" than the latter, but because the Pre-Raphaelites were still idealists, and Courbet was not.

In the 1870s, to evaluate a work in moral terms was still part of the brief of any self-respecting critic of art and literature. Henry James was no exception, for to him the difference between the Pre-Raphaelite detailed realism and the looseness and imprecision of the Impressionist technique was "characteristic of the moral differences of the French and English races. The Impressionists . . . abjure virtue altogether, and declare that a subject which has been crudely chosen shall be loosely treated. They send detail to the dogs and concentrate themselves on general expression. . . . The Englishmen, in a word, were pedants, and the Frenchmen are cynics."[15] To claim, as James does here, that the rough brushwork and lack of painterly detail in Impressionism is cynical, is to say that it is anti-idealist, a deliberate attempt to avoid moral virtues altogether. Although the tone is humorous, the whole article shows that James thought that the moral purpose of art was to produce beauty, and that only the artistic imagination could transform the actual into the beautiful. What he misses in Impressionism is, precisely, the beauty-creating work of the imagination. This is a stunningly perceptive analysis of the impact of modernism on art. Ten years before Nietzsche, Henry James saw that the new movement in art would deliberately situate itself beyond good and evil, *beyond moral judgment.* To become a modernist is not to reject realism; it is to reject idealism. In painting and literature, the ultimate anti-idealist position is not realism, but formalism.

It is a mistake, then, to take Henrik Ibsen's or Henry James's unenthusiastic response to Impressionism for a lack or a flaw. It is, rather, precious evidence that Ibsen and his contemporaries inhabited an aesthetic world that has been largely obliterated by the comprehensive victory of modernism. The challenge is to understand how the first modernists emerged from this aesthetic culture, not to censor them for belonging to it. It is to this task that I now turn.

Ibsen's Visual World as Background

That Ibsen's interest in painting was formative for a dramatist who once declared that to "create (*digte*) is essentially to see" is not news (15: 393). Yet Ibsen has hardly ever been considered in relation to the mainstream nineteenth-century painting that he actually liked.[16] This is surprising, for Ibsen's plays are often highly pictorial. In some cases—the end of *Lady Inger* and *Ghosts* spring to mind, and so do many scenes from *Peer Gynt*—it is obvious that Ibsen must have imagined the stage as a tableau. Ibsen often used painting and other visual arts as a metaphor for art and aesthetics in general, and some of his most important characters are visual artists (painters, sculptors, architects). This is as evident in early programmatic poems such as "I billedgalleriet" ("In the picture gallery") and "Paa vidderne" ("On the heights") from 1859, as it is in *When We Dead Awaken* from 1899.

In this chapter, then, I shall analyze the European visual culture that formed the background to Ibsen's work. By "background" here I don't simply mean static historical context. I use the word, rather, in Simone de Beauvoir's dynamic and dialectical sense, as the cultural world in which Ibsen found himself, the world that defined him, the world he found himself obliged to respond to and intervene in. My topic, however, is *Ibsen's* background, not the whole of nineteenth-century visual culture. I shall focus only on elements broadly relevant for an understanding of Ibsen's theater, as I explore and analyze it in the rest of this book.

Ibsen's visual world is made up both by aesthetic ideals and attitudes that he himself may have been influenced by, and by aesthetic ideals and attitudes that his critics and audiences would most likely have had in mind as they first encountered his works. These aesthetic attitudes were made up of experiences and practices; they were learned by most people not by studying aesthetic theory, but by looking at paintings and sculptures, going to see panoramas and dioramas, watching "living statues" and *tableaux vivants*, going to the theater, and by discussing all these experiences with family and friends.

The account that follows, therefore, has three broad categories: aesthetic theories; visual technologies, spectacles, performances; and the interaction between painting and theater in Ibsen's century. In my discussions of theory, I foreground and define some concepts that will be important for my arguments throughout this book: namely, *absorption, theatricality*, and *antitheatricality* (these are all categories broadly based on Diderot's aesthetics); and *antitheatricalism* (the outright hostility to theater as an art form that began with Plato and found a powerful exponent in Diderot's colleague Rousseau).

Whenever relevant, I relate these discussions to Ibsen's own works. In some cases this leads me to make new connections between Ibsen and art. Towards the end of the chapter, I show how a seemingly traditional idealist painting—namely, the Scottish painter William Quiller Orchardson's *The First Cloud* (1887)—outstrips its own idealist premises, so that it comes to embody a particularly interesting moment in the transition from idealism to modernism. (In Chapter 6, I further theorize such transitional works of art in relation to Ibsen's *Emperor and Galilean*.) The chapter ends with a discussion of a brief scene in *The Wild Duck* that is at once painterly and anti-idealist.

Diderot

The philosopher whose thoughts about theater and painting have been most illuminating and most useful for my own understanding of Ibsen's theater is Denis Diderot (1713–84), and particularly "Conversations on *The Natural Son*" (1757), a text often neglected in favor of *The Paradox of the Actor* (1770–7), perhaps because the former embraces identification, emotion, absorption, and moral education, while the latter applauds distance and irony. (It is no coincidence that ideologues of modernism have preferred late Diderot.[17]) The Diderot who helps us to understand the European stage at the time when Ibsen first started to write and direct plays, however, is the early Diderot, the tearful and emotional one, the one who wanted to be totally carried away by art.

Diderot's aesthetic ideas were in fact first elaborated in relation to theater, in 1757, and then further developed in his long series of *Salons*. His preference for the pictorial led him to break decisively with Aristotle's principles of drama, unchallenged in France since Racine's days. For Aristotle, the plot (*mythos*) was the very "soul of tragedy".[18] The best plots, by far, Aristotle claimed, were plots with sudden reversals (*peripeteia*) and unexpected recognitions (*anagnorisis*). Although Aristotle accepted music as an important "accessory" to the words, he thought that the visual aspects of theater (*opsis*, "spectacle") were irrelevant to the full experience of the dramatic text: "For tragedy fulfills its function even without a public performance and actors," Aristotle proclaims.[19]

The difference between Aristotle and Diderot is the difference between a theater based on words and a theater based on pictures. Diderot preferred spectacle to plot, and would never have agreed that to read a play could be just as powerful an experience as to see it. In "Conversations on *The Natural Son*", the "I" stresses the distinction between *tableaux* and *coups de théâtre*: "An unforeseen incident which takes place in the action and abruptly changes the situation of the characters is a *coup de théâtre*. An arrangement of these characters on stage, so natural and so true that, faithfully rendered by a painter, it would please me on a canvas, is a *tableau*."[20] A *coup de théâtre*, then, is a sudden plot reversal; a *tableau*, as the word indicates, is a painting, a dramatic, arresting, immediately intelligible, and beautiful arrangement of the characters against an equally painterly backdrop. "If a dramatic work were well made and well performed," Diderot writes, "the stage would offer the spectator as many real tableaux as the action would contain moments suitable for painting."[21] The theatrical genre of melodrama, which was born in France in the 1780s, would pick up the idea of making theater visually spectacular, not as Diderot surely would have wished, instead of, but in addition to plots full of sudden reversals and recognitions.[22]

As Michael Fried has shown, Diderot's aesthetics sets up a powerful opposition between *absorption* and *theatricality*. Because Diderot despises theatricality, Diderot's aesthetics in general is *antitheatrical*. (Diderot, however, is not an *antitheatricalist*: if he were, he would be against theater, just like Rousseau.) To be *absorbed* is to be in a state or condition of "rapt attention, of being completely occupied or engrossed . . . in what [one] is doing, hearing, thinking, feeling".[23] If Diderot praised representations of absorption in painting, it was because they appeared to be entirely unconscious of the presence of the beholder. "Diderot's conception of painting rested ultimately on the supreme fiction that the beholder did not exist, that he was not really there, standing before the canvas," Fried writes (*AT*, 103). Art (theater and painting) had to establish the "supreme fiction of the beholder's non-existence" (*AT*, 149). When the fiction of the non-existence of the beholder is broken, the supreme illusion disappears, the beholder or the audience becomes self-conscious, and the result is theatricality.

Theatricality is anything that smacks of calculated effects, any deliberate effort to "act for the camera" (as it were), any attempt to ham it up—in short, any artistic quality that makes the beholder or the member of the audience conscious that he or she *is* a beholder or a member of an audience. Theatrical actors are bad, Diderot writes, because "they seek applause, they depart from the action; they address themselves to the audience; they talk to it and become dull and false."[24] Theatricality in art or acting prevents immersion in the illusion proposed by the work of art: "Whether you compose or act, think no more of the beholder than if he did not exist. Imagine, at the edge of the stage, a high wall that separates you from the orchestra. Act as if the curtain never rose."[25] Ultimately, Diderot's advice to actors is that they should pretend that the theater is not a theater.

Diderot, then, is ferociously *antitheatrical*, in the sense that he is *against theatrical art*. He therefore constantly exhorts painters and actors to be "natural" and "naïve", to represent "absorptive" motifs, to avoid aiming for effect—in short, to act and paint in ways that reveal no awareness at all of an audience or a beholder. Because he found neoclassical tragedy too theatrical with its stylized soliloquies and obvious declamation for the gallery, he also called for a new, more realistic, dramatic genre, *le genre sérieux*, between comedy and tragedy, in which serious, even tragic, situations could be experienced by middle-class characters in "natural" circumstances.

Diderot also wanted art (theater, painting, writing) to *move* us. Here is an example from "In Praise of Richardson", where Diderot describes a "friend" (in reality he is referring to himself), who has just got hold of a recently translated passage left out of the French edition of *Clarissa*: "He promptly grabbed the pages and went off into a corner to read them. I was watching him: first I saw tears flowing, he stopped reading and began to sob; suddenly he got up and walked up and down without knowing where he was going, crying out like a man distressed, and addressing the most bitter reproaches to the whole Harlow family."[26] The tears and rage of the "friend" shows that he has forgotten that he is reading fiction, that he has become so immersed in the novel's illusion that he takes the Harlow family to be real.

It seems to me that for Diderot, maximal emotional engagement in the fiction proposed by the work of art enables the reader or beholder to lose him—or herself entirely in the fictional world proposed in a way that blurs the boundaries between art and life, fiction and reality. (This may not be the case for painting—Fried certainly never says it is—but it does seem to be true for Diderot's experience of Richardson's novels.) I am also struck by the figures of the wholly "held" beholder of a painting, the completely immersed reader of fiction, and the totally transported viewer of a play that we occasionally find in Diderot's texts. It is as if a properly absorptive work of art also produces an absorbed beholder, that there is a parallel between the work of art's representation of absorption and the viewer or reader's ability to lose him or herself in the work of art, to the point of forgetting that she is experiencing art.

In Madame de Staël's *Corinne, or Italy* there is a scene that strikes me as a perfect incarnation of these aspects of Diderot's aesthetics. In Book VII, Corinne takes the part of Juliet in a full-scale performance of Shakespeare's play. That it is Shakespeare and not Racine that is being played is in itself significant. Juliet's death scene inspires Corinne's lover, Oswald, with "the cruel mixture of despair and love, death and ardor, which make this scene the most heart-rending in the theatre".[27] When the play is over, Oswald goes backstage to see Corinne:

Once the play was over, Corinne felt exhausted with emotion and fatigue. Oswald was the first to enter her room and saw her alone with her attendants, still dressed as Juliet and, like her, half lifeless in their arms. In his great disarray, he could not distinguish between truth and fiction, and throwing himself at Corinne's feet, said these words of Romeo in English:

> "*Eyes, look your last! arms, take your last embrace.*"

Corinne, still beside herself, cried, "Good God! What are you saying? Would you want to leave me, would you?"[28]

Here there is a passionate outpouring of emotion, and a complete blurring of the boundary between fiction and reality, to the point that Oswald, who did not act, can only express himself by speaking a line from the play, and when he speaks Romeo's line, Corinne, who did act, takes him to refer to his own intentions. The powerful prolongation of illusion and Oswald's unbroken absorption testify at once to Corinne's authenticity and to her artistic power. It is easy to see why Diderot in many ways can be considered an unwilling theorist of melodrama.

Although Ibsen and Diderot address completely different theatrical situations (Diderot was reacting against stylized neoclassical declamation, Ibsen against the generic poses, intentional overacting, and generally highly melodramatic style of his time), Ibsen's innumerable instructions to actors and directors to be natural and avoid theatricality are reminiscent of Diderot's. Here is a typical example, from a letter to a young actress who had asked for advice on how to play Rebecca in *Rosmersholm*: "No declamation. No theatrical accents. . . . Give each mood a believable, natural expression. Never think of this or that actress you have seen. But stick to the life that pulsates around you, and represent a living, real human being" (18: 131).[29] Such instructions are invariably read as evidence of Ibsen's realism or naturalism; it is salutary to remember that they are also evidence of his antitheatricality, which in this case means his opposition to the style of acting that dominated the European stage for most of the nineteenth century.

Lessing and his Followers

The German playwright and theorist Gotthold Ephraim Lessing (1729–81) was probably the most influential visual theorist in the late eighteenth and the whole of the nineteenth century. As late as 1904, Julius Meier-Graefe, the fiery apostle of artistic modernism, found it worth his while to denounce precisely Lessing as the cause of all the rot in traditionalist European painting. In Lessing's *Laocoön* (1766) we find a predilection for paintings that express one single, pregnant moment that can be taken in at a glance (this is equivalent to Diderot's stipulation that the tableau should be instantly intelligible). Lessing's main concern, however, is the difference between painting and poetry. The domain of painting, Lessing writes, is space; the domain of poetry is time. "Bodies with their visible properties are the true subjects of painting. . . . Actions are the true subjects of poetry."[30] "Painting", Lessing writes, "can use only a single moment of an action in its coexisting compositions and must therefore choose the one which is most suggestive and from which the preceding and succeeding actions are most easily comprehensible."[31] Taken up by Goethe and Schiller around 1800, Lessing's theory of the "fruitful" or "pregnant" moment was to remain deeply influential for well over a century.[32]

"Lessing [invents] the modern concept of an artistic medium," Michael Fried writes.[33] This is entirely true, and read in this way, Lessing anticipates the aesthetics of modernism as well as the theoretical concerns of poststructuralism. No wonder, then, that the question discussed by present-day critics interested in Lessing has usually been whether words can ever fully describe an image. Nineteenth-century painters, however, thought that Lessing told them *how* to make a painting tell a story: namely, by choosing the "pregnant moment", a dramatic moment containing its own past, and pregnant with its own future. They could certainly base their belief on the text of *Laocoön*. Just about every discussion of painting in *Laocoön* is related to passages in Greek and Roman mythology, and in poetry and literature. Lessing simply took it for granted that painters would and should turn to narratives for material. Lessing's crucial idea, then, was not that painters should not turn to narratives, but that poets and painters had to choose different *kinds* of scenes from their favorite narratives.

That romantic painters took Lessing to be encouraging the use of literary and narrative materials is evident from an 1801 lecture given by the enterprising Swiss-born artist Henry Fuseli (1741–1825), one of the first to exploit the increasing interest in the connection between painting and theater. Fuseli was a talented painter and influential teacher, who for a while was the object of Mary Wollstonecraft's passion. Fuseli was also something of a philosopher and well versed in the European aesthetic tradition. Today he is probably best known for his violently erotic painting of a woman having a nightmare beset with ghastly fantasy creatures (*The Nightmare*, 1781).

In *Realizations*, Martin Meisel provides some precious information on and quotations from a March 1801 lecture on "Invention" given by Fuseli to the Royal Academy in London. Rejecting Lessing's preference for paintings of bodies at rest, Fuseli preferred "momentaneous energy", a phrase that resonates with the preference for moments of "passion and action", for the "body in action" that one finds in the works of David around this time.[34] According to Fuseli, Lessing's message to painters was that they should choose for their subject a particularly charged and dramatic moment, one that contains and condenses its own past and future: "Those important moments, then, which exhibit the united exertion of form and character in a single object, or in participation with collateral beings, *at once*, and which, with equal rapidity and pregnancy, give us a glimpse of the past, and lead our eye to what follows, furnish the true materials of those technic powers, that elect, direct, and fix the objects of imitation" (quoted in *R*, 19). For Fuseli, as for Lessing and Diderot, a painting should be *instantly intelligible*: audiences must be able to take it in at a glance, and it should focus on a significant, highly intense, *dramatic* moment.

Here it may be necessary to stress that for Diderot, as well as for the romantics, *drama* was not the same thing as *theatricality*. For Diderot theatricality was the opposite of the sincere, the spontaneous, and the natural; it was *not* the opposite of intense, passionate expressivity. "For Diderot and his contemporaries", Fried writes, "the human body in action was the best picture of the human soul; and the representation of action and passion was therefore felt to provide ... a pictorial resource of potentially enormous efficacy" (*AT*, 75). Eighteenth-century French painting should be *dramatic*, and to achieve this, Fried writes, it had to represent *action* and *passion*, and it should have *pictorial unity*. These demands are as typical of Lessing as they are of Diderot. Thus the demand that a painting should be dramatic meant that it should depict genuine action and genuine passion with intensity and sincerity. (A bad painter might very well render a dramatic subject in a theatrical fashion: if so, Diderot would have hated the result.)

To me, the most striking difference between Lessing's *Laocoöon* and Diderot's art criticism is that Diderot is fundamentally concerned with the relationship between the work of art and the beholder in a way that Lessing is not. Lessing's text does not contain anything resembling Diderot's concern with the difference between theatricality and absorption. Yet Lessing encourages painters to develop the specificity of their own medium, and to do so in striking representations of moments in which the past is about to determine the future. Drama, action and passion, and the instant intelligibility of the painting or theatrical tableau are values common to both of them, and to their followers, such as Fuseli.

In 1806 the Frenchman Anne-Louis Girodet (1767–1824) produced a painting that perfectly illustrates Fuseli's points: namely, *The Flood* (*Le Déluge*) (Plate 1). When the huge canvas was first exhibited at the Salon of 1806, "many critics found the painting unnecessarily horrific", but in 1810 *The Flood* received the Prix Décennal (a prize for the best painting of the decade), beating *Intervention of the Sabines* (1799) of Girodet's old teacher Jacques-Louis David (1748–1825) into second place.[35] Girodet's painting is as dramatic as one could wish for. It is full of action and passion, it can be taken in at a glance, and it is meant to stun its audience into transfixed immersion.[36]

In Ibsen's *The Pretenders* (1864), set in thirteenth-century Norway, there is a passage which describes a strikingly similar motif:

BISHOP NICHOLAS. Did you never see an old painting in the Christ Church at Nidaros? It shows the Flood rising to cover all the mountains, so that there is only one peak left. A whole family climbs up there; father and mother and son and the son's wife and children;—and the son pulls the father down in the flooding waters in order to get a better foothold, and he will pull down the mother and his wife, and all his children too, in order to get to the top himself;—for up there is a foot of land, *there* he can stay for an hour.— *That*, Earl, is the tale (*saga*) of wisdom, and the tale of every wise man.

(5:49)

This is of course intended to be a fictive description of a fictive medieval painting, not a faithful description of Girodet's *The Flood*. Yet the situation described—a family about to be destroyed by the biblical Flood—is the same. The evil Bishop Nicholas is clearly describing the scene according to his own darkly Machiavellian nature, for however horrific it may be, Girodet's *The Flood* is a scene of doomed rescue, not intentional murder.

The *way* in which Bishop Nicholas talks about the painting, moreover, is particularly interesting. Describing an extremely dramatic scene, he immediately inserts it into a narrative, confidently names the family relationships, and imagines the thoughts and motivations of the main figure before drawing out the underlying moral truth of the story. In all these respects, Bishop Nicholas reveals himself to be a typical nineteenth-century art critic. There is no reason to assume that Ibsen's own way of looking at paintings was radically different.

In a letter from 1872, Ibsen shows that he too takes the unity and intelligibility of a painting for granted. Explaining that he can't write journalism, he says that he has no talent for the genre: "What I think and see in pictures takes quite a different form; all of it gathers as particulars around a larger whole, and therefore I need a larger form or frame in order to express myself fully" (17: 37).[37] Seeking pictorial unity within a large frame, Ibsen's imagination was visual in a mode inherited from the tradition after Diderot and Lessing.

The Illusions of Art: Performances, Spectacles, and Visual Technology

Ibsen grew up at a time of increasing demand for arresting visual spectacles, when new kinds of performances and new kinds of visual technologies were being invented. For the purposes of understanding Ibsen's theater, two sets of developments of the late eighteenth and the early nineteenth century are particularly relevant: first, the development of spectacles and technologies (panoramas and dioramas) that attempted to *maximize the illusion of reality*, to produce visual impressions so lifelike that the beholder would forget that they were art and take them to be real, and second, the development of new kinds of performance art, which aimed to *make reality look like art: attitudes* and *tableaux vivants*.

In Europe, from the 1780s onwards, there was increasing public interest in dramatic, arresting, sensational visual scenes. One of the first painters to exploit the new appetite for spectacular sights was the Frenchman Philip James de Loutherbourg (1740–1812), who settled in London in 1771. According to Robert Rosenblum, in 1781, Loutherbourg began to produce "theatrical performances that imitated, with complex light and scenic effects, a vast repertory of wondrous things, from Biblical deluges, modern ship-wrecks, and the Great Fire of London of 1666, to Neapolitan sunsets, the Falls of Niagara and Derbyshire gorges".[38]

Lotherbourgh seems to have drawn on the techniques of the theater to make the display of paintings more dramatic, more arresting, more striking. In 1789, John Boydell's new "Shakespeare Gallery" tried something similar with scenes from Shakespeare. In such spectacles, theater and painting came together to produce a highly dramatic visual experience. In the theater, the melodrama was an expression of the same aesthetic trends.

In 1787 the Scot Robert Barker invented the painted panorama, which in various forms (Alporama, Europorama, cosmora, georama, neorama, and many more) was to flourish across Europe for the next century.[39] The quest for the perfect illusion of reality entirely dominated the form. The first subjects of the new panoramas were cityscapes and landscapes, soon followed by battle scenes. There were representations of exotic cities like Constantinople and Jerusalem, spectacular landscapes from the New World, and countless depictions of Napoleonic battles. In Norway, the landscape painter Johannes Flintoe (1787–1870) painted a series of canvases of Norwegian nature, which he exhibited as a cosmorama entitled "Norwegian prospects" (*Norske prospekter*) in Christiania and Copenhagen in 1835. Today, some of the canvases from Flintoe's cosmorama hang in the National Gallery in Oslo, most notably *Vøringsfossen*, a view of a waterfall in the west of Norway, which Ibsen also painted in the 1850s.

Panoramas were shown in Christiania in Ibsen's time. In July 1863, for example, the great summer attraction in town was the panorama at Klingenberg, which offered "true to life" representations of subjects taken from current affairs, including several from the Civil War raging in the

United States: "The Entrance in London of the Prince of Wales and Princess Alexandra", "The Battle between 'Monitor' and 'Merimak' ", "The Aspromonte Affair", "The Battle of Fredericksburg" ("perhaps almost too horribly true to life"), "The Industrial Palace in London", and "The Sunday Service at Gardermoen". "All of it truly deserves to be looked at by an art loving audience," wrote the newspaper *Morgenbladet*.[40]

The immense panoramic canvases were painted in a kind of hyperrealist style, which lent itself well to propaganda. The Franco–Prussian War of 1870–1 revived the form in France and Germany. In Berlin in the early 1880s, a panorama showing the victory of the Prussian Army over the French in 1871, painted by the official court painter Anton von Werner and a team of fourteen assistants, was an immense success.[41] According to one source, almost 100,000,000 spectators visited panoramas between 1870 and 1900, when they finally started to go out of fashion.[42] Did Ibsen, who lived in Germany at the height of the craze, entirely miss out on the experience?

The diorama was invented in 1822, by Charles-Marie Bouton and Louis-Jacques Mandé Daguerre (the latter, of course, went on to invent photography in 1839). The diorama consisted of painted scenes on a big semi-transparent canvas, which, when suitably illuminated, gave the illusion of temporal change, "in such a way that the same landscape would be seen first by night and then by day".[43] In the diorama, the quest for illusion was allied with the wish to represent temporal change, a wish which surely also fueled the invention of film. Panoramas were essentially very large paintings. The diorama, too, had close connections with painting, for both inventors of this novelty were painters. Bouton had been a student of David's, and Daguerre was a significant member of the French romantic school before he turned to technology. In the 1820s he produced dioramas while still continuing to exhibit at the annual Salons. At the Salon of 1824, for example, Daguerre exhibited a romantic painting called *Ruins of the Chapel at Holyrood by Moonlight*, which one art historian compares to Caspar David Friedrich's Gothic ruins, and describes as "haunting relics of a mysterious civilization viewed by moonlight".[44] A version of the painting had already been exhibited as a diorama in 1823.[45]

All these technologies of vision aimed to maximize the illusion of reality by immersing the spectator in the experience. The viewer was to feel as if he or she were truly present at the scene depicted. The quest for overpowering artistic illusions of reality did not go unchallenged. In the late eighteenth and early nineteenth century, two new kinds of performance arts became fashionable among the European aristocracy: *tableaux vivants* and *attitudes*. Both have left their traces in Ibsen's work. A *tableau vivant* was the theatrical performance of a well-known painting, with costumes, décor, and as many participants as the painting required. In Europe, the fashion for *tableaux vivants* took off after the publication of Goethe's *Elective Affinities* in 1809, in which they play an important role.[46] The *tableau vivant* should be distinguished from the tableau in Diderot's sense, which simply meant any stage arrangement that would have given pleasure as a painting, whether or not such a painting actually existed. Sometimes stage tableaux were inspired by actual paintings, sometimes painters would be inspired by the stage tableaux. In order to make space for as many pleasing tableaux as possible, nineteenth-century theater productions routinely cut large parts of the dramatic text.

Attitudes, on the other hand, were performed by one woman, who in a dancelike performance would freeze into a series of imitations of classical sculptures, usually in an aristocratic salon.[47] Pioneered by Emma Hamilton, Lord Nelson's great love, the origins of attitudes may owe something to her early work as a model for the fashionable English painter George Romney.[48] At the beginning of the nineteenth century, the Danish Ida Bruun, daughter of Frederike Bruun, a close friend of Madame de Staël's, was generally acknowledged as the most refined practitioner of the art. At the age of 13, Ida Bruun performed at Mme de Staël's Coppet (see SA, 104–9). The year was 1805–6, and when she was not engaged in amateur theatricals and watching attitudes, Madame de Staël was busy writing *Corinne, or Italy*.

According to Karen Klitgaard Povlsen, attitudes were part of the early nineteenth century's extensive experimentation with the arts of "mute expression": gesture, mimicry, dance, and music (SA, 97). (Here, too, Diderot was a pioneer, for he was obsessed with gesture and pantomime.) Thus Ida Bruun's attitudes were experienced at once as dance, sculpture, and painting (see SA, 107). Most importantly, the attitude was always allegorical, always alluding to famous works of art. The woman's body performed the allegory; the members of the audience had to join the two together by using their own imagination, sensitivity, and education: "The higher one's cultural level and the greater one's powers of imagination, the higher the ideal perceived. Thus members of the audience virtually competed to be the most deeply moved" (SA, 98). The attitude explored the boundaries between life and death, art and life. When the movement of life froze into the stillness of death, moreover, it embodied pain, Povlsen writes, "attitudes became the living performance of Laocoön's pain" (SA, 100).

Attitudes inspired sculptors such as Canova and Thorvaldsen. They also inspired Ibsen's vision of the female figure in Rubek's sculpture "The Day of

Resurrection" in *When We Dead Awaken.* This enigmatic figure, hovering between life and death, at times appears as a living woman, Irene, at times as dead marble (see also SA, 95). Its model, Irene, is explicitly said to have worked as a living sculpture: "I have stood on the revolving platform in variety shows. Stood as a naked statue in *tableaux vivants*" (13: 233–4).[49]

In the first half of the nineteenth century, the fascination with attitudes and *tableaux vivants* spread from the chateaux and manor houses of the upper classes to popular theaters. In England, "living statues" remained a popular entertainment in theaters until about 1850, and the theatrical use of *tableaux vivants* lasted even longer, not least in Scandinavia. *Tableaux vivants* were hugely popular in Norwegian theatres in the 1850s, and Ibsen not only helped to stage them, but wrote poetry for them too (this will be discussed in the next chapter).[50]

Antitheatricalism and Performing Women: Corinne's Tarantella

Around 1800, then, there was an opposition between bourgeois arts of illusion and aristocratic arts imitating art. If the former were in keeping with the antitheatrical desire to produce absorptive illusions, the latter were self-consciously and evidently theatrical. Women who performed in theatrical arts were often considered theatrical—manipulative, scheming, hypocritical—themselves. In *Elective Affinities* (1809) Goethe disapproves of the beautiful but coquettish and selfish Luciane's desire to display herself in *tableaux vivants*, yet approves of the modest and shy Ottilie's reluctant posing as the Virgin Mary in a Christmas tableau.

The critique of performing women was often based on a general rejection of theater. Following the usage of Jonas Barish in *The Antitheatrical Prejudice*, I shall call the rejection of theater as an art form *antitheatricalism*, in order to distinguish it from Diderot's *antitheatricality*. (In Ibsen's time, antitheatricalism was a dominant position in Norwegian cultural life, and I therefore discuss it at length in Chapter 5.) Antitheatricalists are against theater altogether: their ancestors are Plato and the Church Fathers. The strongest antitheatricalist voice in the late eighteenth century was that of Diderot's colleague Jean-Jacques Rousseau, whose *Letter to d'Alembert* (1758) set out the moral and political case against theater with implacable rigor. One of Rousseau's many arguments against the theater is that simply by showing them onstage, it makes "great villains" impressive, and thus contributes to the moral corruption of the audience.[51] As evidence, Rousseau adduces none other than the Roman traitor Catiline, who was to become the hero of Ibsen's first play.[52]

The difference between antitheatricalism and antitheatricality, then, is that the former considers all kinds of theater bad and corrupting, whereas the latter wants art, including theater, to be unself-conscious, "natural", spontaneous, and absorptive. The prudish Fanny Price in Jane Austen's *Mansfield Park* (1814) strikes me as a typical antitheatricalist, since she objects to the whole idea of staging a play well before she knows what the play is going to be. Antitheatricalists often invoked women's morals in their arguments against theater. Rousseau thought that one of the roots of all social evil was that human beings depend on the opinion of others. This makes us seek to appear other than we are in the eyes of others, and so makes us fundamentally inauthentic. Women are even more inauthentic than men, for their sex makes them intrinsically coquettish, and therefore insincere. The theater, Rousseau concluded, is to be condemned because it serves only to reinforce human inauthenticity, and because it has a particularly bad effect on women.[53]

The great exception to the general chorus of disapproval of female performances can be found in Corinne's tarantella. For Mme de Staël, Corinne's dance is a manifestation of female pride and independence, and of female artistic talent. In a footnote Mme de Staël informs her readers that her description of Corinne's tarantella was inspired by the shawl dance of her close friend Mme de Récamier. In fact, Mme de Staël's description of Corinne's tarantella blends the somewhat orientalist shawl dance with Ida Bruun's attitudes:[54]

Shaking her tambourine in the air she [Corinne] began to dance, and in all her movements there was a graceful litheness, a modesty mingled with sensual delight . . . Corinne knew so well all the poses [*toutes les attitudes*] depicted by the ancient painters and sculptors that, with a slight movement of the arms, placing her tambourine now above her head, now in front of her with one hand while the other ran along the bells with incredible skill, she brought to mind the dancing girls of Herculaneum and aroused, one after another, a host of new ideas for drawing and painting.

As she danced, Corinne made the spectators experience her own feelings, as if she had been improvising, or playing the lyre, or drawing portraits. Everything was language for her; as they looked at her, the musicians made greater efforts to make their art fully appreciated, at the same time an indefinable passionate joy, and imaginative sensitivity, stimulated all the spectators of this magical dance, transporting them into an ideal existence which was out of this world.[55]

Immersed in the romantic idea of the unity of the arts, Mme de Staël represents Corinne's dancing as embodied poetry, a work of art which at one and the same time is an imitation of ancient painters and sculptors, and an absolutely original source of ideas for new paintings. "Everything was language for her," Mme de Staël writes: Corinne is expressivity embodied, and so it doesn't really matter what specific medium she chooses, for she will express the same ideal—the true, the beautiful, and the good—in all of them.

When Ibsen makes Nora dance the tarantella in *A Doll's House*, he pays homage to *Corinne, or Italy*, the novel he read in Rome, and that Georg Brandes had praised to the skies in *Emigrantlitteraturen*. The difference is that when Ibsen's Nora dances the tarantella, there is no trace of Mme de Staël's idealism; instead, we find a path-breaking reflection on the nature of theater.[56]

Theater and Painting as Sister Arts

So far we have looked at aesthetic theories, spectacles, and performances relevant to Ibsen's visual formation. It is time to turn to painting, or rather to the exceptionally close connections between theater and painting. In the period from the French Revolution to the advent of modernism, theater and painting were as intertwined as different arts could be. Throughout the nineteenth century, Martin Meisel writes in *Realizations*, there was "an extraordinary dialogue of literary and pictorial forms, in the exhibition galleries, in the print shops, and in the parlor" (*R*, 32). Seen against this background, Ibsen's wish to become a painter, his practice of painting, and his lifelong love of art is not just a curious fact about him, but evidence that he placed himself right at the center of a living, productive aesthetic tradition in which painting and theater were sister arts.

In keeping with the romantic idea that painting was frozen theater, and theater speaking paintings, nineteenth-century theaters continued to build the stage to make it look as if it were surrounded by a picture frame. Adolph von Menzel's gouache "Festival Performance in the Theatre of the New Palace in 1829" (from the album "The Magic of the White Rose" painted in 1853–4) perfectly illustrates the point. Such a picture frame arrangement is still a conspicuous feature of the main stage at Nasjonalteateret, the Norwegian National Theater, which opened on 1 September 1899 with a gala performance of scenes from Holberg attended by Ibsen and Bjørnson.

Throughout the nineteenth century, paintings were regularly based on literature and drama. The connection between painting and literature was so ingrained that the mere suggestion that painting could be non-literary came to seem absurd. When, in the 1890s, someone finally got around to telling the ageing Pre-Raphaelite Edward Burne-Jones that French painting was no longer based on literature, he was astounded: "What do they mean by that?", he replied, "landscape and whores?" (*R*, 32).

As we have already seen, the British contribution to the Universal Exhibition in Vienna in 1873 contained a great number of literary paintings. Led by Delacroix, the French romantics were particularly given to painting scenes from Byron and Scott, who to them represented modernity. Between 1822 and 1837, nearly 230 paintings of scenes from Walter Scott's novels were exhibited in France.[57] Scenes from Shakespeare remained popular throughout the century. The Pre-Raphaelites seem never to have tired of him. William Holman Hunt exhibited a particularly striking *Claudio and Isabella* in 1853. John Everett Millais's mid-century *Ophelia* (1851–2) is surely the most famous; but Ophelias, Hamlets, Violas, and Isabellas are everywhere in nineteenth-century art. Arthur Hughes's childlike *Ophelia* dates from 1852; and there is a fin-de-siècle one by John William Waterhouse from 1894. (Waterhouse in fact painted three Ophelias, the last as late as 1910.[58]) But painters also chose scenes from poetry and novels. Tennyson was a particular favorite, and just about all the Pre-Raphaelites painted *The Lady of Shalott* (1832, revised in 1842). John William Waterhouse's well-known version dates from 1888, the year of Ibsen's *The Lady from the Sea*. There is even a *Lady of Shalott* from 1913 (Sidney Harold Meteyard, *"I am half-sick of Shadows," said the Lady of Shalott*).

Just as painters painted scenes from plays, so playwrights would write plays based on paintings. As Martin Meisel has shown, around 1830 the English stage was overcome by a vogue for "picture plays" that lasted until the end of the century. Plays would be based on paintings by successful and respected painters such as William Hogarth, Charles Eastlake, David Wilkie, W. P. Frith, and the Pre-Raphaelites.[59] Often, but by no means always, the paintings chosen to become plays were themselves based on well-known theatrical or literary scenes. The interaction between painting, theater, and literature was constant, extensive, and not at all considered aesthetically demeaning to the well-known painters whose works were turned into plays.

A fascinating example of a painting that was turned into a mass spectacle at the same time as it became the basis for a play and an opera is Théodore Géricault's monumental *The Raft of the Medusa* (1819), inspired by the horrendous aftermath of the shipwreck of a French frigate off the coast of West Africa in July 1816 (Fig. 5). This was the beginning of a horror story that included "betrayal, mutiny, starvation and cannibalism, with a collective death toll of over one hundred and forty people".[60] Based on a recent, politically scandalous event, Géricault's painting combined the frisson of political subversion with the grand scale of traditional history paintings. Strikingly,

Géricault's masterpiece still idealizes the bodies on the raft. In real life, the survivors resorted to cannibalism to avoid starving to death. They would hardly have had the beautiful, proportional, well-muscled bodies we see in the painting. However gruesome, political, and topical his subject matter might have been, Géricault still thought that his task as an artist was to provide beauty.

Exhibited at the Salon of 1819, Géricault's painting did not sell. In 1820, therefore, Géricault brought *The Raft of the Medusa* to London's Egyptian Hall, a multipurpose entertainment and exhibition venue, often used for panoramas. The exhibition was a spectacular success: in six months, from June to December, 40,000 people paid to see Géricault's masterpiece.[61] The success of the exhibition had immediate effects on the London theater. Earlier that year, a melodrama called *Shipwreck of the Medusa; or, The Fatal Raft* by the British dramatist W. T. Moncrieff had had a short run in London. Based on news reports of the wreck and its aftermath, Moncrieff's play originally had nothing to do with Géricault's painting. Géricault's *Medusa* exhibition opened for the public on 12 June 1820. On 19 June, Moncrieff's play reopened, now with clear visual references to Géricault's painting. When the play was revived in 1831, the influence of the painting was pervasive (see *R*, 190). In France, the shipwreck of the *Medusa* was long too politically controversial to be the subject of public performances. In 1839, however, there was a play (*Le Naufrage de la Méduse* by Charles Desnoyer), followed a month later by an opera of the same title. Both were based on Géricault's painting rather than on narrative sources, and in part took the form of a spectacular *tableau vivant* (see *R*, 194).

We have seen that paintings were based on plays, and plays on paintings. But playwrights would also write plays consisting of a series of picturesque tableaux suitable for realization as paintings. Ibsen was immersed in this aesthetics, and much of *Peer Gynt*, for example, is one long series of such tableaux. This is not just my interpretation, but Ibsen's own view. After finishing *Emperor and Galilean*, Ibsen decided that he wanted to make *Peer Gynt*, originally published as a closet drama in 1867, suitable for stage performance. In January 1874 he wrote to Edvard Grieg to ask him to compose the music for the play. In this letter, he speaks of leaving out almost all of Act 4, replacing it with a "a big musical tone painting", during which one would see several tableaux (17: 124–5).[62] He also wrote to Christiania Theater about this, and in 1875 he summarized his original plan for the stage version of *Peer Gynt*: "The first time I wrote to Grieg about the music, I developed for him how I had imagined replacing the fourth act with a tone painting suggesting the contents, to be accompanied by a few *tableaux vivants*

5. Théodore Géricault (1791–1824), *The Raft of the "Medusa"*, 1819 (oil on canvas), Louvre, Paris, France/Bridgeman/Art Library.

representing the most suitable situations in the excluded act, for example Peer
Gynt and the Arab girls, Solveig waiting at home by the hut, etc." (17:
195).[63] Apparently, then, as late as 1875, Ibsen did not find the idea of
"levende billeder" (literally: "living pictures", a direct translation of the
French *tableau vivant*) old-fashioned in the least.

The intermingling of painting and theater was strongly encouraged by the
Art Academy in Düsseldorf. According to Wendt von Kalnein, students at
the Düsseldorf Academy were sent to work at the local theater, where they
had to read Shakespeare, Goethe, Ariosto, and Tasso, and regularly appeared
onstage.[64] In the 1840s the Düsseldorf school's literary and theatrical blend
of romanticism and detailed realism was enormously influential in Norway,
since two of the most important Norwegian painters of the period, Adolph
Tidemand and Hans Gude, whose works Ibsen knew and admired, studied
and taught at the academy of Düsseldorf.[65]

In the Düsseldorf milieu it must have felt quite natural to take the step from
painting and theater to *tableau vivant*, the theatrical realization of an existing
painting. In 1849, Tidemand and Gude's joint painting *Bridal Procession
in Hardanger* (*Brudeferden i Hardanger*) became an instant national icon, the
most famous nationalist *tableau vivant* in Norwegian history (Fig. 6). The
iconographic parallels between Tidemand and Gude's *Wedding Procession*
and Emmanuel Leutze's *Washington Crossing the Delaware* are obvious, and
not coincidental, for Tidemand, Gude, and Leutze were colleagues. In fact,
the two first versions of *Wedding Procession in Hardanger* and the first version
of the American national icon were all painted in Düsseldorf in the spring of
the year of revolution, 1848.[66]

Throughout his career, then, Ibsen lived in a world in which images circulated among poets, painters, and playwrights. I think it is likely that the title
character of *Little Eyolf* (1894) is a result of Ibsen's participation in the visual
economy of his time. In the play, little Eyolf is a lame boy, dependent on his
crutch. A visible reminder of his parents' neglect (Eyolf damaged his leg
by falling off a table while his parents were having sex), the crutch is the one
thing left floating after Eyolf, transfixed by the uncanny Rat Wife and her
dog, walks into the fjord and drowns. The parallels to the legend of the rat-
catcher of Hameln have been noted by many scholars. Yet in the original
German tale, which Ibsen presumably knew, there is no child on crutches.
There is one, however, in Robert Browning's "The Pied Piper of Hamelin: A
Child's Story" from 1842. But Ibsen, who was fluent in German, only read
English with difficulty. To get from Browning's boy with a crutch to Ibsen's
little Eyolf, however, we may simply have to look at the pictures illustrating
Browning's tale.

6. Adolph Tidemand and Hans Gude, *Bridal Procession in Hardanger* 1848, Photo by J. Lathion: © The National Museum of Art, Architecture and Design, Oslo.

In 1888 Browning's poem was published in London by Frederick Warne and Co. as a children's book, with Kate Greenaway's famous illustrations. Greenaway draws a poignant picture of a boy on *two* crutches.[67] But Ibsen, who lived in Munich until 1891, probably never saw this edition. A far more likely candidate for a book that Ibsen may have seen is a German translation for children published in Munich in 1889, with illustrations by Arthur C. Payne and Harry Payne (Fig. 7). In this version we find a boy on *one* crutch, isolated from other children.[68] The German text right under the picture of the boy with a crutch reads: "Ein einziger Knabe nur blieb zurück, / Blieb ausgeschlossen von Lust und Glück."[69] ("Only one single boy remained behind, / remained shut out from pleasure and happiness.") In Browning's poem, the little lame boy moves too slowly to keep up with Pied Piper, and the mountain closes before he can reach it. For the rest of his life he laments his fate, for to him the mountain was paradise, where his bad leg would have been healed. As an explanation of why Ibsen's little Eyolf follows the Rat Wife into the fjord, this is hard to beat.

I do not know whether Ibsen saw the page in the German picture book with its strikingly relevant combination of drawing and verse. All I can say is that it is possible that his attention was caught by a picture of a little boy with a crutch who could not keep up with the other children, and perhaps the picture made him look at the words, too. In Ibsen's own text, we find all this, but we also find new haunting pictures: a crutch floating on the fjord and the open, accusing eyes of a drowned little boy.

Orchardson's *The First Cloud*

As I was researching Ibsen's visual culture, I was struck by some late nineteenth-century paintings that seem to make their way towards modernism in a way that reminds me of Ibsen's. If these paintings today come across as traditional, and perhaps as uninteresting, it is because we are no longer capable of looking at them without interference from the ideology of modernism. I shall now look at a painting that exhibits a particularly fascinating tension between idealism and modernism: namely, *The First Cloud* by Ibsen's near contemporary, the Scottish painter William Quiller Orchardson (1832–1910), reproduced on the cover of this book.[70] Painted in 1887, *The First Cloud* is not just interesting in its own right; it is strikingly similar in preoccupation to Ibsen's plays of the same period: *Rosmersholm* (1886), *The Lady from the Sea* (1888), and above all *Hedda Gabler* (1890).

The modern subject matter of *The First Cloud* is trouble in an upper-class

Die Herren, die erst so sicher waren,
    Wie litten sie jetzund Folterqualen,
        Als plötzlich der Spielmann, die Stadt verlassend,
            Zur Weser sich wandte. Zitternd, erblassend
                Sah'n sie die Kinder zum Wasser gehen
                    Und glaubten im Geist schon ihr Grab zu sehen, —
            Als plötzlich die Schaar sich seitwärts schob.
            Dorthin, wo der Koppelberg sich erhob.
    „Das Steigen wird ihm nun den Athem erschweren!
        Jetzt muß er doch auf zu pfeifen hören
        Und unsere Kinder kehren zurück!"
            So riefen sie alle voll hohem Glück. —
                    Steil stehet der Berg; die Kinder davor —
                    Da öffnet sich pötzlich ein weites Thor;

                Hinein geht der Spielmann; die Kinder ihm nach; —
                Dann schließet der Berg sich mit lautem Krach.
        Ein einziger Knabe nur blieb zurück;
            Blieb ausgeschlossen von Lust und Glück,

7. Arthur C. Payne and Harry Payne, Illustration from Robert Browning, *Der Rattenfänger von Hameln*, ca. 1889. University Library of Braunschweig.

marriage. *The First Cloud* was the third and last painting in a hugely successful series on the subject: *Mariage de convenance* (1883) and *Mariage de
convenance—After!* (1886). The very idea of a series of paintings conveying the
story of a loveless and degrading marriage recalls Hogarth's *Marriage à la
mode*, and reeks of moral high-mindedness. Yet Orchardson's marriage trilogy
is not, in fact, a simple allegory of conventional morality.

Mariage de convenance presents the two characters seated at either end of a
very long dining table, which serves as an emphatic visual bar between them.
Leaning back with a bored and impatient expression, the young, attractive
wife is not touching her food; the much older, obviously wealthy husband
appears not to notice, for he has an eye only for the wine being poured by
the butler. There is a spectacular absence of friends, children, family, or other
social relations, and of conversation; the picture conveys a palpable sense
of silence, boredom, and depression. The length of the table reinforces the
sense, quite frequent in Orchardson's paintings, that the characters are
entirely isolated, incapable of conversation, entirely unknown to each other.

Mariage de convenance—After! shows the husband alone in front of the
fireplace in the same room, still dominated by drab brown and olive color
tones, where the only sign of the departed wife is a bunch of strikingly pink
flowers on the dining table behind him.[71] This time, the table is not so much
a bar of separation as the looming shape of a coffin bearing flowers. The two
pictures are also linked by the presence of the wine decanter, signaling the
husband's increasing fondness of drink. The man's anger and depression are
obvious, but it is unclear to me (perhaps because I am a woman writing in the
early twenty-first century) whether we are expected to sympathize with him,
or rather feel that he deserves his fate. There is a certain ambiguity about
Orchardson's paintings, for although they invite moral speculation, the
pictures themselves do not tell us what conclusions to draw.

Although it was painted last, *The First Cloud* represents the beginning
of the narrative sequence. In this painting, the age difference between the
husband and wife is much less marked. Visually, the huge empty space
between the spouses is daring, particularly because the canvas is very large
(135 × 194 cm). The husband looks petulant, strident, possibly somewhat
drunk. The wife looks proud, even arrogant, as if she feels insulted. There
are reminiscences of Gwendolyn Harleth here, and strong premonitions
of Hedda Gabler, not least in the curtains between the two rooms, the
woman's reflection in the mirror in the back room, and the sense that the
woman's most dramatic moment will take place behind a curtain, unseen,
offstage.

The First Cloud is highly dramatic, still based on the idea of the pregnant moment—the first quarrel is a condensed image of past errors of judgment and behavior, as well as of the dire future to come—but the pregnant moment is no longer one of external passion and action; rather, it has become mostly psychological and internal. As a result, the painting is much harder to insert in a narrative, and much harder to interpret morally than, say, Girodet's *The Flood.* The more we look at this painting, at the aggressive stance of the man, the sweeping hauteur of the woman, the less it tells a moral tale. Whose fault is this rift? What could be done to save this marriage? Where do we place moral blame? The painting does not say.

Its interpretative openness, the sheer modernity of its representation of gender relations, makes this painting a natural contemporary of Ibsen's plays of the same period. Yet Orchardson himself appears to have sought to minimize the ambiguity of this unsettling canvas. At the Royal Academy's summer exhibition in 1887, *The First Cloud* was accompanied by two lines of poetry: "It is the little rift within the lute / That by and by will make the music mute." The lines are taken from Tennyson's epic poem "Merlin and Vivien", a part of *Idylls of the King* (1859):

> In Love, if Love be Love, if Love be ours.
> Faith and unfaith can ne'er be equal powers:
> Unfaith in aught is want of faith in all.
> It is the little rift within the lute,
>   That by and by will make the music mute,
>   And ever widening slowly silence all.
> The little rift within the lovers' lute,
>   Or little pitted speck in garner'd fruit,
>   That rotting inward slowly moulders all.

Idylls of the King had been immensely popular, and had been widely used by painters. "Merlin and Vivien" alone had already inspired both Arthur Hughes's *The Rift in the Lute* (1861–2) and Edward Burne-Jones's *The Beguiling of Merlin* (1870–4).[72]

Most viewers of *The First Cloud,* then, would have known that the passage in question is taken from a poem in which a wily temptress, Vivien, ensnares the wizard Merlin, in a plot usually interpreted as the victory of the (female) senses over the (male) intellect. In Tennyson's *Idylls,* moreover, Guinevere's adultery with Lancelot is represented as the cause of the destruction of the brotherhood of the Round Table, and squarely blamed on Guinevere. Orchardson's catalogue text thus enabled spectators to believe, without much hesitation, that the painting represented the first step towards the ultimate destruction of a marriage by female adultery (this interpretation is also cued by the poem's concern with "faith" and "unfaith" in the passage that caught Orchardson's attention).

To our modern taste, this is exactly what we do not need to appreciate *The First Cloud*, for it makes the painting simpler, less ambiguous, less challenging than it actually is. The textual reference to the first rift reduces that daring visual void between the spouses to a mere metaphor for the "rift within the lute", which in its turn is a metaphor for the "unfaith" which eventually will silence the music of love. To late Victorian taste, however, a text like this was exactly what was required to give the viewers the necessary clues about how to interpret the painting. The fact that Orchardson presents a radically modern interpretation of Tennyson's medieval theme could then be applauded as an original, but unthreatening, novelty, perhaps as evidence of the eternal truths contained in good poetry.

Looked at without the accompanying text, *The First Cloud* is not a self-evident illustration of female treachery. Rather, it embodies a threatening sense of distance, distrust, even hatred between the sexes. The misery of this particular couple becomes a representation of the sex wars of the last decades of the nineteenth century, and places *The First Cloud* right at the center of early modernist concerns with sex, sexuality, gender, and marriage. Looked at in conjunction with the text provided by the painter, however, it threatens to degenerate into sexist kitsch. I take this to mean that Orchardson was a better painter than he dared to admit, or in other words, that the painting outstrips the ideology it is supposed to embody.

The First Cloud shows that in the late 1880s, the increasingly outmoded idealist aesthetics did not prevent the representation of modernity; what it prevented was the *acknowledgment and interpretation* of that modernity. To put it differently: by the 1870s and 1880s, idealism remained for most artists and writers a compulsory way of talking about art. This led to an increasing discrepancy between the works of art themselves and the interpretations placed on them. Exhibited in 1887, *The First Cloud* was a huge success. A contemporary reviewer declared it "far finer" than the two *Mariage de Convenance* paintings, adding that the "telling of the story [. . .] could hardly be improved upon", before concluding that "the whole aspect of the picture glowing with harmonious colour compels admiration".[73] It was instantly sold to the National Gallery of Victoria, and Sir Henry Tate liked it so much that he persuaded Orchardson to paint a smaller version just for him.[74]

In the early 1890s, Ibsen's plays unleashed one of the most intense culture wars in British history.[75] Critics who would have enjoyed Orchardson's painting reacted with fear and loathing to Ibsen. But the difference between them is not that absolute. Orchardson's painting is far more modern than the text he appends to it, and conversely, Ibsen felt at home in the visual world that Orchardson inhabited. But had Ibsen been a painter, he would surely never have appended the lines from that Tennyson poem; nor would he have given the painting such a moralizing title. In 1887, the difference between Orchardson and Ibsen, then, is that Orchardson remains entangled in the idealist aesthetics that Ibsen had long since rejected. Refusing to supply the audience with reassuringly conventional moral interpretations of his unsettling themes, Ibsen forced his audiences to come face to face with the painful contradictions of their own modernity.

Böcklin, Ibsen, and Modernism: The Arrival of Formalism

In 1904, a young German art historian named Julius Meier-Graefe (1867–1935) published a path-breaking work entitled *Modern Art*. In the early 1890s, Meier-Graefe belonged to the circle around Strindberg in Berlin, and started his career with a novel entitled *Nach Norden* (1893), inspired by an interest in Ibsen and in Scandinavia. His first art criticism was on Edvard Munch.[76] In 1904, Meier-Graefe's *Modern Art* provided the first serious scholarly account of Impressionism in Germany. In 1905, he published an enraged pamphlet entitled *Der Fall Böcklin* against Arnold Böcklin (1827–1901), one of the most admired German painters of the age, followed in 1906 by a more qualified assault on the equally respected Adolph Menzel (1815–1905).[77] According to Meier-Graefe, Böcklin was simply one of the worst painters in world history: "Even in the worst periods of the history of art no decadence has ever produced such barbarities as his *Cholera*, and other things in the same vein," he declares.[78]

Meier-Graefe's attack on Böcklin shows how the aesthetic era that began with Lessing and Diderot was brought to an end. It also brings out the differences between the new, triumphant modernist aesthetics and Ibsen's visual taste. Until Meier-Graefe entered the scene, a taste for Böcklin had not been incompatible with avant-garde status. In 1907 Strindberg, for example, still had not heard of Böcklin's loss of cachet, for at the very end of *The Ghost Sonata* the stage directions read: "The room disappears; Böcklin's *The Island of the Dead* becomes the backdrop; soft, quiet, pleasantly melancholy music is heard from the island."[79]

Böcklin's *Island of the Dead* was painted in five versions from 1880 to 1886, and instantly became immensely popular (Fig. 8). In 1890, Georg Brandes's friend, the German painter and sculptor Max Klinger made an engraving of the 1883 version, which helped to spread the painting to fans all over Europe.[80] Georges Clémenceau owned one of the Klinger prints. Sigmund Freud had a reproduction in his waiting room, Vladimir Illitch Lenin pinned it up over his bed in Zürich, and after he came to power, the erstwhile painter Adolph Hitler bought one of the five originals.[81]

Ibsen obviously looked at *The Island of the Dead* too, for there are references to the white figure in the painting in the appearance of Irene in Act 1 of *When We Dead Awaken*, where the stage directions read:

A slender lady, dressed in fine, cream-colored white cashmere, followed by a deaconess in black with a silver cross in a chain on her chest, emerges from behind the corner of the hotel and walks through the park over to the pavilion in the left foreground. Her face is pale and her features as if frozen; her eyelids are lowered, the eyes seemingly without the power of sight. Her dress reaches to her feet, falling in even folds close to her body. Over her head, neck, breast, shoulders and arms she wears a large white crepe shawl. She holds her arms crossed high up on her chest. The posture is rigidly immovable. Stiff and measured paces. The deaconess's bearing is similarly measured, and like that of a servant.

(13: 225)

Irene's appearance here is taken straight from *The Island of the Dead*, which also shows us a stiffly erect figure shrouded in white, with arms crossed high up over the chest, assisted by a lesser, servant-like figure in dark clothes. The theme of the living dead is fundamental to the play, and such a transparent reference to Böcklin's painting brings this out. The connection between the sculpture-like immobility of the Böcklin figure and Irene's past as a living sculpture is equally obvious.

Ibsen's preoccupation with Böcklin in *When We Dead Awaken* doesn't stop here. For we also learn that Rubek (whose first name, Arnold, provides another reference to Böcklin) is a sculptor who feels that all his portrait busts are really portraits of animals:

PROFESSOR RUBEK. There's something suspicious, something hidden, inside and behind those busts—something secret that human beings can't see—. . . Only *I* can see it. And that amuses me intensely.—On the outside there is this "striking likeness," as they say, which people stand there and gape at in astonishment— [*Lowering his voice.*] But fundamentally, they are respectable, honorable horse faces, obstinate donkey snouts, flop-eared, low-browed dog skulls, satisfied swine heads—and occasionally some oafish, slack, brutal bull's heads as well—(13: 220)

In 1872 Böcklin made a series of six grotesque, animal-like masks for the façade of the Kunsthalle in his native Basel. Unfortunately for Böcklin, they

8. Arnold Böcklin, *The Island of the Dead* (first version), 1880. Kunstmuseum Basel. Permanent loan of the Gottfried Keller Foundation, 1920. Photo; Kunstmuseum Basel, Martin Bühler.

provoked a great scandal, for he was accused of having used local worthies as his models. The fury mounted to the point that the masks were about to be taken down. Hearing of these developments, the directors of the Art Museum in Strasbourg offered to buy the masks. Such signs of foreign interest apparently inspired a change of heart among the members of the board of the Basel Kunsthalle, and the masks stayed. A satirical postcard from the period, entitled "Master Böcklin and his models", preserves the memory of the occasion.[82] But of course, it is impossible to tell whether Ibsen ever saw this postcard, which certainly provides a striking visual parallel to Rubek's busts with animal faces.

There is another connection between Böcklin and Ibsen. In *The Lady from the Sea*, the painter and jack-of-all-trades Ballested is busy painting a picture of a half-dead mermaid. Later on in the first act, Ellida asks the consumptive sculptor Lyngstrand about his artistic plans: "And what would you model? Will it be mermen and mermaids? Or will it be old vikings—?" (11: 72). First of all: this is probably not supposed to be ironic. Norwegian and European painting in the 1880s was still full of mermaids and Vikings. Ellida's reference to "mermen and mermaids", moreover, brings one specific picture to mind: namely, Böcklin's *Im Spiel der Wellen* (In the Play of the Waves). In the foreground of this painting, there is a happily laughing merman playing with a much younger mermaid, who has a particularly striking look of uncertainty and anguish on her face (Plate 4). As soon as I saw it, Ibsen's Ellida came to mind: the painting is the very expression of her situation at the beginning of the play.

But can we be sure that Ibsen saw it? Here is what I know about this. *Im Spiel der Wellen* was first exhibited in Berlin in 1883. There it created a great sensation, and was immediately bought for a private collection. In January 1888, however, it was given as a gift to the Neue Pinakothek in Munich, where it still hangs. The gift created quite a stir, and the painting was immediately exhibited.[83] In the winter of 1887–8, Ibsen lived in Munich and was preparing to write *The Lady from the Sea*.

With Böcklin the story that started with Diderot and Lessing comes to an end, for Böcklin epitomized everything that the new, bold generation of modernist art critics hated. His art was literary, mythological, allegorical, religious, and existential. Meier-Graefe attacks Böcklin for doing precisely what Lessing recommended: "What Böcklin turned into reality, Lessing praised. . . . The same misjudgment of the flesh and blood of painting that drives Böcklin, is already there in the author of *Laocoön*."[84] The problem with Lessing, Meier-Graefe claims, was above all his *literary* understanding of painting. Modernist painting must be about the eye and the canvas, about

Meister Boecklin und seine Modelle

9. Anonymous, *Master Böcklin with the Ugly Mugs of his Critics*, photographic postcard, ca. 1872. Photo; Kunstmuseum Basel.

the direct spontaneous act of perception and the possibilities of the medium, not about moralizing narrative.

Painting, then, must be purged of literature. But for Meier-Graefe and his modernist comrades, this is not enough. What ultimately has to be overcome is not just certain kinds of representation, but *representation itself*:

Böcklin stands for naturalism in its most blatant form; for naturalism is not merely the bare imitation, however accomplished, of anything we see or know or can conceive. It is any kind of presentation which aims solely at recording the thing seen so faithfully that it has the air of reality. Moreover it is clear that it matters nothing whether the artist has seen the thing in question or not . . . If what he has painted has the semblance of reality without other qualities, that is enough to bring it under the category of naturalism.[85]

Meier-Graefe's attitude condemned almost all nineteenth-century painting to the dustheap of history. Exceptions were made only for painters who through their handling of color, brushwork, or form could be said to anticipate the new aesthetic ideal, which was that the painter's task is to explore the possibilities of his own medium. From now on, interpretation was to be formal and painterly, not literary and ethical.

Modernism is antitheatrical, and Meier-Graefe is as antitheatrical as Diderot.[86] "We expected a philosophy of life, and find nothing but turgid melodrama," he exclaims: "Away with Böcklin!"[87] But the meaning of theatricality has changed since the eighteenth century. Although Meier-Graefe still means to denounce inauthentic art, art made to impress and manipulate the beholder, the criteria for painterly inauthenticity have shifted radically. The new painterly ethics is formalist; the ideal painter is now a saint of formalist purity, single-mindedly pursuing his explorations of his medium without regard to critics, buyers, and audiences.

In the new paradigm, therefore, the nineteenth-century tradition becomes nothing but literary, religious, sentimental, moralizing, didactic twaddle. Meier-Graefe and his followers ensured that idealist aesthetics quickly lost every last shred of intellectual credibility. The millions of readers who still want to be morally improved or religiously uplifted by their aesthetic experiences, as well as all those who want to be totally absorbed in films and books that make them take the fiction they propose for reality, are the last inheritors of a once noble, but now fallen aesthetic tradition.

A Non-formalist Modernism: The Painterly Light of Transfiguration in *The Wild Duck*

The Wild Duck shows that Ibsen realized well before Meier-Graefe that ideal-ism breeds theatricality. Critics have, of course, noticed that this magnificent play is a sustained critique of ethical idealism, embodied in the figure of Gregers Werle and his "ideal demand" (*ideale fordring*). But, as we have seen, aesthetic idealism encompasses ethical idealism. *The Wild Duck* is as much about the demand that *art* embody the ideal as it is about the demand that human beings live up to ideal notions of truth. This becomes clear in the scene in Act 4 when Gregers, the card-carrying idealist, enters the Ekdals' living room for the first time after he has told Hjalmar the truth about Gina's past relationship to Gregers's own father. I quote the scene at some length, for it is crucial to our understanding of Ibsen's modernism:

GREGERS [*advancing with a radiant, joyful expression, reaching his hands to them*]. Now, you dear people—! [*He looks from one to the other and whispers to Hjalmar*]: Isn't it done yet?

HJALMAR [*loudly*]. It's done.

GREGERS. Is it really?

HJALMAR. I have lived the bitterest hour of my life.

GREGERS. But also the most uplifting, I should think.

HJALMAR. Well, it's off our hands for the moment.

GINA. God forgive you, Mr. Werle.

GREGERS [*greatly astonished*]. But I don't understand this.

HJALMAR. What don't you understand?

GREGERS. After so great a confrontation—a confrontation that will lay the founda-tion for a whole new way of life—a way of life, a life together, in truth, without deceit—

HJALMAR. Yes, I know; I do know all that.

GREGERS. I had so certainly expected that when I came in through that door, I would be struck by a transfiguring light shining from both husband and wife. And then I see nothing but this dull, heavy, gloomy—

GINA. If that's how it is.

[*Takes off the lampshade.*]

GREGERS. You don't want to understand me Mrs. Ekdal. No, I can see that you will need time—. But what about you, Hjalmar? *You* must feel you've been con-secrated for a higher purpose by this great confrontation.

HJALMAR. Of course I do. That's to say,—in a way I do.

GREGERS. For there surely isn't anything in the world that compares with *that*—that compares with finding forgiveness for an erring sinner, and lifting her up to you in love.

HJALMAR. Do you think a man can overcome the bitter cup I have just drained that easily?

GREGERS. Not an *ordinary* man, perhaps. But a man like *you*—!

(10: 123–4)

Fantasizing about walking straight into a Victorian genre painting entitled "Forgiven!" (Dante Gabriel Rossetti worked on one entitled "Found"), Gregers, clearly, has imagined that after the revelation of truth, there would be a great idealist scene of reconciliation, in which the husband gloriously forgives the erring wife.[88] (In *A Doll's House* Torvald Helmer speaks in precisely such tones to Nora after he has discovered that he is not threatened by Krogstad's blackmail after all.) Once reconciliation has taken place, idealists imagine, the audience (in this case Gregers) will be filled with an uplifting sense of truth, beauty, and goodness.[89] Gregers, then, resembles a theater director who also writes the script for performances that in the end will benefit himself.

Mixing aesthetics and ethics, Gregers speaks of uplifting moments, transfiguration, and an ennobling consecration to higher purposes, clearly expecting to find the husband ennobled by his self-sacrificing power of forgiveness, and the wife uplifted by the power of the husband's noble love. But instead of painterly light streaming down over their faces, he finds Hjalmar's self-pitying sulking and Gina's justifiable anger. Gregers's idealism is partly represented as grotesquely funny (particularly when Gina removes the lampshade in response to his idealist metaphors), partly as theatrical, and ultimately as murderous, for eventually Gregers's insistence that someone must sacrifice something for the sake of truth, beauty, and reconciliation will kill a child.

The Wild Duck is Ibsen's most savage and most focused attack on idealism. It shows convincingly that truth, beauty, and goodness have come apart. Once idealism is rejected, writers and artists must find new aesthetic ideas. Meier-Graefe and his generation were moving towards formalism. The scene discussed here tells us that Ibsen chose a different direction. The idealist Gregers despises the ordinary, which to him is a realm of life and experience entirely without redeeming powers. To Ibsen, however, Gina's and Hedvig's sense of the ordinary meaning of words held out more hope than Gregers's flowery metaphors.

Part II

Ibsen's Modern Breakthrough

5

The Idealist Straitjacket
Ibsen's early aesthetics

When Ibsen arrived in Christiania in 1850, he found a fairly undeveloped artistic and theatrical world focused on one great project: that of forging a national culture. Romantic nationalism ruled unchallenged. Obsessed with national identity, Norwegian art and literature were churning out ideal Norwegian heroes and heroines. Poems, plays, and genre paintings featured themes and characters inspired by the Icelandic sagas, Norwegian folktales and folk songs, and, not least, Norwegian peasant life. Because Norway never developed feudalism, Norwegian peasants and farmers (*den norske bonden*) were considered the very incarnations of national independence, bearers of the proud traditions of the Viking past, miraculously unsullied by foreign influences for more than 500 years. It is a measure of Ibsen's isolation in Grimstad that he chose a Roman—that is to say, a European and cosmopolitan—subject, rather than a national one for his first play, *Catiline* (1850).

The situation in Norway around 1850 bears out Jonas Barish's claim, in his path-breaking book *The Antitheatrical Prejudice*, that there is a profound parallel between romantic and Puritan attitudes towards the theater: "Romanticism, like Puritanism, leans toward inwardness, solitude, and spontaneity. It shares with Puritanism a belief in an absolute sincerity which speaks directly from the soul, a pure expressiveness that knows nothing of the presence of others. It takes as its models the guileless folk of the earth, who 'know not seems': the peasant, the savage, the idiot, the child—those in whom the histrionic impulse remains undeveloped."[1] However different they were in other respects, around 1850, Norwegian nationalism, idealism, and pietism shared the antitheatrical prejudice: this was a cultural milieu where antitheatrical and antitheatricalist attitudes were rife.

Cherishing authenticity, spontaneity, and natural naïvety, Norwegian national romanticism harbored deep suspicion of anything that seemed staged or contrived. "Romanticism", Barish comments, "fostered a cult of inwardness and privacy which fed the puritanical distrust of qualities like mimicry, ostentation, and spectacle, and was fed by it."[2] Distrust of theater was fanned by the established Lutheran Church, and even more so by the strong lay pietist movement, which had its roots precisely in the rural population extolled by national romantic art. Adolph Tidemand's famous painting *Haugianerne* (1848), depicting a pietist gathering of peasants, perfectly captures the powerful blend of nationalism, idealism, and religion that dominated the arts in Norway. Unless the religious purpose was unmistakable, pietism was hostile to theater, to any kind of performance, and to art itself. Dancing, song, music, and card games were considered the devil's work. In 1856, Bjørnstjerne Bjørnson wrote a series of articles entitled "About Dance, Song, Card Games, Fiddle Playing and Other Kinds of Fun", in which he argued against the strict and joyless pietistic faith and in favor of the joy of life.[3] The pietists were hardly convinced: when film was invented, they immediately added cinema to the list of sinful arts.

Just as aesthetic idealism blended ethics and aesthetics, so it also blurred the lines between the secular and the religious. True art should be beautiful; beauty uplifts us by making us contemplate the highest truth; truth, ultimately, is God, or rather: God is truth. In mid-nineteenth-century Norway, the internal connection between idealism and religion was particularly intense, which explains why Ibsen's modernism emerged not just from the ruins of idealism, but from the ruins of religion (a connection Ibsen himself fully explored in *Emperor and Galilean*).

In 1850, however, the radical revolt against God had not yet arrived in Norway, and there was no clearly defined secular, radical, cultural front for writers and artists to join; above all, there was no alternative to aesthetic idealism. This chapter, therefore, has one overarching aim: to show that Ibsen's early works are records of his struggle to fit into the straitjacket of idealist aesthetics, and that this struggle came to an end in 1862, with the publication of "Terje Vigen" and *Love's Comedy*.

Ibsen's early idealism was not simply literary. I shall begin by showing that Ibsen came of age as a writer and man of the theater in an environment dominated by the visual idealism of the painters J. C. Dahl, Adolph Tidemand, and Hans Gude. Idealist and nationalist aesthetics permeated much of his early thought about art and theater. Yet, however much he struggled to fit the idealist mould, Ibsen's early works end up sounding either too satirical or too ambivalent to produce much of an uplift in the audience. From the point of view of idealist aesthetics, Ibsen's early plays had two flaws: they failed to convey the ideal, and they were too aesthetically conflicted and self-conscious to produce the required degree of transfixed attention in the audience. As examples of his early failures, I shall discuss *St John's Night*

(1853) and *Lady Inger* (1855), before briefly contrasting them with Ibsen's only relative success in the early years, *The Feast at Solhoug* (1856), praised by Bjørnson precisely because it enabled the spectator to experience total immersion in the fiction.

Some of Ibsen's early poems express his early aesthetic conflicts. This is particularly true for the two programmatic poems "I billedgalleriet" ("In the picture gallery") and "Paa Vidderne" ("On the heights"), from the 1850s. The turning point came in 1862. With the publication of the epic poem "Terje Vigen", for the first and only time in his long career Ibsen demonstrated that he was capable of producing an idealist masterpiece. "Terje Vigen" (written in 1861–2) is a glorious piece of poetry, a triumphal expression of the prevailing nationalist, idealist, pictorial aesthetics, rightly celebrated as a major contribution to the Norwegian poetic tradition and to the formation of a Norwegian national identity.

The experience of finally mastering the dominant aesthetic form appears to have been liberating to Ibsen. Above all, it appears to have given him the self-confidence he needed to find his own, original voice as a writer. In his next work, *Love's Comedy*—his first play for five years—he did not try to repeat the undoubted aesthetic success of "Terje Vigen". Rather, he boldly took idealism as his subject matter. I shall show that *Love's Comedy* is an exploration not just of idealist notions of love, but of idealist aesthetics, too. The result is a startlingly radical play, questioning the foundations of art as well as love. Ibsen's meta-aesthetic turn was not appreciated: *Love's Comedy* received the most intensely hostile reception of any Ibsen play before *Ghosts*.

Idealism, Religion, and Theater: Excursus on Bjørnson's *The Fisher Maiden*

How could a young man of the theater find a self-confident artistic voice of his own in a profoundly antitheatrical and antitheatricalist culture? The question was pressing for Norwegian writers and artists of Ibsen's generation, and Ibsen's friend and colleague Bjørnstjerne Bjørnson felt it so keenly that he wrote a much admired story about the conflict between theater and religion, the 1868 novella *Fiskerjenten* (*The Fisher Maiden*). The story of a little country girl who becomes a great actress, *The Fisher Maiden* has been called Norway's first artist's novel.[4] Its deep autobiographical roots were stressed by Bjørnson, who once exclaimed that "The Fisher Maiden! She is of course me!"[5] Explaining why he chose to write about a woman actress rather than about a male writer and theater director, Bjørnson wrote:

I chose the theater because pietism and all the prejudices considers it the lowest: the victory is more palpable when *this* breaks through the wall. . . . I chose a woman to achieve the breakthrough, because there it can happen more freely, in the spontaneous movement of instincts and talents;—it had to happen in art, because it is the child of freedom and also eternally frees us; but woman has no other art that can be given plastic form than the art of acting.[6]

In a small town on the coast of Norway (probably modeled on Molde, Bjørnson's home town, later said to be the setting for *The Lady from the Sea*), the illegitimate Petra is brought up by her mother, who runs a small inn for sailors. Petra's spontaneous and wild nature lands her in much childish trouble, delightfully conveyed in Bjørnson's racy, colloquial style. After Petra has managed to get herself engaged to three young men at once, she is packed off to Bergen, where she goes to the theater for the first time. In a bravura piece of writing anticipating Tolstoy's capacity to make the familiar strange, Bjørnson presents the play through Petra's eyes. Since Petra has no idea what theater is, the reader has to work out for herself that what Petra is actually seeing is Adam Oehlenschläger's popular romantic tragedy *Axel and Valborg*, performed by a troupe of Danish players.

When the curtain rises, Petra thinks she is in a church. Cleverly establishing the parallel between church and theater as the key metaphor of the story, this scene also shows that Petra, like Diderot's reader of Richardson, takes the action onstage to be real. Although she barely understands what the Danish actors are saying, Petra is completely and immediately immersed in the theatrical illusion. "He is deceiving you!", she cries out in a desperate attempt to warn one of the lovers against an evil monk, and when the two lovers are separated, Petra leaps to her feet and cries out in agony, entirely ignorant of the fact that she is creating a scandal.[7]

At the end, the two lovers die, *à la* Romeo and Juliet. Bjørnson follows Petra's reactions with great mastery, in a sequence that gives powerful voice to Bjørnson's own faith that art and religion can be harmoniously reconciled by idealist aesthetics:

The bride looks up from the breast of the dead man and prays that she too may die. The heavens open to that gaze; a wondrous light streams down; the bridal hall is above; let the bride enter! Yes!—she can already look in, for from her eyes there emanates the same peace as in the high mountains. Then the eyelids droop, the struggle had a higher solution; their fidelity a higher crown; now she is with him.
Petra sat long silent; her heart uplifted in faith, filled with strength from this

greatness. She rose high above all that was petty, above all fear and pain; she rose with a smile to all, for they were her brothers and sisters; the evil that separates us did not exist; it lay crushed under the thunder.

(F, 438)

A better account of the uplifting effects that idealism attributes to art would be hard to find. Petra is a better person for having seen the play. She is at peace, in harmony with herself and the world. Her thoughts have been lifted towards heaven. Her radiant joy shines on all who come near her: this is the liberation that art bestows on us; this is why art makes us free.

After her visit to the theater, all of Petra's inchoate longings come together: "This is the greatest thing on earth; this is what I want to be" (F, 439). The next day, she goes to see the Danish company director to ask for a job. Too natural, too ignorant, too shy, and above all too Norwegian, Petra fails utterly to impress. Desperately disappointed, she leaves Bergen and ends up seeking refuge in a deanery in the mountains, where the dean (*prosten*), a widower, and his daughter Signe become her friends and protectors.[8] Petra then spends two happy years, devoted to reading the great works of world literature in this idyllic, pastoral, national, and religious setting.

One day just before Christmas, however, the dean discovers that Petra is consumed by the ambition to become an actress. Appalled and scandalized, he denounces her for deviously exploiting his hospitality. But just as the dean is about to expel her from his mountain paradise, he receives a delegation of pietist mountain farmers, who have come to complain that the dean owns a piano and encourages "wordly singing, music and dancing" (F, 479). Another clergyman, a friend of the family, who once was in love with Petra, Hans Ødegaard, then attempts to prove that art, theater, and music are indeed compatible with the strictest faith in God.

The discussion continues among the dean's Christmas guests without reaching a conclusion. At this point, Ødegaard asks Petra to read a poem about a young boy who was refused leave to go abroad with the Vikings. Challenging the chieftain of a Viking ship, the boy easily defeats him, takes over the ship, and sails it right back to his home village. The poem ends on a note of triumph: "He smiled at them: 'Do I have your permission *now*?' " (F, 493). The parallel to Petra's own situation is obvious, and needless to say, her performance is spellbinding:

The poem had been spoken with intense feeling, solemnly, without the slightest ostentation. They [the audience] stood as if a rainbow-colored stream of light a hundred feet tall had suddenly flashed up from the ground. Nobody spoke, nobody moved; but the captain could no longer stand it, he leapt up, drew his breath, lifted himself up and said: . . . "The devil take me, but now I really must have a song about our fatherland!"

(F, 493)

Petra's greatness as an actress is underwritten by her antitheatrical delivery (she speaks "without the slightest ostentation"), which produces instant and profound attention in the audience, until the captain breaks the spell, and the whole audience bursts into song, spontaneously choosing to sing Bjørnson's beautiful nationalist lyrics "Jeg vil verge mitt land" ("I shall defend my country"). Aesthetic performance and nationalist fervor are one.

The dean has long remained silent. At the dinner table, he suddenly stands up and declares that "I have an engagement to announce!":

"I have an engagement to announce," the dean repeated, as if he had some trouble getting started. "I have to confess that at first I did not like the thought of it . . . I thought, to tell you the truth, that he was unworthy of her. . . . But now," the dean continued, "now that I have got to know him better, I no longer know whether she is worthy of *him*, for so great has he become in my eyes; for he is art, the great art of the stage, and his fiancée is Petra, my foster daughter, my dear child; may you be happy together! I tremble to think of it, but what belongs together, must be together. God be with you, my daughter!"

(F, 495)

The heavy insistence on the metaphor of the engagement turns Petra into a vestal virgin. The figure of the pure woman, beloved by Christian religion and idealist aesthetics alike, is here mobilized to guarantee the sanctity of the theater. The idealist motif of sacrifice is here too: Petra will have to sacrifice her sexuality on the altar of her vocation; the dean's daughter will marry Ødegaard, Petra will marry the theater.

Bjørnson's last chapter is a *tour de force* of idealist reconciliation, for here everyone from Petra's past is united to witness her first triumph in her homeland, playing the lead in Oehlenschläger's *Axel and Valborg*. This is how Bjørnson ends the story: "The overture slowed down, the harmonies became peaceful, melting away as if in sunshine. The overture ended; there was anxious silence. Then the curtain rose" (F, 501). Although idealist aesthetics did not require a happy ending (tragedy is, after all, the quintessentially idealist form), Bjørnson did; his tale ends on a note of peace, harmony, sunshine, and the assured confidence of victory.

The Fisher Maiden appealed to its time; within a year it was translated into Swedish, Finnish, German, and English. Ibsen read it too, and wrote to his publisher: "The first half I like extraordinarily well, but the rest is not worked through; there he has wanted to do something which lies outside his talent"

(16: 213).[9] This was surely a polite way of saying that Bjørnson was no intellectual and ought to stay clear of theology and philosophy (at the time Ibsen himself was considering a return to his most philosophical project ever: namely, *Emperor and Galilean*). Ibsen was right: the first half of *The Fisher Maiden* is a masterpiece, the second degenerates into turgid theological discussion. Yet the novella marvelously conveys that the only publicly acceptable way of defending theater in mid-nineteenth-century Norway was to turn it into an ally of religion and nationalism. The point is that while this was a solution available to a happy idealist like Bjørnson, the conflicted Ibsen simply could not squeeze himself into the mould.

In 1871, three years after Bjørnson published *The Fisher Maiden*, Georg Brandes issued his fiery call for a modern, secular, political literature. The decades that followed were a period of contentious transition. With the advent of naturalism and the slow demise of idealism in the 1870s and 1880s, the enmity between art and religion intensified in Scandinavia, and for a century to come, art, theater, and literature remained at the center of a gigantic struggle between radical secularism and pietistic hostility to the arts. Ibsen left no doubt about what side he was on. In an 1879 letter to his old friend, the art historian Lorentz Dietrichson, he expressed his views with unusual force:

As long as a population considers it more important to build religious meeting houses than theaters, as long as it is more ready to support the Zulu mission than the art museum, art cannot expect healthy well-being; indeed, it won't even be considered an immediate necessity. I don't think it helps to defend the cause of art with arguments derived from its nature, since in our country art is still little understood or thoroughly misunderstood. What we need to do, above all, is thoroughly to stamp out and exterminate all the dark, medieval monasticism that narrows reflection and dulls the mind. My opinion is: for the moment it is no use to take up arms on behalf of art, we need rather to fight the hostility to art. First do away with that, then we can build.[10]

(17: 374–5)

Religious meeting houses against theaters, the Zulu mission against the art museum, medieval religion against the love and understanding of art: for the next century, these oppositions continued to play themselves out in Scandinavian cultural struggles.

An Evening of *tableaux vivants*

In his early, formative years, Ibsen's involvement with painting and the most painterly of performances, the *tableau vivant*, was extensive. Although *tableaux vivants* were all the rage in Norway in the late 1840s and 1850s, historians and critics have written remarkably little about them. In 1836, Welhaven had informed the Christiania public that French theater was leaving classicism behind, and becoming thoroughly pictorial, declaring that "The new French dramas are moving tableaux".[11] As we have seen in Chapter 4, French plays inspired by paintings such as *The Raft of the Medusa* and many others date from the 1830s. After 1848, and throughout the 1850s, however, Christiania Theater also produced actual *tableaux vivants* based on famous paintings.

In Norway the passion for the *tableau vivant* appears to have received a new, patriotic lease on life in 1849. After the February Revolution, a rare constellation of Norwegian artists and musicians who usually worked abroad sought shelter from the European storms in Christiania. Their fervently national and idealist aspirations were memorably expressed in three national *Festaftener* (festive evenings) at Christiania Theater. The performances consisted of music, song, dance, and declamation of poetry, culminating in a *tableau vivant*.

The last *tableau vivant* of the famous festive evenings of 1849 was based on Adolph Tidemand and Hans Gude's *Bridal Procession in Hardanger*. The two painters themselves painted the backdrop for the production, which appears to have been conceived as a veritable *Gesamtkunstwerk*. A choir and orchestra performed a song composed by Halfdan Kjerulf to a poem by Andreas Munch specially written to accompany the painting. The speaker begins by declaring: "Det aander en tindrende Sommerluft / Varmt over Hardangerfjords Vande" ("A sparkling summer air breathes / warmly over the waters of the Hardangerfjord"). He then compares the bride in the painting to a princess of olden days and praises the power of traditional fiddle music, before, finally, with clear reference to the painting, ending by rhapsodizing on the power of painting to capture such a moment of national pride and joy:

> I dette bævende, flygtige Nu,
> Før Draaben af Aaren er trillet,—
> Har Kunsten fæstet med kjærlig Hu
> Det hele, straalende Billed,
> Og løfter det stolt for Verden frem,
> At Alle kan kjende vort herlige Hjem
> Og vide de Æventyr klare,
> Som Norges Fjorde Bevare.[12]

(In this trembling, evanescent Now / before the drop has rolled off the oar,—/ art has fixed with a loving mind / the whole, radiant picture / and lifts it up for the world to

see, / that all may know our delightful home / and learn the bright fairy tales / that
Norway's fjords preserve.)

The violinist Ole Bull, who was later to become Ibsen's first employer (see
Chapter 2), took the part of the fiddler in the boat. The audience was
ecstatic. Originally only one "festive evening" was planned, for 28 March
1849, but the enthusiasm was such that two more had to be scheduled. In a
curious historical coincidence, exactly at the same time as the first production
of the *Bridal Procession in Hardanger* made the Christiania bourgeoisie wild
with national enthusiasm, the pioneering socialist Marcus Thrane gave his
first lecture to workers gathered at Vaterland, on the east side of the capital.[13]

The "festive evenings" laid bare the cultural dominance of painting at the
time: Tidemand and Gude's painting inspired poetry, music, declamation,
and theater. In 1850, it became the source of a ballet choreographed by the
great August Bournonville in Copenhagen. In 1867, the music that Kjerulf
wrote for the original 1849 *tableau vivant* was performed by 500 Swedish
singers at the Universal Exhibition in Paris. The performance was so successful that it was repeated in May 1868, before the French emperor and empress
and an audience of 6,000.[14]

During his stay in Norway, Adolph Tidemand also painted a series of
scenes from Norwegian peasant life for the small royal castle of Oscarshall,
just outside Christiania, completed in 1850. Again, painting inspired poetry,
for Andreas Munch promptly produced a suite of ten poems based on Tidemand's ten paintings.[15] Jan Askeland has rightly compared Tidemand's representation of peasants and farmers to George Sand's peasant idylls: it is
indeed difficult to imagine a more idealized—and in Tidemand's case, a
more nationalist—view of country life than this.[16]

In March 1849 Ibsen had not yet arrived in Christiania. Yet the nationalist
tableau vivant in general, and *The Bridal Procession in Hardanger* in particular, remained popular for another decade, and Ibsen was involved in at least
one theatrical event of which it was a part. In December 1859, the *Bridal
Procession* was performed as part of an evening entertainment at Christiania
Theater consisting of a series of *tableau vivants* performed with music, poetry,
and dance. Included in the evening's fare was a poem entitled "En Aften Ved
Sæteren" ("An evening at the high mountain farm"), written by Ibsen specially
for a *tableau vivant* based on a painting by Knud Bergslien (Fig. 10).[17]

Bergslien's painting shows the wall of a small farmhouse in the high
mountains, with women and children wearing regional dress from Hardanger
(at the time considered the most beautiful and most "Norwegian" of regional
costumes) tending to sheep and goats. A young woman in the foreground

10. Knud Bergslien, *An Evening at the High Mountain Farm.* The Syndics of Cambridge University Library, and Adolph Tidemand from Christian Tønsberg, *Norske folkelivsbilleder efter malerier og tegninger* (1858). Waddleton. bb. 11.17.

flanked by a goat looks thoughtfully away, not towards the mountains and glacier in the background, but sideways out of the picture. Slightly further back on the left, a woman knits, a half-grown girl cleans buckets and containers, and a younger child seems to listen to a story told by the knitting woman. In the background on the right, another half-grown girl feeds a cow.

First advertised under the same title as Bergslien's painting, Ibsen's poem was later published under the title "Højfjeldsliv" ("Life in the High Mountains") (see 14: 265–6). Koht writes that the poem created quite an uproar during rehearsals because of Ibsen's use of Norwegian words. Most offensive was his repeated use of *Sel* and *Kve*, meaning, respectively, "small mountain farm house" and "pen" or "fold" (for sheep and cattle); both are depicted in Bergslien's painting. Apparently, the Danish actor who was to have read the poem declared that the very sound of these words made them unpoetic, and refused to take them in his mouth.[18] This may well be true, for the advertisement for the performances announces that Ibsen's poem was to be declaimed by a Norwegian actress, Miss Svendsen.[19]

The altercation, if it took place, illustrates the potential conflict between idealism and nationalism: if certain words were not beautiful, they could not be art; but if those words represented some of the most idealized national traditions (here the venerated tradition of sending sheep and cattle up to high mountain pastures in the summer), then either nationalism or idealism would have to give. Right from the start of his career, Ibsen was keenly aware of this conflict, and where others would have glossed it over, he chose to expose it (I am thinking of a play like *Sancthansnatten* (*St John's Night*), to which I shall return).

After describing the contrast between the dark summer night of the valley and the golden sunlight reflected in the glaciers of the high mountains, "Høyfjeldsliv", in a clear reference to the theatrical tableau, invites us to *look* at the young woman:

> Se Sætergjenten fager staa
> I Kvældens Skygge svøbt.
> Den Tankealf, hun stirrer paa,
> Har intet Ordlag døbt.
>
> (14: 266)

(Look at the beautiful dairymaid standing / wrapped in the evening's shade. / The thought-elf she stares at / has not yet been baptized by words.)

Returning to the contrast between valley and mountain, the speaker ends by stressing how short the mountain summer is, and ends on a promise, or perhaps a consolation:

> Et syn på Sommerkvældens Guld
> Er vel en Vinter værd!
>
> (14: 267)

(A glimpse of the summer evening's gold / is well worth a winter!)

This ending elegantly incorporates the theater audience watching the *tableau vivant*, for who else is getting a glimpse of the summer evening's gold? It is by no means obvious that the answer is the dairymaid, for she is, as we have seen, staring at a "thought-elf"—that is, she is looking inward, not outward. If we assume that her unformulated but elf-given thoughts are a metaphor for poetry, the speaker is attributing the capacity for poetry to a woman. The contrast between the pedestrian life in the winter valley with the free flight of the imagination of the mountains is typical of the early, idealist Ibsen.

At once describing and interpreting Bergslien's national romantic painting, Ibsen's poem fitted very well with the rest of the evening's program, which, in addition to the *Bridal Procession in Hardanger*, boasted four more *tableaux vivants*, based on, respectively, Charles Auguste Steuben's *Peter the Great Saved by his Mother from the Streliz*, Niels Simonsen's *Bedouins Lying in Wait*, Tidemand's *Night on the Fjord* (*Fishing with Light*), and Louis Léopold Robert's *Reapers in the Pontine Marshes*.[20] *Night on the Fjord* was one of the paintings Tidemand had done for Oscarshall castle, and it was, of course, accompanied by the relevant poem from Andreas Munch's Oscarshall suite. A poem by Munch entitled "Italian Harvesters" illustrated Robert's painting.

Throughout his career, Andreas Munch wrote a great deal of poetry inspired by paintings, sculptures, monuments, and ruins. Did he and other poets do so in the hope that the poems would be used in professional *tableaux vivants*? Or does his predilection for paintings as subjects simply convey how important pictorial imagination was for writers in this cultural moment in Norway? If a Norwegian poem about Bedouins had ever existed, it would surely have been used for Simonsen's painting which was performed without a text. If we are to judge by this program, Norwegians appreciated history paintings and genre paintings—that is to say, narrative, dramatic, pictorial art; they also enjoyed a touch of exoticism (not to say orientalism), as long as Norwegian nationalism was richly represented too.

St John's Night: Nationalism and Idealism in Conflict

St John's Night (*Sancthansnatten*), Ibsen's third play after *Catiline* and *The Burial Mound*, is an extremely interesting effort to conform to the requirements of idealist aesthetics while sounding the right national tone. Ibsen himself repudiated this play, not by denouncing it explicitly, but by refusing to let it be included in the first collected editions of his plays in Norwegian and German.[21] It is curious that *St John's Night* was the only play Ibsen refused to publish in his lifetime, since it is in many ways better than the little one-act play *The Burial Mound*, which he did not hesitate to publish in 1854, and which he was happy to include in his collected works.[22]

So why did Ibsen withhold *St John's Night* from publication? Perhaps he considered it a youthful folly. Perhaps it was because the name of the disputed property in the play and of the character Birk is Birkedalen. (Birk's aunt shortened his name from Birkedalen to Birk, "for that was supposed to sound more urban" (2: 78).) The name Birkedalen may have reminded the ageing Ibsen of an episode in his life that he would prefer to forget, for it was the name of Ibsen's lover and their son back in his Grimstad days.

St John's Night, subtitled "Eventyrcomedie i tre Acter" (fairy-tale comedy in three acts), was created under the influence of Shakespeare's *Midsummer Night's Dream*, which Ibsen had seen in Dresden, and probably also under the influence of Hettner's *Das moderne Drama* (1852), which strongly recommended "fairy-tale comedies" (*Märchenlustspiele*) as a suitable genre for modern playwrights.[23] When *St John's Night* opened in Bergen on 2 January 1853, it was a resounding failure. At the end of the same month, Ibsen found himself directing P. A. Jensen's *Huldrens Hjem* (*The Home of the Hulder*), in which a traditionally melodramatic murder and marriage plot was adorned with a string of folkloric spectacles.[24] For Ibsen this must have been a bitter irony indeed, for in June 1851 he had panned *Huldrens Hjem* on the grounds that it failed to convey the properly national tone:

Our national dramatic literature is therefore just as underdeveloped now as it was before the production of *The Home of the Hulder*. And it will be no different as long as writers do not know how to distinguish between the demands of reality and the demands of art, as long as they do not have sufficient taste to polish off the raw edges of reality before it is reproduced as a poetic work and placed in the frame of art. Then they will also realize that the national in art in no way is advanced by the petty copying of scenes from everyday life; then they will realize that the national writer is he who understands how to give his work the keynote ringing towards us from mountain and valley, from the hills and the coastline, but above all from inside ourselves.

(15: 81)

It is striking, to say the least, to find the young Henrik Ibsen arguing against the "petty copying of scenes from everyday life", insisting instead that writers must strive to "polish off the raw edges of reality" before the work can be framed as art (the whole passage insists on the parallels between writing and painting).

How does Ibsen practice his own idealist theory? In the prologue to *St John's Night*, the speaker begins by stressing the importance of the homeland to travelers who wander far away from its shores. Yet if their art is to flourish, artists must embrace their homeland. This is surely an admiring reference to J. C. Dahl, an artist obliged to live abroad, but who kept his art fresh by constantly painting Norwegian landscapes. Why, the poet asks, should all artists have to take southern lands as their subject?

> Er ei Folkets stille Færd
> Høit i Li og dybt i Dale
> Billeder, som vel er værd,
> At en Kunstnerhaand dem male?

(2: 21)

(Are not the people's quiet ways / high in the wooded hillsides and deep in the valleys / pictures well worth / being painted by an artist's hand?)

Whether writer or painter, only the artist can express and interpret the life of the people:

> Og blir Barmen os for trang,
> Kan den ei sin Fylde gjemme,—
> Maa vi lette den i Sang,
> Fryd og Vemodssuk faa Stemme.
> Da vi søge Kunstens Hjem;
> Thi det er jo der, at Folket
> Kræve kan sit Liv fortolket
> Og forklaret stillet frem.

(2: 21)

(And if our heart becomes too narrow, / if it cannot hide its fullness, / we have to ease it in song, / give voice to joy and wistful sighs. / Then we seek the home of art; / for it is there that the people / can demand to have its life interpreted / and represented in transfigured form.)

There is nothing original here; Ibsen sounds like what he is, a young poet desperately searching for a voice of his own by imitating Munch and Welhaven. The word *forklaret* ("transfigured") nevertheless grabs attention. In the sense used here, *forklare* means to make luminous, to glorify, to transfigure, in the religious sense. It is a key idealist term, also for the young Ibsen.

In 1859, in a review of Tidemand and Gude's last (and worst) joint painting, entitled "I havsnød" ("In danger at sea"), Ibsen still uses *forklare* to convey his æsthetic ideal. Inspired by a maritime disaster off the coast of Norway in which almost thirty fishermen died, the painting depicts a small open boat in which an elderly father and his two young sons are struggling to stay afloat in a horrifying storm. Needless to say, this entirely fails to convey the scale of the disaster it is supposed to commemorate, and Ibsen was distinctly unhappy with the rendering of the subject:

One might ask whether the artists really have comprehended the material as it was formed in the general consciousness after the disaster, or whether it is not true that each one of us comes with a different—perhaps foggy, unclear and confused—but still a different picture in mind, and that we demand to see precisely this vision ideally transfigured in the work of art and presented in the light of day. This objectivity, this artistic instinct, which whispers to the artist beforehand what the people will require from his work, coincides with the national demand.

(15: 222)

The idea is at once Schillerian, Herderian, and Hegelian: art is to give objective form to the longings of the nation, and this objective form is to be better, clearer, higher than our own thoughts, so that it will uplift and inspire us; the artist's highest calling is to be a prophet to his own nation. Thus the artist has to idealize the inner vision of his people: it is his task to turn their vision into an "ideally transfigured" picture. The distance between Ibsen's apparently uncritical use of *forklarelse* ("transfiguration") in the 1850s and his highly ironic handling of the same word in *The Wild Duck* in 1884 is stunning.

Yet, as we shall now see, in spite of its prologue, *St John's Night* itself is no Dahl-inspired paean to the Norwegian mountains. There is a discrepancy between the national ambitions of the prologue, admirably suited to the expectations of the audience, and the play itself, which was not. I shall show that regardless of his declarations in the prologue, in the actual text of *St John's Night*, Ibsen effectively withholds "the light of transfiguration" from his characters, and in so doing undermines the nationalist and idealist project of the prologue.

A prose play with folk songs, poetry, music, and dance, *St John's Night* is set at the farm of the widowed Mrs Berg in Telemark. (Telemark was Ibsen's own home county, at the time specially admired for its natural beauty and rich folkloric traditions.) Mrs Berg's daughter from her first marriage, Juliane Kvist, a narcissistic and superficial young woman, is secretly engaged to Johannes Birk, a student in Christiania. Mrs Berg also has a stepdaughter, Anne Berg, a kind of Cinderella character, derided by her stepmother and stepsister for her fidelity to the Norwegian fairy tales and folk songs she has learned from her old grandfather Berg, who still lives in the old, traditional farmhouse. (Mrs Berg, of course, had a new house built the moment she arrived on the farm.) On midsummer night's eve, Birk arrives at the farm accompanied by his friend, the self-styled wild, dark, Byronic, and national poet Julian Poulsen.

The crucial plot reversal is produced by a *nisse*, here the Norwegian folkloric equivalent of Shakespeare's Puck, who drips the juice of a secret herb into the punch bowl of the midsummer night's party. This makes anyone who drinks it able to see past outer appearances and glimpse the inner truth of the soul:

> Og hvo som smager dens Saft saa sød,
> Hans Blik for det ydre Skin er borte;

(*presser Saften af Blomsten i Bollen*)
De Taager der har sig for Synet lagt
Vil klares i Drømmens spillende Flammer;
Da føles med Sandhed den indre Magt—
Der raader i Sjælens forborgne Kammer;—
Men den som har Intet at grunde over,
Han vandrer i Blinde som ellers og—sover!

(2: 45)

(And whoever tastes its sweet juice, / will lose his eye for outer appearance. / (*squeezes the juice from the flower into the punchbowl*) / The fog that has covered his vision / will be cleared in the play of the dream's flames; / then he will feel truthfully the inner power / ruling the hidden chamber of the soul. / But he who has nothing to ponder / will walk around blindly as usual and—sleep.)

Under the influence of the magic potion, Birk admits to himself that he thinks that Juliane is nothing but "a bombastic, eccentric coquette" and by the end of the play, Birk is engaged to Anne, and Julian to Juliane (2: 50).

A highly contrived subplot reveals that Mrs Berg somehow has managed to swindle the farm Birkedalen away from Birk.[25] The reason why Birk doesn't know this is that, at the age of 10, he suffered a dangerous fever that caused complete amnesia about his childhood. This is also the reason why he entirely fails to recognize the farm and realize that Anne was his childhood playmate. At the end of the play, when Mrs Berg's guilt is revealed, Birk nobly tears up the paper that proves it and everyone is happy.

By far the most interesting character is Julian Poulsen, introduced to the audience as "The Poet". Anticipating characters like Steensgaard in *The League of Youth*, Hjalmar Ekdal in *The Wild Duck*, and even Ulrik Brendel in *Rosmersholm*, Poulsen is spineless, inauthentic, and full of himself. His very name signals his inauthenticity: in nineteenth-century Norway Julian was an extremely rare and foreign-sounding name, inevitably producing associations to the Roman emperor. (Juliane, on the other hand was a quite common name for women.) Poulsen is an ordinary, yet not particularly national name. The fact that Julian's father was a *Landhandler*—the owner of a country store—also fails to provide him with the "national" background he dearly would have liked to have. Born and bred on the old family farm in Telemark, Anne, on the other hand, is a poster girl for nationalist romanticism.

The usual reading of *St John's Night* (in so far as there is one: disavowed by Ibsen, this play is rarely commented on by critics) is that Julian Poulsen is merely a figure of fun, an ironic satire of the tendency to produce inauthentic national plays just to profit from the national romantic vogue. On this reading the prologue expresses Ibsen's genuine project, as it was expressed in 1851:

namely, his "longing to find the right national keynote" (2: 17).[26] Admittedly, in *St John's Night* Ibsen fails to find that keynote, the argument goes, but if he sings flat, it is because he was a young and inexperienced playwright, and because for good historical reasons he knew far too little about the folk traditions he wanted to praise, not because he was uncomfortable with the idea that poets had to sing uplifting national songs.[27]

If this were right, we would have to be able to read the play as a straight-forward satire of inauthentic nationalism. But this is not possible. Whatever Ibsen's intentions were, I shall show that *St John's Night* is full of metatheatri-cal and meta-aesthetic elements, which taken together reveal that this is a play fraught with aesthetic and ideological conflicts. Let us begin with the fact that Julian Poulsen is a poet, albeit one who, *à la* Ulrik Brendel, still has written nothing. By placing a "national poet" at the center of his play, Ibsen clearly signals that the play is going to explore the relationship between nationalism and aesthetics. If anything, the play makes its intentions in this respect all too clear, for under the influence of the *nisse*'s truth serum, Julian explains to Juliane that when he went to Christiania to become a student, he discovered "aesthetics, and criticism and whatever all that unnational trash is called" (2: 54). One day, however, Julian discovered that the university's insistence on an aesthetic education was threatening to dilute his national soul; to purify it, he went for a walk in Norwegian nature, rediscovered his authenticity (*Oprindelighed* (2: 54)) and fell in love with "An ideal!" (2: 43).

Julian's ideal was, of course, the most national creature conceivable: namely, the *Hulder*. The very notion that a poet needs an ideal was the essential point of the "unnational" (i.e., German) aesthetics Julian would have been studying at the university. Imagining the *Hulder* as a beautiful fairy-tale woman, "this lovable, airy creature who sits under the linden trees in the dark spruce-covered mountainsides, singing her delightful ballads in a minor key", Julian unfortunately remains ignorant of a fundamental fact (2: 54). One day, however, while reading a volume of national fairy tales, he discovers to his horror that the *Hulder* is a beautiful woman in every respect but one: she has a cow's tail, a long, ugly, animal tail that simply cannot be hidden: "I cannot describe how I suffered; aesthetics and nationality fought a mortal combat in my breast;—but let me just say it—this time nurture vanquished nature,—I had to renounce my love" (2: 55).

Ibsen clearly expected his audience to know why love for the ideal was incompatible with a cow's tail, or, in other words, why anyone idealizing the *Hulder* would be caught in a conflict between aesthetics and nationalism. In any case, Julian spells out the point: cows' tails, he proclaims, are "abnormal growths conflicting with the idea of beauty" (2: 63). This is not simply a critique of inauthentic nationalism, but an acute diagnosis of a contradiction that eventually would undermine the whole national romantic project. For what if the truth about Norwegian nature, Norwegian culture, Norwegian traditions, turned out not to be beautiful? How could one then uphold one's faith in a national ideal? (What if *Sel* and *Kve* simply *were* "unpoetic" words?) And worse: What if beauty were no guarantee of truth and virtue? Ibsen's send-up of Julian Poulsen's love for the *Hulder* does not fully analyze these issues, but it comes close enough to grate on the nerves of a Norwegian audience in 1853.

In Act 2, the mountainside opens to show the midsummer night revelries of the fairies, *nisse*, and other national creatures: "The Mountain opens", Ibsen writes in the stage directions, "and inside one sees a large and brilliantly illuminated hall; the Mountain King sits on a throne in the background. Elves and the people living inside the mountains dance around him" (2: 64). Completely failing to grasp what he is seeing, Julian Poulsen cleans his glasses to no avail, and calls for more visual aids:

POULSEN [*to Juliane*]. Oh, but this does look delightful; it's a scene taken directly
    from the people's life;—I hope you brought your pince-nez—
JULIANE. Of course!
POULSEN. I just wish that there was a painter present.
JULIANE. Or a daguerreotypist.
POULSEN. You are right; that would be better.

(2: 64–5)

Apparently, Poulsen needs to have his experiences mediated by others. That he readily acquiesces in Juliane's suggestion that a "daguerreotypist" would be preferable to a painter as an interpreter of his own vision indicates that this self-proclaimed poet has no sense of the difference between art and non-art. According to national romantic theory, only a genuine artist—"vor gjæve *Dahl*" ("our noble *Dahl*"), as Welhaven put it—can transfigure ordinary experience; the irony is the more obvious precisely because Poulsen takes himself to be a poet. While Ibsen's prologue is alive with the will to make art the transfigured expression of the soul of the people, this scene reminds us forcefully of the potential for theatricality and bad faith that lies precisely in the romantic faith in the sublime vocation of the writer.

Act 2 of *St John's Night* is also Ibsen's first major metatheatrical scene. The mountainside opens like a theater curtain, and the two watching couples clearly represent contrasting modes of spectatorship. Taking the scene in the mountain to be real, Anne and Birk are transported and transformed by their artistic experience. Recognizing the songs and stories, they rediscover their own identity, and realize that they learned all these things when they were playing together as little children.

By constantly commenting on the form of the proceedings, and also by paying more attention to themselves than to what they are seeing, Julian and Juliane literally turn a real scene into theater. Taking the court of the mountain king to be a spectacle mounted by the local peasants, Julian and Juliane mistake the mountain king for a member of the organizing committee, and the *nisse* for a drunken lout (see 2: 65). Moreover, they can't stop congratulating themselves on their great national and poetic sense. They also constantly watch themselves watching: "while we are sitting here with a keen eye for the poetic aspects of life, Birk and the others are most likely fast asleep, or dreaming some humdrum dream—" (2: 66–7). In short: if Anne and Birk represent antitheatrical spontaneity, Julian and Juliane embody the self-consciousness and constant awareness of artistic artifice that characterize theatricality.

But where does this leave Ibsen's audience? If *St John's Night* is to be read as an uncomplicated nationalist play, Ibsen must have intended the audience to identify with Anne and Birk, and to laugh at Julian and Juliane. But *St John's Night* has so many metatheatrical devices and aesthetic discussions, so much artistic self-consciousness, that it effectively blocks absorption and identification. As a result, Anne in particular comes to look unbelievably naïve, and Julian and Juliane's knowing ways of seeing do not come across as hopelessly inartistic, but rather as a pretty good model for anyone faced with the task of making sense of *St John's Night*. The fact that Julian and Juliane recognize that they too are soul mates, that they too have met before—not at a farm, but at a ball at Madame Olsen's school, where Julian, wearing a yellow vest *à la* Goethe's Werther, stepped on Juliane's foot—produces an unsettling equivalence between the two couples, and thus between authenticity and theatricality, better suited to modernism than idealism.

Almost ten years later, in an 1861 article about the state of the theater in Christiania, Ibsen claimed that Norwegian theater audiences were afraid of losing themselves in a work of art because of their lack of culture and education: "In a society so undeveloped as ours, half-culture (*Halvdannelsen*[28]) produces a ghostlike fear of transgression . . . that rides the people like a nightmare and inhibits spontaneous self-surrender; [and] the audience so thoroughly . . . misunderstands its position that it puts on a distant air and hurries past enjoyment" (15: 255). Surely Ibsen here also speaks of his younger self: *St John's Night* is about the impossibility of producing authentically nationalist art in a society where any artistic endeavor makes artists as well as audiences self-conscious.

As long as he stayed in Norway, Ibsen must have felt forever cut off from true culture. The situation is finely registered in *St John's Night* where there is one true child of nature, a goodly number of half-cultured people, but no true bearer of culture. Birk, who ends up marrying the child of nature, is structurally placed where the fully cultured character ought to be, but although he is decent enough, and has the right instincts, his character is not particularly associated with art, culture, and aesthetics. To me, Birk's peculiar anonymity turns him into an allegory of Ibsen's own position at the time: he is an intelligent and sensitive young writer who has not yet found a voice of his own.

St John's Night is not a good play; it is technically clumsy and structurally lopsided. Just about everything of any importance happens in the two first acts, and there are too many superfluous characters (Anne's brother Jørgen Kvist, for example, runs around onstage for no obvious reason). Yet even in its confused and unsettled form, *St John's Night* is marked by Ibsen's complex sense of irony and depth of thought. Through the play there runs a mostly unformulated, but potentially powerful critique of the aesthetic paradigm that dominated Norwegian culture at the time, and to which *St John's Night* itself ostensibly belonged. No wonder it was a failure with its audience.

Another Idealist Failure: *Lady Inger*

Since authenticity was aligned with the national romantic project, inauthenticity was marked as foreign in mid-nineteenth-century Norway. Thus truth, sincerity, honesty, simplicity, and inner soulfulness were on the side of Norwegian nationalism, whereas play, masks, lies, hypocrisy, ostentation, and spectacle were aligned with foreign treachery. National self-expression was modest, natural, and spontaneous; foreign self-display, on the other hand, was self-conscious and calculated. The former was authentic expression, the latter *acting*, and therefore theatrical.

We have already seen that *St John's Night* muddles the opposition between theatricality and sincerity in ways that would have made it unpalatable to contemporary audiences. Ibsen's next play, *Lady Inger* (*Fru Inger til Østerraad*), subtitled "Historisk Drama i fem Akter" ("Historical Drama in Five Acts"), tries much harder to comply with the ruling idealist paradigm. Ibsen's fourth play, *Lady Inger* was written in 1854, and first performed in Bergen on 2 January 1855. It too was a failure in the theater, but in the spring and summer of 1857 it was serialized in a magazine edited by Paul Botten-Hansen, a good friend of Ibsen's. Later the same year it was published as a special offprint from the magazine, in a print run of 200 copies. (In 1874, Ibsen published a revised version, which I shall not discuss here.[29])

From a formal point of view, Lady Inger is Ibsen's most thoroughly annoying play. Although the characters and the questions they have to deal with are fascinating, the plot is preposterous. Important events happen by complete coincidence; characters mistake each other's identities with alarming frequency, always acting precipitously on conclusions drawn from mistaken premises, and always with disastrous consequences. It is as if Ibsen had set himself the task of writing grand national tragedy by relying exclusively on the plot conventions of farce.[30]

In spite of all this, Lady Inger offers an interesting example of how the still very young Ibsen related to the ideological opposition between ideal national authenticity and debased foreign theatricality.[31] Set in 1528, when Norway was on the point of losing the last vestiges of its ancient independence, the play offers a fiercely melodramatic plot focused on Lady Inger's covert attempts to encourage a movement for national liberation that will place her illegitimate son by the rebellious Swedish count Steen Sture, the young Niels Steenssøn, on the throne of Norway. Brought up by poor peasants, Niels Steenssøn has not been allowed to learn to read. Arriving at Lady Inger's manor house as a simple messenger, he does not yet know who his parents are. Mistaking the young messenger for Steen Sture's legitimate son, Lady Inger has him killed in order to protect her own son's claim to the throne. The play ends with her discovery of her fatal mistake, in an intensely melodramatic scene strikingly similar to the end of Ghosts.

At the end of the play, it transpires that Niels Steenssøn was the only person who might have been able to unite enough support to become king of an independent Norway. Authentic, spontaneous, and natural, he represents an excessive accumulation of Norwegian national romantic ideals: a youth and a peasant, yet born of the highest nobility, he is the bearer of the nation's still undeveloped self-consciousness. Since he has also been spared from exposure to the corrupting influence of print culture, he is more like a Rousseauian child of nature than anyone else in the play (and thus he has much in common with Anne in St John's Night). Although Niels Steenssøn's character may be intended as a paradigm of national ideals, he is so naïve, trusting, and ignorant that he comes across as stupid. Happily handing over a bunch of crucial documents (which he wouldn't have done had he been able to read them) to the first man who comes along (Niels Lykke), he unwittingly seals his own fate.

Against Niels Steenssøn the play pits Lady Inger and Niels Lykke, a

Machiavellian Danish nobleman. Niels Lykke, in particular, is initially represented as a calculating, manipulative, deceptive schemer. Ibsen, however, does not let such stark melodramatic opposites stand unquestioned.[32] Right from the start, Lady Inger is a fiendishly complex character, and the evil Niels Lykke gains in stature as he falls in love with Eline, Lady Inger's daughter. Fierce and heroic, Eline is a precursor of Svanhild in *Love's Comedy* and Agnes in *Brand*, yet she is given nothing to do except to lament the death of her sister Lucia and fall in love with Niels Lykke. Niels Lykke, however, is precisely the man who betrayed Lucia's love, and thus drove her to her early death. Although he is supposed to be a Machiavellian womanizer, Niels Lykke is shown to be capable of passionate love, and comes to regret his worst misdeeds, albeit only when it is too late. Obviously fascinated by the Dane as a figure of masculine erotic power, Ibsen fails to make him truly evil in the way his melodramatic plot would have required.

As for Lady Inger, she is one of Ibsen's most fascinating women characters. Strong, passionate, a natural leader, she cannot be fitted into any simplistic categories. Because nobody knows that she has an illegitimate son, she has been forced to deal in secrets and lies ever since he was born, a fact which makes her come across as inauthentic, and unnational, too. By paying no heed to idealist stereotypes of "femininity", *Lady Inger* singularly fails to produce the noble, pure, self-sacrificing female characters craved by mid-nineteenth-century audiences.[33]

If *Lady Inger* ends up outstripping its own ideological and aesthetic premises, it is not least because the play makes it extremely difficult to distinguish between heroes and villains. Both Lady Inger and Niels Lykke are characters in whom hypocrisy and authenticity coexist. While Niels Steenssøn may have been intended as a kind of national ideal, he comes across as a dolt. His death is sad, but hardly tragic. By the end of the play we have lost sight of anything resembling a national ideal, which is surely why the play was a failure.[34] To put it in aesthetic terms; once again Ibsen had failed to provide sufficiently "ideal" writing. At the end of *Lady Inger* we are neither reconciled nor uplifted, mostly because it is too difficult to locate the sources of beauty, truth, and goodness in this play.

A Minor Success: *The Feast at Solhoug*

By 1855, Ibsen had written four plays, none of which had had any success in print or onstage. His next effort, *Gildet paa Solhoug* (*The Feast at Solhoug*), however, was warmly received. Written during the summer of 1855, this is a poetic tale of medieval love and marriage, full of song and music, yet with a tragic undertone in the story of the proud Margit who, having married a man for money, loses the love of her life to her own sister. *The Feast at Solhoug* was first performed on 2 January 1856 in Bergen. On the opening night, for the first time in his life, Ibsen got to take numerous curtain calls. Later that evening the theater orchestra and a great crowd of people serenaded him outside his lodgings. "I almost think I let myself be moved to make a kind of speech to the crowd; I certainly do know that I felt exceedingly happy," Ibsen writes (3: 27).

Today *The Feast at Solhoug* reads like a trifle, although it does have some excellent moments. Certain scenes between Margit and her husband Bengt, in particular, reveal a relationship anticipating that of Jørgen Tesman and Hedda Gabler. The play is more technically accomplished than *St John's Night*, mixing prose and lyrical song with elegance. The younger sister, Signe, is the quintessentially innocent, pure young woman of idealism (Gudmund falls in love with her "innocent, childlike spirit" (3: 61)); Margit, on the other hand, is a difficult, multifaceted woman; having married for money, she comes close to murdering her boring and somewhat alcoholic husband. The plot offers moments of mistaken identities and melodramatic suspense: a poisoned drink is left untouched at the last moment; the hero, Gudmund, who had been declared an outlaw for telling the truth at court is reprieved by the *deus ex machina* in the shape of the king's envoy, who reestablishes him in his lands and property. Signe and Gudmund will marry; Margit, whose husband has been conveniently killed by a violent neighbor, enters a convent. Although it is an accomplished entertainment, this play does not seem to me to engage with the great aesthetic questions of its day. Perhaps that is precisely why it appealed to Norwegian audiences at the time.

In March 1856 *The Feast at Solhoug* was produced in Christiania. As in Bergen, the audience was pleased, although the capital's critics were not. The only exception was the 24-year-old Bjørnstjerne Bjørnson, who warmly defended Ibsen in *Morgenbladet*. Ibsen's verse was "among the most beautiful, the most melodious ever written in Norwegian":[35]

We sit leaning against the edge of the box; we no longer see; we only listen and dream; soon everything is transformed for our soul; we are no longer in the theater, but in an old medieval castle with towers and archways, a drawbridge and tombs. It is no longer the actor who performs, but a peasant, a traveling troubadour, who has come to the castle and wants to sing a poem for you in the great courtyard.[36]

Absorbed in the spectacle, Bjørnson, like his Fisher Maiden, forgets the theater and enters Ibsen's poetic world. I am reminded of Diderot's habit of imagining himself inside the landscape paintings he liked, or of carrying on imaginary conversations with characters in paintings, plays, and novels. Like Diderot, Bjørnson measures the quality of the play by his own immersion in the fiction proposed by the work, as if the beholder's absorption testifies at once to the quality of the work of art and to the "sensibility" (in Diderot's sense), the sense of poetry and humanity in the beholder's soul.

Conflicted Idealism: "In the picture gallery" and "On the heights"

Unlike Bjørnson, Ibsen continued to agonize over idealism. In 1859 he appears to have spent much time thinking about aesthetic problems. In September 1859 he published a cycle of poems consisting of twenty-three poems (mostly sonnets) entitled "I billedgalleriet" ("In the picture gallery"), declaring in an editorial note that they belong to "an earlier period of his life and poetic development".[37] The picture gallery in question is not named, but it is obviously the Königliche Galerie in Dresden, which Ibsen visited in 1852. Most critics place the composition in 1853–4; it is unknown whether Ibsen made substantial changes later.[38]

This cycle is concerned with a poet who feels unable to write, weighed down by doubts of his vocation. In sonnets IV–IX the depressed poet remembers a visit to a picture gallery, where he once experienced the enthusiasm and faith inspired by eternal art. There are striking parallels between Ibsen's presentation of the uplifting effects of painting and Bjørnson's account of the glorious effect of great acting in *The Fisher Maiden*. In his aesthetic rapture, the poet feels that the silence of the gallery is superior to the silence of the church; when he is looking at the paintings, his soul is filled with hope and faith:

> Ja, her jeg føler, at i mig er Gud;
> Thi jeg formaar at gribes og beruses
> Ved Skjønhedstanken der er foldet ud.
>
> Jeg skuer Gudsideen klar og plastisk;
> Se! derfor svulmer og min Sjæl elastisk,
> Og Tvilens Dæmon i mit Indre knuses!
>
> (14: 242)

(Yes, here I feel that I have God within, / For I can be so moved and so rapt / by the thought of beauty that here unfolds. // I see the idea of God made clear and plastic; /

Look! therefore my soul too swells, elastic / and the demon of doubt in my inner being is crushed!)[39]

Through art, which gives plastic form to the idea of God, the poet is trans-ported, much like Oswald and Corinne in the Vatican Gallery, whose souls were "uplifted to hopes filled with enthusiasm and virtue", because, as Madame de Staël puts it, beauty "always arouses a religious feeling in the hearts of mankind".[40]

The skeptical theme is obvious: the poet's doubts about his vocation, nourished in solitude, hidden in the depths of his soul, are crushed by the aesthetic experience, which places God in his soul, thus undercutting the opposition between inner and outer, soul and other, that otherwise is so noticeable whenever this poem moves to think about lonely, crushed, and frustrated artistic talents. The poet's doubts, I think, also register his sense of being torn between different aesthetic ideals, between idealism and the ordinary, as we shall see. That the idea of aesthetic power is figured as a swelling, adds a sexual undertone emphasizing the poem's preoccupation with the *power* of a poet.

"In the picture gallery" contains references to several paintings that still hang in Dresden: Raphael's *Sistine Madonna*, Correggio's *Night*, and Murillo's *Madonna and Child*. In the 1850s, these paintings were all icons of idealist taste. Raphael, in particular, was "the high priest of beauty" at a time when "beauty bestrode an artistic continent", as one present-day critic puts it.[41] For idealists, Raphael was the perfect painter, the one who knew how to make one feel the presence of the ideal in every brushstroke. With the death of idealism, Raphael was demoted from divine to merely very good. In the very late 1890s, Freud's Dora still "remained *two hours* in front of the Sistine Madonna, rapt in silent admiration", but at that time, this tells us only that she was a well-brought-up young lady of the bourgeoisie sub-mitting to the increasingly old-fashioned standards of taste laid down by her elders.[42]

The three named paintings all have religious themes: there are two Madonnas and one nativity scene. In contrast stands the generic reference to Dutch genre paintings in Sonnet VII, evoking "den trivelige Nederlænder" ("the chubby Dutchman") surrounded by dead geese, ducks, and hens:

> Den ene overskygger ei den Anden
> Violen kan jo dog med Tulipanen
> Forliges nok saa godt i en Bouket;
> Og tør da ikke jeg i en Sonnet,
> Som Annemonen med den gyldne iris

Forbinde Rafael med Jan van Mieris?—

(14: 243)

(And neither painting overshades the other
the violet and tulip, sister, brother,
quite happily bind up in one bouquet;
So can't I use a sonnet in this way,
to bind anemone and gilded iris,
combining Raphael with Jan van Mieris?—)

(N, 143)

Jan van Mieris (1660–90) died young without achieving much as an artist. Both his father Frans and his brother Willem were better known. Only a few of Jan's paintings are known today, and the picture gallery in Dresden never owned any of them. Given the insignificance of Jan van Mieris, critics have wondered whether Ibsen meant to invoke Jan van Huysum, whose famous flower pieces he must have known, not least because one of them was the subject of a well-known poetic text by Henrik Wergeland.[43]

If we assume that Ibsen means what he says, Jan van Mieris represents the unknown and unappreciated artist who will never reach the pinnacle of fame. This reading would fit very well with the sonnet cycle's general preoccupation with artistic failure. Juxtaposed to the Italian Madonnas, the Dutch genre paintings also represent the northern as opposed to the southern artist, and, above all, the desire for realism, the ordinary, and the everyday in art.

This part of the verse cycle, then, is about the poet's wish to reconcile two different aesthetic contents: idealism and realism, or idealism and the everyday. What matters in art, he declares, is form. Art can digest anything (it is "en Strudsemave"—an ostrich's stomach); what makes the work beautiful is the form:

Ja Formen, Formen kun i Et og Alt
Formaar at adle Kunstneraandens Foster
Og Stemple det som stort og genialt.

(14: 244)

(Yes form it is, it's form above all things
that elevates the poet's flight of fancy
and guarantees a mighty genius sings.)

(N, 144)[44]

But if this is so, the poet continues, then there is no need to try to soar into regions "hvor Vingen brister og hvor Stemmen svigter" (14: 244) ("where wings get broken, voices crack and wave" (N, 144)); we might just as well "skabe Billeder med Kjød og Blod / Fra Hverdagslivet, som Stillebens-Digter!" (14: 244) ("shape images from flesh and blood / from everyday life, as still-life poets!" (N, 144; amended)).

Like Balzac and George Sand before him, the young Ibsen thinks of ideal-ism and realism as ultimately compatible aesthetic approaches, united by the ideal of formal beauty.[45] More unsettling is the poet's realization that if both the high and the low, the Madonna as well as a bunch of dead geese, will get him into the higher spheres of art, then there is no reason to worship the Madonna—the ideal—at all. Although this idea is left undeveloped, it con-tributes to the poem's atmosphere of aesthetic doubt, the sense that this poet has not yet found a voice of his own.[46]

An important sequence of "In the picture gallery" tells the story of a woman who wanted to become an artist, but who—like Svanhild in *Love's Comedy*—discovered that although she had an artist's spirit, she lacked the artist's talent. Sitting alone, in the innermost room of the picture gallery, she copies Murillo's *Madonna and Child*. Like Jan van Mieris, the failed woman artist is a touching incarnation of a perennial theme in Ibsen's works: the conflict between the human imagination and will, and human capacity, or, to put it in Kantian terms, the conflict between freedom and necessity.

Another poem published in 1859, "På vidderne" ("On the heights") is also commonly read as a poem about aesthetics.[47] In this epic poem, the poet leaves his mother and lover behind in the valley, and remains on the heights, leading the life of a hunter, at times accompanied by a mysterious, ironic stranger, not dissimilar to Mephistopheles in *Faust*, who urges the poet to leave all human ties behind. From the high mountains the poet sees that his mother's cottage is on fire. While the cottage burns and the mother dies, the stranger from the south holds forth about the unusually picturesque effects of the combination of moonlight and fire in the dark winter night: "Han kikked gennem den hule hånd / til vinding for perspektivet" (14: 398) ("He viewed the scene through his hollowed hand / to gain the correct perspective" (N, 88)). Strikingly, the poem leaves completely unresolved this obvious contrast between ethics and aesthetics. Had the young Ibsen been able to submit to the ideal demand, he would surely have found a way to reconcile this stark opposition.

Later, in a sequence described in picturesque terms reminiscent of Tidemand's painting of a peasant wedding for the Oscarshall castle, the poet watches from afar his lover's wedding. Although he feels pain at these events, he also feels liberated. As the wedding party disappears from his view, he exclaims:

Nu bytted jeg bort mit sidste stev
for et højere syn på tingen.

Nu er jeg stålsat, jeg følger det bud,
der byder i højden at vandre!
Mit lavlandsliv har jeg levet ud;
heroppe på vidden er frihed og Gud,
dernede famler de andre.

(14:400)

(I've traded my last folk-song / for a higher view of things. // I'm clad now in steel, I
follow the commandment / that bids me to wander in high-country! / I've lived out
my lowland life; / up here on the heights there is freedom and God, / down there the
others are groping.)[48]

Another recurrent Ibsen conflict also turns up in this poem: that in which
a man is torn between his vocation and his duties towards his family (it
returns in *Brand, An Enemy of the People, Little Eyolf, John Gabriel Borkman*,
even *When We Dead Awaken*). Women too are caught in this dilemma: in *A
Doll's House*, Nora also makes a choice that has much in common with that
of the poet here, and in *Ghosts*, Mrs Alving discovers that she ought to have
chosen her own desires over her marital duties. In "On the heights" the poet
chooses his vocation. Is it worth the sacrifice? The poem leaves the reader to
draw her own conclusion. Today we may wonder whether art can justify a life
of destructive human relations, but from an idealist point of view, there really
was no question about it: to follow one's artistic vocation is the perfect
reconciliation of freedom and necessity; to reject it is to reject the search for
the ideal which alone gives human life meaning. Although the artist in this
poem suffers much existentially and emotionally in order to sever all ordinary
ties, in the end he finds freedom, and the highest entity of all, God.

But this is not quite the end of the story. The acute sense of bitter choice,
of struggle and loss attached to the choice of the ideal (of the poetic vocation)
undercuts any harmonious reconciliation. To this speaker, the idealization of
art is neither self-evident, nor necessarily a stable achievement. "On the
heights" casts the conflict between art and non-art as a conflict between
the "high" and the "low", between the mountain and the valley, between the
open vistas and nomadic life of the hunter and the enclosed horizon and
everyday toil of the farmer. The everyday is aligned with love, marriage, and
family; artistic vision requires height, distance, and "perspective" on the
everyday.

This reading, however, makes it look as if only the Sistine Madonna, and
not the ducks and geese of the "chubby Dutchman" from "In the picture
gallery", is compatible with the soaring vision from the heights. Comparing

the two poems, we find an an unresolved tension surrounding the place of the everyday—the place of realism—in Ibsen's aesthetics. In 1859, Ibsen was coming to acute consciousness of his aesthetic conflicts, but he was still far from resolving them.

An Idealist Triumph: "Terje Vigen"

In 1862, Ibsen published two radically different texts. First to appear was "Terje Vigen", a pictorial, idealist, national, historical, heroic, and uplifting epic poem. Following hot on its heels was the anti-heroic satirical verse play *Love's Comedy*. Set in contemporary Norway, the play contrasts idealist notions of love with the everyday experience of marriage, offering neither comfort nor uplift. How do we explain such a remarkable and sudden shift of register? The great Ibsen scholar Daniel Haakonsens refers to "Terje Vigen" as the "first completely resolved poem from Ibsen's hand" and *Love's Comedy* as the "first consistently good play he ever wrote".[49] Why are these works so much *better* than the texts that precede them? I shall begin by looking at "Terje Vigen".

An epic poem in forty-three rhymed stanzas, "Terje Vigen" is thoroughly traditional in form. It begins with a glimpse of a strange, gray-haired recluse, living on the outermost island on the south coast of Norway; in the second stanza the narrator tells us that the only time he ever saw Terje, he saw a happy, relaxed older man selling fish from his boat. At the end of the poem we come full circle; the second to last stanza repeats the second, and the last stanza describes the wild and unkempt grass growing on Terje Vigen's grave.

In the third stanza the poem settles down to tell Terje's story. A wild youth, he ran away to Amsterdam; when he came back as a fine young man, his parents and the rest of his family were dead. He married quickly, and although he may initially have regretted his loss of freedom, the birth of his little daughter, Anna, turned him into an exemplary family man. Terje's life is destroyed by history: in 1809, the English blockaded Norwegian waters, cutting off all contact between Norway and Denmark. The resulting famine threatens to kill Terje's family, and Terje rows to Denmark to buy corn. Just as Terje returns home with the life-giving corn, he is caught by an English frigate, commanded by a young lord of 18. Terje's little boat with all his corn is sunk. On the deck of the frigate, the proud Norwegian falls to his knees and begs for mercy for the sake of his wife and child, but in vain. After five years in an English prison, Terje returns home in 1814, the year of national liberation, only to find that his little family had died of starvation and were buried as paupers in an unmarked grave.

Terje then becomes a brave, bad-tempered, and wild pilot. One day, years later, there is a horrendous storm, and an English yacht is in danger. Coming to the rescue, Terje recognizes the owner of the yacht: it is the English lord, accompanied by his wife and child. Terje tells them to board his little boat if they want to survive. Terrified by the tempestuous sea, the English mother cries out, "Anna, my child!" Hearing the name, Terje trembles, but sails on.

Within sight of land, Terje suddenly plunges an oar through the bottom of the boat, exactly on the spot where his rowing boat was sunk. Suddenly, the Englishman recognizes the Norwegian sailor, and now Terje roars out his wish for revenge. Falling to his knees, the noble Englishman begs for mercy, but Terje now gives full vent to his rage. Although they were poor and not particularly remarkable, his wife and his child mattered as much to him as the lord's family now matters to *him*. Now the time has come for the great lord to feel what he himself once felt. Grabbing the little Anna and her mother, Terje threatens to drown them both if the Englishman as much as moves. Realizing that he is defenseless, the aristocrat's hair turns gray in an instant, just as Terje's once had done.

At this moment peace and harmony return to Terje; putting the child gently down, he kisses her little hands and explains that all those long years in prison had made his heart sick. Then he expertly guides the yacht safely to shore. The next day, the lord and lady come to thank him for their salvation; but Terje strokes the little girl's head and replies: "nej, den som frelste, da værst det kneb, / det var nok den lille *der*!" (14: 380). ("No, rescue came in the nick out there / from *this* little mite by me!" (N, 73)). As Terje watches the yacht turning out to sea, he finally sheds a tear:

> "stort har jeg mistet, men stort jeg fik.
> Bedst var det, kan hænde, det gik, som det gik,—
> og så får du ha'e tak da, Gud!"
>
> (14: 381)
>
> ("Great are my losses, but great my prize.
> Perhaps it was all for the best, in some wise,—
> so the thanks, God, are rightly yours!")
>
> (N, 73)

This note of reconciliation is reinforced by the two last stanzas describing Terje's happy old age: "hjem han for / i solskin, den gamle ørn" ("then homeward he sailed with the jib set broad / in sunshine, the aged hawk" (N, 73)), ending with the picture of his grave covered by grass and wild flowers.

Highly melodramatic, deeply nationalistic, thoroughly idealist, and even more pictorial than *Peer Gynt*, "Terje Vigen" offers plenty of tableaux: Terje's wedding, Terje playing with his little daughter, Terje rowing to Denmark for corn, the English sailors destroying Terje's boat, Terje on his knees on the deck of the English frigate begging for mercy, Terje in the English prison, the English yacht in the storm, Terje swinging the English baby over the raging sea, the English lord on his knees before Terje in the wild storm, Terje selling fish on his boat, the wildflowers on Terje's grave.

A perfect allegory of nineteenth-century Norway, the national pathos of "Terje Vigen" is striking: the poor sailor who suffers searing injustice at the hands of the rich English lord shows himself to be nobler than the nobleman, capable of teaching him a lesson about mercy that he will never forget. Here there is no questioning of marriage, no conflict between vocation and family; whether he is rich or poor, the love of wife and child is the center of a man's existence. The parallels and contrasts in the poem are starkly melodramatic. Both daughters are called Anna; the hair of both men turns gray overnight; the innocence of children inspires mercy and salvation. There are plenty of scenes of recognition and naming of guilt and responsibility. The final reconciliation with God provides the right transcendent note, enabling the poem to end, in the last two stanzas, with images of sea, sunshine, and wild flowers.

Remarkably for Ibsen, moreover, there is no trace of irony anywhere. After reading this poem, we are to feel like Bjørnson's Petra felt when she was leaving the theater in Bergen: uplifted, strengthened, happy, and free. No poem, surely, could be more suitable for the inculcation of a politically correct national identity. For generations, Norwegian schoolchildren had to learn long excerpts from "Terje Vigen" by heart. When I was a child, my grandfather, farmer, road worker, and staunch trade unionist, used to recite "Terje Vigen" with almost frightening passion. Here he was following in glorious footsteps: the young road worker Knut Hamsun had once done the same, and Fridtjof Nansen confessed that when he feared the worst on his polar expeditions, reciting "Terje Vigen" helped him through.[50]

Given that it would be difficult to imagine a less modernist text, Ibsen's great poem has not been a favorite with recent generations of literary critics. Even the nationalist Francis Bull felt somewhat disturbed by its melodramatic theatricality.[51] Yet the power of "Terje Vigen" is undeniable, even today. In Norwegian, the verse is strikingly good; the strong, yet rich and varied rhythm, the powerful and concrete imagery, and the gripping story make the poem memorable like few others. Every time I read it, I have to steel myself to face the unbearably moving stanzas where the English sailors catch up with Terje, and sink the boat with his precious corn. As performed by Jørgen Langhelle during the 2002 Ibsen Festival in Oslo, "Terje Vigen" triumphantly rose above critical fashions and moved the audience to tears.

In terms of national and human pathos, this poem is unmatched in Ibsen's production. It is Ibsen's only thoroughly *successful* attempt to master the demands of aesthetic idealism. The only parallel I can think of is the long speech in Act 5 of *Peer Gynt* usually referred to as "The parson's sermon at the graveside", where Peer overhears a parson's powerful, poetic hymn to an ordinary working man, in every respect Peer's antithesis, who sacrificed his reputation for the sake of his family. Yet there is not much nationalism here, and no comfort for idealists. The old man died alone, for his sons had all emigrated to America; the appalling hardship he endured on the mountain farm is hardly a credit to the nation. In any case, Peer's presence onstage, his ironic disbelief, makes the scene metatheatrical and blocks identification.

"Terje Vigen" is a masterpiece, but it is a masterpiece of a kind that Ibsen would never write again. Perhaps "Terje Vigen" is the condition of possibility of *Love's Comedy*. It is as if writing "Terje Vigen" taught Ibsen both what pictorial idealism could achieve, and what its limitations were. Perhaps he realized that although he might master idealism in the form of poetry, he would never be able to write a great idealist *play*. Perhaps writing "Terje Vigen" convinced him, once and for all, that in order to write good plays, idealism could no longer remain in the background, as the silent framework for his work, but rather had to be placed in the foreground, as a subject matter to be analyzed and criticized. This, in any case, is what happens in *Love's Comedy*.

Idealism addressed: *Love's Comedy*

Ibsen's most difficult years in Christiania had taken their toll, for *Love's Comedy* was his first play in five years. Written in verse, it is subtitled "Komedie i tre akter" ("Comedy in three acts"). In Ibsen's eyes, *Love's Comedy* was a "precursor to *Brand*" (16: 162). After the success of *Brand*, Ibsen wrote that the subject matter of *Love's Comedy* was "our time's dominant conflict between reality and the ideal demand in everything that has to do with love and marriage" (4: 115). *Love's Comedy* represents a real turning point in Ibsen's career because it is the first time Ibsen makes idealism not just his subject matter, but the object of critique.[52] The result is a play that is at once an investigation of the conditions of love and marriage in the contemporary world and a profound meditation on the future of idealist aesthetics. In this context, it is, of course, no coincidence that the principal character, Falk ("Falcon"), is a poet.

Although there are a multitude of characters, the action of *Love's Comedy* is simple. Falk rents a room in Mrs Halm's boarding house. Like Julian Poulsen in *St John's Night*, Falk is an unproductive poet in search of a muse. He is more or less in love with Mrs Halm's daughter Svanhild, whom he considers a kindred spirit, mostly on the grounds of her name. In the *Volsunga Saga*, Svanhild is the guiltless daughter of Gudrun and Sigurd, unjustly sentenced to die by being trampled by four horses.[53] Telling Svanhild that her name belongs to "the daughter of the Saga king . . . who, innocent, was crushed beneath the horses' hooves", Falk shows that he takes her to be as pure and innocent as her namesake (4: 160). We should note that there is nothing in the saga to indicate that the original Svanhild distinguished herself by *doing* something particularly heroic. All she had to do to provoke Falk's romantic reverie was to be innocent and die horribly. There is a warning here for Ibsen's Svanhild, one that she (unlike most modern critics) will not fail to notice.

Disgusted by the distance between the official belief in the ideal of love and contemporary practices, Falk and Svanhild both lament the absence of heroism in present-day society:

SVANHILD. . . . Hvem ruster sig for Sandhed nutildags?
   Hvem er Personens Indsats vel tillags?
   Hvor findes Helten?
FALK [*ser skarpt paa hende*]. Og hvor er Valkyrien?

(4: 161)

(SVANHILD. . . . Who puts on armor to fight for truth nowadays?
   Who feels happy risking his whole person?
   Where is the hero?
FALK [*looks hard at her*]. And where is the Valkyrie?)

We note that *truth* is the ideal to be fought for, but in keeping with the idealist tradition, the struggle for truth will take place in poetry, and be expressed in the form of beauty.

As foils to Falk and Svanhild, the play offers us three couples: Lind and Anna, two young people who get engaged in Act 1; Styver and Miss Skjære, who have been engaged for years because they are too poor to get married; and Straamand and Maren, who turn up at the end of Act 1 accompanied by eight of their twelve children. At the end of Act 3, we learn that they are expecting their thirteenth. Once famous for the poems and songs he wrote in praise of his beloved Maren, Straamand is now a prosaic country parson, recently elected as a member of parliament. The sight of Mrs Straamand, once the object of so much poetry and music, stirs Falk to disdainful irony:

FALK. . . . Og Fruentimret med det skidne Skjørt,
   Med Skjæve Sko, som klasker under Hælene,
   Hun er den Vingemø, som skulde ført
   Ham ind til Samfundsliv med Skjønhedssjælene.
   Hvad er igjen af Flammen? Neppe Røgen!
   Sic transit gloria amoris, Frøken!

                                   (4: 175)

(FALK. . . . And the woman with the dirty skirt
   with worn-out shoes slapping under her heels,
   She is the winged muse who was to have led
   him into the company of beautiful souls.
   What remains of the flame? Not even the smoke!
   Sic transit gloria amoris, Miss Svanhild!)

According to Falk, then, only a young and beautiful woman can serve as a muse, even for the oldest and most decrepit poet. Again, as we shall see, this telltale sign of Falk's egocentrism is not lost on Svanhild. Remarkably aware of the sexism involved in Falk's single-minded pursuit of his poetic vocation, *Love's Comedy* is in fact a critique of the position allotted to women in idealist aesthetics as well as in society.

At the very end of the first act, Falk implores Svanhild to love him freely, in the moment, without regard to laws and morality, for only then will he be able to write the poetry of which he is capable. When Svanhild asks what will happen once he has learned all she has to teach, Falk points to a little bird he has just killed with a stone for no reason at all. Clearly the bird is a metaphor for the saga's innocent but horribly murdered Svanhild. Showing her independence and grandeur of soul, the modern Svanhild indignantly refuses the identification: calling Falk a shamelessly egoistic coward, she declares that she will not be the muse of a paper dragon, a poet dependent on her for the life of his writing. If he is to be worth anything as a writer, he needs to grow wings of his own:

SVANHILD. . . . Papirets Digtning hører Pulten til,
   Og kun den levende er Livets Eje,
   Kun den har Færdselsrett paa Højdens Veje;
   Men vælg nu mellem begge den De vil.

                                   (4: 181)

(SVANHILD. . . . To put poems on paper is deskbound work,
   only living poetry belongs to life,

it alone has the right to travel on the roads leading to the heights
But you must choose between them as you please.)

The center point of Act 2 is Falk's famous "tea water speech" (*Thevandstale*), which likens love to the tea plant. Just as tea transported on the great oceans loses its aroma, so love without the fetters of law and morality is despised. But tea also decays on its long journey over land from China to Norway, and so does love when forced to accommodate itself to social demands:

> Hvad blev vel Følgerne,
> Hvad Skrig, hvad Verdens Dom, hvis De, hvis jeg,
> Bar kjækt vor Elskov over Frihedsbølgerne!
> "Gud, den har tabt Moralens Krydderi!"
> "Legalitetens Duft er rent forbi!"
>
> (4: 203)
>
> (What would the consequences be,
> What outcry, what judgment of the world, if you, if I
> Bravely transported our passion across the waves of freedom!
> "God, it has lost the spice of morality!"
> "The aroma of legality is completely gone!")

Outraged by Falk's undisguised praise of free love, Mrs Halm expels him from her boarding house. Declaring his disgust for the petty-minded society that surrounds him, Falk asks Svanhild to join him in his lonely struggle. Agreeing, she accepts his ring.

In Act 3, about to set out for a life in freedom, Falk and Svanhild passionately declare their love, their strength, and their fidelity to the ideal. Precisely at this point, the excellent, good, loving but decidedly unpoetic and seriously rich merchant Guldstad, who has loved Svanhild for many years, decides to test their idealism. His method is simple: he asks Svanhild to marry *him*. Mobilizing Falk's own ideas against him, Guldstad asks how long he expects his love for Svanhild to last. Is Falk alone exempt from the temporal decay of the ideal that he lamented in his tea-party speech? Marriage can be based on passion, Guldstad argues, but it can also be based on loving-kindness, care, duty, and an everlasting concern for the other's well-being and happiness. This is what *he* offers Svanhild.

Admitting that he cannot guarantee that his love will last eternally, Falk can only reply that it will last for a long time. Disdaining such a feeble reply, Svanhild makes her choice: in order to ensure that their love is kept forever young, pure, and ideal, she will leave Falk and marry Guldstad. She has, in other words, discovered that the ideal can only survive if it is removed from every conceivable real world context:

SVANHILD. Slaa Linet over alle Drømmes Lig;
  Vor Kjærlighed, den glade, sejerskjække,
  Skal Sot ei tære paa, ej Ælde svække,—
  Dø skal den, som den leved, ung og rig!

(4: 241)

(SVANHILD. Cover all our dreams with a shroud;
  Our love, our glad, triumphant love
  Shall never be weakened by illness or enfeebled by age
  It shall die as it lived, young and rich!)

To preserve love is to renounce it; the play dissolves on a paradox. Svanhild gets engaged to Guldstad, and Falk joins a group of wandering student minstrels heading for the mountains.

Although Svanhild's renunciation of Falk is genuinely heart-rending, her motivations are complex. On the one hand, she accepts Falk's idealist notions of a poet's vocation. By renouncing him, she can remain ideal in his mind, and thus become the perfect, never-decaying muse (unlike Straamand's Maren). Svanhild clearly knows just as well as the audience, that romantic poetry thrives on absence, loss, and longing. Her choice of Guldstad would be a textbook case of idealist sacrifice, if it were not for the fact that Svanhild also makes it quite clear that she knows that she is not cut out to be Falk's wife:

FALK [*i dyb Smerte*]. Og langt fra Dig—hvad blev mig *der* vel Livet!
SVANHILD. Hvad blev det *nær* mig—uden Kjærlighed?
FALK. Et Hjem!
SVANHILD. Hvor Lykkens Alf med Døden stred.
[*med Styrke.*]
  Til Viv for Dig blev Evnen ej mig givet,
  Det ser jeg nu, det føler jeg og ved!
  Jeg kunde Elskovs glade Leg Dig lære,
  Men tør din Sjæl ej gjennem Alvor bære.

(4: 241)

(FALK [*in deep pain*]. And far away from you—what would life be for me *there?*
SVANHILD. What would it be *near* me—without Love?
FALK. A home!
SVANHILD. Where the elf of happiness would be struggling with death.
[*forcefully*]
  I was not given the ability to be a wife for you,
  I see it now, I feel and know it!
  I could teach you the cheerful play of love,
  But I don't dare to carry your soul through serious times.)

These are not the words of a woman convinced that she is giving up her life's happiness in giving up Falk. On the contrary, she is clear that a life with Falk would mean a life in which she would slowly watch the death of their love and happiness. Her choice of Guldstad, then, is not simply a noble, idealist sacrifice. It is also a perfectly sensible, perfectly realistic decision, given that she lives in a society in which marriage is the only possible career for middle-class women.

As we have seen in Chapter 3, Ibsen's contemporaries, who assessed *Love's Comedy* from the point of view of aesthetic idealism, found it an outrageous and immoral "break with the idea", a demonstration of the author's complete lack of "ideal faith and conviction". Where *The Feast at Solhoug* had struck the young Bjørnson as through and through "poetic", *Love's Comedy* was declared unpoetic and ugly. A Danish critic claimed that Ibsen had not understood that bitter anger could never be poetic.[54] Ibsen himself reinforced the point, in a preface written for the second edition of *Love's Comedy*, published in 1867, after the success of *Brand*: "The poem provoked a storm of ill will, more violent and more widespread than most books can pride themselves on in a society in which the great majority usually considers literary matters completely irrelevant to them" (4: 137).

Modern critics agree with their predecessors that *Love's Comedy* is indeed a stingingly satirical critique of the empty moralism of Scandinavian society, but they are also convinced that *Love's Comedy* is a glorious tribute to the ideal of love. Bjørn Hemmer expresses an extreme version of this view: "A theory of sacrifice inspired by Christianity . . . and a romantic theory of the ennobled life in the world of memory here walk hand in hand. This is Ibsen's perspective in *Love's Comedy*."[55] More moderate, Daniel Haakonsen declares that Ibsen here has become a "faithful believer in romantic love".[56] Even Brian Johnston, who has a sharp eye for the satirical elements in the play, concludes that idealism carries the day: "The inauthentic idealism is demolished so that the authentic can be established. Otherwise, *Love's Comedy* would be only a bitter paradox instead of a tragi-comedy of idealism."[57] The exception to this chorus of male voices is Joan Templeton's claim that the play is a "feminist satire".[58] I think there is much to be said for this, yet the only reason Templeton gives for saying so is that that Svanhild's engagement to Guldstad "fails to convince as a preferable alternative to a love match", for it represents "Svanhild's surrender to society's essential demand for women—a suitable marriage".[59] On this view, the satire is to be found in our awareness of Svanhild's failure to marry for love. This lets Falk and his "poetic" views of love and marriage off the hook rather too easily. In my view, *Love's Comedy* does not praise idealist notions of love; nor does it idealize female sacrifice. As we shall see, *Love's Comedy* is in many ways still deeply ambivalent about the legacy of idealism.[60] The one thing, however, this play is *not* ambivalent about, is the huge, and hugely unfair, gender differences embedded in idealism. In this play, Ibsen becomes the first great writer to see that although idealism may be uplifting for aspiring male poets, it is hugely oppressive to women.

First of all, Ibsen calls his play a *comedy*, a fact that modern idealist readings usually try to get around, either by speaking, with Brian Johnston, of "tragi-comedy", or by declaring, as Hemmer does, that "Ibsen could have chosen the title *Love's Tragedy*. . . . What appears to be clear, is that this is about the tragic and necessary consequences of absolute idealism."[61] What bothers idealist critics, I think, is that the very genre of comedy pulls in the direction of the low and the everyday. The fact that *Love's Comedy* is written in verse, however, pulls in the other direction, towards the soaring heights of idealist flight. Just as Falk has "two natures" in him (4: 162), so *Love's Comedy* is torn in two directions: towards the ordinary and the everyday, represented by marriage, and towards the heroic, the noble, the high, the good, the eternal, and the true, represented by poetry. As so often in Ibsen, these oppositions are so many instantiations of the fundamental conflict between will and capacity, imagination and talent, freedom and necessity.

The character of Falk is a self-proclaimed idealist. Voicing an inflamed defense of heroism, in love as in poetry, he ceaselessly attacks "Tidens usle Lære: / At Idealet er det Sekundære" (4: 228) ("the despicable teachings of the time / that the ideal is secondary"). Since *Love's Comedy* does not invite us to sympathize with its slew of banal, off-putting secondary characters, there can be no doubt that Ibsen, like Svanhild, had deep sympathy for Falk and his version of the "ideal demand". Yet *Love's Comedy* also shows that Svanhild knows the price of such idealism and decides that for her, it is not worth paying. After all, Falk confesses that once he has used her fully, he will kill her off spiritually, just as he killed the songbird in front of her eyes. Moreover, his constant circling around the motif of the innocent woman trampled to death by wild horses indicates that his erotic imagination is not a little sadistic in relation to women.

Insofar as all the idealist readings of the play essentially align themselves with Falk's world view, they completely disregard Svanhild's more complex point of view, and so overlook not just Ibsen's analysis of gender differences, but also the fact that Ibsen never in his life wrote a play in which a single character can safely be taken to embody his own point of view. (If there is an exception, it is *Catiline*.) Why would *Love's Comedy* be the only exception to this rule? Although Falk struggles for truth and beauty, the play makes it abundantly clear that he is no more capable of living a life in keeping with his ideals than anyone else in the play. Nor is it obvious that he will become a great poet at the end of all his struggles, for he is hardly the most original of spirits. At the very least, *Love's Comedy* should inspire its readers to ask what we should make of ideals that are unlivable even by their most ardent proponents.

Falk's project is to unite life and the ideal. But Falk's definition of "life" is quite peculiar, shaped more by idealist notions of beauty than by any sense of what it means for a human being actually to live in the world. Railing against the habit of sending engaged women off to learn how to keep house, for example, he declares that men surely don't fall in love with "en Kogebogsprofessorinde" (4: 206) ("a professor of cookery books"). For his part, he prefers "en Balheltinde" ("a ballroom heroine"):

FALK. Jeg tar ærbødig hatten af, min Frue,
　　For "Balheltinden"; hun er Skjønheds Barn,—
　　Og Idealet spænder gyldne Garn
　　I Ballets Sal, men knapt i Ammens Stue.

$$(4: 206)$$

(FALK. I take my hat off to the belle of the ball,
　　dear Madam; she's the child of beauty,—
　　and the ideal tends its golden net
　　in the ballroom, but hardly in wet-nurse's cottage.)

According to Schiller, the idealist is the "sworn enemy of everything petty and trivial".[62] It is not surprising, then, to find that Falk's poetic notion of beauty is incompatible with cooking, housework, and human reproduction, too. In perfect keeping with Schillerian theory, Falk wants passionate love, but not babies; desiring the soul, he disavows the body. Falk's distaste for the material side of life is so profound that he even appears incapable of idealizing motherhood. Are we to embrace such attitudes entirely uncritically? (Svanhild certainly doesn't.) Shouldn't we rather see in such passages a send-up of the limitations of idealism?

Guldstad pointedly refers to himself as one of life's "unpoets" (*Vi upoeter* (4: 182)), by which he means to say that he renounces all talk of the ideal, in favor of a far more human and practical understanding of life. Is it a coincidence that he represents the best of the everyday and the ordinary? I have difficulty agreeing with the critics who assume that Svanhild is doomed to a Mrs Alving-like existence with him. Is it so obvious that Svanhild would be happier with the selfish Falk? Should we not at least consider the fact that Svanhild herself obviously does not think so? Guldstad's extraordinary respect for Svanhild's freedom has much more in common with Dr Wangel's respect for Ellida's right to choose how she wants to live than it has with Chamberlain Alving's excesses.

Love's Comedy carries in embryonic form the insight that was to revolutionize Ibsen's theater in *A Doll's House*: namely, that idealist aesthetics offers women only a restricted range of roles compatible with its lofty ideal of beauty. The ideal woman is beautiful, pure, and ready to sacrifice all for love. As such, she is fit only for the role as ideal mother, ideal lover, tragic heroine, or supernatural muse. In Norway, as elsewhere, the cult of self-sacrifice in women was often understood in Christian terms, as an act done for the sake of others, intended to provide us all with the hope of redemption. By the time he was writing *Love's Comedy*, Ibsen was clearly questioning his relationship to Christianity. Stripped of Christian underpinnings, the idea that a woman simply has to sacrifice herself for Falk's writing is ludicrous. In Ibsen's later works, the two most obvious parallels are Gregers's fateful idea that Hedvig will somehow regain her father's love if she sacrifices something that is infinitely dear to her, and, of course, Rosmer's ferocious demand for female sacrifice. I am also reminded of Ibsen's ironic handling, in *The Lady from the Sea*, of the sculptor Lyngstrand's wildly egoistic demand that Bollette should sacrifice herself to be his muse. Behind Bollette and Lyngstrand there is the even more troubled and troubling couple of Irene and Rubek in *When We Dead Awaken*, who incarnate the ugly ruins of idealist art and idealist love alike.

At the end of *Love's Comedy*, the audience is left with more questions than answers. Should we flee with Falk or settle down to a livable, but unpoetic, everyday life with Svanhild? Is it right that women do not have the same kind of choice in these matters as men? By giving equal weight to Falk's desperate impatience with the stifling mediocrity that surrounds him, and to Svanhild's severely circumscribed choices, Ibsen indicates his awareness of the limitations of idealist notions of beauty. While he is not yet ready to give up idealism, he is certainly not capable of espousing it uncritically, either.

The ambiguity of *Love's Comedy* is repeated in *Brand*. Both plays are written in verse, as required by the highest notions of idealist beauty. Both plays invite an idealist interpretation: the point would be to denounce everyday accommodations with the demands of the ideal, and to praise the attempt to live up to the demands of stronger, more exacting ideals. There can be no doubt that Ibsen hated narrow-minded, self-serving mediocrity. Both plays are implacable attacks on the petty concerns of small-minded people, embodied more often than not in the figures of officials and politicians. But by the end of each play it is by no means clear whether Ibsen has condemned or embraced the radical idealism of Falk and Brand. Like the end of *Love's Comedy*, the end of *Brand* is ambiguous: does Brand die a hero or a failure? Was his ideal inhuman? Or does his fate show that ordinary people simply cannot live up to the true ideal?

The fact that we cannot provide final answers to such questions goes to show that they were not—and could not then be—settled in Ibsen's own mind. Judging from the evidence of *Love's Comedy*, all we can say is that in this play he finally made idealism his subject matter; for the first time he allowed himself to express a keen awareness of sexism in aesthetics and society, and showed that the theme of contemporary marriage was capable of releasing his most powerful artistic powers. By making idealism a subject for reflection, Ibsen put himself in a position to judge it for himself, rather than simply submitting to it as an unquestioned aesthetic framework.

Ibsen's greatest aesthetic victory in *Love's Comedy* is his handling of the character of Svanhild, which he freely acknowledged was inspired by his own wife, just as the play as a whole was inspired by his own experience of marriage. In *Love's Comedy*, for the first time, Ibsen writes about a contemporary woman character in a way that fully respects her desire for freedom. Ultimately, his wish to write about strong, complex, and free women forced him to break with the idealist framework. Because of its feminism, because of its challenge to established moral norms, and because of its critical investigation of idealism, *Love's Comedy* is the first play in which Ibsen starts to sound like himself.

6

Becoming Modern
Modernity and Theater in *Emperor and Galilean*

Introduction: A Pivotal Play

Emperor and Galilean is pivotal in Ibsen's work, literally as well as figuratively. It stands in the middle of his production: twelve plays come before, twelve plays come after. This enormous double play, a world-historical prose tragedy, also stands alone at the center of Ibsen's *œuvre*. Four years (an unusually long gap for Ibsen) separate *Emperor and Galilean* from its neighbor on either side. In 1869 Ibsen finished *The League of Youth*, an entertaining comedy about politics and inauthenticity. In 1873 he published *Emperor and Galilean*, and in 1877, *Pillars of Society*. Together these three plays constitute Ibsen's transition from being the author of *Brand* (1866) and *Peer Gynt* (1867) to becoming the author of *A Doll's House* (1879). Of these three, *Emperor and Galilean* is by far the most important for an understanding of Ibsen's modernism, for here Ibsen develops not just a full-scale analysis of modernity in Europe, but a new understanding of what theater is and what it can do. It also marks the moment in which Ibsen breaks with Norwegian nationalism and defines himself as a European: the immodest subtitle "A World-Historical Play" says it all. After *Emperor and Galilean*, Ibsen's Norwegians are Europeans.

Ibsen always considered *Emperor and Galilean* his *hovedverk* ("main" or "most important" work).[1] It was, he once said, not just his *hovedverk*, but "without comparison the play that has cost me most work!"[2] Ibsen's choice of word is important: it is always *hovedverk*, never *mesterverk* ("masterpiece"). A *mesterverk* is a masterpiece, "the greatest work of a particular artist or writer", a "person's most eminent or crowning achievement", as the dictionary puts it. *Hovedverk* has no exact English equivalent. A Norwegian dictionary gives this example: "the trilogy stands as a *hovedverk* in his production". Since it is not synonymous with a *mesterverk*, a *hovedverk* is not necessarily an author's most perfect work, but rather a work that is pivotal—central, cardinal, vital—to the understanding of an author's whole production.

When Ibsen said that *Emperor and Galilean* was his *hovedverk*, I think he meant to say that it would be impossible to understand *him*—his works, his thought, his view of the world—without understanding this immense play. My work on Ibsen has led me to the same conclusion. As if to confirm this interpretation, Ibsen, quite unusually, stressed his personal and auto-biographical investment in *Emperor and Galilean*: "I have placed a part of my own spiritual [*åndelig*] life in this book; what I describe here, I have in different forms lived through myself, and the chosen historical theme also has a closer connection to the movements of our own time than one might believe in advance" (17: 61).[3] This play expresses Ibsen's own spiritual and intellectual trajectory, as well as his understanding of his own time.

There is, then, an enormous discrepancy between the attention Ibsen wanted us to pay to *Emperor and Galilean* and the neglect from which it has suffered. Few writers and intellectuals know it. Wittgenstein is an exception, for in 1937 he was reading *Emperor and Galilean* in Norwegian in his cabin by the Sognefjord.[4] Scholars have only been moderately interested. Most books on Ibsen do not have chapters on *Emperor and Galilean*. Even more alarming is the extreme rarity of productions. Because there is no strong, living tradition of producing this play, it is not part of the experience that directors, actors, and theatergoers bring to *other* Ibsen plays. The result is an impoverished understanding of Ibsen's depth and scope.

It is true that Ibsen did not write *Emperor and Galilean* for the stage, but rather thought of it as a closet drama, a play written to be read rather than performed. While nineteenth-century stage conventions and stage technol-ogy made the production of a ten-act play with great narrative sweep and stunningly spectacular scenes unfeasible, today it could be turned into a terrific stage production. After all, *Brand* and *Peer Gynt*, also conceived as closet dramas, have long been in the repertoire of theaters all over the world. In London, the National Theater's productions of David Edgar's *Speer* in 2000 (a play that charts the rise and fall of the Third Reich by focusing on the biography of one man close to power) and Tom Stoppard's *The Coast of Utopia* trilogy in 2002 (the three parts take over nine hours to perform) made it clear to me that the right director and the right theater could work marvels with *Emperor and Galilean*.[5]

Why has there been so little interest in Ibsen's *hovedverk*? When it comes to productions, the obvious answer is the length. *Emperor and Galilean* is twice as long as *Brand* or *Peer Gynt*. It is also true that it is not a perfect play. There are longueurs, repetitions, and, at times, a certain lack of intensity and drive. But I am inclined to think that the main reason for the neglect of *Emperor and Galilean* is historical. Right from the start *Emperor and Galilean* was a favorite with idealists, who read it as a religious and uplifting drama about the necessary, historical victory of Christianity. Although idealists claimed *Brand* for their cause, too, that play was always more obviously open to ambiguous or anti-religious interpretations. In the 1880s and 1890s the Christian and idealist predilection for the play would have made any radical, freethinking defender of Ibsen (Georg Brandes, or George Bernard Shaw, for example) wary. Once the idealist tradition lost its influence, there was nobody left to champion *Emperor and Galilean*. The modernists preferred the later plays, and the realistic and discursive *Emperor and Galilean* could in any case never appeal to the ideologues of modernism. Perhaps we have only now arrived at a moment where this great play can become readable in new and challenging ways.[6]

In this chapter I have two concerns: modernity and theater. I shall show, first, that *Emperor and Galilean* is centrally concerned with the experience of modernity in Europe after 1870. In this respect, it belongs squarely alongside the most important avant-garde responses to European modernity in the second half of the nineteenth century, such as those of Marx and Nietzsche. But this was not a perspective available to the contemporary audiences of the play, who read it in idealist terms. My example of such a reading is the earliest and fullest available: namely, Arne Garborg's 1873 pamphlet on the play.

In the second half of this chapter I turn to the question of theater. I show, first, that *Emperor and Galilean*, often considered hopelessly old-fashioned, in fact is self-consciously reflecting on its own theatrical tradition, in a tremendous effort to develop a new understanding of theater and theatricality. In its reflections on theatricality, we can find almost all the fundamental features of Ibsen's modernism. *Emperor and Galilean* itself, however, is not a full member of the group of plays that constitute Ibsen's modernism. (In my view, Ibsen's first fully modernist play is *A Doll's House*.) One crucial feature is still missing, and one is underdeveloped. The missing feature is a full and radical consideration of women's situation in modernity. The underdeveloped feature is the turn to the everyday and the ordinary. Although *Emperor and Galilean* is in supple everyday prose, and although it has a lot of "everyday people" in it, it is still a kind of tragedy about gods and emperors. On my reading, *Pillars of Society* begins to provide the missing feature and further develops the turn to the everyday. I therefore end this chapter about how Ibsen became a modernist by looking, very briefly, at *Pillars of Society*.

This chapter does not discuss *The League of Youth*. I simply do not find in this play the same intense concern with theater as in the two subsequent plays. Through its form and language, *The League of Youth* nevertheless made an important contribution to Ibsen's transition towards modernism. Nobody has expressed this better than Ibsen himself in a letter to Brandes: "In my new comedy you will find average everydayness (*jævne Dagligdagshed*), no strong movements of soul, no deep moods, and above all no isolated thoughts. . . . It is written in prose, and it follows that it has a strong realistic coloring. I have taken special care with the form, and have among other things pulled off the trick of managing without a single monologue, yes, even without a single 'aside' " (16: 249).[7] Because *The League of Youth* was a comedy, the trad-itional genre of the low and the ordinary, it was surely easier for Ibsen to experiment with the "average everydayness" here than it would have been in a tragedy.

Although *Emperor and Galilean* retains many of the formal elements of romantic tragedy (it is about the ruler of a state, it is full of pictorial tableaux, and it has a tragic end), it is also an experiment in prose. Ibsen was passion-ately convinced that *Emperor and Galilean* had to be written in ordinary, everyday language. In January 1874, Ibsen wrote to Edmund Gosse to thank him for his review of the play, and to take issue with him on one point: Gosse had claimed that *Emperor and Galilean*, like *Love's Comedy, Brand*, and *Peer Gynt*, ought to have been written in verse. Ibsen strenuously objected:

The many everyday and insignificant characters, which I have deliberately placed in the play, would have become indistinct and blurred into each other, if I had let all of them speak in rhythmic cadences. . . . In general the linguistic form must follow the degree of ideality given to the representation. My new play is no tragedy in the sense of older times; I have wanted to portray human beings and that is precisely why I have not wanted to let them speak "the tongue of the gods".

(17: 123)

In the same letter, Ibsen writes that he chose the "realist form", since the "illusion I wanted to produce, was that of reality" (17: 122). The everyday language and realistic form of *Emperor and Galilean*, then, marks an import-ant step towards Ibsen's modernist breakthrough. But if this were its only contribution to Ibsen's modernism, it would not be the pivotal work it is.[8]

Europe after 1871: War, Doubt, and the Death of God

Emperor and Galilean is a play about war, terrorism, religious fanaticism, and religious persecution.[9] Covering the period from 351 to 363, *Emperor and Galilean* sets out to convey the dying moments of the once so brilliant culture of Greek and Roman antiquity and the brutal religious conflicts that shaped the culture of Christianity in Europe.[10] But this is no antiquarian exercise. A play about the end of one era and the dawning of another, about human violence in a world in which all traditional ethical norms have been swept away, it was intended to be a diagnosis of European modernity.[11] In the character of Julian, it shows us a human being desperately seeking truth, beauty, and meaning in an increasingly chaotic and violent world.

Ibsen first had the idea for a play about Julian the Apostate in Genzano, outside Rome, in the summer of 1864.[12] Halvdan Koht writes that at the time Ibsen was going through a spiritual crisis which led first to the publication of *Brand*, and later to *Emperor and Galilean* (see 7: 9). In the end, it was going to take Ibsen nine years to finish the project, and he really did not get going until 1870–1. On 20 December 1870 he wrote in a letter to Georg Brandes that he had just had a clear and striking vision of his new work, but without saying what it was. In the letter, however, the reference to the new vision is followed by a revolutionary and rather upbeat analysis of the Franco–Prussian War:

Besides, the world events occupy a great deal of my thoughts. The old illusory France has been smashed to pieces, when finally the new factual Prussia is smashed to pieces too, then in one leap we shall be in an age of becoming. How the ideas then will collapse around us! And it will truly be high time. Everything we have been living on until today amounts to no more than the crumbs from last century's revolutionary table, and that nourishment has been chewed over for long enough. The concepts need a new content and a new explanation. Freedom, equality and fraternity are no longer the same things they were in the days of the blessed guillotine.

(16: 327)

We should bear in mind that this letter was written during the long siege of Paris, after the devastating French defeat on 2 September that led to the birth of the Third Republic, but before the final German victory and the rise and bloody fall of the Paris Commune in the spring of 1871.

When it was all over, the war had cost the lives of 140,000 French and 47,500 German soldiers.[13] Estimates of the numbers killed in the massacres at the end of the Commune range from a sober 30,000 to a rather incredible 200,000. That two of the most economically and culturally advanced countries of Europe could engage in warfare and slaughter on such a horrendous scale shook the Western world to the core. In 1871 an American observer wrote that this was a "war which, in its rapid movement, its terrible destructiveness, and its stupendous results, is without a parallel in history".[14]

In July 1871, less than two months after the fall of the Paris Commune,

Ibsen began to write *Emperor and Galilean* in earnest. The traces of the events of 1870–1 are not hard to find in the text, for they show up in the play's preoccupation with warfare, revolt, terrorism, dictatorship, and gratuitous death, but also with cataclysmic historical and cultural change, with the transition from one era to another, and with the search for meaning in a world in which God is dead and traditional values have lost their grip on people's soul.[15]

Another important source of inspiration must also be mentioned. In the early spring of 1872, when he was well into the work, Ibsen took time off to read *Emigrantlitteraturen*, Georg Brandes's fiery call for a modern literature, which had just been published. Rarely has Ibsen responded with such violent enthusiasm to a book:

> But I want to turn to the topic that in these days has incessantly been in my thoughts and disturbed my peace at night. I have read your lectures.
>
> A more dangerous book could never fall into the hands of a pregnant writer. It is one of those books that opens a fathomless gap between yesterday and today. When I went to Italy I did not understand how I could have been able to lead an existence before I had been there. In twenty years one will no longer be able to understand how it was spiritually possible to live at home before these lectures. . . .
>
> What will emerge from this struggle to death between two epochs, I do not know; anything rather than the established order is the decisive thing for me. From victory I do not really draw a promise of stable improvement, for all development has so far consisted only in lurching from one error (*vildfarelse*) to another.
>
> (17: 31–2)[16]

Ibsen here speaks of a new age, a watershed, a complete change in spiritual or intellectual (*åndelig*) life. The "struggle to death between two epochs" could be a description of the theme of *Emperor and Galilean*. If we take it in that sense, we should note that although Ibsen is violently in favor of change, he does not have faith in the results: "lurching from one error to another" is hardly a "positive world view", as he had promised his publisher the previous July (16: 371).[17] Because Ibsen is writing to Brandes, the "struggle to death" must also be a reference to the culture wars unleashed by Brandes's lectures— that is to say, to the struggle between religious idealists and the freethinking "men of the modern breakthrough".

When we look at the finished text, it shows that Ibsen is immersed in some of the most culturally contentious issues of its time, for example in its obsession with determinism. Darwinism surely contributed to the general preoccupation with the question, but so did the emerging disciplines of statistics and probability calculation, for they showed that the inexorable necessity of mathematics could be used to predict people's actions. Although it sounds strange to us, "statistical fatalism" actually became a topic of debate in Germany in the 1860s.[18]

Julian constantly worries about freedom and necessity, often in the religious sense of free will as opposed to predestination. What is the relationship between Julian's choices and what he calls the "world will"? Is he, perhaps, an instrument of God's plan for the world? The horrifying alternative—that there is no plan, that human existence is just meaningless—is expressed in Julian's visions of the universe as an ugly, terrifying, slimy void. Recoiling from these visions, Julian desires determinism, for he passionately wants to *discover* rather than *shape* his destiny.[19] In the case of Julian, then, *Emperor and Galilean* explicitly represents faith as a desperate, self-protective recoil from the deepest doubt. He is not the only one who desires determinism, however. So do his Christian opponents, who wish to see in him an instrument of God's will, and Maximus, who wants Julian to be the chosen one, the one who implements the world will and founds the mysterious Third Empire.

Julian's desire for a pre-scripted role in the destiny of the world expresses his fear of freedom. By casting his willful and arbitrary decisions as acts of submission to the world will, Julian forces himself to believe that he is acting in accordance with the signs and omens sent to him by the gods, or by the world will. The scene in I.3, when Julian has to accept or refuse the status as Caesar, is a good example.[20] Although Maximus tells him three times that the signs are contradictory, Julian flatly denies it, picks one "sign" (the messenger's reference to Helena as the "pure woman") and decides that the gods have spoken.

Julian fears freedom because, to him, the very thought of a universe without meaning, a universe in which God is dead, signifies loneliness and isolation. The historical Julian wrote about a youth (pretty obviously himself) devoted to Zeus, Helios, Athena, and Hermes: "The youth [. . .] declares to his gods: 'Do with me what you will,' and Helios replies to him, 'We are your benefactors and friends and saviours. . . . We will be with you everywhere.' "[21] It seems to me that Ibsen must have known this passage. I think we are supposed to have compassion for Julian's doomed wish to hold on to a universe made on the human scale, a world that speaks to him, gods who are his friends and guardians, for the alternative, figured in those horrible visions of the void, is the modern, secular world where the earth is just one small globe in an immense, cold, and silent universe.

Critics have often aligned themselves with determinist readings of *Emperor and Galilean*, particularly with the Christian version.[22] The anti-determinist

Brandes completely misread it, for he thought Julian's determinism was Ibsen's.[23] Yet the play offers no final, unambiguous position; it simply has no spokesperson for Ibsen's "message".[24] At the end, Maximus insists that the Third Empire must come. Basil claims that Julian must have been God's instrument, since his persecutions have brought the Christians together and renewed their faith. As she covers the face of Julian's dead body, Basil's sister Macrina, the pure woman, gets the last word: "Erring human soul—if you *had to* err, you will surely be received with favor on that great day when the mighty one comes in a cloud to judge the living dead and the dead who live!" (7: 336).[25] That this grand drama of freedom and necessity ends with a hypothesis in the conditional tense is exactly in keeping with its refusal to subscribe to determinisms of any kind.

Only in Marx and Nietzsche do we find equally radical diagnoses of European modernity. In their great hymn to the power of capitalism, *The Communist Manifesto*, Marx and Engels also famously describe a culture in the throes of cataclysmic social and historical change: "All fixed, fast-frozen relations, with their train of ancient and venerable prejudices and opinions, are swept away, all new-formed ones become antiquated before they can ossify. All that is solid melts into air, all that is holy is profaned, and man is at last compelled to face with sober senses, his real conditions of life, and his relations with his kind."[26] Although this is intended as a description of Europe in 1848, it is a vision of historical change that fits the world of *Emperor and Galilean* perfectly. But Ibsen is bleaker than his socialist precursors: in Julian's increasingly mad delirium of interpretation, the value of knowledge comes under pressure. At the end of this play, I certainly don't see much faith in "man's" capacity to "face with sober senses, his real conditions of life, and his relations with his kind".

Nietzsche's *Beyond Good and Evil* (published nine years after *Emperor and Galilean*) provides an even closer match, for here there is a stunning passage that reads like a commentary on Ibsen's "world-historical play":

All sorts of new what-fors and wherewithals; no shared formulas any longer; misunderstanding allied with disrespect; decay, corruption, and the highest desires gruesomely entangled . . . a calamitous simultaneity of spring and fall, full of new charms and veils that characterize young, still unexhausted, still unwearied corruption. Again danger is there, the mother of morals, great danger, this time transposed into the individual, into the neighbor and friend, into the alley, into one's own child, into one's own heart, into the most personal and secret recesses of wish and will: what may the moral philosophers emerging in this age have to preach now?[27]

What indeed? The same question resonates at the end of *Emperor and Galilean*.

When I speak of parallels between Ibsen and Nietzsche, I do not mean to say that Ibsen must have read Nietzsche, just that they sometimes work on similar questions and reach similar conclusions. There may be just one exception to this rule: namely, the relationship between *Emperor and Galilean* and *The Birth of Tragedy*, two works written in Germany in the immediate aftermath of the war of 1871.

Critics have often remarked on the differences between Part I ("Caesar's Apostasy") and Part II ("Emperor Julian") of *Emperor and Galilean.*[28] "Emperor Julian" is wilder, freer, and more incoherent than "Caesar's Apostasy". In comparison to the unruliness of Part II, Part I seems almost classical. What caused the differences? One hypothesis is that Ibsen read or got to know about Nietzsche's *The Birth of Tragedy* between writing the two parts.

Originally Ibsen planned a play in three parts:

1. "Julian and the Friends of Wisdom" (3 acts)
2. "Julian's Apostasy" (3 acts)
3. "Julian on the Emperor's Throne" (5 acts)

In the spring of 1872, Ibsen had already written the first two parts according to this scheme. Some time during that summer, however, he changed his plans, and in the early fall he turned the existing Part II into Acts 4 and 5 of "Caesar's Apostasy". Then he wrote all five acts of "Emperor Julian" in one furious outburst from 21 November 1872 to 13 February 1873.[29]

The Birth of Tragedy was published in the spring of 1872. It was reviewed and attacked in the *Norddeutsche Allgemeine Zeitung* in May and June.[30] Ibsen, who lived in Dresden, and was an avid reader of newspapers, might very well have noticed the controversy. Or talked to someone who had. Or he might not: I know of no evidence one way or the other. As usual, Ibsen gives nothing away: "I really did not know much about him," is all he has to say about Nietzsche, in an interview dated November 1900, the year of Nietzsche's death (15: 436).

There is some internal evidence to support the idea that Ibsen read or heard about *The Birth of Tragedy*. But given that the historical Julian is said to have worshipped a whole range of Greek gods, it may be a complete coincidence that both Apollo and Dionysus, the gods who provide their names to Nietzsche's two key terms, turn up right at the beginning of Part II, and that they remain the most frequently invoked gods throughout "Emperor Julian".[31] In II.1, for example, Julian's first public sacrifice is to Apollo, Dionysus, and Fortuna; his first public procession is in honor of Dionysus, and it is characterized by drunkenness and dance, albeit in an ironic mode that strikes me as entirely foreign to Nietzsche's tone in *The Birth of Tragedy*. In II.2, Julian's procession in honor of Apollo dramatically clashes with the long column of Christian prisoners eagerly desiring martyrdom; and the act ends with the spectacular collapse of the Apollo temple in Antioch.

The Dionysus procession in II.1 contains a passage that just might indicate some knowledge of Nietzsche's main idea that there are two kinds of artistic principles: namely, the Apollonian, which stands for individuation, reason, and clarity, and the Dionysian, which stands for ecstasy, communal frenzy, and the loss of individuation, and that true tragedy requires the combination of both:

JULIAN. . . . No god's been so misunderstood—so ridiculed, even—as this bringer of ecstasy, Dionysus, whom the Romans call Bacchus. Do you think he's a god of mere drunkards? Oh, you ignorant ones, I pity you if that's what you believe. Who else do the poets and seers look to for their miraculous gifts? Oh, I know some credit Apollo with this faculty, not entirely without justification; but that's to be understood in a different context—as I can prove from various writings.

(7: 192; *EG*, 109; amended)

That Julian identifies with Dionysus is obvious. He too feels misunderstood and ridiculous. His insistence that Dionysus, not Apollo, is the god of poets and seers serves to underline his wish to communicate with his people. By choosing the god of ecstasy, Julian also expresses his hope that he might overcome his separation from others by losing his painful self-consciousness in ecstasy and mysticism.

It is hard to say whether Ibsen got this from Nietzsche. Reading *Emperor and Galilean* after Nietzsche, it is difficult not to see connections. Yet most of the elements mentioned here could have been derived from historical knowledge about Julian's life, or from fairly superficial accounts of Nietzsche's book. Given the state of the evidence, the only conclusion one can draw is the obvious one, which is that in 1872 Ibsen and Nietzsche certainly shared a preoccupation with Apollo and Dionysus and with the question of what theater is and what it could be in European modernity.

Finally, to turn the question of influence on its head, it is possible that Nietzsche was inspired by *Emperor and Galilean*.[32] In fragment 984 of *The Will to Power*, written in 1884, Nietzsche writes about "the Roman Caesar with Christ's soul", a phrase that Walter Kaufmann considers to be "the very heart of Nietzsche's vision of the overman", and which readers of *Emperor and Galilean* can't fail to associate with Ibsen's *hovedverk*.[33]

A Conflicted Idealist Response: Arne Garborg

As soon as he finished his draft in February 1873, Ibsen set to work on the fair copy, and on 24 May 1873 he sent the final installment of the manuscript off to his publisher. *Emperor and Galilean* was published in Copenhagen in October 1873, and enjoyed excellent sales.[34] Only a few weeks later, the 22-year-old Arne Garborg, later to become a major naturalist writer, rushed a little book about Ibsen's double play into print.[35]

Garborg's response to Ibsen is of enormous interest both because it is the record of a brilliant contemporary reader's passionate response to the text and because it demonstrates that although he still read *Emperor and Galilean* in an idealist aesthetic frame of reference, his idealism exhibits signs of strain. Despising old-fashioned idealism, Garborg refers to it as the "old view of art", and declares that it is falling apart, and rightly so, for it has degenerated into mere entertainment.[36] Poetry shouldn't be mere play and relaxation, Garborg claims; the task of literature is not to "procure for Peter and Paul some 'hours of rest' away from their toil at the office" (AG, 13).[37] Rather, literature ought to teach us something in existentially and philosophically serious and challenging ways.

Garborg was nevertheless all in favor of uplift: "The poet's task is to lift our mind above the narrow conditions of everyday life towards the heights of the realm of beauty . . . to lift the seething struggle of the age up to coherent clarity in the higher light of beauty" (AG, 12–13). To Garborg, in fact, representations of real life are entirely compatible with beauty, not because the everyday is beautiful as it is, but because the task of the poet is to *idealize*:

It is a misunderstanding to believe that real life is the same thing as ugliness (*Uskjønheden*), and that one necessarily has to establish a new world up in the sky in order to find beauty. . . . Real life also contains, albeit in a divided and scattered fashion, all the elements of beauty: the art of the poet is to see them, find them and use them; his task is to create a beautiful whole from the scattered elements—and the work one has named to "idealize" consists precisely in this activity aimed at removing the haphazard, the divided and the confusing, and at linking the disharmonious and confused life of reality to the laws of beauty and harmony. According to these considerations, the greatest fidelity to reality will also become the greatest beauty as long as reality is represented as harmonious and coherent.

Ibsen's treatment of history in "E. and G." provides a handsome illustration of the view of beauty presented here.

(AG, 60–1)

Garborg also praises the author of *Emperor and Galilean* for his ability to see beauty in reality, to turn history into realistic, yet beautiful life: "The external world here becomes really what it should be, one single organic unfolding of the ideal world. . . . We have, in short, in this treatment of the material the closest possible realization of the most important demand one can put to all art: that it should be nature, above all, but nature transfigured by the idea" (AG, 64).

In spite of such praise, however, Garborg begins and ends by stressing Ibsen's skepticism: "What one ultimately is left with as the final result of his poetry, is the discovery—which by the way is not new—that 'everything is vanity'; disappointments and emptiness, emptiness and disappointments,—this is the inner despair we encounter everywhere" (AG, 5). Although *Emperor and Galilean* is an aesthetic masterpiece, its world view—marked as it is by skepticism and despair—fails to satisfy.

When I first read Garborg's pamphlet, I found it almost incomprehensible. I certainly failed to see that the constant invocations of beauty and the ideal had to be taken as an explicit formulation of a strong aesthetic norm. On my second reading, which came after I had rediscovered idealism, I got the impression that Garborg's argument was falling apart, for he seemed to be saying both that the play was a glorious instance of idealist aesthetics, and that it failed to supply reconciliation and uplift. Only on my third reading did it occur to me that Garborg's contradictory reaction to *Emperor and Galilean* might be a sign of an incipient aesthetic conflict that would ultimately make Garborg, and many others of his generation, break with idealism. Garborg, after all, praises Ibsen for the historical and realistic truth and the aesthetic beauty of his work, and excuses his faults on the grounds that the weaknesses—which have to do with Ibsen's "world view"—on the whole have to do with "circumstances outside aesthetics" (AG, 64).

But if this is what Garborg believes, then he is willing to divorce a work's philosophy or its outlook on life from aesthetics. This is the first step on the path leading to a rejection of the fundamental beliefs of idealism. In other words, Garborg may still hold truth and beauty together, but his notion of truth is showing signs of becoming divorced from religion and philosophy (world views), in a way that the early German idealists would have found utterly unacceptable.

While still almost wholly idealist, Garborg's reading also puts him at odds with more traditional and conservative idealists like Wirsén, who read *Emperor and Galilean* as a stellar example of idealist aesthetics. In 1873, then, there were two different idealist ways of reading this play (the "old" and the "new" idealisms, we might call them), but no modern or modernist ones.

The reason for this is historical: Garborg was writing in 1873, only a year and a half after Brandes's *Emigrantlitteraturen* was published. At this time, the aesthetic terms with which to evaluate modern literature that Brandes called for had still not been developed. And how could they be, given that the new literature itself was barely coming into existence. *Emperor and Galilean* itself is surely one of the very first examples of a significant literary work written in self-conscious response to Brandes's lectures.

Reconsidering the Tradition: Ibsen and Hugo, Peterssen and Delaroche

"The essential fact of . . . the modern lies in the relation between the present practice of an enterprise and the history of that enterprise, in the fact that this relation has become problematic," Stanley Cavell writes.[38] The beginning of the modern, he continues, is a "moment in which history and its conventions can no longer be taken for granted; the time in which music and painting and poetry (like nations) have to define themselves against their pasts; the beginning of the moment in which each of the arts becomes its own subject, as if its immediate artistic task is to establish its own existence".[39] *Emperor and Galilean* marks this moment in Ibsen's work. This is the play in which he turns towards his own aesthetic past, not to reject it *en bloc*, but to reflect on it, to consider where he stands in relation to it. Ibsen's transition from idealism to modernism is marked by a reflection on romantic tragedy in its most flamboyant European (as opposed to Norwegian) form. I find the same return to European romanticism in the work of the painter Eilif Peterssen (1852–1928), one of Ibsen's friends in Munich in the mid-1870s, and the first to paint a portrait of Ibsen. Why do these artists need to turn towards romanticism just as they are moving away from it?

When the curtain rises for the fifth act of "Caesar's Apostasy", Julian is in the catacombs under the cathedral of Vienne in the south of France, waiting for a sign. If the right sign comes, he will proclaim himself emperor. The similarity to the fourth act of Victor Hugo's *Hernani*, the 1830 play that launched romantic tragedy in France, is arresting, for Hugo's Don Carlos is also in a vault under a cathedral, and he too is waiting for a sign that will proclaim him emperor.[40] Both scenes, moreover, are equally pictorial and picturesque, with the same Gothic overtones.

In Don Carlos's case, the cathedral is in Aix-la-Chapelle, the vault of which contains Charlemagne's tomb, and the much awaited sign is straightforward enough: when the electors of the Holy Roman Empire have elected a new emperor, they will fire a canon: if they fire three shots, Don Carlos will become Charles V. Eagerly desiring the imperial mantle, Don Carlos prays to Charlemagne for inspiration to carry out his imperial duties with proper idealist dignity and honor:

> Verse-moi dans le cœur, du fond de ce tombeau,
> Quelque chose de grand, de sublime et de beau![41]

(Pour into my heart, from the depths of this tomb, / Something great, sublime and beautiful!)

After an intense period of suspense, three canon shots are fired. Having become the new emperor, Don Carlos immediately shows himself worthy of being Charlemagne's successor by displaying great magnanimity towards his erstwhile enemies.

Julian is also placed in the vicinity of a dead body, but in his case, the body is that of Helena, his adulterous wife, poisoned by her brother, the emperor Constantius. Throughout the act, the background of the action is the sound of the Christians singing hymns and clamoring at miracles worked by the dead woman's coffin in the cathedral above. Rumors are even starting to circulate that Julian killed his saintly wife. Given what the audience and Julian know about the actual life of Helena, the dramatic irony here serves to explain Julian's apostasy, at the same time as it throws any kind of faith in miracles and signs into severe doubt.

The different treatment of the motif of the sign brings out some crucial differences between *Hernani* and *Emperor and Galilean*. In *Hernani*, it is clear what the sign is, and the question of interpretation never arises. In "Caesar's Apostasy", on the other hand, the audience does not even know what kind of sign Julian is waiting for. Only towards the end of the act do we realize that he has been waiting for the mystic Maximus to decipher his future in the entrails of animals sacrificed for the purpose. According to Maximus, how-ever, there are no signs to be had, for the incessant Christian hymns in the cathedral above silence the spirits.

In the end, Ibsen even leaves it unclear whether Julian actually gets his sign. Having refused to take Maximus's advice, "Take your fate into your own hands" (7: 153; *EG*, 83), Julian finds his army on the point of mutiny, and finally decides to descend to the deepest underground vault to carry out the blood sacrifice, spurred by his rage at hearing Helena hailed as the pure woman. Offstage we hear Julian shouting "Helios! Helios!"; shortly thereafter he returns with blood on his hands. Aghast at the sight, Sallust asks Julian what he has done; Julian replies, "Torn away the mists of fear" (7: 161;

EG 88). Exquisitely ambiguous, his reply leaves us free to imagine either that Julian did receive his sign, or that he finally plucked up the courage to choose his destiny, as Maximus had been urging him to do. His ambiguous reply demonstrates his avoidance of responsibility. Instead of speaking of his choices, he will invoke the more or less obscure signs of the gods.[42] The end of "Caesar's Apostasy" reveals that, for Julian, people and things have become opaque, threatening, and potentially meaningless.

Hugo and Ibsen both use a Gothic setting with vaults and tombs to bring out the same motif—namely, the making of an emperor—and both convey the sense that we are present at a moment on which a whole world's destiny depends. But where Don Carlos is all nobility, certainty, and action, Julian is all ambiguity, doubt, and hesitation. Even when he has made his choice, his reasons remain open to interpretation. Whereas Ibsen writes about will, choice, the psychological weight of religion, and the interpretation of signs, Hugo confidently moves ahead with expression and action. Whenever Don Carlos has something to say about his soul, he expresses it in a soliloquy. Julian, on the other hand, loses himself in specious reasoning and metaphysical speculation. In short: where Hugo is all exteriority, Ibsen is all interiority.

What does this tell us about the relationship between Ibsen's incipient modernism and romanticism? To get closer to an answer, I shall look at the way in which Eilif Peterssen's *Christian II Signs the Death Warrant of Torben Oxe* (1875–6) appears to reflect on Paul Delaroche's *The Execution of Lady Jane Grey* (1833) (Plates 2 and 3). Peterssen was working on his breakthrough painting just as Ibsen moved to Munich in the spring of 1875. In 1876, just as *Christian II Signs the Death Warrant of Torben Oxe* was enjoying a remarkable success in Germany, Ibsen chose Peterssen to paint his portrait.[43] That year, Peterssen also gave Ibsen an inscribed photographic print of *Torben Oxe*, which now hangs in the Ibsen Museum in Oslo. On the print, the painting is called "Elisabeth's Intercession for Torben Oxe with Christian II" (*Elisabeth's Fürbitte für Torben Oxe bei Christian II*).[44]

Delaroche responded to the moving story of Jane Grey, proclaimed Queen of England at 15 by her ambitious father. When Queen Mary came to power, Jane, who had ruled for all of nine days, was accused of treachery, imprisoned in the Tower of London, and beheaded on 12 February 1554. Stephen Bann reports that Delaroche's painting was intended to represent the moment when Jane, blindfolded, is supposed to have cried out piteously: "What shall I do now? Where is the block?"[45]

Michael Fried considers that in *Jane Grey* Delaroche embraced the "theatricalization of action and expression".[46] There is indeed a strong emphasis on the externality, or visibility, of dramatic action in this painting. The overwhelming feeling in *Jane Grey* is compassion, figured in the gestures of the priest and the expression of the executioner, and almost forcibly elicited from the spectator, too. Bann convincingly shows that the painting in fact draws on the tradition of paintings of Christian martyrdom, and adds that when it was first exhibited in 1833, some viewers instantly recalled the sight of young aristocratic women going to the guillotine during the French Revolution.[47]

The story that fascinated Peterssen is less well known: Christian II of Denmark–Norway, who ruled from 1513 to 1523, was convinced that Torben Oxe, the governor of Copenhagen Castle, had poisoned his mistress, the beautiful Dyveke. The Queen who intercedes for Torben is Elizabeth of Habsburg, sister of the future Holy Roman emperor Charles V, the Don Carlos of *Hernani*. The execution of Torben Oxe sparked a revolt among the Danish aristocracy that led to the king's downfall and exile. Peterssen may have felt that the future of Norway also depended on this moment, for the next king, Christian III, introduced the Reformation in Denmark–Norway, and did away with the last vestiges of Norwegian self-governance.[48] (His is the reign represented in Ibsen's *Lady Inger*.)

In 1907, the Norwegian art historian Jens Thiis wrote about *Torben Oxe*: "The motif is extremely dramatic, almost *too* dramatic, described with theatrical clarity and tension, but the composition is outstandingly well mastered, and the execution reveals a rare painterly power."[49] At first glance, then, *Torben Oxe* may appear to position itself in something like a reactionary continuity with romantic history painting, just as *Emperor and Galilean* could be mistaken for a belated and futile attempt to write romantic tragedy.

The Execution of Lady Jane Grey and *Christian II Signs the Death Warrant of Torben Oxe* have much in common. Both are highly dramatic history paintings. Painted on a large, but not monumental, scale, both represent a "pregnant moment" chosen from a sequence of acts beginning with the moment a monarch signs a death warrant and ending with the moment of execution. On closer inspection, however, the differences between *Jane Grey* and *Torben Oxe* are just as striking as the differences between *Hernani* and "Caesar's Apostasy". In *Jane Grey*, every eye is averted, and the main point of focus is the blindfold covering Jane's eyes; in *Torben Oxe*, on the other hand, we are besieged by eyes, or, more precisely, by a profusion of glances in every direction. Although his chosen moment is extremely dramatic, Delaroche is still honoring the antitheatrical value of unself-consciousness. Peterssen, on the other hand, deliberately draws our attention to the act of looking. It is as if he wants us to feel that by standing in front of this painting and looking at it, we are behaving just like the silent and suspicious courtiers in the painting.

Instead of the overt, dramatic, physical action of *Jane Grey, Torben Oxe* offers us an entirely internal process: what matters is not what the queen does, but what goes on in the king's soul. As with Julian's moment of decision at the end of Part I of *Emperor and Galilean,* his reasons for action are obscure. What is the king thinking? Why is he taking this fateful step? Are we supposed to feel compassion? But for whom? The doomed Torben? The dead Dyveke? But they are not in the picture. The queen? Surely not for the king about to doom himself and his reign? (There is something unpleasantly willful about his expression that prevents sympathy.) There is no telling: *Torben Oxe* keeps its secrets by blocking easy identifications. If Delaroche's Jane Grey is an icon of wronged innocence, Peterssen's Christian II is a mystery to himself as much as to us.

When we consider Ibsen and Peterssen in relation to Hugo and Delaroche, the relationship between the artists of the 1870s and those of the 1830s begins to emerge. Ibsen and Peterssen feel the need to invoke, and in some ways continue, the tradition created by high, flamboyant romanticism. Their works certainly have the look of the tradition they are reconsidering. Yet, just as Peterssen frustrates the requirement that paintings should be "instantly intelligible", Ibsen resists the idealist demand for clarity. There is a sense, both in *Emperor and Galilean* and in *Torben Oxe,* that human actions have become unintelligible. Obsessed with the difference between the outer and the inner, the surface and the depth, between the human body and the human soul, Ibsen and Peterssen are haunted by the feeling that what a human being says or does is no reliable indicator of what he or she means, thinks, or feels. Both *Emperor and Galilean* and *Torben Oxe* draw attention to the difficulty of understanding another human being by placing problems of interpretation and judgment right at the center, thematically as well as formally, and both make the beholder or the audience experience the loss of intelligibility that haunts them.

It is as if Ibsen and Peterssen look back at a tradition which sought to produce unself-conscious representations of beauty, truth, and goodness with nostalgic disbelief. Although they still signal some formal allegiance to it, their works make this tradition look too blissfully innocent. The explicit thematization of skepticism emerges here as a feature that divides romanticism and modernism.

Julian's Public Sacrifice: Theater and Finitude

"Emperor Julian" begins with a spectacular tableau-like picture, in which Julian watches the arrival of the funeral barge of Constantius, before sacrificing to Apollo, Dionysus, and Fortuna in public:

JULIAN. . . . Here I stand, in the bright light of day; the eyes of all the Greeks are upon me; I expect the voice of every Greek to unite with me in praise of you, immortal gods!
[*During the ceremony of sacrifice most of the Christian onlookers gradually have drifted away; only a little group remains behind. When Julian stops speaking, faint cheers are heard, blended with soft laughter and astonished whispering.*]
JULIAN [*Looking around*]. Aha! What's become of them all? Have they sneaked away?

(7: 176; *EG*, 99; amended)

Characterizing Julian's rites as doomed, formalistic attempts to turn back history, Arne Garborg rightly took these scenes to indicate that Ibsen wanted to stress the absurdity of Julian's attempt to revive the old religion. When they expressed the collectivity of the ancient city or state, the ancient rites were effective, but here they represent only the idiosyncrasy of a misguided individual: Julian's restoration of the Greek world of beauty mercilessly turns into a caricature, and he himself becomes a fool in a philosopher's gown. . . . The sacrifice turns into an absurd spectacle that feels uncanny, because it pretends to be life" (AG 43–4). Garborg's reference to an "absurd spectacle" (*et meningsløst Skuespil*) brilliantly grasps the preoccupation with theater and theatricality that underpins Ibsen's description of Julian's processions and offerings.

Julian has staged an elaborate and spectacular ritual, in which he casts himself quite self-consciously as an actor. His aim is clear: he wants to feel at one with the audience, he wants his voice to merge with theirs. He has just sacrificed to Dionysus, whom he addresses as "God of Ecstasy, who lifts the souls of men from baseness" (7: 175; *EG*, 99). Desiring ecstasy, Julian wants to be transported beyond the petty conditions of ordinary life. (The same distaste for the petty, the ordinary, and the low characterizes Hedda Gabler.) Above all, however, he wants his audience to experience these things *with* him; the point of his public rituals is always to make others join him, share in his experiences. It is his failure to achieve such unity that makes him look so utterly theatrical.

Julian's spectacular extravaganzas are tied up with his sense of human isolation, for he is a devastatingly lonely soul who feels immured in his own particularity. Throughout the play, Ibsen shows Julian begging people to stay, only to have them leave him (I am thinking of Agathon, Basil, and Gregory). We also learn that his whole family, except his brother Gallus, was massacred when he was little. Now that he is a grown-up, Julian would give anything to feel at one with someone else. If he can't achieve unity with others, he will destroy them: "Ah, if I could only lay waste to the world! Maximus, is there no poison, no consuming fire that could shatter creation to what it was when the solitary spirit was moving over the face of the waters?" (7: 321–2; *EG*, 189; amended).

I want to put this in Stanley Cavell's terms: Julian is someone who has never managed to come to terms with his own *finitude*—that is to say, with his own separate, embodied, human existence. For Cavell, the foundation for interaction with others is the acknowledgment that they *are* other. But in order to acknowledge others' separate, finite existence, we must also acknowledge our own finitude: "The choice of finitude . . . for us (even after God) means the acknowledgment of the existence of finite others, which is to say, the choice of community, of autonomous moral existence."[50] Julian's inability to acknowledge his own finitude—which means acknowledging that he is mortal, that he is sexed, and that he is separate—explains why Julian becomes such a completely destructive emperor: he cannot build community, he can only tear it apart.[51]

But what has this got to do with theater and theatricality? On my reading of Cavell's foundational essay on *King Lear*, "The Avoidance of Love", theater is the art of finitude. Theater requires two groups of people—actors and audience—to share a certain space for a certain period of time, while acknowledging that they are separate, and that they have different responsibilities to each other. That theater—any theater, even street theater and happenings—presupposes this separation, is shown in our relationship to characters: "A character is not, and cannot become, aware of us," Cavell writes.[52] "The usual joke is about the Southern yokel who rushes to the stage to save Desdemona from the black man. What is the joke? That he doesn't know how to behave in a theater?" (AL, 327). The yokel's problem, rather, is that he has not understood that *the characters are in our presence, but we are not in theirs* (AL, 332).

Some examples may help to clarify this. I once saw a production of *The Wild Duck* that took place in a ballroom where the chairs were distributed in two rows along the walls. I was seated in the front row, so close that I could easily have touched the actors. After the intermission, the actor playing Gregers Werle came onstage with a long white thread stuck to the back of his dark jacket. The thread was distracting, and the temptation to stretch out my hand and take it off was immense. Yet I didn't. I simply *could not* do it, and the thread stayed where it was.

"They are in our presence, but we are not in theirs": this means that the characters aren't aware of us. They can go up to us, exhort us, speak to us, rush out among us, but when they do so, they are not relating to us as human beings; they are turning us into characters in their play. Since we, as the audience, are not in their presence, nothing we can do can impinge on them. If a character in a play comes up to us, we cannot reciprocate. Or rather: if we reciprocate, we either do so only on their cue and bidding, or we become like the Southern yokel who wants to rescue Desdemona. Phaedra's soliloquies do not place us in Phaedra's presence, they place her in ours. Or in other words: however much Phaedra addresses us, she is not aware of us; we, however, are challenged to acknowledge her words, to acknowledge *her*.

It follows that *whatever* the characters do, they cannot overcome the separation between the audience and themselves. (This is why theater is the quintessential art of finitude.) A long time ago I saw the Théâtre du Soleil's production of *1793* in a huge hangar at Vincennes outside Paris. Spread all over the immense floor, the audience figured the revolutionary crowd. The actors were mostly high up above us on trestle tables connected by planks. From time to time, however, they came down and mingled with the crowd. At one point a revolutionary festival was supposed to be taking place. I remember vividly how embarrassed I was when a huge brown bear insisted on waltzing around the arena with me. I was very young, had hardly ever been to the theater before, and was rather upset by the whole thing, yet I obscurely felt that I had no option but to waltz along as best I could.

Thinking back on the experience, I realize that whether I had waltzed or refused to waltz, I would have had no influence on the theatrical situation. If I had refused to waltz, I would simply have become a *surly* member of the revolutionary crowd. I was not free to rush up on the trestle tables to join the actors, but they could waltz with me as much as they liked. When they did, it transformed me into a character in their play, but I had no power to transform them into anything at all. Had I rushed onto their tables, I would not have become Marie Antoinette or Olympe de Gouges, I would just have turned myself into a Norwegian yokel.

Theater is deeply threatening to Julian because its very condition of existence is to reveal the separation between self and other, between actors and audience. Since he desires ecstatic union and merger with his audience, Julian has to disavow and deny theater. This is why Julian is a hard-line antitheatricalist, a point that is explicitly made in his passionate attack on the poet Heraclius, where Julian disparages theater and insists, like Plato, that all art is lying, that its only reason for existence is to praise the gods (see 7: 232–3; *EG* 135).

Julian desires religious community, but produces theater. His failure to produce passionate ecstasy in his fellow citizens—his fall into theatricality— is deeply painful to him, for it makes him feel lonely and isolated. Julian's theatricality makes him look ridiculous to his subjects; but it also indicates that he is losing touch with any sense of community, that his ascension to the throne is the beginning of that inner exile that will lead to madness. It is no wonder, then, that in II.2 he decides to instruct his subjects and audience (who must obviously have been getting it wrong so far) in the difference between the theater and the temple:

> JULIAN. . . . Let this serve you as a guide to your conduct in the future. In the palace, in the marketplace, yes, in the theatre—if it didn't disgust me to enter such a place of folly—it is suitable that you greet me with shouts of praise and joyous applause. . . . But if you see me enter the temple, that's another matter. It's my wish that you then keep silent and direct your shouts to the gods, not to me, as you watch me advance with downcast eyes and head bowed.
>
> (7: 207; *EG*, 119; amended)

The imagery of theater and temple links *Emperor and Galilean* to Bjørnson's ecstatic, idealist defense of theater in *The Fisher Maiden*.[53] Yet Ibsen takes a far less optimistic view of the possibilities of uniting the two. Here Julian insists that applause, the ultimate acknowledgment of theater, is out of place in the temple. In exemplary Diderotian fashion, Julian stresses the absorptive aspects of his performance: although the audience will be looking at him in the temple, *he* will not be looking at them.[54] Julian's efforts fail. Every single one of his religious productions is booed and jeered. (Booing and jeering, like applause, are also acknowledgments of theater.) Yearning to be one with others, Julian nevertheless casts them as his audience rather than as his fellow human beings, thus reinforcing his separation from them. This is his existential tragedy.

"An unusual and sublime Spectacle": Theatricality and Truth

Emperor and Galilean is obsessed with trust, truth, and faith, and with their opposites: doubt, lies, and skepticism. There is a connection, I now want to claim, between Julian's constant theatricalizing of himself and of others, and

I. Anne Louis Girodet de Roucy-Trioson (1767–1824), *The Flood,* 1806
(oil on canvas), Musée Girodet, Montargis, France, Peter Willi;
Bridgeman Art Library.

2. Hippolyte (Paul) Delaroche (1797–1856), *The Execution of Lady Jane Grey*, 1833 (oil on canvas), National Gallery, London, Bridgeman Art Library.

3. Eilif Peterssen, *Christian II Signing the Death Warrant of Torben Oxe*, 1876. Photo by J Lathion: © The National Museum of Art, Architecture and Design, Oslo.

4. Arnold Böcklin, *Im Spiel der Wellen,* Bayerische Staatsgemäldesammlungen, Neue Pinakothek Munich and Kunstia-Archiv ARTOTHEK, D-Weilheim.

his extreme skepticism, expressed as a corrosive undermining of everyday criteria of truth and an obsession with the interpretation of signs.

After the failure of his first public sacrifice, Julian returns to his palace, and proclaims the freedom of religion. The conclusion of his speech contains the only use of the word *skuespil* ("play" or "spectacle") in *Emperor and Galilean* (apart from the subtitle). Mixing thoughts about flattery, hypocrisy, and spectacle with thoughts about love and harmony, the themes of this passage reverberate throughout the rest of the play:

> JULIAN. . . . In this way we'll live in harmony together. My court shall be hospitable to all distinguished men, whatever their opinions. Let's show the world the unusual and sublime spectacle of a court free of hypocrisy—in truth the only court of its kind—a court in which flattery is deemed the most dangerous foe. We'll condemn and criticize each other whenever appropriate without loving one another any the less.
>
> (7: 177; *EG*, 100; amended)

Julian describes a court without hypocrisy as an "unusual and sublime spectacle" (*det usædvanlige og ophøjede skuespil*). This is a peculiar claim. In Norwegian *skuespil* means a play, but it can also mean an act of dissembling or hypocrisy. Thus, when Julian claims that an honest and non-hypocritical court is a *skuespil*, his wording makes it clear that it is still theater. Given that the anti-theatricalist Julian thinks that theater is synonymous with lies and hypocrisy, his proclamation of an honest court undermines itself as it is being uttered.

By declaring his honest court to be a *skuespil*, Julian is in effect theatricalizing all his courtiers. By this I mean simply that he is turning them all into actors. But how does he then expect to tell the difference between a courtier who is acting and one who is being authentic? Between one who is lying and one who is telling the truth? Whatever they do, whether they are honest or dishonest, hypocritical or sincere, they cannot escape theater: they will be judged on the effects of their performance, not on the truth of their statements.

Immediately after Julian's declaration of religious tolerance and opposition to flattery and hypocrisy, he turns on the good Ursulus, Constantius's old chamberlain, for telling the truth. (In the end, Ursulus is executed.) The contrast between Julian's words of love, tolerance, and respect for truth and his cruel treatment of Ursulus is puzzling. For, whatever his flaws may be, Julian has simply not been portrayed as a cynical monster, deliberately proclaiming one thing while planning to do another. This scene therefore requires closer attention.

His rage at Ursulus is provoked by a difference of interpretation. Immensely flattered by the arrival of ambassadors from the outer edges of the known world, whom he takes to have come especially to court favor with him, Julian makes a highly self-conscious, public display of magnanimity. Before receiving them, he explicitly debates whether or not he should have his hair cut first, and wonders what costume to wear for the occasion (see 7: 178; *EG*, 101). Here, too, Julian is theatricalizing himself (turning himself into an act, a spectacle). Likening Julian to a god, the ambassadors flatter him in the most adroit way possible, and Julian laps it all up, thus inspiring a new round of flattery from his own courtiers.[55]

The only exception to the general chorus of flatterers is the honest Ursulus, who has the temerity to point out that the ambassadors must have been dispatched from their distant lands long before the news of Constantius's death could possibly have reached them; they were sent to see Constantius, not Julian. His evidence is incontrovertible: "Just consider the time involved, my lord; reckon the number of days, and say how it could be otherwise" (7: 183; *EG*, 103), he says to Julian. Julian's response is telling:

JULIAN [*pale with rage*]. Why are you telling me all this?
URSULUS. Because it's the truth, and because I can't bear seeing your young and
   splendid glory sullied with borrowed achievements.
THEMISTEUS. What presumption!
MAMERTINUS. Extreme presumption!
JULIAN. You can't bear seeing . . .! Oh, I know you better. I know all you old guard at
   this court. It's the gods whose glory you want to disparage. For isn't it to the glory
   of the gods that they work great things by means of a man?

                                                              (7: 183; *EG*, 103; amended)

By asking Julian to count for himself, and to reach his own conclusion, Ursulus is assuming that Julian shares his own (and everybody else's) criteria for how one calculates these things. He is, in other words, assuming that Julian is reasonable. Julian, however, never even addresses the question. Instantly flying into a rage, he shifts the ground from truth to motivation. Against Julian's theater stands Ursulus's truth; and theater will win.

In a key passage in *The Claim of Reason*, Cavell writes:

The philosophical appeal to what we say, and the search for our criteria on the basis of which we say what we say, are claims to community. And the claim to community is always a search for the basis upon which it can or has been established. I have nothing more to go on than my conviction, my sense that I make sense. It may prove to be the case that I am wrong, that my conviction isolates me, from all others, from myself. That will not be the same as a discovery that I am dogmatic or egomaniacal. The wish and search for community are the wish and search for reason.[56]

The scene with Ursulus shows that Julian is losing touch with reason. But to say this is to say more: that his loss of reason has to be figured as isolation, as loss of community, as a loss of that sense of attunement with others that we have when we feel that our words make sense. That sense of attunement is produced by criteria, and in this scene, Julian is losing his grasp of the usual criteria of reasonableness—for example, honesty, probity, good sense, and fidelity. Without such criteria, one cannot tell the difference between truth and fiction, flattery and sincerity.

As "Emperor Julian" develops, one increasingly gets the impression that there are no *grounds* for any of Julian's decisions, that he believes exactly what he wants to believe. He is at once far too gullible and far too suspicious. The most spectacular example of this is his unquestioning belief in the Persian spy who advises him to burn his ships in Act 4 of "Emperor Julian", and his spontaneous rage against the faithful Christian general Jovian, who dares to warn him against the Persian. As Julian burns his ships, the Persian flees, and Julian's troops are doomed. No scene demonstrates better the fatal consequences of Julian's extreme skepticism, which by the end of the play floats free of any conceivable connection to reality. (This is also indicated, at several points in the play, not least in II.5, by his visions of the earth as seen from some impossible vantage point in space.)

As the play nears its end, Julian employs an ever increasing number of soothsayers, priests of oracles, and magicians. Helpless in relation to the signs of the world, Julian hopes that the signs from the gods will provide absolute certainty, absolute truth, so that he will be freed from the burden of having to judge for himself. (Judgment requires criteria, hence requires a background of agreement in what Wittgenstein calls forms of life.[57]) *Emperor and Galilean* is a play precisely about changes in the human form of life, hence about the possibility of agreement as such.[58]

Constantly consulting signs, visions, omens, and oracles, Julian eventually realizes that the more divine utterances he gathers, the more interpretations he accumulates, the more likely they are to contradict each other. When this in fact happens, as when Maximus's ominous "Sign against sign" resounds in I.3, Julian simply denies that it is so, and does what he wants (7: 106–8; *EG* 53–4). This pattern does not change until II.5, when Maximus tells Julian that the stars will tell him nothing. Nearing his end, Julian responds in a new, revealing way: "Alone! No longer a bridge between me and the spirits" (7: 315; *EG*, 185). For Julian, the gods were his only friends, and now they have left him. (No wonder he felt that he had to declare himself a god: it is his last attempt at providing himself with something like a family.) Julian is moving because he is so lonely, so lost, so utterly disoriented, so desperately eager to find some clues, some signposts, only to find that he is, after all, alone in a world which steadfastly withholds its meanings, where there are no signs, and where, in the end, "all the omens are silent" (7: 315; *EG*, 185).

Theatricality, Skepticism, and Love

Why is Julian theatrical? I think of theatricality as a skeptical recoil *against* the discovery that we are separate from each other. The skeptic tries to avoid acknowledging finitude, in order to avoid acknowledging the problem of knowing others. This may sound a bit abstract. What exactly do I mean by skepticism? I use the word in the usual philosophical sense. Fundamentally, I mean the overwhelming feeling or the intense intellectual conviction that we simply *cannot know* the other, or, in another version, that we simply *cannot know* the world. (Julian clearly suffers from both.) Usually, skeptics absolutize their terms, in the sense that if I point out that we can, after all, know *something* about the other or about the world, the answer will be that whatever I think I know is not *certain* knowledge or the *absolute* truth, but something else (interpretations, constructions, or some hypothesis that works only for practical purposes).

I am persuaded by Stanley Cavell's argument that skepticism can be understood as an existential experience as well as an intellectual predicament. Existentially, skepticism with respect to other minds (which is the kind that preoccupies me in this book) is a response to the discovery of human separation and finitude. The premise of the skeptical experience is that because we are separate from each other, we are also unknown to each other. But this thought alone is not enough to produce skepticism. Someone who believes that although we are unknown to each other, we can learn to know each other, is not a skeptic. What characterizes the skeptic is the idea that other human beings are *metaphysically unknowable*. Typical for the modernist experience of skepticism is that this conclusion is expressed as a loss of faith in language (this is why Julian's loss of criteria matters so much), which is now experienced as incapable of conveying reliable knowledge about others, as well as of expressing my own feelings and thoughts.

The idea of the fundamental unknowability of the other gives rise to many characteristic fears and fantasies. One important version is the fear that I cannot know whether others are human at all. (In literature and film, this is often figured as a preoccupation with dolls, robots, and aliens.) This version of skepticism is marked by a profound distrust of the human body, now considered as nothing but a cover for inner secrets. (I return to this in my analysis of *A Doll's House* in Chapter 7.) The sharp divide between outer and inner, body and soul, the belief that outer surfaces can tell us nothing about inner depths, is itself deeply skeptical. That Julian *is* a skeptic is obvious. Apart from Faust, I can hardly think of another character in world literature who searches so intensively for certain knowledge and the absolute truth.

Skepticism can take many forms. I can worry that I can never know others, or that others can never know me. I can feel that nothing I can ever say will express my unknown inner depths. In other words, I may feel that my words have nothing to do with my soul (I use "soul" here as a word for what is going on inside a human being). To feel deeply unknown in this way is to feel isolated, unloved, cast out of humanity. Julian is a case in point.

I can also feel that your words are entirely unconnected to your soul, so that I can never know you either. But if I start thinking along these lines, I am beginning to theatricalize you—that is to say, I am turning you into a mere spectacle or performance. The problem with doing this is that I can then always pretend that you are not a fellow human being with the same capacity for joy and pain as myself. (Perhaps you are just an alien masquerading as human: your words, after all, provide no certain clues to anything.) If I think about you in such ways, I absolve myself from any responsibility to acknowledge your pain. That Julian behaves as if the suffering of others makes no difference to him is made obvious in his treatment of Ursulus. Soon he will be persecuting all Christians.

If I theatricalize *myself*, I am at all times performing an act for you. One consequence of this is that I put myself in a situation in which I cannot manage to mean what I say (in Ibsen's works, the quintessential example is Hjalmar Ekdal in *The Wild Duck*). Another is that I turn you into my audience. Then I will be in your presence, but you will not be in mine. In other words, I will be the star of my own performance, and you will be in the dark for me; if you are in pain, I will not perceive it. (In the theater, we do not expect Othello or Desdemona to acknowledge our pain: our task is to acknowledge theirs.) The implication of Julian's constant self-theatricalizing is that Ibsen is seeking a new theater, and a new idea of theater, one that reveals us in our reciprocal concealments, one in which our inevitable everyday theatricalizations are further thematized.[59]

At the end of the play, Ibsen rather unexpectedly places love at center stage. We are in II.5, just before the battle in which Julian will be mortally wounded by his childhood friend Agathon. Julian has started to lose his mind. He has tried to commit suicide; he feels that the "Galilean", Jesus Christ, has won. Maximus tries to strengthen Julian's will, but Julian no longer has the courage:

MAXIMUS. Don't give up, Julian. He who wills, wins.
JULIAN. And what does the victor win? Would it be worth the winning? What did the Macedonian Alexander, what did Julius Cæsar win? Greeks and Romans speak of their fame with cold admiration—but that other, the Galilean, the carpenter's son, reigns as the King of Love in the warm hearts of the faithful.

(7: 320–1; *EG*, 188–9)

In these lines Julian finally discovers the importance of love. If love requires us to be able to acknowledge the pain (and joy) of the other, then a self-theatricalizing character like Julian cannot love. All his life he has been alone and unloved. Even his quest for the "pure woman" was not spurred by love, but by the idea that he was to become the new Adam, destined to found a new Eden with a new Eve.[60] His closest relationships have been with men: if there is any desire beneath Julian's ascetic asexuality, it is homosexual.[61]

In a moving comment on *Emperor and Galilean* made in a speech in Kristiania in 1874, Ibsen strongly stressed the importance of love in *Emperor and Galilean*:

When Emperor Julian reaches the end of his career, and everything collapses around him, then there is nothing that depresses his mind more profoundly than the thought that all he has won was *this*: to be remembered with respectful admiration by clear and cold minds, while his opponent was surrounded by love in warm, living human hearts. This aspect emerged from much that I have lived through, it has its origins in a question that I occasionally have asked myself down there in the solitude.

(15: 395)

In this play, there is only one person incarnating love: Macrina, the pure woman, who is uninterested in sex, loving, forgiving, and the embodiment of mercy. The irony is that when Julian, in the end, does get to the plains beyond the Euphrates with the pure woman, it is not to find the new Eden and found a new earth, but to die in her care.

By placing love at the end of *Emperor and Galilean* Ibsen recognizes that the greatest challenge for a human being is no longer to reach beauty and truth—God knows that Julian tried that—but to be able to love. Macrina's last words are there to exemplify mercy, not to convey the ultimate religious or philosophical message of the whole play. Love, moreover, is incompatible with the theatricalization of self and others, for it requires the ability to acknowledge the other's feelings and perceptions. This is a huge departure from the sublimated and sublime idealist notion of love, which is usually represented as a man worshipping an ideal woman, or as a woman sacrificing her life for the love of a man.

The implications are far-reaching. Most important is the insight that skepticism in general, and theatricality in particular, are the enemies of love. Modern human beings will have to struggle to overcome their skepticism, if they want to love each other. Since skepticism is a key characteristic of Ibsen's modernity (and ours), this will turn out to be a difficult task.

Ibsen's Modernism: Towards a New Theater

Emperor and Galilean is about aesthetic change as much as it is about change in other historical spheres. However beautiful the idealist aesthetic utopia was, *Emperor and Galilean* shows that in the post-1871 world it is doomed to degenerate into derisory theatricality. "Life, life, life in beauty!" (7: 188; *EG*, 106) Julian shouts as he sets off for his first Dionysus procession in II.1. In the very next lines the uncomprehending crowd wonders whether they are seeing "Syrian clowns"[62] or an "Egyptian band" with "monkeys and dromedarian camels" (7: 188; *EG*, 106, amended).[63] Nothing could be more idealist than Julian's dreams of a life in beauty; nothing could be more savagely ironic than his reception by the crowd.

Julian's whole spiritual trajectory has been motivated by his dream of truth and beauty, and Ibsen makes completely sure that it will be crushed. Already in I.2, when he is still studying in Athens, Julian passionately cries out his disappointment:

JULIAN. . . . One thing only did I learn in Athens.
BASIL. What, Julian?
JULIAN. The old beauty is no longer beautiful, and the new truth is no longer true.

(7: 81; *EG*, 36; amended)

When Julian lies dying, he realizes that he should not have been looking for beauty in absolute, abstract, metaphysical notions. His last words indicate that beauty is right here on earth, but that in his frenzied quest to be one with the gods he failed to see it:

JULIAN [*with closed eyes*]. Alexander was granted his entry——into Babylon.——I too will——Beautiful leaf-crowned youths——dancing girls——but so far away.

Beautiful earth——beautiful life on earth——[*He opens his eyes wide.*] Oh Sun,
Sun,——why did you betray me? [*He sinks back.*]

(7: 334; *EG*, 197)

Julian tried and failed to live out the highest utopian vision of idealist aesthetics. He believed that the pursuit of beauty and truth was the pursuit of God.
He tried to turn philosophy into aesthetics, and aesthetics into religion.
Julian's mad ambition was to defeat finitude, to embrace infinity. Julian's
whole life is evidence that idealist aesthetics simply cannot be lived.

But couldn't we say the same thing about *Emperor and Galilean* itself? In
its enormous scope and its world-historical ambitions, this play is surely itself
a last, ritual enactment of the infinite demands of idealism. But would it not
follow that *Emperor and Galilean* is as disastrous a failure as Julian's career? I
can't bring myself to draw that conclusion: the play is far too fascinating, far
too thoughtful, far too *good*. I would say, rather, that in *Emperor and Galilean*
Ibsen is not just reflecting on the past by inserting an extended reference to
Victor Hugo. He is doing something far more ambitious: he is *re-staging* the
past, placing idealism's wildest ambitions onstage, so as to be able to convey
both their beauty and their madness. *Ibsen moves away from idealism by
representing it.* (In this way, *Emperor and Galilean* builds on the achievements
of *Love's Comedy*. This also explains why idealism keeps turning up in his
later, fully modernist plays.) This is brilliant, for to represent idealism is to
grasp it in its finitude, to bring it down to earth. He also elaborates a new
understanding of what theater after or beyond idealism should be.

What, then, does Part II of *Emperor and Galilean* tell us about Ibsen's
emerging modernism? Let me begin with a list. There is an acknowledgment
of theater, and a rejection of antitheatricalism; there is a critique of empty
and debased theatricality (understood historically as the fate of idealism in
modernity, and existentially as skeptical recoil from the discovery of human
finitude); there is a sustained ironizing of idealism; there is a choice of realism
and prose and a deliberate inclusion of the everyday; there is the discovery
that love (understood as requiring acknowledgment and not idealization of
the other) is far more important than the pursuit of the ideal, of absolute
religious or philosophical truth; there is the insight that love is destroyed
by theatricality and self-theatricalization; and, finally, there is a strong
preoccupation with skepticism as the characteristic condition of modernity.

Ibsen, then, is completely aware that theater is not life. His modernist
theater will take this realization as its fundamental starting point. What we
are required to do in the theater is not what we are required to do in everyday
life. "Attendance at a tragedy is not a substitute for attendance at a funeral.

(We need one another's presence for more than one reason)," Cavell writes (AL, 341). We do not expect to be loved by theatrical characters. Would it even make sense to claim to be loved by Brand or Dr Stockmann? (If I claim that Ralph Fiennes or Ian McKellen loves me, I am either mad or mistaken, but the claim as such is perfectly comprehensible.) Although we are in their presence, theatrical characters are fictional, not real.[64] To draw attention to the fact that we are watching theater, then, is always to stress the fact that we are in the presence of art, of illusion, not reality.

In *Emperor and Galilean* Ibsen begins a new and modern exploration of theatricality. Ibsen's later plays are full of self-theatricalizing characters whose skepticism destroys love and condemns them to solitude and death. Obvious examples are characters like Hjalmar Ekdal, Ulrik Brendel, even Gregers Werle. But that is not all. For Ibsen's later theater is also full of meditations on the impossibility of avoiding theatricality, even—precisely—in our most passionate and intense moments. This is true for Nora Helmer, for Rebecca West and Johannes Rosmer, and for Ellida West and Hedda Gabler, too.

With *Emperor and Galilean*, then, Ibsen realized that the greatest gift of theater is its capacity to *be* theater, to bear witness to our finitude, to help us acknowledge our separation from others, and theirs from us. In the plays to come, Ibsen will constantly draw attention to the fact that he is writing theater; there will be a metatheatrical element in all the plays usually considered realist. (This is precisely a way of stressing his awareness that realist theater is *art*.) In this sense, Ibsen's modern plays break completely with Diderot's antitheatrical aesthetics. Because Ibsen's realism is based on the inclusion of the everyday and the insignificant, it also breaks with the idealist notion that any representation of reality would have to idealize and harmonize the everyday.

Some of the features of Ibsen's modernism conform to the requirements of the ideology of modernism: the self-conscious references to theater, the preoccupation with theatricality. There is also, in his later plays, a keen awareness of the skeptical loss of faith in the power of language to represent, express, and communicate, which is so typical of modernism, and of modernity. (*The Wild Duck* and *Rosmersholm* are particularly acute investigations of this problem.) Yet Ibsen is no linguistic skeptic, and no formalist either. Ibsen's realist plays are neither naïvely unself-conscious attempts to "represent reality", nor attempts to *deny* that art can represent reality. Ibsen still has faith in the power of language to express the world and the plight of human beings. Ibsen's modernist theater is not a cultivation of theater for the sake of theater, but an attempt to say something about the world and our place in it, without for a moment denying its own status as theater.

Theater in *Pillars of Society*

I just listed the features of Ibsen's modernism that emerge in *Emperor and Galilean*. *Pillars of Society* contains and develops these features, first by inserting the question of theatricality plainly into the everyday, and second by beginning a radical analysis of women's situation. Among the contemporary plays, this is the one that has the clunkiest plot, and is most strongly beholden to nineteenth-century melodramatic conventions. It has certainly never been suspected of great metatheatrical finesse.[65] For the sake of brevity, I shall limit myself to a quick analysis of the treatment of theater and theatricality in the play, after which I shall add just a few lines about the emergence of a new understanding of women's situation.[66]

As the play begins, the cleric and schoolmaster Rørlund has just come to the end of a book he has been reading aloud for a group of ladies busy sewing. As he closes the book, two of the ladies exclaim: "Oh, what an edifying story! . . .—and so moral!" (8: 34–5). Strongly reinforcing the sentiment, Rørlund adds some comments about the "gilded and painted (*sminkede*) façades" (8: 35) of the great societies of the world, thus implying that their glory is merely a theatrical effect. Later we discover that he is a hypocritical and selfish man, that the sewing circle is working for the improvement of the "morally corrupt" (8: 36), and that the book was called "Woman as the Servant of Society" (8: 39). Soon thereafter, the ridiculous, cowardly, and self-theatricalizing Hilmar Tønnesen speaks about the necessity of "holding up high the banner of the idea" (8: 40). In a few deft strokes, Ibsen has characterized the Christian sewing circle as antitheatrical, idealist, and completely bigoted, and with light irony reminded us that idealism now is ridiculous and theatrical.

The antitheatricalism of the conservative and moralizing pillars of society is strongly underlined. Thus we learn that fourteen or fifteen years earlier, there was a theater society in town, and for several seasons, even a couple of professional actors, Mr Dorf and his wife. They are both long dead, and their young daughter, Dina, now lives in Consul Bernick's house. The leading citizens in town all try to forget that they were ever involved with such a frivolous activity.

In general, *Pillars of Society* shows that the people most ready to admit to being involved in theater are the least theatrical, and the most honest. They also happen to be women: Dina Dorf, the actors' daughter, will elope with Johan Tønnesen, and Lona Hessel, the character who most insistently represents the spirit of freedom, truth, and social change in this play, is the most closely associated with theater and performance. Thus she is said to have "sung for money in taverns" (8: 46), and when she first turns up in town, fresh off the ship from America, she is taken to be a member of a troop of circus artists performing on horseback (see 8: 56–7). Confronted with this misunderstanding, she laughs: "Hahaha! Are you crazy, brother-in-law? Do you believe that I perform on horseback? No; although it's true that I have performed a lot, and made a fool of myself in many ways—" (8: 57).

The most important reference to theater in the play, however, extends through the whole of the last act. The stage directions are particularly detailed, and if read with care, show that Ibsen is imagining the stage set up exactly like a stage, but one turning away from the audience:

A spacious garden room in Consul Bernick's house. . . . The rear wall consists almost entirely of large, clear glass windows, with an open door giving on to a broad flight of steps covered by an awning. Below the steps one can see part of the garden, enclosed by a fence with a small gate. Outside the fence and parallel with it, is a street, lined on the far side with small, brightly painted wooden houses. It is summer and the sun shines warmly. Now and then some people walk by in the street, they stop and chat to each other, buy things from a small corner shop, etc.

(8: 33)

The glass wall has curtains that can be drawn at will (see 8: 56). We note that, at the beginning of the act, the view through the glass wall is an extremely ordinary, everyday scene. As we shall see, the effects of this stage arrangement is to turn the stage into a kind of double theater.

The last act of the play opens on a dark, stormy afternoon. As the curtain rises, a servant is lighting the chandelier, and two maids are bringing in pots of flowers, lamps, and candles. Rummel, the wholesale merchant, is busy directing the servant, with a clear eye to theatrical effect: "Only every other candle, Jacob. It mustn't look too festive; it's supposed to be a surprise. And all these flowers—? Oh, well, just leave them. It can look as if they were there every day—" (8: 120). We learn that Rummel and his colleagues have organized a procession with banners and a brass band to celebrate Consul Bernick. Officially, the procession is a surprise. In reality, Rummel is busy stage-managing their performances: they are to spruce themselves up, change into nice, but not too nice, clothes (if the clothes were too resplendent, the illusion of surprise would be in jeopardy), and above all, the curtains must be drawn closed, so that when the procession arrives, they can be opened to show a happy surprised family in all its glory:

RUMMEL [*over by the windows*]. Damn these new-fangled contraptions. I can't get the curtains down.

MISS HESSEL. They're coming down? I thought on the contrary—

RUMMEL. Down first, Miss Hessel. I suppose you know what's about to happen?

MISS HESSEL. Oh yes. Let me help; [*takes the cords*] I'll ring down the curtain on my
brother-in-law—though I'd rather raise it.

RUMMEL. You can do that too, later. When the garden is filled with the surging
crowd, the curtains will rise, and one will behold inside a surprised and happy
family—a citizen's home should be like a glass cabinet.

(8: 123–4)

As Asbjørn Aarseth has shown, what Rummel has in mind here is a tableau of
a happily surprised family.[67] Rummel himself might have been thinking
about a leading citizen's duty to lead a transparently moral life. But what
he is actually saying is that a bourgeois family should be constantly self-
theatricalizing; not simply by always living as if it were on display, but by
living in full and constant consciousness of the fact. The rest of the act is one
long effort to expose the consequences of this pernicious idea.

Discussing the forthcoming procession, Karsten Bernick envisages the
moment where he will have to go out to receive the applause of the crowd:
"there will be shouts of hurrah outside, and the crowd will cheer until I come
out from that door, and I'll have to bow and thank them" (8: 130). In this
specific situation, the contrast between his inner crime and outer show of
probity is extreme, for Bernick believes that he has just sent the ship called
The Indian Girl on its way to certain shipwreck. Just as he is speaking these
lines, he also learns that Olaf, his beloved son, has stowed away on *The Indian
Girl*. In that very moment, the procession arrives, and Rummel draws the
curtains aside: "Away with the curtains! . . . [*The curtains are drawn aside from
windows and door. One sees the whole street illuminated. On the house opposite is
a big banner reading: 'Long live Karsten Bernick, pillar of our society!'*]" (8: 135).
Bernick's reaction is instant: "Away with all this! I do not want to see it! Put it
out! Put it out!" (8: 135). In a double refusal of theater, Bernick neither wishes
to go onstage nor to watch the illuminated spectacle in front of him.

The Bernicks' garden room, then, works as a two-way stage. First of all,
when the curtains are drawn aside, the crowd is to gaze in at the happy
tableau. At the same time, Bernick and the others in the garden room are
spectators of the brightly illuminated scene taking place outside the glass
windows. Several characters comment on the high turn-out, on the music,
flags, and the bright illumination in the street. "What a procession!" Rummel
exclaims (8: 138). This is a version of the grand spectacles that nineteenth-
century theater loved to present to its audiences, but which here is literally
seen through a glass. The audience sitting in the theater is here placed in a
double position: on the one hand, we witness the back stage preparations of

the tableau of the happy family. On the other, we see the street procession from the same vantage point as the characters onstage. Ibsen is here laying bare the workings of theater. That this is intended as a critique of Rummel's theatricality is beyond doubt, for, as Consul Bernick is about to point out, both the tableau and the procession are fake productions.

Even more important, however, is the ease with which both the members of Bernick's household *and* the inhabitants of the town are turned into willing actors. It is as if Ibsen wants to warn us that our lives can at any time be theatricalized, and that the place to realize this most fully is precisely the theater. Only minutes before his change of heart (how far does that transformation go?), Consul Bernick himself asks his sister and wife to change for the performance: "Listen, Martha, you'd better go and dress up a bit. And tell Betty to do the same. I don't want anything grand, of course, just something that looks nice around the house. But hurry up." Lona Hessel instantly replies: "And a happy and excited face, Martha, make sure your eyes light up" (8: 129). Considering the fact that only minutes before Lona was comforting the poor Martha for the loss of the love of her life, we are surely to see this as an ironic commentary on Bernick's stage-management.

Bernick's speech to the crowd sounds at once like a farewell to the theatricality produced by the unlivable ideals of idealism, and like a manifesto for a new age with a new aesthetics and a new sense of ethics: "But first my fellow citizens must know me through and through. Then let each one of you examine yourself, and then let it be resolved that from tonight we'll begin a new era. The old era, with its make-up, its hypocrisy and its hollowness, its sham propriety and its pitiful calculations, is to be as a museum for us, open for our instruction" (8: 143–4). That Ibsen is still preoccupied with historical transition, is obvious. The "old era" denounced by Bernick is described in terms that apply perfectly to theater. The reference to makeup or greasepaint (*sminke*) is particularly revealing, but so is every one of the following four nouns, each one of which could describe a particularly bad—a particularly theatrical—melodrama.

In *Pillars of Society*, then, Ibsen practically bends over backwards to make sure we realize that we are seeing theater. At the same time, however, he uses the stage and its resources (particularly the set) to expose the concealments of theatricality. Bernick says that his fellow citizens need to know him. As long as he has been playing theater for them, he has made that impossible. But the play also reveals that he is a man who has never tried to find out who his wife is ("I have never really seen you all these years, I think" (8: 147).) His blindness to the pain of others is an inevitable consequence of his self-theatricalization as a "pillar of society". It is difficult to imagine a stronger indictment of men in power.

Lona Hessel instantly generalizes Bernick's realization: "I certainly believe that; your society is made up of bachelors' souls; you don't see women" (8: 147). In these lines, *Pillars of Society* breaks new ground. A new thought with immense political potential emerges here: namely, that men's self-theatricalization prevents them from knowing, or even wanting to know, the women they are with. Insofar as women here emerge as individuals, and as individuals who demand to be seen, known, and understood, and who are not at all inclined to sacrifice themselves for love, *Pillars of Society* gives voice to a pointed critique of the idealist ideal of the self-sacrificing pure woman. Lona Hessel could never have found a place in an idealist play, other than as a target of the most savage mockery.

By turning to the situation of women in modernity, by taking a special interest in the fate of women in a society of self-theatricalizing men, Ibsen completes his modern breakthrough. In the next ten years Ibsen's modernism will produce a series of works that rank among the best in the Western tradition. It is to these revolutionary plays I now turn.

Part III

Ibsen's Modernism
Love in an Age of Skepticism

7

<hr/>

"First and Foremost a Human Being"
Idealism, Theater, and Gender in *A Doll's House*

Introduction

A Doll's House is the first full-blown example of Ibsen's modernism. It contains a devastating critique of idealism entwined with a turn to the everyday, a celebration of theater combined with a fierce analysis of everyday theatricality (*A Doll's House* is teeming with metatheatrical elements), and a preoccupation with the conditions of love in modernity. In *A Doll's House*, Ibsen mobilizes all these features in a contemporary setting, and in relation to a fundamentally modern theme: namely, the situation of women in the family and society.[1] The result is a play that calls for a radical transformation (*forvandling*), not just, or not even primarily, of laws and institutions, but of human beings and their ideas of love.

This chapter explores three major themes: idealism, theater, and gender. Although idealist aesthetic norms were a primary concern for many of the play's first critics, contemporary literary scholars have barely raised the subject.[2] Idealist responses to *A Doll's House* were *embattled* in a way that idealist responses to *Love's Comedy* and *Emperor and Galilean* were not. Defenders of Ibsen's realism nevertheless come across as less sophisticated than their idealist opponents. In fact, by propagating the idea that *A Doll's House* was to be understood as a "slice of life", Ibsen's first admirers entirely missed his protheatricalism, his metatheatrical insistence that what we are seeing is *theater*. Around 1880, then, neither Ibsen's enemies nor his friends were in a position truly to grasp the scope of his aesthetic achievement.

But idealism was not just an important element in the reception of *A Doll's House*. It is also embedded in the play, most strikingly in the character of Torvald Helmer, a card-carrying idealist aesthete if ever there was one.

Moreover, Helmer's idealism and Nora's unthinking echoing of it make them theatricalize both themselves and each other, most strikingly by taking themselves to be starring in various idealist scenarios of female sacrifice and male rescue.

Ibsen's critique of idealism is the condition of possibility for his revolutionary analysis of gender in modernity. In this respect, the key line of the play is Nora's claim to be "first and foremost a human being". Nora's struggle for recognition as a human being is rightly considered an exemplary case of women's struggle for political and social rights.[3] But Nora claims her humanity only after explicitly rejecting two other identities: namely, "doll" and "wife and mother". In order to show what these refusals mean, I first consider the signification of the figure of the doll. "The human body is the best picture of the human soul," Wittgenstein writes.[4] What happens if we take Nora's body dancing the tarantella to be a picture of her soul? Starting from this question, I show that the tarantella scene is revolutionary both in its handling of theater and theatricality and in its understanding of different ways of looking at a performing woman's body.

I read Nora's refusal to define herself as a wife and mother as a rejection of Hegel's theory of women's role in the family and society. Read in this light, *A Doll's House* becomes an astoundingly radical play about women's historical transition from being generic family members (wife, sister, daughter, mother) to becoming individuals (Nora, Rebecca, Ellida, Hedda).

I do not mean to say that Ibsen set out to illustrate Hegel. (No claim would have annoyed him more.) I mean, rather, that Hegel happens to be the great theorist of the traditional, patriarchal, and sexist family structure that *A Doll's House* sets out to investigate. There is no need to posit any knowledge on Ibsen's part of Hegel's theory of women and the family: we only need to assume that Ibsen saw the situation of women in the family at least as clearly as Hegel did, and that, unlike Hegel, he saw it as something that would have to change if women were to have a chance of the pursuit of happiness in modern society.[5] If, as Rita Felski has claimed, modernist literature represents women as outside history and, in particular, as outside the modern, then Ibsen's modernism is a glorious exception, not just because *A Doll's House* is about Nora's painful entrance into modernity, but because all his modern plays contain women who are as radically engaged in the problems of modern life as the men who surround them.[6]

Idealist and Realist Responses to *A Doll's House*

A Doll's House was published on 4 December 1879 in Copenhagen. The first performance took place at the Royal Theatre in Copenhagen on 21 December 1879, with Betty Hennings as Nora. In 1873, Arne Garborg's idealist reading of *Emperor and Galilean* was written in a situation in which alternative aesthetic points of view were unavailable. Six years later, this had changed. Norwegian and Danish reviews of the book and the world premiere show that *A Doll's House* was received in a cultural moment when the war between idealists and realists was already raging.

On 9 and 10 January 1880, *Aftenbladet* in Kristiania published two articles on *A Doll's House*, which come across as exemplary instances of belated and embattled idealism. The author was Fredrik Petersen (1839–1903), a professor of theology at the University of Kristiania, and thus a typical representative of the alliance between idealist aesthetics, established religion, and conservative social views that characterized the opponents of Ibsen in the 1880s and 1890s. It is no coincidence that the character of Pastor Manders in *Ghosts* personifies precisely this social and political constellation.

Explicitly fusing Christianity and idealist aesthetics, Petersen's analysis was based on the idea that "Society needs divine ideality, needs faith in the idea of the good and the beautiful to survive."[7] The glaring flaw of *A Doll's House*, therefore, was the absence of reconciliation: "And yet one does not leave this play in the uplifted mood which already in the time of the Greeks was regarded as an absolute requirement for any artistic or poetic work. Having seen something profoundly ugly (*noget saare Uskjønt*) we are left only with a distressing (*pinlig*) feeling, which is the inevitable consequence when there is no reconciliation to demonstrate the ultimate victory of the ideal."[8] According to Petersen, the defining characteristic of realism in general was the refusal of reconciliation and uplift.

Why was the sense of uplift so important to idealist critics?[9] Starting from the premise that art is a "a child of humankind's creative capacity in its highest ideality, the aspect in which human beings are most like God", Petersen insists that anything that is to be called a work of art has to bear the "creative, idealizing stamp of the human spirit". Pointedly contrasting such idealization to "mere reproduction", he expresses himself in terms that recall Schiller, but also the discussion between George Sand and Balzac: "The ideality of art is beauty, because beauty is the natural external expression of the good. Even when art represents ugliness (*det Uskjønne*), it is not real but idealized ugliness." Reconciliation enables the reader and spectator to leave the work with "ideality awakened in his soul", and this, precisely, is what triggers the sense of uplift. Art is thus crucially important in the world because it empowers and ennobles us.

According to Petersen, realism is the antithesis of true art. By deliberately withholding reconciliation, realism demonstrates that it has lost all faith in the "divine ideality's power in life". In this way, realism is aligned with skepticism and secularism. This is significant, for the culture war that broke out over the Scandinavian "modern breakthrough" was articulated as a battle between Christian idealists and freethinking realists, led by the Jewish Georg Brandes.

Although he was the most interesting and most articulate, Petersen was not the only idealist responding to *A Doll's House*. Other critics, too, lamented the play's lack of reconciliation. In Denmark, M. V. Brun, reviewing the play in *Folkets Avis* on 24 December 1879, even claimed that the absence of reconciliation between the spouses was entirely unnatural, running against common psychological sense. Once Nora understood that she had committed a crime, the natural thing for her to do would be to "throw herself into her husband's arms and say: 'I have erred, but I have erred without knowing it, and out of love for you, save me!' and her husband would then have forgiven and saved her."[10] Throughout the play, Brun writes, the spectator still hopes that Nora will confess, and that her confession will be followed by reconciliation. The audience is therefore completely unprepared for the "revolting break-up" in the third act, which he considers "hideous". Indeed, *A Doll's House* exhibits "such screaming dissonances that no beautiful harmony capable of resolving them exists".

Socialists and radicals, on the other hand, praised the play without reservations, but also without aesthetic sophistication. In the Danish newspaper *Social-Demokraten*, the owner of the signature "I-n" treated the play as a completely realistic, political treatise: "Our own life, our own everyday life has here been placed on stage and condemned! We have never in dramatic or poetic form seen a better, more powerful intervention in the question of women's liberation!"[11] In the radical Norwegian paper *Dagbladet* Erik Vullum used idealist terms to laud the play's aesthetic perfection (he speaks of its "clarity and artistic harmony" and uses beauty as his highest term of praise), a practice that he obviously considered entirely compatible with political praise for Ibsen's radical social thought.[12]

In January 1880, the feminist novelist Amalie Skram published a brilliant commentary on *A Doll's House* in *Dagbladet*. It is a tremendously insightful, sympathetic, and passionate defense of Nora's actions, as well as a clear-eyed registration of the play's radical challenge to the social order. Strikingly combining feminism and idealism, Skram completely identifies with Nora's idealist fantasies: "Like lightning an insight strikes in Nora's soul: too base, his soul cannot understand, let alone nourish, the kind of love that accepts all blame, yes, even offers up its life. [He rages] at the hypocrite, liar, criminal, yet the inner, essential truth is that she has risked everything to save his life."[13] Skram's conclusion practically repeats Schiller's idea that modern poets must either lament the absence of the ideal or glorify its presence: "Marriage is judged here. Its high and holy idea has fled away from earth. The poet can only expose the caricature that has been put in its place, or admonish us by pointing upward."[14]

Around 1880, then, the idealists still monopolized the concepts required for a serious discussion of art and aesthetics. Even in its belated, moralizing form, idealism had intellectual power. Petersen's review of *A Doll's House* gives voice to a highly articulate and sophisticated theory of art, derived from German idealism and infused with a good portion of Lutheran Christianity. (This is precisely the form of idealism expressed by Wirsén, the Swedish literary critic who was the power behind the early Nobel Prizes.)

Cultural modernizers, on the other hand, either treated art as if it were life or simply combined idealist aesthetic concepts (the ideal, beauty, harmony) with radical politics. Insofar as they saw *A Doll's House* as an impressive political tract, a slice of life onstage, they did Ibsen a disservice, for their reactions helped to cement the impression that Ibsen's realism was nothing but the unself-conscious presentation of real life. Although the idealists did not yet know it, they were doomed to historical oblivion. Paradoxically, then, the victorious realists laid the foundations for the still widespread belief that Ibsen's contemporary plays are nothing but unself-conscious and boring realism. Both his opponents and supporters, moreover, completely missed the self-conscious and pro-theatrical use of theater in *A Doll's House*. In this respect, Ibsen's own practice far outstripped the aesthetic categories of his audience.

Late in his life, Ibsen always adamantly declared that he never wrote with politics or social philosophy in mind. Surely these claims should be understood as a reaction against the reductive and, as it were, overpoliticizing reception of his plays, which dominated the 1880s and the 1890s. The most famous instance of such a denial is his speech at the gala evening organized in his honor by Norsk Kvindesagsforening (the Norwegian Association for the Cause of Women) in 1898: "I have been more of a poet and less of a social philosopher than one generally appears inclined to believe. [I] must decline the honor consciously to have worked for the cause of women. I am not even quite clear what the cause of women really is. For me it has appeared to be the cause of human beings. . . . My task has been to *portray human beings*" (15: 417).

Helmer's Sense of Beauty

Throughout *A Doll's House* Torvald Helmer is represented as an aesthetic idealist. I am not the first to notice this. In 1880, the great Danish writer Herman Bang criticized Emil Poulsen, the actor who played Helmer in the first production, for making his character insufficiently refined. Helmer, Bang writes, quoting most of the relevant passages in support, is a "completely aesthetic nature", in fact, an "aesthetically inclined egoist".[15] This is a fine perception: Helmer is an egoist, and a rather brutal and petty-minded one, too. Astute contemporary readers and theatergoers were perfectly capable of noticing the veiled critique of idealism produced by this juxtaposition of idealism and egoism. We should note, however, that Bang never calls Helmer an idealist; the word he uses is always "aesthete".[16] This seems to me to confirm what the newspaper reception of *A Doll's House* also shows: namely, that in 1880, there was still only one way to be an aesthete, and that was the idealist way. To be a realist was to be radical, political, committed: another register of experience altogether.

Torvald Helmer, then, prides himself on his sense of beauty. "Nobody has such a refined taste as you," Nora says to him (8: 306). He enjoys seeing Nora beautifully dressed, but he "can't stand seeing tailoring" (8: 314). He prefers women to embroider, for knitting "can never be anything but ugly (*uskønt*)" (8: 344). In these lines, Helmer also manifests his social class: knitting is ugly because it is useful, embroidery is beautiful because it is a pastime for leisured ladies. Helmer's sense of beauty, moreover, admits no separation between ethics and aesthetics. He has never wanted to "deal with business matters that are not fine and pretty (*smukke*)" (8: 280–1). His love for the good and the beautiful makes him despise people like Krogstad who have sinned against the ideal. Blighted by guilt and crime, they are doomed to bring the pestilential infection of lies and hypocrisy into their own families, and the result is ugliness:

HELMER. Just think how such a guilt-ridden human being must lie and pretend and be a hypocrite to all and sundry, how he must wear a mask even with his closest family, yes, even with his own wife and his own children. And the children, Nora, that's just the most horrible thing.
NORA. Why?

HELMER. Because such a stinking circle of lies brings infection and bacteria into the life of a whole home. Every breath that the children take in such a house is filled with the germs of something ugly.

(8: 307)

Sickness, pollution, infection, pestilence: these are the motifs that regularly turned up in idealist attacks on Ibsen's later plays. Helmer also draws on idealism's characteristically antitheatrical language: hypocrisy, pretense, mask. "No play-acting!", Helmer says to Nora as she is on her way to drown herself (8: 351). Then he calls her a hypocrite, a liar, and a criminal (see 8: 352).

The macaroons are forbidden in the name of beauty too, for Helmer is worried that Nora will destroy her pretty teeth. Nora therefore eats them only in the presence of Dr Rank or when she is alone. At one moment, when she is alone with Dr Rank, she munches some forbidden macaroons, and then announces that she is dying to take in her mouth some "ugly" swearwords. Given Helmer's incessant harping on beauty, it is no wonder that the swearwords Nora wants to say are "Død og pine" ("Death and pain"), and that she says them to Dr Rank (8: 293).

Helmer's refinement cannot deal with death and pain. Dr Rank makes it perfectly clear that Helmer is unwanted at the deathbed of his best friend: "Helmer, with his refined nature, has an intense sense of disgust for everything that is hideous. I don't want him in my sick room—," Dr Rank says when he tells Nora that he will die within a month (8: 320). No wonder, then, that Helmer's first reaction to the news of Rank's impending death is purely aesthetic: "With his suffering and his loneliness, he provided as it were a cloudy background to our sunlit happiness" (8: 274). Helmer speaks like a painter, or perhaps even like a painter of theater décor: all he can think of is surface effects. When prodded by Nora, Helmer is even capable of giving up sex at the thought of something ugly. When she questions whether they really should have sex just after learning about Rank's impending death, he acquiesces, for "something ugly has come between us; thoughts of death and decay. We must try to free ourselves from them" (8: 350).

For Helmer, beauty is freedom; freedom is beauty. Right at the beginning of Act 1 he warns Nora against borrowing money: "No debt! Never borrow! There is something unfree, and therefore also something ugly (*uskønt*) about a home founded on borrowing and debt" (8: 274). If Helmer had not thought of debt as ugly and unfree, he might not have objected to borrowing money for the trip to Italy.

Helmer's constant display of his sense of beauty, then, is responsible for what he calls the "bottomless hideousness" uncovered by Krogstad's letter (8: 352). His refined aesthetic sense does not prevent him from proposing that their life together should now be lived in the mode of theater: "— And in so far as you and I are concerned, it has to look as if everything between us remains just as it was. But of course only before the eyes of the world" (8: 353). The irony is that just when Nora is finally ready to "take off the masquerade costume", Helmer is more than willing to put it on (8: 355).

Idealism and Theatricality: Melodramas of Sacrifice and Rescue

Both Nora and Helmer spend most of the play theatricalizing themselves by acting out their own clichéd idealist scripts. Nora's fantasies are variations on the idealist figure of the noble and pure woman who sacrifices all for love. First she casts herself as a pure and selfless heroine who has saved her husband's life. Her secret is the source of her identity, the foundation of her sense of worth, and makes it easy for her to act the part of Helmer's chirping songbird and playful squirrel. That she has aestheticized her secret—turned it into a thing of beauty—is also clear, for when Krogstad threatens to reveal their dealings to Helmer, Nora replies, on the point of tears: "This secret, which is my joy and my pride, he is to learn about it in such an ugly and coarse way,—and learn it from *you*" (8: 300).

When she realizes that her secret in fact is a crime, she feels besmirched by ugliness. To save her sense of self-worth, she mobilizes the plainly melodramatic fantasy of *det vidunderlige* (literally: the wonderful thing; often translated, somewhat too religiously, as "the miracle", or—better—as "something glorious"). Nora imagines that once Helmer learns about her crime, he will generously and heroically offer to rescue her by sacrificing himself. In an even higher and nobler spirit of self-sacrifice, she will refuse his sacrifice and drown herself rather than let him sully his honor for her sake. This is debased idealism, a melodramatic scenario of the kind that routinely played in nineteenth-century boulevard theaters.

That the figure of the pure and self-sacrificing woman had become no more than a well-worn cliché by the time Ibsen wrote *A Doll's House* is made clear in Krogstad's suspicious reaction to Mrs Linde's offer of marriage: "I don't believe in this. It is nothing but a high-strung woman's sense of nobility, driving her to sacrifice herself" (8: 340). Insofar as Mrs Linde and Krogstad are counterpoints to Nora and Helmer, it is not least because they refuse to build their marriage on theatrical clichés.

Helmer, of course, is also fantasizing. First of all, he thinks of himself as extremely manly, even heroic. Nora is perfectly aware of this: "Torvald with his masculine pride,—how embarrassing and humiliating would it not be for him to know that he owed me anything" (8: 287). Helmer's sense of masculinity depends on Nora's performances of helpless, childlike femininity: "I wouldn't be a man, if just this feminine helplessness did not make you twice as attractive in my eyes" (8: 354). As clichéd and theatrical as Nora's, his fantasies are more frankly sexual, although they represent sexuality in idealist terms (probably to avoid acknowledging what the idealists considered to be mere animal lust). After the masqued ball, for example, Helmer reveals that he has a fantasy about ravishing his virginal child-woman—but only after the wedding: "—[I] imagine . . . that you are my young bride, that we have just come from the wedding, that I am bringing you into my house for the first time,—that for the first time I am alone with you,—completely alone with your young, trembling, delightful beauty!" (8: 346).

Helmer also thinks of himself as the dashing hero coming to the rescue of the pure woman: "You know what, Nora,—often I wish that some imminent danger threatened you, so that I could risk life and blood, everything, everything for your sake" (8: 350). When Nora takes him literally, and urges him to read his letters, the result is a savagely ironic demolition of idealist stage conventions, and a reminder that people who claim to live by idealist clichés are liable to theatricalize themselves and others.

The most destructive expression of Helmer's fantasies comes just as he has read Krogstad's second letter, realizes that he is saved, and suddenly becomes all forgiveness. When Nora says she will "take off her masquerade costume", Helmer completely mishears her tone, and launches into a horrendously self-aggrandizing monologue. The stage directions indicate that he is supposed to speak through the open door, with Nora offstage, changing her clothes. By placing Helmer alone onstage, Ibsen stresses the distancing, estranging effect of his self-theatricalization: "Oh, you don't know a real man's heart, Nora. For a man there is something indescribably sweet and satisfying in knowing that he has forgiven his wife,—that he truly has forgiven her with his whole heart. It is as if she has doubly become his property; as if he has brought her into the world again; as if she has become his wife and his child as well. This is what you will be for me from now on, you little bewildered, helpless creature" (8: 355). This discourse on forgiveness is surely what Gregers Werle had in mind when he urged Hjalmar Ekdal nobly to forgive Gina. This is the moment where the idealist reconciliation ought to be, and Ibsen undermines it completely by having Nora coming back onstage in her *hverdagskjole* (everyday dress).

At this point, with Nora in her everyday dress and Helmer still in his evening clothes, the famous conversation that completely destroyed idealist expectations begins. Ibsen's masterly exploration of the relationship between theatricality, melodrama, and debased idealism here reaches its logical end and high point, for Nora cuts straight to the chase. Requesting—or rather, ordering—Helmer to sit down to talk, she says:

NORA. Sit down. This will take a long time. I have a lot to talk to you about.
HELMER [*sits at the table directly opposite her*]. You make me anxious, Nora. And I don't understand you.
NORA. No, that's just it. You don't understand me. And I have never understood you either—until tonight.

(8: 356)

There is a clear acknowledgment here that both Nora and Helmer have been blinded by their self-theatricalizing fantasies. Without letting Helmer off the hook, Nora acknowledges that she has contributed to this outcome: "I have earned my living by doing tricks for you, Torvald. But you wanted it that way" (8: 357).

Nora's recognition of her own participation in their games of concealment should make us pause. So far, I have written about Nora's and Helmer's theatricalization of themselves and each other in a way that might give rise to the idea that the two of them are, as it were, pure performers. But their fantasies reveal them as much as they conceal them. Because they are fantasies of rescuing the other, of doing something heroic for the sake of love, they reveal that Nora and Helmer love each other as well as they can. They just cannot do any better. Had they known what they were doing when they performed their masquerades, they would have stopped doing it.[17] By showing us their theatrical marriage, Ibsen did not mean to turn these two decent people into villains, but to make us think about the way we theatricalize ourselves and others in everyday life.

If to grow up is to choose finitude, as Cavell puts it, then it is clear that neither Nora nor Helmer have been grown-ups until this point.[18] They have, rather, been like children playing house together. In the final conversation, their performances of adult masculinity and femininity come across as mere impersonations. But perhaps they are not children, or not just children, but dolls: after all, the play in which they appear is called *A Doll's House*.[19]

The doll as a Literary and Philosophical Figure: Corinne and Nora

We have arrived, then, at the figure of the doll. When Nora tries to explain her experience of life and marriage, this is the figure she uses to describe her past self. Her father, she says "called me his doll-child and played with me the way I played with my dolls" (8: 357). And Helmer has done the same thing: "But our home has been nothing but a play-house. Here I have been your doll-wife, just as at home I was Papa's doll-child" (8: 358).[20] She herself has carried on the tradition: "And the children, in turn, have been my dolls" (8: 358). Nora leaves, then, because she no longer wants anything to do with this doll-life.

The figure of the doll is the most important metaphor in *A Doll's House*. In philosophy, the living doll—the doll that moves, that gives the impression of being alive—has been used as a figure for the problem of other minds ever since René Descartes looked out of his third floor window one evening in 1641 and saw people walking around in the street below. Or did he? His moment of vertigo arose when he realized that he could not *with certainty* say that he was watching real human beings. All he could really be sure of seeing were "hats and cloaks that might cover artificial machines, whose motions might be determined by springs".[21] In this sentence the phrase "artificial machines, whose motions might be determined by springs" translates a single Latin word, namely *automata*.[22]

The imagery of automata, robots, dolls—and in modern science fiction aliens—gives voice to a fundamental philosophical question: how do I know that another human being is another human being? That he or she thinks and feels as a human being? How can I tell the difference between the human and the non-human, between life and death?[23] For this reason, the doll easily becomes a figure of horror: in European literature the image of the doll-woman is often found in the borderlands between Gothic horror and romanticism. In E. T. A. Hoffmann's horror story "The Sandman" (1817), the writer Nathanael rejects his real-life fiancée, Clara, for the doll Olympia, who can only nod and say "Oh! Oh!"[24] While still part of a horror story, Hoffmann's doll also serves to criticize some men's preference for subservient women. In Ibsen's own works, the uncanny character of Irene in *When We Dead Awaken*, who is half woman, half statue, also evokes the Gothic and the uncanny. In recent film history, the original *Stepford Wives* articulates the same preoccupation with the horror and uncanniness of the woman-doll, in ways that can't fail to recall *A Doll's House*.[25]

In Madame de Staël's works, the figure of the doll, without Gothic over-tones, is also used to criticize sexist attitudes towards women. In her short satirical play *Le Mannequin* (1811), a German painter called, of all things, Frédéric Hoffmann, helps his beloved Sophie de la Morlière to trick the stupid French count d'Erville, an enemy of "l'esprit des femmes" ("the intel-lect of women"), into preferring a paper doll to a real woman. In the key scene, the count falls in love with the doll precisely because she doesn't say a word. More important to *A Doll's House*, however, is Madame de Staël's use of the figure of the doll in *Corinne, or Italy*, where it certainly has affinities to *A Doll's House*. During a long stay in England, Corinne is forced to remain silent in society just because she is a woman, and complains that she could just as well have been a "doll slightly perfected by mechanics" (*une poupée légèrement perfectionnée par la mécanique*).[26] When Corinne does speak (or dance or sing), the situation does not improve, for then she is accused of being theatrical.[27]

Whether Corinne is forcibly silenced or accused of being theatrical, she is reduced to her body. In the first case she is entombed in it; in the second, it is turned into a theatrical spectacle. Either way, she is not listened to, her words are not heard, and her humanity—what the romantics would have called her soul—remains unacknowledged. Corinne, then, is caught in a sexist dilemma in which she is either theatricalized or forcibly silenced, and in both cases, reduced to a thing. A woman in such a position will struggle to signify her existence, her humanity. This is true for Corinne, but it is true for Nora, too, for she too has to try to assert her existence by finding a voice, by launching into what Cavell elsewhere calls her "cogito performance", an aria-like expression of her soul intended to proclaim, declaim, declare her existence.[28] Losing her voice, Corinne dies misunderstood and unacknowledged.[29] Ibsen's Nora, however, finds her voice, and claims her own humanity: "I believe that I too am first and foremost a human being, just as much as you" (8: 359).

"The human body is the best picture of the human soul": Nora's Tarantella

The tarantella scene in Act 2 is something like Nora's bodily cogito perform-ance: a performance in which she demonstrates her humanity (as opposed to her "dollness") not through song, but through dance. The tarantella scene is melodramatic in all the usual meanings of the word. It provides music and dance, and it is staged in order to postpone the discovery of a secret, a discovery that Nora believes will lead to her death. Nora, moreover, dances her tarantella motivated by fear and anxiety, and gives a performance that is explicitly said to be violent or vehement (*voldsom*) (8: 334).

The exaggerated expressivity of melodrama, Cavell writes, can be understood as a reaction to the fear of the "extreme states of voicelessness" that can overcome us once we start wondering whether we can ever manage to make others recognize and acknowledge our humanity.[30] If this is right, then the melodramatic obsession with states of terror, of suffocation, of forced expression, expresses fear of human isolation, of being reduced to a thing, of death. Such states are at once bodily and quintessentially theatrical, both in the sense that they belong to the traditional repertoire of the stage, and in the sense that anyone exhibiting them will be suspected of overacting, of expressing more than they feel.

This is precisely the reaction that many actresses and directors have had to Nora's tarantella. They have wished to tone down the sheer theatricality of the scene, in the name of realism and in an effort to preserve Nora's dignity. Eleanora Duse was famous for hardly dancing the tarantella at all. Even Elizabeth Robins, the actress who pioneered many of Ibsen's plays in Britain, thought the tarantella was "too stagey", Alisa Solomon writes.[31] But theater and theatricality are central concerns of *A Doll's House*, and if we are to understand Nora's tarantella, we need to see that it is, among other things, an invitation to reflect on the nature of theater. As Solomon brilliantly puts it, the tarantella is "not a *concession* to the old effect-hunting, [but] an *appropriation* of it".[32]

Given all the melodramatic elements of the tarantella, it would be easy to conclude that it simply shows Nora theatricalizing her own body, that she deliberately turns herself into a spectacle in order to divert Helmer's attention from the mailbox, thus acquiescing in her own status as a doll. Although this is surely Nora's main motivation for insisting on rehearsing her tarantella right away, the scene itself exceeds such a limited reading. Feverish with fear, Nora dances extremely fast and violently. This could also be a part of her act, for she wants to persuade Helmer that he needs to instruct her instead of reading his mail. But the stage directions tell us more: "Rank sits down at the piano and plays. Nora dances with increasing wildness. Helmer stands over by the stove regularly addressing instructions to her during the dance; she does not appear to hear him; her hair comes loose and falls over her shoulders, she does not notice, but continues to dance. *Mrs. Linde* enters" (8: 334). We could, of course, link Nora's dancing to Freud's hysteria, to the woman's body signifying the distress her voice cannot speak.[33] But that would be to deprive Nora of agency by turning her into a medical case. It may be better simply to say that Nora's tarantella is a graphic representation of a woman's struggle to make her existence *heard*, to make it *count* (this is what I assume Cavell means by "cogito performance").

During the performance Nora's hair comes undone. Ibsen, I am sure, here deliberately invokes the theatrical convention known as "back hair", which in nineteenth-century melodrama handbooks signifies the "onset of madness".[34] As her hair comes down, Nora no longer listens to Helmer's instructions. Now she dances as if in a trance, as in the grip of madness, as if she genuinely *is* the body Helmer reduces her to. But if Nora is her body and nothing else, then the tarantella would be pornographic, a mere display of a sexualized body. What happens to our understanding of the tarantella if, instead of agreeing with Helmer, we invoke Wittgenstein and say that in this moment, Nora's body is the best picture of her soul?

The first question is, what does this mean? What makes Wittgenstein's "The human body is the best picture of the human soul" pertinent to *A Doll's House*? The sentence appears in section iv of the second half of *Philosophical Investigations*, a section that begins in this way:

"I believe that he is suffering."—Do I also *believe* that he isn't an automaton?

It would go against the grain to use the word in both connexions.

   (Or is it like this: I believe that he is suffering, but am certain that he is not an automaton? Nonsense!)[35]

Here the question of the suffering of others is linked to the picture of the automaton (I take this to be a deliberate invocation of Descartes's skepticism). At stake, then, is the question of the difference between dolls (automata) and human beings. This is reinforced by the next few lines: "Suppose I say of a friend: 'He isn't an automaton'.—What information is conveyed by this, and to whom would it be information? To a *human being* who meets him in ordinary circumstances?"[36] If I imagine a situation in which I would say "He isn't an automaton" to a friend (A) about another friend (B), I find that I would say it if I were trying to tell A to stop treating B as she has been doing, perhaps because I think that A has been cruel to B, that she has behaved as if she did not think that B, too, has feelings. That is what the "soul" means in these passages: the idea of an inner life, of (unexpressed) pain and suffering (but—I hope—joy, too).

To grasp what Wittgenstein is getting at here, it is necessary to understand the skeptical picture of the relationship between body and soul. For one kind of skeptic—let us call her the romantic kind—the body hides the soul. Because it is (literally) the incarnation of human finitude (separation and death), the romantic thinks of the body as an obstacle, as that which prevents us from knowing other human beings. True human communication, the romantic believes, must overcome finitude; thus we get fantasies of souls commingling, of perfect communication without words, and of twin souls destined for each other from all eternity. (These are themes that are particularly intense in Ibsen's *Rosmersholm*, as we shall see in Chapter 9.)

Another kind of skeptic—let us call her the postmodern kind—may impatiently reject all talk of souls as a merely metaphysical construct; she prefers to picture the body as a surface, an object, or even as materiality as such. Considered as pure materiality, the body is neither the expression nor the embodiment of an interiority. To think of the body as a surface is to theatricalize it: whatever that body does or says will be perceived as a performance, not an expression. To think of it as a thing or as pure materiality is to de-soul it, to render it inhuman. While the romantic will deny finitude by rising to high idealist heaven, the postmodern skeptic will deny human interiority ("the subject", "agency", "freedom") altogether.[37]

Wittgenstein's "The human body is the best picture of the human soul" is meant as an *alternative* to such skeptical positions. It is meant to remind us that skepticism ends up wanting either to escape the body or to obliterate the soul. The difference between a "doll perfected by mechanics" and a human being is that the former *is* a machine, while the second has an inner life.

Dancing the tarantella, Nora's body expresses the state of her soul. Nothing could be more authentic. At the same time, however, her body is theatricalized, by herself (her performance is her own strategy), and even more so, perhaps, by the men watching her. For the tarantella scene does not simply show Nora dancing; it also stages two different ways of looking at her dance. First there are the two men. They watch her, I surmise, pretty much in the theatricalized, quasi-pornographic mode. For them, Nora's dance is a display of her body; their gaze de-souls her, and turns her into a "mechanical doll". But as Nora dances, her friend Mrs Linde, who is privy to Nora's secret, also enters the room:

MRS. LINDE [*stands tongue tied by the door*]. Ah—!
NORA [*still dancing*]. Watch the fun (*løjer*), Kristine.
HELMER. But dearest, best Nora, you are dancing as if your life were at stake.
NORA. But it is!
HELMER. Rank, stop it. This is pure madness. Stop it, I say. [*Rank stops playing and Nora suddenly stops.*]

(8: 334)

Nora cries out to Mrs Linde that she should *watch* her. In Norwegian the phrase is "Her ser du løjer, Kristine", which literally translates as "Here you see fun, Kristine". In a nineteenth-century Danish dictionary, *løjer* is defined as "something that is fun, that entertains and provokes laughter, something said or done in jest, without serious intentions". A traditional Norwegian dictionary defines it as "pranks; jest; entertainment; fun; noisy commotion".[38] The word describes what Helmer and Rank think they are seeing. But Nora tells Mrs Linde to watch, look at, *see*, the fun going on: what Kristine is to see is not just Nora, but the relationship between Nora's performance and the men's gaze.

Mrs Linde sees Nora's pain; she also sees that the men do not. They see only Nora's wild body, which they theatricalize in the very moment in which it is most genuinely expressive. The point is stressed by Ibsen, for after the tarantella, Dr Rank asks Helmer, privately, "There wouldn't be anything—anything like that on the way?", which I take as a reference to pregnancy—that is, an attempt to reduce her dance to a mere effect of hormonal changes (8: 335). Helmer replies that it's just "this childish anxiety I told you about" (8: 335). Refusing to consider Nora's bodily self-expression as an expression of her soul (her will, intentions, problems), both men reduce it to a matter of hormones, or the unfounded worries of a child. In either case, Nora is seen as someone who is not responsible for her actions. (Paradoxically, perhaps, the only man in this play who treats Nora as a fully thinking human being is Krogstad, the man who taught her that they were equal in the eyes of the law.)

This scene, then, invites the audience to see Nora both as she is seen by Helmer and Dr Rank, and as she is seen by Mrs Linde. While the former theatricalize her, the latter sees her as a soul in pain. But the scene does not tell us to choose between these perspectives. If we try, we find that either option entails a loss. Do we prefer a theater of authenticity and sincerity? Do we believe that realism is such a theater? Then we may be forgetting that even the most intense expressions of the body provide no certain way of telling authenticity from theatricality, truth from performance. Do we prefer a theatrical theater, self-consciously performing and performative? If so, we may make ourselves deaf to the pain and distress of others by theatricalizing it. If I were asked whether I would call Nora's tarantella theatrical or absorbed, I would not quite know what to say. Both? Neither the one nor the other? Here Ibsen moves beyond the historical frame established by Diderot.

Ibsen's double perspective, his awareness of the impossibility of either choosing or not choosing between theatricality and authenticity, stands at the center of Ibsen's modernism. It is the reason why his theater is so extraordinarily rich in depth and perspective. In Nora's tarantella, then, Ibsen's modernism is fully realized. Here Ibsen asks us to consider that even the most theatrical performance may at the very same time be a genuine expression of the human soul. (But it may not: there is no way of knowing this in advance.)

But there is more. The striking theatricality of the tarantella—the fact that it is such an obvious theatrical show-stopper—reminds us that we are in a theater. Ibsen's modernism is based on the sense that we need theater—I mean the actual art form—to reveal to us the games of concealment and theatricalization in which we inevitably engage in everyday life. I do not base this claim only on Nora's dancing. By placing two kinds of spectator onstage during the tarantella, Ibsen tells us that only the audience is capable of seeing the whole picture: seeing both the temptation to theatricalize others and the possibility of understanding and acknowledging Nora's suffering. Admittedly, the audience's perspective is closer to Mrs Linde's than to the two men's, for Mrs Linde knows more than the men do about Nora's deal with Krogstad. The audience, however, knows even more than Mrs Linde about what is at stake for Nora, for it has just heard that she is determined to commit suicide when Helmer learns the truth:

KROGSTAD. Perhaps you intend to—
NORA. I have the courage now.
KROGSTAD. Oh, you don't frighten me. A fine, spoiled lady like you?
NORA. You'll see; you'll see.
KROGSTAD. Under the ice perhaps? Down in the cold, coal-black water? And then
   float up in the spring, ugly, unrecognizable, with all your hair fallen out—
NORA. You don't frighten me.

(8: 329)

This masterly exchange conveys to the audience what picture Nora has in her head as she dances the tarantella. (Both declare that they are not frightened by the other's words, but surely they are.) The vision of Nora's ugly dead body conveys all the death and pain that Helmer's sense of beauty tries to disavow, and explains why Nora can't help answering "But it is!" when Helmer says that she is dancing as if her life were at stake.

In *A Doll's House*, Nora has seven very brief soliloquies. These have often been read as indicators of Ibsen's still clumsy stagecraft, as unwitting or unwilling breaks in the realist illusion.[39] But, as we have seen in Chapter 6, already in 1869, in *The League of Youth*, Ibsen managed to write a whole play without a single monologue or aside. Had he wanted to, he could have avoided soliloquies in *A Doll's House* as well. Nora's moments alone onstage are there to show us what Nora is like when she is not under the gaze of the man for whom she constantly performs, but they are also there to remind us that we are in a theater.

Nora's fear and horror only appear when she is alone onstage.[40] At one point in Act 2, Helmer dismisses Nora's fears of Krogstad's revenge as "empty fantasies" (8: 319), and claims that he is "man enough to take it all on myself" (8: 318). Left alone, Nora is "wild with fear", whispering almost incoherently to herself: "He would be capable of doing it. He will do it. He'll do it, in spite of everything in the world.—No, never ever this! Anything but this! Rescue—! A way out –" (8: 319). These moments are almost Gothic. This is particularly true for the last one:

NORA [*wild-eyed, gropes about, grabs Helmer's domino, wraps it around herself; speaks in a fast, hoarse and staccato whisper*]. Never see him again. Never. Never. Never. [*Throws the shawl over her head*] Never see the children again either. Not them either. Never; never.—Oh, the icy black water. Oh, this bottomless—; this—. Oh, if only it were over.—He has it now; he is reading it now. Oh no, no; not yet. Torvald, goodbye to you and the children—[*She is about to rush out through the living-room; in that moment Helmer flings open his door and stands there with an open letter in his hand.*]

(8: 351)

In his 1879 review of the book, Erik Vullum wrote that this passage is "too beautiful not to be copied", and quoted it in full. Lear-like, Nora says "never" seven times, using the word "bottomless" to describe the black, icy water she is going to drown herself in; a few lines later, in a deliberate theatrical irony, Helmer uses the very same word to describe the "hideousness" of her crime (8: 352). The moment when Helmer stands there with the letter in his hand is a tableau, a moment of high melodrama that could have been a painting, perhaps even by Orchardson.

By having Nora behave most authentically in what, from a formal point of view, are her most theatrical scenes, Ibsen signals, again, the power of theater to convey the plight of a human being. Sitting in the audience, we are given a precious opportunity. If we will not acknowledge Nora's humanity, then perhaps nobody will.

Wife, Daughter, Mother: Hegel Rebuffed

Nora's claim that she is "first and foremost a human being" stands as an alternative to two refusals. We have already seen that she refuses to be a doll. But she also refuses to define herself as a wife and mother:

HELMER. It's outrageous. That you can betray your most sacred duties in this way.

NORA. What do you count as my most sacred duties?

HELMER. And I have to tell you! Are they not the duties to your husband and your children?

NORA. I have other equally sacred duties.

HELMER. No, you don't. What "duties" might you have in mind?

NORA. My duties to myself.

HELMER. You are first and foremost a wife and a mother.

NORA. I no longer believe that. I believe that I am first and foremost a human being, just as much as you,—or, at least, that I'll try to become one.

(8: 359)

In *Cities of Words*, Cavell gives a bravura reading of this passage, in which he discusses the moral grounds that Nora can claim for the notion that she has duties towards herself: "Where do these distinctions come from in her? These are the opening moments of this woman's claiming her right to exist, her standing in a moral world, which seems to take the form of having at the same time to repudiate that world."[41] On Cavell's reading, Nora is heading for exile (thus imitating Corinne's withdrawal from the world). It is an open question whether she will feel able to return to society, to her marriage, to Torvald, who after all loves her as well as he can. Cavell rightly notes that the "final scene is only harrowing if his live love for her is not denied. I have never seen it played so."[42] Neither have I.

Most critics have not taken this passage as seriously as Cavell. Joan Templeton has shown that many scholars insist that if Nora wants to be a human being, then she cannot remain a woman. Their motivation appears to be the thought that if *A Doll's House* is taken to be about women and therefore, inevitably, about feminism, then it would follow that it is not a truly universal, that is to say, truly great work of art. In support of this idea, such critics usually invoke Ibsen's 1898 speech opposing the cause of women to the cause of human beings.[43]

It strikes me as an overreading, to say the least, to try to turn Ibsen's refusal to reduce his writing to social philosophy to evidence that Ibsen never thought of Nora as a woman, or to a ground for a denial that Nora's troubles have to do with her situation as a woman in modernity. Such claims are fatally flawed, for they assume that a woman (but not a man) has to choose between considering herself a woman and a human being. This is a traditional sexist trap, and feminists should not make the mistake of entering into its faulty premise—for example, by arguing (but can this ever be an *argument*?) that Nora is a woman, and therefore not universal. Such critics refuse to admit that a woman can represent the universal (the human) just as much or just as well as a man. They are prisoners of a picture of sex or gender in which the woman, the female, the feminine is always the particular, always the relative, never the general, never the norm. That Ibsen himself never once opposes Nora's humanity to her femininity is evidence of his political radicalism as well as his greatness as a writer.

Nora, then, refuses to define herself as a wife and mother. This refusal comes just after she has asserted that she has duties towards herself, and just before she says that she is first and foremost a human being, thus aligning the meaning of "human being" with "individual" and opposing it to "wife and mother". To me, this irresistibly brings to mind Hegel's conservative theory of women's role in the family and marriage. To explain why, I need first to look at a key passage in the first act, which establishes Nora's own unquestioned commitment to the traditional understanding of women's place in the world. This is the exchange when Krogstad confronts Nora with her forgery and explains to her that she has committed a crime:

KROGSTAD. But didn't it occur to you that this was a fraud against me?
NORA. I couldn't take that into consideration. I didn't care at all about you. I couldn't stand you for all the cold-hearted difficulties you made, although you knew how dangerous the situation was for my husband.
KROGSTAD. Mrs. Helmer, you obviously have no clear notion of what you really are guilty of. But I can tell you that what I once did, which destroyed my whole status in society, was neither anything more nor anything worse.
NORA. You? Do you want me to believe that you ever did something brave to save your wife's life?
KROGSTAD. The laws don't ask about motives.
NORA. Then they must be very bad laws.
KROGSTAD. Bad or not,—if I present this paper in court, you will be sentenced according to those laws.
NORA. I really don't believe that. Has not a daughter the right to spare her old, dying father from anxiety and worry? Has not a wife the right to save her husband's life? I don't know the laws very well, but I am sure that somewhere in them it must say that such things are permitted. And you don't know about that, although you are a lawyer? You must be a bad legal scholar, Mr. Krogstad.

(8: 303)

Krogstad asserts that there is no difference between what he once did and what Nora did, and that the law and the community will treat them both as criminals. To Nora this is insulting: *she* acted as a good wife and daughter should, for the benefit of her family. Left alone onstage after Krogstad's departure, she says "But—?——No, but it's impossible! I did it for love"

(8: 304). To Nora, then, her forgery was noble and selfless, an example of the highest form of ethics she knows.

What makes the conversation between Krogstad and Nora so Hegelian is the conflict between the law of the community invoked by Krogstad and Nora's sense of her ethical obligations as a *wife* and *daughter*, rather than as an individual. According to Hegel, the family is not a collection of individuals, but a kind of organic unit: "one is present in it not as an independent person, but as a member," he writes in *Elements of the Philosophy of Right*.[44] Within the family, feeling is the dominant principle. For Hegel, words like "wife", "daughter", "sister", "mother" (and "husband", "son", "brother", "father") are, as it were, generic terms. They refer not to this or that individual person, but to a role or a function. Any woman can be Mrs Torvald Helmer, but only Nora is Nora.

This unit of generic members (father, mother, sister, brother, son, daughter) is headed by the father, the family's only connection to the state. Through his interaction with other men outside the family, the man gains concrete individuality: "Man therefore has his actual substantial life in the state, in learning, etc., and otherwise in work and struggle with the external world and with himself, so that it is only through his division that he fights his way to self-sufficient unity with himself," Hegel writes (§166). Men become citizens and participate in public life; women remain locked up inside the family unit.

For Hegel, women never really become self-conscious, concrete individuals (that is only possible if a person enters into a struggle with others through work and conflict outside the family). Enclosed in "family piety", women neither have nor care about having access to the universal (the state, the law) (§166). In family piety we find the "law of woman", Hegel writes; this law is "emotive and subjective", whereas the law of men is the "public law, the law of the state" (§166). The reference to "piety" reminds Hegel of *Antigone*, whom he extols in *The Phenomenology of Spirit* as an example of the highest kind of ethical behavior that a woman can ever reach. (The parallels between Nora and Antigone have often been explored.[45])

Women's exclusion from the universal has two consequences. First, Hegel thinks that women are not really capable of education. (Apparently, he always refused to let women attend his lectures.) Nor can they ever be artists and intellectuals, for their work requires understanding of the ideal—that is to say, of the concept, which in its very nature is universal. Their capricious, contingent, emotional defense of their family interests also makes them entirely unfit to govern:

Women may well be educated, but they are not made for the higher sciences, for philosophy and certain artistic productions which require a universal element. Women may have insights, taste, and delicacy, but they do not possess the ideal. The difference between man and woman is the difference between animal and plant; the animal is closer in character to man, the plant to woman, for the latter is a more peaceful [process of] unfolding whose principle is the more indeterminate unity of feeling. When women are in charge of government, the state is in danger, for their actions are based not on the demands of universality but on contingent inclination and opinion.

(§166)

Second, Hegel thinks that because women's position in the family makes them incapable of relating to the universal, they will always be unreliable and disloyal citizens of the state, an eternal fifth column of the community. The most famous formulation of this idea comes from *The Phenomenology of Spirit*:

Womankind—the everlasting irony [in the life] of the community—changes by intrigue the universal end of the government into a private end, transforms its universal activity into a work of some particular individual, and perverts the universal property of the state into a possession and ornament for the Family. Woman in this way turns to ridicule the earnest wisdom of mature age which, indifferent to purely private pleasures and enjoyments, as well as to playing an active part, only thinks of and cares for the universal.[46]

In her conversation with Krogstad, Nora is the perfect incarnation of the Hegelian woman. Flighty, irresponsible, caring only for her family's interests, she has no relationship to the law (the universal). At the end of the play, however, all this has changed. Nora has undergone a transformation. She began by being a Hegelian mother and daughter; she ends by discovering that she too has to become an individual, and that this can be done only if she relates to the society she lives in directly, and not indirectly through her husband: "I can't be satisfied anymore with what most people say and what's written in the books. I must think about them for myself and get clear about them" (8: 360). Although the law of her day made it impossible for a woman who left her home to keep her children, this is not why Nora leaves them. She makes a point of saying that she *chooses* to leave her children, precisely because she is not yet enough of an independent individual to educate them: "The way I am now, I can't be anything for them" (8: 363).[47]

What Ibsen's Nora wants that Hegelian theory denies her is expressed in her desire for an education. Education is the prerequisite for access to the universal—to participation in art, learning, and politics. As long as marriage and motherhood are incompatible with women's existence as individuals and citizens, Nora will have none of them. It follows that after *A Doll's House*, marriage must be transformed so as to be able to accommodate two free and equal individuals.

Freedom and equality, however, are not enough: Nora leaves above all because she no longer loves Helmer. Picking up the thread from *Pillars of Society*, *A Doll's House* insists that to love a woman, it is necessary to *see* her as the individual she is, not just as a wife and mother, or as a daughter and wife:

NORA. That's just it. You've never understood me.—A great wrong has been done to me, Torvald. First by Papa, and then by you.
HELMER. What! By us two—the two people who have loved you more than anyone else?
NORA [*shakes her head*]. You never loved me. You just thought it was fun to be in love with me.

(8: 357)

Nora, then, demands nothing short of a revolutionary reconsideration of the very meaning of love.

When Helmer asks what it would take for her to return to him, Nora answers that then *det vidunderligste*, the most wonderful thing (sometimes (mis)translated as the "miracle of miracles"), would have to happen: "That our life together could become a marriage" (8: 364). I take the difference between *samliv* ("life together") (what they have had) and *ægteskab* ("marriage") (which Nora now thinks of as an impossible dream) to be love. What will count as love between a man and a woman in a world where women too demand to be acknowledged as individuals? What will it take for two modern individuals to build a relationship (whether we call it marriage or, simply, a life together) based on freedom, equality, and love? These are questions Ibsen will return to. These are questions we all return to.

Losing Touch with the Everyday
Love and Language in *The Wild Duck*

A Doll's House shows how Nora finds a way out of her idealist and melo-dramatic scenarios towards the everyday, dramatized onstage by having her change into her everyday dress and launch into the deliberately non-spectacular conversation that ends the play. In *A Doll's House*, then, the everyday stands for the realm in which words in a conversation begin to make sense, where we can manage to see that language—or, more precisely, our use of language—expresses us.[1] In this chapter I shall show that *The Wild Duck* explores the connection between language and the everyday further than any other Ibsen play.[2]

The Wild Duck is Ibsen's most moving play. In its harrowing exploration of a father who cannot even begin to acknowledge his true relationship to his daughter, *The Wild Duck* reminds me of *King Lear*.[3] Given that the question of paternity is surrounded by doubt in *The Wild Duck*, Ibsen's play also contains a reflection on the meaning of fatherhood. "Perhaps I am not really Father's child," Hedvig says; "Well, I think he could love me just as much anyway. Yes, almost more. We got the wild duck as a present too, and I love it so much all the same" (10: 137). In this masterly play, Ibsen turns the tragedy of Hedvig into a disturbing meditation on the connection between the ways in which words lose their meaning and the ways in which we avoid love.

The Duck

The eponymous wild duck plunges us straight into the question of the mean-ing of words. To its first audiences, *The Wild Duck* was utterly baffling. "The audience does not know which way to turn," the Norwegian writer Henrik Jæger noted, "and from the current reviews it will get no wiser, for one newspaper says one thing and the other another" (10: 29–30).[4] Foreign audiences did not find the play any easier to understand. "Browning was obscure. . . . But Browning at his worst is nought compared with Ibsen," one British critic complained when the play opened in London in 1894.[5] The problem seemed above all to be the so-called symbolism of the wild duck itself. In Paris members of the first audiences at Antoine's 1891 production quacked like ducks every time the poor bird was mentioned.[6] The respected French critic Francisque Sarcey summed it up: "Oh! That wild duck, absolutely nobody ever, no, nobody, neither you who have seen the play, nor Lindenlaub and Ephraim who translated it word for word, nor the author who wrote it, nor Shakespeare who inspired it, nor God or the Devil, no, no one will ever know what that wild duck is, neither what it's doing in the play, nor what it means."[7]

As derision ceased and *The Wild Duck* became generally acknowledged as one of Ibsen's greatest plays, critics went to the other extreme. Far from declaring the duck to be meaningless, they now uncovered ever more subtle layers of meaning in what they took to be Ibsen's profound symbol. But, as Errol Durbach points out, this is simply to repeat Gregers Werle's attitude towards the wild duck. "Ibsen, at the height of his power as a symbolist, assigns no portentous symbolic value whatever to the duck," Durbach writes. "He merely presents it as the vehicle for the ridiculous duck-symbolism of Gregers, for whom all surface reality is a system of transcendental referents."[8]

I agree with Durbach that the idea that the duck has to *mean* something is entirely of Gregers's making. But that is because the word "mean" here is used in a rather special way. Otherwise it would simply be a mistake to blame Gregers for the incessant interpretation of the wild duck, since already in the first act, Håkon Werle, Gregers's rich industrialist father, compares certain kinds of people to wild ducks: "There are people in this world who plunge to the bottom when they get a couple of shots in the body, and then they never come up again" (10: 59). But Sarcey was presumably not driven to intellectual despair by a simple simile, as if he could not grasp the idea that some of the characters are in some respects *like* the wild duck in the Ekdals' loft. Thus old Ekdal has given up the struggle for life after being emotionally destroyed by a prison sentence; Hedvig is innocent, wounded, and fragile; and Hjalmar has, like the duck in her basket, grown contentedly fat in his narrowed circumstances. (The only person in the Ekdal family who has no relationship to the duck is Gina. I shall return to that.) "I do realize all that", Sarcey might well have said to me had I tried to be helpful by pointing out these parallels, "but that's *obvious*, something anyone can see. That's not what I mean by the *meaning* of the wild duck." To which I could reply that if one presses the meaning of "meaning" in this way, pretty quickly nothing will count as the meaning of the wild duck. So the quest comes to seem hopeless.

Sarcey's despair about ever grasping the meaning of the wild duck, then, is fueled by a sense that to "understand" the wild duck must be to grasp something far deeper, altogether more meaningful, more mysterious, than any ordinary comparisons and parallels will yield. Literary critics have followed in his footsteps ever since. This is precisely Gregers's attitude, too. To him, the wild duck cannot be just a wild duck, a bird that some people can be compared to; she has to be a sign of something else, something beyond the surface of everyday phenomena. As we shall see, Gregers is constantly gesturing towards a world of absolutes beyond the veil of appearances, thus revealing that to him, ordinary life and everyday people, things and activities, are worthless unless they can be invested with some great metaphysical drama of sacrifice and forgiveness.

If we get transfixed by the idea that the wild duck must be either a symbol or an allegory, or at the very least some special kind of really deep metaphor, we will fail to notice that the wild duck is just one element in Ibsen's much wider investigation of language.[9] The wild duck tempts us to repeat Gregers's attitude towards meaning. Only if we can manage to resist that temptation will we be in a position to understand *The Wild Duck*. For the most important question in *The Wild Duck* is not at all what the eponymous wild duck means (and certainly not what it "means" in a *deep* sense), but whether it is possible to hang on to meaning at all in a world full of self-theatricalizing cynics, skeptics, and narcissists, who all do their best to empty words of meaning.

The loft: Photography, Theater, and the Negation of Theater

The Wild Duck quite explicitly draws attention to the idea that the word "loft" might mean something else or more than it usually does, in the passage where Gregers asks Hedvig whether she is certain that the loft is a loft (see 10: 99).[10] Separated by a single wall, the Ekdals' combined photographic studio and living room and the adjacent loft are on the same level on the top floor of the building in which the Ekdals live. While the attic studio in the foreground is light, the loft is dark, and the double doors between them must be opened to let in the light from the studio. In this way, the loft in the background comes across as a photographic negative of the attic room in the foreground. Perhaps we could even think of it as an image of a camera, with the double doors functioning as the shutter letting in light on the negative.

On the other hand, the double door opens more like a theater curtain than a shutter. "On the back wall there is a wide double door, designed to slide back to the sides," Ibsen writes (10: 66). Inside the double door, moreover, there is something Hjalmar calls *mekanismen* (10: 93). The "mechanism" is released when Hjalmar pulls a cord: "from inside, a curtain glides down, the nether part of which consists of a strip of old sailcloth, and the rest, above, of a piece of tautly stretched fishing net. As a result, the floor of the loft is no longer visible" (10: 93). Falling down like a drop curtain, the "mechanism" lets in light while at the same time preventing the birds and rabbits from getting out. The invisible floor is not just a haphazard detail: a godsend to producers, it ensures that the wild duck and the other members of the menagerie will never actually be seen by the audience.

This stage arrangement is structurally quite similar to that of the last act of *Pillars of Society*. The difference is that where *Pillars of Society* has a glass wall, *The Wild Duck* has an ordinary wall and a double door.[11] In *Pillars of Society*, the space behind the glass wall is used for a brilliantly illuminated, spectacular, theatrical, torch-lit procession. In *The Wild Duck*, however, the loft is mostly hidden from view. On the one occasion where the loft remains open to view for any length of time, Hjalmar and his old father are seen through the fishing net darkly, happily building a new path to the water trough for the wild duck. In the foreground, meanwhile, Hedvig and Gregers are having the strange and fatal conversation in which Hedvig says that she sometimes thinks of the loft as *havsens bund* ("the bottom of the sea") (10: 98), an expression that links the loft to the sea (and so to the *Flying Dutchman*, and the pictures of the sailing ships in the books in the loft), but also to the wild duck, who would have died at the bottom of the lake had it not been for the dog that brought her up. A book that Hedvig singles out for special attention is Harryson's *History of London*, with its picture of Death, an hourglass, and a virgin. Finally, and most importantly, the loft is the place where Hedvig kills herself, offstage and unseen, but not unheard.

What, then, does the loft mean? As with the image of the wild duck, we should beware of concluding that the loft must have *one*, preferably deep, meaning. It means different things to different characters. The two Ekdals use it as a space to escape everyday reality; for Hedvig it is a place of poetry and dreams; whereas for Gina it appears to be purely a practical problem. Since the set and stage directions connect the loft to theater and photography, we are also being invited to think of the loft in terms of light and darkness, things being seen and things remaining unseen, concealment and theatricality, acknowledgment and avoidance. The loft thus becomes not just a metatheatrical element, but a figure for the thematic concerns of the play it appears in. In this way, Hedvig's death, hidden away in her own place of dreams, becomes a shocking picture of unacknowledged love.

Housework as the Everyday

The Wild Duck is full of housework. Gina cleans and dusts, makes herring salad, coffee, and sandwiches for her self-pitying husband and his guests; she serves the men at the table, and clears up after them, often with the help of Hedvig. Moreover, and in spite of Hjalmar's great proclamations about his responsibilities as the breadwinner of the family, she is the one who earns a living for the family. While Hjalmar digests his copious meals on the sofa, Gina deals with clients, takes photographs, retouches them with the help of Hedvig, and takes care of the household finances.

At the very beginning of Act 3, Ibsen inserts a story that contrasts Gina's housework with Gregers's total lack of practical sense. Strictly speaking unnecessary for the plot, the story contributes crucial elements to the characterization of Gregers, and so to the philosophical concerns of the play. At this point Gregers has just broken with his father, and moved into the Ekdals' spare room. He instantly refuses all help from servants. Here is Gina's account of the ensuing events:

GINA. Well, he wanted to manage for himself, he said. So he was going to light the fire too, and then he closed down the damper so the whole room got full of smoke. Ugh! what a stink! Like a—

HJALMAR. Oh dear.

GINA. But here's the best bit, because then of course he wants to put it out, and so he pours all his washing water into the stove, so the floor's swimming in the worst filth.

HJALMAR. What a nuisance.

GINA. I got the porter's wife to come and scrub up after him, the pig; but it won't be fit to live in until this afternoon.

(10: 90)

In his incapacity to see everyday practices and words as a potential source of value, Gregers resembles Falk in *Love's Comedy*.

Ignorant of his own limitations, Gregers thinks that he can manage without help. Given that he obviously cannot, this scene tells us that he has never in his life paid any attention to everyday chores. To him, housework has been invisible, unacknowledged, a set of tasks that go without saying. The dust and soot and dirt he produces comprise an ironic commentary on his misbegotten pursuit of the ideal.

Some readers of this scene have found it utterly unrealistic, and have concluded that it was included purely for comic effect. Such critics take Gregers's talk of his fifteen years of solitude up at the ironworks at Højdal to mean that he has lived a solitary life in the woods. Surely, they say, such a man would know very well how to make a fire.[12] But we should not take Gregers's talk about solitude too literally. Although Gregers speaks of himself as a brooding and ungregarious man, incapable of marriage, he did not actually live alone in the woods at Højdal, for in the first act we learn that during all those years he has worked in some supervisory capacity for his father, the owner of the ironworks. Later on, Dr Relling informs us that Gregers also spent considerable time and effort going around trying to elevate the souls of the workers at the ironworks.

Compared to the high social life of his industrialist father (exemplified by the party scene in the first act), Gregers led a simple and relatively solitary life in self-imposed exile from fellow members of the bourgeoisie. We can nevertheless safely assume that, at the very minimum, he has had a woman to cook and clean and make fires for him. When Gregers speaks of his solitude, then, he means something like spiritual and social, but not literal, isolation.

Ibsen's deliberate foregrounding of cooking and cleaning is not just a critique of Gregers's idealism. It is also a metatheatrical statement, which tells us that the last thing Ibsen wants to write is grand tragedy, whether classical or romantic. We cannot imagine Doña Sol in *Hernani* dusting and sweeping, and a well-placed offer of coffee and sandwiches would hardly make Phaedra forget all about Hippolytus. To traditional nineteenth-century theatergoers Ibsen's use of the everyday (soot, sandwiches, beer, and butter—the whole lot) would come across as elements belonging to farce or folk comedy.[13]

Late in life, Ibsen complained precisely about the tendency to turn *The Wild Duck* into a farce, and insisted on the double nature of the play: "It must be tragicomedy", he said, "otherwise Hedvig's death becomes incomprehensible."[14] In *The Wild Duck*, the challenging juxtaposition of the deadly serious and the utterly ridiculous unsettles traditional categories of genre (farce, comedy, melodrama, tragedy) and blocks identification, in ways that make the play truly difficult to interpret. Ibsen clearly knew this, for he practically issued a challenge to his critics: "This new play occupies in some ways a place apart in my dramatic production. The method is in various respects different. But I do not wish to say more about this. The critics will hopefully find the points, in any case they will find much to disagree about, much to interpret" (18: 32–3).[15]

Fleeing the Ordinary and the Everyday

Both Gregers's metaphysical skepticism and Hjalmar's narcissistic and self-pitying theatricality are forms of rejection of the everyday. In the character of Gregers, the connection between idealism and theatricality is strongly stressed. Gregers's metaphysical absolutism drives him towards melodrama in the most ordinary sense of the word: namely, as Peter Brooks puts it, the tendency to "pressure the surface of reality", the drive to create "drama—an exciting, excessive, parabolic story—from the banal stuff of reality".[16] Gregers is like the man in Wittgenstein's *Philosophical Investigations* who becomes theatrical in his effort to stress his own unique, isolated interiority: "I have seen a person in a discussion of this subject strike himself on the breast and say: 'But surely another person cannot have THIS pain!'"[17] This man is a skeptic: someone who feels that nobody else can know what he knows about himself. This is precisely Gregers's position. Throughout the play, Gregers goes around lecturing others, convinced that he knows who they are, and what they need and want. His loneliness, his self-declared love of solitude, and unfitness for marriage tell us that he is equally convinced that nobody could ever understand *him*. (The same is true of Dr Relling.)

Turning his back on the ordinary and the everyday, Gregers looks for ideals to worship. His fatal mistake is to take Hjalmar to be that ideal. To him, Hjalmar is extraordinary, unique, special: "No, an *ordinary* man; that may well be. But a man like *you*—!" (10: 124). There may be more than a touch of homoerotic libido in the unmarried Gregers's starry-eyed idealization of Hjalmar. But whatever its source, his idealization of Hjalmar is based on the conviction that Hjalmar is *not* ordinary. Hjalmar too is convinced that he is extraordinary, certainly too extraordinary to do any actual work. After his father's catastrophic imprisonment for theft, Hjalmar had to learn the craft of photography. But, as we have seen, he does not actually take any pictures. Photography will always be beneath him, unless he manages to lift it out of its humdrum everyday existence:

HJALMAR. As you can imagine, when I decided to devote myself to photography, it
   was not in order to go around here and take portraits of all sorts of everyday people.
GREGERS. No, of course not, that's what your wife just said too.
HJALMAR. I swore that if I was going to dedicate my powers to this craft, then I
   would raise it so high as to make it both an art and a science. And so I decided to
   make this astonishing invention.
GREGERS. And what does the invention consist in? What's the idea behind it?

HJALMAR. Oh, well, you mustn't ask for details just yet. It all takes time, you know.

(10: 102–3)

Despising the ordinary people to which photography exposes him, Hjalmar dreams of art and science, fame and recognition, theatricalizing himself by imagining a melodramatic scenario in which he, the poor misunderstood inventor, dies unrecognized by all. Shortly after his death, however, his invention wins the fame it deserves, so that his family is restored to bourgeois life, and the name Ekdal is again without blemish. The irony is that Hjalmar's refusal of the ordinary guarantees that he will never invent anything at all, for only someone who actually practiced photography with some passion and respect for the medium would be in a position to discover ways to improve its techniques.

Gregers's and Hjalmar's rejection of the ordinary is also an exercise in sex and class prejudice. For them, to reject the ordinary is to refuse to acknowledge the humanity of "ordinary people". There is in both of them a strong romantic streak, a faith in the power of the exceptional person, the prophet, the seer, the savior. They, the chosen ones, the exceptional ones, cling to the belief that they are different (superior) in kind to the rest of humanity. This is how they endow themselves with an identity. The problem with returning to the everyday, then, is that it would mean returning to a life in which they were no longer special, no longer singled out as more valuable than anyone else.

Gina, on the other hand, doesn't think of herself as extraordinary at all. Her class background, however, predisposes her to share Gregers's conviction that Hjalmar is extraordinary:

GINA. Yes, and it really isn't anything for a man like Ekdal to go here and take pictures of the hoi polloi.[18]
GREGERS. That's what I think too, but once he's gone in for that kind of thing, then—
GINA. Surely you can understand that Ekdal isn't like any of your ordinary photographers, Mr. Werle.

(10: 100)

Gina, however, does not use her heroization of Hjalmar to support her own sense of identity and importance. Brought up to be self-effacing and fatalistic, she underestimates her own worth. Although she knows that she is good for her husband, she feels entitled to nothing, and so becomes the perfect mate for Hjalmar, who feels entitled to everything.

Strange Talk: Dogs, Lofts, and Criteria

Gregers's and Hjalmar's rejection of the everyday becomes evident when one listens to the way they use words. In the second act, Gregers visits the Ekdals for the first time, and sees the loft with the wild duck sleeping in her basket. Old Ekdal tells him that when the duck was winged by Gregers's father, it plunged to the bottom to die as ducks do, but that Old Werle's exceptionally good dog plunged after it and brought it to the surface. A little later on, Gregers says that he hates his own name, and that he does not know what to do with himself in the world anymore:

HJALMAR[*laughs*]. Ha! ha! If you weren't Gregers Werle, what would you like to be?
GREGERS. If I could choose, I'd most of all like to be a clever dog.
GINA. A dog!
HEDVIG [*involuntarily*]. Oh, no!
GREGERS. Yes, a really excessively clever dog, the sort that goes to the bottom after
   wild ducks when they dive down and bite on to the seaweed in the mud.
HJALMAR. No, really, Gregers,—I don't understand a word of all this.

(10: 86–7)

Of course Gregers does not want to be just any dog. Only a really extraordinary dog will do. And of course he is speaking in metaphors. To him, a dog is not a dog, a duck not a duck: they must both be symbols of something else. Here he is presumably trying to say something about "rescuing those wounded by life". Translated thus, his project sounds as rhetorically hollow as Hjalmar's wish to "save the shipwrecked man", by which he means restoring his father's good name (10: 103). But Hjalmar's metaphor is quite different. Old Ekdal is not a shipwrecked sailor, but he is a broken man. Although it is exaggerated, excessive, unconvincing, Hjalmar's metaphor is not particularly mysterious. Gregers's metaphors, however, are so obscure as to become, at least in the minds of many critics, deep symbols. The alternative is to wonder whether they mean anything at all.

   Gina and Hedvig have no experience with people who speak in riddles. Hedvig immediately notes that Gregers uses language strangely: "it was as if he meant something different from what he said—all the time," and generally manages more clearly than anyone else to expose Gregers's bizarrely symbolic language (10: 87). It would be easy to leap to the conclusion that Hedvig is Gregers's polar opposite. Yet Ibsen also makes her share something with Gregers. It turns out that they both use the phrase *havsens bund* ("the bottom of the sea"), and Hedvig reveals that she sometimes thinks of the loft in that way. While not being outlandish, this expression, with its old-fashioned genitive case, has poetic and fairy-tale-like overtones. (There is a Norwegian fairy tale about a mill that churns and churns at the bottom of the sea, for example.) Hedvig's poetic talents, her love of the loft, her willingness to give it a beautiful name, make her feel a kind of community with Gregers when he uses the very same words. Yet in this case, the same words are used very differently. Hedvig can be poetic without losing touch with the everyday, while Gregers cannot. (Poetic language is not the opposite of ordinary language.[19]) This becomes evident at the very end of their bonding over *havsens bund*:

HEDVIG. . . . I always think that the whole room and everything is called "the bottom of the sea". But that's just silly.
GREGERS. You shouldn't say that.
HEDVIG. Yes, because it's only a loft.
GREGERS [*looking steadily at her*]. Are you so sure of that?
HEDVIG [*astonished*]. That it's a loft!
GREGERS. Yes. Do you know that for certain?
HEDVIG [*says nothing and looks at him, open-mouthed*].

(10: 99)

When Gregers strays into explicit skepticism, Hedvig can only stare at him. Baffled, she can think of nothing to say. Gregers must seem almost mad to her, yet curiously seductive too. How can she be *certain* that a loft is a loft? Well, if the question were about its being a loft, as opposed to a cellar, there would be no mystery. But Gregers is not asking about identity. This is why his question seems so bizarre. To speak in Wittgensteinian terms: he has taken a completely ordinary expression ("How can you be certain that it is a loft?") and placed it outside the language games where it would normally be at home. In other words: he has taken a question that is usually used about identity, and turned it into a question about existence. Because he is not asking about anything we can define with the help of criteria, there can be no answer to Gregers's question.[20] Hedvig's baffled silence is the only possible response, unless she were to cast loose from the everyday too.[21]

Hedvig thinks that the loft could be called "the bottom of the sea". To her this is a poetic metaphor, an expression of similarity. It has never occurred to her that saying so entails that there is no way of telling the difference between the bottom of the sea and the loft. In fact, poetic metaphors *rely* on differences for their effect. The art of metaphor is the art of seeing likenesses, but it is no art unless the likenesses are unexpected, striking, suddenly illuminating, or thought-provoking. Hedvig's metaphor is excellent because it is allusive, interesting, and original. If there truly were no way of telling a loft from the bottom of the sea, however, the "bottom of the sea" would not *be* a metaphor. Exploiting Hedvig's poetic talents, Gregers takes her metaphor and turns it into outright skepticism. He is, in short, cutting words loose from their ordinary criteria of meaning. But without criteria, words can mean anything or nothing. That way chaos lies.

Gregers thus leaves Hedvig with no way to tell the difference between metaphorical and literal ways of speaking. How will she now be able to tell whether a loft is a loft? Or whether a wild duck is a wild duck? If Gregers thinks he can become a dog, is it not possible that *she* could become a wild duck? In this fatal conversation Gregers shows Hedvig the way out of the ordinary, and so lays the foundation for her ultimate suicide.

Hedvig dies offstage. She has gone inside the loft, with Hjalmar's pistol, possibly in order to shoot the wild duck as a "sacrifice" to Hjalmar. (The absurdity and cruelty of Gregers's idealism are nowhere more obvious than here: outside the idealist faith in self-sacrifice, it is difficult to understand why the killing of an innocent duck would appease Hjalmar's craving for absolute proof of love.) Through the thin partition wall she overhears the onstage conversation between Hjalmar and Gregers. Hjalmar hits his most self-pitying rhetorical high, and declares that since he has come to doubt that he is Hedvig's father, he can no longer trust Hedvig's love for him. Why would Hedvig love a poor man like him, if she could return to the person Hjalmar now takes to be her real father, the rich Håkon Werle?

HJALMAR. Suppose the others came, those whose hands are laden with fruit, and they called to the child: "Leave him! We can offer you life—"
GREGERS [*quickly*]. Yes, then what?
HJALMAR. If I then asked her: "Hedvig, are you willing to give up life for me?" [*laughs scornfully.*] Oh yes,—you'd soon hear her answer all right. [*A pistol shot is heard in the loft.*]

(10: 156)

Hedvig dies because she takes Hjalmar's histrionic language literally. He speaks of "life" metaphorically, in the sense of "rich, interesting, socially elevated daily life". Hedvig thinks he means life itself. Gregers's contribution to Hedvig's death is obvious. By depriving her of criteria, he has made her incapable of dealing with metaphors. But his responsibility goes further than this. For Gregers has also been preaching sacrifice to Hedvig. His idea is that an act of sacrifice is far more powerful than words. He has therefore told Hedvig to shoot the wild duck, the thing she cherishes the most in the world, in order to prove to Hjalmar that she loves him.

Gregers here espouses exactly the same theory as Johannes Rosmer at the end of *Rosmersholm* when he asks Rebecca to kill herself in order to rescue him from his doubt. In both plays the same words are used. Rosmer asks for *vidnesbyrd* ("testimony", "proof", "evidence"), and so do Hjalmar and Gregers (see 10: 431). Hjalmar has just said that he suffers from "this horrible doubt—; perhaps Hedvig has never really and truly loved me" (10: 154). That it never once occurs to Hjalmar that the question just may be whether *he* is capable of truly loving Hedvig is the scandal of this play.

Again we have to remember that Hedvig hears what the two men are saying from inside the loft:[22]

GREGERS. [. . .] I tell you that you might get proof that your poor, misjudged Hedvig loves you!

HJALMAR. Oh what proof can she give me! I don't dare to believe in assurances from that quarter.

GREGERS. Hedvig surely does not know deceit.

HJALMAR. Oh, Gregers, *that* is precisely not so certain.

(10: 155)

In both *The Wild Duck* and *Rosmersholm* a girl or a woman is asked for testimony or proof in a situation where a man is racked with doubt. In these plays *vidnesbyrd* turns out not to mean what it usually means—namely, a speech act—but an act of self-sacrifice. Whatever Hedvig says will be insufficient, Hjalmar claims. When words have come to seem empty, actions must be substituted. A woman must pay with her life for the man to regain his self-confidence and inner peace. Hjalmar's monstrous narcissism makes him accept the idea of Hedvig's sacrificing the duck for his sake with alacrity, but Hjalmar is no Rosmer. Where Rosmer is desperately serious, Hjalmar's skeptical crisis is mostly sham. He is theatricalizing himself, and would surely get over his doubts in a few days whatever Hedvig does. It is significant, therefore, that it is Gregers, the idealist, who introduces the idea of the ordeal, of self-sacrifice, as testimony of love. It is Gregers, not Hjalmar, who has lost faith in words, which is another way of saying that he is disappointed with criteria, and therefore puts his faith in action. It is as if he thinks that he can conjure forth the transcendental reality he always dreams of by making someone else commit an act of sacrifice. As we shall now see, Hjalmar's problem is different, but equally death-dealing. If Gregers constantly gives the impression that he means more than he says, Hjalmar constantly says more than he can manage to mean.

Broken Promises: Hjalmar Ekdal's Way with Words

Hjalmar's language is taken straight out of nineteenth-century romantic and melodramatic prose. As many critics have pointed out, the very name Hjalmar has a grandiose sound to it, reminiscent of national romanticism and its admiration for heroic Vikings. It is not for nothing that we learn that Hjalmar in his youth was a popular declaimer of poetry. Ibsen must have been chuckling as he gave Hjalmar lines such as these: "[*gloomily*]: Gregers, I want to go. When a man has felt the crushing blow of fate on his brow, you see—" (10: 57); "I am a man besieged by the host of sorrows" (10: 76); and "Happy and carefree, chirping like a little bird, she flutters into life's eternal night" (10: 78).

It is difficult to imagine that nineteenth-century actors would manage to speak such lines without striking what were then considered the appropriate melodramatic poses. Yet that was precisely what Ibsen wanted to avoid. In a letter to theater director Schroeder at Christiania Theater, Ibsen wrote, "I would really prefer to be entirely free of Isachsen, since he always goes around gesticulating like a strange actor and not like an ordinary human being" (18: 47).[23] Ibsen's contrast between a "strange actor" and an "ordinary human being" could not be more striking. Right from the start, Ibsen also protested against the temptation to turn Hjalmar Ekdal into a buffoon.[24] In the same letter he is quite explicit: "This part [Hjalmar] must absolutely not be acted with anything like parody in the expression; nor with the slightest trace of awareness in the actor that there is any thing at all comic in his utterances. He has this heart-winning quality in his voice, Relling says, and that needs above all to be maintained. His sensitivity is honest, his melancholy beautiful in form; not the slightest touch of affectation" (18: 47).

Hjalmar's invocation of God just after Hedvig's death, which Ibsen, in his stage directions, provides with the kind of gestures one might expect from a melodramatic actor, exemplifies the point: "And I drove her from me like an animal! And then she crept terrified into the loft and died for love of me. [*Sobbing*]. Never be able to make it up to her! Never be able to tell her—! [*clenches his fists and cries to heaven*]: Oh, you up there—!—If you exist—! Why hast Thou done this to me?" (10: 159). Ibsen's letter tells us to believe that Hjalmar honestly has these feelings, that he is not affected, that there is something heartwarming about him. Let us furthermore assume that the actor playing the part knows how to convey this. Why do we still feel that there is something theatrical and morally wrong about Hjalmar's behavior?

The obvious answer—namely, that Hjalmar can be understood as a straight-forward case of Diderotian theatricality—does not work.[25] For Ibsen tells us that Hjalmar's behavior is not calculated; that he does not strike these poses simply in order to impress his audience. There is nothing in the scene itself, either, to produce that impression. Peculiarly enough, then, Hjalmar's theatricality is not self-conscious. We have to look at it from a different angle.

The problem, first of all, is that Hjalmar's feelings do not last, as Dr Relling points out at the very end of the play: "We can discuss it again when the first grass has withered on her grave. Then you'll hear him regurgitate phrases about 'the child so untimely torn from her father's heart' " (10: 160). In the passage just quoted, Hjalmar shakes his fist at God, behaving like Job, or an Old Testament prophet. The tone and gestures promise a grandeur and a depth that Hjalmar simply cannot provide. This is crucial. The fact that his language constantly makes promises the man cannot keep is the key to Hjalmar's theatricality. This has nothing to do with Hjalmar's subjective intentions, and everything to do with the way he fails to live up to the meaning of his words. Hjalmar's most fundamental psychic structure is disavowal (avoidance, Cavell might call it), which here means the capacity not to notice this, and so not to notice that he will never be a prophet or a great inventor, or—worse—a good father.

Hjalmar's narcissism surely exacts all this self-inflation in compensation for the steep social fall he has experienced. But the effect on Hedvig is disastrous, for she grows up in a household where her father's grandiose phrases are invariably followed by huge letdowns. Hjalmar's language always promises more than it can keep. This point is established right at the beginning of the second act, in the very first interaction between Hjalmar and Hedvig. The scene, which I am going to quote at length because it is so important, shows us what is wrong with Hjalmar's language. The poignancy, sadness, and horror of it tell us how we are supposed to feel about it. Here, then, we are right at the ethical, emotional, and philosophical center of *The Wild Duck*.

Gina and Hedvig are alone at home, waiting for Hjalmar to return from the splendid dinner party at Håkon Werle's house. Hedvig says to her mother: "I'm looking so immensely forward to father coming home. He promised he'd ask Mrs. Sørbye for something nice to eat for me" (10: 67). We also learn that Gina and Hedvig have skimped on dinner in order to save money, and Hedvig confesses to feeling a little hungry. When Hjalmar arrives, Hedvig waits patiently for a long time. But in the end she cannot bear it any longer:

HEDVIG [*after a moment, tugs at his jacket*]. Father!

HJALMAR. Well, what is it?

HEDVIG. Oh, you know what it is.

HJALMAR. No, I really don't.

HEDVIG [*laughing and whimpering*]. Oh father, you mustn't torment me any longer!

HJALMAR. But what *is* it then?

HEDVIG [*shaking him*]. Oh, stop it! Just give it to me, father. You know, all the nice things you promised me.

HJALMAR. Oh—no! How could I forget!

HEDVIG. Oh, you just want to fool me, father! You ought to be ashamed! Where have you put them?

HJALMAR. No, I really did forget. But wait a minute! I have something else for you, Hedvig.

[*Walks across and searches in his coat pockets.*]

HEDVIG [*jumping and clapping her hands*]. Oh, mother, mother!

GINA. You see, if you just are patient, then—

HJALMAR [*with a piece of paper*]. Look, here it is.

HEDVIG. *That?* That's just a piece of paper.

HJALMAR. It is the bill of fare, you see, the whole bill of fare. Here it says "Menu". That means bill of fare.

HEDVIG. Haven't you got anything else?

HJALMAR. I told you I forgot the other things. But take my word for it: all that sweet stuff isn't really much fun. Go and sit at the table now and read the menu, then I'll tell you afterwards what the different courses taste like. There you are, Hedvig.

HEDVIG. Thanks.

[*She sits down, but doesn't read; Gina makes a sign to her, Hjalmar notices.*]

HJALMAR [*pacing the floor*]. It really is incredible, all the things a breadwinner has to think about, and if one forgets the slightest little thing,—at once there are sour faces. Well, one gets used to *that*, too. [*Stops by the stove, by old Ekdal.*] Have you looked in there tonight, father?

(10: 73–4)

Discussing the wild duck with his father, Hjalmar forgets all about Hedvig, who never reads the menu (just a few minutes earlier, incidentally, she was told that she must not read at night, since it will damage her weak eyes), but who soon comes to offer him beer to cheer him up. Hjalmar hugs her, Hedvig sheds tears of joy, and calls him her kind father, and Hjalmar replies: "No, don't call me that. There I sat, helping myself at the rich man's table,— gorging myself at the groaning banquet—! And still I could—!" (10: 76).[26] Here, for once, Hjalmar goes straight to the heart of the matter, which is, precisely, whether he deserves to be called *snille far* ("kind father").

That this scene is literally one of a broken promise makes the point abundantly clear: Hjalmar's theatricality can be defined as the constant production of empty language, of language that cannot keep the promises of meaning it makes. There are, then, two kinds of empty language in *The Wild Duck*: Gregers's obscurely metaphysical formulations and Hjalmar's histrionic exaggerations. The parallel between them is made quite explicit by the fact that Hedvig reacts in exactly the same way to both men. Here, when Hjalmar offers her words for food, she replies: "It's just a piece of paper." When Gregers talks to her about the loft, she says, "It's just a loft."

In both cases, Hedvig is struggling to hang on to criteria, to the idea that words can be used in meaningful ways, to the idea that it is possible to mean what one says and say what one means. She would like a loft to be a loft, and a piece of paper to be a piece of paper, not because she is a closet positivist, but because she is a poet at heart. As we have seen, if criteria disappear, nothing can be defined as different from anything else, and that makes metaphors impossible. But, even more crucially, without criteria, words lose their meaning. If loft and paper can go that way, so can more crucial words, such as father, daughter, and, ultimately, love.

If Hedvig is driven by her desperate need to hang on to criteria (another way of saying that she needs language to make sense, that she needs language to be *ordinary*), it explains why she is so reluctant to believe that Hjalmar has forgotten all about his promise. For Hedvig's absolute faith in her father in this scene is puzzling, to say the least. She has lived with Hjalmar for almost fourteen years. This is surely not the first time he has forgotten a promise, yet her behavior throughout the scene shows that she will not even let herself *think* that he might be unfaithful to his words. She thinks he is joking when he says he has forgotten her treat, even though he has already said so several times. The sweet, excited jumping and clapping of hands bear the mark of disavowal. Hedvig is about to turn 14, not 8. Is she not just a little too old to behave in this way? Does she really believe in a last-minute surprise at her age, and at this point? In her mind she surely does. But in her heart?

Hedvig's constant attempts to flatter and please her moody father by showering him with compliments about his hair and looks, by running to get him beer and sandwiches, show that she knows very well what he is like. Yet she has steadfastly refused to learn that her father usually does not mean what he says, because it would make it impossible for her to love him as a daughter should, and if she cannot love him, she has no other ground of existence. Because language use is at once the practice and the ground of all human meaning—a "thin net over an abyss", Cavell calls it—this is not just a linguistic, but an existential disaster.[27] *The Wild Duck*, then, is specifically about

Hedvig's struggle to uphold the meaning of the words "daughter" and "father", and Hjalmar's betrayal of that struggle.

But there is more. Hjalmar gives Hedvig words instead of food, and expects her to be as delighted with the one as with the other. This brings us back to our discussion of metaphors. Everything conspires to undermine Hedvig's faith in words. The words he gives her, moreover, are of a particular kind—namely, a bill of fare, a menu—not of the kind one gets in restaurants, but of the kind one gets at a banquet or a private dinner. Such a menu is itself a promise. The promise to Hjalmar was kept: he has eaten all the food listed on the menu. To hand the menu to Hedvig in *this* situation, however, is simultaneously to make and break the menu's promise. This is a perfect allegory of Hjalmar's way with words.

Hjalmar, who is a good-natured fellow, obscurely feels that there is something wrong with his gesture. To make up for it, he makes another promise: if she will read the menu, he will describe how the food tastes. Of course he never does. To cap it all, he tells her to "believe him at his word". The irony of it! Except that Hedvig cannot afford to discover the meaning of the word "irony", for if she does, her faith in her father will not survive.

Hjalmar, moreover, will not let Hedvig feel her own disappointment. He instantly gets cross with her and invokes his role as the breadwinner in the family. But this act opens with a scene where Gina counts the money *she* earned from taking photographs that day. At this point the audience already suspects that Hjalmar is not much of a breadwinner. Hedvig, however, *knows* that he is not. Again she is confronted with words empty of meaning, and again she must pretend that she does not notice. For Hedvig, Hjalmar simply *must* mean what he says, or she will not know what the word "father" means anymore.

Hedvig is exposed to two different kinds of attack on meaning. Gregers deprives her of criteria by removing words from their everyday context, and making even simple questions quite unanswerable. But Hjalmar also deprives her of criteria by constantly using words in ways he cannot mean. If Hedvig is to survive, she needs to love her father. To love him is to believe him at his word. So she must make herself take everything Hjalmar says literally. Then she will have to bear her disappointment, but that is better than not to be the daughter of a loving father. Hedvig's desperate suicide is caused by Hjalmar's rejection. She cannot live except as a loving daughter, and she cannot bear to hear that her beloved father knows her—knows her love—no better than to think that she would betray him for the kind of life money can buy. Hedvig does not die because she mistakenly takes Hjalmar's talk about her "life" literally, but because she understands only too well what he is accusing her of.

But, ironically, if she were not so deeply identified by her need to believe in Hjalmar, she would have known that he could not possibly mean what he was saying about her, just as he cannot really mean most of his theatrical proclamations. But if she let herself know that, Hjalmar would no longer be the father she needs and loves. And she is just a little girl. So she has to make a choice: refuse to understand metaphors, or become cynical, knowing, lost to love. (This sounds like a good description of Dr Relling.)

"All her words are words of love; to love is all she knows how to do," Cavell writes of Cordelia. "That is her problem, and at the cause of the tragedy of King Lear."[28] Hedvig is a modern Cordelia. All her words are love, and her death too, for Hedvig dies to show Hjalmar what love means. Every time I get to the bit where Hjalmar says, "There is this horrible doubt—; perhaps Hedvig has never really and truly loved me," and Gregers eagerly replies, "But you might very well get proof that she does" (10: 154–5), the same pity and the same fear grip me. Hedvig does what Gregers has been telling her to do, and sacrifices the dearest thing she has for her father, except that he did not mean it *that* way. She takes Hjalmar at his word, and gives up her life for him, and of course he never meant it *that* way either. By her death, Hedvig tries to teach them how to mean what they say. They will not heed her lesson.

The Need for Skepticism: Why Gina Lacks a Voice

The Wild Duck, then, is about the threat of skepticism and the ways in which skepticism reveals itself in our words. But it is also, and this may be more surprising, about the *need* for skepticism. Wittgenstein himself experienced the threat of skepticism more keenly than most. His constant struggle to find a philosophical voice, his desire for silence, his sense that nothing can be said, that human knowledge might not be enough, are well known.[29] To find a voice is to affirm one's existence.[30] But before one can do this, it may be necessary to have felt it to be threatened.

The question that Wittgenstein and Cavell both raise is whether it is possible to find a way back to the everyday once one has lost one's way. A different problem, not much discussed by our philosophers, is the plight of those for whom skepticism has never been an option. I get the impression that *The Wild Duck* tells us that to doubt the world and the people in it is a privilege as well as a plight. This is brought out in the figure of Gina, who appears never to have felt the threat of skepticism. In many ways, Gina is completely admirable. She is certainly no idealist; she is neither theatrical nor narcissistic; she is, rather, a veritable saint of the everyday, the incarnation of women's ordinary heroism, an oasis of practical sense and human consideration in the midst of the wild schemes of the madmen around her.

Yet even so, Gina is no existential heroine. It is difficult to get a sense of her personality, beyond an even, almost fatalistic temper, and an enviable capacity to deal with things as they come. Gina's use of words is striking: her working-class background is revealed in her frequent mispronunciations, or mistaking of one word for another. Although this is a source of benign comedy, there can be no doubt that Ibsen means us to notice that, unlike Hjalmar and Gregers, this uneducated woman always makes sense, always says what she means and means what she says. At the same time, however, Ibsen never grants Gina a voice of her own, in the sense of giving her own "cogito performance", her own aria of existence.[31]

What, then, does the admirable Gina lack? What is her flaw? The answer has to be sought in her relationship to Hedvig. When Hjalmar drives Hedvig to the depths of despair, Gina is the one who screams to him to look at the child:

HJALMAR. Don't come near me, Hedvig! Go far away! I can't bear the sight of you. Oh, those eyes—! Goodbye.
HEDVIG [*clinging to him and screaming loudly*]. No! No! Don't leave me!
GINA [*shouting*]. Look at the child, Ekdal! Look at the child!
HJALMAR. I won't! I can't! I must get out, away from all this!

[*He tears himself away from Hedvig and exits through the hall door.*]

(10: 136)

Hjalmar's horrifying refusal to *look* at Hedvig is a figure for his refusal to acknowledge her love. This scene shows that Gina, who loves her daughter passionately, sees—and is appalled at—what Hjalmar is doing to Hedvig, but also that she is powerless to stop it.[32] What does this tell us?

After Gregers's first visit to the Ekdals, in the second act, Hjalmar accompanies his friend down the stairs. Left alone onstage, Gina and Hedvig comment on Gregers's strange talk:

GINA [*gazing into space, her sewing in her lap*]. Wasn't that strange talk, that he really wanted to be a dog?
HEDVIG. I'll tell you one thing, mother,—I think he meant something different by that.
GINA. What would that be?
HEDVIG. I don't know, but it was as if he meant something different from what he said—all the time.
GINA. Do you really think so? Yes, it certainly was strange.

(10: 87)

Here Gina rightly finds Gregers's metaphorical speech "strange". But it is Hedvig who has to explain to her that perhaps Gregers's words meant something more and something different: unlike her mother she has grasped the thought that language can be used in ways that break with the ordinary. In reply, Gina can only repeat that it "certainly was strange". Unable to expand on Hedvig's brilliant observation, she doesn't really take in what it means, and therefore can't help her daughter to deal with Gregers's seductive and dangerous way with words, because she doesn't realize how dangerous it is. Hedvig, on the other hand, has the soul of a poet; although she cannot yet formulate it, she intuitively grasps both the glory and the fragility of the meanings that bind us to others.

  Gina's hardworking life has taught her the value of things and actions, but it has not taught her the danger of words. Gina is practical, down to earth, reliable, caring, loving, but she lacks a sense of poetry, and so of tragedy, too. Perhaps this is what it might mean to speak of the need for skepticism: that unless we are capable of experiencing for ourselves the plight of skepticism, the fear that we will be unable to make sense, to ourselves or to others, we will be unable to understand how easy, and how fateful, it is to tear apart the thin net over the abyss that is constituted by the meaning of our words.[33]

Dr Relling and the Life-Lie

I cannot leave *The Wild Duck* without taking a quick look at Dr Relling's contribution to Hedvig's tragedy. His most famous line is the one about the "life-lie": "Deprive the average human being of his life-lie, and you deprive him of his happiness as well" (10: 145). What exactly is a life-lie? Some story, some fantasy that endows quite ordinary and inglorious pursuits with melodramatic grandiosity: another flight from the ordinary. Hjalmar's future invention, Molvik's "demonic" nature, perhaps Gregers's belief that his destiny is to "save" people by telling them the truth and exhorting them to live up to his ideals.

  Ibsen does not believe that everyone has to have a life-lie.[34] Dr Relling is Gregers Werle's counterpoint. Gregers goes around foisting the ideal onto people; Relling goes around supplying them with life-lies. Both men are lonely, unmarried, and unhappy. (In Ibsen's contemporary plays, the capacity for happy marriage is an almost infallible gauge of a person's relationship to the ordinary.) Compared to Gregers, Relling is more human, far better at listening to others, and a much better judge of people (he can see what

Hjalmar is like, and knows that Hedvig is in danger), but his willing support of Hjalmar's life-lie, his total cynicism, and his far-reaching and explicit skepticism make him the accomplice of those who conspire to deprive Hedvig's life of meaning. As Helge Rønning puts it in a different context, "Dr Relling prescribes drugs for the soul."[35]

Dr Relling appears to be a Benthamite promoting the greatest happiness for the greatest number, yet he himself is not happy. When his lost love Mrs Sørbye marries Håkon Werle, all he knows to do is to go on a binge. In the same way, Gregers is an idealist who believes that from truth, goodness and beauty spring, yet he himself is described as ugly. It is of course possible that Dr Relling does not believe in the value of happiness at all. If so, he is simply a cynical manipulator of others, a nihilist whose enduring message to mankind is the play's famous last line: "Å fan' tro det" ("The devil believe it") (10: 160).[36]

Dr Relling and Gregers both refuse to acknowledge the freedom of others. They are both utterly convinced that they know only too well what other people need. Dr Relling's prescriptions are more pleasing to the recipient than Gregers's, but the fact is that the doctor's provision of Hjalmar's life-lie has enabled Hjalmar to live without the slightest need for self-criticism and change. He has confirmed and strengthened Hjalmar's worst tendencies, and thus helped to make him a disastrous father to Hedvig.

Gregers, on the other hand, has made the mistake of believing in Hjalmar's phrases. In a sense, then, Gregers's behavior is more excusable than Dr Relling's, insofar as Gregers acts in mystified ignorance (while believing he is the apostle of truth), whereas Relling acts in full knowledge of the situation. Relling does not have the guts to stand up for the meaning of words, just as he never had the guts to do what it took to win the woman he loved. Hjalmar's death-dealing theatricality has received nothing but support from Dr Relling.

There is no mouthpiece for Ibsen in *The Wild Duck*. In a letter written while he was working on *The Wild Duck*, Ibsen wrote that "Long ago I ceased to posit universal demands, for I no longer believe that one can posit any such with any inner right" (18: 29).[37] Instead of lecturing us, he made us look at the child. At the center of *The Wild Duck* there is a frightened, loving child struggling and failing to make sense of words and the world. "We learn language and learn the world *together*."[38]

9

Losing Faith in Language
Fantasies of Perfect Communication
in *Rosmersholm*

Introduction

In *Rosmersholm* there are two major plot lines enacted onstage (as opposed to recounted from the past):

—two men wish to become public speakers; both fail.
—a man ends up doubting the word of the woman he loves; in the end, only action can redeem her in his eyes.

The play is also packed with references to voice and expression, suffocation and silence, to hearing and not hearing, to understanding and not understanding others. This tells us that the major concerns of *Rosmersholm* are human expression and its failures, how we can come to doubt the power of words in general, and within a relationship between a man and a woman in particular. In short, *Rosmersholm* is about linguistic skepticism, and its consequences for love.

A linguistic skeptic is someone for whom the road to the skeptical conclusion (that the other is metaphysically unknowable; that I am metaphysically unknowable) goes through a deep disappointment in language. If I am a linguistic skeptic, I am convinced that language fails in its tasks of expression. Then words lose their value; I come to feel that I can never hope to know others, or be known by them, as long as words are all I have to go on.

In *Rosmersholm* the outer is progressively abandoned for the inner: the action and the characters move away from the public and towards the intensely private, away from the body and towards the soul. If we take the ceremony of marriage to represent the moment of public recognition of private desires—that is to say, a moment when the public and the private intersect—then the mock marriage ceremony at the end of the play (no public authority is vested in Rosmer; there are no witnesses) is a figure for the ultimate rejection of human community. After this ceremony, just as they are about to die together, Rebecca and Rosmer declare that they are *one*. This claim marks the end point of their journey away from the body towards the soul. (Only souls can merge: bodies remain desperately separate, even—or, rather, most palpably so—in the act of sex.) *Rosmersholm*, then, shows us how linguistic skepticism can lead to a rejection of externality and a privileging of interiority (figured as secrecy, isolation, exile from all community) so extreme that death is its only possible outcome.

At the same time, however, *Rosmersholm* is a play. Theater is the art of finitude, the art form that most strongly embodies human separation; it is also the most external of arts, the one that challenges us most intensely to acknowledge human expressions.[1] Sitting in the audience watching *Rosmersholm*, we too have to listen to Rosmer's and Rebecca's words, and in this play we have no more to go on than the characters onstage when it comes to understanding them. By accepting our separation from these characters, by acknowledging their plight, we do what they cannot do for each other. The constant emphasis on theater and theatricality in the play is the counterpoint to Rosmer's and Rebecca's journey out of the human condition.

Theatricality in the Melodramatic Mode

Even the most cursory look at *Rosmersholm* reveals plenty of melodramatic elements. Among the most obvious are political power struggle, two women's rivalry for a man, adultery, incest, madness, murder, suicide, and—not least—Beata's "ungovernable, wild passion" (10: 377) and Rebecca's "wild, uncontrollable desire" (10: 426). The house called Rosmersholm, moreover, is a melancholy old manor house in the Gothic tradition, a place where ghostly white horses, harbingers of death, race through gloomy rooms where children never cry and adults never laugh.[2]

Melodrama is a mode of insistent, exaggerated theatricality, an effort to push human expression to its most intense limits. Thus Peter Brooks has suggested that melodrama embodies the "desire to express all", and Cavell has shown that the register of melodrama is above all a register of *voice*.[3] It readily gives rise to images of suffocation and strangulation, of singing, shouting, and crying, and to images concerned with the ear, hearing, sounds, and silence. These are all dominant images or motifs in *Rosmersholm*.

In *Rosmersholm*, moreover, melodrama becomes metatheatrical: in its very theatricality it reminds us that we are in a theater. This effect arises not just from the expressive intensity of the melodramatic mode, but from the fact that *Rosmersholm* almost stridently draws attention to its own use of melodramatic and theatrical devices. The best example is the very last scene, where Mrs Helseth, looking out of the window, reports to the audience what happens in Rebecca's and Rosmer's last moments on earth: "Oh, sweet Jesus! Over there, the white—! My Lord, it's them, both, on the bridge! God have mercy on the sinful creatures! They are embracing each other! [*Screams loudly.*] Oh! Falling—both of them! Into the waterfall. Help! Help! [*Her knees shaking, she is trembling as she holds on to the back of a chair, barely able to form her words.*] No. No help now.—The dead wife got them" (10: 438).

A powerful concoction of sinful passion, the dead wife's revenge, and the ghostly white horses of Rosmersholm, sprinkled with a good measure of invocations of higher powers, Mrs Helseth's tale is pure melodrama. Even an ideologue of modernism like Atle Kittang acknowledges that this scene is "Ibsen at his most melodramatic".[4] But these lines are also a soliloquy, intended to remind us that Rosmer's and Rebecca's deaths are *theatrical*, that they are happening in a theater.

That this is a deliberate effect is beyond doubt. For in *Rosmersholm* there is a brief soliloquy at the end of *every* act.[5] In modern, realist theater, soliloquies are the very sign of stylized, "unrealistic" writing, reminding us of operas and classical tragedy. *Rosmersholm* at once evokes and rebuffs such associations, for its soliloquies barely deserve the name: they serve almost exclusively to draw attention to the fact that this is theater, precisely as each act is drawing to a close. Mrs Helseth's final soliloquy is by far the longest. The others are neither particularly long, nor particularly intense. At the end of Act 1, for example, Mrs Helseth mutters to herself: "Sweet Jesus! That Miss West. The way she talks sometimes" (10: 371).

Just before the end of Act 3, Rebecca watches Rosmer take the long way around the waterfall, yet again: "[*Speaking softly to herself.*] Not across the bridge today either. Goes around. Will never cross the millrace. Never. [*Leaves the window.*] Yes,—yes, then" (10: 420). This is an important moment, for it is here that she decides to give up on Rosmer and leave Rosmersholm. (In her next line she asks Mrs Helseth to bring her trunk down from the attic.)

The final example is Rosmer's puzzled "What—is—this?" at the end of Act 2 (10: 398). Since Ibsen has made sure that audiences and readers share Rosmer's point of view as he stands there alone and bewildered onstage at the end of the act, the question gains maximal urgency. Because it turns the last two acts into a slow unveiling of guilt and innocence, this is a genuinely melodramatic strategy, further enhanced by Kroll's Conan Doyle-like reference to the "riddle of the millrace", which has already drawn our attention to the mystery that is being constructed (10: 384).[6] In this way, Rosmer's soliloquy serves to thicken the sense of enigma surrounding Rebecca as the act closes, and to keep us on tenterhooks until the next opens.

Rosmer's Idealist Project

Rosmer embodies Schiller's idealism. As we have seen in Chapter 3, Schiller thought that art should ennoble us by embodying or pointing to the ideal, which ultimately was the full and free expression of human nature. Human nature, we remember, came in two forms: "actual" (*wirkliche*) human nature and ideal, or "genuine" (*wahre*) human nature. True beauty—and therefore true human freedom—is incompatible with the vulgar and the crude, not least with sexuality, which Schiller considered to be part of actual, but not of true human nature. By recommending the extreme idealization of women (seen as bearers of sexuality), Schiller's idealist aesthetics strongly inspired the proliferation of nineteenth-century literary fantasies about the "pure woman".

That Rosmer was considered to be an idealist in Ibsen's time is borne out by George Bernard Shaw, who in 1891 proposed that the end of *Rosmersholm* should be read as a straightforward critique of the idealist demand that the pure, true, and good woman sacrifice all for love: "[T]he thin veil of a demand for proof with its monstrous sequel of asking the woman to kill herself in order to restore the man's good opinion of himself, falls away. What is really driving Rosmer is the superstition of expiation by sacrifice."[7]

What is Rosmer's project? At the beginning of *Rosmersholm*, it appears to be the same as that of Schiller and the romantics: to work for the advent of a new world through a transformation of the human spirit. Refusing to side with any of the existing factions, Rosmer will participate in the "work of liberation": "to create true democracy in this country" (10: 366). "The true task of democracy", Rosmer continues, is "to make every human being in this country a noble human being." This is to be achieved "by liberating the mind and purifying the will" (10: 366).

When Rosmer is besieged by doubts in Act 2, Rebecca gives voice to the project she has worked so hard to inspire in him:

REBECCA. . . . You wanted to intervene in vibrant life (*levende liv*),—in the vibrant life of today,—as you used to say. You would go as a liberating guest from one house to the other, winning over hearts and minds. Create noble human beings everywhere,—in ever wider circles. Noble human beings.

ROSMER. Joyful and noble human beings.

REBECCA. Yes,—joyful.

ROSMER. For joy ennobles the mind, Rebecca.

(10: 394)

For Rosmer, true nobility of the soul is proved by the presence of the supremely romantic values of *freedom* and *joy* (*glede*).[8] In high idealist fashion, he also stresses the need for peace and reconciliation: "People are becoming evil in the struggle now taking place. Peace and joy and reconciliation must enter their minds. This is why I now step forward and openly confess who I am" (10: 369).

The verb *træde frem*, which I have translated as "step forward", also means to "appear" and has strong connotations of the New Testament's description of the emergence of Jesus as a leader and prophet. This particular verb, then, signifies a public revelation of formerly private or concealed qualities. Rosmer, moreover, immediately connects it to the idea of confessing one's identity. Rosmer, it appears, intends to ennoble others by *revealing himself.* This idea is at once outrageously arrogant (by "stepping forward" he will save humankind: does Rosmer take himself to be Christ?), and astonishingly democratic (for Rosmer has complete faith that the masses can change, that every single person on earth can become an aristocrat).[9]

If this is true, then Rosmer understands his own project in the same terms as idealist aesthetics understands the work of art. Just as the work of art, by embodying beauty, uplifts us, so Rosmer's self-revelation—of his inner beauty? of his very soul?—will uplift the men and women he will visit in their homes, filling them with joy, peace, and harmony (again, I think of Bjørnson's Petra after her first experience of the theater). This also explains why Rosmer feels unable to go ahead once he has started to feel guilty about Beata's death in Act 2, for if his understanding of his mission is that he is to reveal himself as an exemplar of ideal human nature, then guilt and sin have to be banished; otherwise he would simply be presenting a mask: instead of intimate self-revelation, there would be theater.

Ultimately, then, Rosmer's project is about *being*, not *doing*. But Rosmer can't just exhibit himself like another idealist painting. He still needs to reach the souls of men and women by speaking to them. The question of what exactly Rosmer will *say* once he visits the houses of those in need of ennoblement (there are echoes here of Gregers Werle foisting the "ideal demand" on the workers up in Højdalen) remains unanswered in *Rosmersholm*. This tells us something quite significant about Rosmer's relationship to language. To get clearer on the role of language in *Rosmersholm*, it is necessary to turn to Ulrik Brendel, Rosmer's uncanny double.

Ulrik Brendel: Theatricalizing Language

Rosmer's fantasy of self-revelation is placed in an ironic frame by the arrival of Brendel, on his way to deliver his message—his ideals—to the masses. Brendel too wants to "step forward". In his case, however, the expression is immediately linked to the idea of theater: "I want to intervene in life with an energetic hand. Step forward. Step up / Perform" (10: 362).[10] The sense of performance is also there in Brendel's intention to speak in big halls, whereas Rosmer sees himself as a guest in people's homes. Brendel, moreover, is associated with poetry, theater, and the powers of the imagination: at the beginning of the play, his self-image is that of an externally somewhat extinguished, but inwardly still incandescent, romantic poet-prophet.

When Brendel turns up in Act 1, we learn that he is dressed like a tramp, that he is a sometime author, that he used to be a member of a traveling theater company, and that he has done time in the workhouse (see 10: 359). More importantly, he was the young Johannes Rosmer's teacher until he was chased away by Rosmer's strict father because of his radical opinions. There is also a strong suggestion that he has a drinking problem. Brendel is at once an artist, a tramp, and a clown; the humor he brings to *Rosmersholm* reminds me of the comedy in *Waiting for Godot.*

Brendel speaks in set phrases and fragments of quotations. For Brendel, the very act of speaking to another person is an exertion, an effort, a kind of performance. He certainly theatricalizes his own attempts at communication. Thus, after having explained his project to Rosmer, Rebecca, and Dr Kroll in the living room at *Rosmersholm*, Brendel calls them his "audience" and explicitly notes the effect he is having on them: "The audience is moved. That soothes my heart—and strengthens my will. And now I shall proceed to action" (10: 363).

All intent on making his big speech in town, Brendel presents himself as a man of vision, imagination, and insight. His project is a complete break with his past, for until now he has always preferred the solipsistic enjoyment of his own thought: "I like to enjoy my pleasures in solitude. For then I enjoy them twice as much. Twenty times as much. You see,—when golden dreams would drift over me,—daze and bewilder me,—when new, dazzling, far-reaching ideas were born in me,—fanning me with their soaring wings,—then I formed them into poems, visions, images. In rough outline, you understand" (10: 362).

As he develops this theme, the narcissistic references to the laurels of poetry are unmistakable, but so is the imagery of swallowing, eating, and nausea:

BRENDEL. Oh, how I have enjoyed my pleasures and gulped it all down (*svælget*) in my time, Johannes! The mysterious bliss of creating form,—in rough outline, as I said,—the applause, the gratitude, the fame, the laurel wreath,—all this my full hands trembling with joy have received. Sating myself in my secret imaginings with such rapture,—so huge, so dazzling—!

KROLL. Hm—.

REBECCA. But you never wrote anything down?

BRENDEL. Not a word. The tedious task of scribbling has always inspired nauseous revulsion in me.

(10: 363)

In Norwegian, the verb *svælge* ("swallow") sounds quite strange here. The connotations are to oral greediness, to something like a babyish wallowing in food. Brendel also talks about "sating himself". Here Ibsen writes *mætte sig*, a verb that usually means to sate oneself by eating. Psychoanalytically speaking, these are oral images.[11] The same, unusual use of *svælge* turns up once more in the play, this time spoken by Rosmer (see 10: 395; I shall return to this passage in a different context).

The verb *svælge* connects Brendel and Rosmer, stressing the parallels between their ambition and failure. Emphasizing the throat, the area where we take things into the body and expel things from it, the verb connects the sense of enjoyment in fantasy with Brendel's nausea at the thought of writing. Given that it is impossible to swallow and speak at the same time, this reminds us that the throat is also the site of voice and breath, and so the place of suffocation and strangulation. There are also two strikingly unusual uses of the verb *kvæle* ("strangle"), first in Rosmer's proposal to Rebecca, where he speaks of "strangling" the memories of Beata (see 10: 397), and then at the end of the play, when Rebecca says that she can think of nothing that can "strangle" Rosmer's doubts (see 10: 435).

The verbs *svælge* and *kvæle* evoke ideas of forced or silenced expression. In a discussion of the melodramatic drive to "express all", Cavell writes: "I am led to stress the condition that I find to precede, to ground the possibility and the necessity of, 'the desire to express all,' namely the terror of absolute inexpressiveness, suffocation, which at the same time reveals itself as a terror of absolute expressiveness, unconditioned exposure, they are the extreme states of voicelessness."[12] In a further exploration of these fears, he mentions that "One fantasy may appear as a fear of having nothing whatsoever to say—or worse, as an anxiety of there being nothing whatever to say".[13] Brendel is a textbook case, for he thinks of his inner self as his "locked money-box", which, when the time has finally come to unlock it, turns out to be completely empty: he truly had nothing to say, no meanings to share with others (10: 432).

The image of the locked money-box spells out the idea that underpins the fear of having nothing to say: namely, the idea that the soul, the inner self, is something secret, something hidden away, unavailable to others.[14] From here it is easy to move to the idea that the human body is an obstacle to the understanding of the human mind. The next step is to consider language as a curse: as a highly flawed instrument we have to use to connect with others because of the opaqueness of the body. Brendel is a perfect example of this logic, for he dreams of being understood—even adored—without having to write a word: his is a fantasy of perfect communication without the intermediary of language.

Quintessentially skeptical, the fantasy of perfect communication between two souls devalues the body, but it devalues language, too, for it deprives words of all value: human speech can only ever be second best in relation to the true, wordless communion of souls. Again, Brendel is the perfect case in point, for he thinks of his ideals as treasures locked up in his inner money-box, and imagines that sharing them with others will degrade them: "Why would I profane my own ideals when I could enjoy them in their purity and on my own?" (10: 363).

The fantasy of perfect communication of souls clashes completely with the idea of making speeches in public. Public speeches not only require words, they confront us with the freedom of response of others. We simply cannot take for granted that the audience will understand our words the way we do: speaking out, we run the risk of being rebuffed. In comparison, the fantasy of perfect communication from soul to soul comes to look coercive, for it does not open any space for the other's freedom of response: beneath the fantasy of the harmonious merger of souls lurks a refusal to acknowledge the otherness of others.

Brendel, then, is a linguistic skeptic. "The tedious task of scribbling" may be good enough for Ibsen, but it is not good enough for Brendel. Simply by having precise meanings, words degrade and destroy: Brendel could never enjoy his thoughts were he to go beyond the "rough outline". Brendel's project is doomed by his own distrust in language; his fate is a perfect, and darkly comic, allegory of the meaning of *Rosmersholm*.

When he returns to Rosmersholm after his failure, Brendel asks Rosmer if he has any spare ideals, for he has none left. Launching into a scathing condemnation of Mortensgård, he claims that Mortensgård's very subjectivity has been polluted by the degraded social circumstances he aspires to govern: "Peder Mortensgård has the capacity for omnipotence. He can do anything he wants. . . . For Peder Mortensgård never wants more than he can do. Peder Mortensgård is capable of living life without ideals" (10: 433). A man who genuinely can't imagine anything beyond his own powers, Mortensgård is the polar opposite of Rosmer. If Rosmer's ideal is to ennoble others by revealing his innermost soul, Mortensgård is a man whose innermost personality *is* the expression of social forces. If the future belongs to Mortensgård, bourgeois modernity has no place for souls.

After his resounding failure, Brendel's fantasies of plenitude are transformed into fantasies of emptiness; now, he claims, he suffers only from "homesickness for the great void" (10: 431). Rife with references to negativity and nothingness, Brendel's last lines are spoken in his usual theatrical style. But if Brendel remains theatrical in his moments of extreme distress, it is because he now speaks knowing that he has nothing to express. (What can be more theatrical than a performance of nothing?) Like idealism itself, he has survived himself: he is a ghost on its way to extinction.

Rebecca's Refusal

At the end of Act 2, Rebecca violently refuses Rosmer's proposal of marriage. What is more, she refuses to explain why. If he ever again asks why she won't marry him, it is over between them, she says, and Rosmer is left alone onstage to utter his melodramatic "What—is—this?" (10: 398).

Critics and audiences have shared Rosmer's bewilderment. "Rosmer cannot understand this rejection," Freud writes in his famous 1916 essay on *Rosmersholm*, "and still less can we, who know more of Rebecca's actions and designs."[15] Freud's theory is that Rebecca refuses Rosmer because she suffers from guilt over a previous sexual relationship with her late adoptive father, Dr West. This explains why Kroll's revelation in Act 3—that Dr West in all probability was her real father—comes as such a shock to her. I think this is right. But, as Freud readily admits, the trouble is that he still has not explained why Rebecca refuses to marry Rosmer at the end of Act 2—that is to say, well *before* she learns that Dr West may be her real father. Since I do not find Freud's attempt to solve this problem particularly convincing, I shall try to suggest another reading of Rebecca's refusal.[16]

First of all, it is worth noting that Ibsen himself did not find Rebecca's motivation all that puzzling: "I don't think Rebecca's character is difficult to penetrate and understand," he wrote to a young actress in 1887 (18: 131).[17] I take this to mean that all we need to do to explain her refusal is to take her own explanations seriously. After all, at the end of Act 2, she knows something we do not: namely, that she used her charms to make Beata fall in love with her—Ibsen uses the term *desperat forelskelse* ("desperate love or infatuation") to describe Beata's feelings for Rebecca—only to manipulate the credulous, unstable, and infatuated woman into the millrace (10: 409).

In Act 4 Rebecca explains that she couldn't accept Rosmer's proposal because by the time he proposed, he had already succeeded in ennobling her. When she arrived at Rosmersholm, she was free, energetic, and ready to commit crimes to reach her goals, but life with Rosmer changed her, removing her wild sexual desire, and filling her with pure, forsaking love instead. In spite of all this, Rebecca admits that this transformation has destroyed the one thing she wanted in life: happiness:

REBECCA. The Rosmerian view of life ennobles. But—[*shakes her head*]—but,—but—
ROSMER. But? What?
REBECCA. —But it kills happiness, you know.

(10: 429)

Living at Rosmersholm, Rebecca has been transformed from an amoral Nietzschean to a guilt-ridden, post-Christian idealist. She too has come to consider sexuality as a fall, as second-rate compared to the intense purity cultivated by Rosmer. "Everything else,—that ugly, sensual desire, drifted so far away from me. . . . Then love arose in me. A great, self-renouncing love that contents itself with the way we two have been living together" (10: 428).

Rebecca is here revealing powerful, even compelling, reasons to refuse Rosmer's proposal. Idealists might have found them entirely sufficient (the very thought that Rebecca should "profit from her crime" would have been anathema to them), yet Freud (and all the other critics who have followed in his footsteps) have found them emotionally shallow. Even if we fully believe Rebecca, the play still gives the impression that there is more to her refusal than this. This becomes apparent if we consider it in the light of the main theme of *Rosmersholm*: namely, expression, communication, and language, or, more concretely, the many signs that Rosmer, for one reason or another, does not listen to Rebecca.

Rosmer's Deafness

Rosmer constantly shows himself guilty of a certain deafness in relation to Rebecca. This is highlighted in the very first scene of the second act, which opens with a piece of apparently banal conversation. Rosmer is in his study with his back to the audience, leafing through a pamphlet from his library, when there is a knock on the door:

ROSMER [*without turning*]. Come right in.

> [*Rebecca West, in a dressing-gown, enters.*]

REBECCA. Good morning.
ROSMER [*looks through his pamphlet*]. Good morning, dear. Is there anything you want?
REBECCA. I just wanted to hear if you slept well.
ROSMER. Oh, I have slept so soundly, so delightfully. No dreams—. [*turns around.*] And you?
REBECCA. Yes, thank you. Towards morning, at least—
ROSMER. I don't know when I last felt so easy at heart as now. Oh, it was truly good to get it said.
REBECCA. Yes, you shouldn't have kept silent for so long, Rosmer.

(10: 372)

This is precisely the kind of conversation that has made many critics believe that Ibsen is nothing but a dreary representational realist, reproducing banalities onstage to no purpose other than to imitate everyday chit-chat. But this passage does much dramatic work: it contrasts Rosmer's political naïvety with Rebecca's more realistic assessment of the situation, and tells us a number of things about their relationship. First of all, it is obvious that Rebecca is not telling the truth when she says that she has come simply to ask whether Rosmer has slept well. For if she herself had great difficulty in falling asleep, it was presumably because there was something on her mind, something she now wants to discuss with Rosmer. But she doesn't say that, at least not right away.

Rosmer, on the other hand, doesn't pause to ask her why she slept so badly. Moreover, because Rosmer keeps his back turned to her for the first half of the conversation, he blocks out her expression, her gestures, and her general body language, which might have helped him to hear what she is not saying. Interrupting Rebecca's brief mention of her own bad night, he eagerly expands on his own easy happiness. It is as if he does not want to know that

Rebecca does not share his joyous mood. This is important, for the next time Rosmer shows his peculiar deafness in relation to Rebecca, it is at a more important juncture: namely, just before the proposal, at the point when he complains that guilt makes his big political project impossible (we should also note the verb *svælge* ("swallow") in this passage):

ROSMER. . . . There will always be a lingering doubt. A question. I'll never again be able to bask in (*svælge i*) that which makes life so wonderfully delightful to live.

REBECCA [*leaning over the back of his chair, more slowly*]. What kind of thing is it you mean, Rosmer?

ROSMER [*looking up at her*]. Quiet, joyous freedom from guilt.

REBECCA [*takes a step back*]. Yes. Freedom from guilt.

[*Brief pause.*]

(10: 394–5)

Rebecca's reaction to Rosmer's emphasis on freedom from guilt is striking. Although she *says* nothing, her body moves. Her step back is a recoil, the result of a shock, certainly a graphic embodiment of new insight. In this crucial moment, if not before, Rebecca feels the weight of her own past. By making her repeat Rosmer's exact words, Ibsen shows that they have a profoundly different meaning for her. Yet Rosmer takes none of this in. In particular, he does not see Rebecca's body: what he takes to be the free exchange of thoughts between them is far more one-sided than he wants to admit. This brings us to the proposal scene:

ROSMER [*comes closer*]. Rebecca,—if I asked you now,—will you be my second wife?[18]

REBECCA [*speechless for a moment, then cries out in joy.*] Your wife! Your—! Me!

ROSMER. Good. Let us try it. We two will be *one*. There must no longer be an empty space left by the dead.

REBECCA. Me—in Beata's place—!

ROSMER. Then she will be out of the story. Completely out of it. For ever and ever.

REBECCA. [*in a slow trembling voice*]. Do you think so, Rosmer?

ROSMER. It has to happen! It has to! I can't—I won't go through life with a corpse on my back. Help me cast it off, Rebecca. And then let us strangle all memories in freedom, in pleasure, in passion. You shall be to me the only wife I have ever had.

REBECCA [*composed*]. Don't ever mention this again. I will never be your wife.

ROSMER. What! Never! Oh, don't you think you could come to love me? Is there not already a touch of love in our friendship?

REBECCA [*covering her ears with her hands, as in fear*]. Don't talk that way, Rosmer! Don't say that kind of thing!

(10: 397)

First we should note the striking use of the verb *kvæle* ("strangle"): "And let us then strangle all memories in freedom, pleasure and passion," Rosmer says. The verb turns Rosmer's memories of Beata into throats to be squeezed, voices to be silenced. This is appropriate, for this scene turns on Rosmer's violent and Rebecca's terrified wish *not to hear* certain things. For Rosmer, the voice that must be strangled, the corpse that has to be cast off, is Beata's. For Rebecca, the words that must be screened out are Rosmer's words of love, which she treats rather like Odysseus treats the sirens' song.

Rosmer's proposal also contains a fairly explicit reference to sex: in Norwegian *lidenskab* ("sensual passion") is a strong, sexual word. The only other time the word turns up in the text is in his reference to Beata's sexuality, which Rosmer experienced as frightening and abnormal. To him, Beata's "ungovernable, wild (sensual) passion" only confirmed his belief that she was mad (10: 377). For Rosmer, then, sex has been connected to fear, madness, and a sense of complete estrangement from the desiring other.

Rosmer has started to think of sex as a solution because he believes that celibate cohabitation, what he calls a "pure life together", is possible only in "quiet, happy peace" (10: 396). The political turmoil that now lies ahead means that he will have to lead a "life of struggle and unrest and strong emotions" (10: 396). Debasing sex by linking it with unethical political warfare, this logic makes sex second-rate compared to the joyous, guilt-free, and sexless life he truly aspires to. Above all, however, the proposal scene exhibits, once again, Rosmer's strange deafness to Rebecca's voice. Rosmer does not ask whether *Rebecca* will be able to "strangle all memories" by marrying *him*. It is as if it doesn't occur to him that Rebecca might have memories of her own to deal with. Rosmer's frequent deafness to Rebecca's reactions strikes me as the effect of a profound refusal to acknowledge Rebecca's difference from himself, by which I mean her separate human existence.

"Acknowledgment of the other calls for recognition of the other's specific relation to oneself, and . . . this entails the revelation of oneself as having denied or distorted that relationship," Cavell writes in *The Claim of Reason*.[19] What is it about his relationship to Rebecca that Rosmer does not want to see? I am sure that it is his obvious denial of her body, of her palpable, wild, irrepressible desire for him. This is what he has avoided, and the result is tragedy. At the very end, at the exact point where Rebecca explains that Rosmer has transformed her, that her original wild desire has disappeared, and that she now contents herself with loving him in a self-renouncing way, Rosmer replies, "Oh, if only I had had the faintest notion of all this!" (10: 428). In what tone does Rosmer speak his last line? Is he blaming himself or Rebecca? Or just wishing for a different fate? I can't tell. My point is that

Rosmer *ought* to have had *some* notion of "all this". His specific avoidance is the avoidance of the sexed and sexual human body; the tragedy at the end of *Rosmersholm* is caused by his denial of the "vulgar" and the "low", in the name of an Edenic ideal of innocence.

No wonder, then, that Rebecca covers her ears when Rosmer speaks words of love in the proposal scene. She does not want to hear them because they come too late, because they increase the pain of renunciation, and because they are so utterly naïve. For when Rosmer says "Oh, don't you think you could come to love me?", he reveals his bottomless ignorance and complete blindness. If he hasn't seen that she loves him already, that she has done so ever since she first met him, to the point of being willing to kill for his sake, then Rebecca can't fail to feel profoundly unacknowledged.

In short: in the very way he proposes to her, Rosmer disappoints her.[20] It is as if Rebecca thinks that although she has *said* nothing, Rosmer should have been able to read her soul. The worst part of it is that she knows that she herself has colluded in Rosmer's deafness, by her silences, her secrets, by her deceit, by her calm, gentle talk about helping Rosmer to ennoble people. But this would not prevent her from feeling that he ought to know more about the woman he is proposing to.

Rebecca has something in common with Brendel: just as he wants adulation without the work of writing, so she wants to be understood without having to use words to reveal herself. (In Act 1, Rebecca is the only character who appears fully to believe in the riches of Brendel's unwritten works.) Her version of this fantasy is nevertheless different from Brendel's solipsism, for hers is the romantic dream of true love, of the two twin souls destined for each other from all eternity.

The moment of Rosmer's proposal is the moment of breakdown of conversation, the moment when it becomes clear that Rosmer simply will not acknowledge Rebecca's separation and otherness, and when Rebecca realizes that she will never be able to share her innermost feelings with Rosmer. Since the purpose of the marriage is to help Rosmer feel free from guilt in relation to Beata, it follows that if Rebecca marries Rosmer, she will have to remain forever silent about her crime. Rosmer may throw off Beata's corpse, but her dead body will be forever entombed in Rebecca. The very solution that will enable Rosmer to "strangle all memories" will also strangle Rebecca's voice. At this point, these two are not one; they are separated by an abyss. Rosmer's puzzled soliloquy at the end of the act enacts this separation. The difference is that Rebecca already knows this, while Rosmer still has no clue.

Rosmer's Illusions: Language and Finitude

In Act 3, Rosmer starts to wonder about the nature of his past relationship with Rebecca:

ROSMER [*puts his hat down on the table*]. The question I've been wrestling with is—whether the two of us weren't deceiving ourselves all the time when we called our relationship a friendship.

REBECCA. You mean we could just as well have called it—

ROSMER. —a love relationship. Yes, that's what I mean. Even when Beata was living, I gave all my thoughts to you. I was longing only for you. It was with you that I felt this quiet, joyous, desireless bliss. If we really think about it, Rebecca—our life together began the way two children fall in love, secretly and sweetly. No demands, and no dreams. Didn't you feel that way, too? Tell me.

REBECCA [*struggling with herself*]. Oh—I don't know how to answer you.

ROSMER. And it's this intense life in and for each other that we took for friendship. No, Rebecca—our relationship has been a spiritual marriage—perhaps from the very first days. This is why there is sin on my part. I had no right to it—I wasn't allowed, for Beata's sake.

(10: 406)

Rosmer's criterion for love, the passage reveals, is that he has always been able to express his soul to Rebecca. Taking his own openness for a genuine communion of souls, he felt ecstatically happy. He also felt childish—that is to say, sexually undefined—and so, above all, he feels *unfallen*. Projecting these feelings onto Rebecca, taking her to be the pure woman, he is overjoyed and delighted. Again, Rosmer appears to be curiously uninterested in Rebecca's responses. We never learn, for example, what *she* might have wanted to call their relationship. Strangely inattentive to her non-verbal reactions, Rosmer does not notice Rebecca's "struggle with herself", nor her less than enthusiastic response to his demand that she mirror his own feelings. Instead, he takes her reticent and half-hearted words as unqualified assent, and carries on as if she had warmly embraced his view.

Rosmer, in short, speaks as if the two were already one. Here, then, is his version of the fantasy of perfect communion without words, and again we see that this fantasy hides a destructive element: the negation of the other's difference, which is easily turned into aggression and violence, a violence that surfaces in Rosmer's wish to strangle voices he doesn't want to hear, not to mention the outrageous demand that Rebecca kill herself for his sake.

Until the nasty rumors about Beata's death and about himself and Rebecca started to circulate, Rosmer lived in his own private little Eden. The sweet unspoken, unacknowledged childlike love described by Rosmer is without sex, without self-consciousness, and without sin. The expulsion from Eden happens right here, in the very moment Rosmer starts wondering what words to use for this relationship. Was their relationship friendship or childlike love, or even a spiritual marriage? It doesn't really matter, for once language becomes necessary, we are fallen. The power of language to define, describe, to make us self-conscious, to give us knowledge, is undeniable, but it comes at the price of separation and loss. The very existence of words opens up a gap between words and things, or so a skeptic would say. Now that Rosmer has to speak about their relationship, the original state of guiltless and guileless innocence is lost forever: nothing he can *say* can recapture his lost bliss.

The fantasy of communication without words is at work both in Rebecca and in Rosmer, but it takes a different form in each of them. Rebecca's fantasy starts from the fact of her isolation, her separateness, and takes the form of wishing to be known by Rosmer without having to use words. She wants Rosmer to be able to read her soul. Rosmer's fantasy, on the other hand, starts with the disavowal of human separation, and takes the form of imagining that the other is a part of himself.

The ordeal: Losing faith in language

In Act 4, Rebecca claims that Rosmer has transformed her, that his spiritual influence has made her a purer, nobler being. In her view, this ought to give him back his faith in himself, in his power to "ennoble people". But Rosmer is consumed by doubt. She has hidden so much from him before, why should he believe her now? Perhaps she's just saying this to further some kind of agenda of her own. His response distresses Rebecca:

REBECCA [*wringing her hands*]. Oh this murderous doubt—! Rosmer,—Rosmer—!
ROSMER. Yes, it's appalling, isn't it, Rebecca? But I can't help it. I'll never be able to free myself from this doubt. Never know for certain that I have you in whole and pure love.
REBECCA. But isn't there something deep inside you that testifies (*vidner for*) that a transformation has taken place in me! And that the transformation has come from you—and only you!
ROSMER. Oh, Rebecca—I've lost faith in my power to transform people. I have no faith in myself at all any more. I don't believe in myself or in you.
REBECCA [*looking at him somberly*]. Then how can you go on living?

(10: 430–1)

At other times Rebecca uses the word *omslaget* ("shift", "change"). Here, however, she uses Nora's word from the last lines of *A Doll's House: forvandlingen* ("the transformation"). Nora doubts that the transformation necessary for marriage to be possible could ever happen; Rebecca claims that it has already taken place, that she *is* profoundly changed. But how does one *prove* to another that one is a changed person? This is a question Nora doesn't have to confront; it is *the* question at the end of *Rosmersholm*.

Appealing to Rosmer's own, inner understanding of the matter, Rebecca asks whether there is nothing in his inner self that *vidner for*—testifies to, bears witness to—the fact that she has changed? That Rosmer cannot find anything inside himself to support her claim is not surprising, for he truly doesn't know her. When the image of Rebecca as an extension of himself, his narcissistic mirror image, is shattered by Rebecca's confession of her crime in Act 3, the bewildered Rosmer has no image of her at all. From now on, he doubts everything she says. The underlying logic is one of absolutes: if Rosmer can't read Rebecca as an open book, he will conclude that he can't know her at all. For him, there is no middle ground. This is the position of radical skepticism, and when it permeates an extremist such as Rosmer, everyday life and ordinary human interaction become impossible. No wonder that Rebecca asks, "Then how can you go on living?"

Errol Durbach's comments on this moment strike me as exactly right: "But how does one prove a condition of spirit, an alternation of consciousness? And how does one convince when language itself has lost all credibility?"[21] Rebecca is here put in the position of the person who is trying to convince the skeptic that he *can* have knowledge of the world or others. This is a futile endeavor. But now that Rebecca has revealed herself as other, as a consciousness separate from his own, Rosmer too is confronted by the problem of how one can know what other people think and feel, or even *that* they think and feel. Rosmer thought he was one with Rebecca, which is to say he thought the problem of other minds did not apply to her. Now he realizes that it does, and the result is bone-chilling loneliness.

After the passage just quoted, Rosmer says that he doesn't think he can live without faith in himself and in Rebecca:

REBECCA. Oh, life—life has renewal in it. Let's hold on to it, Rosmer.—We're out of it soon enough.

ROSMER [*leaps restlessly to his feet*]. Then give me my faith again! My faith in *you*, Rebecca. Faith in your love! You must bear witness! I've got to get you to bear witness!

REBECCA. Bear witness? How can I bear witness for you—!

ROSMER. You *must*! [*Pacing the floor.*] I can't bear this desolate—this awful emptiness—this—this—[*Sharp knocking on the hall door*].

(10: 431)

Here Ulrik Brendel enters on his way to the great void.

Rosmer is asking for *vidnesbyrd*. The importance of the word is obvious: it is repeated four times in a row. Most translations settle for "proof" or "evidence". But in Norwegian there is a distinction between *vidnesbyrd* ("testimony", "the act of bearing witness") and *bevis* ("proof", "evidence"). In *Rosmersholm* this distinction is important. First of all, *vidnesbyrd* has to do with a person, and designates a particular kind of speech act: that of bearing witness. To bear witness, it is necessary to give voice to one's own perceptions of something; proof, on the other hand, often refers to things or facts (think of Othello's taking Desdemona's handkerchief to be the "ocular proof" of her betrayal). Rosmer's absolute doubt echoes Othello's. Othello's doubt makes him characterize Desdemona as a "closet, lock and key of villainous secrets".[22] Rosmer has come to experience Rebecca in exactly the same way. Nothing Rebecca can *say* will give Rosmer his faith back. So we get to the idea of the ordeal, not by fire, but by water.

Here it is relevant to note that *vidnesbyrd* also evokes *jernbyrd*, as in *bære jernbyrd* ("to carry iron"). *Jernbyrd* is a version of the medieval ordeal by fire, a test of truth and innocence in which the person tested had to carry red-hot iron in her hands. In Ibsen's *The Pretenders*, set in thirteenth-century Norway, the ordeal by fire is associated with a woman risking her body and her life for a man. The curtain rises on a square in front of a church. Hymns are heard, the assembled crowd wonders what is happening, and Bishop Nicholas enters to announce that "Now Inga from Vartejg is carrying red-hot iron for Håkon the Pretender" (5: 23). Inga is Håkon's mother, and her *jernbyrd* proves that Håkon is the legitimate heir to the Norwegian throne. Throughout the play, Håkon's rock-solid faith in his vocation and right to be king is related to the *jernbyrd*, and contrasted with the doubt of the other pretender, Duke Skule.[23]

When Rosmer makes his fatal demand, moreover, he explicitly invokes Brendel. "Have you the courage to—are you willing to, joyfully, as Ulrik Brendel said,—for my sake, now, tonight—joyfully, to go the same way,—that Beata went?" (10: 436). I read the reference to Brendel—the man who discovered that he was empty inside, that he had nothing whatsoever to say—as an indication that when language has failed, action is the only option. That Brendel uses the image of Rebecca cutting off her little finger and her left ear for Rosmer's sake reinforces the parallel (see 10: 433).

In the passage we are still concerned with here, both Rosmer's language and the stage directions have a strong melodramatic flavor. He "leaps . . . to his feet", and every single line he utters ends with an exclamation mark, before he runs out of words to signify his feelings ("this desolate—this awful emptiness—this—this—"). Here Rosmer is literally losing his voice. This passage is the inscription of a struggle between expressiveness and muteness, between voice and silence.

If I start believing that I cannot express myself at all, I may be overcome by the fear that I have fallen out of human community: that nobody will ever acknowledge me as a fellow member of the human race. Then I can become overcome by fear, the fear of being inhuman, monstrous, alien, mad. First projected onto the poor Beata, Rosmer's fear of monstrosity and madness here resurfaces in himself. His wildly egocentric and melodramatic demand that Rebecca kill herself for his sake is a madman's attempt to recover something like an identity, something like a voice. At the very end of the play, Rosmer for a moment (but only for a moment) registers the sheer madness of their behavior: "All this—it's insanity," he exclaims (10: 436). Then they continue as before.

Consciousness of the finitude of human existence, of our separation, our sexuality, our mortality, is the fruit of the tree of knowledge. It is the knowledge that expels us from Eden and gives us the idea that we need redemption, that the world and everyone in it need to be made over. This has been Rosmer's project. When it fails, all he can do is to follow the lure of the millrace, the whirling waters of madness. As Rosmer and Rebecca near their end, they have become monstrous in their mad, incandescent forswearing of the world.

"Now we two are one": Voices for Death

Rereading the end of *Rosmersholm* I am struck by the fact that the text moves with extreme rapidity from the idea that *Rebecca* is to kill herself to restore Rosmer's *tro* ("faith", "belief"), to the idea that they are to die *together*.[24] Why does Rosmer change his mind? Why does it suddenly become necessary for him to go with her to the millrace? Critics have not always paid attention to Rosmer's change of heart. Atle Kittang goes so far as to speak of "the Rosmer who in the final scene persuades Rebecca to go with him into the millrace", which implies that Rosmer had decided to commit suicide all along.[25] A careful look at the passage where Rosmer makes up his mind shows that the situation is more complicated:

REBECCA [*slowly picks up her shawl, throws it over her head, and says calmly*]. You'll get
  your faith back.

ROSMER. Have you the courage and will—for this, Rebecca?

REBECCA. You'll have to judge that tomorrow—or later—when they fish me out.

ROSMER [*with his hand to his forehead*]. There is a fascinating horror in this—!

REBECCA. For I don't want to lie down there—any longer than necessary. Take care
  that they find me.

ROSMER [*springs to his feet*]. But all this—it's insanity! Leave—or stay! I'll believe you
  on your word alone this time too.

REBECCA. Empty talk, Rosmer. No more cowardice and evasions now! How can you
  believe me on nothing but my word after this day?

ROSMER. But I don't want to see your defeat, Rebecca!

REBECCA. There will be no defeat.

ROSMER. Yes, there will. You'll never have the mind to follow Beata.

REBECCA. You don't think so?

ROSMER. Never. You're not like Beata. You're not ruled by a warped view of life.

REBECCA. But I am under the Rosmersholmian view of life—*now*. For the crimes I
  have committed—it behooves me to atone.

ROSMER [*looks fixedly at her*]. Have you come to *that*?

REBECCA. Yes.

ROSMER [*with determination*]. I see. Well, *I* hold by our liberated view of life. There
  is no judge over us, therefore we have to ensure that we carry out justice ourselves.

REBECCA [*misinterpreting him*]. Yes. Yes, that too. My going will save the best in you.

(10: 437)

The question of whether it is possible to believe Rebecca "on [her] word
alone" is here explicitly discussed and rejected. Words are decidedly no longer
acceptable at Rosmersholm. The stage is thus set for Rebecca's ordeal by
water. If she dies, she is pure and worthy of Rosmer; if she decides to live, she
is not. The parallel to witch dunking is obvious. Earlier in the play there are,
in fact, many indications that there is something witch-like about Rebecca, as
when Kroll alludes to Rebecca's erotic powers over himself and Beata by
saying "Who could you not bewitch—when you put your mind to it?"
(10: 409).

At the end of this conversation, it is clear that Rosmer has changed his
mind and decided to die too. The first sign that he has done so is to be found
in the stage direction "*with determination*", before his conclusion: namely,
that we have to "carry out justice ourselves". In the next line, the stage
directions specify that Rebecca *misinterprets* him when she takes this to refer
to her death and his survival. After this point in the text, Rosmer explicitly
declares that he will go with Rebecca.

What is it in this conversation that pushes Rosmer in this direction? The stage directions show that he reacts extremely melodramatically ("*with his hand to his forehead*"; "*springs to his feet*") at two specific points: namely, when Rebecca refers to her own dead body lying in the water. There is something new about Rebecca's voice in those lines. For the first time she issues orders to Rosmer. Her concrete, powerful language is strikingly ordinary, clear, and decisive. There is an authority about her, a certainty that must seem compelling to the doubtful and hesitant Rosmer. Refusing spiritual and metaphysical generalities, she issues instructions about finding and disposing of her corpse, in strikingly concrete terms: "when they fish me out"; "Take care that they find me." In this way she brings home the material, bodily aspect of death in a way that must sound completely shocking to Rosmer.

In my view, then, it is only when Rosmer hears Rebecca's explicit and forceful references to her own dead body, that he decides to die, too. This is the moment when he has to acknowledge Rebecca's separation from himself, the moment when he fully understands that Rebecca's death will not give his faith and his project back, for that faith and that project were based on an Edenic disavowal of the difference of others. Standing there while they "fish out" her corpse, he will finally be confronted with his own human body, his own finitude. Rosmer decides to die because he cannot bear to live as an ordinary mortal human being in an ordinary world of difference and separation.

Rosmer's Edenic fantasies of spiritual marriage were an attempt to make two one without sex. The decision to die with Rebecca is Rosmer's last attempt to salvage the fantasy that two can be one. In *Rosmersholm* death is the other side of sex. This is why he pronounces the words of the marriage ritual before they leave for the millrace: their marriage is the negation of ordinary marriage; they are married not for life but for death.

Their very last conversation is a discussion of a question that has often bothered critics: namely, who bears the greater responsibility for this double suicide:

REBECCA. But tell me this first. Do you follow me? Or do I follow you?
ROSMER. We'll never get completely to the bottom of that.
REBECCA. Still, I would really like to know.
ROSMER. We two follow each other, Rebecca. I you and you me.
REBECCA. That's what I believe too.
ROSMER. For now we two are *one*.
REBECCA. Yes, now we are *one*. Come! Let's go gladly then.

[*They leave hand in hand through the front room . . .*]

(10: 438)

Ibsen's language here is a masterpiece of economy. Here is the desire for knowledge, the frustrated search for absolute answers (*grunde ud tilbunds* is more philosophical than the English "get completely to the bottom of"), but both expressions contain an allusion to the bottom of the millpond), and above all that stunning sequence of personal pronouns: "I you and you me", which tells us, again, that this whole play has been about self and other, identity and the loss of it, the dream of merger and the fact of separation. By choosing to die, they are rejecting separation, finitude, the everyday, the world.

Leaping into the millrace, Rebecca and Rosmer consider the world well lost. In fact, the theme of the loss of the world has been there from the very start, for it is implied in the very setting and name of Rosmersholm. In Norwegian a *holme* is a tiny island or large rock surrounded by water. Rosmersholm, a manor house some way outside the town, is Rosmer's island. The world is out there, but as the action unfolds, it recedes further and further away. The last person to visit Rosmer's island is Ulrik Brendel, and he is heading for the great void.

Floating free of the rest of society, Rosmersholm is increasingly given over to the fantastic. The intensification of Gothic and melodramatic elements at the end of *Rosmersholm* shows us that Rebecca and Rosmer could not manage to "transcendentalize the domestic", could not find meaning in everyday life, could not find a way back to the ordinary, the everyday.[26] So the ghosts of *Rosmersholm*, the deadly white horses, come rushing in at the very end, reincarnated in Rebecca's white shawl, transformed from domestic handiwork to harbinger of death.

Are They One?

In Rosmer and Rebecca's last lines, there is happiness. Twice Rebecca stresses the joy of her last act on earth, and there is no reason to disbelieve her. The question is no longer one of belief: it is whether we can follow them in their decision to sacrifice their lives for a dream of absolute purity. As the curtain falls, we are left with Mrs Helseth's image of Rebecca and Rosmer falling into the millrace. Are we to venerate it as an icon of romantic love, or consider it a declaration of failure?

On this point, critics have always been sharply divided. Some find that Rebecca's and Rosmer's final declaration that they are one expresses the deepest truth of the play, and take the end to exemplify the lovers' sacrificial, expiatory unity.[27] "They . . . die as a fusion of autonomous spiritual powers, a single consciousness, a genuine cosmology of two," Errol Durbach claims.[28] Such interpretations are possible only if one idealizes the protagonists, and espouses a fairly idealist view of life and literature. Vigdis Ystad, for example, writes, "Because of the tragic conflict structure in the very nature of life and love, perfect realization of love can only occur through complete self-abandon: through sacrifice."[29] Others beg to differ. Readers who, like George Bernard Shaw, prefer a political reading of *Rosmersholm*, refuse to idealize the protagonists. To such readers, Rosmer's "Now we two are *one*" expresses his own deluded view, and Rebecca's assent is motivated by disillusionment and self-hatred: "When Rebecca agrees to kill herself in the millstream it is not expiation but a furious disappointment in Rosmer and disgust with herself," Elisabeth Hardwick claims.[30]

My own view is that *Rosmersholm* is a pessimistic analysis of the condition of politics and love in modernity, incompatible with the idealism of the traditional tragedy. First of all, I think it is a mistake to idealize the kind of love that Rosmer and Rebecca reach at the end: their relationship, after all, has been based on Rebecca's explicit lies and Rosmer's failure to acknowledge her difference from himself.[31] Their fantasies of merger and union are unlivable, destructive, and death-dealing, for they are built on a vision of the body as an obstacle to the merger of souls, a vision that can lead only to desperate skepticism when confronted with the most fundamental aspects of the human condition: that we have separate, sexed, and mortal bodies; that we need to use language to understand others and to make them understand us. In this play, Rosmer's and Rebecca's rejection of the everyday stands as a figure for their skepticism.

Why, then, do I still say that there is something tragic about the end? Ibsen has placed his protagonists in a world disfigured by egoism, self-aggrandizement, and cynicism. At the end of the play, Brendel's scathing condemnation of Mortensgård stands uncorrected. It is *this* modern world, filled with despicable political maneuvers in equally despicable media, that Rebecca and Rosmer reject. In such a world, Rosmer's naïve and unlivable idealism shines like a beacon. No wonder Rebecca is attracted to him: he must be the only thoroughly good and decent man she has ever met.

It is well known that Ibsen himself shared some of Rosmer's ideals. In a famous speech to the workers of Trondheim on 14 June 1885 (the summer before he started work on *Rosmersholm*), he expressed his disappointment with the new parliamentary regime: "A majority of those who govern us grant neither freedom of belief nor freedom of expression to the individual, beyond an arbitrarily fixed limit. There is then still much to do before we can be said to have reached true freedom. But our present democracy will probably not be equal to those tasks. A noble element must be introduced into the life of the state, in our government, in our representatives, and in our press" (15: 407).

The nobility he seeks, Ibsen adds, has nothing to do with birth or money: "I am thinking of the nobility of character, mind and will. It alone can liberate us. This nobility . . . will come to us from two sides. It will come to us from two groups, which have not yet been irreparably damaged by the pressure of political partisanship. It will come to us from our women and our workers" (15: 408). Yet Ibsen himself never tried to "step forward" and reveal his inner beauty to the masses, and he certainly never disdained the "tedious task of scribbling" (10: 363). Strongly in favor of radical change, he was convinced that it would never come about through the squalid dealings of parliamentary democracy. Rosmer's mistake is a noble one: he wants to engage in politics in order to ennoble the world; yet this is a project that Ibsen must have considered hopeless from the start. Rosmer's judgment is here at fault. His project is hardly without flaws, either. At the end of the play, Rosmer says to Rebecca, "Human beings can't be ennobled from outside, Rebecca," and she replies, "Not even through quiet love?" (10: 430). Like Julian before him, Rosmer tried to change the world by talking about joy and beauty, while forgetting about love.

Again, we have reached a point where the complexity of Ibsen's vision is striking. Politically and humanly, he has sympathy for Rosmer. But that sympathy only goes so far. At the end of the play, Rebecca represents the spirit of Rosmersholm not as something joyful and liberating, but as something dark and crushing, something that weighs her down, something that deprives her of happiness. This is dystopia, not utopia. Rosmer's idealism has turned into its own negative mirror image, just as Rosmer and Rebecca's "marriage" is the negation of the life in society that marriage ordinarily represents. The death of the protagonists does not bring about reconciliation, for their claim of union represents an extreme withdrawal into their own private world: that way madness lies. At the end of the play, it is impossible to return to Rosmer's doomed project of ennoblement, and equally impossible to espouse either the protagonists' suicidal incandescence or the debased values of the society that surrounds them. *Rosmersholm*, then, is a play about the noble and lamented, yet inevitable and necessary, death of the romantic project in the post-Nietzschean world. The play conveys in equal measure Rebecca's and Rosmer's grandeur and their monstrosity and madness. They are heartbroken romantics (not moralizing idealists) who cannot bear the world that bourgeois democracy has produced. That is why Ibsen asks his audience to fully acknowledge their plight.

In its obsession with doubt, proof, and testimony, and its subtle analysis of the wreckage produced by linguistic skepticism, *Rosmersholm* is one of Ibsen's most pessimistic analyses of modernity. This is a world in which even the best men and women can't find a way to have livable relationships, a world in which the deepest expressions of the pain of the soul will go unheard and unacknowledged, where language has come to seem untrustworthy, and where the search for absolute truth will drive us mad. *Rosmersholm* is Ibsen's darkest and most complex play. It is a masterpiece.

10

The Art of Transformation
Art, Marriage, and Freedom in *The Lady from the Sea*

Introduction

The middle play of the so-called Munich trilogy, *The Lady from the Sea* (1888) follows *Rosmersholm* (1886) and precedes *Hedda Gabler* (1890). Whereas *Rosmersholm* and *Hedda Gabler* end with suicide, *The Lady from the Sea* has a happy ending. For this reason this remarkable play has often been treated as one of Ibsen's least convincing and most light-weight works. Errol Durbach rightly comments that "the positive ending of *The Lady from the Sea* has opened it to 'charges of artistic deficiency, of being somehow not *echt* Ibsen'—defying, as it does, the stereotypical image of Ibsen as the prophet of doom, while affirming the bourgeois carp-pond of marriage and family and distressing those modern Romantics for whom the *dénouement* betrays the vigorous Romantic spirit".[1] (I take it that romantic here means something like the dramatic, existential, heroic, and idealist, as opposed to the ordinary and the everyday.) Examples of the dismissive attitude provoked by the play's happy ending abound. Maurice Valency, for example, claims that "[The optimistic outcome] was an unusual departure for Ibsen, and the result is singularly unconvincing".[2] The last act, in particular, he claims, is "quite without vitality".[3] Bjørn Hemmer adds that many critics of *The Lady from the Sea* try to reinterpret the offending end, for they "prefer to consider Ibsen's choice of a harmonizing end as ironic, or at least as clearly ambiguous".[4] Coincidentally or not, irony and ambiguity are core aesthetic values of the ideology of modernism: it would seem that the specific kind of modernism and modernity that we find in *The Lady from the Sea* has the power to annoy ideologues of modernism as well as romantic idealists.

Since *The Lady from the Sea* remains a relatively neglected play in Ibsen's *œuvre*, I shall briefly introduce it here. The protagonists are an estranged couple, Dr Wangel and his wife Ellida. The local parson used to refer to her as "the heathen", because her father, the lighthouse-keeper out in Skjoldvigen, did not give her a "Christian name of a human being" (11: 66), but named her after a ship instead. Precisely because there is no self-martyrizing saint Ellida in Christian history, the name may perhaps be read as a hint that Ellida herself will refuse to conform to Christian-idealist demands for female self-sacrifice.[5] The Wangels' newborn son died three years before the play opens, and since then, Ellida has lived in her own fantasy world, completely withdrawn from family life, neither noticing how much her husband loves her nor how much her younger stepdaughter Hilde yearns for her affection. Leaving the household duties to her grown-up stepdaughter Bolette, Ellida spends her time taking sea baths and dreaming about the ocean and about the Stranger, a mysterious sailor and a murderer, to whom she feels bound as if in marriage. Further stressing Ellida's connection with the sea, Ibsen tells us that the people in their little town call her *fruen fra havet* ("the lady from the sea"); the name is a deliberate transposition of *havfruen* ("the mermaid"), which for a while was Ibsen's working title for the play (see 11: 170).

In *The Lady from the Sea* the fantasmatic intensity of Ellida's inner life coexists with a starkly realist analysis of marriage, not least in the subplot concerning Ellida's stepdaughter Bolette and Arnholm, a headmaster who now lives in the capital, but who once was her teacher. The play also contains a comedy of art and artists involving Ballested, painter, musician, choir-master, hairdresser, and general jack-of-all-trades, and Lyngstrand, a consumptive sculptor full of idealist illusions about art and women, constantly teased and taunted by Bolette's wild younger sister, Hilde. All this is enfolded in Ellida and Wangel's conversations about her life, her dreams, her aspirations, often read as a striking anticipation of Freud's psychoanalytic therapy.

In *The Lady from the Sea* the shadowy figure of the Stranger is surrounded by uncanny, melodramatic elements. Ever since her baby died, Ellida has been obsessed by the memory of the moment when, as a young girl, she willingly let the Stranger—a man she knew to be a murderer—throw their two interlinked rings into the ocean, in a wedding-like ceremony. Although she sent him three letters breaking off the relationship as soon as he had left, he never acknowledged receiving them. (The Stranger's deafness to Ellida strikes me as an extreme version of Rosmer's deafness to Rebecca.) Ellida is convinced that her baby had the eyes of the Stranger, a sign, I think, that she feels that the baby ought to have been his. Since the baby's death she has refused to share Wangel's bed: I take this to be an act of absurd and terrified fidelity to the Stranger, an effort to protect herself against further revenge for her unfaithful behavior, an expression of her fear that any future children will also be stricken by the Stranger's revenge.

Through a tale told by Lyngstrand, a tale which is never fully corroborated, we get the impression that Ellida's psychic suffering started on the very night the Stranger (or someone who could have been him), on board a ship on the North Sea, learned that she had married another man. Ellida herself insists that when she was with him, the power of his will completely overwhelmed her own. For her, the power of the Stranger and the power of the sea are intertwined: the Stranger is "like the ocean", she says to Wangel (11: 112). The Stranger and the sea, then, are barely disguised metaphors for Ellida's yearning for the infinite and the absolute. Stressing her desire for the endless and the unbounded, the play sets up a series of oppositions between the closed and the open (the fjord/the sea; the carp pond/the ocean; the small town/the wide world), and between the outer and the inner (the body/the soul or the mind; reality/dreams), all of which help to establish the play's two most fundamental thematic oppositions: finitude and infinity, necessity and freedom.

The Lady from the Sea, then, continues the exploration of the melodramatic register that began in *Rosmersholm*. When *The Lady from the Sea* was first produced in London in 1891, Clement Scott, the Ibsen-hating theater critic of *The Daily Telegraph*, ironically commented that Ibsen could only save this boring play from disaster by drawing on the most hackneyed theatrical tricks: "It was not until the 'master' became absolutely conventional; it was not until the apostle of originality borrowed without blushing the stalest tricks of despised melodrama; . . . it was not until Ellida, in true old-world Surrey transpontine fashion, flung herself between her spouse and the cocked revolver, that the audience woke up from its despondent lethargy."[6] What Scott failed to see is that all these uncanny elements are there to contrast with the everyday and the ordinary, and thus to convey Ellida's neurotic fears.

Ellida, then, hides secrets in her soul, secrets that she feels incapable of expressing. Ever since her baby died, she has been haunted by *det uutsigelige* ("the inexpressible", "the unsayable", "the unutterable"), and terrified by *det grufulde* ("the horrible or terrible thing"). The main action of *The Lady from the Sea* consists in the conversations between Ellida and Wangel, during which Ellida comes to realize that she can in fact find words for her feelings, and—even more importantly—have those words acknowledged by her husband. By Act 4 she has become capable of boldly inviting Wangel to listen to her: "Wangel, come and sit down here with me. I have to tell you all my thoughts" (11: 127). Through her own version of Freud's "talking cure" she comes to find human society (the theme of acclimatization) and marriage (including sex) possible again.

The Lady from the Sea contains all the principal features of Ibsen's modernism that I have established in this book, but in a new and challenging combination. Thus idealism, which was such an enormous preoccupation in *Rosmersholm*, is here ironically reduced to the sculptor Lyngstrand's egocentric ravings about the pleasures of having a woman sacrifice her youth for him. Ibsen's rejection of idealism, however, also surfaces in the play's pointed rebuttal of two famous romantic texts: Richard Wagner's *The Flying Dutchman* and Hans Christian Andersen's "The Little Mermaid".

Like *Rosmersholm*, *The Lady from the Sea* is profoundly concerned with theater and theatricality, but here the investigation of theater is connected with the other arts: painting, sculpture, and, in a minor way, music. The play's concern with skepticism also emerges in the same way as in *Rosmersholm*: as a preoccupation with the possibilities of expression, the power of language and the acceptance of human finitude. The parallels between the two plays do not stop there: both deliberately explore the melodramatic mode; both plays tell us that the inability to find a voice, to make sense to others, leads to madness; both plays focus on the contrast between outer and inner, body and soul; both explore the consequences of trying to escape human finitude.

Although *Rosmersholm* and *The Lady from the Sea* have much in common, the outcome of the respective protagonists' confrontation with skepticism could not be more different. At the end of *A Doll's House* Nora considers that she has never been married to Helmer. Nora tells Helmer that she would only return if they both were *forvandlet* ("transformed") to the point that their life together could become a marriage. In *Rosmersholm* Rebecca declares that she is transformed, but Rosmer's skepticism makes it impossible for him to believe her. *The Lady from the Sea* returns to the question left unanswered by Nora: namely, what constitutes a marriage? If legally binding ceremonies, the birth of children, or the fact of living together do not suffice, then what will it take for Ellida to recognize herself as married to Wangel? *The Lady from the Sea* shows, among other things, that the agents of the transformation that will make marriage possible are freedom and choice, particularly for women. In this way, *The Lady from the Sea* closes the investigation of marriage that began in *A Doll's House*.

In this chapter, then, I shall discuss the most striking aspects of Ibsen's modernism in *The Lady from the Sea*: the critique of idealism, the play's reflections on theater and the other arts; the relationship between love and skepticism. I shall also show that this play is a self-conscious meditation on the power of art to express the plight of the soul. Above all, however, I shall pay attention to Ibsen's investigation of love, marriage, and the everyday, and his radical analysis of freedom and choice.

Faithlessness or Freedom? Idealism Rebuffed

Set on the west coast of Norway, *The Lady from the Sea* features a heroine haunted by her fear and longing for a half-ghostly, half-real sailor. Richard Wagner's opera *The Flying Dutchman* is also set on the coast of Norway and tells the story of a ghostly sailor doomed to sail the oceans of the world until he finds true love. Like Ellida, Wagner's heroine, Senta, dreams of a mysterious sailor. One day, her father, a sea-captain, returns with the Flying Dutchman, who turns out to be the man she has been dreaming of, and Senta immediately and joyfully agrees to marry him. After a silly misunderstanding, her Dutch fiancé wrongly concludes that she is unfaithful to him, and immediately sails away on his ghostly ship. In despair, Senta throws herself off a cliff to prove her faith and her love. Her noble self-sacrifice lifts the curse on the Dutchman's soul, and the opera ends with the image of the two lovers' entwined souls ascending up to heaven.

Senta, then, is the quintessentially idealist heroine: she is young, she is pure and virginal, and, above all, she is heroically ready to give up her life to save the man she loves. Wagner's opera was first performed in Dresden on 2 January 1843. It is difficult to believe that Ibsen, who by the time he wrote *The Lady from the Sea* had lived in Germany for almost twenty years, had managed to remain entirely ignorant of this famous work. (In the *Wild Duck*, Hedvig says that the old sea captain who once owned the strange things kept in the loft was called "The Flying Dutchman" (10: 97).) *The Lady from the Sea* can certainly be read as a deliberate, and quite ironic commentary on Wagner's unbridled idealism, as a strong statement of Ibsen's difference from the famous composer.

The titles of *The Lady from the Sea* and Hans Christian Andersen's "Den lille Havfrue" ("The Little Mermaid") (1837) already signal a connection. As we have seen, Ibsen even considered calling his play *Havfruen*, and Ellida is explicitly compared to a mermaid on several occasions. In Andersen's tale, the pure and innocent mermaid falls in love with a human prince on her fifteenth birthday. In order to be with him, she willingly exchanges her fish tail for human legs even though it means letting the sea-witch cut out her tongue and accepting that she will suffer horribly whenever she uses her lovely legs. Deprived of speech, the little mermaid nevertheless expresses herself by dancing in spite of the excruciating pain of every step.

One day, however, the handsome prince marries a beautiful princess. Because he did not marry the little mermaid, she will never have an immortal soul. At his wedding, she dances more beautifully than ever, but she "laughed and danced with the thought of death in her heart", for she had decided to kill herself once the party was over: "She knew it was the last evening she saw the man for whom she had left her family and her home, given up her beautiful voice and daily suffered infinite agonies, without him ever having realized it".[7] Ellida is not unlike the little mermaid: she has left her home out in Skjoldvigen, lost her capacity to express herself, and suffers daily agonies of which her husband knows nothing.

Ibsen's allusions to these two romantic tales of female sacrifice, however, have a deeper point. Senta and the little mermaid are both absolutely pure, absolutely loving, absolutely faithful. The evidence of their love and their faith is their willing death for the sake of the man. (Rosmer's gruesome demand that Rebecca die for his sake is clearly related to this idealist tradition.) In response to these tales, *The Lady from the Sea* also foregrounds the theme of faithful and faithless women, but in a radically different way. Already in Act 1, Lyngstrand tells Ellida about his plan for a great sculpture:

ELLIDA. And what would you model? Will it be mermen and mermaids? Or old Vikings—?

LYNGSTRAND. No, nothing like that. As soon as I get the chance, I'll try to do a large work. A group, as they call it.

ELLIDA. Well—but what will the group represent?

LYNGSTRAND. Oh, it's supposed to be something I have experienced.

ARNHOLM. Good—better stick to that.

ELLIDA. But what will it be?

LYNGSTRAND. Well, I had thought that it would be a young sailor's wife who is strangely restless in her sleep. And she is dreaming too. I definitely think I will be able to manage it so one can actually see that she is dreaming.

ARNHOLM. Won't there be more?

LYNGSTRAND. Oh, yes, there is to be another figure. More like a shape or appearance. It is to be her husband, to whom she has been unfaithful while he was away. And he has been drowned at sea.

ARNHOLM. How do you mean?

ELLIDA. He has been drowned?

LYNGSTRAND. Yes. He was drowned while away at sea. But the strange thing is that he has returned home anyway. It is night, and now he stands by the bed and looks at her. He is to stand there as soaking wet as if he had been dragged out of the sea.

ELLIDA [*leans back in her chair*].   That is extremely strange. [*Closes her eyes.*] Oh, I can
   see it so vividly before me.

                                                                        (II: 72)

Later, Lyngstrand refers to his characters as the "faithless sailor's wife" and the
"Avenger", and claims that he can see both of them clearly, as if they were
alive before him (II: 74). At that point, Ellida is overcome by a sense of
suffocation and gets up to leave (II: 75). Lyngstrand's motif exactly translates Ellida's unspoken fears: that the Stranger will return to exact his revenge
for her infidelity to him.

   While Lyngstrand considers his story of faithlessness and revenge as something like a morality tale, Ibsen shows us that Ellida has been driven to the
brink of madness precisely by such idealist notions of a woman's absolute
fidelity. When the Stranger turns up for the first time in Act 3, he goes
straight for the jugular, as if he knows how guilty she feels for breaking her
vows to him: "Both Ellida and I agreed that this business with the rings
should remain in force and be as binding as a wedding ceremony," he says to
Wangel. Ellida's instant response to this line is revealing: "But I don't want
to, you hear! Never in the world do I want to have anything more to do with
you! Don't look at me in that way! I said I don't want to!" (II: 108). Against
the Stranger's insistence that she owes him her faith, Ellida insists on her *will*.

   Where Ellida breaks off, the Stranger continues. In the next few lines, he
says two crucial things: that he has kept his word to her: "I have kept the
word I gave you," and that if she is to come with him, it has to be of her own
free will: "If Ellida wants to come with me, she has to come of her own free
will" (II: 108). Here the Stranger offers Ellida precisely the concept she
needs: namely, freedom. At the same time, he highlights the key philosophical and ethical question at stake in this play: namely, the relationship
between a promise—specifically the kind of promise we call a wedding
vow—and freedom. Does a solemn promise of the marriage-like kind always
bind us for life? Under what circumstances is a woman justified in breaking
such a promise?

   Such questions were simply not thinkable for idealism: Senta and the little
mermaid are *absolutely* faithful. In 1888, however, divorce was rapidly
becoming a legal option all over the Western world, and, as *The Lady from the
Sea* shows, the time of idealist heroines was definitely past. Neither Bolette
nor Hilde feels inclined to do anything but laugh when the naïve Lyngstrand
reveals that he would like Bolette to spend her youth faithfully waiting for
him to become a great sculptor abroad, but that when he returns as a famous
artist, he will discard her for someone younger, perhaps someone like Hilde.

The very fact that Ibsen's investigation of marriage in *The Lady from the Sea* fully incorporates the question of when a woman may be justified in breaking her vows to a man tells us how far beyond idealism he has moved. In this context Wagner's sublime Senta and Andersen's selfless mermaid come across as old-fashioned masculinist fantasies. By raising the question of women's emotional, sexual, and economic freedom, by investigating the destructive power of absolute promises (including the vows of marriage), *The Lady from the Sea* shows how dangerous idealist absolutism can be when it is allowed to distort the relationships of modern men and women.[8]

"Externalizing the inner mind": Theater and Other Arts

To James McFarlane, one of the finest Ibsen scholars of his generation, *The Lady from the Sea* is the drama of Ellida's mind, and so, fundamentally, a play about an intense, obsessive, half-mad love triangle involving Ellida, Wangel, and the Stranger. If one looks at the play in this way, the presence of all other characters appears puzzling, even clumsy; the two artists appear entirely superfluous, the subplot involving Bolette and Arnholm becomes a heavy-handed parallel to the marriage of Ellida and Wangel, an obvious illustration of the "traffic in women", or the kind of sordid bargaining and trade-offs imposed on women in a sexist society; the character of Hilde serves only as a foil for Lyngstrand's unbridled sexism:

[Ibsen] weight[s] the drama with such naturalistic solidities as his stuttering odd job man, his consumptive artist, his careworn schoolmaster. . . . Translate the action of the play into choreographic terms . . ., and one discovers that the central conflict in Ellida's mind is of a kind that can, using techniques akin to those of the expressionist theatre, be successfully and economically communicated without any great need of these subsidiary characters. Here is perhaps an index of how firmly, despite his innovations, Ibsen was rooted in the naturalistic tradition.[9]

The technical problem facing Ibsen, McFarlane writes, is to "externalize this kind of inner drama of the mind", and he could have succeeded only by choosing a more thoroughly expressionistic form.[10] In other words: if Ibsen had been capable of abandoning his old-fashioned allegiance to naturalism (or realism), he would have written a better play.

But this logic is flawed. Ever since Hamlet declared that "I have that within which passes show", Western playwrights have dealt with the question of how to "externalize the inner drama of the mind". Unless we want to claim that Shakespeare entirely failed to show us what was going on in Hamlet's mind, expressionism can hardly be the only correct formal solution. As I have tried to show in this book, Ibsen's modernism offers us a long series of self-conscious explorations of the powers of theater to express and to make us acknowledge the pain and joy of the human soul. (It is unnecessary to speak of "inner" pain or about the "inner" drama of the mind. Is there an "outer" joy or an "outer" pain that we have no trouble perceiving or trusting?)

Ibsen's modernism shows us that there is nothing wrong with the powers of expression of the theater; it is modern skepticism that makes us feel that ordinary language and everyday actions fail to provide good enough expression of pain and joy. Even the formulation used by McFarlane—the inner drama of the mind—shows that he shares the skeptical picture of the soul as a mysterious inner realm, one that is, as it were, hidden by the body. (I discuss this picture in Chapter 7, in relation to Nora's tarantella.) McFarlane really poses the skeptical problem: how can I trust a person's attempts to express (to say or to show through gesture or action) what he or she thinks, feels, or believes? The question of how to "externalize" the human mind is really a question about how we can know others, and how we can trust that knowledge. This is not just a question that arises in connection with the theater, it is a question for all of us, for it is surely no easier to read other people's minds in everyday life than it is onstage.[11]

In *The Lady from the Sea*, however, Ibsen does not just reflect on the powers of theater to "externalize the inner mind", he also turns to other arts. Are the references to art in *The Lady from the Sea* superfluous attempts at providing local color, a deplorable effect of Ibsen's naturalism, as McFarlane implies?[12] If so, the opening scene of *The Lady from the Sea* is particularly likely to produce offense, for the first thing it offers us is a conversation between the two artists, the jack-of-all-trades Ballested and the consumptive sculptor Lyngstrand, concerning Ballested's unfinished painting:

LYNGSTRAND. There's to be a figure as well?

BALLESTED. Yes. In here by the reef in the foreground there is to be a half dead mermaid.

LYNGSTRAND. Why is she to be half dead?

BALLESTED. She got lost and can't find her way out to the ocean again. And now she lies dying here in the brackish water, you see.

LYNGSTRAND. Yes, right.

BALLESTED. It was the lady of the house who made me think of painting something of the kind.

LYNGSTRAND. What will you call the picture when it is finished?

BALLESTED. I intend to call it "The Mermaid's End".

LYNGSTRAND. That sounds good.—I think you really can make something good out of this.

(II: 54)

Ballested's dying mermaid will strike most modern readers as a quite absurd motif. Surely, we think, Ibsen must be intending this to be an ironic illustration of amateur painting at its worst. If so, this scene is, as McFarlane assumes, mere comic relief, of no importance to the main plot. But we should not leap to conclusions. When Ellida asks Lyngstrand about his work, she begins by asking, "And what would you model? Will it be mermen and mermaids? Or old Vikings—?" (II: 72). In Europe in the late 1880s, artists still commonly painted Vikings, mermaids, and mermen—that is to say, historical and mythological motifs requiring narrative explanation, based on Lessing's theory of the "pregnant moment". As we have seen in Chapter 4, it is even possible that Ibsen was inspired by Arnold Böcklin's anguished mermaid in *The Play of the Waves* (*Im Spiel der Wellen*) for his conception of Ellida.[13]

Ballested, moreover, is not just an amateur. When he arrived in town seventeen or eighteen years earlier, we are told, it was as a painter for Skive's traveling theater company. His name, as well as that of the theater company, reveals that he is Danish, thus a stranger in the true sense of the word, yet one who has "acclimatized himself", as he keeps repeating. There is, surely, a distance between Ibsen's point of view and Ballested's, but there is no need to imagine this as hostile or disdainful, for Ballested represents something of Ibsen's own past: the Danish traveling theater companies that toured the south coast of Norway in his childhood and youth, and perhaps also his encounter with the theater painter in Bergen in the 1850s, Johan Ludvig Losting, himself quite a jack-of-all-trades.[14] Ballested's painting, moreover, echoes *his* theatrical past, for he explains that although he has painted the background, he has yet to place the figure in the foreground. It is as if he is waiting for the actress playing the mermaid to turn up, just as we are waiting for the actress playing the lady from the sea to turn up.

The problem with Ballested's painting, then, is not that it is of a mermaid, or that it is narrative and mythological, but that he is not bringing the tradition after Lessing to its fullest potential. It would seem that he has chosen a fairly undramatic moment, which explains why his narrative about the lost mermaid is more than a little flat. At the same time, however, the absence of dramatic tension and the emphasis on the brackish water in the inner reaches of the fjord indicate hopelessness, stagnation, and closure. Whatever its aesthetic flaws, Ballested's painting is a pretty effective rendering of Ellida's state of mind, and is intended to be taken as such by the audience, since we learn that it was Ellida who gave Ballested the idea for the painting in the first place.

Lyngstrand's planned group uniting the "Unfaithful Sailor's Wife" and "The Avenger", on the other hand, is squarely melodramatic, even Gothic, and reminds me not a little of Fuseli's famous *Nightmare* paintings. Like Ballested's painting, it presupposes a narrative, but Lyngstrand has an altogether firmer grasp than Ballested of how to choose a maximally dramatic moment. We should note, too, that neither the painter nor the sculptor strives for everyday realism: Ballested has a mermaid, Lyngstrand a ghostly avenger. In this respect, there are obvious parallels between these works and the play in which they appear.

Tormented by the thought that the death of her child was punishment for her faithlessness, Ellida is like both Ballested's half-dead mermaid and Lyngstrand's dreaming, unfaithful wife about to be confronted by the Avenger. It is significant, moreover, that both works are described right at the beginning of the play: they express Ellida's feelings at a time when she cannot yet express them herself. In so doing they set in motion the process that will transform her from a woman threatened by suffocation to a woman with a voice of her own.

There is also another art present in *The Lady from the Sea*: namely, music. Even in her depressed and neurotic state, Ellida often goes up to the view point to hear the local brass band (*hornforeningen*) (see 11: 56 and 11: 79). Only in Act 5, however, is music given a relatively strong theatrical presence, for there the very last moments of the play take place to the accompaniment of the brass band playing to salute the departure of the English steamer, the last tourist ship of the season.[15]

The Lady from the Sea, then, begins with painting and sculpture, and ends with music. Although it is difficult to judge this precisely from Ibsen's text, I get the impression that the audience never sees Ballested's painting, which in any case remains only half-finished throughout the play. Describing it to Lyngstrand in Act 1, Ballested is at once describing his actual canvas and telling us what it is going to become (11: 53–4). Existing only as a projection into the future, Lyngstrand's sculpture remains purely linguistic. The music at the end of the play, on the other hand, is a finished composition, heard by all the characters and the audience, too. As long as the visual works remain projected and unfinished, they remain enclosed in the fantasy world of their creators (completely so in the case of Lyngstrand, partly so in that of Ballested). The music, on the other hand, is shared by all. Thus the transition from project to work, from vision to hearing, from painting and sculpture to music that accompanies Ellida's transformation, signifies a transition from isolation and inwardness to community and externality.

Painting and sculpture, moreover, are static—I mean atemporal—arts. Theater and music, on the other hand, unfold in time. The reason why the half-dead mermaid and the unfaithful sailor's wife express Ellida's inner state at the beginning of the play is that, like them, she has remained frozen in a desperate, more or less melodramatic, moment. Perhaps we can see her immobility and stasis as profoundly antitheatrical, as a negative version of the immutable Ideal. Against this, *The Lady from the Sea* posits the idea of acclimatization, adaptability, changeability, and—ultimately—transformation. There are shades of *The Winter's Tale* here: like Hermione, Ellida is transformed so as to again become part of the ordinary course of time, and an ordinary marriage. Perhaps Ibsen wants to tell us that only theater can give life and voice to human transformation. At the end of *The Lady from the Sea*, we celebrate not just Ellida's powers of transformation, but the powers of theater, too.

Disavowing Finitude: Ellida and the Stranger

In *A Pitch of Philosophy*, Cavell notes that "in seeking for the representativeness of your life you have to watch at the same time for your limitedness, commemorating what is beyond you".[16] If we cannot acknowledge our own limitedness, our finitude, we will not be able to acknowledge the existence of others. Ellida knows no boundaries. To her, the ocean is boundless, and so is the Stranger. "That man is like the ocean," she says after seeing him again for the first time (11: 112). He represents infinity, absolute freedom that tolerates no human limitations.[17] In the ceremony that keeps haunting her, he compelled her to marry both him and the ocean by throwing their entwined rings into the sea. In his presence she feels as if she has no other will than his: the Stranger comes across as a Nietzschean creature of compelling will, a murderer beyond good and evil. Ellida's achievement is that she comes to realize that she has the power to defy this will, not by mobilizing some superhuman effort of resistance, but by choosing finitude. (I shall return to this.)

But if the Stranger is like the ocean, so is Ellida. "Ellida—your mind is like the ocean," Wangel says to her at the end of the play (11: 154). The Stranger, then, is both internal and external to Ellida; he is her, she is him; he is a figment of her imagination, as well as a real man. If the audience has trouble deciding whether the Stranger is real or imagined, it is because Ellida herself cannot quite work this out. Whatever he is, he is not *other* to her (I use the word in the ordinary sense of acknowledging that other people are—well, *other*: not identical with us, not a part of us, not an extension of us). In this respect it is significant that when Ellida first sees the Stranger in Act 3, she does not recognize him at all: he has existed so much in her mind that she has no recollection of what he looks like. But Dr Wangel is not an other to her either, for he simply doesn't figure in her imagination: "When he isn't here, I often can't remember what he looks like. And then it is as if I truly had lost him" (11: 103). It is as if Ellida has not fully discovered Wangel's existence, so that she perceives him either as pure externality or as a void.

The Lady from the Sea, then, is about a woman driven to the edge of madness by her refusal of finitude. She is unable to acknowledge the separate existence of others; she takes refuge in melodramatic fantasies about the Stranger's revenge so as not to have to acknowledge death (the death of her baby); she avoids sex so as not to have to acknowledge sexual finitude. The result is a sense of being completely lost, an increasing sense of isolation from human community, a conviction that she is fundamentally unable to make herself known. As long as she remains bound up in her fantasy about the freedom of the unbounded horizons of the ocean, Ellida will remain a stranger in the world of everyday commitments. No wonder we find it difficult to tell whether the Stranger is inside or outside Ellida's mind.

Towards the end of the play, in the highly dramatic scene in which Ellida makes her choice, Dr Wangel finally comes up with his diagnosis: "Your craving for the boundless and the infinite,—and for the unattainable—it will drive your mind completely into the darkness of night in the end." His acknowledgment of her state of mind appears to come as a liberation and a relief to Ellida, for she replies, "Oh yes, yes,—I feel it—like black, silent wings above me—." This exchange enables Dr Wangel finally to acknowledge Ellida's freedom to choose: "It won't come to that. There is no other salvation for you. I can't see any at least. So therefore—therefore I let—let our bargain be unmade, right now.—Now you can choose your path—in full—full freedom" (11: 153). (The reference to the "bargain" is to Ellida's claim that her marriage to Wangel was a commercial transaction, in which she traded her freedom for economic security.)

Wangel acknowledges Ellida's freedom because he sees that if he doesn't, she will surely go mad. Against the Stranger's absolute, infinite, unbounded, mad freedom, he offers concrete, finite, ordinary human freedom. This is a stroke of genius, for to choose is to embrace finitude, to accept that we are no more, but also no less, than human. Not to choose is to refuse definition,

much of a liberation. But this is a misreading. At the beginning of Act 5, just before the Stranger is to return for the last time, Wangel and Ellida have the following exchange:

ELLIDA. I *must* speak to him myself. For I am supposed to make my choice freely.

WANGEL. You have no choice, Ellida. You won't be allowed to choose. I won't let you.

ELLIDA. You can't prevent my choosing. Neither you nor anyone else. You can forbid me to go away with him—to follow him—if that's what I choose. You can keep me here by force. Against my will. You can do that. But that I choose—choose in my innermost mind—choose him and not you,—in case I will and must choose that way—you can't prevent that.

WANGEL. No, you are right. I can't prevent that.

(II: 137–8)

Ellida, then, knows perfectly well that she is free to choose. What she requires of her husband is that he should *acknowledge her right to choose*. That is what it takes for her to recognize that he too is transformed, that he has learned to consider her a free and equal human being, that he is qualified to be her husband:

WANGEL. . . . Now you can choose your path—in full—full freedom.

ELLIDA [*staring at him, as if speechless, for a while*]. Is it true,—true,—what you are saying? Do you mean it—in your innermost heart?

WANGEL. Yes, I do mean it—in my innermost, suffering heart.

ELLIDA. And *can* you do it, too? Can you let this *happen?*

WANGEL. Yes, I can. I can—because I love you so much.

ELLIDA [*slowly, tremulously*]. I have come this close—so deeply inside (*så inderligt*) your heart?

WANGEL. The years and our life together brought it about.

ELLIDA [*clasping her hands*]. And I never noticed it!

(II: 153)

Ellida's questions are quintessentially skeptical: Are you really speaking the truth? Do you really mean it? In your innermost heart? And even if you say you mean it, and really think you do, you may still be mistaken, so the question is, can you really let it happen? Can you let me go off with this stranger standing here with a gun in his hand? When Wangel claims that he does and he can, Ellida strikingly replies by talking about closeness and intimacy, about having come "close and deeply inside [his] heart". Like the German *innerlich*, *inderlig* is notoriously difficult to translate, for it means internal, but also heartfelt. This closeness, this intimacy, is established by the years, their life together (*samlivet*). This is closeness, but it is not merger. The love that is here being acknowledged has nothing to do with the romantic absolute. It is finite and human, and certainly will not rescue us from failures and misunderstandings, as the very last lines of the play show:

ELLIDA [*smiling, but serious*]. Well, you see Mr. Arnholm—. Do you remember—we talked about it yesterday? Once one has become a land creature, it is impossible to find a way to return to the ocean. And not to the life of the ocean, either.

BALLESTED. But that is just like my mermaid!

ELLIDA. Well, more or less.

BALLESTED. Except for the difference that *the mermaid dies of it*. Human beings, on the other hand—they can acclam-acclimatize themselves. Yes, I assure you, Mrs. Wangel, they *can* acclimatize themselves!

ELLIDA. Yes, if they are free they can, Mr. Ballested.

WANGEL. And responsible, dear Ellida.

ELLIDA [*quickly, takes his hand*]. That's exactly right.

[*The great steamer glides silently out over the fjord. The music can be heard closer to the shore.*]

(II: 156–7)

Ballested here pronounces Ellida's humanity: to him, as to us, she is no longer like his mermaid; she is truly transformed. But how are we to take Ellida's last line? I read Wangel's "and responsible" as a rather over-eager and slightly thoughtless rejoinder, a line that demonstrates his wish to say something, perhaps a moment where he falls back into his usual role as the unquestioned *pater familias* who always gets the last word. Yet his line is harmless: human freedom does entail responsibility; there is no choice without consequences. But surely there is no point in telling Ellida this now, for she has just demonstrated that she knows all this by embracing her family, and particularly by opening her heart to the young Hilde's need for love (Ellida addresses her as "dear Hilde" (II: 156) when she announces that she will stay with them after all). Wangel's last line, in short, is not his finest moment, and Ellida knows it. She rescues him from saying more silly things by quickly claiming to agree, perhaps with a smile that at once conveys her understanding, her judgment, and her love. But more importantly, she gives him her hand. They are together. They acknowledge each other's freedom. They understand each other. They are close. But they are not one. There is still plenty of space in which to disagree, to quarrel, and to make up. This, Ibsen tells us, is what it takes to have a marriage. This is why Ellida and Wangel are the antithesis of Rebecca and Rosmer.

The Meaning of Freedom: Bolette's Choice

This reading of the end of the play may sound naïve. Do I really believe that Ellida chooses freely? Should I not at least consider that Ibsen may here be pushing a liberal ideology that wildly exaggerates the possibilities of free choice in modern society? This question might have some force were it not for the fact that the very question of what might count as free choice receives close attention in *The Lady from the Sea*. Let us begin by recalling that this is a play fundamentally concerned with the force of a woman's promise of marriage. In a key exchange in Act 4, in which Ellida tries to explain how she came to marry Wangel after the death of her father, the issues at stake are brought out:

ELLIDA. And I for my part—. There I was, helpless, not knowing where to turn, and so completely alone. So it was only reasonable to accept—when you came and offered to provide for me for the rest of my life.

WANGEL. I didn't see it as providing for you, dear Ellida. I asked you honestly if you would share with me and the children what little I could call mine.

ELLIDA. Yes, you did. But I shouldn't have accepted it anyway! Not for any price should I have accepted! Not have sold myself! Rather the most wretched work and the most miserable circumstances—freely—and by my own choice!

WANGEL [*gets up*]. Then the five–six years we have lived together have been completely worthless to you?

ELLIDA. No, don't ever think that! I have been as content here with you as any human being could wish for. But I did not enter your home of my own free will. That's the point.

WANGEL [*looks at her*]. Not of your own free will!

ELLIDA. No. I did not go with you of my own free will.

(II: 128)

Ellida here challenges the notion of "free choice" just as profoundly as Nora challenges the notion of marriage. "I asked you honestly if you would share with me and the children what little I could call mine," Wangel says. He means that Ellida can hardly say he forced her: she *chose* to marry him. By rejecting this idea, Ellida shows that to her the verb *ville* ("will" or "would") is not at all synonymous with "i frivillighed—og efter eget valg" ("freely—and by my own choice"). If a promise has been made under coercion, it is worthless. This is precisely why Ellida is inclined to think that only her *first* promise (to the Stranger) could have turned out to be a "complete and pure marriage", for, as she puts it, "a promise freely given is just as binding as a wedding ceremony" (II: 129).

To figure out exactly what *The Lady from the Sea* has to say about these crucial issues, I shall turn to the scene between Bolette and Arnholm in Act 5. Arnholm has just offered to help Bolette to get out in the world, to travel, to get the education she is longing for. Although she is a little dubious about whether she can receive such a great gift from *noget fremmed menneske* ("a stranger", in the sense of someone who is not a member of the family; literally: "some strange human being") (II: 142), she soon expresses her delight: "Oh, I could both laugh and cry for joy! For happiness and bliss! Oh, then I'll really get to live after all. I was beginning to be afraid that life would pass me by" (II: 142). But her joy is short-lived, for Arnholm quickly explains what he has in mind:

ARNHOLM. . . . Well—since you are free, Bolette, since no relationship binds you—. So I ask you then—if you could want (*kunde ville*)—could want to join me—for life?
BOLETTE [*recoils in horror*]. Oh,—what are you saying!
ARNHOLM. For your whole life, Bolette. If you will (*vil*) be my wife.
BOLETTE [*half beside herself*]. No, no, no! This is impossible! Completely impossible!

(II: 143)

Twice Arnholm says not just *ville*, but *kunde ville* ("could will", which here means something like "could you bring yourself to want")—as if he knows that Bolette will have to overcome a resistance in order to want to marry him. The third time, however, his proposal has come to sound like a simple choice ("will you"), and Bolette recoils in horror. But Arnholm does not give up: stressing the economic and sexual facts, he reminds Bolette that when her father dies, she will need money (just like Ellida once did), and that if she refuses him, she may one day have to accept someone she likes even less. These are scare tactics, and it is not surprising that in the end, Arnholm's proposal sounds more like a threat than a promise:

ARNHOLM. Then will you (*vil De*) rather remain at home and let life pass you by?
BOLETTE. Oh, it is so terribly painful to think of it!
ARNHOLM. Will you (*vil De*) renounce the opportunity to see something of the world outside? Renounce taking part in all those things that you say you have been yearning for? . . . Think carefully, Bolette.
BOLETTE. Oh yes,—you are so completely right, Mr. Arnholm.

(II: 145)

Playing the phrase *vil De* ("do you want to", "will you") like a virtuoso, Arnholm makes it look as if, by refusing him, Bolette freely chooses to renounce all her dreams and ambitions. His final "Think carefully, Bolette" is pure menace. And it works: a moment later, he gets his wish. In this sequence, Ibsen handles all the different expressions for choice and will in a particularly masterful way:

ARNHOLM. Do you mean that you perhaps nevertheless could be willing to (*kanske dog kunde være villig til*)—? That at least you could want to allow me (*kunde vilde unde mig*) the pleasure of helping you as a faithful friend?

BOLETTE. No, no, no! Never that! For *that* would be completely impossible now.— No,—Mr. Arnholm,—then you'd better take me.

ARNHOLM. Bolette! You will, after all!

BOLETTE. Yes,—I think—I will.

ARNHOLM. Then you will be my wife!

BOLETTE. Yes. If you still feel that—that you ought to take me.

(II: 146)

As the dialogue develops, Arnholm moves from his hesitant *kunde vilde* ("could bring yourself to want") to the triumphant *vil*. The repetition of "will" reinforces the ideology, making it look as if Bolette here freely chooses to marry him. Her repetition of the phrase "take me", on the other hand, signals not only that she feels sexually threatened, but also that she knows that she is here agreeing to commodify herself. Does Bolette freely choose to trade her body and her life for financial security, travel, and an education? What powers does she have to ensure that Arnholm keeps his part of the bargain? Ibsen's subtle and striking analysis of the ways in which what looks like free choice may be the result of coercion embedded in a particular social situation is matchless.

The juxtaposition of the brutality of Arnholm's proposal and the individual happiness achieved by Ellida and Wangel is unsettling, to say the least, for it provides a glimpse of the sexist power relations with which any marriage in this culture will have to deal. The juxtaposition, moreover, has a double edge. Because Ellida, who also sold herself when she married, chooses Wangel all over again, we know that there is hope. (Human beings *can* acclimatize themselves.) On the other hand, we have just seen that Arnholm is a man capable of using barely veiled threats to get his way, something that Wangel shows no signs of ever having done. We also note that Bolette prefers not to announce her engagement before the end of the play. This is not, so far, a marriage made in heaven. Perhaps love, good will, and infinite patience can save this marriage; but given this beginning, one has to question whether there is going to be enough love.

Whatever we think Bolette and Arnholm's future will be, *The Lady from the Sea* asks whether we want a society which regularly stacks the odds against marriage in this way. If the answer is no, then *The Lady from the Sea* tells us that the only way to improve the conditions of marriage is to improve women's social and economic situation. In 1888, then, both Ibsen and Ellida realize that until marriage ceases to be women's only way of earning a living, it will never be a genuine choice. Ellida's understanding of what counts as a marriage is that she should have chosen the man, freely and knowingly.[18] As we have seen, "freely" here does not mean absolutely freely: as I have shown, Ellida's "responsible choice" is posited precisely as the only alternative to the demand for the absolute, which may drive us mad. Ibsen understands that one always chooses in a human situation, not in the abstract and the absolute. The contrast between Ellida's and Bolette's choices tells us that even within a sexist society there are degrees of freedom and degrees of responsibility. Ibsen, then, is alert to the social and economic pressures that undermine women's freedom of choice. That Ellida chooses to reconfirm her commitment to Wangel is not incompatible with such critical insights: Wangel has earned her respect, and her love. Had Wangel been anything like Arnholm (whom Ellida herself once rejected), the outcome might have been very different.

Make It New

In September 1887, half-way between *Rosmersholm* and *The Lady from the Sea*, Ibsen gave a brief speech at a dinner in Stockholm:

It has been said that I too . . . have contributed to the creation of a new era in the world.

I believe, on the contrary, that it would be just as reasonable to designate the era we now find ourselves in as an end, from which something new is now about to be born.

In fact, I believe that the scientific theory of evolution is also valid with regard to the spiritual elements of life. . . .

One has on different occasions said about me that I am a pessimist. And so I am, in so far as I do not believe in the eternity of human ideals.

But I am also an optimist, in so far as I fully and firmly believe that ideals are capable of reproduction and evolution. . . .

I for my part will be content with the yield of my life's work, if this work can serve to prepare the mood for tomorrow.

(15: 410–11)

Destroyer of the old, fervent believer in the new: this is a quintessentially modernist attitude. As in his 1870 letter to Brandes about the Franco–Prussian

War, Ibsen sounds positively cheerful about the destruction of old regimes and old ideals.[19] Like the dinosaurs and the do-do bird, they are doomed to extinction: this is cause for joy, not sorrow. What matters to Ibsen is the birth of the new, which he explicitly compares to the utopia of the "Third Empire" in *Emperor and Galilean* (see 15: 411), but which he also—as usual—refrains from defining more closely. Whatever the new will be, however, it will contain the "conditions of humanity's happiness" (15: 410).

Many features of this speech are echoed in *The Lady from the Sea*, which, as we have seen, is a play finely balanced between the constructive and the destructive, between utopia and critique. In *The Lady from the Sea*, Ibsen demolishes the old, idealist clichés of love, marriage, and female self-sacrifice. From his acute analysis of freedom and choice, we learn that the new, modern kind of marriage that is about to be born will only come about when women are given full freedom, concretely as well as abstractly, in social and personal life. This, surely, is one ideal that might have the power of further evolution, as Ibsen put it in his Stockholm speech. But *The Lady from the Sea* also tells us that this apparently simple idea has enormous ramifications. For if the key insight of the play is that love requires the acknowledgment of the other's freedom, the play also tells us that we will never get that far unless we are willing to think through a host of other questions: the necessary destruction of idealism; the relationship between freedom and constraint; the force of promises and marriage vows; madness, skepticism, and the desire for infinity; the power of art and theater; and—not least—the healing power of ordinary human conversation.

Epilogue
Idealism and the "Bad" Everyday

Hedda Gabler: Anachronistic Idealism and the "Bad" Everyday

Like *The Lady from the Sea, Hedda Gabler* contains a reference to *Emperor and Galilean,* the pivotal play of Ibsen's modernist breakthrough, for the vine leaves that Hedda wishes to see in Ejlert Løvborg's hair are worn by Julian in his fake, theatrical Dionysus procession. For Julian the vine leaves signify his quest for truth and beauty, for he thinks of Dionysus as the god not of drunkards, but of poetry and sublime ecstasy; Hedda clearly connects vine leaves to similarly exalted states. What an irony, then, that Løvborg, in whom she wishes to see a poet and a prophet, is an alcoholic who dies as a result of a brawl in a brothel.[1]

When Hedda learns that Løvborg has not shot himself in the head, as she had wished, she first believes that he chose the chest instead, which she also finds acceptable, and exults, "I say that there is beauty in this," a line that is met with blank incomprehension by her husband ("Beauty! Just think!") and with moral recrimination by Thea Elvsted ("Oh, Hedda, how can you speak of beauty in this kind of thing!") (11: 385). A little later, Judge Brack tells her that Ejlert actually died from a more or less accidental gunshot wound in his genitals (*underlivet*).[2] Hedda is appalled, not so much for Ejlert as for herself: "Oh, the ridiculous and the low, it covers like a curse *everything* I touch" (11: 388).

Hedda's horror of *det lave* ("the low") is a horror of the ordinary and the everyday, which she here associates with farce (the ridiculous combined with the low). The theatrical reference is not coincidental: throughout the last two acts of the play, Hedda has behaved like a producer and director trying desperately to stage a sublime idealist tragedy entitled "Løvborg's Death". The distance between tragedy and farce conveys the distance between Hedda's dreams of aristocratic beauty and her sense of being besmirched by the petty, lower-class environment in which she finds herself. (Jørgen Tesman and his aunts are, of course, solidly middle class; Hedda, however, considers their social status to be ludicrously out of keeping with the style to which she feels entitled.)

Faithful to Schiller's description of the idealist, Hedda is the "sworn enemy of everything petty and trivial".[3] That this woman finds herself married to a stolid, pedantic, and profoundly unimaginative academic whose doctoral thesis dealt with the medieval handicrafts of Brabant is indeed surprising. Tesman, moreover, is deeply attached to his domestic comforts, a man whose moment of greatest joy comes when his aunt gives him back his old embroidered slippers. It is as if a comfortable old dog had married a tigress. When Ejlert Løvborg exclaims, "Oh, Hedda, Hedda—how could you throw yourself away in this way!" (II: 345), the audience feels the same way. All Hedda says by way of explanation is "Yes,—that's how it goes." Later she indicates, in keeping with social conventions, that she was getting old, and had to settle down. The choice of Tesman, however, comes across as a moment of desperate acting out: when there are no heroes anymore, it doesn't matter who one marries.

Hedda's horror of sex and sexuality, including her own pregnancy, is entirely in keeping with idealist aesthetics, which venerated Raphael's Madonnas, but did not want to know how ordinary babies come to be born. Since having babies is something any woman can do, Hedda surely feels that her pregnancy drags her down into the ordinary and the everyday. Jørgen's Aunt Julie does nothing to make her feel better, for she appears to think of Hedda as nothing but an incubator for future little Tesmans. In the same way, her marriage to Tesman is nothing but a source of irritation: every time she sees her husband, she is reminded of her own fall into the ordinary. This is why she idly wonders whether Tesman might perhaps have a political career:

HEDDA. . . . Do you think, then, that it would be quite impossible for Tesman to become prime minister?
BRACK. Hm,—you see, dear Mrs. Hedda,—for *that* to happen, he would first of all have to be a fairly rich man.
HEDDA [*gets up impatiently*]. That's it! It's these shabby circumstances I have ended up in—! [*Walks across the floor.*] They make life so wretched! So totally ridiculous!—For *that's* how it is.

(II: 337)

The word *latterligt* ("ridiculous") connects her dismay at her lowered social status to her disappointment at the absence of beauty in Løvborg's death.

Throughout the play, Hedda identifies with heroic masculinity and despises domestic femininity. In the end, she kills herself (and her unborn child) in the way Ejlert Løvborg did not: courageously, cleanly, with a bullet through the temple. Hedda here behaves like a man; that is to say, she breaks completely with the idealist opposition between female sacrifice and male heroism. Once Hedda is gone, there is nobody left to admire the idealist heroism of her deed: her husband can only repeat his eternal "Just think!", and Judge Brack's famous last line, "But God have mercy,—one simply doesn't *do* that kind of thing!", reveals his incapacity even to imagine horizons other than those of the social conventions of his milieu (11: 393). In the world of *Hedda Gabler* the everyday has turned poisonous, and idealism has become an incomprehensible anachronism.

Apart from Hedda, nobody in this play appears to know what it might mean to have high ideals. Løvborg might have been an exception, but if so, his erstwhile idealism has not survived his self-destructive tendencies. *Hedda Gabler* thus inaugurates a new phase in Ibsen's modernism, one in which idealism comes across as a baffling anachronism, yet, as in the case of Hedda, as an anachronism that has more splendor than the mediocrities that surround her. In *Hedda Gabler*, moreover, the everyday is a negative force. More than anything else, Hedda's constant and intense sense of *boredom* signals the change. Her boredom easily turns into aggression: although the scene in which she makes fun of Aunt Julie's hat gives us an early warning, the burning of Løvborg's manuscript is nevertheless shocking in its astounding ferocity.

In *Hedda Gabler*, then, Ibsen radically changes his representation of the everyday. In the sequence of plays from *A Doll's House* to *The Lady from the Sea*, the everyday is represented as the sphere where *forvandling* ("transformation") must be sought. This is true even for *Rosmersholm*, where Rebecca insists that she has been transformed simply by sharing everyday life with Rosmer. That Rosmer refuses to believe this testifies to the connection between idealism and skepticism, but it does not turn the everyday into something negative. Rather, it stands as an opportunity that the protagonists of *Rosmersholm* are unable to take. In *Hedda Gabler*, on the other hand, the everyday is no longer represented as the only sphere where we have a chance to find acknowledgment and love; here the everyday is no longer potentially redemptive; it has become, rather, a petty and banal sphere of routinized, conventional, and empty interactions. In Ibsen's previous plays marriage stands as a figure for the redemptive everyday: in *Hedda Gabler*, marriage and the everyday are equally empty. It would simply make no sense to suggest to Hedda that she should follow Ellida's example and seek to reaffirm her choice of Jørgen Tesman as her husband. Tesman is no more capable of listening and responding to Hedda in a loving and authentic way than Hedda is to him: an abyss separates this marriage from that of the Wangels.

In his fascinating book *Menzel's Realism*, Michael Fried distinguishes between the "good" and the "bad" everyday—that is to say, between the everyday considered as a sphere of potential meaning and redemption and the everyday considered as a routinized realm of inauthenticity, alienation, and boredom. By suggesting that we think of Wittgenstein as theorizing the "good" and Heidegger as theorizing the "bad" everyday, Fried reminds us that both perspectives on the everyday are intrinsic to modernity and modernism.[4]

Ibsen's Late Modernism

In *Hedda Gabler*, the waning of idealism coincides with the emergence of the "bad" everyday. This is surely no coincidence. In this book, I have tried to show that although Ibsen was idealism's greatest critic, he also admired its radical utopian vision. I get the impression that for Ibsen, the energy to turn the everyday into a sphere of transformation and redemption originates in the idealist utopia. In its early phase, Ibsen's modernism is finely poised between utopia and critique. In its late phase, however, Ibsen shows what the world looks like when we truly have to "live life without ideals", as Ulrik Brendel puts it (10: 433). Without the utopian energy of radical idealism, everyday life in modernity becomes incapable of generating meaning, energy, passion, or hope.

Ibsen's last plays investigate the various ways in which a human life can become frozen, static, immobile, meaningless. Hedda's boredom expresses her sense that she lives in a world in which nothing at all is worthy of her energy, her interest, her love. In *The Master Builder*, Aline Solness is forever frozen in the moment when her dolls burnt and her children died. Her husband, the master builder himself, fears that his creative and sexual life is finished. So does Arnold Rubek in *When We Dead Awaken*. After being released from prison, John Gabriel Borkman imprisons himself in his house for eight years, and when he finally ventures out, it is to a landscape of frozen ice and snow, where he dies. In all these plays, the frozen protagonists are opposed to characters representing youth, desire, vitality, and energy: Hilde Wangel, Fanny Wilton, Maja, and Ulfhejm. (*Little Eyolf* may be an exception to this rule.[5]) We have seen that the theme of stasis first surfaces in *The Lady from the Sea*. But, unlike Hedda, Solness, Borkman, Rubek, and Irene, Ellida finds her way back to the everyday. This possibility is blocked when the theme of immobility and emptiness is connected with the "bad" everyday, for then the result is living death: a life dominated by complete stasis, as if fixed in an eternal tableau, or, as in *When We Dead Awaken*, in a sculpture.

The transition from the "good" to the "bad" everyday, then, is the great difference between Ibsen's early and late modernism. But what about the other key features of Ibsen's modernism? Do they still apply to Ibsen's late phase? It seems to me that they do. The most difficult feature to analyze is the first: Ibsen's modernist commitment to realism and prose. The late plays are obviously still written in prose, but is this still realism? Critics who think that the late plays are not realistic, often draw the line between *Hedda Gabler* and *The Master Builder*, and declare that the last four plays are symbolist, or protomodernist.[6] But if realism simply means the representation of reality, then none of the five late plays is less realistic than *The Lady from the Sea* or more symbolist than *The Wild Duck*.

I think critics have recourse to terms such as "symbolism" to convey their sense that Ibsen's characters get harder to understand in the late plays. But the sense of heightened obscurity of motivation and purpose is not caused by a departure from realism (surely it is not always that easy to understand people in real life either), but rather by Ibsen's ever deepening interest in the skeptical problem of "expressing the inner mind", a problem that is absolutely central in all his major modernist works (and in *Emperor and Galilean*, too). In the late plays, characters have increasingly lost their faith in language; there is less love and more skepticism, which means that more characters feel radically isolated, misunderstood, and unacknowledged. The audience is given no privileged access to their minds: late Ibsen obliges us to experience the difficulty of human expression as deeply as the characters do.

As for the other features of Ibsen's modernism, they are all more or less powerfully present in the late plays. (Since we are talking of a bunch of features, one would not expect them all to be equally present in every single play.) Thus idealism is important in *Hedda Gabler* and *When We Dead Awaken*, but recedes into the background in the plays in between (again, *Little Eyolf* may be an exception). Skepticism, on the other hand, is everywhere, more insistently than ever; and for that reason, love is almost nowhere. The situation of women is strongly foregrounded in *Hedda Gabler*, and, in part, in *Little Eyolf*. Marriage remains a crucial theme in all five late plays, but it is now placed in the middle of the "bad" everyday, with predictably dire consequences. Finally, the late plays are if anything more meta-aesthetic and metatheatrical than the ones that precede them, and "late" Ibsen is as interested in everything from obvious self-theatricalization to subtle masquerades as he ever was.[7]

When We Dead Awaken: Ibsen's Dramatic Epilogue

No Ibsen play is more meta-aesthetic than *When We Dead Awaken*, and few are more explicitly concerned with idealism.[8] The subtitle "A Dramatic Epilogue" already indicates that this text is concerned with its own relationship to Ibsen's earlier works. When asked whether this meant that his new play would be his last, Ibsen vigorously denied it. He intended the play, he said in December 1899, to be the "epilogue to the series of my dramatic works that begins with *A Doll's House* and now comes to an end with *When We Dead Awaken*. This last work belongs to the experiences I have wanted to depict in the whole series. This forms a whole, a unity, which I now have finished. If I write something after this, it will all be in a completely different context, and perhaps in a different form, too" (19: 226).

In March 1900, he wrote to Count Moritz Prozor, his French translator: "You are actually right when you say that the series that is completed with the epilogue, really began with *The Master Builder*. But I don't want to go more deeply into this. I leave all comments and interpretations to you" (18: 447). Whether Ibsen thought that the "series" began with *A Doll's House* or with *The Master Builder*, the fact is that *When We Dead Awaken* ends with an avalanche that sweeps the two protagonists away—that is to say, with an obvious reference to *Brand*, the first play Ibsen wrote after leaving Norway (and which he saw performed for the first time in Copenhagen in April 1898, just as he was beginning work on *When We Dead Awaken*).[9] Readers and audiences should surely make up their own mind about what "series" Ibsen here is completing.

My candidate for what it was that Ibsen thought he had finished with in *When We Dead Awaken* is his long investigation of idealism. Whatever the truth of the matter, it is possible to read *When We Dead Awaken* as Ibsen's final judgment on idealism.[10] In this play, the world-famous sculptor Arnold Rubek explains to Irene, who was his model when he worked on his masterpiece called *The Day of Resurrection*, how he felt when he met her. He had long had the idea for a work representing a young woman arising from death: "The woman awakening was to be the noblest, purest and most ideal woman on earth. Then I found *you*. I could use you for everything. And you submitted so gladly and willingly. And you gave up your family and your home— and followed me" (13: 238). The young Rubek was a passionate idealist, placing women on the highest pedestal, thinking of sex as degrading, and art as capable of justifying existence: "You became for me a high and sacred creature, to be touched only by thoughts of adoration. I was still young then, Irene. A superstition filled me: that if I touched you, if I desired you sensually, then my spirit would be profaned so that I would be unable to create what I was striving for" (13: 238).

However he tries to explain it away, the young Rubek's relationship to the young Irene was a denial of love. Rubek is Pygmalion in reverse: by not kissing Irene, he turned her into stone. When the sculpture was completed, Rubek said farewell to Irene, calling their work together an "episode". Irene never recovered. She disappeared, and spent her life posing naked in *tableaux vivants* and living sculptures: the pure woman fallen, the madonna turned whore. She has, she says, killed her first husband, or at least inspired him to kill himself. She has spent time in a mental hospital and now travels with her nurse, a nun who carries a straitjacket in her suitcase. Thus Rubek's idealism completely theatricalized Irene, turning her into a spectacle, a mere surface. By refusing to love her, and—even more damaging to Irene—by refusing to acknowledge that *she* loved him—he de-souled her, and turned her into a statue. (This is the extreme version of the tendencies implicit in the men's gaze on Nora's tarantella.) Rubek's sin, one might say, is not that he couldn't distinguish between the woman and the sculpture, but that he preferred the sculpture.

When Rubek confesses that he actually changed his masterpiece after Irene left, Irene is rightly outraged. Now, Rubek says, Irene stands in the background, surrounded by other figures, whereas he has placed himself in the foreground as the incarnation of something he calls "remorse over a forfeited life" (13: 263). Irene has sacrificed her life for his art, yet Rubek feels free to turn himself into the central figure in the sculpture. There is a savage denunciation of the idealist myth of female sacrifice here: Irene's sacrifice has not lead to redemption, but to sex-work and madness. Rubek's treatment of Irene is strikingly similar to the way the poet Falk intends to use Svanhild in *Love's Comedy*, and the parallel is brought out in Irene's contemptuous response to Rubek's description of the changed sculpture: "Poet!" (13: 263).

After Irene left, Rubek has not been able to create. Like Ulrik Brendel, he refers to his imagination as a locked box. Tapping his chest, he tells Maja, his trophy-wife, that "In here, you see,—I have a tiny little casket with a lock that can't be picked. And in that casket all my pictorial visions are kept. . . . And she had the key,—and she took it with her" (13: 254). When Maja tells Rubek that he clearly regrets marrying her, he defends himself by saying, "You really have no clear notion of what an artist's nature looks like inside," to which Maja ripostes, "Good Lord, I don't even have a notion of what I look like inside" (13: 252–3). In his condescending way, Rubek takes this as evidence of Maja's frivolousness. We, however, are free to see it as her rejection of Rubek's unilateral demand for complete acknowledgment of his soul and of his narcissistic self-idealization in the name of art.

Rubek, then, does not want a woman; he wants a muse figure able to read his mind and entirely unconcerned about having her own mind read by him: unless he finds such a creature, he cannot express himself artistically. Rubek's desperate wish for unity with a woman completely dedicated to his creative project (there are shades of Rosmer here) makes him easy prey for Irene's insane idealism: together they will ascend the mountain, go beyond the fog and into the sunshine, where they will finally have sex:

IRENE [*enraptured in passion*]. No, no—up into the light and all the glittering glory. Up to the promised mountain peak!

RUBEK. And up there we'll celebrate our wedding feast, Irene—my beloved.

IRENE [*Proudly*]. The sun may look at us, Arnold.

RUBEK. All the powers of light may look at us. And all those of darkness, too. [*Grasping her hand.*] Will you now follow me, my bride of redemption (*min benådelses brud*)?[11]

IRENE [*as if transfigured*]. I follow my lord and master willingly and gladly.

RUBEK [*pulling her upwards*]. Through the fog first, Irene, and then—

IRENE. Yes, through all the fog. And then all the way up to the top of the tower that gleams in the sunrise.

(13: 283)

As they disappear from sight, we hear Maja's joyful song of freedom from the lowlands below; the avalanche comes thundering down, and the nun appears just in time to see Rubek and Irene disappear in the snow. Making the sign of the cross, she says "Pax vobiscum!" ("Peace be with you"), and the curtain falls. Here we should probably not forget that "Irene" is Greek for peace.

Rubek speaks of their "wedding feast" and calls Irene his bride, before Irene declares that she follows Rubek willingly and gladly. There is an insistent echo here, not just of the end of *Brand*, but of the end of *Rosmersholm*, where Rosmer speaks the words of the marriage ceremony before Rebecca and Rosmer follow each other (no lord and master there) out to the millrace. Both these plays show admirable idealists (I mean Brand and Rosmer) ending their lives as apparent failures. In both cases, the audience is left to wonder whether they should consider these men tragic heroes or deluded egoists. In my view, the end of *When We Dead Awaken* is less ambiguous. Irene is described as being "as if transfigured". Is it possible that Ibsen has forgotten the irony with which he described Gregers Werle waiting for the "light of transfiguration" (*forklarelsens lys*) (10: 123) to come streaming down on Gina and Hjalmar in *The Wild Duck*? In *When We Dead Awaken*, moreover, after Rubek and Irene have disappeared from sight, we hear Maja singing as she makes her way down from the cold heights of idealist ecstasy to the valleys and plains of ordinary life:

> Jeg er fri! Jeg er fri! Jeg er fri!
> Mit fangenskabs liv er forbi!
> Jeg er fri som en fugl! Jeg er fri!

(I am free! I am free! I am free! / My life in captivity is over! / I am free as a bird! I am free!)

Readers who tend to idealize Rubek, invariably overlook his belittling treatment of Maja.[12] But Maja is right to feel free as she leaves her horrible marriage. Her song is not great poetry, but that may be the point: Maja is not interested in art, but in life and love.

At the end of *When We Dead Awaken* Ibsen bids a characteristically unsentimental farewell to idealism and its ecstatic celebration of art and artists. Idealism took it for granted that art could justify life; for what could be higher than a life devoted to unveiling the beautiful, the true, and the good? Ibsen saw that without idealism, it is hard to feel *that* sanguine about a life spent in the service of art. At the end of his writing life, Ibsen left us with a question we have not finished with: what is the value of theater, and art, and literature, in our own terrifying modernity?

APPENDIX 1

Synopsis of *Emperor and Galilean*

PART I: *Caesar's Apostasy (AD 351–361)*

Act 1. Constantinople. The 20-year-old **Julian** (b. 331) at the imperial court of the Christian emperor **Constantius**. Julian and his brother **Gallus**, both Christians, are young princes, cousins of the emperor, the only survivors of a bloody massacre of their family carried out on the emperor's orders. It is Easter night, and the court is about to attend midnight mass. A street scene reveals how divided and belligerent the Christians are. Julian's childhood friend **Agathon** boasts of massacring heathens, and tells Julian he has had a vision that "Julian is to fight with lions". Gallus is proclaimed "Caesar"—that is to say, the crown prince, the designated inheritor of the imperial crown. Julian gets the emperor's permission to leave Constantinople, and sets off for Athens in search of philosophy.

Act 2. Athens. The restless and disenchanted Julian has seen through his philosophy teacher **Libanius**. The lonely Julian's closest friends are the future Christian leaders **Basil from Caesarea** and **Gregory of Nazianzus**. Julian is interested in hearing about Basil's sister **Macrina**, said to be a holy and pure woman, devoting herself entirely to good works. Yet Christianity no longer holds Julian: "The old beauty is no longer beautiful, and the new truth no longer true," he declares, and takes off for Ephesus, where he hears that the great mystic **Maximus** is making statues move.

Act 3. Ephesus. **Basil** and **Gregory** arrive. They are shocked at Julian's pagan mysticism. Julian has cosmic visions, and learns that "what is, is not, and what is not, is". The high point of the act is a mystical experience organized by **Maximus**, in which Julian has a vision in which he sees the figures of Cain and Judas, and surmises that he, Julian, is the absent third, called to follow them. A voice tells him to found the "Third Empire" (*det tredje rike*). Julian believes that he is the chosen one, that a "pure woman" will be given him, so that he can found a new earth, and a new human lineage. The emperor's envoy **Leontes** arrives: Julian's brother **Gallus** is dead, and the emperor chooses Julian as his successor. Julian discovers that Gallus was executed on the emperor's orders. Basil and Gregory implore him not to accept worldly power. Maximus tells him that the spirit world gives no clear sign as to what Julian should do, speaking the famous line: "Sign against sign." Julian suspects the emperor of plotting his death. Then Leontes reveals that the emperor offers Julian the princess **Helena**, the emperor's sister, in marriage. Julian instantly believes that Helena is the "pure woman" that has been promised him, takes it as a sign, and accepts the purple robe and the title of Caesar.

Act 4. *Lutetia* (today's Paris). Julian has enjoyed great military success, and has beaten the barbarians. Returning after his campaign, he learns that the emperor has proclaimed Julian's victories to be his own. Nubian envoys arrive from Rome with exotic fruits and other gifts. **Helena** eggs Julian on to revolt. Suddenly Helena is taken ill: the peaches from Rome were poisoned. Helena dies uttering fearful imprecations, which reveal that she finds Julian sexually unappetizing, that she was in love with Gallus, and that she has had an affair with a priest in Lutetia, who has made her pregnant. Apparently, everyone except Julian knew of her pregnancy, for the emperor, who is planning to marry again, poisoned his own sister to prevent Julian from producing an heir to the empire. Disgusted and afraid for his life, Julian, who is now entirely alone, manipulates the army to revolt against Constantius, and proclaim Julian as emperor.

Act 5. *Vienne*, a small town in the south of Gaul (today's France). The whole scene is set in the catacomb under the Christian cathedral in the town. In the cathedral above, hymns are heard, for now miracles happen at Helena's casket. The army is restless, for Julian has been in the catacombs for five nights and days. Julian has to take command or lose their support. Julian seems powerless to make a decision. **Maximus** finds no signs, for the hymns silence the spirits. Finally, after hearing that Helena is referred to as the "pure woman", Julian goes down in the crypt to sacrifice. We have no idea what he sees in the entrails of the animal, but whatever it is, he ascends, shouting "*Helios!*" The breakthrough is made, he is no longer a Christian, and he will march on Constantinople with his army to seize power. The end of the act, and of this part of the play, takes place in counterpoint with the Christian hymns above, where they are singing the Lord's Prayer. Julian ascends up into the light, proclaims that he is finally free, and claims the kingdom for himself.

PART II: *The Emperor Julian (AD 361–363)*

Act 1. *Constantinople*. **Constantius** is dead. We see his magnificent funeral barge. Julian performs a spectacular public sacrifice to Apollo and Dionysus. Julian proclaims total freedom of religion, and then instantly turns around and starts to persecute all those who disagree with him, all those who tell him the truth, and refuse to flatter him, exemplified by the old, faithful chancellor **Ursulus**. There is a highly theatrical Dinoysus procession through the streets of Constantinople. Hypocrisy and flattery now become the order of the day.

Act 2. *Antioch*. Julian persecutes Christians. The Christians destroy Julian's Greek temples. **Gregory of Nazianzus** now becomes a bishop of glowing faith and power. The high point of the act is the clash between the procession of singing Christian martyrs in chains (among them **Agathon**) and Julian's procession in honor of Apollo. Increasingly hirsute and disheveled, Julian appears mad, sometimes as a figure of fun. He is also increasingly desperate, increasingly lonely, and increasingly unable to distinguish between truth and lies. At the end of the act the old and frail **Bishop Maris** curses Julian.

Act 3. *Antioch*. The persecutions increase. The people are increasingly opposed to Julian. Even former flatterers now declare their Christian faith. Julian has sent **General Jovian** to Jerusalem to rebuild the temple of the Jews. The Christian God has said this cannot be done. Jovian returns and reports that fires and earthquakes prevented the rebuilding. Julian and **Maximus** talk about the Third Empire again.

Act 4. *On the empire's eastern borders. Wild mountain landscape.* The army is marching eastwards to fight the Persian King, **Sapores**. Julian has innumerable philosophers and priests from different religions forecast the outcome of the war. Omens, warnings, signs are scrutinized. They all give different advice. Julian now declares himself God, and orders all the soldiers to worship him. **General Jovian** reveals that he is a Christian, and refuses to do so. The army rounds up **Basil of Caesarea** and his sister **Macrina**, and Julian orders them and their followers to follow the army, as a kind of medical corps. **A Persian** who claims to have escaped from Sapores' persecution is brought to Julian. He advises Julian to burn his ships (on the adjacent river) and set off across the plains, to surprise the Persian army. Although all the army's supplies are on board the ships, Julian decides to trust the Persian, burns his ships, and sends his army off across the plains beyond the Tigris. But the Persian turns out to have been a spy, he has misled Julian, and the army is now in a dire situation.

Act 5. *The plains beyond the Tigris (ancient Mesopotamia; present-day Iraq).* Julian is losing his mind and tries to commit suicide. Desperate for a sign, an omen, Julian turns to **Maximus**, who can tell him only that "all omens are silent". Julian is killed by his childhood playmate **Agathon**, who appears fanatically deranged himself, only too ready to die for the cause of killing Julian. He kills Julian with what he claims is the spear that pierced Jesus' side on the cross. The Christian general **Jovian** is proclaimed emperor, and Julian expires, surrounded by **Maximus, Basil**, and **Macrina**. His last words are: "Beautiful earth, beautiful life on earth—[*He opens his eyes wide.*] Oh Sun, Sun, why did you betray me?"

APPENDIX 2

Translating Ibsen

Why does Ibsen so often come across as flat-footed in English? Books and articles have been written on the question. Just about everything I shall say here has been more brilliantly conveyed by Inga-Stina Ewbank in her 1998 article "Translating Ibsen for the English Stage".[1] Ewbank's article was based on her own experience of translating for London stage productions directed by two of the leading British directors of Ibsen: Peter Hall and John Barton, and I strongly recommend it. I shall begin by conveying some of Ewbank's general comments on Ibsen's language. Then I shall look at one example from *Rosmersholm*. I hope that this will give interested readers at least some sense of what is at stake in the difficult business of translating Ibsen into English.

Ewbank on Ibsen's Prose

"An Ibsen translation into English is still expected to sound as if Ibsen had written in a standard English idiom, when in fact the Norwegian of his dramatic texts is more inventive than standard," Ewbank writes (p. 66). This is an important reminder, for Ibsen was not a writer of standard Norwegian. He helped to shape the modern Norwegian language; in some ways Ibsen is to Norwegian as Shakespeare is to English: one constantly discovers that he invented expressions that are now part of the language.

"Ibsen's prose texts tempt the translator to expand and explain, because he creates his own language—his unique 'sprogtone'—by packing with suggestion an apparently flat and colourless style," Ewbank writes (p. 59). Ibsen's suggestiveness is achieved by the use of the most ordinary and everyday words. The challenge is to convey the same intensity and suggestiveness in English without losing the colloquial everydayness of the language. When a translation fails to convey this, Ibsen's incomparable mastery of the everyday is turned into flat, pedestrian prose.

Ewbank points out that Ibsen often makes "his speaker refer to something very important in the simplest and vaguest kind of phrase" (p. 58). Often the word conveying the vagueness is "det" ("it") or "dette" ("this") or "slik" ("thus", "the way", "in this way"), used in a way that makes the whole phrase quite untranslatable in English. Ewbank's examples are from *The Master Builder*: "dette med oss to", Solness says to Hilde ("this with us two"); "slik som De har det" ("the way you have it") (p. 58); and then Aline Solness's famous line, spoken to her husband: "Men det forfærdelige som branden drog efter sig—Det er det! Det, det, det!" (12: 71). ("But the horrible [thing] that followed in the wake of the fire—It is it! It, it, it!") (p. 58).

As we can see, the so-called literal translations are not translations at all; they are not

English. In such cases, a translator has to rewrite in some way. Ewbank rightly says that in an Ibsen play "characters will use a 'det' or a 'dette' or a 'slik' as a sign of something he or she cannot, or will not, understand or bear. It is a matter not so much of inarticulateness as of deferral of meaning" (pp. 58–9). Working with Peter Hall, Ewbank herself decided to translate Aline Solness's line as "But the terrible things that followed in the wake of the fire . . . Terrible . . . Terrible . . . Just terrible," but she still wonders whether this was not a mistake.

An example from Rosmersholm

I shall now try to convey, through a brief example, some of the difficulties involved in turning Ibsen's spare, subtle, and suggestive language into something equally good in English. My example comes from Act 3 of *Rosmersholm*, the scene where Rebecca confesses to Rosmer and Kroll that she drove Rosmer's wife, Beata, to commit suicide by leaping into the millrace. I shall supply the original text, my own "literal" translation (insofar as there is no such thing as a literal translation, what I mean is an attempt to stay as close to the original as possible without regard to style and speakability onstage), and then four published versions of the same passage.[2]

Ibsen's text

[1.] REBEKKA [*heftig*]. Men tror I da at jeg gik her og
[2.] handled med kold og kløgtig fatning! Jeg var da ikke
[3.] slig, dengang, som nu, da jeg står og fortæller det. Og
[4.] så er der da vel to slags vilje i et menneske, skulde jeg
[5.] mene! Jeg vilde ha' Beate væk. På den ene måden
[6.] eller på den anden. Men jeg trode aldrig at det skulde
[7.] komme alligevel. Ved hvert skridt, som jeg fristed og
[8.] voved fremad, syntes jeg ligesom noget skreg indeni
[9.] mig: Nu ikke længer! Ikke et skridt længer!—Og
[10.] så *kunde* jeg ikke la' det være endda. Jeg *måtte*
[11.] friste et bitte lidet gran til. Bare et eneste et. Og så
[12.] et til—og altid et til.—Og så *kom* det.—Det er
[13.] på den vis, sligt noget går for sig.

(*Rosmersholm*, Act 3; 10: 419)

"Literal" translation

[1.] REBECCA [*vehemently*]. But do you then believe that I
[2.] acted with cool and clever composure! I was not
[3.] then as I am now, standing here and telling it. And
[4.] then surely there are two kinds of will in a human being, I should
[5.] think! I wanted Beata gone. In one way
[6.] or in another. But I never thought that it would

[7.]   come anyway. At every step I tried and
[8.]   dared to take forward, I almost felt as if something screamed inside
[9.]   me: No further now! Not one step further!—And
[10.]   still I *couldn't* let it be. I *had*
[11.]   to try just one tiny little bit more. Just one. And then
[12.]   another one—and always another one.—And then it *came.*—This is
[13.]   the way that sort of thing happens.

Translation 1: Rolf Fjelde (USA)

REBECCA [*fervently*]. You think I went through all this with ice in my veins? That I
    calculated every move! I was a different woman then than I am now, standing here,
    telling about it. Anyway, I think a person can be of two wills about something. I
    wanted Beata out of here, one way or another. But even so, I never dreamed it could
    happen. With every step ahead that I gambled on, it was as if something inside me
    cried out: 'No further! Not one step further!' And yet I *couldn't* stop. I *had* to try for a
    tiny bit more. Just the least little bit. And then again—and always again—until it
    happened. That's the way these things *do* happen.

Translation 2: Brian Johnston (USA)

REBECCA [*vehemently*]. Do you think I set to work with cold, calculating composure? I
    wasn't the same, then, that I am now, standing here telling you about it. Besides, I
    think there are two kinds of will in a person. I wanted Beata gone—one way or
    another. But at the same time, I never believed it would happen. With each step
    forward I ventured, it was as if a voice inside me cried in terror, "No further now! Not
    one step further!" And yet I couldn't hold back. I had to risk just that tiny bit more.
    Just that one. And then one more—and always only one more—. Until it happened.
    That's the way such things come about.

Translation 3: James McFarlane (UK)

REBECCA [*vehemently*]. But do you think I set about these things deliberately in cold
    blood! I was different then from what I am now, standing here talking about it. And
    besides, it seems to me a person can want things both ways. I wanted to get rid of
    Beata, one way or another. But I never really imagined it would ever happen. Every
    little step I risked, every faltering advance, I seemed to hear something call out
    within me: "No further! Not a step further!" ... And yet I could not stop. I *had* to
    venture a little bit further. Just one little bit further. And then a little bit more ...
    always just a little bit more. And then it happened. That's the way things like that do
    happen.

Translation 4: Michael Meyer (UK)

REBECCA [*vehemently*]. But do you think I did all this calculatedly and in cold blood?
    No, I was different then from what I am now—standing here and talking about it.
    And besides—I think a person can have two wills. I wanted to be rid of Beata.

Somehow or other. But I never thought it would happen. Every step that I ventured forward, I felt as though a voice cried within me: "No further! Not an inch further!" But I *couldn't* stop! I had to venture another inch. Just one. And then another—just one more. And then it happened. That's how such things happen.

Notes on the original language

The extraordinary everydayness of the language contrasts strongly with the dramatic event that Rebecca is talking about. Here are some of the more characteristic features of this passage. (1) There is the characteristic use of a very high number of short adverbs: *da, så, vel, alligevel, endda.* (2) There are also some extremely colloquial, everyday verbal expressions, which also consist of short, common words: *ha' Beate væk, la' det være, går for sig.* (3) There are some vivid verb combinations, also very colloquial: *gik her og handled, står og fortæller.* (4) There are a number of fairly vague pronouns that fall under Ewbank's warning against turning them into something too concrete: *det, noget, sligt noget.* (5) For the translator, perhaps the most difficult and challenging thing in this passage is Rebecca's two references to Beata's suicide as "something" (*det*) that "came" ("*at det skulde komme*", "*Og så kom det*").

Short Norwegian adverbs are notoriously hard to translate into English. They are typical of Norwegian everyday speech, and provide great scope for actors, who can use them to vary the tone, emphasis, and rhythm of the language. This becomes a problem for translators in lines 3–5. Here Rebecca's claim about the two wills in a human being is introduced by "Og så er der da vel" and ends with an emphatic "skulde jeg mene!", which reminds us that Rebecca is a woman of strong intellectual passions. This has given all our sample translators a great deal of difficulty:

> *Ibsen:* Og så er der da vel to slags vilje i et menneske, skulde jeg mene!
> *Literal:* And then surely there are two kinds of will in a human being, I should think!
> 1. Anyway, I think a person can be of two wills about something.
> 2. Besides, I think there are two kinds of will in a person.
> 3. And besides, it seems to me a person can want things both ways.
> 4. And besides—I think a person can have two wills.

Of the four examples, the first ends lamely on two empty words. Since there isn't, in my opinion, an empty word in *Rosmersholm*, the overall stylistic effect produced is unfortunate. Although it is imaginative, the third example conveys quite misleading connotations in this context. The second and fourth are not wrong, but they do sound very flat compared to the Norwegian. The question is why.

First of all, "I think" is far more tentative than Rebecca's emphatic "skulde jeg mene!". In fact, in Norwegian the emphasis is repeated twice, partly through the adverbial "da vel" and partly through "skulde jeg mene!". In Norwegian, moreover, Rebecca does not use the personal pronoun "I" to introduce her claim about the two wills. This turns her statement into something like a philosophical maxim, more than just a personal opinion. To this, she then adds her emphatic, personal "skulde jeg mene!". Both the second and the fourth examples use "person" for "menneske", which means "human being". This makes Rebecca's statement less obviously anthropological or philosophical than it is. In the play, we learn that Rebecca had already read all the new, anti-idealist and anti-traditional books when she came to Rosmersholm, and that she influenced Rosmer deeply, intellectually and spiritually. These two translations give actors less scope for a wide range of nuanced interpretations than the original Norwegian. They also fail to convey Rebecca's passion and intellectual self-confidence. This is why there is not the same *life* in them as in the original. Unfortunately, it is not easy to do much better and still produce a good, speakable text.

"Og så *kom* det"

Rebecca speaks of an unspeakable act that she never can bring herself to name. In lines 12–13 "det" ("it") and "sligt noget" ("that sort of thing") are there, as Ewbank points out, to convey the profound, unnamable horror of what she has done.

> *Ibsen*: Og så et til—og altid et til.—Og så *kom* det.—Det er på den vis, sligt noget går for sig.
> *Literal*: And then another one—and always another one.—And then it *came*.—
> That is the way that sort of thing happens.
> 1: And then again—and always again—until it happened. That's the way these things *do* happen.
> 2: And then one more—and always only one more—. Until it happened. That's the way such things come about.
> 3: And then a little bit more . . . always just a little bit more. And then it happened. That's the way things like that do happen.
> 4: And then another—just one more. And then it happened. That's how such things happen.

Rebecca's "Og så *kom* det.—" is not quite standard Norwegian. The sentence builds expectations that it might finish in some other way: my associations are to "Og så kom det over meg" ("and then it came over me") and "Og så kom det jeg hadde ventet på" ("and then that which I had been expecting arrived/happened"), both of which help to explain why Rebecca chose the verb *kom*. There is a case, therefore, for rendering it in slightly non-standard English.

The translations here all use the verb "happen" to convey Rebecca's meaning. That is understandable. But examples 1, 3, and 4 use "happen" not once, but twice. This surely is too much, for it makes the whole confession sound stylistically pedestrian, and too concrete. Example 2 is not really better, since the final "come about" sounds almost jaunty, and undermines the sense that Rebecca is speaking of *one*, sudden, horrifying event.

The challenge here is to convey that although Rebecca is confessing to it, she cannot bear actually to say what she did to Beata. Ideally the translator should preserve Ibsen's punctuation, which indicates Rebecca's breathing pattern, and he or she should preserve the sense of extreme intensity, which Ibsen indicated by underlining *kom*. The language of this shocking confession is as ordinary and untheatrical as it can possibly be; yet Ibsen's choice of words suggests a world of criminal passions, and guilt, too. The passage conveys with great precision an important theme in *Rosmersholm*: namely, that the most melodramatic horror, crime, and madness can and will take place in the everyday.

Notes

INTRODUCTION

1. Without Stanley Cavell's generosity of spirit and willingness to engage in many friendly conversations about Ibsen, this summary would have been less succinct, and much less lucid.
2. Kuhn, *Structure*, 74–5.
3. Miller, "Ibsen and the Drama of Today", 228–9.
4. Latter-day idealists who read *Emperor and Galilean* in various Platonic and Christian ways would violently disagree. See, e.g., Wyller, *Ibsens Keiser og Galilæer*, and Hoem, *Henrik Ibsens hovedverk*, the main points of which are translated in Hoem, "*Emperor and Galilean.*"
5. For more information, see Dauber and Jost (eds.), *Ordinary Language Criticism*.

CHAPTER 1 IBSEN AND THE IDEOLOGY OF MODERNISM

1. See <http://www.ibsen.net/index.db2?id=441> for a partial list of current productions.
2. See Mori, "Staging Ibsen's Realism," and Nilu, "Staging Ibsen in Bangladesh."
3. Lebowitz, *Ibsen and the Great World*, 1.
4. Only the maverick Harold Bloom appears to have time for Ibsen, for he includes *Peer Gynt* and *Hedda Gabler* in his *Western Canon*.
5. For more on the concept of distinction, see Bourdieu, *Distinction*.
6. Adorno, *Minima Moralia*, 92. The remarks on Ibsen appear in a section dated 1945.
7. Auerbach, *Mimesis*, 520. *Mimesis* was written in Istanbul between May 1942 and April 1945, and was first published in Switzerland in 1946.
8. Atkinson's review is quoted in Bentley, *Search*, 13. Bentley's own remark appears in "Ibsen, Pro and Con," first published in 1950 (see *Search*, 365).
9. Williams, *Drama from Ibsen to Eliot*, 97.
10. Williams, *Drama from Ibsen to Brecht*, 74. Williams himself presents *Drama from Ibsen to Brecht* as a major revision and rewriting of *Drama from Ibsen to Eliot*, which was first published in 1952.
11. McCarthy, "Will and Testament," 178.
12. Ibid. 174.
13. Ibid. 177.
14. There are no negative references to Ibsen in Tynan's theater criticism from the 1950s, and quite a few truly perceptive observations (see *Curtains*).
15. Billington, "The Troll in the Drawing-Room." Billington's quotation comes from Guthrie, *A Life in the Theatre*, 53. The web text misprints "chenille hobbles" for "chenille bobbles."

16. See Jameson, *Singular Modernity* (hereafter quoted in the text as *SM*), particularly esp. Part II: "Modernism as Ideology".

17. Billington, "Troll".

18. On this point, Jameson might disagree.

19. Its editorial manifesto, in particular, uses the word modernism in a self-evident way (see Rainey and Hallberg, 1–3).

20. Diamond, *Unmaking Mimesis*, 4–5.

21. Ibid. 7.

22. In a thoughtful essay on Barthes, Balzac, and S/Z, Knight takes issue with the "claim that realism as artistic form is inherently reactionary" ("S/Z", 134) and declares herself unconvinced that "sexism is more than a historically contingent feature of the realist paradigm, or that mimesis actually obliges its readers to confuse reactionary social orders with reality" ("S/Z", 121). But hers is a lonely voice among a chorus of critics persuaded that realism is politically reactionary and philosophically naïve.

23. Moe, "Hvor god", 24.

24. Fried argues along similar lines, stressing that his understanding of Courbet is "at odds with the formalist-modernist assumption that a fundamental opposition exists between painting as illusion or representation and painting as material object" (*Courbet's Realism*, 284).

25. See Diderot, "Conversations on *The Natural Son*", 10.

26. Guthrie, *A Life in the Theatre*, 202. The "cup-and-saucer" reference is to T. W. Robertson's 1867 play *Caste*. Part of the tea scene from *Caste* is reprinted in Innes (ed.), *A Sourcebook on Naturalist Theatre*, 9.

27. See Barthes, "The Reality Effect".

28. Letter to Edmund Gosse, 15 Jan. 1874.

29. In *SM*, Jameson also fails to mention theater.

30. For a much needed corrective to the prevalent neglect, see Shepherd-Barr, *Ibsen and Early Modernist Theatre*. The most obvious exception to the general rule is Bradbury and McFarlane's much used anthology *Modernism*, but then McFarlane was Britain's leading Ibsen scholar for a generation.

31. Fried, *Art and Objecthood*, 153.

32. Ibid. 163.

33. Ibid.

34. Innes, "Modernism in Drama", 131–2.

35. Lund, "Da Nora gik og kom hjem igen".

36. See Bjørneboe, "Endelig—hun skjøt ham!"

37. I am grateful to Inga-Stina Ewbank for information about the London performance of this production.

38. Fried, *Art and Objecthood*, 163.

39. Artaud, *Artaud on Theatre*, 14, a text written in 1923 and published in 1924.

40. Brecht, *Brecht on Theatre*, 66.

41. When Brecht speaks of "dramatic theater" as old-fashioned, and opposes it to his

own "epic theater", he means to include Ibsen in the "old-fashioned" category. For the opposition between epic and dramatic theater, see *Brecht on Theatre*, 33–42.

42. Puchner, *Stage Fright*, 8.

43. Szondi's pro-theatrical critique of Ibsen's realism is an example of the avant-gardist factions within the ideology of modernism. Szondi famously argues, in *Theory of the Modern Drama*, that *John Gabriel Borkman* is too narrative to be true theater. He also thinks that *Rosmersholm* never rises to the level of true tragedy, because the play is held back by Ibsen's allegiance to realism (see p. 17).

44. Even Puchner, who does much to untangle different attitudes towards theatricality, never imagines that the author of the closet dramas *Brand*, *Peer Gynt*, and *Emperor and Galilean* might be relevant to his study of modernist closet dramas (see ibid. 82–3).

45. The quotation is taken from the subtitle of Auerbach's *Mimesis: The Representation of Reality in Western Literature*.

46. See Haakonsen, *Henrik Ibsens realisme*, 21–6. Further references will be given in the text, abbreviated *IR*.

47. A brief, pioneering study of Ibsen's modernity was published in this period: viz. Tjønneland, *Ibsen og moderniteten* (1993).

48. Helland, *Melankoliens spill*, 28 and 491.

49. Ibid. 491.

50. Kittang, *Ibsens heroisme*, 372.

51. Ibid.

52. Both Helland and Kittang tend to forget that they are writing about theater: for them, Ibsen's plays are simply *texts*. The point is forcefully made by Ewbank, "Første opponent", 170. For my own disagreements with Kittang, see Moi, "Menns titaniske streben".

53. See Petersen, "*Peer Gynt*, dramatisk Digt".

54. Helland, *Melankoliens spill*, 21.

55. Letter, Rome, 28 Dec. 1867.

CHAPTER 2 POSTCOLONIAL NORWAY? IBSEN'S CULTURAL RESOURCES

1. Published in 1888, the first Ibsen biography was written while Ibsen was still at the height of his powers. Jæger's otherwise slight book remains precious as a source of opinions that may have been acceptable to Ibsen himself. So far, the best biography of Ibsen remains Koht's *Henrik Ibsen: Eit diktarliv*, written in the 1920s, and revised in the mid-1950s. (A somewhat abridged translation entitled *Life of Ibsen* was published in English in 1971.) The most comprehensive biography in English is Meyer's three-volume biography, 1967–71 (an abridged one-volume version was published by Penguin in 1974), but this is an accomplished compilation of research rather than a new interpretation. Ferguson's 1996 *Henrik Ibsen* added little to Koht and Meyer. A new biography by Ivo de

Figueiredo is to be published by Aschehoug in 2006, to mark the centenary of Ibsen's death.

2. Haakonsen's *Henrik Ibsen* points to some connections between Ibsen's reading of European literature and his plays. There is, for example, a discussion of possible connections between Staël's *Corinne* and *Ghosts* (see pp. 145–51).

3. Conversation with Felix Philippi in 1886, quoted in Meyer's 1974 *Henrik Ibsen*, 17.

4. Meier-Graefe, *Modern Art*, ii. 191.

5. Ibid. 193.

6. Bourdieu always spoke of a writer's "trajectory". Although mine is not an orthodox Bourdieuian analysis, this chapter owes much to Bourdieu's sociology of culture.

7. Bulyovszky, *Reiseminner fra Norge 1864*, *passim*.

8. Information in this paragraph is based on Pryser, *Norsk historie*, esp. chs. 8 and 10.

9. Information in this paragraph is based on Nerbøvik, *Norsk historie*, esp. chs. 10, 11, and 12.

10. For a history of the first Norwegian theater, see Blanc, *Christiania Theaters historie*.

11. See Dinesen, *Anecdotes of Destiny*.

12. See Ansteinsson, *Teater i Norge*, for information about Danish theater troupes and Norwegian dramatic societies on the south coast of Norway 1813–63.

13. Koht, *Henrik Ibsen*, i. 57.

14. For a presentation and reprint of the three reviews of *Catiline* that appeared in 1850, see Haugholt, "Samtidens kritikk".

15. Botten-Hansen in Haugholt, "Samtidens kritikk", 76.

16. Bø, "*Nationale subjekter*", discusses all the national romantic plays, and *Brand* and *Peer Gynt*, with a view to clarifying Ibsen's understanding of Norwegian national identity.

17. For the Norwegian reception of *The League of Youth*, see Meyer, *Farewell to Poetry*, 115–18. For Fjørtoft's politics, see Nerbøvik, *Norsk historie*, 182.

18. In "Den umulige treenighed" ("The Impossible Trinity"), Per Dahl writes that "The relations between Norway and Denmark have surely never been closer than during the so-called 'modern breakthrough' in the 1870s and 1880s. The connections criss-crossed: they were political, artistic, literary and personal." (Dahl's excellent lecture text also alerted me to Bjørnson's cultural condescension towards Ibsen, to which I shall return.)

19. Rottem, interviewed in Wold and Haagensen, "En ny dansketid?"

20. The information about art in Christiania in this paragraph is based on Askeland, *Adolph Tidemand*, 86–97, and on Malmanger's account in Berg *et al.* (eds.), *Norges Kunsthistorie*, iv. 126–9.

21. Munch, *Ephemerer*, in *Samlede Skrifter*, i. 104.

22. For an account of this offer, see Aubert, *Maleren Johan Christian Dahl*, 165–77.

23. See P. T. Andersen, *Norsk litteraturhistorie*, 197.

24. For a detailed account of how this came about, see Monrad, "Andreas Munch: Livsskizze", 11–12.

25. Munch, *Lord William Russell* (1857). Ibsen's discussion of Christiania Theater's production was published in *Illustreret Nyhedsblad* on 20 and 27 Dec. 1857 (see 15: 160–83). Brandes's review of the Copenhagen production was originally written in 1869; the text in Brandes, *Kritiker og Portræter*, is a revised version.

26. Malmanger, "Maleriet 1814–1870", 129. The first 25 years of the Norwegian National Gallery are documented in a web exhibition, providing an excellent overview of the taste of discriminating citizens of Christiania in the period: <http://www.museumsnett.no/nasjonalgalleriet/NG25aar/index.htm>. Since the National Gallery became part of the National Museum for Art, this fabulous web resource is no longer to be found.

27. Information in this and the preceding paragraph is based on Askeland, *Adolph Tidemand*, 97–101.

28. Welhaven, *Samlede Verker*, i. 231.

29. Ibid. 232.

30. Quoted by Westergaard, in "J. C. Dahl og Danmark", 21.

31. All of Ibsen's paintings and drawings, including his costume sketches for Olaf *Liljekrans*, are available at <http://www.ibsen.net>.

32. See Koht, *Henrik Ibsen*, ii. 146–7.

33. Bergliot Ibsen, *De tre*, 40–1.

34. See Edvardsen, *Gammelt nytt*, 20. See also Edvardsen, *Henrik Ibsen om seg selv*, 50–1.

35. Quoted in Høstmælingen, "Den evangelisk-lutherske", <http://www.hf.ntnu. no/din/hostmalingen.html>.

36. For an analysis of folkloric motifs in *The Lady from the Sea*, see Alnæs, *Varulv om natten*, 286–331.

37. In *Nordic Orientalism*, Oxfeldt reads Act 4 of *Peer Gynt* as a critique of orientalism.

38. To spell out the point: had Ibsen been born a woman in the same economic, social, and geographical circumstances, it is extremely unlikely that he would have become a writer, simply because such a girl would probably have received even less education than Ibsen did. Rather than working in a pharmacy, she would have been married off at a young age, without any chance of going to Christiania on her own to make her fortune. Of course, had this woman also given birth to an illegitimate son, all avenues would have been closed to her.

39. For details, see P. K. H. Dahl, *Streiflys*, 83.

40. There is an unsubstantiated account of a meeting between father and illegitimate son in Kristiania in 1892, finely explored in Byatt's *The Biographer's Tale*.

41. Woolf, *Room*, 47.

42. Werenskiold's painting does not, of course, show Ibsen seated in his apartment: the background is mountains. My point is that it is impossible to imagine the man in this painting as someone who is not "bourgeois" in the usual meaning of the word.

43. P. K. H. Dahl, *Streiflys*, 86.

44. Ibid. 11–52.

45. Bull, *Tradisjoner og minner*, 195.

46. See Koht, *Henrik Ibsen*, i. 219.

47. Letter, Oct. 1866. I should stress that Ibsen's papers and manuscripts were not sold at the auction: Ibsen was upset by the fact that they were in the hands of strangers, most likely the solicitor Nandrup.

48. Koht, *Henrik Ibsen*, i. 17.

49. Ibsen once claimed that he arrived in Grimstad in the summer of 1843, but this appears to be wrong. Koht believes that he arrived in Grimstad on 3 Jan. 1844 (see Koht, *Henrik Ibsen*, i. 29). After much hesitation, Dahl concludes that he must have arrived on 29 Nov. 1843 (see P. K. H. Dahl, *Streiflys*, 121).

50. Koht, *Henrik Ibsen*, i. 29–30.

51. Ibid. 32–5.

52. Ibid. 41.

53. According to the Central Bureau of Statistics in Norway, in 1865 the population of Norway was 1,700,000. In 1906, it had grown to 2,300,000. See <http://www.ssb.no/emner/historisk_statistikk/>.

54. Askeland, *Adolph Tidemand*, 86.

55. Jæger, *Henrik Ibsen*, 159–60.

56. As the editor of *Norsk Tidsskrift*, a magazine that published a fairly negative review of *Catiline*, Monrad took the rather unusual step of adding his own dissenting postscript to the review, in which he lauds the "poem's beautiful fundamental idea" (repr. in Haugholt, "Samtidens kritikk", 93).

57. See Koht, *Henrik Ibsen*, i. 75–6.

58. In "Arbeiderføreren Marcus Thrane", Noreng claims that Ibsen used elements of Thrane's life in many different characters. See <http://museumsnett.no/ibsen/Noreng/mthrane.html>.

59. This paragraph is based on information in Koht, *Henrik Ibsen*, i. 79–81, and in Meyer, *Making*, 100–2.

60. I am summarizing some of the fine findings in Ewbank, "Ibsen in Wonderful Copenhagen".

61. Ibid. 70.

62. See Meyer, *Making*, 81.

63. Ibsen mentions his limited and self-taught English several times. See, e.g., his letter to Edmund Gosse, 15 Jan. 1874 (17: 122).

64. Georg Brandes and Edvard Brandes, *Brevveksling*, i. 313.

65. Brandes, *Breve til Forældrene*, i. 82. See also Christensen, *Henrik Ibsens realisme*, i. 47.

66. Information in this paragraph is based on Moisy, *Paul Heyse*, 46.

67. Letter to C. J. Salomonsen, 10 Aug. 1873, in Brandes and Brandes, *Brevveksling*, 297.

68. Moisy, *Paul Heyse*, 168.

69. Ibid. 165.

70. Letter, 2 May 1875.

71. Letter, 13 July 1875, quoted in Moisy, *Paul Heyse*, 213–14.

72. Letter, Rome, 16 Sept. 1864.

73. See Moisy, *Paul Heyse*, 214.

74. One of Ibsen's best friends in Munich was the Bergen painter Marcus Grønvold. In his memoirs, he confirms that Ibsen got to know Heyse and the members of the idealist literary society *Krokodil* during his first period in Munich, and that he was far less sociable after 1885 than he had been from 1875 to 1879 (see *Fra Ulrikken til Alperne*, 136).

75. Bjørnson, *Kamp-liv*, ii. 244.

76. Ibid. 245.

77. See Brandes, "Paul Heyse". (A slightly different version is translated in Brandes, *Eminent Authors*, 1–60.)

78. See Brandes, "Paul Heyse", 319.

79. Brandes, *Emigrantlitteraturen*, 15.

80. Anonymous, "Preface", in Heyse, *Children of the World*, i. p. vi.

81. Letter, 25 May 1879.

82. Like most other Norwegian writers at the time, Ibsen wrote in Dano-Norwegian, which was basically written Danish, albeit often mixed with Norwegian words and expressions. Although it would have been pronounced quite differently from spoken Danish, Ibsen's spoken Norwegian would have been entirely comprehensible in Copenhagen.

83. For further information, see the memoirs of the two Bergen natives, Didrik Grønvold (*Diktere*) and his brother, the painter Marcus Grønvold, one of Ibsen's best friends in Munich (*Fra Ulrikken*).

84. See Nerbøvik, *Norsk historie*, 22.

85. Kenner explored the relationship between Joyce and Ibsen as early as 1951, but shows such condescension towards Norwegian culture that his analysis is deeply flawed (see "Joyce and Ibsen's Naturalism"). A more sober assessment of Ibsen's importance for Joyce can be found in Tysdahl, *Joyce and Ibsen*, esp. chs. 1 and 2. Finally, there is Richard Brown's thoughtful "James Joyce between Ibsen and Bjørnson". See also Joyce's own writing on Ibsen, included in *Occasional, Critical, and Political Writing*.

86. Recently, Casanova has written about the parallels between Ibsen and Irish writers. See "La Production de l'universel littéraire" (devoted to Ibsen in Europe), and the immensely ambitious *La République mondiale des lettres*, esp. 219–26.

CHAPTER 3 RETHINKING LITERARY HISTORY: IDEALISM, REALISM, AND THE BIRTH OF MODERNISM

1. For a polemical account of modernist elitism, see Carey, *The Intellectuals and the Masses*.

2. "Idealism" or "idealist aesthetics" is not an entry, e.g., in Cuddon, *A Dictionary of Literary Terms and Literary Theory*, or in Baldick, *Concise Oxford Dictionary of*

Literary Terms. "Idealism" is an entry in Childers and Hentzi (eds.), *Columbia Dictionary of Modern and Cultural Criticism*, but the entry never mentions the aesthetic meaning of the word.

3. Discussions of idealism in Ibsen are usually about idealism in the political, psychological, or moral sense. There are some good ones dealing with *Emperor and Galilean*: viz. Madsen, "Tanken om Det tredje rike"; Rønning, "Ond idealisme"; Rønning, "The Unconscious Evil of Idealism"; and Wærp, *Overgangens figurasjoner.*

4. Ystad's brief discussion of the aesthetics of idealism in "Dikterens syner" is an exception to this rule. Rightly connecting Danish and Norwegian idealism to a certain classicism, Ystad's discussion of Monrad is particularly interesting. But she also defines idealism as an aesthetics that emphasizes the "hidden, metaphysical, inner life behind the forms that the senses can perceive" (p. 180), and thinks of Ibsen's modern plays as subjective, passionate incarnations of this aesthetics. I find both these claims intensely problematic.

5. See Bell, "Metaphysics of Modernism", 18–20.

6. Schor, *George Sand and Idealism*, 4.

7. On this point, my approach is very different from Schor's.

8. The fragment is attributed to Hölderlin, but the manuscript version is in Hegel's handwriting, and Bernstein writes that "it is more plausible to regard the fragment as the result of an exchange of ideas amongst the three friends" (Bernstein (ed.), *Classic and Romantic*, 185 n. 1).

9. Hölderlin, "Oldest Programme", 186.

10. Ibid. 186–7.

11. Schlegel, "From *Ideas*", 263.

12. The first book version was published in 1800.

13. Wirsén, *Kritiker*, 124. Stefan Jonsson helped me with the translation.

14. Johnston has, more powerfully than anyone else, set forth the case for Ibsen's Hegelian heritage (see, e.g., *To the Third Empire*, 3–27). Ystad has discussed the connection between Ibsen's poem "I billedgalleriet" ("In the picture gallery") and the "classicizing, idealist aesthetics of contemporary men of taste like Heiberg, Welhaven and Monrad" ("Dikterens syner", 177).

15. For Hegel's treatment of truth and beauty, see, e.g., "The Idea of Artistic Beauty, or the Ideal", in *Hegel's Aesthetics*, i. 91–115.

16. Deutscher, *The Prophet Armed*, 54. Ascherson also quotes this passage ("Victory in Defeat", 3).

17. Lukács's idealist humanism is eloquently expressed in essays like "The Ideal of the Harmonious Man in Bourgeois Aesthetics" and "Marx and Engels on Aesthetic", collected in *Writer and Critic and Other Essays.*

18. Schiller, "On Naive and Sentimental Poetry", 196. Further page references will be given in the text, without any identifying abbreviation.

19. "In terms of reality the naive poet has the better of the sentimental poet;" Schiller writes (p. 234).

20. Satire has two subcategories, the pathetic and the mocking, which appeal, respectively, to sublime souls and beautiful hearts, but I shall not go further into these distinctions here (see p. 207).

21. C. Petersen, "*Peer Gynt*, dramatisk Digt af Henrik Ibsen", <http://www.ibsen. net/index.db2?id=229>.

22. Quoted by Bull in his introduction to *Love's Comedy* (4: 134).

23. Monrad, "Om Henrik Ibsen som Digter", 1.

24. Monrad, "Om Ibsens *Brand*," <http://www.ibsen.net/index.db2?id=69783>.

25. Kant, *The Metaphysics of Morals*, 178.

26. Ibid. 179.

27. Ibid.

28. Kant, *Lectures on Ethics*, 149.

29. Ibid. 150.

30. After being stabbed, Emilia kisses her father's hand in thanks, and dies (see Lessing, *Emilia Galotti*, 81).

31. For an interesting discussion of idealism before romanticism, see Pavel, *La Pensée du roman*. Like me, Pavel considers Flaubert as an anti-idealist novelist (see esp. pp. 281–90). But Pavel's understanding of nineteenth-century idealism is very different from mine, both because he does not discuss the German idealist tradition, and because he does not mention the theater.

32. I am not here going to engage with the vast literature on the death of tragedy, on the question of whether one can have a modern tragedy, and so on.

33. Keats, "Ode on a Grecian Urn", in *The Complete Poems*, 186.

34. See his letter to Brandes, 4 April 1872 (17: 30–3).

35. Brandes, *Emigrantlitteraturen*, 15 (hereafter cited in the text as *EL*). Brandes's works are notoriously difficult to cite, for he substantially cut and rewrote his works in every subsequent edition. Students of Ibsen—or anyone who wants to understand why *Emigrantlitteraturen* struck Scandinavian culture like a bombshell—need to read the 1st edn., published in 1872. The edition I use is a modern reprint of the 1872 edn. published in Oslo in 1971, which preserves Brandes's original spelling, but not the original pagination. For a fascinating account of the difficulty involved in editing Brandes's texts, see Per Dahl, "Det kritiske tekstvalg".

36. In a critique of the state of the theater in Norway, Ibsen claimed that Norwegians applauded Oehlenschläger's romantic tragedies in 1861 just because they were applauded in 1814. Norwegian theatergoers were so anxious at the thought of having to make up their own minds that they preferred to stick to the received opinion: namely, that Oehlenschläger is a great classic. The truth, Ibsen argued, was that Oehlenschläger's "saga style" and "heroic scenes" were thoroughly passé, no longer expressing a satisfying understanding of Norwegian history (see 15: 255–6).

37. Summarizing her works, Brandes writes that her aim is "neither revolutionary nor reactionary, but *reformist*" (*EL*, 147.)

38. See Ibsen's letter to Brandes, 4 April 1872 (17: 30–3).
39. For information about Ibsen's use of *Corinne*, see Haakonsen, *Henrik Ibsen*, 86 and 145.
40. Staël, *Corinne, or Italy*, 139.
41. Sand, *Story of My Life*, 922.
42. Ibid. 922–3.
43. Ibid. 923.
44. For the critical reception of French realism from 1830 to 1870, see Weinberg's illuminating *French Realism*.
45. See Schor, *George Sand and Idealism*, 29.
46. See Weinberg, *French Realism*, 141 and 192–9.
47. Poovey, "Forgotten Writers, Neglected Histories", 443.
48. Weinberg writes that Balzac criticism became markedly more hostile in the 1840s. I am inclined to interpret this as a sign of the breakup of the union between idealism and realism described by Sand (see Weinberg, *French Realism*, 32–90).
49. For a succinct overview of the two trials, see LaCapra, "1857: Two Trials".
50. Letter to Brandes, 1 July 1880, quoted in Moisy, *Paul Heyse*, 216.
51. Letter to Hans Bröchner, Munich, 1 Aug. 1873, reprinted in Brandes and Brandes, *Brevveksling*, 188.
52. Letter to Brandes, 3 March 1882, quoted in Moisy, *Paul Heyse*, 216–17.
53. Monrad, "Hvad man kan lære", 194.
54. Ibid. 200.
55. Moisy, *Paul Heyse*, 215.
56. Skram, "Mere om *Gengangere*", 355.
57. Anonymous editorial comment, *The Daily Telegraph*, 14 March 1891, 5; repr. in Egan (ed.), *Ibsen: Critical Heritage*, 190, 192.
58. See Shaw, *Quintessence*, 3–5.
59. Ibid. 30.
60. Nietzsche, *Beyond Good and Evil* (sect. 39), 49–50.
61. Nietzsche, "Attempt at Self-Criticism", 22 (a text written in the same year as *Beyond Good and Evil*).
62. For examples, see Carey, *The Intellectuals and the Masses*.
63. Quoted in Buss, "Introduction", p. viii.
64. Tissot, *Le drame norvégien*, 1–2.
65. Ibid. 22.
66. Ibid. 207.
67. Ibid. 113.
68. In 1897, a German book entitled *Ibsen als Idealist* (Ibsen as Idealist) argued the exact opposite. Invoking Schiller's aesthetics, Hanstein claimed—apparently in an attempt to rescue Ibsen from his idealist critics—that Ibsen was and always had been an idealist, which is why all the attacks on him for his naturalism were mistaken.
69. Espmark, *Nobel Prize*, 1; hereafter cited in the text as E.

70. From the Nobel committee's report of 1905, when the prize went to Henryk Sienkiewicz (E, 9).

71. The web pages of the Nobel Prize for Literature are full of valuable information and documents. See <http://nobelprize.org/literature/>.

72. The quotation about Sully-Prudhomme is the official Nobel Prize citation for 1901, available on <http://nobelprize.org/literature/laureates/1901/index.html>; the quotation about Zola comes from the Nobel committee's internal report cited in E, 17.

73. For the quotations in this paragraph, see Wirsén, *Kritiker*, 117, 120, and 121.

74. Wirsén's presentation speech to Bjørnson, <http://nobelprize.org/literature/laureates/1903/press.html>.

75. Presentation speech by Harald Hjärne, <http://nobelprize.org/literature/laureates/1908/press.html>.

76. Woolf, "Character in Fiction", 421.

77. Presentation speech by Wirsén, <http://nobelprize.org/literature/laureates/1910/press.html>.

78. Ibid.

79. What Brecht actually wrote, in the 1940s, was this: "While Ibsen was writing *Ghosts*, Ehrlich was working to find a cure for syphilis. The devil that Ibsen painted on the wall for the hypocrites, was wiped out by Ehrlich. . . . The bourgeoisie had become a greater evil than syphilis, its hypocrisy was not interesting because it threatened the bourgeoisie, but because it threatened humanity" (*Werke*, xxiii. 42).

80. For an interesting discussion of Thomas Hardy's hybrid form, see Daleski, "Thomas Hardy: A Victorian Modernist".

81. Wirsén complained about James's "lack of concentration" (E, 25–6).

82. Ellmann writes, "Wilde did not underrate his Norwegian rival; he allowed that *Hedda Gabler* was Greek in its power to generate pity and terror. But his own goal, he saw, was to make dialogue as brilliant as possible, while Ibsen confined his characters to ordinary words in ordinary life. . . . One probed a situation to uncover an infection; the other relied on verbal ricochet, to express a 'conflict between our artistic sympathies and our moral judgment.' For Wilde, unlike Ibsen, the setting had to be in the leisure class, people with time, money, and education, proficient in conversation" (*Oscar Wilde*, 333).

83. Wilde, *Dorian Gray*, 10.

84. "You were to me such an ideal as I shall never meet again. This is the face of a satyr," Basil says to Dorian when he sees the picture (ibid. 157).

85. Ibid. p. xxiii.

86. Wilde, "The Critic as Artist", 393.

87. Wilde, "The Decay of Lying", 299–300.

88. Wilde, "The Critic as Artist", 380.

89. Wilde, "M. Caro on George Sand", 87.

90. Ibid. 87–8. Among Sand's artists' novels, Wilde recommends *Consuelo, Horace,*

Les Maîtres Mosaïstes, Le Château des Désertes, Le Château de Pictordu, and *La Daniella.*

91. This is the famous catchphrase from Brandes's breakthrough lectures on main currents in European literature delivered in Copenhagen in the winter of 1871–2 (*EL*, 15).

92. The classical work on mass culture as modernism's other is Huyssen, *After the Great Divide.* I can't help noticing that Huyssen's book has plenty of discussions of Baudelaire, Flaubert, and Manet, but not a single reference to Ibsen.

CHAPTER 4 IBSEN'S VISUAL WORLD: SPECTACLES, PAINTING, THEATER

1. For his daily routines during the stay, see his letter to Suzannah, 25 June 1873 (19: 317–18).

2. Meyer, *Farewell to Poetry,* 178–9.

3. Summarized from *The British Section at the Vienna Universal Exhibition, 1873* (no pagination).

4. Gould, *G. F. Watts,* 119.

5. Both the quotation from Watts and the critical comment appear in Duguid, "Whispers".

6. I owe great thanks to Erik Henning Edvardsen, the director of the Ibsen Museum in Oslo, for allowing me to look at the paintings in Ibsen's apartment, and for sharing with me his knowledge of other paintings that Ibsen may have owned.

7. All quotations from Ibsen to this point in this paragraph are from the same letter to Suzannah, 12 March 1895.

8. Koht, *Henrik Ibsen,* ii. 250.

9. Meyer, *Farewell to Poetry,* 178 n.

10. See Langslet, *Henrik Ibsen, Edvard Munch,* and Templeton, "The Munch–Ibsen Connection".

11. James, *Parisian Sketches,* 131.

12. Ibid. 131–2.

13. Ibid. 132.

14. Meier-Graefe, *Modern Art,* ii. 188.

15. James, *Parisian Sketches,* 132.

16. Interest in Ibsen and painting has focused almost entirely on painters active at the very end of Ibsen's career, most frequently Munch. Only Durbach ("The Romantic Possibilities of Scenery") turns to the potential influence of J. C. Dahl's romantic landscape paintings, relating them to the winter scenery in *John Gabriel Borkman.*

17. See, e.g., Versini's clear preference for the later Diderot ("Introduction", 1076).

18. Aristotle, *Poetics,* 51.

19. Ibid. 52.

20. Diderot, "Conversations on *The Natural Son*", 12.
21. Ibid. 13.
22. Meisel, *Realizations* (hereafter cited as *R* in the text), and Brooks, *The Melodramatic Imagination*, are the best starting points for the history of melodrama.
23. Fried, *Absorption and Theatricality*, 10; hereafter cited in the text as *AT*.
24. Diderot, "De la poésie dramatique", 1336. This translation appears in *AT*, 95.
25. Ibid. 1310; translation in *AT*, 95.
26. Diderot, "In Praise of Richardson", 94.
27. Staël, *Corinne, or Italy*, 127.
28. Ibid.
29. Letter to Sofie Reimers, 25 March 1887.
30. Lessing, *Laocoön*, 78.
31. Ibid.
32. For an excellent account of the influence of Lessing's theory of the pregnant moment, see Andersen and Povlsen, "Det sublime øjeblik".
33. Fried, "Foreword", p. vii.
34. The phrase "passion and action" comes from *AT*, 75; Fuseli is quoted in *R*, 19.
35. S. N. Brown, "Girodet", <http://www.groveart.com>.
36. By the time he painted *The Flood*, Girodet had long experience of literary paintings: he had illustrated Racine and Virgil, had done a series of "Ossian" paintings, and was to go on to paint "Atala's Burial", based on Chateaubriand's novel. He nevertheless insisted that *The Flood* was not based on the Bible.
37. Letter to Ludvig Lund, 11 April 1872.
38. Rosenblum and Janson, *19th-Century Art*, 76.
39. The list of different "ramas" is taken from Comment, *The Painted Panorama*, 57.
40. *Morgenbladet*, 15 July 1863, 2. I am grateful to Erik Henning Edvardsen for finding this notice and other information about panoramas in Norway.
41. Comment, *The Painted Panorama*, 70.
42. Ibid. 66.
43. Ibid. 57.
44. Rosenblum and Janson, *19th-Century Art*, 127.
45. See Noon's catalogue text to this painting in Noon (ed.), *Constable to Delacroix*, 102.
46. A pioneering source on the *tableau vivant* is Holmström, *Monodrama*.
47. In her brilliant article on the subject, Povlsen further defines the "attitude" as a "tableau for one person" ("Standsningens attitude", 93; hereafter cited in the text as SA).
48. Holmström, *Monodrama*, 126.
49. Freud continued Ibsen's fascination with the woman as a "living sculpture" in his 1906 essay on Wilhelm Jensen's 1903 novel *Gradiva*, in which the protagonist believes that an ancient Roman sculptural relief depicting a walking woman has come alive. See Freud, "Delusions and Dreams in Jensen's *Gradiva*". For a

foundational study of Danish nineteenth-century preoccupations with life, death, and sculpture, see Sanders, *Konturer*.

50. There is little material on the *tableau vivant* in Norway. A precious source, therefore, is Rudler, "Levende bilder".

51. Rousseau, *Politics and the Arts*, 28.

52. Ibid. 29.

53. For Rousseau's views on dissembling women and coquetry, see Book 5 of *Emile*.

54. For this point, see also Holmström, *Monodrama*, 140–5.

55. Staël, *Corinne, or Italy*, 90–1.

56. I discuss Nora's tarantella in Ch. 7.

57. See Noon, "Colour and Effect", 18.

58. See Trumble, *Love and Death*, 104.

59. The interaction between painting and stage is one of the main concerns of Meisel's admirable *Realizations*.

60. I am quoting Riding's excellent summary of the events and their repercussions ("*The Raft*", 66). Riding also provides a thorough account of the exhibition of *The Raft of the Medusa* in Britain. Meisel relates Géricault's painting to British and French theater in *R*, 190–5. The chapter called "Shipwreck" in Barnes, *A History of the World*, shows a modern writer's fascination with Géricault's painting.

61. For details, see Riding, "*The Raft*", 71–2.

62. Letter to Edvard Grieg, Dresden, 23 Jan. 1874.

63. Letter to Hartvig Lassen, Kitzbüchel in Tyrol, 16 Aug. 1875.

64. See Kalnein, "De tyske Düsseldorfere", 8.

65. From 1845 to 1847, so did the Swiss painter Arnold Böcklin, whose work Ibsen would later come to admire.

66. The 1848 original version of *Washington Crossing the Delaware* was damaged by fire; the version now in the Metropolitan Museum of Art (New York) was painted in 1851.

67. The Greenaway picture is available at <http://www.indiana.edu/~librcsd/etext/piper/44.html>.

68. See Browning, *Der Rattenfänger*. I am grateful to Erik Edvardsen for the reference, and to the helpful staff at Duke University Library, not least Sara Seten Berghausen, who managed to get me a digital version of the book. Cyndie Burgess, librarian at the Armstrong Browning Library at Baylor University, supplied the name of the illustrators and explained that although the book was printed in Munich, it was published in London and New York as well.

69. Ibid. n.p. Browning's original text also tells us that the boy remained sad for the rest of his life, for just as he had glimpsed the "joyous land" where he "felt assured / My lame foot would be speedily cured", the mountain door slammed shut. I quote from the online version of "The Pied Piper" at <http://eir.library.utoronto.ca/rpo/display/poem2750.html>.

70. For an excellent presentation of *The First Cloud*, to which I am much indebted,

see Trumble, *Love and Death*, 136. Trumble quotes the original catalogue text that accompanied the painting at the Royal Academy Exhibition in 1887.

71. *Mariage de convenance* (1883) is in the Glasgow Kelvingrove Art Gallery and Museum, and *Mariage de convenance—After!* (1886) is in the Aberdeen Art Gallery. For anyone interested in seeing these paintings without going to Scotland, reasonable pictures of them turn up on a simple Internet search. *The First Cloud* is by far the best of the three.

72. See Trumble, *Love and Death*, 136.

73. Anonymous, "The Royal Academy Exhibition", 248.

74. I am grateful to Heather Birchall, Assistant Curator at Tate Britain, for helping me to establish these facts.

75. Egan's thorough edition of Ibsen reviews from the early British reception of Ibsen shows that after the first important production of *A Doll's House* in 1889, the true year of breakthrough was 1891, when five different Ibsen plays were staged in London (see *Ibsen: The Critical Heritage*).

76. See Moffett, *Meier-Graefe*, 10.

77. Meier-Graefe, *Der Fall Böcklin* and *Der junge Menzel*. Fried tells us that Menzel gave some paintings to his good friend Paul Heyse, the German idealist and Ibsen's friend discussed in Chs. 2 and 3 (see Fried, *Menzel's Realism*, 101).

78. Meier-Graefe, *Modern Art*, ii. 132.

79. Strindberg, *Spöksonaten*, 225.

80. For more information about the Klinger prints, see Holenweg, "*L'Ile des morts*", 20.

81. I base my account on Rival, "Le roman de *l'Ile des morts*", 30.

82. See Moirandat, "Der Plastiker Böcklin", 82–3.

83. See Lindemann and Schmidt (eds.), *Arnold Böcklin*, 280.

84. Meier-Graefe, *Der Fall Böcklin*, 164.

85. Meier-Graefe, *Modern Art*, ii. 131.

86. "Theatricality begins in Böcklin already in the 1860s" is the first sentence of the chapter entitled "Böcklin's stage" (Meier-Graefe, *Der Fall Böcklin*, 222).

87. Meier-Graefe, *Modern Art*, ii. 133.

88. Rossetti's "Found" (1854–81) was left unfinished at his death. There is also an ink drawing of the same subject matter from 1853. They are reproduced as Figs. 169 and 65, respectively, in Prettejohn, *The Art of the Pre-Raphaelites*.

89. I discuss the idealist requirement of reconciliation, leading to a sense of "uplift" in the audience, in Ch. 7, in relation to the reception of *A Doll's House*.

CHAPTER 5 THE IDEALIST STRAITJACKET: IBSEN'S EARLY AESTHETICS

1. Barish, *The Antitheatrical Prejudice*, 326.

2. Ibid. 299.

3. See Bull, "Indledning", p. xxxvii.

4. Francis Bull writes, "The intention with the story was to show the development of an artistic nature, until the vocation is found, and everything that has been scattered gathers in one clear line" (ibid. p. xxxv).

5. Ibid. p. xxxvi.

6. Letter, 7 May 1868, quoted in Bull, *Norges litteratur*, iv. 568.

7. Bjørnson, *"Fiskerjenten"*, 434; hereafter cited in the text as *F*. There are several Victorian and Edwardian translations of *The Fisher Maiden*, none of which is very faithful to the original.

8. As dean (*prost*) in the Norwegian church means a clergyman who heads a *prosti* (deanery, i.e., a larger subdivision of a diocese).

9. Letter to Frederik Hegel, 28 July 1868.

10. Letter to Lorentz Dietrichson, Munich, 19 Dec. 1879.

11. Welhaven, "Om det franske Theater", 254, an article originally published in the newspaper *Den Constitutionelle* in 1836.

12. The poem was published in Munch's 1851 collection *Nye Digte* under the title "Brudefærden" ("The Bridal Procession") (pp. 297–8).

13. All information about the "festive evenings" comes from Askeland, *Adolph Tidemand*, 219–22.

14. Ibid. 224.

15. See Munch, "Norsk Bondeliv".

16. See Askeland, *Adolph Tidemand*, 225–31.

17. The full program was published in *Morgenbladet*, 11 Dec. 1859. I am deeply grateful to Erik Henning Edvardsen, who found the advertisement.

18. See Koht, *Henrik Ibsen*, i. 145–6.

19. *Christianiaposten*, 343 (13 Dec. 1859). Erik Henning Edvardsen found the advertisement.

20. The painting by Louis Léopold Robert (Switzerland, 1794–1834) was a sensation at the Paris Salon in 1831, and was bought by Louis Philippe. Niels Simonsen (1807–85) was a well-known Danish history painter. In 1839 he traveled in Algeria, and his Algerian subjects became very popular in Scandinavia. One of Nasjonalgalleriet's first commissions went to Simonsen, whose painting *En karavane overfalt af storm i ørkenen* ("A Caravan Surprised by Storm in the Desert") was bought by the National Gallery in Christiania in 1855. Charles Steuben (1788–1856), a student of David and Gros, was a well-known French history painter.

21. For the publication history, see 2: 9.

22. *Kjæmpehøien* (*The Burial Mound*; sometimes also called *The Warrior's Barrow*) was written in 1850, and rewritten in 1853. When it opened at Christiania Theater on 26 Sept. 1850, it was the first Ibsen play ever to be performed. The revised version opened at Den Nationale Scene in Bergen on 2 Jan. 1854. For more information, see 1: 245–52.

23. For details, see Ewbank, "Ibsen in Wonderful Copenhagen".

24. The most frequently performed play at Det Norske Theater in Bergen in the

period was C. P. Riis's nationalist romantic idyll *Til Sæters* (*To the High Mountain Pastures*), with twenty-nine performances (see Gatland, *Repertoaret . . . 1850–63*).

25. As mentioned in Ch. 2, Birkedalen was the name of the mother of Ibsen's illegitimate son.

26. This is Bull's argument in 2: 9–17.

27. Bull points out that most of the folk songs in *St John's Night* are Danish or Swedish, since Ibsen's play was written just before Landstad's famous collection of Norwegian folk songs was published in 1853 (see 2: 15–16).

28. *Halvdannelsen* means something like "semi-culture". *Dannelse* is the equivalent of the German *Bildung*, and means "education", "culture", "breeding", "refinement".

29. See Koht's introduction in 2: 113–20.

30. Johnston says as much: "Lady Inger's plans go astray owing to circumstances so freakish that they could be tolerable only in farce" (*To the Third Empire*, 69).

31. In *Norske naturmytologier*, Witoszek also writes that Norwegian national authenticity is founded on a fear of theatricality (see p. 105).

32. Wilkinson makes a similar point: "Ibsen's play [*Lady Inger*] is a melodrama about melodrama, both in the sense that it catalogues and criticizes a number of popular melodramatic conventions and in the sense that it suggests the ways in which melodrama and its conventions can shape—and distort—one's view of the world" ("Gender and Melodrama", 169).

33. In *Ibsen's Women*, Templeton notes the strength of *Lady Inger*, and concludes that she is an "androgynous character" (p. 330). More convincing is Templeton's suggestion that Lady Inger has much in common with Mrs Alving in *Ghosts* (pp. 34–5). This is a point also made by Van Laan ("*Lady Inger* as Tragedy", 39).

34. Bø writes that in *Lady Inger* Ibsen made romantic ideas so complex that the audience must have been unable to follow him (see "*Nationale subjekter*", 103).

35. Bjørnson, "Gildet paa Solhaug", 104.

36. Ibid. 105.

37. The poems were published in two installments in *Illustreret Nyhedsblad*, 18 and 25 Sept. 1859. The accompanying note is quoted in full in 14: 482.

38. An excellent discussion of various theories concerning the date of composition can be found in McFarlane, "Ibsen's Poem Cycle", 32–7.

39. This is my translation. In general, I shall be quoting Ibsen's poetry in Northam's verse translations, but in this particular case, I needed something a little more literal, to bring out the Schillerian theme. Northam's translation of Ibsen's poems will hereafter be quoted in the text, abbreviated to "N".

40. Staël, *Corinne, or Italy*, 139.

41. Hall, "Passion", 18.

42. Freud, "Fragment of an Analysis", 96.

43. For an interesting analysis of Wergeland's poem in relation to Jan van Huysum's painting, see Helland, *Voldens blomster?*

44. Northam's translation is a little free. A more literal version would be: "Yes form, form alone / can ennoble the embryonic creation of the artist's spirit / and guarantee its greatness and genius."

45. As we have seen, the same idea turns up in Ibsen's 1851 review of Jensen's *Huldrens Hjem*.

46. Ystad would disagree. She considers the speaker's praise of artistic form to be purely ironic, and takes him to be unambiguously committed to idealist aesthetics, which she defines as art that has "a deeper meaning" because it represents an "underlying ideality" ("Dikterens syner", 170).

47. In Northam's translation this poem is called "On the Moors".

48. Based on N, 90; but I have butchered Northam's verse to render Ibsen's words as literally as possible.

49. Haakonsen, *Henrik Ibsen*, 61.

50. See Heidem, "Fiksjon og virkelighet", 70. This article also discusses the transformations of "Terje Vigen" into opera, play, and, famously, into Victor Sjöström's 1917 Swedish film.

51. "There is undeniably something theatrical about the famous scene where the 'proud English nobleman falls on his knees before the Norwegian pilot'; but Terje's words afterwards have a personal tone" (Bull, *Norges litteratur*, 329).

52. "There is nevertheless a kind of agreement among literary historians that [*Love's Comedy*] marks an important stage in Ibsen's artistic development, although this appears not to have inspired many thorough readings," Hemmer writes (*Ibsen: Kunstnerens vei*, 88).

53. There are various versions of the story of Svanhild. In a rejected draft, Ibsen stressed that the innocent Svanhild was sacrificed by her guilty family (see 4: 263).

54. The first quotation is by Monrad, the second by Botten-Hansen. The Danish critic is Clemens Petersen. The source of all quotations in this paragraph is Bull's introduction to the play (4: 134).

55. Hemmer, *Ibsen: Kunstnerens vei*, 115.

56. Haakonsen, *Henrik Ibsen*, 63.

57. Johnston, *To the Third Empire*, 115.

58. Templeton, *Ibsen's Women*, 58.

59. Ibid. 64 and 65.

60. Northam comes some way towards my view, for he writes that *Love's Comedy* "inhibits simple judgment" (*Ibsen*, 18).

61. Hemmer, *Ibsen: Kunstnerens vei*, 89.

62. Schiller, "On Naive and Sentimental Poetry", 255.

CHAPTER 6 BECOMING MODERN: MODERNITY AND
THEATER IN *EMPEROR AND GALILEAN*

1. Already on 12 July 1871, just as he was beginning work on the first complete draft, Ibsen wrote to his publisher Frederik Hegel that "This book will become

my most important work (*hovedverk*)" (16: 371). He repeated the claim in another letter to Hegel from Dresden dated 26 Sept. 1871 (see 16: 376).

2. Conversation with Arnt Dehli, Ibsen's masseur for the last five years of his life (19: 229).

3. Letter to Edmund Gosse, Dresden, 14 Oct. 1872.

4. On 16 April 1937 Wittgenstein was in Skjolden in Norway, and wrote in his diary that he was deeply impressed by Ibsen's *Emperor and Galilean* (*Den ukjente dagboken*, 119). In the same diary, he also quotes *Peer Gynt* (see p. 93).

5. Both *Speer* and *The Coast of Utopia* were directed by Trevor Nunn. In Norway, Hilda Hellwig directed a fascinating production of *Emperor and Galilean* at Den Nationale Scene in Bergen in 2000, and Norwegian Broadcasting (NRK) turned it into a successful radio play in 2003.

6. Interest in the play may be increasing. Wærp devotes half of *Overgangens figurasjoner* to *Emperor and Galilean*, and Kittang includes a substantial chapter on the play in *Ibsens heroisme*.

7. Letter, Dresden, 26 June 1869.

8. I shall not discuss two questions that usually preoccupy scholars in relation to *Emperor and Galilean*: what the vision of the "Third Empire" actually means, and whether Ibsen here really presents a "positive world view", as he claimed just as he was beginning work in earnest (see 16: 371). Were I to look for the roots of Ibsen's utopian vision of a Third Empire, I would begin by returning to the idealist vision of a realm uniting aesthetics and ethics, philosophy and religion, the sensuous and the spiritual, in a way that ultimately produces human freedom.

9. For a synopsis of the plot, see Appendix 1.

10. In *Henrik Ibsen's "Keiser og Galilæer"*, Garborg wrote that the "peculiar characteristic of this time" was its "lack of calm and harmony" (p. 16).

11. Ystad describes the play as a "diagnosis of the times", in "Om angst og despoti".

12. For an entertaining account of how Ibsen got the idea, see Dietrichson, *Svundne Tider*, 336. Also available online at <http://www.dokpro.uio.no/litteratur/dietrichson/>.

13. "Franco–Prussian War", in Hutton (ed.), *Historical Dictionary*, 397.

14. Brockett, *The Year of Battles*, 1.

15. In "The Unconscious Evil of Idealism", Helge Rønning writes about the impact of 1870–1 on Ibsen.

16. Letter to Georg Brandes, Dresden, 4 April 1872.

17. Letter to Frederik Hegel, Dresden, 12 July 1871.

18. In *The Taming of Chance*, his thought-provoking account of the emergence of modern statistics, Ian Hacking shows that "statistical fatalism" became a particularly prominent subject of debate in Germany after the publication of Henry Thomas Buckle's *History of Civilization in England* (1857–61), which argued that theories of predestination and free will are worthless, for statistics prove that human actions are governed by laws just like natural phenomena (see pp. 125–41).

19. Here I disagree with Kittang, who thinks of Julian as a classically romantic hero desiring freedom and autonomy (see *Ibsens heroisme*, 124). While Kittang is quite right to say that Julian wishes to free himself from the yoke of Christianity, Julian also constantly tries to discover his own identity in non-Christian signs and omens.

20. I.3 means Part I, Act 3. Similar abbreviations will be used throughout this chapter.

21. Quoted in Bowersock, *Julian the Apostate*, 41.

22. For a religious reading of the play, see Wyller, *Ibsens* Keiser og Galilæer.

23. See Brandes, review of *Kejser og Galilæer*, <http://www.ibsen.net/index. gan?id=110586&subid=0>.

24. I agree with Wærp, who writes, "The *text*, moreover, does not really take a position on whether some divine power has or has not manipulated events, although the dramatic characters do" (*Overgangens figurasjoner*, 111).

25. Ibsen, *Emperor and Galilean*, 198 (trans. amended). English quotations from *Emperor and Galilean* come from Johnston's fine translation. Further references to this translation will be given in the text, preceded by *EG*. The words translated as "erring" and "err" here are *vildfarende* and *fare vild* in Norwegian, which mean to lose one's way, literally as well as metaphorically. Far more concrete than the English *err*, the expression is composed by *fare* ("travel", "voyage", "go"), and *vild* ("wild(ly)", "astray").

26. Marx and Engels, *Communist Manifesto*, 223.

27. Nietzsche, *Beyond Good and Evil* (sect. 262), 211.

28. For an overview of critical responses to *Emperor and Galilean*, see Wærp, *Overgangens figurasjoner*, 27–49. Critics have usually preferred "Caesar's Apostasy" to the far more complex "Emperor Julian". Part II, Kittang writes, has been thought to have "far too many longueurs, far too many processions and grand spectacles, and the dialogue often comes across as stiffer and more stilted than in the first part" (*Ibsen's heroisme*, 83). Idealists were disappointed with Part II because they thought that Julian's increasingly erratic and cruel behavior made his character incoherent, even grotesque, and thus undermined his status as a tragic hero. Even Brandes, who reviewed it while he was still in his transitionally idealist mode, preferred Part I, because it showed Julian as "warm, wise and powerful", as opposed to Part II, which makes him seem small (review of *Kejser og Galilæer*). Others have simply found Part II obscure, or too full of philosophy, or too messy and disjointed. Wærp, on the other hand, commends Part II for its "literarity, poetic complexity and polysemy", thus reiterating some of the most cherished concepts of the ideology of modernism (Wærp, *Overgangens figurasjoner*, 29–30).

29. The information in this paragraph is based on Koht's introduction in 7: 16–17.

30. See Kaufmann's introduction in Nietzsche, *The Birth of Tragedy*, 6–7.

31. Bowersock tells us that among the historical Julian's favorite gods and goddesses were Cybele, Zeus, Helios, Athena, and Hermes (see *Julian the Apostate*, 17, 48,

62, 82). In connection with Julian's sojourn in Antioch, he also mentions Apollo quite frequently. Dionysus, however, is entirely absent from Bowersock's study of Julian. In II.1, Apollo is mentioned four and Dionysus eight times.

32. I owe this suggestion to Stanley Cavell.

33. Nietzsche, *The Will to Power*, 514 n. 59. According to Kaufmann, Karl Jaspers also found this phrase to be crucial. In *The Rebel*, Camus quotes it in a discussion of why Nietzsche's philosophy would make one consent to murder and crime (see pp. 76–7).

34. According to Janss, *Emperor and Galilean* was published in five editions in Ibsen's lifetime. The first print run of 4,000 copies sold out right away, and 2,000 more copies were printed. In comparison, *The League of Youth* had a print run of 2,000 in 1868 (see review of *Overgangens figurasjoner*).

35. Arne Garborg (1851–1924) was to become one of the great Norwegian writers, but in 1873 he was still unknown.

36. Garborg, *Henrik Ibsen's "Keiser og Galilæer"*, 10. The text of the first edition from 1873 is available on the web (see <http://www.ibsen.net/index.db2?id=58922>). I am quoting from the 2nd edn., published early in 1874. Further references will be given in the text, denoted AG. The general critique of the "old aesthetics" can be found in AG, 10–12.

37. This is a belated echo of Ibsen's rebuff to the smug sheriff (*fogden*) in *Brand*, who declares that he really likes poetry because it provides such a relaxing uplift between seven and ten in the evening, "naar man, af Dagens Gerning trætt / kan trænge till en Løftnings-Tvætt" (5: 249) ("when tired of the day's work / one sorely needs a cleansing uplift").

38. Cavell, "Foreword", p. xxxiii.

39. Ibid. p. xxxvi.

40. Did Ibsen know *Hernani*? The obvious textual echoes make it virtually certain. The play was in the repertoire of Norwegian theaters in the 1850s, and in 1857 Ibsen mentioned the title role in *Hernani* as one of the actor Anton Wilhelm Wiehe's many claims to fame (see 15: 157). Ibsen owned a 3-vol. study by P. A. [pseudonym for Pauline Kronberg, *née* Ahlberg], entitled *Victor Hugo och det nyare Frankrike* (*Victor Hugo and the New France*), published in Stockholm in 1879–80 (see Reistad and Grevstad, "Ibsen's private Bibliotek", 69). In an 1897 interview with the Paris newspaper *Le Figaro*, Ibsen said that although he much admired Victor Hugo, he was not nearly as influenced by him as Bjørnson was (see 19: 209).

41. Hugo, *Hernani*, 128.

42. A very similar sequence of events happens in I.3, when Julian has to choose whether or not to accept the status of Constantius's heir.

43. According to Thiis, Peterssen's painting won a prize in Stuttgart, sold for much money to the city of Breslau, and people flocked to see it in Kristiania (*Norske malere*, ii. 175).

44. The photographic print is inscribed "Mr. Henrik Ibsen. In friendly remembrance

of Eilif Peterssen 1876". I am grateful to Erik Edvardsen for transcribing the
dedication for me.

45. Bann, *Paul Delaroche*, 122.

46. Fried, *Courbet's Realism*, 35.

47. Bann, *Paul Delaroche*, 124 and 127.

48. Most of my information about this painting comes from Lange and Ljøgodt
    (eds.), *Svermeri*, 204–5.

49. Thiis, *Norske malere*, ii. 175.

50. Cavell, *Claim of Reason*, 464.

51. Human finitude thus has three interconnected aspects. In this chapter I focus on
    Julian's denial of finitude in the sense of human separation. But Julian denies
    finitude in the most comprehensive way: by staying away from sex altogether, he
    denies or disavows his sexual finitude; by proclaiming himself a god, he is surely
    denying death.

52. Cavell, "Avoidance of Love", 332; hereafter cited in the text as AL.

53. For a discussion of *The Fisher Maiden*, see Ch. 5.

54. See Ch. 4 for a discussion of Diderot's antitheatrical aesthetics, and Fried's terms
    "theatricality" and "absorption".

55. Psychologically, the persecution of Ursulus is motivated by Julian's narcissism,
    vanity, and megalomania, which make him unable to tolerate criticism. He simply
    has not got the ego strength required to sustain the conflicts and disagreements
    he piously calls for in the passage we are concerned with here.

56. Cavell, *Claim of Reason*, 20.

57. See Wittgenstein, *Philosophical Investigations*, §241 (hereafter *PI*).

58. Stanley Cavell helped me to see this clearly.

59. I owe this formulation to Stanley Cavell.

60. After meeting Maximus, Julian became convinced that he was to become the
    new Adam, that he was to be given the pure woman, go to the East, to find the
    New Eden and produce a new human race (see I.3, 7: 92–3; *EG*, 43–4).

61. Julian addresses Agathon as "my beloved (*elskede*) possession" at 7: 38 (*EG*, 9,
    has "dearest friend"). He calls Maximus "beloved" at 7: 160, 267, 319 (*EG*, 88,
    156, 188), and refers to Gregory with the same term (7: 197; *EG*, 112). Basil
    addresses Julian as "beloved brother" on his deathbed (7: 333; *EG*, 196).
    Maximus addresses Julian as "beloved" at 7: 156, 265, 335 (*EG*, 85, 155, 197).
    Although such terms did not have the same implications in the nineteenth
    century as today, I note that Julian also refers to Basil as the "gentle-hearted man
    with the girlish eyes" (*EG*, 164, amended; 7: 280).

62. The Norwegian *gjøgler* has two principal meanings: (1) comedian, clown, juggler,
    or fool; (2) mountebank, hypocrite.

63. The Norwegian *apekatt* ("monkey") contains the verb *ape*, which means to
    imitate in a ridiculous or grotesque way.

64. Cavell has an excellent discussion of the status of a character in relation to the
    actor in AL, 326–44.

65. The exception is Aarseth, who shows that the stage directions reveal much about Ibsen's aesthetic aims, and also stresses the importance of the "glass cabinet" scene in the last act of *Pillars of Society*, rightly noting that it can be read as a tableau, set up to be seen both from the garden and from the audience, thus introducing a metatheatrical element (see *Ibsens samtidsskuespill*, 48–9).

66. Although I have substantially developed the general argument, parts of the analysis that follows were first published in Moi, "Ibsen's Anti-Theatrical Aesthetics".

67. Aarseth, *Ibsens samtidsskuespill*, 48.

CHAPTER 7 "FIRST AND FOREMOST A HUMAN BEING": IDEALISM, THEATER, AND GENDER IN *A DOLL'S HOUSE*

1. Although I shall show that *A Doll's House* contains most of the features of Ibsen's modernism, as defined in Ch. 6, I shall try not to dwell on the obvious. It can hardly be necessary, for example, to *show* that *A Doll's House* is intended to produce an illusion of reality. The extensive references to acting have also been much analyzed, both in relation to Nora's performance of femininity and in relation to their implications for a reassessment of Ibsen's realism. I recommend Solomon's excellent chapter on *A Doll's House* ("Reconstructing Ibsen's Realism"), which stresses Ibsen's self-conscious use of theater in the play, and Kamilla Aslaksen's analysis of Ibsen's use of melodramatic elements in *A Doll's House* ("Ibsen and Melodrama"). For a general presentation and analysis of the play, I recommend Durbach, *A Doll's House: Ibsen's Myth of Transformation*.

2. Shatzky and Dumont begin by invoking Bernard Shaw's claim that "Ibsen's real enemy was the idealist" (" 'All or Nothing' ", 73), but they also follow Shaw in reducing idealism to a moral and political position.

3. Socialists and feminists from Eleanor Marx Aveling to Lu Xun and Simone de Beauvoir have praised *A Doll's House* as a breakthrough for women's rights. For a general overview of Ibsen and feminism, in which *A Doll's House* figures centrally, I have found Finney's "Ibsen and Feminism" to be very useful. In *Ibsen's Women*, Templeton reviews an important part of the reception of *A Doll's House*.

4. Wittgenstein, *PI*, 178.

5. That Cavell begins a book entitled *Pursuits of Happiness* with a brilliant reading of *A Doll's House* strikes me as profoundly right (see pp. 19–24).

6. See Felski, *Gender and Modernity*, 30.

7. Petersen, "Henrik Ibsens Drama '*Et Dukkehjem*'", quoted from <ibsen.net>.

8. Two words in this quotation often recur in idealist reviews: *uskjønt* and *pinlig*. *Uskjønt* literally means *unbeautiful*. The word also turns up in *A Doll's House*, usually in relation to Torvald Helmer. It is generally translated as "ugly", although the most common word for "ugly" today is *stygt*. (In Ibsen's time, *stygt* often had a clear moral meaning.) *Pinlig* means embarrassing, painful, distressing; the word is derived from *pine* ("pain", "torture").

9. The same views are expressed in Anonymous, review of Henrik Ibsen, *Et dukkehjem*, available on <ibsen.net>.

10. Brun, "Det kongelige Teater". Quoted from <ibsen.net>.

11. I-n, "Et Dukkehjem", quoted from <ibsen.net>.

12. Vullum, "Literatur-Tidende", quoted from <ibsen.net>.

13. Skram, "En Betragtning over *Et Dukkehjem*", 309.

14. Ibid. 313.

15. "He was, as Helmer, not sufficiently refined." My quote is from Bang, "Et Dukkehjem", <http://www.ibsen.net/ index.gan?id=355&subid=0>. The text is also available in a modern critical edition (see Bang, *Realisme og Realister*).

16. Bang also calls Nora and Ibsen himself idealists, but in those contexts, the word is not used primarily in an aesthetic sense.

17. Postmodern readers might find this a little too simplistic. (Can we just stop performing our masquerades?) As I shall show, Ibsen's play is anything but simplistic on these matters. But right here I am not trying to say anything general and theoretical about the "performance of gender" in modernity. Rather, I am trying to say something about the depressing consequences of Nora's and Torvald's lack of insight into their own motivations and behavior, and particularly to draw attention to the fact that it is because they do not understand themselves that they do not understand others either.

18. See Cavell, *Claim of Reason*, 464.

19. Americans sometimes ask me whether *Et dukkehjem* should be translated as *A Doll House* or *A Doll's House*. As far as I know, both terms designate the same thing: a small toy house for children to play with, or a small model house for the display of miniature dolls and furniture. If this is right, the only difference between them is that the former is American and the latter British. In Norwegian, the usual word for a doll['s] house is *en dukkestue* or *et dukkehus*. (*Hjem* means "home", not "house".) *Et dukkehjem* is thus far more unusual than either the British or the American translation. What did Ibsen mean by the title? To indicate that Nora and Helmer were playing house? To signal that Nora's and Helmer's home life is made for display only (this would be the theme of theatricality)? That both of them are as irresponsible as dolls? As unaware of the real issues of human life as dolls? Or simply that both Helmer and Nora's father have treated Nora as a doll? (Durbach's *A Doll's House* contains an interesting discussion of the problems involved in translating the play into English; see esp. pp. 27–39.)

20. "Play-house" is a translation of *legestue*, which means a small house for children to play in. It does not mean playpen, as many translators suggest.

21. Descartes, *Discourse*, 84.

22. For the French 1647 text and the 1641 Latin original, see Descartes, *Méditations*, 49.

23. I am speaking of the doll in the philosophical imagination. It doesn't matter to my argument whether or not mechanical dolls or automata actually existed. The

link between the figure of the artificial human body and skepticism was first explored in Cavell, *Claim of Reason*, esp. 400–18.

24. The story of "The Sandman" was also told in a popular 1851 French play by Jules Barbier and Michel Carré called *Les Contes fantastiques d'Hoffmann*. Offenbach's opera *The Tales of Hoffman* did not open until 1881, two years after *A Doll's House*.

25. By turning *The Stepford Wives* into a light-hearted comedy, Frank Oz's 2004 remake gutted the doll motif of its potential horror.

26. For the French text, see Staël, *Corinne, ou L'Italie*, 369. The published English translation is slightly different: "a delicately improved mechanical doll" (p. 249).

27. Explaining her hostility to Corinne, Lady Edgermond says to Oswald, "She needs a theatre where she can display all those gifts you prize so highly and which make life so difficult" (*Corinne, or Italy*, 313).

28. In his analysis of *Gaslight*, Cavell writes of Ingrid Bergman's character launching into "her aria of revenge" at the end of the film (*Contesting Tears*, 59–60). See also Cavell's discussion of the unknown woman's cogito performances as singing, in "Opera and the Lease of Voice", in Cavell, *A Pitch of Philosophy*, 129–69.

29. I analyze Corinne's death in "A Woman's Desire to Be Known".

30. Cavell, *Contesting Tears*, 43.

31. Solomon, "Reconstructing Ibsen's Realism", 55. Solomon also describes Duse's low-key performance of the tarantella.

32. Ibid.

33. See the discussion of "Realism's Hysteria", in Diamond, *Unmaking Mimesis*, 3–39. A similar claim is made in Finney, "Ibsen and Feminism", 98–9.

34. Meisel, *Realizations*, 8.

35. Wittgenstein, *PI*, 178.

36. Ibid.

37. Langås's brilliant analysis of *A Doll's House* is deeply attuned to the ambiguities of the tarantella. We agree on many details in the analysis of Nora's dance. But in the end Langås reads the play as a "play about the feminine masquerade" ("Kunstig liv", 66), and turns Nora into a postmodern performative heroine: "Nora is so good at performing 'woman' that we do not see that she is performing. In her performance she cites established ways of being a woman which at the same time confirms those ways. By doing this, she confirms and strengthens the idea of femininity, and at the same time her reiteration legitimates this way of being" (p. 76). Her postmodern perspective makes it impossible for Langås to take Nora's claim that she is first and foremost a human being quite seriously: "It is possible that she thinks she will find this 'human being' in her new life, but given the premises established by the play, her only option will in my view be to explore and shape new parts to play" (p. 67). In my view, Langås's ahistorical reading fails to grasp the revolutionary aspects of this play.

38. I am grateful to Vigdis Ystad for providing these definitions.

39. Solomon writes that "if students learn anything about Ibsen, it's that his plays follow a clear progressive trajectory from overwrought verse dramas to realistic paragons, the prose plays themselves evolving like an ever more fit species, shedding soliloquies, asides, and all the integuments of the well-made play as they creep, then crouch, then culminate in the upright masterpiece, *Hedda Gabler*" ("Reconstructing Ibsen's Realism", 48).

40. Northam lists all of Nora's monologues, and considers that they "lack the illustrative power of comparable passages in poetic drama". As they stand, he claims, they provide but a "small opportunity of entering into the souls of [Ibsen's] characters" (*Ibsen's Dramatic Method*, 16). I truly disagree.

41. Cavell, *Cities of Words*, 260.

42. Ibid. 258.

43. See Templeton, *Ibsen's Women*, 110–45.

44. Hegel, *Philosophy of Right*, §158. Further references will be given in the text.

45. For a good account of various comparisons between Nora and Antigone, see Durbach, "Nora as Antigone".

46. Hegel, *Phenomenology of Spirit* (§475), 288.

47. In her excellent study of Ibsen's revisions of the manuscript of *A Doll's House*, Saari shows that Ibsen began by thinking of Nora as "a modern-day Antigone, one in whom the sense of duty was grounded in a specifically feminine conscience", and that he was thinking in terms of writing a tragedy about a "feminine soul destroyed by a masculine world". This, she stresses, was not the play he actually wrote ("Female Become Human", 41). To me, this shows that although Ibsen may have begun by thinking in Hegelian terms, he ended up breaking with them entirely.

CHAPTER 8 LOSING TOUCH WITH THE EVERYDAY: LOVE AND LANGUAGE IN *THE WILD DUCK*

1. I should perhaps stress that by "language" I do not mean language as a system or structure, but language as use.

2. Although *The Wild Duck* clearly contains the features of Ibsen's modernism established in Ch. 6, I shall, as usual, not go through them systematically. I discuss Gregers Werle's idealist aesthetics at the end of Ch. 4. This chapter is a revised version of an essay first published in 2002 (see Moi, "It was as if").

3. Since it reminds me of *King Lear*, it also, inevitably, reminds me of Cavell, "Avoidance of Love".

4. Quoted in Bull, "Innledning" (10: 29–30).

5. From an unsigned notice published in *Theatre*, 1 June 1894, reprinted in Egan (ed.), *Ibsen: The Critical Heritage*, 323.

6. I am relying on Bull's account (10: 38).

7. Sarcey, "Le Canard sauvage", in *Le Temps*, 4 May 1891, as quoted and translated by Marker and Marker, *Ibsen's Lively Art*, 28. Whether Ibsen ever read this, I do

not know, but he did know the French critic's name, for in Paris in 1883 his son Sigurd Ibsen went twice to hear Sarcey lecture, and reported very positively to his father about the experience. On 26 April, Sigurd wrote, "Moreover, this week I have listened to two lectures by the critic Francisque Sarcey, which in form, contents and diction must be counted among the very best of their kind" (Sigurd Ibsen, *Bak en gyllen fasade*, 40).

8. Durbach, "*Ibsen the Romantic*", 93.

9. Tjønneland provides an interesting critique of the opposition between symbol and allegory in relation to *The Wild Duck*, but still seems to feel that one has to choose one or the other (see "Organisk symbolikk").

10. Some elements of this analysis of the loft can be found in an earlier essay (see Moi, "Ibsen's Anti-Theatrical Aesthetics").

11. See the end of Ch. 6 for an analysis of the stage arrangements in the last act of *Pillars of Society*.

12. Høst quotes Anders Wyller, who thinks that a man who has lived a "solitary life in the woods" for fifteen years would know very well how to make a fire. Høst agrees, and reads the scene as a comic exaggeration (*Vildanden*, 72). Tjønneland thinks that Wyller may be right, but if so, then Gregers's mess is the result of a mistake (not ignorance, as I am assuming), which might be read as a Freudian parapraxis. Tjønneland further links this to what I consider an overly symbolic reading of the meaning of the damper in the stove (*spjeldet*), which has been rightly criticized by Aarseth (see Tjønneland, "Organisk symbolikk", 234–5, and Aarseth, *Ibsens samtidsskuespill*, 141 n. 73).

13. In order to defend *The Wild Duck* against the accusation that Ibsen's realism here ended up as a *hjemve til sølen* (*nostalgie de la boue*, or "longing for the mud"), Haakonsen insists that Ibsen's surface realism hides a deeper, tragic level, which—unfortunately, in his eyes—is not fully realized. Haakonsen thus repeats the flight from the everyday embodied in the character of Gregers. It is not surprising, then, to find that Haakonsen considers Gregers to be a kind of idealist hero (see *Henrik Ibsens realisme*, 27–62).

14. Quoted in P. A. Rosenberg's account of a conversation with Ibsen in Copenhagen, 3 April 1898 (19: 219).

15. Letter to Frederik Hegel, Gossensass, 2 Sept. 1884.

16. Brooks, *Melodramatic Imagination*, 1–2.

17. *Philosophical Investigations*, §253.

18. My translation does not really convey Gina's many linguistic mistakes. In Norwegian she says "potrætter" for "portrætter", and "kreti og preti" for "kreti og pleti". Ibsen's point, surely, is that although Gina speaks throughout the play as a woman with no education, she makes a great deal more sense than the men who surround her.

19. In the sense that I use the word (inspired by Cavell, Austin, and Wittgenstein), the opposite of the ordinary is not the unusual, the technical, the scientific, or the literary, but metaphysics, or language that means nothing.

20. The distinction between criteria of identity and criteria of existence is established in the three first chapters of Cavell, *Claim of Reason*.

21. "Everything has conspired to make Hedwig distrust the *ordinary* way of looking at things," Mary McCarthy writes in a particularly perspicacious analysis of the play, where she goes on to quote the "it's only a loft" conversation before concluding that "Gregers preaches mysteries. Hjalmar's daily conversation is a flow of oratory" ("Will and Testament", 170).

22. Immediately before the passage I am about to quote, Gregers and Hjalmar hear the wild duck through the partition wall, and comment on hearing her. Ibsen clearly wanted us to know that Hedvig can hear their conversation. Høst (*Vildanden*, 133) and Aarseth (*Ibsens samtidsskuespill*, 142–3) make the same point.

23. Rome, 14 Nov. 1884.

24. According to Marker and Marker, this was particularly common in English-speaking productions: "In England at mid-century [around 1950], meanwhile, the chief and insuperable obstacle to a satisfactory production of *The Wild Duck* remained Hjalmar, who had been portrayed as a buffoon ever since Granville Barker first showed off his "Shavian" Hjalmar at the Court Theatre in 1905" (*Ibsen's Lively Art*, 143).

25. Østerud discusses Hjalmar in the light of Fried's categories. Although I agree with many of his specific interpretations, I think he is too ready to cast Hjalmar as a generally self-conscious calculator: "His style is melodramatic, his effects well-calculated," Østerud writes (*Theatrical and Narrative Space*, 32).

26. As we have seen the word *bugnende* returns in the very line that causes Hedvig's death, precisely to describe the riches of Håkon Werle. *Bugnende* basically has two related, yet different meanings. It can be used about fruit trees, meaning "laden with fruit", and it can be used in the expression "det bugnende bord", as here, meaning a festive table overflowing with good food.

27. Cavell, *Claim of Reason*, 178.

28. Cavell, "Avoidance of Love", 292.

29. For a philosophically insightful account of Wittgenstein's life, see Monk, *Ludwig Wittgenstein*.

30. Cavell writes beautifully about this in "Opera and the Lease of Voice", in *Pitch of Philosophy*, 29–69.

31. I discuss these concepts in relation to Nora's tarantella in Ch. 7.

32. Gail Finney writes of "the powerlessness associated with motherhood" in *The Wild Duck* ("Ibsen and Feminism", 99).

33. The expression "thin net over the abyss" comes from Cavell's astounding analysis of Wittgenstein's vision of language in *Claim of Reason*, 178.

34. In 2000 I saw an American production of *The Wild Duck* in which the word "average" was left out. This inevitably gave the impression that Ibsen thought that everyone needs a life-lie. If so, I wonder what Old Werle's or Mrs Sørby's life-lies are supposed to be.

35. Somewhat freely translated from Rønning, "Ond idealisme", 226.

36. Ewbank brilliantly discusses the meaning and effect of this line ("Translating Ibsen", 61).
37. Letter to Theodor Caspari, Rome, 27 June 1884.
38. Cavell, "Must We Mean?", 19.

CHAPTER 9 LOSING FAITH IN LANGUAGE: FANTASIES OF PERFECT COMMUNICATION IN *ROSMERSHOLM*

1. For a full analysis of these claims, see Ch. 6.
2. I discuss the dense web of references to the melodramatic register more thoroughly in the essay "Expressive Freedom: Melodrama in *Rosmersholm*", which overlaps slightly with this chapter.
3. Brooks, *Melodramatic Imagination*, 4; Cavell, *Contesting Tears*, 43.
4. Kittang, *Ibsens heroisme*, 236.
5. To be exact, there is a brief soliloquy at the end of Acts 1, 2, and 4. In Act 3, Rebecca's moment of speaking alone onstage comes a few lines before the end.
6. Although I can't agree that *Rosmersholm* is a comedy, Hagen deserves credit for stressing the detective story-like aspects of the play (see "Ibsens forsoning").
7. Shaw, *Quintessence*, 120.
8. These are key themes in *Natural Supernaturalism*, Abrams's classic study of English and German romanticism.
9. In one way, then, Rosmer's project anticipates the title of Brandes's 1889 essay on Nietzsche's "aristocratic radicalism". In another, the difference between Rosmer and Nietzsche is striking, for, according to Brandes, Nietzsche thought that the "noblest and highest does not affect the masses at all". In *Rosmersholm*, it is Kroll who despises the masses (Brandes, *Friedrich Nietzsche*, 611).
10. In Norwegian, *fremtre* and *opptre* (*fremtræde* and *optræde* in Ibsen's Dano-Norwegian spelling) can mean "appear" and "perform", or "step forward" and "step upward". Clearly Brendel is playing on both meanings.
11. Hageberg is surely right to link this passage to disavowed oral pleasures (see " 'Møllefossens gåte' ", 158–9).
12. Cavell, *Contesting Tears*, 43.
13. Cavell, *Claim of Reason*, 351.
14. Ibid. 156.
15. Freud, "Some Character-Types", 325.
16. Ibid. 328–9. Freud solves the problem by speaking of Rebecca's *unconscious* guilt. This is oedipal guilt, the guilt every girl child is supposed to feel at having wanted to kill her mother so that she could keep her father to herself. Unless we assume that all women always reject proposals from the men they love because of their unconscious oedipal guilt, Freud would still have to figure out what *specific* reasons Rebecca has for refusing Rosmer.
17. Letter to Sofie Reimers, Munich, 25 March 1887.
18. Fjelde's widely used American translation leaves out "second" in the question

"Will you be my second wife?" (see pp. 545–6). According to Janet Garton, so does the Oxford Ibsen edition (Garton, "The Middle Plays", III–12).

19. Cavell, Claim of Reason, 428.

20. Garton has reached a similar conclusion by pointing to Rosmer's rather insulting formulation "will you be my *second* wife?" (ibid. 112).

21. Durbach, "*Ibsen the Romantic*", 186.

22. Shakespeare, *Othello*, IV. ii. 22.

23. Besides *Rosmersholm, The Pretenders* is the only other Ibsen play that shows a unusually high frequency of words for doubt and faith.

24. There is an excellent discussion of the concepts of *lykke* and *tro* ("happiness" and "faith" or "belief") in Goldman, *Ibsen: The Dramaturgy of Fear*, 115–54.

25. Kittang, *Ibsens heroisme*, 221.

26. Cavell writes that in literature the "domestication of the fantastic and the transcendentalizing of the domestic [may be called] the internalization, or subjectivizing, or democratizing, of philosophy" (*In Quest*, 27).

27. As early as 1892, Andreas-Salomé invoked "Now we two are *one*" in support of the claim that death was a release for the two lovers (*Henrik Ibsens Kvindeskikkelser*, 104).

28. Durbach, "*Ibsen the Romantic*", 190.

29. Ystad, "*Rosmersholm* og psykoanalysen", 162.

30. Hardwick, "The *Rosmersholm* Triangle", 83.

31. On this point I agree with Kittang, who writes that the "final scene only *looks like* a tragic end of the classical type", and who goes on to claim that "if the two are one, then they have become one precisely in *negativity*" (*Ibsens heroisme*, 230 and 232).

CHAPTER 10 THE ART OF TRANSFORMATION: ART, MARRIAGE, AND FREEDOM IN *THE LADY FROM THE SEA*

1. Durbach, "*Ibsen the Romantic*", 154. Durbach quotes Fjelde, "*The Lady from the Sea*", 379.

2. Valency, *Flower*, 188.

3. Ibid. 190.

4. Hemmer, *Ibsen: Kunstnerens vei*, 367.

5. In *Text and Supertext*, Johnston takes the reference to Ellida as a "heathen" to mean that she must be named after a Viking ship (see p. 196). Fjelde also thinks the name refers to a Viking ship (see "*The Lady from the Sea*", 390). *Ellide* [old Norse *Elliði*] is the name of the exceptionally good ship owned by Fridtjov den frøkne ("Fridtjov the brave"), in the saga of that name, first translated into Norwegian in 1858. In the second half of the nineteenth century, several Norwegian ships were named Ellida, and the name, which was—and still is— used as a man's name in Iceland, began to be used as a woman's name in Norway. (I am grateful to Inge Særheim from the University of Stavanger for this information.)

6. From an unsigned review by Clement Scott, *Daily Telegraph*, 12 May 1891, 3; repr. in Egan (ed.), *Ibsen: Critical Heritage*, 247.

7. Andersen, "Den lille Havfrue", 90.

8. I note that Hemmer in *Ibsen: Kunstnerens vei* declares that *The Lady from the Sea* really argues for "fidelity as an ideal" (p. 371), because Ibsen here lets "longing and sexual drives find their natural and satisfying place within the safe framework of marriage" (p. 400). I hope this chapter will show that although I think Hemmer is right to bring up the theme of fidelity, I think his conclusions are completely wrong.

9. McFarlane, *Ibsen and Meaning*, 277–8.

10. Ibid. 277.

11. In *Fangs of Malice*, Wikander makes the mistake of beginning from the premise that theater has a special problem (i.e. one not present in ordinary human relationships) when it comes to expressing the soul.

12. In her Lacanian reading of the play Rekdal argues that the play's concerns with art and with psychoanalytic therapy are unified by the concept of *sublimation*, but the implications of this suggestions are not pursued (see *Frihetens dilemma*, 226).

13. My argument is *not* that Ballested's painting of the half-dead mermaid is intended to be Böcklin's mermaid; it is rather that the anguish of Böcklin's mermaid, her isolation from the merry mood of the other mermen and mermaids, may have played a role in Ibsen's conception of Ellida.

14. See the brief discussion of Losting in Ch. 2.

15. I get the impression that we are to imagine that the band is in a boat that accompanies the ship for a while before turning back towards town, for first we learn that Hilde and Lyngstrand are going down to the quayside to listen to the music (11: 151), and then, in his very last stage directions, Ibsen writes that while the steamer glides soundlessly away, the music is heard closer to the shore (11: 157).

16. Cavell, *Pitch of Philosophy*, 12.

17. Many critics have noted that Ellida is yearning for the absolute. Although Johnston's Hegelian readings of Ibsen usually strike me as problematic, on this point his approach is consonant with mine, for he sees in *The Lady from the Sea* "a contrast between consciousness of the limitless and of the humanly limited, . . . of the lure of an absolute freedom, which at once terrifies and attracts and which will be relinquished for a freedom with responsibility" (*Text and Supertext*, 197).

18. *The Lady from the Sea* has much in common with Cavell's remarriage comedies, as discussed in *Pursuits of Happiness*. Yet it also contains many of the features of Cavell's melodramas of the unknown woman as they are set forth in *Contesting Tears*. I am inclined to think that Ibsen, particularly in *A Doll's House* and in *The Lady from the Sea*, produced something like the common prototype of *both* these Hollywood genres.

19. I quote the letter in Ch. 6.

EPILOGUE: IDEALISM AND THE "BAD" EVERYDAY

1. The secondary literature on *Hedda Gabler* is vast, and in this brief epilogue I cannot engage with it. An excellent collection of varied views on *Hedda Gabler* can be found in Rekdal (ed.), *Et skjær av uvilkårlig skjønnhet*.

2. Most English translations miss the meaning of the word *underlivet*, which is the usual word for women's internal and external reproductive organs, and which also signifies the "lower belly". That Judge Brack uses the term as a euphemism for the genitals is beyond doubt.

3. Schiller, "On Naive and Sentimental Poetry", 255.

4. See Fried, *Menzel's Realism*, 159. When Ibsen turns his attention to the "bad" everyday, he becomes more palatable to ideologues of modernism, probably because most of them are more familiar with Heidegger than with Wittgenstein.

5. Just as *The Lady from the Sea* stands out in the series of plays from *A Doll's House* to *Hedda Gabler*, so *Little Eyolf* stands out among the late plays. It has a lot in common with *The Lady from the Sea*: the idea of *transformation* (*forvandling*) is a major thematic concern; the play has something like a reconciled ending, in which a married couple on the verge of separation finds a way to continue the marriage. But on what terms? This couple has lost a child, and their love for each other is not obvious. Like *The Lady from the Sea*, *Little Eyolf* also has supernatural elements: the Rat Wife with her uncanny little dog who entice their crippled son Eyolf to drown himself in the fjord. It is also a play about a married woman who defines herself as a lover rather than as a mother, and about the incestuous desire of a brother for a sister.

6. Helland, who thinks that the four last plays break with realism, has an interesting discussion of the recent resurgence of interest in Ibsen's four last plays (*Melankoliens spill*, 13–23).

7. In *Melankoliens spill* Helland pays close attention to meta-aesthetic and metatheatrical references. Aslaksen writes well on metatheatricality in *John Gabriel Borkman* (" 'Mændene er så ubestandige, fru Borkman' ").

8. Some critics claim, unconvincingly, that in *When We Dead Awaken* Ibsen acknowledged that he ought to have remained a strict idealist all along (see Gvåle, "Henrik Ibsen"). Ustvedt thinks that Ibsen wants to say that, like Rubek, he regretted his turn to realism ("Professor Rubek"). Olivarius believes, rightly, in my view, that one should not take Rubek's high evaluation of himself to be the same as Ibsen's ("Henrik Ibsen: Idealismens svanesang").

9. For Ibsen's presence at *Brand*, see 13: 191 and Meyer, *Top of a Cold Mountain*, 291–2.

10. Of course the play can't be reduced to this one concern. For anyone interested in criticism of the play, I recommend beginning with Wærp (ed.), *Livet på likstrå*, a lively, multifaceted anthology of essays on *When We Dead Awaken*.

11. Rubek's *min benådelses brud* is hard to translate. In a legal context *benådelse*

means a pardon, and the word thus connects his mock marriage to Irene to the line where he describes his sculpture of himself as a man sunk in remorse over a *forbrudt* ("forfeited") life, for *forbrudt* is the past tense of *forbryte*, which means to commit a criminal act—that is to say, an act which may require a pardon. But *benådet* also means something like "divinely inspired" and is often used about artists. Irene is here represented both as Rubek's redemption and as his chance of renewed creativity.

12. The only convincing reading I know of Rubek's relationship to Maja, and of Maja's relationship to him as well as to Ulfhejm, the bear hunter, is Ottesen's brilliant "Om at finde sin stemme".

APPENDIX 2 TRANSLATING IBSEN

1. Further references will be given in the text. For a more specialized analysis, see Smidt, *Ibsen Translated*.

2. The translations are as follows: Ibsen, *An Enemy of the People, The Wild Duck, Rosmersholm*, trans. McFarlane; Ibsen, *The Complete Major Prose Plays*, trans. Fjelde; Ibsen, *Ibsen, Volume II: Four Plays*, trans. Johnston; Ibsen, *Plays Three*, trans. Meyer.

Bibliography

AARSETH, ASBJØRN, *Ibsens samtidsskuespill: En studie i glasskapets dramaturgi* (Oslo: Universitetsforlaget, 1999).

ABRAMS, M. H., *Natural Supernaturalism: Tradition and Revolution in Romantic Literature* (New York: Norton, 1971).

ADORNO, THEODOR W., *Minima Moralia: Reflections from Damaged Life*, trans. E. F. N. Jephcott (London and New York: Verso, 1974).

ALNÆS, NINA S., *Varulv om natten: Folketro og folkediktning hos Ibsen* (Oslo: Gyldendal, 2003).

ANDERSEN, ELIN, and POVLSEN, KAREN KLITGAARD, "Det sublime øjeblik", in Andersen and Povlsen (eds.), *Tableau*, 7–23.

—— —— (eds.), *Tableau: Det sublime øjeblik* (Århus: Klim, 2001).

ANDERSEN, HANS CHRISTIAN, "Den lille Havfrue", in *Samlede Eventyr og Historier*, 3 vols. (Oslo: Gyldendal Norsk Forlag, 1977), i. 71–92.

ANDERSEN, PER THOMAS, *Norsk litteraturhistorie* (Oslo: Universitetsforlaget, 2001).

ANDREAS-SALOMÉ, LOU, *Henrik Ibsens Kvindeskikkelser*, trans. Hulda Garborg (Kristiania and Copenhagen: Cammermeyer, 1893).

ANONYMOUS, "Preface", in Paul Heyse, *Children of the World*, 3 vols. (London: Chapman & Hall, 1882), i: pp. v–viii.

ANONYMOUS, "The Royal Academy Exhibition", *Art Journal*, 1887, 245–48.

ANONYMOUS, review of *A Doll's House*, in *Fædrelandet (Copenhagen)*, 22 Dec. 1879, <http://www.ibsen.net/index.gan?id=19567&subid=0>.

ANSTEINSSON, ELI, *Teater i Norge: Dansk scenekunst 1813–63. Kristiansand—Arendal—Stavanger* (Oslo: Universitetsforlaget, 1968).

ARISTOTLE, *Poetics*, trans. James Hutton (New York: Norton, 1982).

ARTAUD, ANTONIN, *Artaud on Theatre*, ed. Claude Schumacher and Brian Singleton, trans. Claude Schumacher *et al.* (London: Methuen Drama, 2001).

ASCHERSON, NEAL, "Victory in Defeat", *London Review of Books*, 2 Dec. 2004, 3–6.

ASKELAND, JAN, *Adolph Tidemand og hans tid* (Oslo: Aschehoug, 1991).

ASLAKSEN, KAMILLA, " 'Mændene er så ubestandige, fru Borkman. Og kvinderne ligervis': Problemer omkring genre, teatralitet og identitet i Ibsens *John Gabriel Borkman*", *Agora*, nos. 2–3 (1993), 112–29.

—— "Ibsen and Melodrama: Observations on an Uneasy Relationship", *Nordic Theatre Studies*, 10 (1997), 36–47.

AUBERT, ANDREAS, *Maleren Johan Christian Dahl: Et stykke av forrige aarhundredes kunst- og kulturhistorie* (Kristiania: Aschehoug, 1920).

AUERBACH, ERICH, *Mimesis: The Representation of Reality in Western Literature*, trans. Willard Trask (Princeton: Princeton University Press, 1953).

BALDICK, CHRIS, *The Concise Oxford Dictionary of Literary Terms* (Oxford: Oxford University Press, 2001).

BANG, HERMAN, "Et Dukkehjem", <http://www.ibsen.net/index.gan?id=355-&subid=0>. Also available in *Realisme og realister: Kritiske studïer og udkast*, ed. Sten Rasmussen (Copenhagen: Det Danske Sprog- og Litteraturselskab / Borgen, 2001).

BANN, STEPHEN, *Paul Delaroche: History Painted* (Princeton: Princeton University Press, 1997).

BARISH, JONAS, *The Antitheatrical Prejudice* (Berkeley: University of California Press, 1981).

BARNES, JULIAN, *A History of the World in 10 1/2 Chapters* (New York: Vintage Books, 1990).

BARTHES, ROLAND, "The Reality Effect", in *The Rustle of Language*, trans. Richard Howard (Oxford: Basil Blackwell, 1986), 141–8.

BELL, MICHAEL, "The Metaphysics of Modernism", in Michael H. Levinson (ed.), *The Cambridge Companion to Modernism* (Cambridge: Cambridge University Press, 1999), 9–32.

BENTLEY, ERIC, *In Search of Theater* (New York: Alfred A. Knopf, 1953).

BERNSTEIN, J. M. (ed.), *Classic and Romantic German Aesthetics* (Cambridge: Cambridge University Press, 2003).

BILLINGTON, MICHAEL, "The Troll in the Drawing-Room", *The Guardian*, 15 Feb. 2003, <http://www.guardian.co.uk/arts/critic/feature/0,1169,895763,00.html>.

BJØRBYE, PÅL, and AARSETH, ASBJØRN (eds.), *Proceedings: IX International Ibsen Conference, Bergen 5–10 June 2000* (Øvre Ervik: Akademisk Forlag, 2001).

BJØRNEBOE, THERESE, "Endelig—hun skjøt ham!", *Norsk Shakespeare og teater-tidsskrift*, no. 2 (2002), 44–5.

BJØRNSON, BJØRNSTJERNE, "Fiskerjenten", in *Samlede Digter-Verker* (Kristiania and Copenhagen: Gyldendalske Boghandel, 1919), ii. 375–501.

—— "Gildet paa Solhaug", *Morgenbladet*, 16 March 1856, in Christian Collin and H. Eitrem (eds.), *Artikler og taler*, 2 vols. (Kristiania and Copenhagen: Gyldendalske Boghandel Nordisk Forlag, 1912), i. 103–7.

—— *Kamp-liv: Brev fra årene 1879–1884 med innledning og opplysninger*, ed. Halvdan Koht, 2 vols. (Oslo: Gyldendal, 1932).

BLANC, THARALD, *Christiania Theaters historie 1827–1877* (Christiania: Cappelen, 1899).

BLOOM, HAROLD, *The Western Canon* (New York: Harcourt Brace, 1994).

BØ, GUDLEIV, *"Nationale subjekter": Ideer om nasjonalitet i Henrik Ibsens romantiske forfatterskap* (Oslo: Novus Forlag, 2000).

BOURDIEU, PIERRE, *Distinction: A Social Critique of the Judgment of Taste*, trans. Richard Nice (London: Routledge & Kegan Paul, 1980).

BOWERSOCK, G. W., *Julian the Apostate* (Cambridge, Mass.: Harvard University Press, 1978).

BRADBURY, MALCOLM, and McFARLANE, JAMES (eds.), *Modernism 1890–1930* (Harmondsworth: Penguin Books, 1976).

BRANDES, GEORG, *Breve til Forældrene, 1872–1904*, ed. Torben Nielsen, på grundlag af Morten Borups forarbejder, 3 vols. (Copenhagen: Det danske sprog- og litteraturselskab / C. A. Reitzel, 1994).

—— *Emigrantlitteraturen* (1872; vol. i of *Hovedstrømninger i det 19de Aarhundredes Litteratur*) (Oslo: Gyldendal Norsk Forlag, 1971).

—— *Friedrich Nietzsche: En Afhandling om aristokratisk Radikalisme* (1889), in *Samlede Skrifter*, vii. 596–664; trans. by A. G. Chater as *Friedrich Nietzsche* (London: William Heinemann, 1914).

—— "Paul Heyse" (1874), in *Samlede Skrifter*, vii. 314–58; trans. by Rasmus B. Anderson as "Paul Heyse", in *Eminent Authors of the Nineteenth Century: Literary Portraits* (New York: Thomas Y. Crowell, 1886), 1–60.

—— review of *Kejser og Galilæer* in *Det nittende århundre* (1874–5), <http://www.ibsen.net/index.gan?id=110586&subid=0>.

—— review of *Lord William Russell* by Andreas Munch (1869), in *Kritiker og Portræter*, 2nd rev. edn. (Copenhagen: Gyldendalske Boghandels Forlag, 1885), 349–56.

—— *Samlede Skrifter*, 18 vols. (Copenhagen: Gyldendalske Boghandels Forlag, 1899–1910).

—— and BRANDES, EDVARD, *Brevveksling med nordiske forfattere og videnskabsmænd*, ed. Morten Borup, under Medvirkning af Francis Bull and John Landquist, 8 vols. (Copenhagen: Gyldendal, 1939).

BRECHT, BERTHOLT, *Brecht on Theatre: The Development of an Aesthetic*, ed. and trans. John Willett (New York: Hill and Wang, 1964).

—— *Werke*, 31 vols. (Berlin: Aufbau, 1988–2000).

British Section at the Vienna Universal Exhibition, 1873 [Fine Art Galleries, Industrial, Agricultural and Machinery Halls, and Park]: Official Catalogue with Plans and Illustrations (London: J. M. Johnson & Sons for the British Royal Commission, 1873).

BROCKETT, LINUS PIERPOINT, *The Year of Battles: A History of the Franco-German War of 1870–71. Embracing also Paris under the Commune; or the Red Rebellion of 1871. A Second Reign of Terror, Murder, and Madness* (New York: H. S. Goodspeed, 1871).

BROOKS, PETER, *The Melodramatic Imagination: Balzac, Henry James, Melodrama, and the Mode of Excess* (1976; New York: Columbia University Press, 1985).

BROWN, RICHARD, "James Joyce between Ibsen and Bjørnson: *A Portrait of the Artist* and *The Fisher Lass*", in Inga-Stina Ewbank, Olav Lausund, and Bjørn J. Tysdahl (eds.), *Anglo-Scandinavian Cross-Currents* (Norwich: Norvik Press, 1999), 280–93.

BROWN, STEPHANIE NEVISON, "Girodet (de Roussy-Trioson) [Girodet-Trioson], Anne-Louis", in L. Macy (ed.), *The Grove Dictionary of Art Online*, <http://www.groveart.com>.

BROWNING, ROBERT, *Der Rattenfänger von Hameln*, trans. Marie Schweikher, illustrations Arthur C. Payne and Harry Payne (London and Munich: Lithogr.-artistische Anst., [1889]).

BRUN, M. V., "Det kongelige Teater", review of *A Doll's House*, *Folkets Avis*, 24 Dec. 1879, <http://www.ibsen.net/index.gan?id=61882&subid=0>.

BULL, FRANCIS, "Indledning", in Bjørnstjerne Bjørnson, *Samlede Digter-Verker* (Kristiania and Copenhagen: Gyldendalske Boghandel, 1919), ii: pp. i–xxxix.

—— *Norges litteratur: Fra februarrevolusjonen til første verdenskrig* (vol. iv, part i, of Francis Bull *et al.* (eds.), *Norsk litteraturhistorie* (Oslo: Aschehoug, 1963).

—— *Tradisjoner og minner* (Oslo: Gyldendal, 1946).

BULYOVSZKY, LILA, *Reiseminner fra Norge 1864*, trans. Mária Fáskerti, with Randi Meyer (Oslo: Pax, 2000).

BUSS, ROBIN, "Introduction", in *L'Assommoir* by Emile Zola (London: Penguin Books, 2000).

BYATT, A. S., *The Biographer's Tale* (London: Chatto & Windus, 2000).

CAMUS, ALBERT, *The Rebel: An Essay on Man in Revolt* (1951; New York: Alfred A. Knopf, 1971).

CAREY, JOHN, *The Intellectuals and the Masses: Pride and Prejudice among the Literary Intelligentsia, 1880–1930* (London and Boston: Faber & Faber, 1992).

CASANOVA, PASCALE, "La Production de l'universel littéraire: le 'grand tour' d'Ibsen en Europe", in Eveline Pinto (ed.), *Penser l'art et la culture avec les sciences sociales* (Paris: Publications de la Sorbonne, 2002), 63–80.

—— *La République mondiale des lettres* (Paris: Le Seuil, 1999).

CAVELL, STANLEY, "The Avoidance of Love: A Reading of *King Lear*", in Cavell, *Must We Mean*, 267–353.

—— *Cities of Words: Pedagogical Letters on a Register of the Moral Life* (Cambridge, Mass.: Belknap Press of Harvard University Press, 2004).

—— *The Claim of Reason: Wittgenstein, Skepticism, Morality, and Tragedy* (1979; New York: Oxford University Press, 1999).

—— *Contesting Tears: The Hollywood Melodrama of the Unknown Woman* (Chicago: University of Chicago Press, 1996).

—— "Foreword: An Audience for Philosophy", in Cavell, *Must We Mean*, pp. xxxi–xlii.

—— *In Quest of the Ordinary: Lines of Skepticism and Romanticism* (Chicago: University of Chicago Press, 1988).

—— *Must We Mean What We Say?* (Cambridge: Cambridge University Press, 1969).

—— "Must We Mean What We Say?", in Cavell, *Must We Mean*, 1–43.

—— *A Pitch of Philosophy: Autobiographical Exercises* (Cambridge, Mass.: Harvard University Press, 1994).

—— *Pursuits of Happiness: The Hollywood Comedy of Remarriage* (Cambridge, Mass.: Harvard University Press, 1981).

CHILDERS, JOSEPH, and HENTZI, GARY (eds.), *The Columbia Dictionary of Modern Literary and Cultural Criticism* (New York: Columbia University Press, 1995).

CHRISTENSEN, ERIK M., *Henrik Ibsens realisme: illusion katastrofe anarki*, 2 vols. (Copenhagen: Akademisk Forlag, 1985).

COMMENT, BERNARD, *The Painted Panorama*, trans. Anne-Marie Glasheen (New York: Harry N. Abrams, 1999).

CUDDON, J. A., *A Dictionary of Literary Terms and Literary Theory*, rev. C. E. Preston, 4th edn. (Oxford: Blackwell, 1998).

DAHL, PER, "Den umulige treenighed: Bjørnson—Brandes—Ibsen", unpublished lecture, 2002.

—— "Det kritiske tekstvalg: Problemer og perspektiver", in Jørgen Hunosøe and Esther Kielberg (eds.), *I tekstens tegn* (Copenhagen: Det Danske Sprog- og Litteraturselskab / C. A. Reitzels Forlag, 1994), 96–124.

DAHL, PER KRISTIAN HEGGELUND, *Streiflys: Fem Ibsen-studier* (Oslo: Ibsen-museet, 2001).

DALESKI, H. M., "Thomas Hardy: A Victorian Modernist", in Lawrence L. Besserman (ed.), *The Challenge of Periodization: Old Paradigms and New Perspectives* (New York: Garland Publishing, 1996), 179–95.

DAUBER, KENNETH, and JOST, WALTER (eds.), *Ordinary Language Criticism: Literary Thinking after Cavell after Wittgenstein* (Evanston, Ill.: Northwestern University Press, 2003).

DESCARTES, RENÉ, *Discourse on Method and the Meditations*, trans. John Veitch (Buffalo: Prometheus Books, 1989).

—— *Méditations métaphysiques* (1641), ed. and trans. Florence Khodoss (Paris: Quadrige / PUF, 1956).

DEUTSCHER, ISAAC, *The Prophet Armed: Trotsky, 1879–1921* (New York and London: Oxford University Press, 1954).

DIAMOND, ELIN, *Unmaking Mimesis: Essays on Feminism and Theater* (London and New York: Routledge, 1997).

DIDEROT, DENIS, "Conversations on *The Natural Son*" (1757), in *Selected Writings on Art and Literature*, trans. Geoffrey Bremner (Harmondsworth: Penguin, 1994), 4–79.

—— "De la poésie dramatique" (1758), in *Œuvres*, iv: *Esthétique—Théâtre* (Paris: Robert Laffont, 1996), 1271–1350.

—— "In Praise of Richardson" (1761), in *Selected Writings on Art and Literature*, trans. Geoffrey Bremner (Harmondsworth: Penguin, 1994), 82–97.

DIETRICHSON, LORENZ, *Svundne Tider: Af en Forfatters Ungdomserindringer*, i: *Bergen og Christiania i 40- og 50-Aarene* (1896; rpt. Oslo: ARS, 1984).

DINESEN, ISAK, *Anecdotes of Destiny* (New York: Random House, 1958).

DUGUID, LINDSAY, "Whispers of the Minotaur", *Times Literary Supplement*, 17 Dec. 2004, 18–19.

DURBACH, ERROL, *A Doll's House: Ibsen's Myth of Transformation* (Boston: Twayne, 1991).

—— *"Ibsen the Romantic": Analogues of Paradise in the Later Plays* (Athens, Ga.: University of Georgia Press, 1982).

—— "Nora as Antigone: The Feminist Tragedienne and Social Legality", *Scandinavian-Canadian Studies*, 5 (1992), 29–41.

—— " 'The Romantic Possibilities of Scenery': Ibsen's Mountain Kingdoms and the Dresden School of Landscape Art", *Annals of Scholarship*, 9 (1992), 279–92.

EDVARDSEN, ERIK HENNING, *Gammelt nytt i våre tidligste ukeblader*, Norsk Folkeminnelags Skrifter 147 (Oslo: Norsk Folkeminnelag / Aschehoug, 1997).

—— *Henrik Ibsen om seg selv* (Oslo: Genesis, 2001).

EGAN, MICHAEL (ed.), *Ibsen: The Critical Heritage* (London and Boston: Routledge & Kegan Paul, 1972).

ELLMANN, RICHARD, *Oscar Wilde* (New York: Alfred A. Knopf, 1988).

ESPMARK, KJELL, *The Nobel Prize in Literature: A Study of the Criteria behind the Choices* (Boston: G. K. Hall, 1991).

EWBANK, INGA-STINA, "Ibsen in Wonderful Copenhagen 1852", *Ibsen Studies*, 1/2 (2001), 59–78.

—— "Første opponent til Frode Helland: *Melankoliens spill*", *Edda*, no. 2 (1999), 170–5.

—— "Translating Ibsen for the English Stage", *Tijdschrift voor Skandinavistiek*, 19/1 (1998), 51–74.

FELSKI, RITA, *Gender and Modernity* (Cambridge, Mass.: Harvard University Press, 1995).

FERGUSON, ROBERT, *Henrik Ibsen: A New Biography* (London: Richard Cohen Books, 1996).

FINNEY, GAIL, "Ibsen and Feminism", in James McFarlane (ed.), *The Cambridge Companion to Ibsen* (Cambridge: Cambridge University Press, 1994), 89–105.

FJELDE, ROLF, " *The Lady from the Sea*: Ibsen's Positive World-View in a Topographic Figure", *Modern Drama*, 21 (1978), 379–91.

FORBES, BRYAN (dir.), *The Stepford Wives* (Columbia Pictures and Palomar Pictures, 1975).

FREUD, SIGMUND, "Delusions and Dreams in Jensen's *Gradivá*" (1907), in Freud, *Standard Edition*, ix. 1–95.

—— "Fragment of an Analysis of a Case of Hysteria [Dora]" (1905), in Freud, *Standard Edition*, vii. 1–122.

—— "Some Character-Types Met with in Psychoanalytic Work" (1916), in Freud, *Standard Edition*, xiv. 309–33.

—— *The Standard Edition of the Complete Psychological Works*, 24 vols., ed. and trans. James Strachey (London: Hogarth Press, 1953–74).

FRIED, MICHAEL, *Absorption and Theatricality: Painting and Beholder in the Age of Diderot* (Berkeley: University of California Press, 1980).

—— *Art and Objecthood: Essays and Reviews* (Chicago: University of Chicago Press, 1998).

—— *Courbet's Realism* (Chicago: University of Chicago Press, 1990).

—— "Foreword to the Johns Hopkins Edition", in Lessing, *Laocoön*, pp. vii–viii.

—— *Menzel's Realism: Art and Embodiment in Nineteenth-Century Berlin* (New Haven: Yale University Press, 2002).

GARBORG, ARNE, *Henrik Ibsen's "Keiser og Galilæer": En kritisk studie* (1873; Christiania: Aschehoug, 1874).

GARTON, JANET, "The Middle Plays", in James McFarlane (ed.), *The Cambridge Companion to Ibsen* (Cambridge: Cambridge University Press, 1994), 106–25.

GATLAND, JAN OLAV, *Repertoaret ved Det Norske Theater 1850–63* (Bergen: Universitetsbiblioteket i Bergen, 2000).

GOLDMAN, MICHAEL, *Ibsen: The Dramaturgy of Fear* (New York: Columbia University Press, 1999).

GOULD, VERONICA FRANKLIN, *G. F. Watts: The Last Great Victorian* (New Haven: Yale University Press, 2004).

GRØNVOLD, DIDRIK, *Diktere og musikere: personlige erindringer om noen av dem* (Oslo: Cammermeyer, 1945).

GRØNVOLD, MARCUS, *Fra Ulrikken til Alperne: En malers erindringer* (Oslo: Gyldendal, 1925).

GUTHRIE, TYRONE, *A Life in the Theatre* (New York: McGraw-Hill, 1959).

GVÅLE, GUDRUN HOVDE, "Henrik Ibsen: *Når vi døde vågner.* Ein epilog til eit livsverk", in Daniel Haakonsen *et al.* (eds.), *Ibsenårbok* (Oslo, Bergen, and Tromsø: Universitetsforlaget, 1969), 22–37.

HAAKONSEN, DANIEL, *Henrik Ibsen: Mennesket og kunstneren* (1981; Oslo: Aschehoug, 2003).

—— *Henrik Ibsens realisme* (Oslo: Aschehoug, 1957).

HACKING, IAN, *The Taming of Chance* (Cambridge: Cambridge University Press, 1990).

HAGEBERG, OTTO, " 'Møllefossens gåte' ", in *Frå Camilla Collett til Dag Solstad: Spenningsmønster i litterære tekstar* (Oslo: Det Norske Samlaget, 1980), 152–65.

HAGEN, ERIK BJERCK, "Ibsens forsoning: Eller hvorfor *Rosmersholm* egentlig er en politisk komedie", in *Litteratur og handling: Pragmatiske tanker om Ibsen, Hamsun, Solstad, Emerson og andre* (Oslo: Universitetsforlaget, 2000), 203–29.

HALL, JAMES, "Passion beyond the Pedestal", *Times Literary Supplement*, 10 Dec. 2004, 18–19.

HANSTEIN, ADALBERT VON, *Ibsen als Idealist* (Leipzig: Verlag von Gg. Freund, 1897).

HARDWICK, ELISABETH, "The *Rosmersholm* Triangle", in *Seduction and Betrayal: Women and Literature* (New York: Random House, 1974), 69–83.

HAUGHOLT, KARL, "Samtidens kritikk av Ibsens *Catilina*", *Edda*, no. 6 (1952), 74–94.

HEGEL, G. W. F., *Elements of the Philosophy of Right*, trans. H. B. Nisbet (Cambridge: Cambridge University Press, 1991).

—— *Hegel's Aesthetics: Lectures on Fine Art*, trans. T. M. Knox, 2 vols. (Oxford: Clarendon Press, 1975).

—— *Phenomenology of Spirit*, trans. A. V. Miller (Oxford: Oxford University Press, 1977).

HEIDEM, KNUT, "Fiksjon og virkelighet—Terje Vigen som norsk selvbilde", *Nytt Norsk Tidsskrift*, no. 1 (1998), 61–75.

HELLAND, FRODE, *Melankoliens spill: En studie i Henrik Ibsens siste dramaer* (Oslo: Universitetsforlaget, 2000).

—— *Voldens blomster? Henrik Wergelands "Blomsterstykke" i estetikkens lys* (Oslo: Universitetsforlaget, 2003).

HEMMER, BJØRN, *Ibsen: Kunstnerens vei* (Bergen: Vigmostad Bjørke / Ibsen-museene i Norge, 2003).

HEYSE, PAUL, *Children of the World*, 3 vols. (London: Chapman & Hall, 1882).

HOEM, GUNHILD, "*Emperor and Galilean*: The Problem Child of Literary Scholars", in Bjørbye and Asbjørn (eds.), *Proceedings*, 309–14.

—— *Henrik Ibsens hovedverk* Keiser og Galilæer: *litteraturforskernes "problembarn"* (Oslo: Solum, 2000).

HÖLDERLIN, FRIEDRICH, "Oldest Programme for a System of German Idealism" (1796), in Bernstein (ed.), *Classic and Romantic*, 185–7.

HOLENWEG, HANS, "*L'Ile des morts*: Histoire", in Le Cieux, Peyrolle, and Jacquinot (eds.), *Hommage*, 11–21.

HOLMSTRÖM, KIRSTEN GRAM, *Monodrama, Attitudes, Tableaux Vivants: Studies on Some Trends of Theatrical Fashion 1770–1815* (Stockholm: Almqvist & Wiksell, 1967).

HØST, ELSE, *Vildanden av Henrik Ibsen* (Oslo: Aschehoug, 1967).

HØSTMÆLINGEN, NJÅL, "Den evangelisk-lutherske Religion forbliver Statens offentlige Religion", *Din: Tidsskrift for religion og kultur*, no. 4 (2001), <http://www.hf.ntnu.no/din/hostmalingen.html>.

HUGO, VICTOR, *Hernani* (1830; Paris: GF-Flammarion, 1996).

HUTTON, PATRICK (ed.), *Historical Dictionary of the Third French Republic, 1870–1940* (New York and Westport, Conn.: Greenwood Press, 1986).

HUYSSEN, ANDREAS, *After the Great Divide: Modernism, Mass Culture, Postmodernism* (Bloomington, Ind.: Indiana University Press, 1986).

IBSEN, BERGLIOT, *De tre: Erindringer om Henrik Ibsen, Suzannah Ibsen, Sigurd Ibsen* (Oslo: Gyldendal, 1949).

IBSEN, HENRIK, *The Complete Major Prose Plays*, trans. Rolf Fjelde (New York: Plume Books, 1978).

—— *Emperor and Galilean: A World Historical Drama*, trans. Brian Johnston (Lyme, NH: Smith and Kraus, 1999).

—— *An Enemy of the People, The Wild Duck, Rosmersholm*, trans. James McFarlane (Oxford and New York: Oxford University Press, 1988).

—— *Hundreårsutgave: Henrik Ibsens samlede verker*, ed. Francis Bull, Halvdan Koht, and Didrik Arup Seip, 21 vols. (Oslo: Gyldendal, 1928–57).

—— *Ibsen*, ii: *Four Plays*, trans. Brian Johnston (Lyme, NH: Smith and Kraus, 1996).

—— *Ibsen's Poems*, trans. John Northam (Oslo: Norwegian University Press, 1986).

—— *Plays Three: Rosmersholm, The Lady from the Sea, Little Eyolf*, trans. Michael Meyer (London: Methuen Publishing, 2004).

IBSEN, SIGURD, *Bak en gyllen fasade: Sigurd Ibsens brev til familien 1883–1929*, ed. Bodil Nævdal (Oslo: Aschehoug, 1997).

"I-N", review of *A Doll's House, Social-Demokraten*, 23 Dec. 1879, <http://www.ibsen.net/index.gan?id=19569&subid=0>.

INNES, CHRISTOPHER, "Modernism in Drama", in Michael H. Levinson (ed.), *The Cambridge Companion to Modernism* (Cambridge: Cambridge University Press, 1999), 130–56.

—— (ed.), *A Sourcebook on Naturalist Theatre* (London and New York: Routledge, 2000).

JÆGER, HENRIK, *Henrik Ibsen 1828–1888: Et literært livsbillede* (Copenhagen: Gyldendalske Boghandel, 1888); trans. by William Morton Payne as *Henrik Ibsen: A Critical Biography* (Chicago: A. C. McClurg, 1901).

JAMES, HENRY, *Parisian Sketches: Letters to the New York Tribune 1875–76*, ed. Leon Edel and Ilse Dusoir Lind (New York: New York University Press, 1957).

JAMESON, FREDRIC, *A Singular Modernity: Essay on the Ontology of the Present* (London and New York: Verso, 2002).

JANSS, CHRISTIAN, review of *Overgangens figurasjoner* by Lisbeth Pettersen Wærp, *Norsk Litteraturvitenskapelig Tidsskrift*, no. 1 (2004), 45–57.

JOHNSTON, BRIAN, *Text and Supertext in Ibsen's Drama* (University Park, Pa.: Pennsylvania State University Press, 1989).

—— *To the Third Empire: Ibsen's Early Drama* (Minneapolis: University of Minnesota Press, 1980).

JOYCE, JAMES, *Occasional, Critical, and Political Writing*, ed. Kevin Barry (Oxford: Oxford University Press, 2000).

KALNEIN, WEND VON, "De tyske Düsseldorfere", in Jan Askeland (ed.), *Düsseldorf og Norden* (Bergen: Bergen Billedgalleri, 1976), 5–12.

KANT, IMMANUEL, *Lectures on Ethics*, ed. Peter Heath and J. B. Schneewind, trans. Peter Heath (Cambridge: Cambridge University Press, 1997).

—— *The Metaphysics of Morals*, ed. and trans. Mary Gregor (Cambridge: Cambridge University Press, 1996).

KEATS, JOHN, "Ode on a Grecian Urn", in *The Complete Poems of John Keats* (New York: The Modern Library, 1994), 185–6.

KENNER, HUGH, "Joyce and Ibsen's Naturalism" (1951), in Charles R. Lyons (ed.), *Critical Essays on Henrik Ibsen* (Boston: G. K. Hall, 1987), 53–67.

KITTANG, ATLE, *Ibsens heroisme: fra* Brand *til* Når vi døde vågner (Oslo: Gyldendal, 2002).

KNIGHT, DIANA, "S/Z, Realism, and Compulsory Heterosexuality", in Margaret Cohen and Christopher Prendergast (eds.), *Spectacles of Realism: Gender, Body, Genre* (Minneapolis: University of Minnesota Press, 1995), 120–36.

KOHT, HALVDAN, *Henrik Ibsen: Eit diktarliv*, 2 vols., 2nd rev. edn. (Oslo: Aschehoug, 1954); trans. and abridged by Einar Haugen and A. E. Santaniello as *Life of Ibsen* (New York: B. Blom, 1971).

KUHN, THOMAS S., *The Structure of Scientific Revolutions*, 3rd edn. (Chicago: University of Chicago Press, 1996).

LaCapra, Dominick, "1857: Two Trials", in Denis Hollier (ed.), *A New History of French Literature* (Cambridge, Mass.: Harvard University Press, 1989), 726–31.

Langås, Unni, "Kunstig liv: Simulasjon og sykdom i *Et dukkehjem*", in Gunnar Foss (ed.), *I skriftas lys og teatersalens mørke: Ein antologi om Ibsen og Fosse* (Kristiansand: Høyskoleforlaget, 2005), 51–79.

Lange, Marit Ingeborg, and Ljøgodt, Knut (eds.), *Svermeri og virkelighet: München i norsk maleri* (Oslo: Nasjonalgalleriet, 2002).

Langslet, Lars Roar, *Henrik Ibsen, Edvard Munch: To genier møtes / Two Geniuses Meet*, trans. Palmyre Pierroux, bilingual edn. (Oslo: Cappelen, 1994).

Lebowitz, Naomi, *Ibsen and the Great World* (Baton Rouge, La.: Louisiana State University Press, 1990).

Le Cieux, Laurence, Peyrolle, Pierre, and Jacquinot, Armelle (eds.), *Hommage à l'Ile des morts d'Arnold Böcklin: Exposition à Meaux au musée Bossuet du 13 octobre 2001 au 13 janvier 2002* (Paris: Somogy Editions d'art, 2001).

Lessing, Gotthold Ephraim, *Emilia Galotti: A Tragedy in Five Acts*, trans. Edward Dvoretzky (1772; New York: Frederick Ungar Publishing, 1962).

—— *Laocoön: An Essay on the Limits of Painting and Poetry*, trans. Edward Allen McCormick (1766; Baltimore: Johns Hopkins University Press, 1984).

Lindemann, Berndt Wolfgang, and Schmidt, Katharina (eds.), *Arnold Böcklin* (Heidelberg: Edition Braus / Wachter Verlag, 2001).

Lukács, Georg, *Writer and Critic and Other Essays*, ed. and trans. Arthur Kahn (London: Merlin Press, 1978).

Lund, Me, "Da Nora gik og kom hjem igen", review of *A Doll's House* at Ålborg Teater, *Berlingske Tidende*, 15 Dec. 2002, <http://www.berlingske.dk/artikel:-aid=239748>.

Madsen, Kjell, "Tanken om Det tredje rike: en 'positiv verdensanskuelse' fra Ibsens hånd?", *Edda*, no. 1 (1997), 28–36.

Malmanger, Magne, "Maleriet 1814–1870: Fra klassisisme til tid lig realisme", in Knut Berg, Peter Anker, Per Palme, and Stephan Tschudi-Madsen (eds.), *Norges Kunsthistorie*, 7 vols. (Oslo: Gyldendal Norsk Forlag, 1981), iv. 126–289.

Marker, Frederick J., and Marker, Lise-Lone, *Ibsen's Lively Art: A Performance Study of the Major Plays* (Cambridge: Cambridge University Press, 1989).

Marx, Karl, and Engels, Friedrich, *The Communist Manifesto*, ed. Gareth Stedman Jones, trans. Samuel Moore (1848; London: Penguin, 2002).

McCarthy, Mary, "The Will and Testament of Ibsen", in *Sights and Spectacles 1937–1956* (New York: Farrar, Straus and Cudahy, 1956), 168–78.

McFarlane, James, *Ibsen and Meaning: Studies, Essays & Prefaces 1953–87* (Norwich: Norvik Press, 1989).

—— "Ibsen's Poem Cycle 'I Billedgalleriet': A Study", *Scandinavica*, 17/1 (May 1978), 13–48.

Meier-Graefe, Julius, *Der Fall Böcklin und Die Lehre von den Einheiten* (Stuttgart: Verlag Julius Hoffmann, 1905).

—— *Der junge Menzel: Ein Problem der Kunstökonomie Deutschlands* (Leipzig: Insel-Verlag, 1906).

—— *Modern Art: Being a Contribution to a New System of Aesthetics*, 2 vols., trans. Florence Simmonds and George W. Chrystal (London: William Heinemann; New York: G. P. Putnam's Sons, 1908).

MEISEL, MARTIN, *Realizations: Narrative, Pictorial, and Theatrical Arts in Nineteenth-Century England* (Princeton: Princeton University Press, 1983).

MEYER, MICHAEL, *Henrik Ibsen* (Harmondsworth: Penguin Books, 1974).

—— *The Farewell to Poetry 1864–1882*, vol. ii of *Henrik Ibsen* (London: Rupert Hart-Davis, 1971).

—— *The Making of a Dramatist 1828–1864*, vol. i of *Henrik Ibsen* (London: Rupert Hart-Davis, 1967).

—— *The Top of a Cold Mountain 1883–1906*, vol. iii of *Henrik Ibsen* (London: Rupert Hart-Davis, 1971).

MILLER, ARTHUR, "Ibsen and the Drama of Today", in James McFarlane (ed.), *The Cambridge Companion to Ibsen* (Cambridge: Cambridge University Press, 1994), 227–32.

MOE, JON REFSDAL, "Hvor god er egentlig Henrik Ibsen?", *Norsk Shakespeare- og teatertidsskrift*, no. 3 (2004), 23–5.

MOFFETT, KENWORTH, *Meier-Graefe as Art Critic* (Munich: Prestel Verlag, 1973).

MOI, TORIL, "Expressive Freedom: Melodrama in *Rosmersholm*", in Gunnar Foss (ed.), *I skriftas lys og teatersalens mørke: Ein antologi om Ibsen og Fosse* (Kristiansand: Høyskoleforlaget, 2005), 81–107.

—— "Ibsen's Anti-Theatrical Aesthetics: *Pillars of Society* and *The Wild Duck*", in Bjørbye and Aarseth (eds.), *Proceedings*, 29–47.

—— " 'It was as if he meant something different from what he said—all the time': Language, Metaphysics and the Everyday in *The Wild Duck*", *New Literary History*, 33/4 (Autumn 2002), 655–86.

—— "Menns titaniske streben etter transcendens", review of *Ibsens heroisme* by Atle Kittang, *Norsk Litteraturvitenskapelig Tidsskrift*, 6/1 (2003), 67–77.

—— "A Woman's Desire to Be Known: Expressivity and Silence in *Corinne*", in Ghislaine McDayter (ed.), *Untrodden Regions of the Mind: Romanticism and Psychoanalysis*, Bucknell Review 45/2 (Lewisburg, Penn.: Bucknell University Press, 2002), 143–75.

MOIRANDAT, ALAIN, "Der Plastiker Böcklin", in Susanne Burger *et al.* (eds.), *Arnold Böcklin: 1827–1901: Gemälde, Zeichnungen, Plastiken: Ausstellung zum 150. Geburtstag, 11. Juni–11. September 1977* (Basel and Stuttgart: Schwabe, 1977), 81–4.

MOISY, SIGRID VON, *Paul Heyse: Münchner Dichterfürst im bürgerlichen Zeitalter. Ausstellung in der Bayerischen Staatsbibliothek 23. Januar bis 11. April 1981* (Munich: C. H. Beck, 1981).

MONK, RAY, *Ludwig Wittgenstein: The Duty of Genius* (London: Jonathan Cape, 1990).

MONRAD, M. J., "Andreas Munch: Livsskizze", in Andreas Munch, *Samlede Skrifter*, i. 3–17.

—— "Hvad man kan lære af Ibsens *Gengangere*" (1882), in Tom Christophersen (ed.), *Norsk Litteraturkritikk 1770–1890* (Oslo: Gyldendal, 1974), 194–201.

—— "Om Henrik Ibsen som Digter", *Morgenbladet*, 28 March 1875 (no. 85A), 1.

—— "Om Ibsens *Brand*", *Morgenbladet* 2, 9, 16 and 23 Sept. 1866, <http://www.ibsen.net/index.db2?id=69783>.

MORI, MITSUYA, "Staging Ibsen's Realism", in Bjørbye and Aarseth (eds.), *Proceedings*, 111–17.

MUNCH, ANDREAS, "Brudefærden", in *Samlede Skrifter*, i. 297–8.

—— *Ephemerer*, in *Samlede Skrifter*, i. 21–112.

—— *Lord William Russell: Historisk Tragoedie i fem Akter*, in *Samlede Skrifter*, iii. 51–183.

—— "Norsk Bondeliv", in *Samlede Skrifter*, i. 355–69.

—— *Samlede Skrifter*, 5 vols., ed. M. J. Monrad and Hartvig Lassen (Copenhagen: Universitetsboghandler G. E. C. Gad, 1887–90).

NERBØVIK, JOSTEIN, *Norsk historie 1860–1914* (Oslo: Det norske samlaget, 1999).

NIETZSCHE, FRIEDRICH, "Attempt at Self-Criticism" (1886), in *The Birth of Tragedy and The Case of Wagner*, trans. Walter Kaufmann (New York: Vintage Books, 1967), 17–27.

—— *Beyond Good and Evil: Prelude to a Philosophy of the Future* (1886), trans. Walter Kaufmann (New York: Vintage Books, 1989).

—— *The Birth of Tragedy and the Case of Wagner*, trans. Walter Kaufmann (New York: Vintage Books, 1967).

—— *The Will to Power*, ed. Walter Kaufmann, trans. Walter Kaufmann and R. J. Hollingdale (New York: Vintage Books, 1968).

NILU, KAMALUDDIN, "Staging Ibsen in Bangladesh: Relevance and Adaptation", in Bjørbye and Aarseth (eds.), *Proceedings*, 119–25.

NOON, PATRICK, "Colour and Effect: Anglo-French Painting in London and Paris", in Noon (ed.), *Constable to Delacroix*, 10–27.

—— (ed.), *Constable to Delacroix: British Art and the French Romantics* (London: Tate Publishing, 2003).

NORENG, HARALD, "Arbeiderføreren Marcus Thrane: Lærling av Wergeland, lærer for Ibsen og Bjørnson", *Ibsen-huset, Grimstad Bymuseum*, <http://museumsnett.no/ibsen/Noreng/mthrane.html>.

NORTHAM, JOHN, *Ibsen: A Critical Study* (Cambridge: Cambridge University Press, 1973).

—— *Ibsen's Dramatic Method: A Study of the Prose Dramas* (London: Faber & Faber, 1953).

OLIVARIUS, PETER, "Henrik Ibsen: Idealismens svanesang", in Aage Henriksen, Helge Therkildsen and Knud Wentzel (eds.), *Den erindrende faun: digteren og hans fantasi* (Copenhagen: Fremad, 1968), 192–208.

ØSTERUD, ERIK, *Theatrical and Narrative Space: Studies in Strindberg, Ibsen and J. P. Jacobsen* (Århus and Oxford: Århus University Press, 1998).

OTTESEN, SOFIE GRAM, "Om at finde sin stemme: Melodrama som skepticisme i Ibsens *Når vi døde vågner*", in Lisbeth P. Wærp (ed.), *Livet på likstrå: Henrik Ibsens Når vi døde vågner* (Oslo: LNU / Cappelen Akademisk Forlag, 1999), 149–78.

OXFELDT, ELISABETH, *Nordic Orientalism: Paris and the Cosmopolitan Imagination 1800–1900* (Copenhagen: Museum Tusculanum Press, University of Copenhagen, 2005).

OZ, FRANK (dir.), *The Stepford Wives* (Paramount Pictures, 2004).

PAVEL, THOMAS, *La Pensée du roman* (Paris: Gallimard, 2003).

PETERSEN, CLEMENS, "*Peer Gynt,* dramatisk Digt af Henrik Ibsen", *Fædrelandet*, 30 Nov. 1867, <http://www.ibsen.net/index.db2?id=229>.

PETERSEN, FREDRIK, "Henrik Ibsens Drama *Et Dukkehjem*", review of *A Doll's House, Aftenbladet*, 9 and 10 Jan. 1880, <http://www.ibsen.net/index.gan?id=106188&subid=0>.

POOVEY, MARY, "Forgotten Writers, Neglected Histories: Charles Reade and the Nineteenth Century Transformation of the British Literary Field", *ELH* 71 (Summer 2004), 433–53.

POVLSEN, KARIN KLITGAARD, "Standsningens attitude i krop og tekst: Lady Hamilton, Ida Brun & Friederike Brun", in Andersen and Povlsen (eds.), *Tableau*, 93–116.

PRETTEJOHN, ELIZABETH, *The Art of the Pre-Raphaelites* (Princeton: Princeton University Press, 2000).

PRYSER, TORE, *Norsk historie 1814–1860* (Oslo: Det norske samlaget, 1999).

PUCHNER, MARTIN, *Stage Fright: Modernism, Anti-Theatricality, and Drama* (Baltimore: Johns Hopkins University Press, 2002).

RAINEY, LAWRENCE, and HALLBERG, ROBERT VON, "Editorial/Introduction", *Modernism/Modernity*, 1 (1994), 1–3.

REISTAD, GUNNHILD RAMM, and GREVSTAD, RAGNFRID, "Ibsens private bibliotek og trekk ved hans lesning", in Daniel Haakonsen (ed.), *Ibsenårbok 1985–86* (Oslo: Universitetsforlaget, 1986), 9–186.

REKDAL, ANNE MARIE, *Frihetens dilemma: Ibsen lest med Lacan* (Oslo: Aschehoug, 2000).

—— (ed.), *Et skjær av uvilkårlig skjønnhet: Om Henrik Ibsens Hedda Gabler* (Oslo: LNU and Cappelen Akademisk Forlag, 2001).

RIDING, CHRISTINE, "*The Raft of the Medusa* in Britain: Audience and Context", in Noon (ed.), *Constable to Delacroix*, 66–73.

RIVAL, PIERRE, "Le roman de *l'Île des morts*: mythe et fascination", in Le Cieux, Peyrolle, and Jacquinot (eds.), *Hommage*, 27–35.

RØNNING, HELGE, "Ond idealisme", *Agora*, nos. 2–3 (1993), 220–30.

—— "The Unconscious Evil of Idealism and the Liberal Dilemma: An Analysis of Thematic Structures in *Emperor and Galilean* and *The Wild Duck*", in Vigdis Ystad (ed.), *Ibsen at the Centre for Advanced Study* (Oslo: Scandinavian University Press, 1997), 171–201.

ROSENBLUM, ROBERT, and JANSON, H. W., *19th-Century Art* (New York: Harry N. Abrams, 1984).

ROUSSEAU, JEAN-JACQUES, *Emile or On Education*, trans. Allan Bloom (1762; New York: Basic Books, 1979).

—— *Politics and the Arts: Letter to M. d'Alembert on the Theatre*, trans. Allan Bloom (1758; Ithaca, NY: Cornell University Press, 1960).

RUDLER, RODERICK, "Levende bilder på scenen i Henrik Ibsens tid", *Kunst og kultur*, 48 (1965), 1–16.

SAARI, SANDRA, "Female Become Human: Nora Transformed", in Bjørn Hemmer and Vigdis Ystad (eds.), *Contemporary Approaches to Ibsen* (Oslo: Norwegian University Press, 1988), vi. 41–55.

SAND, GEORGE, *Story of My Life: The Autobiography of George Sand*, A Group Translation, ed. Thelma Jurgrau (Albany, NY: State University of New York Press, 1991).

SANDERS, KARIN, *Konturer: Skulptur- og dødsbilleder fra guldalderlitteraturen* (Copenhagen: Museum Tusculanums forlag, Københavns Universitet, 1997).

SCHILLER, FRIEDRICH, "On Naive and Sentimental Poetry", in Walter Hinderer and Daniel O. Dahlstrom (eds.), *Essays*, trans. Daniel O. Dahlstrom (New York: Continuum, 1993), 179–260.

SCHLEGEL, FRIEDRICH, "From *Ideas*" (1796), in Bernstein (ed.), *Classic and Romantic*, 261–8.

SCHOR, NAOMI, *George Sand and Idealism* (New York: Columbia University Press, 1993).

SHAKESPEARE, WILLIAM, *Othello*, in Stanley Wells and Gary Taylor (eds.), *The Complete Works* (Oxford: Clarendon Press, 1994), 819–53.

SHATZKY, JOEL, and DUMONT, SEDWITZ, " 'All or Nothing': Idealism in *A Doll House*", *Edda*, no. 1 (1994), 73–84.

SHAW, GEORGE BERNARD, *The Quintessence of Ibsenism* (1891; New York: Brentano's, 1905).

SHEPHERD-BARR, KIRSTEN, *Ibsen and Early Modernist Theatre, 1890–1900* (Westport, Conn.: Greenwood Press, 1997).

SKRAM, AMALIE, "En Betragtning over *Et Dukkehjem*", *Dagbladet*, 19 Jan. 1880, in *Samlede Verker*, 7 vols. (Oslo: Gyldendal, 1993), vii. 300–13.

—— "Mere om *Gengangere*", *Dagbladet*, 27 April 1882, in *Samlede Verker*, 7 vols. (Oslo: Gyldendal, 1993), vii. 352–9.

SMIDT, KRISTIAN, *Ibsen Translated: A Report on English versions of Henrik Ibsen's* Peer Gynt *and* A Doll's House (Oslo: Solum, 2000).

SOLOMON, ALISA, "Reconstructing Ibsen's Realism", in *Re-Dressing the Canon: Essays on Theater and Gender* (London and New York: Routledge, 1997), 46–69.

STAËL, GERMAINE DE, *Corinne, or Italy*, trans. Sylvia Rafael (1807; Oxford: Oxford University Press, 1998).

—— *Corinne, ou l'Italie*, ed. Simone Balayé, Collection Folio (1807; Paris: Gallimard, 1985).

—— *Le Mannequin* (1811), in *Œuvres complètes de Mme. la baronne de Staël*, ed. Auguste Louis Staël-Holstein, 17 vols. (Paris: Treuttel et Würtz, 1820), xvi. 478–91.

STRINDBERG, AUGUST, *Spöksonaten* in *Kammarspel*, ed. Gunnar Ollén (1907; Stockholm: Norstedt, 1991), 159–225.

SZONDI, PETER, *Theory of the Modern Drama* (1965), trans. Michael Hays (Minneapolis: University of Minnesota Press, 1987).

TEMPLETON, JOAN, *Ibsen's Women* (Cambridge: Cambridge University Press, 1997).

—— "The Munch–Ibsen Connection: Exposing a Critical Myth", *Scandinavian Studies*, 72 (Winter 2000), 445–62.

THIIS, JENS, *Norske malere og billedhuggere: en fremstilling af norsk billedkunsts historie i det nittende århundrede med oversigter over samtidig fremmed kunst*, 3 vols. (Bergen: John Griegs Forlag, 1907).

TISSOT, ERNEST, *Le drame norvégien: Henri Ibsen—Biörnstjerne Biörnson* (Paris: Libraire académique Didier Perrin, 1893).

TJØNNELAND, EIVIND, *Ibsen og moderniteten* (Oslo: Spartacus Forlag, 1993).

—— "Organisk symbolikk kontra allegori i Vildanden", *Agora*, nos. 2–3 (1993), 231–43.

TRUMBLE, ANGUS, *Love and Death: Art in the Age of Queen Victoria* (Adelaide: Art Gallery of South Australia, 2001).

TYNAN, KENNETH, *Curtains: Selections from the Drama Criticism and Related Writings* (New York: Atheneum, 1961).

TYSDAHL, BJØRN J., *Joyce and Ibsen: A Study in Literary Influence* (Oslo: Norwegian University Presses; New York: Humanities Press, 1968).

USTVEDT, YNGVAR, "Professor Rubek og Henrik Ibsen", *Edda*, 67 (1967), 272–87.

VALENCY, MAURICE, *The Flower and the Castle: An Introduction to Modern Drama* (New York: Grosset & Dunlap, 1966).

VAN LAAN, THOMAS F., "*Lady Inger* as Tragedy", in Bjørn Hemmer and Vigdis Ystad (eds.), *Contemporary Approaches to Ibsen* (Oslo: Universitetsforlaget, 1994), viii. 25–46.

VERSINI, LAURENT, "Introduction", in Denis Diderot, *Œuvres*, iv: *Esthétique—Théâtre* (Paris: Robert Laffont, 1996), 1061–78.

VULLUM, ERIK, "Literatur-Tidende", review of *A Doll's House*, *Dagbladet*, 6 and 13 Dec. 1879, <http://www.ibsen.net/index.gan?id=13689>.

WÆRP, LISBETH P., *Overgangens figurasjoner: En studie i Henrik Ibsens* Kejser og Galilæer *og* Når vi døde vågner (Oslo: Solum Forlag, 2002).

—— (ed.), *Livet på likstrå: Henrik Ibsens Når vi døde vågner* (Oslo: LNU og Cappelen Akademisk Forlag, 1999).

WEINBERG, BERNARD, *French Realism: The Critical Reaction, 1830–1870* (New York: Modern Language Association of America; London: Oxford University Press, 1937).

WELHAVEN, JOHAN SEBASTIAN, "Om det franske Theater", in *Samlede Verker*, iii. 253–7.

—— *Samlede Verker*, 3 vols., ed. Ingard Hauge (Oslo: Universitetsforlaget, 1991).

—— "En Tribut til Kunstforeningen", in *Samlede Verker*, i. 230–5.

WESTERGAARD, HANNE, "J. C. Dahl og Danmark", in *J. C. Dahl og Danmark: Nasjonalgalleriet, Oslo, 3. febr.–11.mars 1973; Statens museum for kunst, København, 1. april–13. mai 1973* (Oslo: Nasjonalgalleriet, 1973), 17–23.

WIKANDER, MATTHEW H., *Fangs of Malice: Hypocrisy, Sincerity, & Acting* (Iowa City, Ia.: University of Iowa Press, 2002).

WILDE, OSCAR, *The Artist as Critic: Critical Writings of Oscar Wilde*, ed. Richard Ellmann (New York: Random House, 1968).

—— "The Critic as Artist" (1890), in *The Artist as Critic*, 371–408.

—— "The Decay of Lying" (1889), in *The Artist as Critic*, 290–320.

—— "M. Caro on George Sand" (1888), in *The Artist as Critic*, 86–9.

—— *The Picture of Dorian Gray* (1891; Oxford: Oxford University Press, 1992).

WILKINSON, LYNN R., "Gender and Melodrama in Ibsen's *Lady Inger*", *Modern Drama*, 42/2 (Summer 2001), 155–73.

WILLIAMS, RAYMOND, *Drama from Ibsen to Brecht* (New York: Oxford University Press, 1969).

—— *Drama from Ibsen to Eliot* (1952; London: Chatto & Windus, 1961).

WIRSÉN, CARL DAVID AF, *Kritiker* (Stockholm: P. A. Norstedt & Söners Förlag, 1901).

WITOSZEK, NINA, *Norske naturmytologier: Fra Edda til økofilosofi*, trans. Toril Hanssen (Oslo: Pax, 1998).

WITTGENSTEIN, LUDWIG, *Philosophical Investigations*, trans. G. E. M. Anscombe, 3rd edn. (New York: Macmillan, 1968).

—— *Den ukjente dagboken*, trans. Knut Olav Åmås (Oslo: Spartacus, 1998).

WOLD, BENDIK, and HAAGENSEN, NILS-ØIVIND, "En ny dansketid?", interview with Øystein Rottem, *Klassekampen*, 5 March 2003, <http://www.klassekampen.no/kultur/2955/2971?view=print>.

WOOLF, VIRGINIA, "Character in Fiction", in Andrew McNeillie (ed.), *The Essays of Virginia Woolf*, iii: *1919–1924* (New York: Harcourt Brace Jovanovitch, 1988), 420–38.

—— *A Room of One's Own* (1929; London: Grafton Books, 1990).

WYLLER, EGIL A., *Ibsens* Keiser og Galilæer: *En løpende kommentar* (Oslo: Spartacus Forlag / Andresen & Butenschøn, 1999).

YSTAD, VIGDIS, "Dikterens syner: Ibsen og den moderne sanselighet", in *"—livets endeløse gåde"*, 167–201.

—— *"—livets endeløse gåde": Ibsens dikt og drama* (Oslo: Aschehoug, 1996).

—— "Om angst og despoti—Ibsens Julian som tidsdiagnose", programme note for Hilda Hellwig's *Kejser og Galilæer* (Bergen: Den nationale scene, 2000), no pagination.

—— "*Rosmersholm* og psykoanalysen", in *"—livets endeløse gåde"*, 153–63.

Index

To avoid long strings of entries under 'Ibsen' and 'idealism,' entries have as far as possible been alphabetized under other subject headings. Thus references to idealist views of beauty will be found under 'beauty,' to idealism and romanticism under 'romanticism,' and so on. Merely referential endnotes have not been indexed. Other endnotes have been only lightly indexed. References to illustrations are set with ***bold italics***.